Very Exceptional Soldiers

A catalogue record of this book is available from the British Library

First Edition: April 2005

ISBN: 1-84375-161-5

To order additional copies of this book please visit:
http://www.upso.co.uk/franksteer

Published by: UPSO Ltd
5 Stirling Road, Castleham Business Park,
St Leonards-on-Sea, East Sussex TN38 9NW UK
Tel: 01424 853349 Fax: 0870 191 3991
Email: info@upso.co.uk Web: http://www.upso.co.uk

Very Exceptional Soldiers

by

Frank Steer

John

Best wishes

Frank Steer

3 June 2005

UPSO

They are......very exceptional soldiers.

General d'Infanterie Hans von Zwehl
Commander
VII Rheinisch Westfälischen Reserve Corps
August 1914

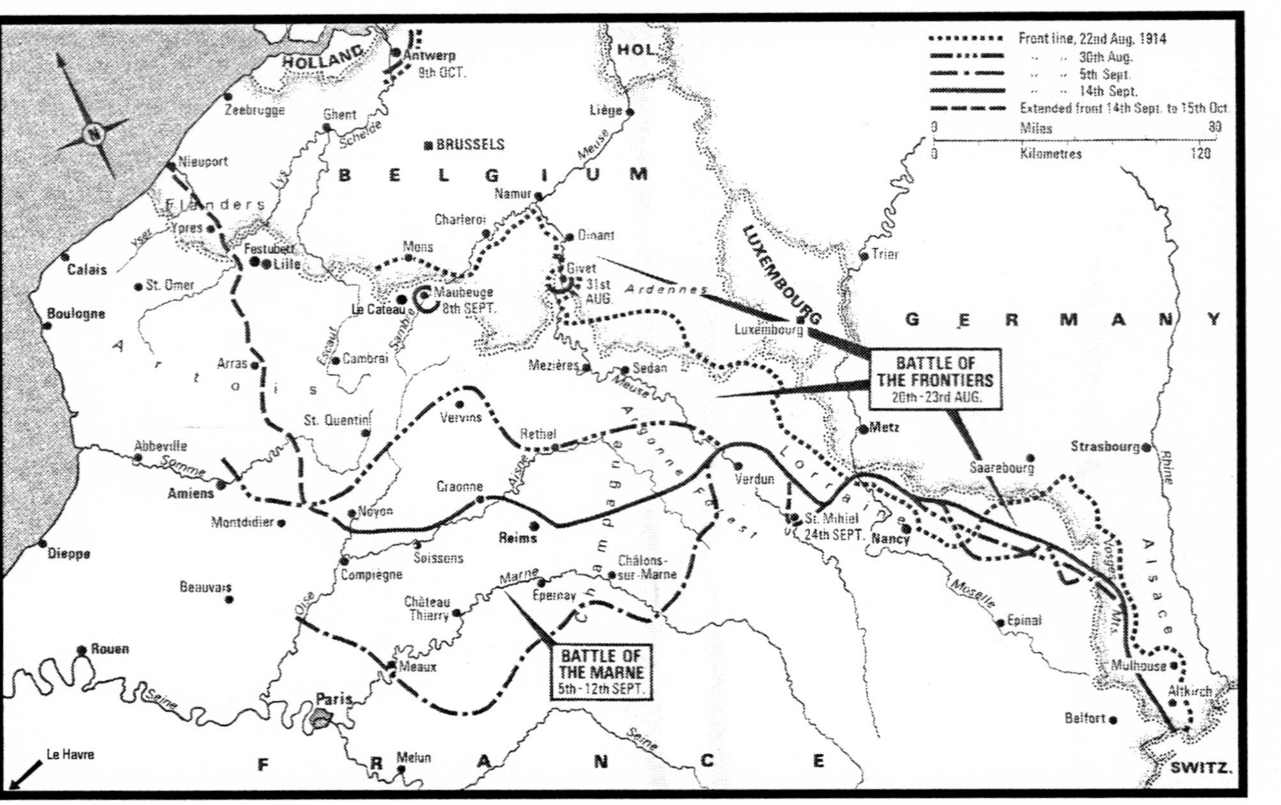
Front line, 22nd Aug. 1914
" " 30th Aug.
" " 5th Sept.
" " 14th Sept.
Extended front 14th Sept. to 15th Oct.
0 Miles 30
0 Kilometres 120
HOLLAND
Antwerp 9th OCT.
HOL.
Zeebrugge
Ghent
Scheldt
BRUSSELS
Liège
Meuse
Nieuport
BELGIUM
Namur
Flanders
Ypres
Yser
Lys
Charleroi
Dinant
Festubert
Lille
Mons
Givet 31st AUG.
Calais
St. Omer
Maubeuge 8th SEPT.
Le Cateau
Sambre
Ardennes
LUXEMBOURG
Trier
Boulogne
Escaut
Cambrai
Luxembourg
GERMANY
Artois
Arras
Mezières
Sedan
Meuse
BATTLE OF THE FRONTIERS 20th - 23rd AUG.
St. Quentin
Vervins
Rethel
Argonne Forest
Metz
Strasbourg
Rhine
Abbeville
Somme
Amiens
Aisne
Craonne
Verdun
Lorraine
Saarebourg
Noyon
Montdidier
Reims
St. Mihiel 24th SEPT.
Nancy
Champagne
Dieppe
Soissons
Châlons-sur-Marne
Compiègne
Marne
Epernay
Vosges Mts.
Alsace
Beauvais
Oise
Château Thierry
Moselle
Epinal
Rouen
Meaux
BATTLE OF THE MARNE 5th - 12th SEPT.
Mulhouse
Seine
Paris
Altkirch
Belfort
Le Havre
Melun
FRANCE
SWITZ.

Prologue

The Beginning of the End

The weak sun lay low on the horizon, its thin, watery light casting long shadows from the skeletal boughs of defoliated Horse Chestnut trees onto the ground below; the branches reaching out in supplication, silhouetted against the pale blue of a November sky as if pleading for release from the downward march into hell that lay in the winter to come.

Fallen leaves lay thick on the unruly green grass, their natural colour darkened by dampness where the sun had found a way through the trees to melt the hoar frost that still coated their brethren lying in the shadows; welding together in thick, soggy masses as they rotted slowly in company with the browning husks of their seed pods, broken open by schoolboys in the annual autumnal search for conkers. The breeze rustled the Viburnum hedgerow that separated the memorial cross, with its fading list of names, from the narrow grey strip of road that ran the length of the village in an unbending line and on out into the flat open Norfolk countryside; it moved the tree tops, catching the uppermost reaches with the black outline of abandoned Rooks' nests clinging tenaciously as they swayed from side to side with shifts in the wind pattern; it fluttered at the trousers of the little girls shivering in their new style Brownie uniforms, it whipped at the scarves worn by the scouts and the cubs as insignia, and by the older men as protection against the damp and biting cold. It was Remembrance Sunday 1994.

He looked slowly around him as the silence hung heavy in the small gathering, the final sobbing, crying notes of the Last Post drifting into the distance, lost in the sound of a motor cycle engine as it roared away from the pub forecourt opposite; its owner unaware, uninterested, uncaring about the small and solemn ritual being enacted in memory of events which his generation certainly couldn't remember, and which so few could.

But he could remember, he'd been there after all. Wasn't the aching pain in his right leg a regular reminder of a time that had begun with such hope and promise, and had ended in cynicism and misery for so many; and death for so many more. When it was all over and the battalion had paraded on Armistice Day 1918 there had been just one officer, the quartermaster and six warrant officers and non commissioned officers left of those thousand or more who had left for France in August 1914.

His head jerked round as the young trumpeter from the Boys' Brigade band began to sound reveille. A smile twitched at the corner of the old man's mouth as he hoped the kid made a better job of this than he had the Last Post. Those high notes at the top of the scale were always a sod to get right, and on a cold day with a cold instrument it could be impossible for the inexperienced. Still, at least the boy tried and he could forgive a great deal for that.

"They shall grow not old....." the words began to spill from the lips of the middle-aged representative of the British Legion.

"Too bloody right they won't, poor bastards."

As his head flopped down, his neck, wrinkled with age, too weak to support it properly, his Adam's apple now more prominent with the advancing years, a sea of images washed across his consciousness. Faces crept up on him from the depths of a memory that had difficulty coping with last week's events, but which had engraved upon it with startling clarity the images of almost a century ago.

"As we that are left...."

"And there's not too many of us; and what would he know about it anyway. Couple of tours in Northern Ireland and a few years in the TA and he thinks he knows it all. Those TA lads, mind, they hadn't done a bad job. Not so good as us regulars, mind, but not too bad for........."

"Come on then, time to go home."

The sharp voice, with its hint of antagonism, broke through the shell of his thoughts. He felt the hands, briskly tucking the blanket around his knees, patting his overcoat into neatness, touching the row of four medals on his chest as if to straighten them despite them being perfectly straight already. Out of the corner of his eye, as a blur, he saw the whiteness of a handkerchief pass across his vision on its way to wiping the clear dewdrop that hung irritatingly from the end of his creased and slightly bulbous nose. He heard the brake release click as she freed the rubber blocks from the rims of the wheels, and felt the first surge as she pressed down on the back of the wheelchair to overcome the inertia of the machine and to set it off on its bumpy ride across the grass towards the road.

"Poor old sod," she thought as she wheeled him down the road, past the derelict row of four cottages set back along the left hand side of the road, and the Bull, the only pub still left in the village now the King's Head down by the old school had closed down. She didn't mean to be hard on him, but she was by nature brisk and direct. She got that down her mother's line, although old Granma had been able to combine it with a benign serenity which allowed her to appear efficient rather than unfeeling.

She ought not upset him. After all, he was all she had left. Granma'd been gone these twenty years now, and Gramps and Granma had brought her up as their own when Mum and Dad had gone in that stupid charabanc crash just after the war. She owed them, and she knew it, but the obligation she felt gnawed away at her and, mingled with the bitterness of her spinsterhood, created a depressive self pity which put up barriers between her and the outside world.

He wished she could be a bit softer. He felt so lonely, his sense of isolation heightened by the physical resemblance between his granddaughter and his Thurza. She was thinner, of course, his granddaughter, the sharp lines of her features thrown into stark relief by the severe hair style pulled tight back into a bun. Ah, Thurza'd had long hair too, but when she'd piled it up on her head it became a reddish, tousled frame around her face that looked soft, and gave way under the gentle caress of his hand. There'd be no gentle caressing of Jenny's hair; be no one that he knew with the courage to get that close.

The nose was straight, a little too long perhaps, but in her case it had an inherent sharpness that matched so well her character. The lips were thinner too, but that slightly offset front tooth was so remarkably similar that on the rare occasions when Jenny smiled he could almost believe Thurza was standing before him.

"Marnin' Jenny, 'e's looking well for such a cold day."

He heard the voice as if from a great distance, with the patronising edge to it that people reserve for the very young and the very old; but he knew the owner at once. Her granpa's name was one of the fourteen on that memorial. "A gunner 'e'd been. Gassed at Loos in 1915. Ah, that gas, my but that had been....."

"Yes, yes 'e is."

He heard her respond, impatient as ever, always in a hurry to get away from folk; as if she had anything to go to. "If only she'd stop and talk decently to people from time to time."

The wheelchair swung left as they reached the path leading up to the modern bungalow that he and Thurza had bought for their retirement, and which he now shared with Jenny. He heard the latch click on the black wrought iron gate, and the slight creak as it swung open.

"Could use a drop of oil, and a lick of paint wouldn't go amiss," he thought, but didn't dare say.

He heard the grunted expellation of air as she pressed down on the handles of the chair, and anticipated the backwards tilt that would come as she heaved the chair over the small step that led up the path, past the dead blooms of the roses that needed removing, towards the orange berries of the Pyracantha that framed the primrose painted half glass door leading into the small hallway of the house.

More grunts and lifts as she negotiated the obstacle course that was a house neither designed nor adapted to a wheelchair, until he found himself in the large room that served both as a living and a dining room. She wheeled him over to the chair by the fire, into which he knew she would lift him once she had gone through the ritual of putting on the kettle, hanging up her coat and putting on the long pinafore that was her hallmark around the house. He didn't mind the delay; she always kept the temperature in the house a bit lower than he liked it. A little longer staying warm inside his overcoat wouldn't hurt.

She reached down and turned on the gas fire that burned to look like a real log fire.

"My," he thought "that's different. Maybe she's going soft on me; more likely someone's coming to visit. Can't think who. Never mind."

"I'll just put the kettle on, Gramps," he heard her say. "Then I'll get you out of that coat and into your chair. You just stay there and I'll be back in a minute."

"And where the 'ell does she think I might go before she gets back?" The thought flashed uncharitably through his mind, and for the briefest instant he felt a touch of shame.

His head lifted and he looked at the artificial logs gradually appearing more and more realistic as the terracotta began to glow in the heat of the gas flames. He glanced at the mantelpiece, seeing the telegram perched behind the little statue they'd bought all those years ago on a trip to Yarmouth. From the Palace that'd come, four months ago. A hundred years old, and congratulations from the Queen.

"Hundred years old....aye, but there were a few who would have given everything for just another ten years....ten years more than they'd 'ad...cut down before they'd the chance to live any kind of a life; to have children; build a home; fulfil the dreams of youth. All that had gone for them, and yet he'd survived for eighty more. How...what right did he have to have been able to....."

His mind had often gone back over the years, wondering why he'd been spared. He'd never forgotten, and perhaps that was why the Lord had left him to live on; so that someone could carry on the memory; someone wouldn't let it all be forgotten; someone could honour the sacrifice.

"Or maybe I were just bloody lucky."

He looked at the fireplace, into the flames that flickered blue and red and yellow and orange around what now looked very much like the logs they'd burnt every winter through the long years of their marriage.

"She'd liked a log fire 'ad Thurza. If w'ed 'ad a pound for every one I split for that big open fire in the old cottage.... Couldn't do that now, not at this age; not in the state I'm in now."

The flames licked higher, his head drooped a little as the warmth began to work its way into him, as the eyelids grew heavier. His right hand slipped out from under the blanket that she kept wrapped round his knees whenever he was out in cold weather. It wasn't a young man's hand any more. The veins stood out starkly, blue against the alabaster white of his ancient skin, wending their way like the rivulets of some great river as it emerges into its estuarial flood plain, twisting and turning between the brown liver-worts towards the knuckle joints knarled with arthritis. The nails were longer than he'd normally kept them, slightly hooked and in need of cutting.

The hand shook slightly, trembling not just with age but also with the effort of pushing against the stricture of the heavy over-coat material. Gently, the tips of the fingers brushed against the second from the left of the four medals, the red, white and blue running from right to left in columns on the water silk; tapering down towards a point just where it joined the bronze, pointed medallion of the Mons Star. They touched the little bronze bar halfway down the ribbon with its dates: 5th August 1914 - 22nd Nov 1914.

To wear it you needed to have been a member of the British Expeditionary Force that had gone to war in France at the start of the Great War, you needed to have fought at

Mons, down through France, back up through France and into Belgium.

There were less than thirty left alive now, less than thirty who had sweated, sworn, starved, fought, killed, withdrawn, advanced, fought, killed, sweated and starved some more; and then stopped, at Ypres.

Old Contemptibles. Old they certainly were, and so few, so very few, of the eighty thousand who'd gone to France in August 1914 were left. Contemptible they were not.

The flames crackled and flickered around the joists in the roof of the small cottage, sparks swirling and twisting into the sky, mingling with the smoke that joined with that rising from the artillery shells that exploded around them as they advanced across the open, muddy, pock marked ground. Water swirled in the shell holes which grew deeper and deeper as more and more shells landed in the devastation. The heat from the flames was all down the right hand side of his body. To his left he could see shapes, peculiar shapes with great humps on their backs, falling, twisting, turning, hands raised reaching out as if to hold onto life even as it was being ripped away from them.

He heard the sounds, the crackling of the flames, the crack of the bullets as they flew past, the cough as the shrapnel burst overhead. He smelt the wood smoke from the fire, the peculiar sharp smell of high explosive once it has detonated, the smell of wet woollen uniform and damp web equipment, the smell of his own fear; and above it all the pungent stink of rotted bodies that had lain too long under the mud, only to be exhumed and ruptured yet more by the constant shellfire.

His legs felt like lead, the weight on his back was pushing him down, the cloying mud gripped around his ankles, his thigh muscles burned with the effort of pushing himself forward, further and further forward. Then he was falling, deeper and deeper, down into the muddy, water-filled depths. The scum-covered oily mess came up to meet him as he turned his head away, but it was too late. He was trapped, fighting to drag his face above the filth, reaching up for air as the water sought to push its way down into his lungs. Fighting for his life, his leaden legs screamed for relief as the muscles strained to push him back upwards, his arms moved slower and slower in the glutinous mud that threatened to envelop him.

And then he had made it. His face was clear of it, looking upwards into a clear blue sky, his lungs filling with clear sweet air, his breath coming in short pants as he sought to recover what he had so nearly lost. He would get out of this, he was going to be all right, he would get back, he......

The movement to his right and above him caught his eye, caused him to look and in looking gave him time to recoil in horror as the side of the hole began to cave in, oozing down towards him. As it split and slid the earth disgorged stones, mud, shell fragments, an old steel helmet. And inside the steel helmet the head moved round as if to look at him, sockets where the eyes had once been, a grey, green jelly where once a brain had functioned; and then the rest of the body sliding and slithering like some messenger from hell, a handmaiden of the devil sliding, slurping, stinking with the torso ripped open exposing rotted lungs, entrails that twisted and interwove in a foul smelling glutinous mass.

On it came, irrevocably unstoppable towards him. His arms trapped in the unyielding mud, he could do nothing; nothing to stave off the horror, nothing to move away from it. He screamed as it struck him, the vileness of it enveloping him, his face feeling the cold, clammy compress of dead flesh and internal organs swamping him, pushing him back down; foul liquids running into his mouth, choking as they hit the back of his throat. He fought against swallowing, but it was too much. He could no longer hold his breath, he had to swallow, he was drowning....deeper and deeper he went, the vomit rising in his throat as his body rebelled against.......

He felt the hand shaking him as he came out of the dream, heard the voice, impatiently telling him to wake up. The images disappeared from his vision; the horror vanished as it had so many times before as he woke from the nightmare.

But this time he didn't want to wake, didn't want the cup of tea he knew she would have for him. He was tired, wanted to sleep as the fire in the grate warmed the right hand side of his body, wanted to think about something else other than the horror of his worst imaginings...wanted to be alone with himself.

As he quietened she knew the bad dream had gone. She put the cup and saucer down on the small Formica topped table beside him, a water biscuit propped in the saucer, and left to go back to the kitchen; left him to his thoughts and his memories......

Chapter 1

The Life That Was

Life for an eighteen year old unemployed weaver, himself the son of an unemployed weaver, in a small village in Norfolk in 1912 carried few joys and even fewer prospects for anything other than a life of considerable poverty. The weaving industry that had been a mainstay of employment in the area for hundreds of years was in terminal decline. There were just two looms in the village now. There had been four in 1910, but Jed Atkinson had taken his machinery north to Lancashire over two years ago in the hope of improving his living, and now Charlie Woolford was doing the same. No one ever heard what happened to Atkinson, but his and Charlie's going was almost the last nail in the coffin of weaving in the village. For Ted Ludgrove and his father the impact was devastating.

The Ludgroves had worked for Mr Woolford for three generations. As jobs disappeared with the decline, from fifteen looms down to two in less than fifteen years, the Ludgroves had felt a modicum of security in Charlie Woolford's constant reassurances that he would stay on; and keep them on. The family's dependence on him extended to their home, in a small row of workers' cottages set back about fifty yards from the main road which ran through the village, and very close to the Bull, one of five public houses which tried to survive the ever decreasing demands for the services they offered from a gradually impoverishing community.

The cottage was very small, by any standards. One of a group of four in a terrace, with the other three derelict and used as storage for machinery and raw materials for the Woolford looms, it provided the Ludgroves with as good a home as any in their station in life, and better than some. There was a single room at ground level with a small storeroom that could be reached by a low door that required anyone other than a seven-year-old child to bend as they went in. Cooking was at its most basic, and was conducted over an open fire that fed into the central chimneystack in the dividing wall with the next-door cottage. A set of open slatted wooden stairs climbed the wall at about a forty-five degree angle leading to two small rooms upstairs. One was just large enough for Ted's father, also called Ted, and his mother Martha to have a bed. The second, and smaller, room was barely large enough for one, let alone two, but Ted's sisters, Eliza and Ruth, used it.

Since he could remember, Ted had slept on a straw filled palliasse in the corner of the downstairs room. It was actually fifteen years since the two girls, twins, had arrived in a sickly and weakened state from a premature birth that had almost killed his mother. Peace and quiet had been the watchwords for care for the three of them after the birth, so father and son had taken to sleeping downstairs. When Martha became well and strong enough to welcome old Ted back upstairs he had gone, but with the twins now firmly installed in the other room, and still weak and fractious, he had left his son to the loneliness of the bottom of the cottage, which teemed with a community of insects and small rodents using the inky blackness of the night to conduct their normal business, much to the physical discomfort of Ted junior.

Some clouds, however, have a silver lining, and the dreadful difficulties of the twins' birth had rendered Martha incapable of conceiving, thereby keeping within manageable limits a family which, were it to follow the norm for working class families in East Anglia at the time, would have seen up to twelve births, of which somewhere between five and eight would have survived. As it was she had already miscarried two before young Ted arrived, and a brother born a year later had lived for only six months before the cold and damp of a Norfolk winter had seen him in his grave.

Life had been hard, but they had got by. But, the blackest day of all had been the day the two Teds came home to confirm that the rumours they had heard about the possible move of the Woolford loom were true, and that they were out of work. For old Ted, the gut-wrenching horror when Charlie Woolford had told him had been like a physical blow to the diaphragm, a sickening sense of despair that had swept over him, manifested in great shuddering reaction that seemed to shrink his body. His heart rate rapidly shot up, the saliva drained from his mouth leaving it dry, but with the sour taste of adrenaline as his fear showed in the pallor of his face, the sweat on his shaking hands and the sudden weakness at his knees which caused him to grab the back of a chair for support.

Young Ted felt the pang of concern, but really had no appreciation of the emotions running through his father's brain and the physical reactions they were causing in his body. Quite simply, the implications for the family as a whole did not strike him as they did the older man.

"Sit yerself down, Ted."

Charlie Woolford had always been a good boss, basically a kind man whose inherently generous and genuinely Christian approach to life had not been entirely blunted by the strain of keeping his business going as markets diminished and the orders fell away with increasing rapidity.

"Listen, I know its not goin' to be easy. God knows there's little enough work around, especially with so many weavers about lookin' for somethin' now the bottoms dropped out of the business round 'ere. I can't offer you anything to go for, you'll 'ave to look out for yourself, but I 'ave 'ad a word with Mr Snell an' told 'im 'ow well you both work and 'e said 'e'd look out for you when there's somethin' goin'."

Snell was a local landowner. Any work for him meant agricultural labourers wages, lower than they had been earning, but better than nothing.

"And I know that means a cut in your wages, and I can't help that. But you can keep on livin' in the cottage......."

Young Ted saw his father's head lift, saw the surprise in his eyes, saw the relief begin to spread across his face, saw the hope light in his eyes. It was only then that the truth of their predicament had hit him, the realisation that the cottage went with the job and the clear implication that loss of job meant the roof disappearing from over their heads. Now he understood, and his features contorted as the horror at the realisation coupled with the sense of relief that it might not be a problem competed for room in the expressions that developed on his face.

For both of them the last part of Charlie Woolford's offer went unheard in the tumble of thoughts and emotions running through their minds.

"I'm sorry guv'nor," Ted heard his father say "I'm sorry, I didn't catch all of that. Did I 'ere you say we could..."

"Aye, Ted. You've worked 'ard for me these past twenty years or so, an' young Ted 'ere these last four years since school; an' then your Dad before you for my old man. I owe you a bit, an' the way things are now I could never sell off that cottage, there's no one with the money or the interest, 'specially with the state of the other three in the row, an' you may as well stay on in there. I'll be back sometime, and we can sort where we go from then on."

They walked home in silence, past the flint stone church with its square tower and the single stemmed weather vane, its arrowhead pointer showing that the light wind was blowing from the east; round the sharp left hand turn, with the school next to the King's Head on the outside edge of the bend and into the mile long straight which bisected the village; past the small shop which served the needs of rich and poor alike; past the village green bordered on two sides by fledgling Horse Chestnut trees which had been planted by the Parish Council; and on home.

Old Ted thought briefly of carrying on a few more yards into the Bull for a glass of ale before going home and breaking the news to Martha. The idea left his mind almost before it arrived. She was a good wife, and tolerant; and he played his part by remaining sober and keeping his spending on personal pleasures within the bounds of their limited income. If, however, she smelt ale on his breath with the news he was bringing home she would get very angry, very quickly, and life for the next few days would become very difficult.

Young Ted entertained a similar idea, but his purpose in visiting the Bull was to see his uncle, the landlord, who had from time to time allowed him to earn a bit of extra money working as a pot boy on busy nights. There was a chance that more work might be forthcoming, and with the vision of not much more than half his weaver's pay being the best he could expect, assuming work was available, he knew he was going to need all he could get.

Henry Johnson was his mother's brother, and he had been back in the village about six months having completed his twenty years service in the Army. He had finished his time as a Battery Sergeant Major in the Royal Artillery, and had returned with his wife and two children to take over the Bull which had coincidentally, and in the view of Henry Johnson very conveniently, become available due to the untimely death of the incumbent.

"Hallo Ted." The voice was deep and seemed to originate from way down within his uncle's barrel chest. "What're you doin' 'ere at this time of the day? Shouldn't you still be at work?"

It took him only a few minutes to explain what had happened. It took Henry precisely the same length of time to realise the seriousness of the situation, to guess what the young man would be seeking once he had finished his explanation, and to work out his answer. The pub was doing all right, but not well enough to become a charitable institution; even for his sister's family. But, the boy was a good worker and given a choice he would prefer to have him than anyone else.

"I'm really sorry to hear that, young feller, really I am, an' I'll do what I can; but life ain't easy and you know that. I'll promise you that when there is work it'll go your way, but it's more than I can do to offer you anythin' regular. You understand...?"

Ted acknowledged the questioning tone with a nod. It wasn't good, but it was better than nothing and he was grateful for that. It would help out, and there was nothing else.

".....don't do what I've been tellin' you for weeks now."

He heard his uncle's voice as if from a distance as it worked its way through his subconscious. He knew what he was talking about, but couldn't stop himself apologising for not having heard and asking him to say it again. He regretted it the instant he said it, for Henry launched forth, as Ted had known he would, on the virtues of Army life, the regular pay, the high standard of the food which appeared regularly three times a day, the excitement of foreign service and the escape from the monotony of life in a small Norfolk village. After all, it hadn't done him any harm, had it, and here he was with a good business and a secure future.....

Ted endured the monologue for as long as was necessary to remain polite, then excused himself on the basis that his mother would need him at home at a time like this, there was a lot to talk about and he would see Uncle Henry soon, and if in the meantime any work.....

He lifted the rusted, cast-iron latch and opened the door to the Ludgrove cottage outwards, stepping backwards as he did before moving round the door and into the dim living area, which was also his bedroom, pulling the door, with a protesting creak, shut behind him. They were all there, sitting round the table; his mother's face blotched with redness against the pallor of a skin rendered white with shock. A handkerchief was clutched tight in her left hand, damp from the tears it had mopped. Dad had both his hands wrapped securely around her right, holding it tightly, as much to offer himself a sense of security as her. The two girls were quiet, sitting side by side and from the looks on their faces aware that something dreadful had happened, but not understanding the implications.

His mother was talking about getting extra work to make ends meet. Taking in washing was always a good way to make money, 'cept there were others doin' that in the village and there might not be enough to go round.

He heard himself apologising, and explaining briefly where he had been. Martha looked up and acknowledged him with a grateful smile. He was a good boy, an honest young man; she knew that, and she appreciated the way his first thought had been for the family.

"We'll have to do somethin', Ted," she said to her husband. "We've still got five mouths to feed, and that's the most important thing, apart from keepin' a roof over our heads; an' Charlie Woolford's seen to that, for the time bein' anyway."

The conversation ebbed and flowed. At some point they ate a meal of bread, some cold salt beef and cabbage left over from the day before. The two girls went to bed, their heads having drooped with tiredness, and Ted remained up and about until his parents retired for the night, the discussion not having progressed any further than thankfulness about the cottage and the need to feed five people on a regular basis.

The next morning dawned bright and clear. A Saturday would normally have been a working day, but that would not be for some time again, unless Snell came up with something. It was, after all, mid-July and the harvest would be under way soon. He would need the extra labour; so there was some hope. His mother and father were still talking, and he knew they had been for much of the night. He took the two girls and they all went across the track that ran behind the cottages to the small vegetable garden that provided them with much of their sustainment during the year. At around midday a familiar deep voice boomed out from the back wall of the Bull, only about fifty yards away, and the result of the long range, but brief, conversation that took place was that he had work in the pub that night.

He was glad to get out of the house. There was nothing that could be done about the situation they were in except to get on and make the best of it, and he was unable to understand the deep-rooted fear which drove his parents incessantly to discuss their current plight. As he left, they were debating yet again the pros and cons of Martha taking in washing to supplement the family income in a village that already had more than its fair share of washerwomen.

The Bull was unusually full that night, and most of the faces were familiar. There were two main rooms in the pub, both of which served as bars, separated by a dividing wall in which there was a back-to-back fireplace. Popular among the villagers who patronised the place was the local brew of cider; a powerful concoction which was very much an acquired taste, needed experience borne of long practice to judge the pace at which it should be drunk, and which would trap the unwary as swift and sure as a poacher's snare. The resultant hangover was not a happy experience.

Unusually for him, Henry seemed to spend much of his time in conversation with one individual. Actually it was a couple, but it was the two men who did almost all the talking. Ted didn't know them, well at least he certainly didn't know the woman; but the man might be familiar. Yes, the more he thought about it the more he realised he must know the man, but for the life of him he couldn't work out from where.

"Who's that?" he enquired of his uncle, grabbing the opportunity when they were both in the cellar heaving a fresh barrel into position to replenish that which had already been consumed.

"Who'd yer mean?" was the grunted response from a man under pressure and feeling the weight of the barrel about to slip away from him.

"Y'know," said Ted, once they had recovered the situation and the barrel was in place, "them two y're talkin' to."

"Oh, them. Thought you'd know 'im at least. That's John Allsop an' 'is missus. 'E's just finished 'is seven years with the colours and 'e's back in the village now. In the Bedfords 'e were, made Lance Corporal."

"Why'd 'e leave then, if its so good an all, like you told me it is, why'd 'e come back 'ere where there's no work when 'e 'ad it all goin' for 'im in the Army?" Ted's voice contained an unnatural note of belligerence.

His uncle glanced up from his efforts to tap the barrel. The look in his eyes was of sympathy; the kind of patronising sympathy reserved by the wise and experienced for those who are neither wise nor experienced.

"It can be difficult for a family man, see," said Henry. "He didn't want to come back." The emphasis lay heavy on the "he", and Henry followed up the implication by explaining that it was the wife, and not the man, who had insisted on leaving.

"Can be an 'ard life for a woman, see." Henry's voice was softer now, his breath coming easier after the exertions of the past few minutes. "He married 'er about two year ago, and they want kids and all that an' she wouldn't 'ave any of it while 'e was in the Army an' so 'e 'ad to come out." His tone became accusing as he spoke. "Aye, many a good man gone to the wall for the wants of a woman. I could tell you a tale or two. There was this Lance Sergeant, Guardsman 'e was. Well, we was in...."

"Henry!"

The sound of his wife's voice, tinged with a hint of impatience, echoed in the cellar and stopped him in mid flow.

"Coming dear."

"Aye," thought Ted, "many a good man." He smiled, thankful for the intercession which had saved him from one of his uncle's tales.

Upstairs again he worked around the bars and tables, moving out of curiosity nearer and nearer the two people occupying the table towards the far end and to which his uncle continued to pay a disproportionate amount of his attention. John Allsop was a well-built man, his hair cut short and his moustache bristling and swept upwards in the fashion of the military. His face was marked by a star-shaped scar high on the left cheekbone; no doubt the result of a wound collected in a feat of arms in some far flung corner of the Empire. He got up to go to the toilet, and as he moved he naturally slipped into that erect posture with the slight swing of his shoulders that showed a man had done his time with the colours.

Mrs Allsop was a nice enough looking lady. A bit younger than her husband, she was probably around 24 years old. She was neatly dressed, sitting upright as was the fashion of the time; she displayed a figure that was shapely, yet comfortably proportioned.

"You can do a lot these days with corsets, though." The thought flashed, uncharitably, through his mind.

The hands, resting in her lap, looked strong and capable, but nonetheless feminine. Her face was round, softly moulded, the mouth was wide, but not overly so. Her nose was perhaps a little too long, but not out of proportion, and the eyes were a delicate shade of brown. A soft pile of hair framed it all, brown with just a subtle hint of reddishness, beneath which a delicate pair of ears were on partial display.

"You finished with that," he heard himself say as he pointed towards her glass.

"Yes thanks." The voice had a nasal quality to it, but not harsh or unpleasant. As she spoke she smiled; a white, attractive smile, revealing as she did so a slightly offset front tooth.

"Nice lady," he thought as he moved away towards the bar; and then thought no more of it as he carried on his evening's work.

The Allsops had just finished with the Army. It might be truer to say that the Army had finished with them, or more properly him. John Allsop had not been a great success as a soldier; indeed, he had not been a great success at anything in his life. Something of a confidence trickster, he had gone south from the village as a young man to seek his fortune in or around London. Several attempts at work in a variety of offices in a range of clerical jobs had not met with any great success, and money was not being earned at a rate that suited his aspirations. Regrettably, whilst his clerical talents were enough to sustain him in routine work, his knowledge and expertise in the keeping of accounts was not sufficiently good to prevent the very early detection of his first attempt at embezzlement. The judge was a martinet, with firm views on the treatment of the criminal fraternity; but as a first offender was prepared at least to offer a choice between prison and the Army.

The Bedfordshire Regiment had the nearest depot, and it was to there that John Allsop was delivered to begin his military career. As had been the case in civilian life, the impression he created was, initially, good. Officers and NCOs marked him out as a man with potential, and someone who might rise to senior rank in due course. It was this same good initial impression that had captured the interest of Thurza Jackson, a seamstress from a small village near Aldershot.

They met on a Saturday, at a market where she was offering tailoring services and where John Allsop, having moved to the shadow of a tent where no one would see him, ripped his shirt and took the damaged garment to her seeking its repair. He wooed and won her heart, coincidentally over a period of time when the Bedfordshire Regiment had realised that they had on their hands not a potential senior NCO, but a potential liability. Efforts by a number of his superiors to catch him out had failed, he did just enough to keep out of trouble, and had grown wise enough to know how much he could bend the rules without breaking them.

Neither was he very popular with his peer group. The star shaped scar on his left cheekbone was the result of a colleague's attempt, with a bottle in the canteen, to assist the officers and senior NCOs of the Bedfordshires by removing John Allsop from the Regiment without recourse to the normal disciplinary or administrative procedures.

Having survived his service, although only a Lance Corporal at the end of his seven years with the colours, he was able to convince himself that the blame for his lack of advancement lay not with him, but with the Army; and that he was forced to leave so that his true potential could be realised in the outside world.

Thurza, having fallen for his charms, had accepted his analysis of his future in the Army, had explained to her mother that the family reservations about marrying a soldier were unfounded as John would be leaving in a couple of years and accordingly had wed the man in the parish church in Fleet. At the end of his service they had returned to Norfolk to embark on the successful career denied him in the service of the King.

Sunday in the Ludgrove household was a ritual that even the news of the unemployment of the two breadwinners could not disrupt. After breakfast the whole family, all dressed in their best clothes, headed for the church for morning service. It was as much a social event as a religious occasion. Everyone who mattered in village life was there, and those who did not attend, some sixty percent of the parish, were probably not worth knowing.

As they approached the church they heard footsteps running behind them, changing tempo as the runner slowed his pace to come in alongside the family group.

"I had to get to you before you went into church!" The words came in rushes, between the gasps as he sought to recover his breath. The Ludgroves smiled their welcome at Charlie Woolford's son, James. Old Charlie was a bit of a rough diamond, but James showed the obvious benefits of his father's investment in the boy's education. The accent, the poise, the manners were all those of a well bred young gentleman, but to young Ted he was still Jim Woolford, and his reception from the Ludgroves was not the formal acknowledgement to an employer's eldest son, but genuine pleasure at seeing him.

"I'm so terribly sorry all this has happened. I can't tell you how much of a strain it has been. Father's had the most awful time trying to decide what to do for the best, it's really been most terribly difficult for him. He hasn't...."

The words tailed off as Martha's hand came to rest on his

forearm, the gentle pressure of her fingers through the folds of his jacket stilling the tumble of words.

"It's all right, James, it's all right," the soft, rounded tones of her Norfolk accent calming the agitated young man. "We unnerstand. It's been comin' for years, and we've all known it." The words, stating the obvious that may have been known, but which had been dismissed from the mind as being too painful to contemplate, masked the stomach-churning worry felt by both Ted and Martha.

"Yes, I know, but....," James' earnest voice was still pitched high from a mixture of the haste with which he had chased through the village, and the anxiety that the Ludgroves would be rendered destitute by his father's decision.

"But nothin'." Martha's voice displayed a calm that betrayed her true feelings. "C'mon now, we'll be late if we don't get a move on. And anyway, where's your father? It's not like Mr Woolford to miss the Sunday service."

"Oh, he'll be along. I ran on ahead of him because I wanted to talk to you before he got to church. I just wanted to say, you know... how much I realise...."

"Jim," young Ted's voice was gentle as he guided his friend by the elbow, "there's no more to be said, there really isn't." They moved up the short path that led from the road into the church porch and waited as a number of people spoke briefly to the vicar, standing by the church door in company with Bert Chalmers, a church warden who ran, with the help of his wife Agnes, the village store. Agnes would already be inside, in the Chalmers' usual pew, with their daughter Betty.

Ted knew what would happen as soon as he walked into the Church. Betty Chalmers would be on the watch, and as she saw him she would glance into his eyes, then demurely lower her eyelids, turning her head away to look to the front. It happened precisely as he expected, and he moved with James Woolford, together with his father, who had arrived, flustered and a little dishevelled, at the last minute, to a pew level with the Chalmers from where he could keep glancing at Betty.

She was a pretty girl, and the apple of her father's eye. Bert and Agnes knew, as did most of the congregation, that Betty had developed a very large soft spot for the young Ludgrove. It was the generally accepted wisdom that the young man would be a fool not to capitalise on the situation, for he would wed an attractive and pleasant young lady and would benefit from her parents' ownership of the only shop in the village.

Generally accepted wisdom it might have been, but the potential long-term association of his daughter with a weaver's son was not a prospect which brought great pleasure to Bert Chalmers. He had his eyes on something better, and anyway he was certainly not going to let her waste herself, and his hard-earned money, by making a bad match. Agnes took a more sanguine view. The boy was honest, hard working and loyal. He was a well-built young man with no physical defects, he had sober habits and he would probably make her happy; and she could do a lot worse.

Ted was oblivious to all this as the strains of the processional hymn creaked from the worn pipes of the small organ, a cacophony of coughing spreading throughout the building as throats were cleared and untrained voices prepared to give praise to God. His glances to the left took in a slim young girl with dark, soft hair dressed in ringlets beneath a wide brimmed hat, a mouth that was small, red and inviting, and a pair of dark brown eyes that met his from beneath lowered lashes. He felt stirrings within which he did not really understand, but which he knew made him want to be with her.

Martha, in the pew behind, saw the electricity passing between them and wondered, not for the first time, at what the future might hold for her son.

Edward Snell stared straight ahead as the vicar sought to explain to an uncomprehending congregation the hidden significance of the words used by St Paul in his letter to the Ephesians, and its importance for them in their daily lives.

Twenty-five years of age, he was a man racked with

frustration at the cards dealt to him by the hand of fate. He should have been born to the aristocracy, he should have lived as part of the land owning classes from the outset, he should have had sophistication bred into him from the beginning, he should have been endowed with natural charm and good looks. Instead, he found himself the son of a ship owner whose own father had made the family fortune in trade with India; he had lived the early part of his life in Boston and Kings Lynn making his childhood acquaintances from amongst the children of his father's business associates. He had suffered terribly at the school to which his father's money had sent him, taunted horribly by the other boys for his provincial dress, and middle to working class attitudes.

He found it difficult to form personal relationships. Inconsequential small talk did not come easily and the deep-seated resentment at his origins and the treatment he had received at the hands of his student contemporaries contributed to make him standoffish and arrogant; and domineering towards those he considered to be less than his equal.

His character was not helped by his looks: he was slightly built, with a small frame and stood only five feet seven inches tall. Thin lips sat beneath a hooked nose and deep set eyes, a combination which had drawn many allusions to Mr Punch, the aggressive and unpleasant glove puppet that was a feature of side shows on every beach in every seaside resort in the land. When he revealed his teeth in what passed for a smile, or more usually a grimace, they were very small, set in a disproportionately large expanse of pink gum, and they were discoloured slightly brown by the incessant smoking of cigarettes.

And by heaven, a cigarette was something he could use now. God alive, would the bloody man not stop talking and let them all get away within a decent time. He reconciled his own presence that morning with the fact that being seen in church was part of the price he had to pay for achieving the place in the community and the status he craved.

It had probably been a mistake for him to go into the

Army from school. He knew, or at least he should have known, that the Royal Military Academy at Woolwich, where he learned his trade as a Gunner, was going to be an extension of the hell that had been his boarding school. He would never know what it was that had made him do it, and he had no idea why he had withstood it. Whatever it was inside him that drove him had been sufficient to overcome the loneliness and the social alienation for which he blamed his fellow Gentleman Cadets.

He had sought solace in his work, and had achieved high marks. He felt he should have passed out as the top cadet, and blamed his social background when he failed to achieve it. He took no part in the social affairs of the College, save those events that the rituals of the military life meant he had to attend. These events he could cope with, for they were structured and followed a natural form and he did not need to make special efforts. It was the house parties, the boating trips, the shooting weekends, the visits to London clubs, the afternoons of tennis that he had shunned. Not only did he find it difficult to mingle with brother officers, but also he felt awkward and ill at ease in the presence of women. He was only too aware of his physical shortcomings, and that he was talked about with distaste behind his back. His frustrations extended beyond his social status and his physical attributes to the more elemental human functions. His need to dominate fellow human beings meant he desired women with a passion that was heightened by the inaccessibility of those who moved in the social classes to which he aspired.

His first visit to a prostitute had been an unsatisfactory affair. He had taken to going alone on the train from Woolwich Arsenal to Waterloo at the weekends, whereupon he would seek to lose himself in the public houses, shops, theatres and clubs which abounded in the city, hoping against hope that he would not meet anyone he knew. It was on one of these early visits that he had met, on leaving a theatre in Shaftesbury Avenue, a woman of uncertain years, but attractive nonetheless in a rounded, comfortable sort of way. Her offer had taken him by surprise, and he found hard at first to understand the words she used, but overcome by curiosity he accepted and followed her. Once they arrived in her small room, an untidy hovel at the top of a steep, worn staircase and smelling of cooked cabbage, stale beer and urine, he began to wonder what it was he was doing there. He thought of leaving, of putting down his money and running, he thought of disease and the social disgrace if anyone discovered what he was doing.

But he had never seen a woman naked, and his curiosity at what might take place in the physical act of love overcame his revulsion and fear and the smell of ale on her breath, and he allowed her to remove her clothes and most of his. The coupling, when it eventually happened, had ended swiftly and unsatisfactorily, the climax occurring much more quickly than it ever had during the frequent bouts of masturbation in which he had indulged over the years.

As time went on he had improved his choice of women and had been more particular about what he had asked them to do. He had also realised with some satisfaction that it was not they who controlled him, but he, with his money, who could control them. He had at last found something he could dominate on terms of his choosing, and drew great satisfaction from it.

His head jerked up as he realised that the vicar had come to the end of his sermon. He felt a twinge of embarrassment at the stirring in his loins which had resulted from his daydreaming of the women he had bought for pleasure on his trips to London. Having glanced around him to ensure that no one was watching him, or had noticed the physical manifestation of his feelings, he allowed his thoughts to drift away to how he might assuage his sexual appetite in a small village so far from civilisation as he had come to know it in the Army he had left some six months ago now.

"..... and may the blessings of God Almighty...."

The closing words of the service penetrated Edward Snell's thoughts, bringing with them a sense of relief that the routine ordeal of Sunday morning was coming to an end.

"...be among you and remain with you always, amen."

The congregation stood for the recessional hymn, singing the words without thinking, uttering phrases of deep significance without any realisation of their true meaning; and looking ahead already to the things that needed to be done as soon as the service was over. In the crush that followed the move towards the door, young Ted found himself walking alongside Betty, forced enticingly close to her by the press of people around them. His hand brushed the bare flesh of her forearm, and he felt a tingling shudder pass through him. She looked up, caught his eye and simultaneously they felt a surge of longing, neither thinking about or knowing whether it was love or lust, but simply realising that they needed to see each other alone, and the sooner the better.

Behind them, Edward Snell's thin little mouth twisted in a sneer, demonstrating an outward contempt for love's young dream, whilst inwardly fantasising about what he would like to do to Betty Chalmers if he had just half the chance. He dismissed the thoughts from his mind almost as they entered, knowing full well that with her father's place in the village she was untouchable short of the marriage bed, and that was not a prospect he had in mind for someone from the lower social orders. His frustration boiled over, and forcing his way past the two youngsters he barged his way out of the church, quite careless of the disruption he caused to the orderly, slow moving crush of people wending their way to the door and the vicar's handshake.

Ted felt himself falling as something straight and hard caught him across the back of the knees, and not knowing where he might land reached to grab at anything which might support him; which happened to be Betty Chalmers' soft and gentle left hand. He sat down hard with a thump on the parish chest. Made of good English Oak and already three hundred years old it bore the weight of the young Ludgrove with equanimity, and subsequently, and very shortly after, the combined weight of the young Ludgrove and the young Chalmers as Betty took the opportunity to fall, quite by chance of course, into place alongside the boy who had been almost the sole occupant of her thoughts for many months now.

"Rude bugger!" was the thought in Ted's mind, but by the time it reached his mouth, and mindful of the close proximity of a very pretty young lady of gentle manners in whom he had more than a passing interest, it had translated to: "Not a nice thing for a genn'lman to do, were it?"

"No," she responded, "not very nice at all really." The voice was well modulated and nicely rounded by the local accent; and he was smitten yet further.

They had about fifteen seconds to complete the conversation before propriety would force them to stand and continue the progress to the door, where family obligations would force them into separate groups. Too late, James Woolford appeared beside them, remarked on the rudeness of Snell and, ever the gentleman, offered a hand to Betty as she made to stand.

"Any plans for today, Ted," he enquired. "Dad's thinking of a trip to Norwich and I'm sure he wouldn't mind if you came along."

Ted's mind was working very fast indeed. He had almost lost the opportunity once, and here was just a glimmer of hope that he might yet recover the situation.

"No," a pause, "no, sorry. I'm workin' in the Bull this lunch time, and then I've got things to do for dad that'll take me up by Woodman's Copse from three o'clock onwards."

As well as being pretty, Betty was bright and alert; and the significance of his words was not lost on her. A flash of her eyes met Ted's, and he knew the message was passed and had been understood, and his heart surged inside his chest.

Lunchtime on Sunday in the Bull was not an occasion where women were normally found. They were at home, organising whatever there might be for the midday meal. The menus would vary from goose or chicken or joints of meat at one end of the scale to broth and bread at the other; but in most cases it was the main family gathering of the week and its preparation was women's work.

Ted was pleased to be helping out in the pub yet again. The more work he could get the better, and it kept him away from the cottage where a depressing air of hopelessness was beginning to pervade.

"I'll have a pint of ale, and a half for the girl." Ted, bending over a barrel to check its position, jumped at the sound of a woman's voice coming at him unexpectedly, and there was no suggestion of "please" as she spoke, but rather a hint of belligerence.

He looked round. "Sorry Missus." He used the only comfortable form of address he could think of to Mary Bartram. "Mrs" was inappropriate since she was not a married lady. "Miss" seemed equally out of place as the girl for whom she had ordered the half pint, and who was standing beside her, was her daughter Alice. "Missus" with plenty of Norfolk wound into it bridged the gap nicely.

"Sorry, could you say that again please?"

"I could, but I don't see why you couldn't listen proper in the first place. If you're goin' to work 'ere you might as well learn 'ow to do it right." The hint of belligerence was now a touch stronger, and he still had no idea what she had ordered.

"A pint of ale, and a half pint, please." Alice's voice was softer than her mother's, and the little smile on her face showed that she understood Ted's discomfort and wanted to help; and anyway, he was a nice lad and a girl could do worse. Ted blushed. He knew full well that in a small village, and at the age he was, there was constant jousting for position among the young folk as to who would pair off with whom, and he recognised the look on Alice's face. Alice was nice enough, but remembering his forthcoming meeting with Betty his mind was on higher things and he turned away to fill their order before moving to the other end of the bar.

From the other side of the pub, looking through from the saloon, another customer saw the mischievous smile and the twinkle as Alice flirted at Ted. His mind cast back over the stories he had heard about the Bartrams. They survived in the village by taking in washing and cleaning from some of the bigger houses. Indeed, if Martha Ludgrove were to pursue her plan to undertake this form of work the Bartrams would be among her stiffest competition. The rumours in the village also reflected a belief that something more than washing and cleaning was a source of income in that household, and that gentlemen from elsewhere in the county could from time to time be seen arriving at or leaving the isolated cottage at the northern tip of the village. Furthermore, so it was said, the daughter helped her mother with the family workload, and that assistance also extended beyond washing and cleaning.

Edward Snell left the pub to wend his way home whereupon he would join his father in a lunch prepared by their housekeeper, and to which his father would have invited a number of guests from among the local community. He would endure this weekly event with as much good grace as he could muster before taking to his horse for as much of the afternoon as possible. His thoughts as he rode home were with the Bartrams, either of whom would do for the purposes he had in mind. His preference might be for the older woman, who might smell a little, but who would bring experience to the proceedings. On the other hand, there were attractions in younger flesh, and whilst thin and pale, Alice was not without her good points.

The sun shone down, darkened gold set in a sky of cobalt blue. There was a red flash of colour as a Green Woodpecker, startled by the approach of a human being, flew straight and low out of the coppice and away to a neighbouring strip of woodland. It was joined by a Blackbird which, in its self appointed role as the sentry for the rest of the wildlife in the area, departed noisily with its familiar alarm call echoing out for all to hear. Swarms of small flying insects gathered in the shade of the trees, and every footstep along the track from the main road raised its own little cloud of dust.

Suddenly, there was a crack as something trod on a branch just beyond the thick bramble hedge that marked the south-western edge of the small clump of trees. A pair of

Wood Pigeons clattered noisily out of the topmost branches of an Elm tree, and Betty Chalmers' head snapped round, partly in apprehension, partly in anticipation.

"Darn," thought Ted, as he removed his foot from the broken remnants of some long-felled tree left behind many years ago by the careless, and anonymous, woodman for whom the copse had been named.

"Sorry," he said, "I didn't mean to startle you."

She smiled as he emerged from the shadows.

"That's all right. Why were you hiding anyway?"

Always tell the truth, his mother had told him. It's always easier to tell the truth, no matter how painful or embarrassing, than it is to try and sort out the pain and difficulties caused by lies, however small they might be.

"I wanted to be sure it was you, and that you didn't have anyone with you in case me bein' 'ere might embarrass you."

There was no hesitation in his voice, just a certainty that he was right to have said what he had, and a mature calmness beyond his years which sent her heart fluttering and clattering; just like the Wood Pigeons that had startled her only seconds before.

There was a silence. What to do? Neither of them had thought beyond meeting, and had no idea what the next move should be or ought to be. A man had to take the lead in these circumstances and despite a dry mouth redolent with the bitterness of flowing adrenaline, sweating hands and a heart rate significantly higher than normal he managed to suggest that they might walk a little.

Given that her only desire was to be with him, and that an invitation to walk over broken glass barefoot was something with which she would happily have complied, Betty turned onto the track, and, inserting her own contribution to their decision making headed north, away from the village. As they fell in beside each other they both simultaneously felt the burning urge to touch each other, to hold hands; whereupon Ted's were thrust deep into his pockets and Betty clutched her small handbag tightly in front of her with both her's and they walked on in a somewhat embarrassed silence. Ah, but courtship was a slow process.

A hot, sunny July Sunday afternoon in Norfolk could be very boring. It could be especially boring when you were seventeen, something of a social outcast among the local population and of an income sufficiently low not to allow for visits to more exciting places further afield. So it was, with nothing to do except to watch her mother sleep off the effects of a couple of pints of lunch-time ale, that Alice Bartram walked disconsolately to the end of the garden. She passed through the wicket gate that led on to the open fields beyond and onto the track that allowed visitors to reach the cottage without being seen too easily by the prying eyes in the rest of the village.

She thought for a moment about the men who had passed through the gate from time to time, how she had lain in her room listening to the grunts and sighs as her mother earned a few extra shillings to keep them from the poor house; and even as she wondered what it might feel like, she gave thanks to God for a mother who, despite her faults, wanted better for her daughter than she herself had, and protected her as much as she could from the less savoury aspects of life. Marriage was what Alice sought, and she was going to hang on to what she had until the right man appeared. Not that she would necessarily wait for the matrimonial bed before sacrificing her purity; just as good to get hold of the right man and then put him in a position where he had no choice but to marry. Many were the families in the village, across all the social divides, where comparison of marriage certificates and the birth date of the first-born showed a difference that was something less than the normal gestation period for the creation of a full term human infant. No disgrace in that, and people had very short memories.

Sitting out here in the sunshine on a grassy bank at the edge of the trees wouldn't achieve anything, however. She needed to make serious inroads into some young man's life, and Ted Ludgrove was high on her list of potential suitors;

indeed, he was at the top of it. But the means, ah the means whereby she might set and trip her snare?

Her thoughts wandered as she drifted in and out of a light doze, the combined effects of a half pint of ale, a lunch of bread and cheese and the warmth of the sun taking its toll. Suddenly, with dreams of a young man of five feet eleven inches tall, light blond hair, blue eyes and a slim young body, and a nice tingly feeling spreading its way up towards her tummy from somewhere between her thighs, she was brought to wakefulness by the sound of a single horse approaching from the south.

Ted and Betty were scarcely able to believe their luck. They had spent almost an hour in each other's company, and after the first few awkward moments had overcome their shyness and were chattering nineteen to the dozen. They were reaching the stage when they knew she would have to return home, and both were sensing the longing for time to stand still so that they would not have to separate. Moving back south, towards the village, and deep in discussion about how they might arrange their next meeting, Ted had just plucked up the courage to reach out and clasp her left hand as gently as he could, had just time to feel a surge of excitement as she accepted his advance and began to reach out with her right hand, turning so that they would be facing each other, had just begun to wonder what might happen next when the scream pierced through the sultry quiet of the afternoon.

Ted ran, following the direction from which the noise had come, homing in on the next two or three screams in the series before something happened to cut them off; but by then he had the direction. Pausing only to glance over his shoulder as Betty gasped out an exhortation for him to be careful, he pushed his way through the undergrowth towards the eastern edge of Woodman's Copse, towards the point where it joined the northernmost tip of the village.

He saw the horse first, a chestnut mare which he seemed to recognise, but could not remember from where. Then he saw the couple on the ground, the man on top. He saw the man sit up astride the woman, watched as she struck up at him with clawed hands and kicked with her legs in a futile attempt to throw him off and recoiled as the man grabbed both her hands and then drawing back his right hand smashed his fist into her face, spitting out "bitch" as he did so.

It did not take a genius to realise that the lady was unimpressed by the attentions being forced on her, and that something needed to be done. As the woman slumped backwards, half stunned by the blow with her legs having stopped kicking Ted heard his own voice calling out.

"'Ere, stop that!"

By now he was only ten feet from the struggling couple. The man turned his head up to the left to see the source of the interference and Ted recognised the deep-seated eyes and the hooked nose, and saw the spittle dribbling from the thin lips of Edward Snell.

"Bugger off you little bastard, this is nothing to do with you."

"I'm sorry," Ted's voice was a mixture of concern generated by what he was witnessing, and by the fact he was in confrontation with a member of the village hierarchy who was potentially going to be both his and his father's employer; but who nonetheless should not have been doing what he was doing to a woman. Alice looked up towards Ted, and he gasped in recognition of the little face with the swelling developing on her left cheek from the blow she had received. The pleading look in her eyes told its own story and he decided he must help her as best he could. For her own part, Alice could not believe that her knight in shining armour had appeared out of nowhere in her hour of need and was clearly bent on rescuing her from the attentions of the awful creature that even now straddled her stomach.

She had stood up at the approach of the horse, and had politely answered up when Edward Snell had spoken to her. She had not been concerned, not even when he had dismounted and approached her. However, the questions and the suggestions had then gone beyond those that a young girl with her background could comprehend, although his desires were clear and obvious. It was her refusal that had made him angry, and her turning away to go home that had caused his frustration to boil over; and that was when he had grabbed her by the arm and she had screamed in pain and fear.

"I said bugger off!" By now Edward Snell was in a half crouch, his left leg still crooked, lower half flat on the ground alongside Alice's body, the right bent with his hand resting on the knee ready to lever himself up.

"No, I won't, not 'till you get up an' leave 'er alone." He could hardly believe it was him speaking, but the clear distress of the girl and the arrogance of Snell, especially following on the incident in Church earlier that day, angered him, and made him determined to allow his own sense of justice to take its course.

By now Snell was on his feet, with the riding crop dangling by its strap from his right wrist. Suddenly, and quite unexpectedly, he grasped it firmly in his right hand and with a rapid sweeping slash brought the crop round in the direction of Ted's face.

The young weaver's background did not suit him for fighting. He had no experience of it, and certainly had no schooling in it. But, he did have good reactions, and a natural strength of the sort to be found in any young man of his upbringing in that part of the world. Consequently, Edward Snell's attempt to lay Ted's face open to the bone was unsuccessful. Instead, the crop cut a sharp weal on young Ludgrove's left forearm, raised in self-protection, at which point Ted's concern at Snell's social status, his potential as an employer and his own sense of justice were subsumed by a blind rage as the pain cut through him.

Snell's attempt to strike Ted had thrown him off balance and left undefended his face and the upper part of his body. Untutored in fighting he might have been, unskilled on the pugilists art he certainly was, but the opening offered by Snell's exposed position gave Ted the opportunity to strike out with his free right fist.

The first blow was into the shoulder, more of a push than an actual punch since the timing was all wrong. The second was more effective and took Snell square in the chest, about six inches below his chin; and at this point Alice made her own small contribution simply by being there. As he stumbled backwards Snell's heel caught against her prostrate body and he fell in an undignified heap on his backside, his discomfort made worse by the fact that in reaching out to break his fall he plunged his arm into a bed of tall and virulent stinging nettles.

Ted's rage was such that he would not let matters rest. He followed up, and stepping across Alice was in time to catch Snell as he rose to a half crouch and smashed his fist down into the mouth that only a few seconds ago had been drooling with lust at the prospect of what Alice Bartram might offer, willingly or otherwise. He grunted in pain as his fist crashed against Snell's teeth, cutting his own knuckles, but allowing him the satisfaction of seeing blood spurt from torn lips and the pleasure of watching the creature he now despised fall further into the nettles which brushed against his injured face and his neck, causing yet more agony.

It was obvious the fight was over. Breathing heavily, Ted looked down on his victim, no longer sure what to do now his rage was subsiding when the decision was made for him by a gentle, sobbing moan coming from behind him, somewhere near his feet. He turned, and knelt beside Alice.

"It's all right, 'e can't 'urt you now. Come on; let's get you 'ome."

He stood, and held out his hand to pull her up. As he did so he was aware of a movement behind him and looked round in time to see Snell, having picked himself out of the nettles, lurching past them both and towards his horse.

"Ted, whatever's happened?"

"What's going on here?" Two separate female voices coming at him from left and right.

He looked down at the sheer adoration on Alice's face as she gazed longingly at her rescuer; looked up to his right in time to watch the concern on Betty's face change to anger as she saw the unmistakable expression on the face of "that little strumpet"; then to his left to see Mary Bartram like a galleon under full sail marching to the rescue of her daughter; and then up and back round to his right in time to see Edward Snell riding off whilst bestowing upon him a look of malevolence that made it clear he would be making life for the young Ludgrove as hard and unpleasant as he could, as soon as he could.

"Oh bugger," muttered Ted, resignedly. "That's done it."

Chapter 2

Gone For a Soldier

"C'mon, get a move on!" Impatience showed clearly in Alfie James' voice and on his normally cheerful face as he waited by the barrack room door for his two friends. It was a warm, July Sunday and the bus from Palace Barracks, Holywood, on the eastern edge of Belfast, to the nearby seaside resort of Bangor would be leaving shortly. Carefully laid plans for an afternoon drinking the odd pint, eating some of the traditional delicacies of a British seaside resort and casting an eye over the local female population were being placed at risk.

"Ted, we'll miss the bloody bus if you don't get a move on." Peter Dakin's voice held the same note of urgency as his friend's. The one chance they'd managed for some time of their own for weeks now, and the prospect of Private Ted Ludgrove wrecking it was putting a serious, albeit probably temporary, strain on their friendship. Ted had seemed unnaturally morose during the course of the day, and his two mates really couldn't understand it. All right, so nobody really liked Church Parades, but there were worse ways of spending a Sunday morning, and the prospect of the forthcoming outing should have been enough to lift his spirits.

"I'm coming, I'm coming." He was pushing at the ill-fitting door of his locker, trying to make it close. Why couldn't the bloody Army even provide a simple thing like a locker that worked? In a fit of bad temper he bashed his fist against the latch and whilst he was successful in his objective of securing the door he paid the price of a bleeding knuckle on the second finger of his right hand.

The steel horseshoe surround on the heels of his leather ammunition boots clacked on the linoleum floor of the barrack room as he marched swiftly along to join his impatient friends. He held up his right hand to look ruefully at the damage. It was two years to the day now that a similar injury had been caused by another punch; the one that had split Edward Snell's lip and changed his life beyond recognition.

His thoughts that Sunday evening two years ago had been in turmoil. His world since the Friday afternoon in that fateful week had stood on its head. In two days he had found himself out of work, in love with a pretty girl who now harboured suspicions about his motives and loyalty, adored by another girl in whom he had no interest and hated by a man who had the power fundamentally to do him and his family serious damage. And the Ludgrove family still had five mouths to feed.

By the Monday morning he had made his decision. Calmly and with careful precision he had explained it to his parents, following his mother's dictum that to tell the truth was better than to lie; although he didn't go into all the details about his feelings for Betty and the complications introduced into his life by the fact that it was Alice Bartram whose virtue he had preserved. He could reduce the number of mouths to be fed by one, bring some much needed money into the household by sending home some of his pay and perhaps make life easier for his family by simply not being there for a while. And so it was, having promised his mother that he would write regularly, his father that he would work hard and send money and his sisters that he would be careful he set out on the road to Norwich, twenty-five miles to the north, to offer his services to His Majesty's Ninth Regiment of Foot, The Norfolk Regiment.

"Ah, bugger it. Alfie and Peter were right. No sense in broodin' over it. What's done is done." His voice rang the length of the barrack room. "All right, keep yer 'air on. I'm comin'."

The warmth of the sun hit them as they left the cool shadows of the barrack block. It would certainly be hot today, and they anticipated with some pleasure the smoothness with which the ale would slide down. As they walked round the edge of the parade square in the direction of the guardroom, past which they must go to catch the bus on the main Belfast to Bangor road just outside the encampment, they glanced at, and spared a thought for, three of their colleagues marching at the ludicrously fast one hundred and forty paces to the minute, complete with rifle and pack, sweat streaming down their reddened faces, and with so much moisture escaping from their overheating bodies that even under the rough serge of their field uniforms the dark stains of sweat could be seen under their armpits.

"Lup, jack, lup, jack, lup jack!" The orderly sergeant's voice shouted the time, adapting the English language, in this case "left, right," as NCOs in the British Army are wont to do, to his own particular vernacular. "Wot are you three lookin' at? If you're enjoyin' this so much you can come and join us. No? Then get about yer business. Lup, jack, lup jack....Maaark Time!"

The three friends very quickly looked away, quite certain that they did not wish to take up the orderly sergeant's kind offer to join their three colleagues in part of the daily routine associated with time spent in clink; and determined not to give him the opportunity to repeat it.

"Why does Ned do it?" asked Alfie James, of no one in particular; a note of exasperation in his voice. His obvious concern ran counter to the facade of cheerful fatalism that was his hallmark.

"Blowed if I know," said Peter Dakin, his slow Norfolk drawl rounding out the words, in response to a question that actually required no answer.

The object of their discussion was Private Ned Preece, citizen of Walthamstow in the north-eastern part of London; fugitive from the parents of a young lady who now pushed his infant daughter on her daily outing for fresh air through the park at Hoe Street; resenter of discipline and, consequently, somewhat out of place in an organisation which was a by-word for exerting it in its most petty and irritating form; and consumer of alcohol in gargantuan proportions when the money and the mood took him. It was his reaction to discipline that got him into trouble on a regular basis, but it was his behaviour when drunk that put him in the guardroom, as it had done three times already in the first seven months of 1914. And Ned was the smallest, thinnest and scruffiest of the three young men nearing exhaustion on the square.

They signed out at the hatch window in the guardroom wall, their booking out to Bangor causing Lance Corporal Joseph Floyd a passing twinge of envy as he surveyed his own prospects as second-in-command of the guard for the twenty hours leading up to eight o'clock the next morning.

"'Bye lads. 'Ave a good time then."

"We will, Corporal, we will." Ted's voice carried the subtle intonation which demonstrated not only his own avowed intent to enjoy himself, but the clear knowledge that Lance Corporal Floyd would not be doing so and that this was something which caused him considerable personal satisfaction.

They moved off, three minutes to the bus stop and four before the bus was due; Peter Dakin's left arm brushing and smudging the chalk writing on the blackboard on the guardroom wall which delineated the routine for Sunday the twenty-sixth of July 1914. He wiped at the white marks standing out on his uniform sleeve, and they had all but disappeared by the time the double decked omnibus ground to a halt in front of them.

Several pints of stout and a couple of plates of cockles, and three young soldiers of the King were in a state of relaxed contentment. However, their plans for devastating the local female population with their charm and joie de vivre had, as usual, fallen by the wayside. They had played on a few of the seaside amusements, one in particular being a depiction of red-coated soldiers fighting off avenging Zulus with the accuracy of their rifles controlled by an ingenious system of hidden rods. For a penny it offered several minutes of boisterous and competitive fun, usually culminating in victory for the soldiers of the Queen Empress. Its particular attraction to the soldiers of the Ninth Regiment of Foot was the brass plate informing players that the source of their amusement had been manufactured in Dereham in Norfolk.

The amusement over, and aware that, with beer at a ha'penny a pint, they were denting severely the money they had saved over the past few weeks, and remembering that the next weekend included a Bank Holiday on the Monday, the three friends decided that a walk along the seafront, a cup of tea and a return to barracks was the best option for the last part of the afternoon.

"Bit of a bastard last week, weren't it?" Alfie turned the conversation round to one of the more common topics amongst the military community: the ongoing difficulties with the Irish population.

"What were that then?" Peter Dakin could be vague, and had little interest in affairs outside the daily routines of the military life he had come to love; although this was not an emotion to which he would ever have admitted. His options prior to joining, however, had been limited. Like Ted he had been a victim of the collapse of weaving in Norfolk just after the turn of the century. However, he was also an orphan, and on leaving the orphanage with no prospect of work and no prospect of a home other than to sleep in a ditch, the Army had offered a very inviting alternative. He had moved from one form of institution to another and had found the transition easy, compared to many. He and Ted had joined about the same time, and it was Peter Dakin's calm approach to institutional trivia and his warm friendship that had helped Ted overcome his own loneliness on leaving home, and his frustration at the pettiness at which the Army could be so adept whenever it chose.

"That poor sod in the shipyard. Catholic 'e were, an' they pushed 'im in the water an' threw that shipyard confetti stuff at 'im till 'e wen' under an' drowned." He referred to the local name for the scrap metal and rivets that were a by-product of the ship building industry.

"No reason, just cos' 'e were a Catholic."

Ted was only half listening to his two chums, not so much bored by the topic as knowing enough about it to be able to listen with only half an ear whilst being consumed with some of his own thoughts. His mother's letters had kept him in touch with life in the village, and with the family fortunes. They had only come about once a month, to save postage and to try and preserve some secrecy as to his true whereabouts, but when they did they were long and full of news.

It had been a year after he left before his father had found regular work. If ever Alfred Snell had intended to honour his word to Charlie Woolford, he certainly wasn't going to after his son returned home, his face streaming blood, complaining that he had been assaulted, for no reason, by one of the local hooligans; someone called Ludgrove. The boy could thank his lucky stars that he had run off before the constable could be brought down from Norwich to place him in arrest.

Old Ted had kept the family going by a mixture of odd jobs, and improving the garden not only to sustain the family better, but also to make a surplus that he could sell. Added to the money from young Ted's Army wages and a bit from Martha taking in what washing she could, they had got by. Then came the news that Bert Chalmers was expanding and moving into fruit and vegetable production. He would use this to support the village shop, and two others in neighbouring villages, and sell off the surplus to a number of outlets he had identified. Bert might not have wanted the younger Ludgrove as a son-in-law, but he knew a loyal and conscientious worker when he saw one and the older Ludgrove certainly came into that category. Accordingly, he had offered old Ted a position that brought him up something above his former wages as a weaver.

The letter from his mother that told him his contribution to the household income was no longer required came as a great relief. The pay of a private soldier in a line infantry regiment was a basic one shilling a day, with a messing allowance of an additional three pence a day. After stoppages his net weekly pay was some two shillings a week less than the wages of an agricultural labourer in Caithness, and in 1914 this was deemed to be the poorest paid job in the whole of mainland Britain. Sending as much as he could home had left him with virtually nothing for himself. Life had been hard enough without having anything with which to seek relief even in the canteen, let alone out of barracks.

Furthermore, with the arrival of his twentieth birthday the previous week Ted had increased his income by electing to serve for a minimum of nine years, which would give him another four pence a day Service Pay. Life, therefore, was now very much better.

There had been another letter, one that he had kept and read from time to time. He had done so this morning, the second anniversary of his forced departure from the village and his subsequent enlistment; and it accounted for his moodiness. The words were very familiar, he'd read them often enough:

"My dear son

It grieves me that I must be the bearer to you of news which I know will cause you to be upset, but you will wish to know that Betty Chalmers has given her promise of marriage to a young man from Thetford. He works in the bank there. The wedding is to be shortly, and I know that Mr and Mrs Chalmers are very pleased."

There had been much more in the letter, but for some time he had read and read again that first paragraph. Stupid, really. He couldn't've expected 'er t' do anythin' else. After all, 'e'd just buggered of without so much as a word, and then 'e 'adn't written to 'er with so much as an explanation.

".....them stupid sods." Alfie's voice penetrated back into his consciousness. "Ted, what was the name of that boat they used back in April to bring in the guns from Germany? The Fanny, weren't it; yeah, that was it, the Fanny. I 'eard that they got over thirty thousand rifles in from that boat. What 're the mad sods goin' t' do with thirty thousand bloody rifles?"

The conversation continued in similar vein as they made their way to the bus stop. The Home Rule Bill received a mention, having just been discussed at the Buckingham Palace conference during the preceding week. It was, however, a very brief mention, the deep political significance of the statesmanlike moves being made in an attempt to assuage the problems of the troubled land in which they were stationed being too much for them. Theirs was a more simplistic perspective, revolving around the levels of security and the amount of mucking about they would suffer because of the benighted Irish; Protestant and Catholic alike.

There was no mention at all in their conversation of the murder in Sarajevo almost a month before, on the twenty-eighth of June, of the Archduke Francis Ferdinand of Austria-Hungary and his wife. It was an event far removed from anything that might affect them, and which had disappeared some time ago from the newspapers they read; when, that is, they chose to read them.

Neither were they aware of the political and strategic ambitions of the Germans, pursued by the Kaiser with a style that sought to imitate the mailed fist approach of the great Bismark, but without the intellectual capacity to underpin bellicose utterances and aggressive action with a sound policy. Nor did they know that His Majesty's Government were concerned at the Kaiser's attitude, or that the Kaiser for his part perceived the British as being weak.

They had no knowledge of the Franco-Russian alliance that had replaced a Franco-Prussian alliance engineered by Bismark, and rendered asunder by the Kaiser. Nor were they aware that the terms of the alliance meant that an attack on either France or Russia would cause the other to mobilise; and that Russia's neighbours, especially the Germans, were afraid of her.

The difficulties faced by the Austro-Hungarian Emperor as his domain continued to crumble about him were not matters of which they had heard or read. They had no idea that the military in Austria, with the Empire beset by a range of debilitating nationality problems, were determined that the time had come to deal with Serbia once and for all. Austria's request to Germany for safeguards against Russia, bearing in mind the Russian association with the Serbs, was a cause for concern in Downing Street, but not in the barracks occupied by the First Battalion of the Norfolk Regiment; and probably not among the soldiers in any barracks anywhere in the Empire. They might have been more concerned had they known of the almost cavalier fashion with which the leaders of some of the European powers, and in particular Kaiser Wilhelm ll of Germany, were prepared to commit their armies to war for what they assumed would be a short term military adventure in order to achieve the political objectives they were seeking.

In fact, the day before the Sunday outing to Bangor was the day upon which the Kaiser had declared himself in favour of Austrian plans for Serbia, and the Austrians had been told they could depend on the complete support of Germany. The Austrians had already drafted and sent an ultimatum to Serbia which, if accepted, would give Austria an overpowering degree of control over Serbian affairs. It was an ultimatum deliberately designed so that the Serbs would surely find it unacceptable. Furthermore, it was an ultimatum that would also be unacceptable to Russia; and its rejection would lead inevitably to war. The Kaiser's men did not even read the Austrian terms, but sent a note to Paris, St Petersburg and London supporting the Austrian ultimatum and pointing out that any interference would be followed by incalculable consequences. In the event, the Serbs capitulated almost entirely, but when the Austrians received the Serbian note agreeing to the terms of the ultimatum it was not read; it wasn't even opened. It was simply assumed to be a rejection, and war was declared on the Serbs.

And so it was, with an insouciant disregard for the unleashing of Armageddon, that the fuze was lit and massive continental armies began to mobilise as part of a self-fulfilling prophesy rapidly developing an unstoppable momentum of its own.

In a panelled room, somewhere in the complex of offices that lie behind the facade of the Admiralty on Whitehall, just opposite the War Office, senior members of the Establishment sat round a highly polished Oak table, surrounded by the portraits of their illustrious forebears frowning down on them from the walls, and discussed the rapidly deteriorating situation. It was the view of Winston Churchill, the First Lord of the Admiralty, supported by the First Sea Lord, the most senior officer in the Royal Navy, that the dispersal of the Home Fleet following the recently completed major exercise upon which it had been embarked should be halted; and they advised the Naval Staff that they would be most grateful if the necessary instructions could be communicated as swiftly as possible to the Fleet. It was a decision taken unilaterally, without reference to the Cabinet, but it retained a homogenous fleet, ready instantly for sea and at war establishment with the reservists who had been attending the exercise.

In the meantime, in barrack rooms throughout the land soldiers prepared their kit for morning inspection; polished their boots so they would gleam in the bright July sunshine; rubbed at brasses and applied blanco to webbing belts; groused as they read the company detail that saw them in the cookhouse on kitchen fatigues or gave them a guard duty which was one more than they felt they should be doing; and generally looked forward to a week which showed little prospect of being much different from its predecessor. But there was the saving grace that waiting at the far end was the first weekend of August, with the advantage that it included as part of it, on the third of August, a Bank Holiday. Unless, of course, you were pinged for a bloody guard duty.

"Stand still." Sergeant Paul Cooper's voice, pitched deliberately high, whipped through the humid air of a late

July morning that was already uncomfortably warm and stuffy.

It was six-fifteen on the morning of Monday the twenty-seventh of July 1914. The barrack room had been awake for fifteen minutes, and had been ready for roll call, a routine that took place with men stood at the foot of their beds. Normally, this was a chore that would be undertaken by the most senior of the junior Non Commissioned Officers living in barracks, but something had caused Sergeant Cooper to rise early that morning and to grace this small ritual with his presence. The shock of his appearance at such an early hour was bad enough, but the ill humour induced in the sergeant by his enforced early rise from the warmth of his bed and the tempting arms of his young wife added to the concern felt by every man in the room.

He was a slim, well-proportioned individual. His dark hair was trimmed smartly in accordance with regulations and his powerful jaw line demonstrated a strength of character and firmness which bred confidence in his ability, whilst at the same time generating that little bit of awe in his subordinates which acted as an inducement for them to do precisely as he told them, without argument. There had been some amusement in the platoon when, some eighteen months earlier, he had met the young lady to whom he was now married. She was not enamoured of moustaches generally and in particular on any man who thought he might have some chance of developing any sort of a relationship with her. It had only been a couple of days before the previously hirsute Sergeant Cooper had become clean-shaven; and he had remained that way ever since.

The platoon's amusement, however, was not something they dared communicate to the Sergeant.

"I want no mucking about this morning. Things are happening and I want you on the square sharp at twenty-five past eight. The Company Commander's coming in this morning and he's got something to say to you all. I want you in working dress, no frills; but you'd better be on the ball. Lance Corporal Floyd!"

The last few words cracked through the room like a rifle shot.

"Sergeant!"

Joseph Floyd squared his shoulders back a little more and looked slightly above the Sergeant's head, wearing the blank expression that soldiers eschew when they are about to be told something they don't want to hear.

"You make sure this lot are in good order, clear?" The question snapped out.

"Yes Sergeant!"

And with that Paul Cooper left them to go to breakfast, returning to the small terraced cottage on the edge of the square to which his rank and status entitled him; and to the wife who had fired him with the extra ambition to become the Regimental Sergeant Major in the Ninth before his twenty-one years were up. Three years as a drummer boy and fourteen years in the Army had seen him advance at a steady pace. He was brighter than the average, and had a degree of poise that set him apart from his peer group. He was not to know it, but promotion to colour sergeant was not far away, and the Commanding Officer had demonstrated his confidence by giving him command of a platoon, thereby offsetting the shortage of junior officers in the battalion. He was one of three sergeants so honoured, and was the most adept at treading the difficult path of being both platoon sergeant and platoon commander. Given a fair wind, and knowing the ages of those ahead of him, he reckoned he could be a company sergeant major within about eighteen months.

Sergeant Cooper's future in the Army was of no concern to the members of his platoon as they left for the cookhouse to collect breakfast. The parade ground was already filling up with the miscreants from the guardroom, joined by those undergoing the slightly, but only slightly, less onerous punishment of "Confined to Barracks", or CB. This was a particularly unpleasant form of disruption inflicted on soldiers for quite small offences, and one of its more unlovely aspects was an hour's close order drill fitted in between six and seven thirty in the morning, together with the occupants of the guardroom cells, wearing a forty pound pack and carrying a rifle.

"I wonder what all this is about."

Private Colin Baxter's well-modulated tones voiced the question that was in all their minds. One thing was for sure, there was embuggerance in the wind, and they were the likely recipients of large slices of it.

Reinforced by tea, bread, jam and some cold bacon the platoon cleaned the barrack room, prepared for whatever the day might bring, reserved some food for two of their number who were on CB and endured Lance Corporal Floyd's pre-inspection before heading for the parade ground.

"What's goin' on Sarge?"

Corporal Fred Smith was the one man in the platoon who could claim to be close to Paul Cooper. They both displayed above their left breast pockets the splash of colour that marked them out as veterans of the South African war; and there were only a few of them left in the battalion. They shared an experience that set them apart from the rest, and it created between them an unspoken bond that neither of them could have defined, even supposing they'd thought about it.

"You'll find out in good time, Fred."

His voice raised as he turned to his platoon, modifying his tones in the presence of the other platoon commanders whose own sergeants were busy chivvying their men into the hollow square that the Major preferred to use when he was addressing the company.

"Corporal Smith, will you sort this lot out!"

He used his senior corporal as his deputy on many occasions, allowing him to stand back a little from his men, and giving him the chance to mix at work with the other platoon commanders whilst knowing that someone he trusted was addressing the basic administration of his small sub-unit.

"If the officers would please move to one side!"

The Company Sergeant Major's voice, drawn from deep

inside his chest, stilled the last remnants of noise from the assembling platoons, carrying with it an authority that demanded instant response, and with just sufficient politeness for the young officers to believe that they had been invited to do something rather than having been given an order. Nonetheless, there was no thought that they might not do as he had suggested.

Paul Cooper took up his place in front of his platoon. The officers moved to one side, waiting formally to be fallen in. This was done by the company Second-in-Command who then stood everyone at ease, awaiting the arrival of the Company Commander.

"Cumpny!" The warning was sharp and one hundred and forty three all ranks assembled in four platoons braced themselves in anticipation.

"Atteeeeeeen", the long drawn out cautionary word of command was the final warning of what was to come: the exhortation to stand to attention.

"Shun!" One hundred and forty three pairs of hands swept from behind backs to be held vertically downwards at the side, thumbs pressed down to lock the elbow, and held against the seam of the trouser, thereby properly squaring the shoulders. Simultaneously, one hundred and forty three left feet, which had been placed with the heels twenty-seven inches apart with the toes pointed outwards at a forty-five degree angle, were raised, left thighs brought parallel to the ground and then driven in hard, in perfect unison, alongside their right hand companions.

A pause, to make certain all was well, and the second-in-command turned about to present the company to its master.

"Stand them at ease, please George." The Major's languid tones demonstrating all the breeding of generations born to lead, and who had over the centuries served the Monarch in positions of authority throughout the Empire.

"Stand easy." The company relaxed. "Gather round." They moved in towards the Major, forming the hollow circle around him that he preferred to use when he really wanted to communicate with them.

"What I have to say to you is very serious and I want you to pay close attention."

Hearts sank. This was it: "serious" meant embuggerance.

"Yesterday, there was a very unpleasant incident in the South. The Nationalists attempted to smuggle in arms by sea from Hamburg in Germany."

"Bloody 'ell," thought Alfie James. "We were talkin' about this yesterday. Bloody Prots it was then, and now the bloody Taegs are at it."

"They attempted to land two thousand five hundred rifles and one hundred and twenty-five thousand rounds of ammunition from a ship called the Howth, which sailed from the port of Hamburg. We received intelligence of their intentions and the police, accompanied by the Scottish Borderers, were sent to investigate."

He had captured completely the interest of the whole company. Speculation was already rife in the minds of the soldiers surrounding him about the likely outcome of the story, but most reckoned it wouldn't be good news, and bad news usually meant pain and grief for them in some way.

The major went on to explain how the Nationalists, on being discovered, had run off and the detachment of the Kings Own Scottish Borderers had set out to march back to Barracks in Dublin. On the way some stones were thrown, and the situation had turned ugly. The officer in command of the detachment had ordered his men to prepare to fire. Regrettably, they had misunderstood him, and had actually opened fire. The consequence of this misunderstanding was that two men and a woman were killed and a further thirty-two people were wounded, none of whom had been even remotely involved in the unsuccessful smuggling attempt.

They were warned that the story would be in that morning's newspapers, and that there was bound to be strong feeling roused in the Nationalist community. Security would be increased, travel would be reduced except on essential duty and there would be limits on walking out and other recreational activity.

The more he spoke, the more they realised that the anticipated pleasures of the long weekend to come were becoming decreasingly likely to manifest themselves. The coming week, it seemed, was going to be just like any other; filled by the monotonous chores that were a feature of life in barracks and with little prospect of anything exciting happening at the end of it.

But the story never did make the headlines, at least not in the main national daily newspapers. There was instead a gradual awakening to the looming crisis in Europe; a crisis that until then had lain beneath the surface of what was perceived to be the murky waters of Balkan politics. Once, however, the news of the non-dispersal of the Home Fleet circulated, public opinion began to wake up to the dangers of the situation. At eleven o'clock on the morning of Tuesday the twenty-eighth of July 1914, Austria declared war on Serbia; and French and German generals began to press their respective governments for authority to commence mobilisation.

By the Wednesday the European crisis had even replaced the perennial discussion of the Irish and their unseemly behaviour in the messes and barrack rooms of the Norfolks.

By that evening the telegraph had passed the message from the War Office in London, via the Headquarters of the Fifth Division at the Curragh, which in turn had informed the Commander of the Fifteenth Infantry Brigade in Belfast, that the tension was such that leave should be cancelled and officers and men on courses should be returned to their units. Brigadier General Count Edward von Gleichen, in directing that the message be passed on to the Commanding Officers of the Bedfordshires, Cheshires, Dorsets and Norfolks, also instructed his Brigade Major to invite those Commanding Officers to join him the next day for luncheon in order that they might discuss the situation; and the Brigade Major, who, paradoxically, was a Captain, should also attend in order to take notes and issue any orders that might emanate from their meeting.

Wednesday was not a dining-in night in the Officers' Mess, so it was only the bachelor officers of the Norfolks who were at dinner to discuss what was going on, and to speculate on the possibility of war; a war that might involve the United Kingdom. The Company Commanders congregated in the CO's house for a glass of port, after he had finished dinner, to be told the news, to be told what to tell their soldiers and to be told that they should be prepared to join him in his office upon his return from the Brigadier's meeting the following afternoon.

"We don't yet know what is happening," said the Major.

"Nothin' new in that," was the uncharitable thought that flashed through the mind of more than one man in the company, standing round him in a half circle for the second time that week.

The CO's advice to his officers the previous evening had been that they should not overly complicate the explanation to their men of the implications of current events. The precautions being taken by the Government were entirely sensible given the prevailing situation in Europe, but a war between the European powers was not an indication that the British Army was about to take part. In any event, the situation in Ireland was sufficiently serious to require the presence of the Norfolks and it was very unlikely that the battalion would be going anywhere.

But, as the soldiers of the Norfolks, and the rest of the Fifteenth Infantry Brigade, returned to fatigues, drill, weapon cleaning, guard duty and the plethora of trivia that marked peacetime soldiering at home, there were others whose thoughts were turning to the implications of events across the Channel, and who were removing plans from shelves and updating the details therein. In the War Office in London, Colonel the Honourable A R Stuart-Worsley of the Royal Engineers, the Assistant Director for Movements, turned to his very small staff and instructed them to examine and, where necessary amend, the plans for the deployment of an expeditionary force to the continent. This process was to be conducted in great secrecy, and not a hint of their preparations was to be communicated to anyone who did not need to know what they were doing.

It would not be long before the British Army would give

thanks for the foresight that, in December 1912, had seen the establishment of the Movements Directorate of the War Office. It was an accident of history that had placed the responsibility for planning and executing strategic movements with the Royal Engineers, and Colonel E M Percival had set up the fledgling department less than two years before it was to be used in anger.

The management of British railway companies had been, very secretly, brought into the confidence of the War Office to assist with the planning, and with the co-ordination when necessary, of the move by rail of army formations, stores and equipment to disembarkation ports. By the end of 1912 co-operation had been organised with a Railway Executive Committee and the London and South Western Railway had been given the role of co-ordinator. At the same time, arrangements were being resolved with the Admiralty to provide the necessary merchant shipping in the right place and in the right sequence to meet the deployment priorities of the commander of the expeditionary force, whoever he might be.

Having told wives and families that the picnics, boating trips, tennis parties and other pleasures which had been keenly anticipated over the holiday weekend to come would have to take place without them, and blaming it on the quite unnecessary alarm being created by the situation in Ireland together with the Government's precautionary measures, a small group of dedicated men turned their attention to the minutiae of railway schedules, shipping availability and the capacity of a number of ports around the Kingdom to accept a sudden influx of troops, their equipment and their ammunition; to embark the same upon a number of ships and to despatch them to France in a predetermined order.

By Saturday the first of August 1914, the soldiers of the Norfolks were beginning to feel just a tiny bit fed up. It was obvious that something was going to happen in Europe, but very unlikely that they would be involved. The tension in Ireland, following the previous weekend's shooting incident, meant that they couldn't walk out safely, and were being encouraged to remain in barracks. For those who had been dragged, protesting, back from leave there was the double insult of having been mucked about severely with nothing to show for it.

It was a quiet, uneventful start to a Bank Holiday Weekend with a boring three days stretching ahead towards another week of peacetime soldiering. They'd cracked all the annual training by now, up to and including brigade training. All they had to look forward to were the divisional exercises which would take place in the damp and cold of an Irish Autumn, somewhere around the end of September. That was another fortnight of messing about, but at least it would make a change. Mind you, there was the rumour going round the barrack rooms of a foreign service posting in the offing. Now that would be something; but then, anything would be better than this bloody place.

And then, that very evening, Germany declared war on Russia. France immediately began to mobilise.

At once the pace of events changed. Speculation about what might happen and their possible part in it became the main topic of conversation in barrack rooms and messes throughout the Army. Wise and cautious men began to think about family affairs and putting matters in order. Bored young officers and soldiers fantasised about the excitement of war and the chance to bash the Hun. The Commander of the Fifteenth Infantry Brigade and his Commanding Officers began to think about possible future events, and gave thanks that the summer training period, just completed, had included a trial mobilisation. Consequently, they were completely up do date with the equipment state of their battalions, knew the deficiencies and knew how they were to be resolved should it ever prove necessary; and it was beginning to look as if it might.

On Sunday the second of August the German Government issued an ultimatum to Belgium, demanding that the German Army be permitted transit though Belgium in the event of the need for them to attack France. Tiny Belgium, a neutral country with its territorial integrity guaranteed by Prussia, the United Kingdom and France, was the key to German success. By attacking France's eastern border with Germany they would hold a large part of the French Army on that line, and then attacking from the north through Belgium with a far stronger force they could take the French in the flank and rear, roll up her armies against the eastern border and win a crushing victory.

Once achieved, within a few days, victory in France would leave Germany free to deal with Russia, whose mobilisation process was so much slower and more cumbersome than her French ally's.

However, although a small nation and militarily weak, there was no lack of courage in the Belgians. On the third of August, even as the Germans were accusing France, quite dishonestly and simply to have an excuse to start the war, of having bombed Karlsruh and Nurembeurg, Albert King of the Belgians' response to the Germans regarding passage through his country had been an unequivocal "Non!"

By this time the process of mobilisation had begun in the United Kingdom. Colonel Stuart-Worsley and his staff had already put procedures in place with the Railway Executive Committee to begin the gathering and pre-positioning of trains. This produced probably the first tangible effect of war on the British population as it resulted in the cancellation of almost all Bank Holiday Monday excursion trains. Many parents were left with the task of explaining to rebellious offspring the reasons for their picnic taking place in the local park, or in some cases at the railway station, rather than at the seaside; not that they really understood the reasons themselves at that stage.

As the British Government sent out tens of thousands of telegrams to mobilise the reserves, it also sent a stiff note to Germany, warning of the protected status of Belgian neutrality and the likely effect of its violation. At half past eight on Tuesday the fourth of August 1914 the German Army crossed the Belgian border, en route to France. An ultimatum to Germany from the British Government left the Germans in no doubt as to the consequences if they had not withdrawn by midnight back behind German borders.

The actual order to mobilise was given at four-thirty p.m. that day, arriving by telegram in the Headquarters of the Fifteenth Infantry Brigade at five-thirty. Immediately, the well-oiled machine that the Count Edward von Gleichen had trained and honed during his time in command swung into action and the orders to mobilise and to prepare to move were issued.

At eleven o'clock that evening, the Germans not having withdrawn from Belgium, the United Kingdom declared war.

The actual impact of this last momentous happening in the whole series of events which had led the Great Powers in Europe to war was lost on the soldiers of the First Battalion the Norfolk Regiment. They had more immediate and pressing matters with which to deal.

"Your personal kit will be inspected by the Company Commander tomorrow morning immediately after breakfast. There will be no deficiencies whatsoever. Have I made myself quite clear? Is there anyone who does not understand? Any questions? ..No ..right, carry on Corporal Smith."

Had there been any questions it would have been a foolish man who asked one. Sergeant Cooper's tone and manner had made it quite clear that he was not in a mood to be trifled with. His own kit was clearly in perfectly good order and there was no point at all in even considering seeking his advice and guidance on how the dented mess tin, the missing water bottle cork or the broken bootlace might be set to rights. No, there were other methods of resolving these matters, but, since the announcement had only come at seven o'clock that evening, time was short.

That night there was a constant murmuring and shifting throughout Palace Barracks as men pored over their equipment and field uniforms, identifying things that needed putting right and then remedying the problem in negotiation with their colleagues. Barter was the preferred method, and most had a few buckshee bits of kit secreted away; but when this failed money or cigarettes changed hands.

Fred Smith had made it quite clear that he was going home to the missus at midnight, and if anyone had not got themselves sorted by then he was taking their kit state as at that time and for deficiencies or inadequacies noted there would be a Show Parade at six o'clock the next morning, after which they would be reported to Sergeant Cooper. Consequently, at the moment that His Majesty's Government declared war upon the German nation he was staring very closely at the studs on Ted Ludgrove's ammunition pouches to ascertain whether there was any sign of fraying of the webbing around them; and Ted's mind was very much on the implications of him finding anything, and not on momentous historical events.

He had already undertaken the closest possible inspection of Ted's mess tins and entrenching tool and had failed to find a trace of dirt, despite the enormous difficulty of keeping them all spotlessly clean. Neither could he now find anything wrong with anything else, and the smug, self-satisfied look on Ludgrove's face was beginning to irritate. He was moving away towards Alfie James when he turned, suddenly, on an afterthought. Reaching down to where the equipment was laid out in neat and orderly fashion on the bed he took a corner of one of the blankets, inspected it minutely and pronounced judgement.

"Idle end on the blanket." He referred to a loose piece of wool which was becoming detached from the material at the edge.

"Aw, Corporal," the pleading tone in his voice seeking the sympathy he already knew would not be forthcoming, "this was supposed to be just our kit for....."

All too late. The system would have its victory, it would ensure he knew his place, and the rest of them would gain some small enjoyment from his discomfiture.

"Idle end, Corporal Floyd." Fred Smith might be a very old soldier of limited intelligence who was not going to rise above the rank of Corporal; but 'e knew how to deal with smart young things like Ludgrove and 'is mates and the words fairly snapped out. There was no further debate on the matter.

"Show idle end removed, Corporal." Joseph Floyd wrote the offence in his notebook, smiled knowingly at Private Ludgrove and stepped smartly along behind his superior as he moved towards the dissection, piece by piece, of Alfie James and his offering.

It was finally well past midnight before they eventually finished the inspection and Fred Smith had departed to the comforts of the small married quarter he was fortunate enough to share with the lady who had been his wife this past twelve months, together with their three month old baby daughter. No one had escaped without something to show the next morning, but then none of them had really expected to. This was the Army at what they felt to be its most trivial and irritating, and there was a deal of grousing.

"'Ere they were, on the edge of great and momentous events, and the bloody Army was muckin' 'em about again, and that silly old sod, Smith, was pissin' about over nothin'. The sooner they got off to the bloody war the better, and stop all this fartin' about." The general mood was not helped by the fact that most of them decided to sleep on the floor, in fairly acute discomfort, rather than disturb the bed upon which they would have to show the remedied deficiency or fault.

Fred Smith, however, slept soundly; satisfied that he had done a good job well. He knew about the grousing, and it bothered him not a bit: did they really think 'e'd forgotten what it were like to be where they were? But he knew, he'd been there before, in South Africa, and he knew that attention to minute detail and proper drills saved lives in a crisis. If there really were to be war in Europe then the young men in the barrack room would find that out soon enough for themselves. In the meantime, it was up to him and to people like him to see to it that they learned those lessons as painlessly as possible, and before it was too late; and time was probably running out fast.

Paul Cooper also slept soundly, sharing Fred Smith's

views and knowing what would have happened at the inspection. He would have very little to do the next morning.

"Private Ludgrove, show idle end removed from blanket Corporal." Joseph Floyd read in a monotone from his notes of the previous evening. Ted Ludgrove was the third soldier in the platoon to be inspected at that morning's Show Parade, both Peter Dakin and Colin Baxter having had a pretty hard time over their inability, in one case, to replace a belt buckle and, in the other case, properly to repair a frayed puttee.

They were already in a foul mood generally, tired and irritable after a night of discomfort and the prospect of a missed breakfast if the silly old bugger didn't get a bloody move on. But Fred Smith was no fool, and he knew when enough was enough and the point had been made. Time to relax it a bit.

"Where is it then?" The slight note of incredulity in Fred Smith's voice ringing an alarm bell in Ted's consciousness.

"Where's what, Corporal?" Ted's tentative response.

"The idle end, Private Ludgrove, the idle end to which Lance Corporal Floyd 'as just referred, which he wrote down in 'is note book last night and about which I presume you 'ave not forgotten."

The note of incredulity had slipped to gentle sarcasm, the impact of which was heightened by the Corporal's semi-formal use of English. The alarm bells rang louder. Fred Smith's nose, at this moment, was a mere two inches from Ted's own proboscis, having drawn ever closer as the Corporal had been asking his question. Ted was very conscious that the Corporal had consumed toast and marmalade for his breakfast, and equally conscious that breakfast was something he, Ted Ludgrove, might not see that morning.

"Well, I've removed it Corporal, like you said, show idle end removed, so I 'ave, its gone."

"It says 'ere show idle end removed. I can see you've removed it, but you were told to show it removed and I can't see it. Is that because you 'aven't got it?" Fred's voice was now faintly patronising, the rest of the platoon were beginning to smile, although trying not to show it, and Ted was becoming confused even as he realised he was being had.

"Well no Corporal. It's gone." Hurt and confusion competed for room in the tone of his voice.

"Show again, idle end removed!" Joseph Floyd's voice was brusque and unsympathetic. Fred Smith moved on, toning down the intensity and increasing the pace of his inspection, the platoon was amused, the more so when they were only five minutes late for breakfast, and Ted became slightly cross as he took, for most of the rest of the day, the brunt of their humour at his misfortune.

Twelve hours later he was to parade with defaulters at the guardroom with a small piece of wool in his hand to show to the orderly sergeant that he had indeed removed the idle end and here was the evidence to prove it. The real nuisance was the long time he had to spend ensuring he was immaculately turned out, lest the orderly sergeant find anything to his own dissatisfaction and young Ludgrove be bidden, yet again, to attend Show Parade.

Before that, however, he was to gain, together with the rest of the battalion, the first inkling of what was to befall them.

The Times banner headline that morning, the fifth of August, was: "Britain at War"; and for a penny you could read all about it.

"We are at war with Germany, together with our allies, the French and the Belgians!"

The Commanding Officer's voice send a shiver of anticipation through the ranks of the battalion; and in the minds of those who had seen war there may also have been a tinge of apprehension.

"There is nothing to fear in this. You are as well trained as any regiment in an army that is better trained than probably any other in the world. You are professionals in a regular army; you will be fighting conscripts. You are almost at the end of this year's training cycle, and consequently are as well prepared as it is possible to be."

"Nonetheless, we shall spend some of our mobilisation time polishing those small areas we identified as needing some improvement. Your company officers will give you details...."

His words drifted away. So this was it. "Bloody 'ell, off to war." A jumble of thoughts flashed through their minds. Ted Ludgrove's pious hope was that he would not let himself or his friends down by being scared and doing something stupid, and that was probably the dominant thought in the majority of heads that morning, including Peter Dakin's and Colin Baxter's.

For some there were other thoughts: if you were Fred Smith there was concern at leaving a wife and baby who had given you a whole new perspective on life; if you were Joseph Floyd you were glad to escape even further from the wife who had become a nag at your failure to obtain promotion and get married quarters and who lived with her family in Norwich, and perhaps improve your chances of getting your hands on other women; if you were Alfie James and Paul Cooper you felt some excitement at the opportunity a short military adventure represented for your future career; if you were Ned Preece you thought about a thin faced, wistful young girl with straw-like hair who pushed your baby around a park in north-east London and wondered, not for the first time, about setting up an allotment for the kid - and what about a will?

The Company Commander's briefing was very clear. He had passed the detail of what he wanted done to the platoon commanders, and they would pass that on and get things sorted. He made just three points: be prepared to accept reservists and perhaps some soldiers from the Special Reserve into the platoons to bring them up to full war strength; be aware of the deficiencies in the company's equipment which had been identified on the recent mobilisation exercise; be prepared to embark upon a short, sharp training programme to polish up the individual skills which they had practised in the spring, at the start of the annual training cycle. Shooting and weapon training would be receiving special attention, and this would be particularly important for the reservists.

"Who the bloody 'ell are you?" Peter Dakin's voice was unnaturally belligerent, and was directed at the prone figure lying on his bed, with its feet encased in none too clean boots resting upon the boxed blankets he had so carefully folded.

The figure turned its head to the left, towards the door through which Alfie and his three friends had just entered. The left eye opened, surveyed them and closed again.

"What's it got to do with you?" The voice held a patronising belligerence.

"'Cos its my bloody bed, that's what. Get off, and bloody well get off now!"

"What is goin' on here and....." Sergeant Cooper was, by now, just behind the small group at the door. His voice paused as he surveyed the figure on the bed. "Private Hayes, as I live and breathe; well, well, well, this is a surprise. On yer feet!" The last few words dripped with ice.

John Hayes, opened his eyes, surveyed the angry Sergeant and slowly, deliberately, stood up from the bed. He did not, however, stand to attention, or defer in any way to his military superior.

"Corporal Cooper, well I suppose I had to end up in the same push as you." His voice held a note that stopped short of insubordination, but left no one in doubt as to his feelings.

"It's Sergeant Cooper to you Hayes, and forgetting that will do you no good at all. Outside, I wanna talk to you."

Those who had witnessed what took place were more than curious at the obvious antipathy between the two men.

"None of your bloody business," was Fred Smith's response to Ted's question, and his tone left no doubt in anyone's mind that to pursue the matter further would be useless to the point of being counterproductive. They were even more curious about the conversation that was taking place at that moment out of their earshot at the far corner of the barrack block's outside wall. Conversation was actually not an accurate description of what was a very one-sided discussion indeed; with Paul Cooper doing all the talking.

"What busted you was your own stupid fault, not mine; and you bloody well know it. You broke the rules and you paid for it, and I'm buggered if I was ever goin' to go down with you just so you could be a stupid bugger in company and not alone."

"I don't 'ave to listen to this from you!" John Hayes spoke with a belligerence that more than transcended the normal mores of military discipline and the relationship between NCOs and the soldiers for whom they were responsible.

"Yes you bloody well do, and you will if you know what's good for you." There was a firmness in Cooper's voice that brooked no argument.

"We are goin' to war, and the rules change." The words were snapped out with a staccato rhythm and emphasised each by a poke with Cooper's right forefinger into the left shoulder of the reservist; and John Hayes' face flinched with each one as if they were whiplashes. "Desertion, absenteeism, insubordination and disobedience to orders will be bloody well hammered. Just you remember that, and if I even think you're even dreamin' about disruptin' this platoon I'll bounce you in for crucifixion so bloody fast your bloody feet won't touch the ground. Do I make myself clear?" The last sentence emerged as a hiss of pure venom.

"Yes, you do."

"Yes what?"

"Yes Sergeant."

"And don't you bloody forget it, not ever Hayes!"

Chapter 3

Mobilisation

Preparation for war focused the minds of politicians and soldiers alike on the unpleasantness that was about to befall the nation. The nation itself went about its business as usual, albeit with a greater interest in the outpourings of the newspapers. Across the Army and the Navy, from the War Office and the Admiralty to the lowliest soldier and sailor, the week of the third to the tenth of August vanished in a blur. The much vaunted Bank Holiday Monday, which had been looked forward to with such keen anticipation, vanished without trace. Suddenly, there were simply not enough hours in the day.

Getting a battalion ready to go to war was no easy task, even when successful rehearsals had taken place only a few weeks earlier in a trial mobilisation as part of the annual training cycle. The fact of actually deploying to war concentrated the mind much more closely on the little things that might have passed by in a peacetime exercise. Now was the time that the little extras were thought of, and ideas that had not been implemented because of peacetime restrictions on money, time or interest suddenly became urgent.

There was also the aftermath of restructuring, the effects of which were still being felt to some extent, for British infantry battalions had been reorganised only a year or so earlier. The old eight company organisation which had existed since Wellington's day was no longer suitable for the modern battlefield where there was a need for increased dispersion. Consequently, there were now four companies, usually, but not always, commanded by a major with a captain as second-in-command. These were further broken down into platoons, commanded in war by a junior officer: a lieutenant or second lieutenant. In peacetime, however, these young men were more often than not absent from the battalion for a number of reasons which might include long training courses or special leave; and there were always shortages. Within platoons there was a sergeant and there were four sections of eight men, each commanded by a corporal with a lance corporal as his deputy.

Each battalion also had a machine gun platoon with two guns, serviced by eighteen men; six on each gun and six in reserve to handle ammunition and to replace casualties. Such was the importance of these guns to the commanding officer that this platoon was commanded by an experienced captain, and it normally came under the CO's direct control until he delegated his authority. Battalion headquarters itself was quite large, totalling some eighty-one men, but this included the signallers, the quartermaster, the medical officer and the other supporting staff necessary to ensure the efficient working of the whole organisation.

To prepare the battalion for war, equipment had to be drawn up from reserve pools, or requisitioned, or recovered from other units to whom it had been lent, officially or unofficially, as a peacetime expedient. The thirteen riding horses, thirty-four draught horses and nine pack horses had to be gathered together, inspected by the veterinary surgeon, be passed fit and then prepared for their tasks. The twelve carts, or wagons which might be issued in lieu, required inspection and last minute maintenance before loading with the contents of the quartermaster's store. This would include the four mobile kitchens, and the nine bicycles which would be used, at the discretion of the commanding officer, to assist the speedy transmission of information.

The Norfolks had only one of their two Vickers Machine Guns in Belfast on the third of August, the other being in

Dublin where it was being used as part of a training programme. It would be the last of Fifteen Brigade's important pieces of equipment to be in place and ready to go, but that would be achieved by Monday the tenth of August.

During that same week, the House of Commons authorised an increase in the regular Army of five hundred thousand. A further Army Order was issued allowing ex-regulars to enlist in the Special Reserve for one year or the duration and Kitchener became Secretary of State for War.

Kitchener did not trust the Territorial Army, or Special Reserve, to be able to undertake the tasks that would be required of them. He felt very strongly that they were week-end, social soldiers and that they were ill-prepared for what might befall them. Unlike most of his contemporaries, politicians and populace alike, he was sure the war would be a long and costly affair. Consequently, he developed the idea that a new Army should be created, building up to seventy-five divisions over three years; and by Friday the seventh of August posters appeared all over the country, together with notices in the newspapers, announcing the call to arms of one hundred thousand men for six divisions.

All this passed by the barrack rooms of the Ninth, where soldiers slept at night the sleep of the dead. Working daily from six in the morning to nearly midnight would stretch the stamina of anyone, but the work in which they were involved was heavy and demanding. Their individual circumstances had not been improved by the sudden influx of reservists, of which John Hayes had been the precursor. Suddenly, a barrack room designed for twenty was holding almost forty; and they had become uncomfortable, stuffy, chaotic and grossly overcrowded. If sleep came easily due to exhaustion, waking was not a pleasant experience. It was a process which involved listening to the snuffles and snorts of others as they gradually awoke, and putting up with the smells emanating from beneath blankets as the gastro enteric systems of the reservists came to terms with their change of diet. Almost overpowering, and certainly the predominant feature, was the smell of stale socks, discarded in stiffened heaps beside bed spaces.

"Sooner we get out of 'ere and off t' bloody war the better!"

When the preparation for embarkation allowed, particular attempts were being made to pack in as much training as possible. Musketry was given a special place in the timetable, and attempts were also made to improve fitness, especially amongst the reservists, but apart from physical training in the barracks there was little that could really be done. Certainly, there was no time to embark on route marches which would have built stamina and helped the breaking in of newly issued boots; not that this would have helped one of the other reservists who had recently arrived in Fred Smith's section to join John Hayes.

Alfred Arbuckle was a large, strong man who required size eleven boots, of which, together with the popular size ten boots, there was an acute shortage across the Army. It was not an easy matter to resolve, and various attempts were made by the War Office to hasten production from factories and to distribute boots to regiments which were swelling rapidly in size from a peacetime strength of around six hundred men to over one thousand. Alfred would eventually receive his boots on the morning of disembarkation, and in the meantime he would have to make do with the brown ones he had worn in civilian life, as a carpenter.

The reservists had to come to grips with a number of difficulties, not least of which was the reorganisation of the battalion itself, and the new tactics that the regulars now accepted as part of their daily routine. Suddenly, the old sweats who thought they were coming back to teach the young 'uns a thing or two were faced with the embarrassment of having to ask these same young men how things now worked. This transcended even down to basic equipment. The Army was now equipped with the new 1908 Pattern webbing which had replaced the buff leather Slade-Wallace equipment which had come into service in 1888. Consequently, the older the reservist soldier the less likely he was to be versed in its assembly and packing, and the greater was likely to be his embarrassment.

John Hayes, in particular, was finding this difficult, and if he bothered to analyse his thoughts at all he would probably have acknowledged that his arrogant know-all approach to his return to the Army might not have been sensible. He had, in fact, forgotten the first basic rule of survival: that bullshit might, as was often alleged, baffle brains, but it cut no ice at all with professional soldiers.

"Come on." Hayes looked round at the sound of the voice as he felt a hand on his shoulder.

"Yer've gorn and twisted it. Look it goes like......oh, take the bloody thing off." Ted's voice held no hint of confrontation, only of mild frustration that so simple an operation as the assembly of webbing could be undertaken in so complex a way.

He sat on Alfred Arbuckle's bed, it being the nearest, and unfastened the two shoulder straps from the buckles on the back of the webbing waist belt. His deft, well-practised hands swiftly reassembled the equipment, and he looked up to Alfred standing above him - watching every move with keen interest.

"You've seen this before, ain't yer?"

"Yup, it were just comin' in when I went out." The voice was slow and ponderous, each word emerging as if it had been individually considered before it was allowed to escape. "But it don't 'urt to look over it again 'case its changed or summat." Alfred was nothing if not a perfectionist. You couldn't be in his trade and do a proper job back home at work without making sure every thing was properly lined up, secured and in its place. And Alfred, honest and straight, could never complete a job until it was to the absolute satisfaction of the customer.

"T'asn't really, Alf" said Ted, by now fastening the reassembled basic set onto a John Hayes who, in response to a raised eyebrow and a flick of the head, had lifted his arms for it to be slipped on.

"Alfred, please," came the deep voice.

Ted looked up, smiled and nodded in acknowledgement

before turning back to Hayes and his webbing. From the back of the waist belt, two cross straps passed over the shoulders and fastened onto the tops of two ammunition carriers which were themselves clamped onto the front of the waist belt; one each side of the buckle. These carriers comprised five small pouches, each of which could hold fifteen rounds of ammunition in three clips of five, with the pouch fastened by a press-stud.

"Turn t' yer left then." Compliance with Ted's instruction brought John Hayes' right side round to face him and he fastened the two-pint capacity water bottle onto the overlap hanging down back and front from the shoulder straps. He had already slipped the bayonet frog and the entrenching tool pouch onto the left hand side, and thus all was complete."

"Good thing about this new stuff is that it all comes off in one piece."

Alfie James voice came in from the next bed.

"Means you don't 'ave to 'ave it on every minute of the day, but you can chuck it on and be on yer way in no time. Them studs is a bit of a bugger though, in the rain like. Can't get 'em shut see 'cos the webbin' shrinks an' they don't fit too well; an' if yer do get 'em shut they're a bugger to open. But you'll get used to it."

"Right then." Ted's voice interceded. "The large pack. There's a list 'ere of what you 'ave to 'ave in it. Can't tell yer too much about 'ow you do that, but it's a sod to get it all in. All I can say is keep the heavy stuff at the bottom 'cos that makes it sit on yer back better."

"Thanks."

The response was genuine, but Hayes voice was muted as he stared down intently at his newly assembled equipment, embarrassed to look the others in the eye. Ted was about to offer a cup of tea in the canteen, for reasons which he really did not understand, except the bloke wasn't all that bad, when Fred Smith's head appeared round the door to announce that their attendance was required the next morning at the medical centre.

"Bloody 'ell, not again!"

"Think yerself lucky, Private Preece. You lot 'ave only got the second Typhoid to come. These other buggers," by which he meant the reservists, "get the first one and Smallpox together; and you'd better make sure you get in the right part of the line or you'll end up gettin' the double dose all over again."

The expression on his face made it clear that such an error on the part of anyone would be a cause of considerable amusement to him. The memory, still clear in their minds, of the stiff arm and mild fever engendered by the cocktail of inoculations at the beginning of the last week gave rise to winces of anguish on the faces of a number of the occupants of the barrack room.

"Is it true, then, corp?" It was the following morning, and Ned Preece's nasal twang rang above the sounds of bed making and preparation for breakfast that filled the barrack room on Monday the tenth of August. "Yer know, about us gettin' an officer?"

"It's Corporal to you, Private Preece, and I'll thank you to remember that!" Ned tried it on every few weeks, the use of a more familiar form of address, and each time Fred knocked him back. "As for a new officer, I don't know; and even if I did it isn't my place to tell you about it until someone tells me they want me to."

Ted Ludgrove looked up from the letter he was trying to finish, a purpose for which he had risen especially early that morning. God knew there'd been precious little time this last week. He thought briefly about joining the conversation, the subject of which concerned them all intimately, and decided against it. His letter to his parents was the most important thing at the moment. It was couched in his usual, slightly formal, style and, in accordance with instructions, included nothing about what they were doing. He certainly did not include mention of the soldier's will he had made in his Pay Book, bequeathing all his worldly possessions to them. No sense in worrying them, and they'd find out soon enough if it ever became necessary.

"Right," Fred's voice raised a little louder. "On the square at eight o'clock sharp."

"What are we doing today, Corporal, apart from getting inoculated?" Colin Baxter's civilised, well-modulated voice always stood the best chance of getting an answer from Corporal Smith. The platoon thought it was because he sounded like an officer, and Fred's immediate reaction was to show respect. That might have had something to do with it, but it was more likely that he was a nice bloke who was always polite and reasonable, and it was easy to be polite and reasonable back to him. There were never any challenges in his questions.

"More of the same, Private Baxter, more of the same." Fred failed to put any enthusiasm into his voice and as such spoke for them all. They were ready to go, everything was packed, the initial excitement had been dissipated in the plethora of trivia that had been involved in the preparation and the anti climax which came with being fully prepared, but with an unexplained delay in their departure.

They were not to know that the British Expeditionary Force was, in fact, already on the move. In due course the Fifth Division, based in Ireland, would join it, taking the Thirteenth, Fourteenth and Fifteenth Infantry Brigades, the latter comprising the first battalions of the Norfolk, Bedfordshire, Cheshire and Dorset Regiments. Within the overall divisional strength of the Fifth Division of eighteen thousand and seventy three all ranks and five thousand five hundred and ninety two horses were 17 and 59 Field Companies of the Royal Engineers, 5 Signals Company, also of the Royal Engineers, 5 Division Train of the Army Service Corps and 13, 14 and 15 Field Ambulances of the Royal Army Medical Corps; and all this fitted into the loading plan.

This was a plan which would transport the eighty thousand men of six infantry divisions and the Cavalry Division, formed into two army corps, to concentration areas between Avesnes and Le Cateau in Northern France in fifteen days. Troops on mainland Britain were sailing from Southampton, whilst motor transport and petroleum products left from Avonmouth. Newhaven, on the south coast in Sussex, saw the loading and despatch of vast quantities of stores and supplies bound for the Ordnance Depot which was even then being set up in Le Havre by Number One Company of the Army Ordnance Corps. More motor transport and frozen meat left from Liverpool. All of Fifth Division would leave from Ireland, from Dublin, Cork and Belfast, but this would be in due time in order to fit with the order in which the staff wished them to arrive in France.

The young soldiers of the Ninth were learning one of the first lessons of war: that they would be rushed to be prepared for a range of eventualities, only to have to wait until the right time came for them to execute the orders given to them; or more likely to rush off somewhere else or to do something else, only to wait again.

The married men in the battalion were mostly grateful for the lull, whilst at the same time being anxious to go. There had been little time for them to undertake the additional tasks involved in preparing their wives for what was to come; or just simply to spend time with them. This in itself could, however, also be galling. Sitting around, waiting to go, not knowing the details and getting edgy was not the way they wished to remember their last few days together. In the hearts and minds of many, husbands and wives alike, was the feeling that they wanted the battalion to be on its way, and yet did not want it to go at all.

Ned Preece had been interviewed by the company commander regarding the allotment he was thinking of making. The major had spoken about responsibility and duty and had used other words that had passed over Ned's head. He simply remembered the final statement, "permission granted, march out" as he went to bequeath six pence a day from his pay to a young lady in Walthamstow for whom the sudden arrival of money she could call her own would allow her to begin building a life of her own which was less dependent on overbearing and disapproving parents.

And now she had an address she could send Ned a picture of their daughter, like she'd always wanted to 'cept 'e'd never told 'er where 'e was.

"Silly bugger, runnin' off like that, but then the old man would probably 'ave beaten the livin' daylights out of 'im if 'e'd caught 'im." Still, she 'adn't looked at anyone since, and she'd always known 'e wouldn't ferget 'er, or the babe.

"This morning you are goin' t' meet your new platoon commander!"

Paul Cooper was confirming the rumour that had already spread throughout the platoon, and forming them up in open order ready for inspection had confirmed in the minds of most of them that the rumour of a new officer was about to become reality.

"I don't know who it is, but two new officers arrived in the battalion last night and I presume it will be one of them."

He was about to remind them to behave properly, to answer up and to look the officer straight in the eye when answering any questions he might have when he caught sight, out of the corner of his left eye, of the look on Fred Smith's face: first of surprise, then of pleasure and then back to formal parade face as he raised an eyebrow in Paul Coopers direction.

"Platoon," the warning command that a drill movement would very shortly be expected of them.

"Atteeeeeen.....shun!"

A pause, then he turned about smartly, clockwise, pausing as he reached a point facing the opposite direction before bringing up his trailing left foot and stamping it smartly in beside the right to bring him to the position of attention, facing the figure which was approaching and was by now some fifty yards away.

He smiled. So it was true. He'd come back and it was Paul Cooper's platoon he was to get. Well, he wouldn't find a better one in the battalion, and he, Paul Cooper, would ensure that it stayed that way. He marched forward to a point where he would be in front of the approaching officer some twenty yards from the platoon. He halted and the lieutenant stopped five paces in front of him, anticipating not just the salute, but the smart one pace forward that would follow it. Behind the sergeant, heads remained facing to the front, but curiosity got the better of most of them and eyes swivelled in their sockets, attempting to gain a first impression of the young man who would have such a profound effect upon their lives.

Those who actually managed to get a glimpse were surprised. The face was older than they had expected, belonging as it did to a man in his early thirties. The uniform was not the perfect fit of a newly commissioned officer's expensively tailored masterpiece; and above the left breast pocket was the same splash of colour exhibited by Sergeant Cooper and Corporal Smith. He was a veteran of South Africa.

They were also surprised by the reaction of the two men as they met. They could only see the officer's face, but it wore a look of pleasure and anticipation. The handshake was not the perfunctory greeting of two men meeting for the first time, but the long, firm clasp of two hands that were renewing a friendship. A bond, a link from the past that had been forged in some way that joined the two men together in a relationship which cloaked them in a common understanding and offered a barrier to the outside world lest it consider seeking to join the small club they had formed.

"I thought it might be you, sir." Paul Cooper was delighted, but he remembered, nonetheless, not to cross the line which divided the non-commissioned from the commissioned; not to break the faith. His voice was soft, but infused with enthusiasm.

"God, but it's good to see you again!"

Almost reluctantly he released the lieutenant's right hand from his own, and resumed the position of attention. The officer spoke, the pleasure in his voice mirroring that of the sergeant.

"It's been a long time, and I'd be lying if I said you don't look a day older. But sergeant, and commanding a platoon; that's good."

"Your platoon now, sir, all yours."

His emotions were mixed as he spoke. They were his, and they were well drilled and in good order and he had to fight down a feeling of resentment that someone else would be benefiting from his work; and he would now have to subordinate himself. However, the tinge of resentment was offset by a sense of relief that the decisions would be someone else's; the responsibility would not be his for the lives of the men in the platoon; he could turn to someone else during the difficult times. But he was the platoon sergeant, and of course he would look after the officer. After all, it'd been thirteen years since Matthew Jenkins had served in the Army, and he would need to be brought up to date, and kept out of trouble. All this passed through his consciousness in a flash.

"Would you like to meet them, sir?"

"Yes, yes of course. We'll talk later" Matthew Jenkins moved forward as Paul Cooper saluted, side-stepped and fell in behind the officer as he approached the platoon; by which time they both wore the formal expressions that befitted a serious and important moment.

He felt awkward and stiff in his uniform. It fitted reasonably well, and he'd been in the Special Reserve since it formed. Consequently, he'd had the time to get it adjusted, but it certainly did not hang as well on him as it might have done. He also felt awkward and stiff standing formally in front of his platoon. He'd never really enjoyed all this parade ground stuff, but knowing the importance of good drills and instant responses in action he could accept the need for it.

"Stand them at ease, please, Sergeant Cooper."

"Sir!" Seconds later the word of command lashed out, followed instantly by "asyouwere"; the exhortation for them to return to their previous position, thereby bringing them in an instant from standing to attention to standing at ease and back again - all in one breath.

Matthew Jenkins permitted himself an inward smile of

contentment as Sergeant Cooper was explaining to the platoon the error of their ways; highlighting the awful sloppiness of a drill movement that to the outside world would have looked perfect, which it had been; pointing out how it ought to be done, and would be done in the future; and advising them of what might happen if there was not an immediate improvement in their approach to life in general and simple drill movements in particular

"God, but it was good to be back. He hadn't realised how much he'd missed it all; and to have Cooper as his platoon sergeant....."

"Right sir!"

The platoon was now in a state with which the sergeant was satisfied, and the officer could now inspect if he so wished.

"Look this way!" Forty pairs of eyes swivelled and forty heads inclined in his direction.

"My name is Lieutenant Jenkins and I am your new platoon commander. I shall be getting to know you all over the next few days, as you will be getting to know me. I am not certain yet when it is we shall be leaving or where we shall be going, but we will use the time to best effect to ensure that we can work together properly and well, and not disgrace either ourselves or the regiment."

"More bullshit. Why the 'ell don't 'e let us get away and get these bloody injections bloody well finished with."

He moved away towards his half left, heading for the front man on the right hand end of the front rank.

"Look to yer front!"

Paul Cooper's command had the forty pairs of eyes in the forty heads back where he wanted them; facing their front.

"And you are?"

"Private Arbuckle, sir. Nice to meet you sir."

"Private Arbuckle!" Paul Cooper's voice hissed in his right ear. "When an officer speaks to you, you stand to attention, don't you Private Arbuckle?"

"Yes sergeant."

"Then bloody well do it Private Arbuckle, and do it now." And as the left foot crashed in beside the right the conversation continued: “And when the officer speaks to you and asks you questions you can answer them, but until he does you keep your opinions and your questions to yourself; do you understand?”

“Yes sergeant!”

“Good, very good indeed.”

Matthew Jenkins waited while the ritual was carried out before his eyes, before pursuing his conversation with the huge, slightly cumbersome looking man with the slow, deep voice. The procession continued along the front rank and part way along the centre until suddenly there were three in the group wearing the same medal ribbons.

“Hallo Smith,” said Matthew. “I’m sorry.... Corporal Smith. It’s good to see you again. His right hand reached out, as did Fred Smith’s, quite spontaneously; and he was the only man, apart from Paul Cooper, that morning to shake the officer’s hand.

“It’s good to see you too, sir. Been too long it ’as.”

“Indeed, indeed; but the years have been kind to you, as has the Army.” He pointed at the chevrons sewn on the sleeve.

“Which section do you command?”

Paul Cooper started slightly. So he knew about the new organisation. Perhaps he had been studying the books, or someone had told him a bit.

“Number three sir.”

“Is it complete? Do you have all nine men?”

“Yessir!”

“And your second-in-command?”

“Lance Corporal Floyd, sir.”

“Ah yes, I met him.” He half turned. “That’s him, the third file in the front rank?”

“Yessir.” Fred Smith responded to the questioning tone in the officer’s voice, confirming with a quick glance towards his right that Joe Floyd was where he thought he was.

“And you, Corporal Smith, how are you? Are you married?”

“Oh yes sir, married a year ago now sir. Got a little girl sir.

Amy 'er name is. Three months old she is." The pride in his voice was clear, and he managed to respond despite the lump rising swiftly in his throat as he thought yet again of the pain that would come as he left them for the war.

"Good, good, that's wonderful." A pause. "We'll talk again later."

"Yessir, look forward to it sir." Fred was positively grinning; and there was no rebuke from the sergeant, for Fred Smith was one of the small club to which the three of them belonged.

Matthew Jenkins moved on, speeding up now; conscious that the platoon had been standing on the square for over half an hour, and it was a very hot August day. Ten minutes later, he was finished.

"Right, what's the form Sergeant Cooper? Where to now?"

"Medical Centre, sir, but only the platoon sir, not the officers. I'll take 'em if your happy with that, sir."

"Yes.....yes, of course." He hesitated. He'd never been happy with this business of sending off the soldiers whilst the officers went through a different door for special treatment. One thing in the mess, but not in preparation for war.....or in war itself. Still, now was not the time.

"Yes, carry on please."

"Right, time for a cup of tea before the medical centre. When I dismiss you, remember there is an officer on parade, and cut away to the canteen; and be outside the medical centre for ten o'clock. Look sharp now, atteeeeeenshun!"

"Officer on parade, diiiiismiss. Turn to your right," a pause, "salute," a pause, "left, right, left, right, left!" As they completed the five marching steps they broke ranks and moved individually off the square, shoulders swaying slightly with a swagger, still swinging their arms the regulation height, parallel to the ground with the thumb pressed down to lock the elbow straight."

Paul Cooper fell in alongside Matthew Jenkins as they left the square.

"Corporal Smith!" Matthew's voice raised just enough to catch Fred's attention, turn his head and, realising who had called, to break away and march towards him. Not for the first time did the rest of them wonder what there was between these three.

"Sir!" Just as Paul Cooper had before him, he observed all the niceties with a crashing halt, a smart salute and a crisp extra one pace forward.

"Corporal Smith, are we wearing socks?"

"Sir?" Fred was aghast. He was aghast because Matthew Jenkins had remembered from thirteen years back that he, Fred Smith, did not wear socks. It was a legacy of his childhood, where such luxuries had been unaffordable, and when given the opportunity by a grateful Queen and country to wear the issued sock he had found it uncomfortable. He was also aghast because he was not, on that day, wearing socks. And he was aghast, because he knew he'd been caught out and there was no escape.

"No sir." They knew each other too well for him to even think of trying a wet excuse.

"Sergeant Cooper, if we are going to keep this lot up to scratch we really can't go round interpreting the rules to suit ourselves can we?"

"No sir." He was seething. He'd been caught, Fred was the cause of it....and it was bloody unnecessary.

"Well, I rely on you and" turning to Fred "the experienced NCOs to keep these young men on the straight and narrow. So we'll maintain the necessary standards ourselves, shall we?"

"Yessir." Two voices in unison.

"Thank you. Well, carry on. I'll see you......when? Eleven o'clock outside the officers' mess. Then you can take me to the barrack room and we can get started."

In just a few brief moments he had succeeded in establishing his place at the head of the platoon; in making it clear that despite the common bond they shared he was in charge; and in placing them at a slight disadvantage that they would strive tooth and nail to redress. And he had done it all simply by creating a small embarrassment; without fuss and bombast or great statements about who was in charge. He had done it whilst at the same time gaining respect and a tacit acknowledgement that the status quo, the relationship between the officers, the NCOs and the men, was intact.

"Right sir. Leave to carry on sir please?"

"Yes please."

Salutes were exchanged. Paul Cooper and Fred Smith turned smartly, in unison, to their right and marched five paces before walking, less formally, on their way.

"Fred, I could bloody kill you!"

"I'm sorry, sarge. 'Ow the bloody 'ell was I supposed to know it was 'im? An' even if I did 'ow was I supposed to know 'e'd remember summat like that? I mean......" His voice tailed off.

"Well, bloody well sort it out, and lets not 'ave another bloody cock up. Jane's got the kettle on. Fancy a cuppa?"

Fred smiled at his friend. "Thanks, but I'd like to see Aggie an' the girl. I'll be at the medical centre at five to ten."

That same morning, in an office across Belfast, Count Edward von Gleichen stood at the window, his hands clasped behind his back, looking out over the barrack square below his Brigade Headquarters building at soldiers busying themselves with the final packing of equipment. Everything they did was configured in such a way that the headquarters could be established in the field as quickly as possible, ready to conduct operations.

Von Gleichen's tall slender frame fitted perfectly the uniform of a Brigadier General of the Grenadier Guards. His greying hair was immaculately groomed, the moustache perfectly trimmed, the leather of his Sam Browne belt and of his riding boots gleamed, and his jodhpurs exhibited not a single crease, despite the fact that he had been seated for most of the morning at his desk going again and again over the detail of his Brigade's mobilisation.

He turned as the door opened, expecting his servant with a cup of tea, but instead saw his Brigade Major wearing a look of excitement on his normally imperturbable face.

"We have our movement orders, sir. Over the telegraph just a few moments ago."

"And?" The calmness in the Brigadier's tone belying the quickening of his heart.

"We go on Friday, sir, the fourteenth. The Norfolks embark from Belfast Quay, from the York Dock. Half the battalion on the SS Anthony, with Brigade HQ and the Dorsets. The other half of the Norfolks are on the third ship, SS Massilion, with the Bedfords and some of the divisional transport. The Cheshires sail on the second ship, but we don't have a name for that yet."

His briefing was just a little more rushed than usual, despite his trying very hard to maintain his normal, restrained composure.

"Thank you. You will see to it that the necessary orders are despatched?" He knew that it went without saying, but it was a polite way of allowing his Brigade Major to leave and get on with his work.

"Yes, of course, Brigadier." He closed the door quietly behind him, paused briefly on the other side, squared his shoulders and headed purposefully towards his superintending clerk's office.

Meanwhile, the Count returned to his examination of the square below.

So this was it. At last, no more waiting. "My God, but I hope I get it right!"

"Come on Corporal." Colin Baxter rubbed a left arm that was already going stiff, recalling ruefully the black humour of the medical orderly who, in choosing which arm for the typhoid injection, had made it clear that, regardless of whether they wrote with their left or right hand, his only interest was that their ability to salute was not impaired. It had been left arms for everybody, and not a few hard men had felt faint as the large syringe had forced the treacle-like serum into the muscle.

"Tell us what's going on. How is it that they know each other, and very well if I'm any judge?"

The platoon was in the barrack room, awaiting the arrival of their new platoon commander. There was a low hubbub of conversation as they put finishing touches to things that had already had finishing touches put to them half a dozen times.

Fred sat down on Ted Ludgrove's bed. "Got a cuppa tea, then?"

An enamel mug appeared, strong brown tea lapping at the lip.

"Sugar?"

"Already in, Corporal." Alfie Jame's voice held a note of reassurance.

So it was that Fred Smith began to talk. As he did so the group around the bed grew larger, but he did not notice. As he continued the hubbub of conversation began to die out as more and more of them in the rest of the barrack room realised what was happening and joined the gathering, but still he did not notice. His eyes were looking somewhere into the middle distance, into his past, into something that had lain hidden for a long while.

He described vast, open plains and a scorching sun, dust rising as long columns of soldiers marched into the interior from the coast of South Africa. He talked about an aching thirst that was barely quenched by the overheated liquid contained in their metal water bottles; a thirst that having been slaked was as bad again within only a few minutes.

He spoke of the dust which pervaded everything: their clothes, their equipment, their food, their rifles and their skin. There was the soreness in the crotch as rough serge rubbed against the soft areas inside the thighs. There were the aching feet, the rawness of blisters that had split, and which were surrounded instantly by swarms of flies whenever they were exposed for treatment. These were the same flies that formed in clouds around food, even as it was on the spoon on its way to the mouth; the flies that spread the bugs which caused the stomach infections which led to diarrhoea and dysentery. It was the dysentery they feared the most. There wasn't enough water to cope with it, it weakened its victims terribly and could result in them being left behind on the march; at the mercy of Boer, native marauder or wild animal. And it was bloody uncomfortable having the shits every five minutes and nothing to wipe yer arse with.

Then there were the Boers; excellent soldiers whose tip and run tactics presented so many difficulties to an unwieldy column of conventional infantry, still fighting with the tactics of Wellington's day in a vast open country where mobility held the key to success. And they were very skilled, those Boers; and their shooting was terrific. Ah yes, the shooting was the key; good, accurate and fast, very accurate. And if we do the same to the bloody Germans as the Boers did to us they won't know what's 'it 'em.

It had been the assault on the hill that had done it. They'd been ordered to advance straight up this bloody 'ill, kopjes they called 'em; well, we copped it all right. There'd been no cover, no artillery, and the General didn't want to use the machine guns in the assault; probably didn't bloody well know 'ow to, 'cept we could've told 'im if 'ed asked. The attack hadn't started until midday, the hottest part of the day. Scarcely a half hour had passed before it was hopelessly pinned down, the fierce and accurate fire of the Boers having stopped it before it was half way to the summit. Lying in the sun with bullets whipping around was no fun at all. The heat was relentless, any exposed flesh becoming painfully burned and blistered within a very short time. Attempts to move, no matter how small, brought down that dreadful rifle fire, and more would be added to the casualty list. A man couldn't even raise a water bottle to his lips without risking death or wounding.

And the wounded suffered. Not daring to cry out, for that attracted yet more fire, they lay in agony, many crying to themselves with the pain of untended injuries, of flesh torn open by the Mauser bullets of the Boers, of internal bleeding creating swelling and pain, of bones broken by hits which shattered legs, arms, ribs, spines and pelvises. The gasping of those whose chest wall had been penetrated, sucking to draw in air to compensate for that being lost through the hole and by damaged lungs, with the taste of blood ever present in their throats. And everywhere were the flies, buzzing and whirling round, crawling over exposed wounds, dipping their proboscis into blood and mucus, guzzling what they could before moving on to the next victim, transmitting the filth they brought with them from the animal dung or carcass which had been their last resting place.

Men died, and many more wished they could.

When the night came there were no orders. The company had been on the right flank, and they had been on the right of the company. They had become separated as they sought to move on up the hill. Dozens, or at least it seemed like dozens, had been killed or wounded around them; and most of those wounded seemed to have succumbed. But with the fall of night there was the coolness; the sun was gone as was the withering fire of the Boers. Then had come the Hyenas, prowling among the dead and wounded, salivating jaws ripping into flesh and crunching through bone; and there were the screams, for some of their defenceless victims were not quite dead. It was time for the living to depart the scene of the carnage.

The young second lieutenant was very young indeed, and he was alone. Most of the NCOs were gone, and those who had survived were not to be seen, lost somewhere in the confusion that always prevails on a battlefield. He gathered around him those he could find. The young drummer boy had been found lying beside the body of a sergeant whom he had been trying to protect from the sun and the Boers, until the sergeant had gasped his last breath with the setting of the sun. There were four or five other privates who were unwounded and two men who had not been so lucky. One had been hit in the shoulder, and what remained was a tattered patchwork of torn ligaments, shattered bone and raw, bloody flesh. The other had been hit in the stomach, and did not have long left.

One private, a noisy unpleasant man who was not much liked, had begun to insist that one of the wounded, if not both, should be left so that the rest could escape with a better chance of success. The young second lieutenant, however, was made of sterner stuff, the private was put firmly in his place, and stretchers were made from tunics and equipment straps.

He spoke of the long march; of the soldier with the stomach wound dying, mercifully, before they had gone a mile; of the shallow grave they had scraped for him; of lying up during the day to escape the marauding Boer patrols, flushed with their victory over the British soldiers; of surviving that long day on very little water, and the aching hunger straining at the bellies of men who had barely eaten for thirty-six hours and were conserving their few biscuits. He told of the second night, marching in what they hoped was a southerly direction, carrying the second wounded soldier who was by now delirious; too delirious to smell the sickly, sweet stench of gangrene that was being emitted from his suppurating wound.

They listened with rapt attention. There was no sound in the barrack room. The tea went cold in the enamel cup in Fred Smith's hand as he talked of things which had been buried inside him for so many years, things he thought he had forgotten. Alfie James reached over and gently removed it from his hand. Fred smiled, his gratitude a subconscious thing, as he continued talking.

The end of the second day laying up, and by now they were in a desperate state. The wounded soldier had lost so much fluid that he would never recover, and he died at around midnight on the third night; by which time the smell of gangrene was overpowering, permeating deep into the stomachs of the rest of them and inducing a permanent feeling of sickness. His passing had been a relief to them all.

Thirst and dehydration were driving them mad. Two of the group, one being the noisy private, refused to move when the burial in a shallow, scraped grave of their dead comrade had been completed. It was too much, and they would take their chances with the Boers, and with anything else that came their way. The second lieutenant, the drummer boy and the three remaining privates moved on, until dawn when they again went into hiding.

It had been the dust that had caused the drummer boy to look into the distance at around midday. He'd been on sentry go for about an hour, trying desperately to keep his eyes open, terribly conscious of the enormous responsibility on his young shoulders for his sleeping colleagues, when he saw the plume rising away towards the line of some nearby hills. Swiftly, they had taken up the defensive positions which had been set out by the officer when they had settled down. Throughout it all he had maintained proper standards, and had never let discipline slip. With the last of the biscuits long gone, and only a mouthful of water each, God knew they were in no state to fight anybody; but he wouldn't accept that and he made sure they didn't.

As the plume had drawn closer he had given the fire control order, quietly and firmly, ensuring that they would hold their fire until he gave the final executive command. Even the young drummer boy had armed himself, quite against regulations, and was squinting along the barrel of the Lee Metford rifle, ready to sell his young life as dearly as he could.

But it was a command that was never given, for it was not the irregular horsemen of the Boer Commandos that came into view. It was the cavalry, and British cavalry, not native troops.

The water their rescuers had eased gently into the throats of the five of them had been like nectar, but it had been so frustratingly slow. The soldiers all knew the danger of suddenly pouring water into dehydrated bodies, but that didn't make it any easier to bear when it was happening to you; and food was given gently and in small quantities. Shelters were made, picquets were posted, a troop was detached to take the exhausted, dehydrated men back to safety; and a day later the final part of their journey began.

By the time Second Lieutenant Matthew Jenkins, three privates and a drummer boy were back with the regiment they were all able to walk on their own two feet, although Private Fred Smith had found it necessary to take Boy Drummer Cooper to one side and smarten him up a bit before the RSM saw him.

As Fred's voice tailed away the silence became a tangible thing, a blanket around them all, creating an atmosphere of togetherness which no one wished, consciously, to break. Partly, it was because Fred was drained by the memories that had been resurrected and was content just to sit, staring into his hands, but also because young men had learned one of the great lessons of life: that a book ought never to be judged by its cover. Suddenly, Fred Smith was no longer the silly old sod who nit-picked over a frayed puttee; suddenly people felt a mix of shame and admiration; suddenly there was respect not for the Corporal, but for the man.

As the silence seemed it would go on forever, the door crashed open.

"On yer feet!"

Paul Cooper had met his new Platoon Commander at the appointed time just in front of the officers' mess, and they walked in step in the direction of the block.

"Tell me," said Matthew, "that young man in the third rank, in Corporal Smith's section, the one with the educated voice. What's his story?"

"Ah, Private Baxter. Yes, he's an odd one. It took us some time to find out what he was up to, and why he joined; but a few glasses of ale loosened 'im up one night."

"And.....?"

"Came from Yarmouth we think. 'Is father works as an accountant or something. 'E was under a deal of pressure to join the family firm, but that wasn't what 'e wanted. There was also a problem with a young lady."

"Oh yes." And it wouldn't be the first time a young lady had driven a man into the Army. Matthew Jenkins smiled a knowing smile.

Paul Cooper grinned.

"No sir, it's not like that. Baxter's old man seems to have been something of a tyrant, and 'e wanted young Colin to help with the expansion of the firm's interests by marrying the daughter of the boss of some other firm in the town. I can't speak about the young lady sir, or why young Baxter didn't want anythin' to do with it all, but 'e left home and joined the Ninth. He never gets any mail. Bit of a loner really."

"Does that mean.......good heavens, who on earth is that?" Matthew cut short his question and gasped as he watched an extremely fat lady walking towards the married quarters area, pushing a perambulator which seemed like a toy beside her massive frame. But it was not simply the size that caused him to gasp; the face surmounting the huge frame was not attractive in any sense of the word. Facial hair, moles and poor teeth were just three things he noticed before he realised he was staring and turned away to look at his platoon sergeant.

"Oh," Paul Cooper smiled, "that's Aggie, Fred Smith's wife; and that'll be little Amy in the pram. Pretty little thing she is."

"But why, how, I mean, what made him......." He stopped speaking, realising that he was about to speak derogatorily about the wife of one of his soldiers. "But, what on earth........?"

"Not the prettiest is she?" Paul Cooper was still smiling. "But you need to understand. You see, Fred lived in barracks for all his service, and after... what....fourteen years or so he'd had enough. But he'd also seen how the wives of some of the blokes behave when the men are away. Not exactly lady-like, some of 'em; and there's always the rear party or blokes from some other mob sniffin' round tryin' it on. Well, Fred decided he was goin' to get married and he went home on leave to find a wife; and his idea was to find someone so ugly that no one else would want to look at her, ever. So he'd always be safe."

"You're not serious?"

"It's the honest truth, really it is. He told me before he went away that he would come back married and he did."

"But, ...well.....I mean, really."

"Don't knock it sir. He has a cooked breakfast every morning, the house is spotless, and he goes home to a cooked tea and a warm bed every night. He's not lonely any more; in fact, he's a changed man in many ways. They've both got smiles on their faces, and while Fred's no oil paintin', and Aggie certainly isn't, little Amy's a smasher.

They were nearly at the barrack room door.

"And you're married as well?"

"Aye, sir, and you'll meet Jane sometime before we go."

It would happen that they would somehow "accidentally" meet on neutral ground, and Matthew Jenkins knew that Cooper would arrange it thus.

The two men entered the room, following the noisy crash of the door and the sergeant's exhortation for them all to stand up. They were in time to see that the entire platoon had gathered near the centre of the room, surrounding someone on one of the beds.

The men in the group started and broke away to stand facing the officer and the sergeant. More slowly, Fred Smith rose from the bed, saw Matthew and stood rigidly to attention.

"Sir!" The senior corporal used, as was so often the case with soldiers, the single word as acknowledgement of his presence. The officer smiled at him and saluted. Both the greeting and the return of the compliment were the marks of mutual respect; and this time the platoon understood.

"We're off!" The voice echoed through the barrack block, as a runner from company headquarters appeared suddenly in the open doorway.

"We're off. The orders are through. We're sailin' on Friday!"

Chapter 4

Off To War

Friday the fourteenth of August 1914 dawned warm and sunny. The battalion marched from Palace Barracks during the middle of the morning, covering the distance to the nearby Belfast Quay in very short order. Although the move was relatively brief, it was an experience that would remain with every man who took part for the rest of his life; and in many cases that would be less than three weeks.

The streets were lined with crowds, cheering and waving frantically, singing impromptu versions of Land of Hope and Glory and Rule Britannia. They were assisted in this latter endeavour by the regimental band crashing out rendition after rendition of their regimental march which, coincidentally, was Rule Britannia. The centrepiece of the cap badge being worn by the soldiers of the Ninth was Britannia herself, seated proudly upon her throne; and they were quite certain that their Britannia would rule, no matter what came their way. There were great outbursts of clapping and applauding as each sub-unit passed by. Union Jacks were much in evidence, clutched in the hot sweaty little hands of small children who cheered as they were told neither knowing nor caring about the reason. They were also in the hands of young women, to whom the soldiers they had rejected on the sea front and in the local dance halls suddenly seemed so much more attractive and to whom they blew kisses, flirting with their eyes. Young men were also in the crowd, their feelings a mixture of emotions, mainly envy. They were envious of the other young men they saw marching; envious of the adoring looks of the women in the crowd; envious of the great adventure upon which the soldiers were embarking; and envious of the obvious pride and comradeship which was transparent on the face of every man who marched past in the long column of just over one thousand men.

Many of those young men in the crowd would be in the recruiting offices within forty-eight hours. Many of them would be dead before Easter the following year, some seven months away.

There were also the old ones in the crowd. Those who had been there before, who remembered the pride and great feeling of togetherness as they marched off to war. And old eyes watered just a little, which may have been the product of a wistful memory of times gone by, of the good old days. Or maybe they were recalling the horror those young men were about to face, the suffering of long marches in foul conditions, the soldiers' illnesses which could reduce a man to a shivering, vomiting wreck, the agony of wounds as flesh and bone were torn asunder, the pain of seeing friends die. Maybe they were just remembering it as it really was and were sad that yet again British soldiers had to march to the sound of the guns.

It was the ones who remained behind in Palace Barracks who did not cheer: the wives who had said their goodbyes, and who could not face the cheerful celebration in the streets outside. For Aggie Smith the agony was almost unbearable. Dragged from a life of misery, from being the butt of jokes and unpleasantness everywhere she went, she had found with Fred a fulfilment she could never have dreamed possible. As she sat and cuddled her baby close to her; she cried a flood of tears, borne on a welling physical pain that developed deep inside her stomach and roared up though her chest as if to tear her heart from her body. She sobbed deeply and uncontrollably until, exhausted, she fell asleep holding Amy to her as if both their lives depended upon it.

Elsewhere other wives held close to their children, keeping a tight grip as if to draw security from their touch. Some cried, some proceeded determinedly to undertake the routines of housework and others gathered in small groups in their houses to drink tea and talk. The officers' wives kept their public faces determined and calm, and began to organise support for wives, children and the departed men; and, behind the scenes, some of them cried too. Meanwhile, in a small Norfolk village, a young, unmarried woman thought wistfully of a young man who was marching off to war, and wondered what might have been; and in the market town of Thetford the young wife of a banker placed her hand upon her tummy, pondered the implications of her delayed period, and she too wondered what might have been. And she prayed.

So it was the Ninth marched to war, rifles held at the slope, the free right arm swinging up and back, the right thumb pressed down to lock the elbow and keep the arm nice and straight, the shoulders swaying jauntily, revelling in the roars and the applause of the crowds lining the streets. The regimental band led them through the streets of Belfast, interspersing their renditions of Rule Britannia with a range of good, patriotic British marches; several of which, paradoxically, had their origins in good patriotic German marches. Sometimes they played something more up to date: "Swanee River," "Tipperary," "The Girl I left Behind Me" and "Who'll Come to France With Me" were also on the list. Chests swelled with an overpowering sense of pride and occasion. What a bloody marvellous thing to happen, especially since it would only be for a short while. They had been promised that the whole thing would be over in time for Christmas, whereupon they could return and take up with some of the adoring young women who were lining the streets to see them off.

The same reception had greeted the Cheshires and the Dorsets as they disembarked from trains that had brought them from Derry and Mullingar and marched to the docks to join the rest of the brigade. The Bedfords too. At the York Dock on Belfast Quay the SS Anthony was drawn up alongside with the SS Massilion, and it was between these two ships that the Norfolks were to be distributed for the voyage to Le Havre in France.

"You will be travelling on the steamship Massilion." Matthew Jenkins had briefed his platoon that morning. "We shall be sharing it with the First Battalion of the Bedfordshire Regiment, and there will also be some of the Alley Slopers' Cavalry from the divisional transport." His uttering of the uncharitable slang always used in connection with the Army Service Corps had caused a smile among his assembled soldiers.

"Cumpneeeeey Halt!" The sergeant major's word of command, issued as the combined left heels of the company hit the ground, was followed by a short checking pace to slow down the speed at which they were marching, followed by the smart "one-two" of a perfectly executed halt; and stillness.

"Cumpney will advance..........leeeeeeft turn!" In an instant they were facing him, drawn up in three ranks.

"Ordeeeeer......arms!"

"Standat ease! Stand easy! Right, you can relax here. It will be about thirty minutes before you're called forward to embark. You can break ranks, but you will not leave this immediate area and you will not smoke while you have that lot looking on." He referred to the civilian population of Belfast, many of whom were gathered at nearby railings, jostling to get the best possible view.

"Clear? Any questions? No? Good. Right, settle your packs on the ground, and keep yer bund'ooks with you." And with that the sergeant major marched swiftly away to where his company commander was talking quietly to the platoon commanders.

It wasn't very many minutes before the attractions at the railings drew many of the soldiers in that direction. Packets of cigarettes, pipe tobacco, sweets and cakes, whisky, beer and brandy were being proffered by young and old alike. Hands were reaching out to shake those of the soldiers, to pat them on the arm or the shoulder.

"I think," said Colin Baxter, "it would be foolish if we

failed to capitalise on the situation. If we play our cards right we could collect enough booze and cigarettes to last us until we come back."

"Just make sure yer keep yer bund'ooks safe, and don't wander too far." Fred Smith's warning voice followed them as they headed for the fence.

"Here ye go lad, take it, it'll keep yer warm in the noit!" There was genuine warmth in the voice, despite the harsh Belfast accent, as the elderly man passed a bottle of Bushmills whisky to Alfie James. It was a flat bottle, which would make it easier to carry. Very considerate.

"Thanks pop, thanks very much."

"Don't thank us laddy," said the old man's even older companion. "Jus' keep it safe, drink it when ye need it, an' keep yer bloody head down when yer doin' it." Alfie looked up, surprised by the tone of gruff affection in the old man's voice.

"Aye lad," said the younger of the two. "Keep yer bloody 'ead down, an' yer arse too, and watch out for them sneaky buggers."

"But 'e's too young t' be doin' this, so 'e is!" The large middle-aged lady was talking about Peter Dakin as she handed him a box of home made cakes. If the box felt a little heavy it had something to do with the bottle of gin packed into the middle. "Y'll look after yerself young man. If yer mother was here she'd be saying the same, so she would. Wouldn't she, Joseph?" She turned for support to her husband.

"Aye, she would that laddie. You take care now." Her diminutive husband responded on cue.

"And write t' yer mother as well. Ye'll do that, won't ye? She'll want ye to do that, so she will." The note of genuine concern in her voice came through very clearly to Peter, blushing furiously at the grins on the faces of his friends nearby who were hugely amused at his discomfort.

"'Avn't got a ma, missus," he heard himself say for a reason he did not understand. It wasn't something he'd thought about for many years. "Nor a da' neether."

"Joseph, pencil and paper!" Her imperious command

had her husband fishing in his pockets in order to comply. She began writing. "Well, you have now, so ye have. Ye'll write to me when ye need to an' I'll be yer ma. An' oi'll be here when ye get back, so oi will."

Her hand reached out and crammed the piece of paper with her name and address into his left hand breast pocket, he being disadvantaged with a rifle in one hand and a box of cakes, and gin, in the other. She kissed the tips of her fingers and touched her hand against his cheek.

"An' ye'll take care now, so ye will?"

"Aye,....aye, I'll take care," he said, barely able to speak for the lump in his throat.

A few feet away Ted Ludgrove had found himself funnelled into position against the railings by the press of his friends, facing a woman in her early twenties. Her brown hair with a hint of red framed a pretty face, with a full red mouth and startling blue eyes.

"Cigarette?" She offered him the packet, and he noticed that she wore wedding and engagement rings. He remembered the sergeant major's last words.

"No thanks, not just now."

"D'ye moind if oi do?"

He fished in his pocket, pulled out a box of Swan Vestas and held out a burning match to light the cigarette she had just put between her lips. She cupped his hand in hers, soft white hands with scarlet painted fingernails. He felt a tremor pass down to his nether regions, and his mouth suddenly became very dry.

"This'll be your first toime, then. Goin' of t' foit, I mean?"

"Aye." He didn't really know what to say.

"Scared?" She raised an eyebrow and looked at him quizzically, her mouth slightly twisted open to reveal a hint of white even teeth.

It was something that had bothered him, but was not a matter that was ever discussed. Nonetheless, he felt the familiar pang of concern deep in his stomach. Confused, he mumbled a response.

"Don't know, really."

"Well oi bloody well would be, an' that's fer sure. Anyway,

take these with ye," she pressed the rest of the cigarettes into his hand. "And this."

With that she reached through the railing with her left hand behind his neck and pulled his face towards her. He jerked back in surprise, but then allowed the pressure of her hand to pull him forward. He'd kissed girls before, but it had always been a hastily snatched peck after a dance or an evening out. He was not prepared for what followed as her right hand reached forward and with gentle pressure on his chin opened his mouth slightly. Her warm, moist lips caressed his own with a gentle, firm pressure. He could smell the perfume she wore, and the taste of tobacco on her breath, in a heady, sensuous mix.

Suddenly, he felt the soft touch of her tongue around his lips and then its gentle insertion, three or four times, into the entrance to his mouth. He was prevented from jerking back in surprise by the pressure of her hand on his neck, the nails gently scratching as she probed with her tongue. Slowly she drew back, just a few inches, looking straight into his eyes, her breath warm and seductive against his face; he still caught the residue of tobacco smoke. The pressure in his loins had increased swiftly and substantially and the tingling excitement spread throughout the lower part of his body in a surging wave.

"Sorry there isn't time to offer you more. Take care now." The voice soft, the eyes tender. Once more the kiss, brief this time, and she was gone into the crowd leaving behind a very confused Ted Ludgrove trying to wipe lipstick from his mouth and to ensure that no one could see the evidence of his instantaneous arousal.

"Some people get all the luck." Joseph Floyd wore a lascivious grin which caused Ted's temper to rise instantly, he having just undergone an experience that had affected him deeply; and he had just been beginning to wonder what he had been missing. He was prevented from saying anything by Paul Cooper's voice instructing them to "get fell in."

It was lunchtime as they boarded the SS Massilion, and at three o'clock in the afternoon she cast off her moorings and sailed out into Belfast Lough. As they boarded, they had been shown to their cramped accommodation where they had dumped their kit before proceeding up on deck.

When he arrived at the ship's rail Peter Dakin instantly began searching for Joseph and his wife, whom he now knew to be Ethel. They were exactly where he had left them, and as soon as he began waving they spotted him and responded. They remained, looking at each other throughout all the preparations for sailing and as the ship moved out through Belfast Lough to the open sea. Joseph and Ethel stayed by the railing, waving until the Massilion vanished out of sight and a local band ceased playing rendition after rendition of Auld Lang Syne. That evening Ethel sat in the front room of her terraced house in New Lodge and wept for a young man she barely knew, but whom she loved; and for the other young men who had neither mother nor father, who would die never having known a mother's love.

Peter stayed at the ship's rail, flanked on either side by Alfie and Ted, each consumed with his own thoughts concerning events at the dockyard railings, each respecting the silence they all sought, staying together as they had since they first joined up.

Thus it was that the Fifteenth Infantry Brigade went off to war, with one hundred and twenty seven officers, three thousand nine hundred and fifty eight men, two hundred and fifty eight horses and seventy-four wagons. They left behind in Northern Ireland those reservists who had become somewhat too flabby in civilian life to be capable of undertaking arduous work or who had medical disorders. They would follow later when a regime of fitness training and less luxurious food would reduce their weight and harden their muscles; and when those with minor ailments were completely healthy. These people were not too unhappy with their lot, but there was another group whose demeanour could easily be described as miserable. Those who were too young to go to war, which was something over one hundred men in the Ninth, had remained as rear party or had been given travel warrants to Norwich where they would join the special reserve battalion at the regimental depot. They were furious. Here was a great adventure of which they could have been a part, and it would be over long before any of them was old enough to partake.

Dinner on board had been far from luxurious for the soldiers, crammed together below decks in a ship which was battened down in complete darkness as a defence against marauding German warships. The Royal Navy was master of the seas, and everyone knew about its first victory with the sinking on the fifth of August of the Konigen Louise, which had been laying mines in the North Sea. Nonetheless, despite their confidence it was best to be on the safe side.

The officers had fared rather better, with a meal prepared by the ship's cook, with beer as an accompaniment and a glass of the Captain's brandy to finish it off. Matthew Jenkins continued to find this different treatment difficult to cope with, and his mind had been on the meal his men would be eating: cold meat, bread and cheese drawn from the cookhouse that morning and carried with them throughout the day. It was a ration that would have to last them the two days until they disembarked, at which point they would revert to the iron rations of bully beef and biscuit that each man carried with him.

"Right, listen in!"

The sergeant major called them to order. The company was gathered in part of a hold with port-holes blacked out and the light from electric lamps fixed onto the bulkhead casting shadows across the assembled soldiery.

"I have called you together to pass on some orders which the brigade commander wishes to have communicated directly to each one of you." The company commander's well modulated voice echoed eerily off the metal walls of the hold, his tone pitched up in order to overcome the throbbing of the engines which pervaded every corner of the ship.

"I want you to pay particular attention to what I am

about to say, and to bear in mind Brigadier General von Gleichen's words as we prepare to do battle with the Hun."

He coughed, cleared his throat and began to read.

"The German fallacy that determined men in sufficient numbers can do anything has been proved a fallacy in fighting around Liege. Their apparently terrifying masses of men can be swept away by steady fire of much smaller numbers. Therefore, keep cool, shoot straight and don't waste ammunition. When you are on the move remember to keep your intervals. The Germans apparently hate cold steel. Therefore, use the bayonet whenever you get the chance."

This last remark produced grins from the young soldiers, and grim looks from the more experienced.

"Pick off the officers. Germans have little initiative and lose their heads once the officers have fallen. Remember, they are not on the lookout for ambushes and traps. And finally, no man in the Fifth Division ever surrenders - we fight to the finish, everyone to the last man."

The company commander looked up from the sheet of paper from which he had read. They were silent, the banter wasn't there. The brigade commander's last instruction had struck a chord. This was war, and some of them would not survive it.

"Right," a firm authoritative voice. "Fifteen minutes to lights out."

"Wot's 'e know abaht it anyway?" Jack Waters had been the last reservist to join the platoon. He had been released from remand, where the police had been discussing with him a series of petty thefts around the market place in Norwich, by a magistrate who thought he would be more use to his country back in the ranks. His arrival had been delayed, and he had reported to Palace Barracks only two days before departure. Kitting him out and preparing him generally had taken considerable effort, and created some acrimony in the section, partly evinced by his unfortunate manner. He was a moaner, always criticising, and very quickly got under the collective skin of a group of soldiers, regular and reservist, who had begun to come together as a team.

His remark was addressed to Ned Preece as they moved towards their accommodation. “Whadyemean, wot does ’e know about it. ’E’s a bloody German ’imself ain’t ’e? ’E’s bound t’ bloody know abaht it?” Ned was not especially pleased that Waters seemed to see in him a kindred spirit, and latched himself on at every conceivable opportunity. His response was, accordingly, hostile.

“An’ that’s another thing.” Waters was not to be put off. “Wot’re we doin’ goin’ t’ war against the bloody Germans an’ the bloody bloke in charge is a bloody German ’isself? Don’t seem right, not t’ me it don’t!”

“Shut yer gab Private Waters and get t’ yer pit, and do not talk disrespectful about yer senior officers!” Fred Smith put an end to the conversation, and earned a grimace of gratitude from Ned Preece.

Brigadier General Count Edward von Gleichen would have permitted himself a wry smile had he heard Jack Waters’ question. A lifetime of regimental soldiering as an officer of the Grenadier Guards had left him with a clear understanding of what motivated his soldiers and how their minds worked. Indeed, he was aware that the question of his name had probably crossed many of those minds since Germany had suddenly become the enemy.

In fact, his family home was in Langenberg, in Wüttemburg in southern Germany. His father, a man of limited income, had been an officer in the Royal Navy at a time when relations between German royal houses and that of the United Kingdom had been rather more cordial than was the case in the summer of 1914. This had come about because Count Edward’s paternal grandmother had been Queen Victoria’s half sister, and the Queen had been very fond of her “half nephew”; Count Edward’s father. When she heard that the boy was unhappy at his school in Dresden and had run away from it she had induced her half sister to send him to England and had put him into the Navy in 1848. In 1866 his father had been forced to leave the Royal

Navy due to ill health and had remained in England, taking up sculpture to supplement his income. Subsequently, the young Edward von Gleichen had undergone his education at Charterhouse and went from there, in 1880, to the Royal Military College Sandhurst. He had been commissioned into the Grenadier Guards in October 1881.

Every inch an officer of one of the world's elite regiments, the first regiment of foot in the household troops of the British sovereign, and a quintessential Englishman, there was no doubt whatsoever where his loyalty lay. Nonetheless, he knew "Thomas" only too well and understood perfectly that his origins, or "Thomas'" version of it, would give his soldiers something to talk about on the troop decks and in the canteens; and it bothered him not one jot.

It was one of his idiosyncrasies to refer to the soldiers under his command, collectively, as "Thomas," after the fashion of calling British soldiers "Tommy Atkins", "Tommy" or "Tommies." In fact, he could be considered to be the more correct bearing in mind the origins of the nickname which allegedly lay with the Duke of Wellington some seventy years or so earlier. Towards the end of the Iron Duke's life in the middle of the previous century, so the story goes, the British Army had sought to create a new accounting sheet for soldiers' pay. In developing an example to show where soldiers should sign it, they had wished to put on the signature block a name which represented the British soldier. On being asked what he felt the name should be the Duke's thoughts had gone back to his time in command of the Thirty Third Regiment of Foot, by 1914 known as the Duke of Wellington's Regiment, during the Flanders campaign at the end of the eighteenth century. It was from this experience that he was to make his choice.

In the aftermath of what had been his first battle he had ridden past a group of his wounded soldiers and had stopped by one who was in great pain, a sabre cut having split his head, a bayonet wound in his chest and a musket ball in his stomach. He was the right hand man of the Grenadier Company and he lay at the spot where he had fallen. A six foot three inch soldier with twenty years service, he was the best handler of weapons in the regiment, and he could neither read nor write. He had looked up, had seen the expression of concern on the Duke's face and had said: "It's all right, sir. It's all in the day's work." And then he had died.

His name was Thomas Atkins.

The weather on Saturday the fifteenth of August was perfect, especially for those who had feared the onset of mal de mer the instant the ship set sail. A blazing sun shone out of a clear blue sky on calm placid waters as the ship made her way south through the Irish Sea towards the English Channel. She hugged the coastline as a precaution against marauding German warships with the added protection of a screen of Royal Naval destroyers to shepherd the small convoy, of which she was a part, safely on its journey.

For most of them it was completely uneventful. Weapons were cleaned, kit was sorted yet again, some reservists undertook revision under the guidance of NCOs and a number suffered the trials of inoculations they had missed before departure. Jack Waters was one of these, and his misery at the perceived injustice was communicated, unreservedly, to the rest of the section. For their part, they became very bored very quickly, and drifted up on deck to enjoy the summer sunshine and the sea breezes.

Ted was staring out to sea, watching, but not seeing, the wheeling seagulls following in the ship's wake, the extraordinary affair by the railings still dominating his thoughts, when his peace was interrupted.

"It's young Ludgrove, ain't it?"

He started and turned, not recognising the voice. The sight of the man talking to him, however, sent a pang of homesickness through him as he remembered home and family. The face was puffier than he remembered it, and the figure was somewhat stouter than it had been when last he saw it, but the star shaped scar on the left cheekbone told him at once that it was John Allsop. Instantly, Ted's mind went back to the fateful weekend when he had first seen

Allsop and his wife, and had last seen his mother, father and sisters.

"I thought it was you. I only saw you the once, in the Bull that night just before you left an' I weren't sure I'd got the right chap; but it is you isn't it?"

"Aye, it's me. Mr Allsop innit. Sorry, Lance Corporal Allsop." He corrected himself, noting the stripes on his sleeves and the Bedfordshire flashes on his epaulettes. "Called you up for this did they?"

"Aye. Seven years with the colours and they can still get you for five years afterwards. Still, I don' mind. Bit of an adventure really. Gets you away from the daily grind, if yer know what I mean." He nudged Ted, and winked conspiratorially. Ted felt embarrassed.

"Not bad really. Quite a lot of the blokes I knew in the regiment are back, and some of the others is seniors. Bit like comin' 'ome really. All me mates an' that." He did not sound convincing.

They stood by the ship's rail, talking for some time before Fred Smith walked by and broke into their conversation. Within a few minutes John Allsop bade his farewells, citing a duty elsewhere as the reason for his departure and promising to stay in touch once they got to France. Maybe to go out for a beer or two when it was quiet and they'd settled down over there. His departure caused no regret in Ted, who found his obsequious manner and overly friendly approach embarrassing and disturbing. The man seemed constantly to be seeking to justify himself; and if he was as popular and proficient as he claimed why was he just a bloody lance corporal?

Ted was clearly unsettled by the meeting, and after a few cursory politenesses Fred Smith moved on, leaving him alone with his thoughts. He gazed back out to sea, his mind in a turmoil and oblivious to the high jinks going on around him as his mates enjoyed their cruise in the sunshine and laughed and joked about the great adventure to come. Alfie James approached him once, trying to get him to join in. One look told him to leave well alone.

Really, Allsop had not told him much he did not know

already from his mother's letters, but it had brought home to him the life he had left behind and the change in his fortunes that had been brought about by his meeting with Edward Snell. One thing was for sure, he wouldn't now be going off to war if it had not been for the events of that weekend. He had, however, learned for the first time that his whereabouts had remained a mystery in the village for a full eighteen months after he had left. He had often wondered why he had not been pursued by the constable to Norwich and taken to task for his assault on Snell. He had known that his actions had been correct, and that he had prevented Snell from doing something awful, but no one would have believed him. Alice was hardly a reliable witness and he could not have let it be known that he and Betty Chalmers had been together, alone in the woods, that day, no matter how innocent it had been. Her honour was at stake.

But his parents had kept the secret, and allowed him the time he needed completely to escape. It had not been until his sister Eliza had let it drop to one of her friends in the village that the news had got out. Reactions had, according to Allsop, been mixed. Inevitably, Henry Johnson had expressed his pleasure, telling anyone who would listen that it had been his idea in the first place. Some had said it was a good thing and would be the making of him. For many others, bearing in mind that the average working man of the day often viewed the Army with disapproval, he had broken the faith and his decision had been viewed with distaste. No one really expected to see him back for as long as Edward Snell retained his position in the community and would probably have him arrested the minute he set foot in the place. His sense of loneliness was almost overpowering.

By midday on Sunday the sixteenth of August the novelty of the sea cruise had begun to wear off, and boredom was setting in. It was another beautiful day, and they really could not have asked for a better crossing, but cramped living conditions, dull food and a general lack of space had taken their toll. From the early afternoon, however, the search was on for the coastline of France and the first sight of the harbour at Le Havre.

Eventually, the signs of land began to appear and men slowly crowded onto the decks, their kit already packed and ready to go despite the fact that it would be several hours before they disembarked. At about three-fifteen the white buildings of the port began to take shape and the SS Massilion headed straight for her berth. Such was the planning and careful staff work that had gone into the execution of the deployment of the BEF there was no delay as the ships containing the Fifteenth Brigade moved into their allotted berths. The Massilion tied up alongside at four o'clock, fractionally over two days after she had left Belfast.

The men disembarked at once, although there was to be a delay whilst the horses were unloaded by sling. They were scarcely able to comprehend the welcome they received. If the farewell from Belfast had been memorable, this was absolutely unforgettable.

Flags of red white and blue waved yet again, this time the French Tricoleur. The yelling and cheering continued unabated as they walked down the gangplank and formed up on the dockside. Attempts to keep the crowd back were not terribly successful, and very soon those who had made it to the waterside were surrounded by French people of all shapes, sizes and types. Language should have been a barrier, but seemed not to be. Officers tried to recall their schoolboy French and made attempts to talk to the grave old men who wore sashes of red, white and blue and, in some cases, the ribbon of the Legion d'Honneur; and who approached them, saluting slowly and formally in the French style, bidding their allies welcome. Bienvenue en France.

Fred Smith sought to use the linguistic skills he had developed in South Africa. This consisted of speaking loudly and slowly in English, and putting the sound "ee" at the end of key words. It was a similar technique to that used by other old soldiers, be they veterans of Burma, India, the Middle East or South Africa. It seemed to work, as they collected bottles of wine, cheeses, packs of ham, flasks of cider and sundry other good things; all of which were a lot more attractive than the bully beef and biscuits which were on their menu for that evening.

Eventually, the senior NCOs managed to get the battalion into some semblance of order. The officers had long ago given up and left them to it. It was a good hour and a half before they managed to march off in the direction of the camp to which they had been assigned, Rest Camp Eight at Graville on the heights above the harbour. However, marching through the cobbled streets of Le Havre they continued to suffer the attentions of the local population. Small children ran alongside the marching men, jumping and skipping and emulating their marching with swinging arms, high steps and looks of mock seriousness. Girls and young women reached out to hold the arm or the hand of a soldier. Some touched as many as they could, others chose an individual and walked alongside him as he marched. Lipstick on their cheeks bore witness to the number of kisses they had received. The major had received a great cheer from the company when a very large middle aged lady had identified him as a man of some importance, had approached him like a galleon under full sail and had enveloped him in her enormous bosom, followed by a large wet kiss, three times, once each on alternate cheeks. He had managed to extract himself with dignity, to thank her most graciously for her welcome and to offer, in flawless French, his best wishes to her and her family. He then moved swiftly to the head of his company where he was able to regain his composure, fully aware that he had given his soldiers something with which they would keep themselves amused for some time to come.

"Amazing really," he said to Matthew Jenkins standing nearby. "We are by no means the first to arrive. They must have been doing this for days. Heaven only knows what it must have been like for our predecessors, poor devils."

It was ten o'clock that night before the Norfolks reached their overnight accommodation, and it was there they discovered that they would be sleeping twelve to a large tent. Because it had been raining heavily in that part of

France for the previous two days the ground was wet underfoot. There was no bedding and, to add to their misery, the battalion's transport was stuck on the steep hill up which they had just marched, blocked by a broken down lorry. They would sleep that night on wet ground in the clothes in which they stood. Not only that, but the march up the steep hill from the port had shown the early manifestation of a problem that was to beset them over the next few days: the reservists were simply not fit. They had experienced difficulties with new boots and with webbing chafing at their shoulders. The sheer physical effort of marching, fully laden with the sixty pound weight of complete Field Service Marching Order, or FSMO, on cobbles up a testing incline had almost been too much in some cases. Neither had the after effects of the inoculations been of great help.

Albert Carter, who had arrived in the same call-up batch as Alfred Arbuckle, had found it particularly testing. He had been down on his luck since leaving the regular Army, and poor diet had been a major factor in him lacking the stamina necessary to keep up with his fitter colleagues. He had been close to dropping out, even over that short distance, and trying to cadge a lift on the transport. He was not relishing the prospect of what might be to come, but at least he was earning a little money which would enable him to send something home to his wife to help her with the children. He remembered vividly the hours leading up to his departure. She had not wanted him to go, she would not be able to cope without him, what was she expected to do when one of the children was sick, how would she manage the vegetable garden, how would she drag the shopping back home, what would happen if............? It had not been a happy parting, and he could remember very clearly the accusing look on her face as she stood in the doorway of their small cottage, hair straggling round her thin, pinched face, baby Enid held on her hip and their small son David clutching at his mother's skirt, mucus dripping from his constantly runny nose, watching his father walk down the garden path to rejoin the colours.

"Right, listen in!" Paul Cooper's voice brought them back from the tents into which they had begun to dump their kit to form a group around him.

"You will sleep in these tents tonight. There is hot tea in the cookhouse, over there." He pointed behind him. "Your ration for the night is the beef and biscuit you were issued in Belfast. I am well aware that you have collected large amounts of food from the natives and the medical officer has advised that there is no problem with you eating any of it. However, there is a Force Order which forbids the drinking of the local milk as it can cause Enteric Fever."

"Wot's that then, sarge?"

"It's Sergeant to you Private Waters, and that is the last time I will tell you that. I don't know what it is, but it gives you the shits, so stay off the milk. Clear?" There was a mumbled response.

"Anyway, given the booze you've collected I doubt that milk will be a major problem. Which brings me to my next point. Any man the worse for drink in the morning is in deep trouble. We are at war and there is to be no nonsense. Clear?" Another mumbled response.

"Finally, if any of you have any idea of going back down into the town you can forget it. It is out of bounds to anyone below the rank of sergeant. You remain here. Understood?" Yet another mumbled response, but this time a little louder and with more than a hint of resentment.

"Right, I will see you in the morning, six o'clock; at which time I will tell you about pay, canteen and camp routine. I do not know how long we shall be here, but as soon as I know anything you will be told. Any questions? No? Good. Goodnight."

"Well, this is a right turn up I must say." Alfred Arbuckle did not often comment on the situation in which the section found itself from time to time. He was a stoical man, normally content to accept life as it was and to make the best of things, but he was not happy with his present circumstances. "First night in a foreign country and I'm sitting in a cold tent with a wet backside and no kit." He spoke for them all.

"And no chance to go into the town. Looked nice down there, didn't it? All them cafés an' shops an' that." Alfie James added his four pennorth.

"Yer, an' crumpet too. Did yer see some of them girls that were chasing us? A man could get well in there, an' no mistake." Joseph Floyd was on to his favourite topic.

"Funny lot too, the French." Heads turned to look at Colin Baxter in anticipation of the story to come. "You remember in the harbour when I needed to find a toilet and I went to that café?" Nods from the assembled group confirmed the corporate memory. "Anyway, the patron, that's what they call the landlord out here, gave me a very large brandy and then showed me to the little room. Well, it wasn't just a gent's, but it was for ladies and gents, you know, either could use it; and there was a little old lady looking after it." Murmurs of astonishment from the rest of the section. "Anyway, as I got in there she saw me coming and wiped the seat for me before I sat down."

"Didn't wipe yer arse afterwards did she?" Joseph Floyd could be relied upon to take the coarse view in any situation.

"No Corporal, she did not," Colin's tone conveying his displeasure at the interruption. "Anyway, as I left she was outside the door and she came straight in and wiped it again, and there was this young lady waiting to go in. Remarkable really."

"Hey lads, come and see this."

They followed John Hayes out of the tent, into a darkness lit only by a few hurricane lamps.

"See what?"

"Well, listen I mean." Their tents were pitched quite close to the camp perimeter and out of the darkness they could hear voices. "Tommee, Tommee." Girls voices calling out of the darkness. "Souvenir Tommee. Venez ici Tommee."

"They are offering souvenirs, although quite what they might be I am not sure, and they are asking people to go and join them."

Without pausing to think how Colin Baxter had known

what was being said Alfie James, Joseph Floyd, Ned Preece and John Hayes headed towards the sound of the feminine voices. The rest went back into the tent to consume some of the brandy they had been given and to try and sleep. It wasn't easy given the conditions and they huddled together for warmth. As he drifted off, images began to float through Ted Ludgrove's mind: white, soft hands, red nails, a warm, moist mouth and the gentle probing of a soft little tongue; and the tingle spread through his loins as he put both hands down between his legs, stretched and finally slept.

Three of the adventurers returned within the hour, Alfie James wearing a grin, lipstick and a tricoleur ribbon in his buttonhole, the other two carrying more brandy and some cheese. Joseph Floyd was very much later, and the rest were asleep as he lay down in the group. All, that is, except Fred Smith, who watched him return and then settled himself to sleep. "Deal with that in the morning."

"Good Morning." Matthew Jenkins reviewed his somewhat dishevelled platoon as they sought to prepare themselves for breakfast.

"Stand up!" Fred Smith's command brought them all to attention in various states of dress and undress. "Morning sir!"

"Stand them easy please, Corporal Smith." As they relaxed he continued. "I have news for you before Sergeant Cooper briefs you on some camp detail. We shall not be here very long. In fact we received orders last night to report to the railway station in Le Havre some time this afternoon or this evening in order that we can entrain for the front. However, whilst you are here I want you to take every opportunity to sort out your basic administration, clean and launder your kit as best you can and prepare yourselves fully for the move since we cannot be certain what awaits us at the other end."

"Right!" Paul Cooper stepped in and took over the briefing in response to the raised eyebrow of his officer. "Keep your eyes on me and not on that lot over there." He referred to members of the brigade headquarters staff gathering the headquarters' horses which the previous evening had panicked, torn up their piquet pegs and run off. Their misfortune had been providing some early morning amusement as people began preparing for the day.

"Breakfast will be available in the cookhouse at seven o'clock. Next to the cookhouse is an Army Post Office and you can send your letters home before you leave if you want to. They will remain open until five o'clock tonight. Pay parade will be at ten o'clock for those of you who do not have the money for stamps. Payment for stamps can be in English or French money. French money is called the Franc, and you will get twenty-five of them for a pound. There are one hundred centimes to the Franc and in each centime there are ten sous. I will tell you now that the pay people will not be changing pennies, ha'pennies and thrupenny bits. The minimum they will accept for exchange is eight pence. Lunch will be at one o'clock, at which time you will also draw your rations for the move. Any questions?"

They remained silent. Most of them were trying to do the mental arithmetic involved with converting their money into French currency. None of them would be drawing as much as twenty five francs, and several realised that they would have to combine resources with someone else in order to make up the eight pence minimum for exchange.

"Good. Right, finally let me remind you of what Mr Jenkins has just said. I want all dirty socks and underwear washed and dried before we go, and you will wear a clean set of each as we leave this camp. Section commanders, see that it happens."

"Sir!" Four voices in unison, answering "sir" rather than "sergeant" as there was an officer present on whose behalf the sergeant was speaking.

It was eventually six o'clock in the evening before they formed up to march down to the town, the order having arrived at two-fifteen, giving them plenty of time to prepare. They were carrying one day's cooked ration for the journey, one day's preserved meat and biscuit for the day after and iron rations as an emergency reserve.

As they marched through the town they saw dozens of motor vehicles carrying boxes and crates of stores to a recently constructed gigantic shed known as the Hangar au Cauton. It was in a part of this shed that Number One Company of the Army Ordnance Corps had first established itself to begin setting up a depot. Numbers 2, 3, 4 and 7 Companies had joined them a couple of days earlier, and Colonel Egan, the Army Ordnance Department officer in charge, was striving valiantly to create some kind of order from the massive flow of stores that were heading his way.

The Norfolks approached the main railway station past the Ordnance Workshops which had been established in the town. They were to entrain at nine o'clock that evening, and on arrival found that they were to travel in boxcars. They were astounded when Colin Baxter translated the markings on the side. They had all, by now, realised that he could speak French. "40 Hommes. 8 Cheveaux", Forty men or eight horses. There was considerable grumbling about the French, their railways, the country in general and the fact that if this was how they were to be treated the bloody French could fight their bloody war on their own.

In fact it made perfect sense for the French railways to assemble standard sets of trains capable of carrying men, animals or stores in unit loads. Reconfiguring rolling stock to suit each cargo being carried would have imposed such delay on the deployment of the French and British Armies that it would have handed victory to the Germans.

In the end, their journey did not begin until one o'clock the next morning; the eighteenth of August. It continued throughout the night, hot stuffy and uncomfortable, with only one stop of an hour for coffee, in Rouen; and for most it was their first experience of the beverage. The journey was painfully slow, with the weight and configuration of the trains limiting their speed to twenty miles per hour. In practice, they rarely got above ten miles per hour. En route they crossed, without noticing, the River Somme.

Grumbling grew apace. Much was made of the view that it would probably have been quicker to walk, that the French were clearly incapable of organising anything and that this was no way to run a proper war. Joseph Floyd spent the journey avoiding Fred Smith. He had not enjoyed their conversation the previous day. Fred had come upon him early in the morning picking and scrubbing at the crotch of his uniform trousers, trying to remove an encrusted, white stain.

"I know what you've been at, Joseph Floyd. I know bloody well. You keep yourself to yourself while we're out 'ere. I'm not 'aving you causing trouble with wimmin, d'you unnerstan'? An' remember, catchin' a dose of the clap is a disciplinary offence with which I would be very 'appy to see you charged." Floyd had looked up, grimaced and bent back to his work without saying a word.

In Le Havre, a twenty-two year old woman regretted that she had flirted in the dark near the British camp hoping for a little fun, for it had gone further than she had planned. The rape had not been violent, just uncomfortable for he had not removed his trousers which had caused itching and scratching and he had dribbled onto her face as he was approaching his climax. She would never report it because she should not have gone there and because of the shame it would bring. Her husband had only gone to join his regiment a couple of weeks earlier, and any result from her encounter with the British soldier could be laid at the foot of their last night together.

The Norfolks were on their way to a concentration area near Le Cateau, where the Fifth Division was to form part of the Second Corps. The original plan for the six divisions and the Cavalry Division in the BEF had been that command would be exercised directly by General Headquarters, to be commanded by General French. There were to have been no intermediate corps headquarters, although the nucleus of one had existed in peacetime in Aldershot. However, it was decided to create Corps HQs for the BEF in order to conform to the French organisation for war. Consequently, the embryo headquarters in Aldershot was activated as First Corps, commanded by Lieutenant General Haig. The Second Corps HQ was swiftly put together from scratch with Lieutenant General Grierson in command. The BEF would enter the line, in two corps, on the left of the French Fifth Army and with the remnants of the Belgian Army to its left, in the south of Belgium.

The first blow to this new structure was that, on the seventeenth of August, the commander of the Second Corps died suddenly of a heart attack in the train on his way to the concentration area.

"Bloody French railways again. Probably drank the bloody milk!" Thomas could be uncharitable when the mood took him.

After a short march from the railway station the Norfolks found themselves in the small town of Pommereuil, where they were billeted with the Cheshires and the Bedfords. This was their first experience of billeting in the local community, and it was not unpleasant. The billeting allowance of twenty centimes for straw and shelter for a soldier or NCO bought the platoon a dry clean barn with plenty of straw in which to make themselves comfortable. There was a water pump in the farmyard of which the barn formed one extremity. Matthew Jenkins fared rather better on his allocation of one franc, with a bed in a small room which he shared with the company second-in-command. The farmer was happy to offer the Colonel free use of the guest bedroom in the farm, refusing the offer of the standard two francs a day which the Colonel's seniority attracted.

"Make yourselves comfortable. We are likely to be here for a couple of days." Morale had improved significantly at the news.

It was not very long before barter and banter were improving the state of their rations, their knowledge of the language and the feeling of being welcome; which had taken something of a dent on the train journey. A cap badge would put a chicken in the pot, a button with a regimental crest was worth a good portion of butter and a few sous bought them bread of a quality they had never experienced. They were also beginning to learn that the French attitude to alcohol was different to that to which they were used, and that drinking wine with food was perfectly normal. They soon began to get the taste for "ving blong" and "ving roodge."

Officers dined in homes and restaurants, the meals cooked by beaming French ladies determined to ensure that those who had come to their rescue would not go to the front without proper feeding. For those who paid at all, the value far outstripped the cost.

A good night's sleep in the barn did them all the world of good. Stiffened limbs began to relax, aching backs began to ease, sore feet began to adjust to the pounding they had begun to take. By ten in the morning breakfast had been completed, laundry was being brought up to date and hung out to dry in the sunshine, rifles were being cleaned and ammunition was being checked.

Each of the ten ammunition pouches on their webbing, five each side of the belt buckle, carried fifteen rounds in three five round clips; a total of one hundred and fifty rounds per man. Additionally, the commanding officer had directed each man to carry an extra fifty rounds in a cotton bandolier which could be slung, conveniently, across the shoulder.

Each of the clips was removed and each round taken out of the clip to be laid on a rag or cloth on the ground. Each round was then cleaned and the clip checked for grit, dirt or damage which might affect speed of loading. Once satisfied, each man would then reload the clip, ensuring that the rim of each cartridge alternated up or down with its neighbour. This offsetting of the rims was vital if the rounds were to feed properly into the ten round magazine on the rifle and allow them to maintain the rate of fire they would need in order to defeat the massed attacks they were about to face.

And rapid, accurate fire was something at which British infantry was very proficient. As is so often the case, it was the vision of one man that brought this about. In 1912 the Chief Instructor at the Small Arms School in Hythe was Lieutenant Colonel McMahon. He believed there was a need to retrain the infantry, to change the focus of its shooting from that which it had used in the colonial wars and to develop it for Europe, where there would be shorter ranges and more, and less fleeting, targets. His recommendation was to give each battalion six machine guns, but this was rejected on grounds of cost and the number was fixed at two. Consequently, he concentrated on improving the speed of fire of the rifleman.

The result was the "mad minute": fifteen aimed shots into a two foot circle at three hundred yards in one minute. This formed the basis of the regular soldier's shooting test, although there were many who could achieve twenty-five rounds per minute; and the odd legend who could manage thirty. The formula for success was a stable firing position, a firm grip on the rifle, speed of taking aim, slick bolt action and rapid reload using the charging clip; hence the importance of proper preparation of clips and ammunition.

It was a regime that could be practised not only on ranges using live rounds, but also in barracks using drill ammunition. And they had practised; oh how they had practised. And they had complained and grumbled about the amount of practise, but soon they were to be grateful for it.

Everything complete, and all preparations done, Ted and Alfie had been sent off by Fred Smith to scrounge up some firewood. The weather was very warm, but they needed to brew tea independently of the cookhouse, and there were a couple of chickens which needed cooking. It was a balmy August day, the sun beat down from a cloudless sky and, despite the fighting to the north, all seemed at peace with the world. They had good food, a warm, dry place to sleep and they were not being buggered about. It really was a truly bloody marvellous war and it was hard to see how life might improve.

"This'll do." Alfie's cheerful voice broke into Ted's thoughts. He was pulling at a couple of old warped planks lying at the foot of a garden wall. They were smothered in long grass and brambles, and the vegetation seemed reluctant to give up its hold as the two men tugged and pulled at the split and decaying timber.

"Qu'est ce que vous faites!" They didn't understand what had been said, but the anger in the shrill voice was plain to both of them. They looked up over the wall to see a small, elderly lady approaching them, waving her fist and shouting unintelligibly. Clearly they had done something wrong, but they knew not what it was. Alfie, seeking to emulate Fred in communicating with the natives, smiled his most winning smile.

"Wantee wood for fire. Hotee water." He waved his hands to simulate flickering flames. However, all the charm in the world was not going to divert the lady from her purpose. She carried on berating them in a loud, high pitched voice and began pushing the wood back into its original place, dirtying her hands on its damp, mossy surface. Alfie continued trying to explain, but her voice simply rose higher as she turned to wag a bony finger under his nose.

"Just what precisely is going on here?" Alfie's and Ted's heads each jerked round at the sound of what was quite clearly a senior officer's voice, to see the resplendent figure of their brigade commander standing in the doorway of the old lady's cottage, his uniform immaculate, his Sam Brown belt with its leather pistol holster and sword frog gleaming in the August sunshine. They had chosen to forage for wood outside his billet. Just their bloody luck. Frozen into silence, they stood rigidly to attention, staring just above Edward von Gleichen's head and doing what all soldiers seek to do in such circumstances: nothing.

"I asked what is going on?" Alfie, knowing this was real trouble, was about to divert his soldierly charm onto the brigadier with a potentially long and convoluted story when madame stepped in and began berating him as she had been berating his soldiers. Count Edward's French was good, but the speed at which his landlady was gabbling was simply too much for him to bear. He turned for assistance.

"Captain St André!" He called for the French officer who had been appointed to his brigade staff as the liaison officer and who had been involved in the small conference of brigade and divisional staff officers that the brigadier had been holding in his quarters.

"Oui, mon general." A small, rather ordinary little man, wearing pinc nez spectacles which made him look very prim and proper, stepped out into the garden and into the fray. In fact, he was anything but ordinary. Intelligent and cultured, he was a protestant pastor from Tours. He had studied theology at Edinburgh and spoke perfect English. However, he had an excellent sense of humour, which drove him to invent words and to go out of his way to put the accent on the wrong syllable.

His conversation with madame lasted several minutes, involving much waving of hands on her part, and several Gallic shrugs on his part as he expressed his desolation and deep regret at the difficulty in which she found herself. Ted and Alfie stood still, said nothing and looked into the middle distance. Finally, it ended. He kissed madame on both cheeks and with a final, withering "bon, alors," in the direction of Ted and Alfie she headed inside.

"Well?" The brigadier looked at his liaison officer. Alfie and Ted did not look anywhere other than straight ahead, but were even more interested than the brigadier in the outcome.

"She claimed that the wood your men were removing was part of a stand of new timber that had been by the wall and that some of it had already been stolen by other soldiers. She was demanding fifty francs in compensation." Alfie did a quick sum, worked it out at two quid and was unable to prevent himself from saying: "but......" He was stopped from saying anything else by a look from the brigadier that would have frozen mercury.

"That," said Edward von Gleichen, "is utterly ridiculous. It is perfectly clear to anyone that the wood has been there for ages, and I am certainly not......"

The French officer held up his hand, palm outwards towards the brigadier. "Mon general, calm yourself. I discussed the matter with madame who agreed with me that given the assistance you are offering to my country, the need to maintain good relations and the hardships we are all about to suffer, a few pieces of wood to help your men cook is a small matter which should not cause her to distress herself. She agreed, and reduced the price to two francs. I will pay her myself, later."

"My dear chap, you don't have......"

"Mon general, it is the least I can do." He lowered his eyes in deference and mild embarrassment; or perhaps it was amusement.

"Leave to carry on, sir please?" Sensing the moment Alfie spoke up to the brigadier. A pause, "yes, of course....yes please." The brigadier nodded at the two young men, his face still firm and forbidding, before turning back towards his lodgings; and with his back to them and his face hidden from their sight he permitted himself a huge grin.

Thomas was clearly on form, and it was good to see.

As he approached the door, the artillery liaison officer from divisional HQ stepped politely out into the light to make way for the brigade commander, and looked at the two soldiers. Ted stood riveted to the spot as Edward Snell stared straight into his eyes with an expression of pure hatred on his face.

"Oh bugger!"

On that same day, Wednesday the nineteenth of August, the Kaiser ordered General von Kluck to "walk over General French's contemptible little army." General von Kluck commanded the German First Army, on the right of the German advance. It was his army that had been ordered to swing round at the edge of the long right hook that the strategist, von Schlieffen, had determined was necessary to defeat France before moving on to Russia. It was his army of which the sleeve of the right hand grenadier was to brush the English Channel as it moved to envelop Paris and the French armies. It was his army, however, which on the orders of von Moltke, Chief of the German General Staff, had already turned southwards before reaching the Channel. This was a move caused by von Moltke's diversion of resources to the eastern French border and towards Russia, and by the delays and casualties imposed by the stout defence put up by the Belgians. It was a move that was to have far reaching consequences; and it would bring the German First Army face to face with the BEF.

It was unfortunate for General von Kluck that his name rhymed with an epithet in common use in the day-to-day vernacular of British soldiery; and it was to form the basis of several songs, all on the theme that the BEF really did not give a fuck for General von Kluck.

In fact, the actual adjective used by the Kaiser to describe the tiny BEF translates more correctly from the German as "insignificant." Contemptible, however, had more appeal to Thomas' black humour. Thus were a name and a legend created. Those who bore the name did so with great pride, and within a few days they would show the Kaiser's soldiers the extent of his contemptuous error of judgement.

Chapter 5

North To Belgium

By Thursday the twentieth of August the British Expeditionary Force was complete in its concentration area between Le Cateau and Mauberg in northern France, a few miles south of the Belgian border. Its line of communication was stretched out in its wake, with bases having been established not just at Le Havre, but also at Boulogne. On its right was the French Fifth Army, with whom it was planned to link up prior to a concerted push to the north to drive the invading Germans from Belgium.

The fact that eighty thousand men had been deployed from a standing start from throughout the United Kingdom to a point where, in just fifteen days, they were poised to move into their battle positions was quite remarkable. It remains a testament to foresight, planning, excellent staff work and meticulous execution. The enormous success of the deployment, however, was not something that was in the forefront of the minds of the soldiers of the Ninth Regiment of Foot. They were warm, snug and dry, but they already knew that they would shortly be on the move. Consequently, they were involved in the basics of their personal administration and in preparing themselves, finally, to fight.

The company was centred on the farm, and each of the four platoon commanders had chosen his particular spot to conduct business. The company commander sat in the sun in an old deck chair, reading, for the fourth time since they had left Belfast, a copy of Punch and apparently paying no attention to the proceedings going on around him. Indeed, for most of the time he appeared to be dozing, but only those who did not know him would have believed that to be true.

His eyes swept the scene before him, watching the way his young officers handled their men, learning from what he saw, trying to judge how they might behave in circumstances of great danger. A strong believer in the view that there were no bad soldiers, only bad officers, he was determined that the leadership in his company would be right, and that he would place each of his officers where he, and with him his men, was best suited. Three of the platoons were lined up in different parts of the farmyard in three ranks, standing easy in the sunshine with their platoon commanders, platoon sergeants by their side, addressing their men. The fourth platoon was harder to see. They were in the shade of a Horse Chestnut tree at the edge of the farmyard, its broad, kite shaped leaves casting a gentle, cooling shadow in which the platoon sat, nursing mugs of tea in their hands and sipping occasionally as they listened to their platoon commander. Matthew Jenkins was not addressing his men, he was talking with them; attaching as much importance to what they had to say as he did to what it was he was trying to tell them. The platoon sergeant was off to one side; there, but not obviously so. The company commander smiled, and went back to his magazine.

Matthew Jenkins had left the Army whilst the regiment was still in South Africa. He had not been entirely comfortable with some of the attitudes of his fellow officers, and with what he felt to be the short sighted approach of the Army to tactics, organisation and equipment. With all the clear sightedness of youth, he felt strongly about the deficiencies he saw. However, he retained an abiding affection for his soldiers, and would probably have remained in the Army had it not been for the untimely death of his father, for it would have been impossible for his mother or sister to manage the farm. The Colonel had been most understanding and his letter to the Military Secretary, expressing his regret at the loss of such a promising young officer yet acknowledging the difficulties faced by the family, had secured Matthew's release.

When Richard Haldane, the Minister for War, had reorganised the militia and created the Special Reserve, Matthew had seen his opportunity to return to a life he had enjoyed, whilst continuing to run the family farm. The purpose of the Special Reserve was to provide drafts for regular units, to fill officer vacancies on mobilisation and to find men for the rear echelons. Volunteers could enlist in the Special Reserve of the regiment of their choice, and there was normally one battalion of Special Reserve for each regiment of the line. It was based upon the regimental depot, where recruits carried out six months basic training, and many recruits used the Special Reserve as a means of sampling army life without signing on as a regular. From Matthew Jenkins' perspective, not only did the Special Reserve offer something more professional and demanding than the militia, but also its inauguration came at a point where he was satisfied with the way things were going on the farm and he felt he could spare the time. Consequently, by the time he rejoined the First Battalion The Norfolk Regiment after an absence of around fourteen years he had been involved for some time in training recruits and preparing them to join the Regular Army in time of war.

Bearing in mind that they were planning to be part of a major advance, they were discussing the employment of the company in this phase of war and their place in it. Matthew's easy, yet firm, manner drew from his regular soldiers every detail of what they had been trained to do and how they had been told to act. He listened to them, as did the reservists, all trying to picture their part in what was to come. The basic tactics they would employ continued to be based on the late nineteenth century three-tier formation of a Firing Line, Supports and Reserves, but modified to suit the infantry's new four-company organisation. This was an enormous help to the reservists, as they could visualise the structure on the ground and it precluded the need for low-level tactical exercises; for which there wasn't time anyway.

The patch of earth cleared by Paul Cooper beneath the tree, suitably decorated with twigs, leaves and a couple of spare boot laces, provided enough of a training medium upon which they could focus their discussion.

The old tactics had, however, been enhanced by the improvements in musketry, better individual and sub-unit field craft and much greater use of covering fire, co-ordinated with the movement of individuals and small groups. The broad principle was that an attack would go forward until the leading troops, in the Firing Line, were fired upon. At this point the Firing Line would push forward in small rushes, using covering fire with movement within sections and platoons and with additional cover from machine guns and artillery. Once they were within assault distance, some one to two hundred yards from the enemy, they would make the final rush to overwhelm them, with the aid of the bayonet.

The role of the Supports was to advance to replace casualties and thicken up the Firing Line until the enemy had been subdued by the effects of musketry and other supporting fire. This was known as "winning the fire fight". Reserves, meanwhile, would have been ready to guard the flanks, give additional fire support and assist with or exploit the final assault. In a battalion it would be normal to have two of the four platoons in a company as company Supports, and one or two of the battalion's four companies as Reserves.

The company commander had discussed with his officers how they might fight the battle upon which they were about to embark. It was his view that the concept for use of the Supports was wasteful and inefficient. To reinforce a line that had already been stopped, or was in danger of being stopped, was, he believed, simply to add to the casualties. Much better to use them in a reserve role, to exploit local success, to throw an enemy off balance, to protect a flank or to cover a withdrawal.

Matthew's platoon was to fill the role of a company reserve. The company commander was taking advantage of his age and experience to place with Matthew the most demanding tasks that were likely to befall the company. He also commanded the platoon which, thanks to Paul Cooper, was the best drilled and most competent in the basic individual skills of the soldiers. Another platoon would take the role of Supports, but would probably be used in a reserve role in conjunction with Matthew's, and probably under his command. The other two platoons would form the Firing Line.

Matthew, for his own part, was happy with the way things were developing. He was getting to know his men and was largely content with what he found. He had decided very early on to extract Colin Baxter to be his runner. It was a vital job, requiring a man of intelligence who could transmit messages verbally when necessary, and who had the courage under fire to get any message through to its destination. Colin continued to live with his chums in Fred Smith's section, but Matthew had accepted that Fred would be below his wartime establishment of ten. Reinforcement would have to wait the arrival of reservists. As platoon commander, Matthew's small HQ also comprised a batman to act as personal servant, in addition to the sergeant and the runner. Despite Cooper's protests he had chosen not to fill the batman appointment; he would do without.

"Right, I think its time for lunch." Matthew had decided that the long morning had gone on long enough. "Take an hour and be back here at two thirty. We have to be on parade with the brigade at five so that will give us plenty of time to cover the rest of the things on my list. I haven't been given any orders yet, but I am pretty certain we shall be on the move tomorrow. I really have no idea where to or for what purpose, so I suggest that you complete all your personal administration before you go. Don't forget, there will be a ration delivery this evening, and therefore the battalion's mail will go back down the line to the Army Post Office. If you want to write letters I suggest you do so now. Good. See you in an hour."

Fred Smith had already written. He had been bothered by some of the things he had heard as they moved up through France and he wanted to be sure that Aggie was all right. His letter was couched in the slightly formal tone that was common at the time, and after the opening sentences enquiring about Amy and what it was they were both doing during his absence he got to the point that had been worrying him:

> *"Do not be tempted to take in billets whilst I am away. I give you enough money to look after yourself and our daughter and there is no need to try and make more. There is a danger that if you make such an arrangement you will be thrown out of our married quarters for misconduct and could lose your entitlement to allotments and a pension."*

He was not to know that it would not be long before wives were to be evicted from married quarters to make room for the mass of men joining Kitchener's new army.

When the mail left that evening it also carried a letter to a small terraced house in the New Lodge area of Belfast. Peter Dakin had begun it with the words "Dear Ma."

Ted Ludgrove had been morose since his meeting the day before with Edward Snell. Nothing had been said and Snell had returned to the conference in the brigadier's billet without so much as a backward glance at him; but he was deeply disturbed, imagining all kinds of unpleasantness that could be brought to bear upon him. Alfie, Peter and Colin all knew the situation. They had been discussing, one night in the canteen in Belfast, the reasons for their joining. It was the night on which Colin Baxter had, for the first and last time, exposed the chink in his armour; and Ted had told, amidst great hilarity, the story of Woodman's Copse.

"Don't worry, Ted," Alfie said, not for the first time. "'E can't touch you 'ere. C'mon, 'ave a cuppa an' forget about 'im for a bit."

"I've found the answer to the Hayes situation," said Colin Baxter in a conspiratorial voice. He had managed to get the story out of Fred Smith the night before, having plied him with a little brandy. Despite promising not to tell anyone, he was bursting to reveal the details, and decided to salve his conscience by convincing himself that it would divert Ted's mind from his troubles, and consequently was in a good cause.

"Well........?" Peter Dakin looked his friend straight in the eye. "Y' gonna tell us, then, or are ye too high an' mighty now y're Mr Jenkins' runner?" His cheerful grin made it obvious that there was no bad feeling concerning Colin's new responsibilities. They all knew how important was the job, and they trusted him, and therefore potentially their lives, with it absolutely.

"Well, it's like this."

"Tea? Sandwich?" Alfie could be irritating at times when he interrupted.

Colin took the proffered food and drink, and began again. "Right, well it all goes back about four years, when they were both corporals. They were inseparable friends, and Hayes was young and every bit as good as Sergeant Cooper." They nodded, a tacit acknowledgement that whilst it was not the done thing to like a sergeant they all knew quality when they saw it. Colin continued, his voice somewhat muffled as it made its way through a mouthful of beef and baguette.

"Anyway, there was this girl, very pretty I'm told, and Hayes fell in love with her. He was, according to Corporal Smith, besotted with her and wanted to marry her. She, for her part, fell for him and agreed that they would marry. I believe, and here Corporal Smith was not clear, that he purchased an engagement ring which she was wearing when Hayes last saw her."

"Where was all this?" Alfie again.

"I'm coming to that." The mildly offended tone in Colin's voice reflecting the fact that he enjoyed telling tales, knew he was good at it and didn't need help from Alfie James. Alfie just grinned, disarmingly, at his friend. "They had met whilst Hayes and Sergeant Cooper were on a long course at the School of Musketry at Hythe. Once they got back to the battalion Hayes was making arrangements to go back and see her when he got a letter from her telling him it was all off."

"Why'd she do tha' then?" Peter Dakin looked up from his sandwich.

"We are not certain," a conspiratorial note in his voice. "Corporal Smith is of the view that her parents did not approve and she was forced to reject him. Anyway, Hayes was not to be put off, and determined to return to Hythe in order to redress the situation."

Peter Dakin paused in his chewing and looked at his chum, thinking hard. "My, but Colin don' arf use long words at times."

"He sought permission to take leave, but it was denied to him because the battalion was about to go on exercise and he was needed. He, apparently, felt this to be unjust since he heard the news on a Thursday and the exercise did not begin until the Monday. He had the weekend, and could be back in time. Well, he went, and by the Monday morning he had not returned. He was posted absent, and subsequently court martialled, reduced to the rank of private and sentenced to three months' clink. He left after his seven years, still a private."

By now, Ted had forgotten his woes and was involved in the story. "So where does the Sergeant come into it?"

"He was the orderly corporal that Sunday and into the Monday morning. He posted Hayes absent without so much as blinking an eyelid. Hayes never forgave him. He actually made it back by the middle of the morning and he reckons Sergeant Cooper could have covered for him and he'd have got away with it. Sergeant Cooper, apparently, thought he was being bloody stupid and wasn't prepared to risk his own career."

Silence. They all pondered the morality of the situation. Always a problem that, when to help a bloke and when enough was enough. Hmmmmmmm.

Meanwhile, the subject of their conversation was leaning on a section of the dry stone wall that linked the various farm outbuildings, staring into the distance. Private Hayes was confused. He was, to some extent, enjoying being back and much of his bitterness had dissipated, almost despite himself. He'd often wondered what he would really have done in Paul Cooper's place, with his own driving ambition easily as powerful. Bloody woman hadn't been worth it anyway. Certainly, this platoon was in good order, but then Cooper was good at his job; and they had been lucky with the platoon commander. Jenkins and his long escape march in South Africa had still been a legend in the regiment when Hayes had joined.

However, he was also entertaining significant moments of self-doubt. He had often wondered what it might actually be like to go to war, and the prospect now facing him was not one he found rewarding. Furthermore, it clearly appeared to everyone that he was a good soldier with a deal of experience, and people were beginning to turn to him. But, this was serious stuff they were embarked upon and a man could get killed if he buggered about; and taking responsibility for others, which meant taking more risks, did not really appeal. He was finally about to face his ghosts and test the nagging concern that had gnawed at him throughout his service: that he was scared, and that he might actually be a coward.

"I have called you together in order to tell you........" The divisional commander's voice rang out across the ranks of the Fifteenth Infantry Brigade, drawn up by battalions. They knew why they'd been "called together": to be fed more bullshit. They stood at ease as Major General Fergusson told them they would be moving the next day and gave some tips on the Germans. He talked of their wiles, their machine guns and their methods of mass attack. The brigade remained silent throughout, with the exception of the Bedfordshire Regiment who from time to time shouted "ear ear" and clapped. The general carried on, unperturbed by these interruptions. Count von Gleichen permitted himself the occasional frosty look in the direction of the Bedfords, and wondered whether he needed to discuss form with the commanding officer.

The next morning the BEF was off on its way north; on its way to face a massive German Army that had been prepared and equipped to deal with the large forts that formed part of the defensive networks in Belgium and France. Consequently, they were equipped with a wide range of artillery with a high percentage of high explosive shells in the arsenal; the infantry carried trench mortars which could lob small bombs over ramparts and walls; and they had lots of grenades, both offensive and defensive. For its own part, the BEF had rifles, two machine guns and a handful of grenades in the infantry battalions. The cavalry fared no better, substituting swords, sabres or lances for grenades, a weapon for which they felt they had no real use.

British artillery had been re-equipped between 1906 and 1914 with Quick Firing, or QF, guns, the brass cartridge case and precision engineered breech offering greatly improved rates of fire and accuracy. The Royal Horse Artillery was equipped with the 13-Pounder Field Gun, a lightweight piece with a range of only six thousand one hundred yards, whilst the Royal Field Artillery had the 18-Pounder, weighing just over a ton and firing a heavier round than its smaller cousin in the RHA, but effectively only out to the same range. The 4.5 inch Howitzer gave the RFA a little more range and punch at seven thousand yards, and a much higher trajectory than the other two guns which allowed it to project its fire over obstacles and to descend directly on the target.

The guns themselves were well designed, durable and simple to operate, but the 4.5 inch Howitzer was the only one for which high explosive shell had been provisioned, and then less than half the total stock. The rest was all shrapnel which was only effective against troops who were unprotected and in the open. It had neither the power, the disruptive capability nor the shattering effect of high explosive.

The Royal Garrison Artillery with its 60-Pounders was the only heavy artillery, firing both shrapnel and HE from a five inch calibre barrel; but only fifty percent of its ammunition scale was high explosive. With a range of twelve thousand three hundred yards and built in 1904 to an Elswick Ordnance Company design it was one of the best guns of its type in 1914. Its four tons and eight hundredweight were towed by a team of twelve horses, and it was serviced by a crew of eight. But however good it was, there were only four for each of the six British divisions. The German Army had the equivalent of twenty for each of its one hundred and four divisions; and this imbalance was replicated across all types of artillery. And it wasn't simply the numbers of guns and the preponderance of shrapnel over high explosive in the BEF's artillery: the overall quantity of ammunition was woefully inadequate.

The British General Staff had assumed that only an expeditionary force of limited size would ever be deployed on the continent, and provision should be made for four intense battles in the first two months, each lasting three days. This was the basis of the calculation for the provision of munitions, and for stocks of other essential stores.

Furthermore, the Royal Ordnance Factory at Woolwich, the Royal Gunpowder Factory at Waltham Abbey and the Royal Small Arms Factory at Enfield had been run down following the end of the South African Wars. Equipment was in place, but only fifty percent manned. Successive Government policy and a reducing Army meant that no arrangements had been made for a force larger than six divisions within the limits of twelve days of fighting determined by the General Staff. There had been an all round disinclination among the military and the politicians to face the costs of investing in ammunition, or in the transport required to carry it.

The Norfolks, however, slept the night unaware of the implications of those policies, or of the potential shortcomings resulting from them in the fire support that was to be crucial to their survival and to their ability to fight effectively. They were to be on the move the next morning, to somewhere utterly unpronounceable, and a couple of glasses of wine or a snort of brandy had seen them to their beds for a good night's sleep.

The morning of the twenty-first of August dawned thick and misty. Edward von Gleichen peered from the window of his billet, barely able to see the end of the garden where the incident with the wood and the two soldiers had taken place the previous day, and unable to discern what it was the soldiers of his headquarters were doing, although he could hear the noise of their preparations. It would not be the last time that he would be unaware of what was going on around him other than in his immediate vicinity. The "fog of war" was destined to envelope him in its clammy grasp on many occasions in the weeks and months to come.

As Matthew Jenkins looked out across the farmyard he could barely see the barn where his soldiers slept. He folded his elbows onto the sill, taking care to avoid the small spigot protruding upwards and designed to hold the latch in place, hunched his shoulders forward and reviewed the scene before him. The only sign of movement was Private Preece, seated with his back to the barn wall, his rifle beside him, the bolt in his hand being cleaned for the umpteenth time, lightly oiled and placed back into the weapon. His kit was beside him, complete and neatly packed, and although his skin retained its spotty, unhealthy appearance he was as ready as any other man in the platoon to do what was necessary.

Matthew smiled. He and Cooper had discussed Ned Preece at some length. The sergeant's view had been quite clear: Preece was trouble, a drunkard, ill disciplined and unreliable; and he should be left in Belfast. But the officer had seen something behind the facade: nothing he could have put into words, but just a feeling that the man ought to be given a chance. To his certain knowledge, Preece had not touched a drop since the Battalion had left Belfast, his kit had always been in first class order and he had pulled his weight throughout. So far so good; it remained to be seen how he would perform under fire, but Matthew had no real doubts.

The subject of his platoon commander's scrutiny sat, unaware that he was being watched. He'd risen early, unable to sleep any longer. His thoughts were a long way off, in a smog-blackened terraced house near the railway line that ran through Walthamstow from the leafy suburbs out towards Chingford whence it carried commuting businessmen into Liverpool Street station to work in the City of London. He'd been a junior porter at Hoe Street station when he'd first seen her. He'd helped her with her bag as she descended from the train, she'd smiled at him and he had looked away, embarrassed and uncertain. His thin, weedy body, acne covered face and poor teeth made him feel terribly awkward when faced with members of the opposite sex. His physical shortcomings had also made him truculent, stubborn and difficult, especially when he felt put upon. To have someone his age smile at him, and look as if she meant it, had come as something of a shock.

It hadn't taken him long to realise that she was a regular on that train, coming in from the clothing factory in which she worked as a machinist in Bethnal Green. He smiled as he remembered his attempt to ask her out, the way she had helped him by saying yes before he was half way through the question and the brief courtship that had followed. Neither of them had meant things to go as far as they did on that fateful evening, but with her parents out at the pub, an empty house to go back to and a moment of high passion and mutual weakness the result had been pregnancy.

He had fled in panic, knowing he would be blamed for everything as he always was and unable to face the retribution that would come his way. He knew that her father would beat the living daylights out of him, and so would his own father, but it wasn't the physical effects of that which bothered him; God knew he'd had enough hidings during his unhappy childhood. No, it was the prospect of a lifetime of accusing looks and moral condemnation.

Having run, and then thought about it, he had known that he should have gone back really, but the longer he stayed away the harder it had become. He had travelled by train into Liverpool Street, and caught the first one going anywhere out of London; which had been to Norwich, travelling free as a railway employee. After three nights sleeping rough and hungry, for he had no money, he had presented himself at the guardroom of the Norfolks. The rest was history.

News of the birth of his daughter, now just a year old, had reached him through a friend he'd arranged to meet in London shortly before joining the battalion in Belfast. He remembered as if it were yesterday the confused feelings of pride, hurt, jealousy, concern and panic which he had experienced. The uncertainty about what he should do had remained with him for the whole year, swinging between a determination to go back and face his responsibilities and a refusal to do anything, knowing that he had been stupid and not wishing to face the reality. It was the prospect of war that had finally decided him to acknowledge his child and to send the money; he hoped more than he could say that it was not too late.

"What the bloody 'ell are you looking for? Can't you see we're goin' t' be late?"

The platoon was forming up on the road outside, and Alfie James was attempting to encourage Ted Ludgrove to join them.

"They were 'ere yesterday."

"Wot were?"

"Me fags, that's wot. I swear there was a packet of twenty Woodbines in 'ere." He was rummaging in his pack, looking up at Alfie as he spoke.

"Well, you'll 'ave to look for 'em later. C'mon, for God's sake get a bloody move on."

"Oh, sod it!" Ted was speaking as he fastened the buckle of his pack and swung it onto his back. Muttering, he stepped outside into a morning where the early mist was fast disappearing under the effects of a sun which promised to make the rest of the day uncomfortably warm.

The battalion formed up on the long road which led into the village from the south, turned to the right as ordered and began the march which would take it to Gommignes, a small village, still in France, but much closer to the Belgian border, and only fifteen miles south of the Mons canal. It was along the line of this canal that the BEF was forming a defensive line. The left wheel at the cross-roads in the centre of the village, out along the Rue des Forêts, took them westwards, before they turned north through pleasant, green open countryside dotted with small farms. The buildings had a strange appearance to most of them, built as they were in a distinctly Flemish style. High, slate-roofed barns and farm buildings towered over the smaller single story dwelling houses with their tiny windows and castellated gable ends to the buildings. From time to time there was something larger and grander, showing that there was money in the region, although much of the machinery and many of the farms had a depressingly run down appearance.

"Don't bloody look after it proper, they don't!" Ted was scathing as he passed yet another small walled farm. Peering through the grey painted wrought iron railings the evidence of lack of attention was plain to see. Ploughs gathering both rust and dust were dumped in the corner of the yard among an untidy pile of old fencing wire and stakes.

"Can't expect it to work properly if 'tain't looked after." Alfred added his own note of disapproval to the proceedings. "An' these buildin's could use a lick o' paint; an' there's work to be done on that barn roof there. Look Ted, can you see it, that 'ole......?"

"Would you two mind cuttin' the cackle!" There was an edge to John Hayes' voice. He, like many of the reservists, was still feeling the effects of the march with heavy loads, new boots and the after effects of the inoculations in the final stages of their unpleasantness. His predicament was not helped by the roads, known locally as pavé, but best described as cobbled. They were narrow, only really a cart's width, with a steep camber inclining down left and right from the centre towards muddy strips running alongside the edge. Not only was the placing of feet on the uneven surface painful, but the permanent lean either left or right depending on a man's position on the road made the whole business of marching very uncomfortable.

As the morning wore on the sun dispersed the mist, and, as forecast by the pundits over breakfast, the day turned hot and became very sultry.

They approached Gommegnies at midday, having passed the small town of Le Quesnoy, fortified for another war in another time - two hundred years earlier - by Vaubin. On their way through the small villages and past the little farms they had been offered fruit, milk, coffee and even wine. Edward von Gleichen had issued strict orders about the acceptance of these gifts, concerned that men should, first of all, not fall out of the march without permission and, secondly, they should not drink more than was good for them. Such gifts as were accepted were only permitted during the ten minute halts in each hour's marching, and then only under supervision.

"Ta missus."

Colin Baxter raised an eyebrow to the heavens, a pleading look on his face. Any attempt to get Peter Dakin to say mademoiselle, or anything that sounded remotely like it, was doomed to failure. The "missus" to whom Peter had referred, as she offered him a large glass of water, was an elfin faced sixteen year old with a shy smile and the largest brown eyes he, Colin Baxter, could recall ever having seen. Anything less like a "missus" it would be hard to imagine.

Ted Ludgrove lay back against a grassy bank on the edge of the road where they had been told to wait whilst billeting arrangements were sorted out. Some pretty uncharitable remarks had been made about the Army in general, lack of organisation especially and the unfortunate billeting officer in particular. It was not his fault that the mayor was away at a cattle auction and no one in the village would take responsibility for anything until he returned. And anyway, it was a nice warm day and after a long march it was quite pleasant to sit in the sun eating and drinking some of the offerings pressed on them by friendly, and somewhat apologetic, villagers.

The march had taken its toll, and as they sat back some of the stragglers began to trudge in. Albert Carter was among them, feeling awfully the effects of the heavy weight he was carrying, the new boots he was wearing and the inoculations which were still affecting him.

"Sit yerself down."

Ted Ludgrove felt a twinge of sympathy for the man. God knew it had been hard enough for the regulars and these poor buggers must be sufferin' terrible. What had surprised them all was the difference it made carrying a full complement of rifle ammunition. Not something they did in normal training, it had a significant effect. Ted offered him the remains of the carafe of cider he had been drinking, and lay back looking at the sky. That march had been hard work, and his back and feet ached in unison. He wriggled his toes, or tried to; glued lightly together as they were by the grease and sweat emanating from his feet. His socks were stuck by the same sweat and grease to the bottom of his feet, and he tried arching the instep by pressing down hard on his toes in order to detach flesh from wool. He failed, became irritated and felt an overpowering desire to remove his boot and free the sock.

"Fancy a game of cards then?" Alfie James voice broke into his thoughts.

"Aye."

Ten minutes later and the game was still not under way.

"If you was better organised you'd know where you put 'em." Alfred Arbuckle's deep, sonorous voice held a note of disapproval.

Before Alfie had time to rise to the implied criticism he was interrupted by Paul Cooper's voice, informing them that billets were ready, and inviting them to follow him to where they would sleep that night. As they moved off Colin Baxter glanced more than once over his shoulder at large brown eyes set in a pale elfin face, and thanked Heaven he had learnt French at school. It was going to make life a great deal more pleasant once they had settled down a bit and stopped all this marching about.

It would not, however, be very long before his skill as a linguist would be put to the test. The platoon had barely settled into the barn it had been allocated when they were approached by a lady of indeterminate years, her complexion so wrinkled by long exposure to the sun and her hands so toughened by years of hard work on the farm that any guess between forty and sixty-five might have been close to the truth. She approached them nervously, looking from one to the other as if seeking a friendly face among young men who were unlikely to speak her language, and she knew not a word of theirs. They were as apprehensive as she. Her left hand brushed self consciously at the cheap muslin scarf, tied with a knot under her chin, the dull gold of a single band glinting on the third finger as it caught a ray of sunshine knifing through one of the many gaps in the roof. For their own part they looked at her, not certain how to act. Alfie and Ted, the memory of their last encounter with a French woman still fresh in their minds, decided by mutual, unspoken consent not to get involved.

"Can I please help you?" Colin Baxter stepped forward, conscious that his spoken French was about to be put to the test; and this was much harder than reading it or understanding what was being said. He prayed that he had got the words in the right order, and that she would not place too many demands on him. He was wrong, she seized on him as if she were drowning and he was the only straw available, gabbling in rapid and indecipherable French.

"Madame, Madame." He held up both hands, palms outwards towards her in a gesture of supplication. "Lentement s'il vous plait. Je ne suis pas interpreteur."

She smiled at him, expressing her regret with feeling, her words, softer now, accompanied by a delightful Gallic expression of desolation on her face. Years seemed to lift from her, and it was as if she realised for the first time that she was surrounded by an audience of young men. Almost coquettishly she began again, this time more slowly, but not patronisingly so. They gathered round, utterly bemused, watching comprehension dawn on Colin Baxter's face, and eagerness register in her voice and attitude. Apart from the fact that it didn't seem to be bad news they had no clue what was going on. At last Colin Baxter, who had prolonged the conversation in order to wring out every possible ounce of acclaim for his skill as a French speaker, turned to his assembled colleagues.

"It appears that all the men have left to go to the war, and there is no one left here but this lady and her two daughters.

They can only do so much, and you will realise that this is a critical time of the year on the farm." Impatience showed on the faces of many. Colin was a bit of a townie, and "'e don' 'ave t' tell a Norfolk man tha' this'ns a bad time t' be down on numbers on a farm."

"What's she wan' us t' do then?"

"There are two orchards which require harvesting, there is hay for winter feed which has been bound, but needs bringing in and she has a quantity of sugar beet that needs pulling together ready for the sugar factory."

This was standard fare for most of them, a daily routine which at one stage had been the likely outcome of the rest of their natural lives. Having left home, in many cases, to escape such a fate they now viewed with relish the chance to return, albeit briefly, to the life they once knew. It was just three o'clock in the afternoon, and in the six hours of daylight left to them a great deal could be accomplished.

Twenty minutes later, when Matthew Jenkins and Paul Cooper returned to the barn, they found it empty, save for Ned Preece. Someone had to guard the kit, and if them stupid turnip 'eads was 'appy t' go an muck about in them fields then that was all right with him. Anyway, he had a letter to write.

"Where are they?" There was a note of aggression in Cooper's voice which drew Ned to his feet.

"Out there, Sergeant." He pointed into the middle distance, just beyond a gap in a stone wall, a rotting three-bar gate hanging drunkenly from a dislodged hinge, half into the field beyond; a dense patch of nettles indicating that it had been a long time since it had been used. A glance along the line of Ned's finger showed men stripped to the waste, their white torsos, unaccustomed to exposure to the sun, contrasting starkly with their surroundings.

"I'll..............."

"It's OK." Matthew Jenkins placed a hand on his sergeant's forearm. "Leave them." As he spoke he was looking away from the group of men heaving stooks of hay towards the direction of the orchards where apples were being loaded into barrels for shipment to the barn.

Suddenly, behind them, a cart, towed by Alfred Arbuckle and Peter Dakin, full of sugar beets hove into view en route to the storage area being pointed out by the farmer's wife. Beside her stood Colin Baxter, revelling in his role of interpreter and, consequently, organiser of his platoon's efforts. In each location, be it field or orchard, stood one man, armed and watchful, with his colleagues' weapons nearby. Those towing carts and moving about had their rifles with them. They were in good order, and very happy.

"No, leave them. Better they have this to do than think about what might be to come. Plenty of time for that later."

That night the platoon dined as many of them had not dined before. Coq au Vin they could barely pronounce, but several chickens from the coop had that evening made the ultimate sacrifice in support of the French war effort and the cementing of the entente cordiale. Accompanied by salt pork and onions, flavoured with garlic and a bouquet garni of fresh herbs and the farm's own red wine they had gone into the pot and stewed gently for a couple of hours. Washed down with yet more wine, plates mopped with endless supplies of bread and they were content. As if they had not already done enough to win the hearts of the lady and the two young girls who shared her home, they insisted on washing up and clearing away when they had finished.

It had transpired that the two "daughters" were in fact granddaughters, Colin's French not yet being as good as he might have wished. Their mother was dead, and their father had gone to the war. Consequently, some having entertained lascivious thoughts at the prospect of two maidens in the vicinity, attitudes had changed to a more paternalistic viewpoint, many of them remembering sisters of a similar age back home.

They slept the deep sleep of men who had worked hard, eaten well, drunk just enough and had good reason to be satisfied with what they had done. The sleep of the dead one might almost say; except that it would be a sleep shortly to come to so many of them. A cold, unfeeling, lonely sleep, quite unlike that they were enjoying on the night of the twenty-first of August 1914.

As they dreamed their dreams Fred Smith walked across the farmyard to keep the appointment he had made with Paul Cooper.

"What's the problem, Fred?" Paul offered his friend a cigarette.

"No thanks." He declined politely, holding up a hand, and watched Paul Cooper place a cigarette between his lips and light it, waving his hand to extinguish the match before discarding it with a flick into the blackness of the night. In response to Cooper's raised eyebrow he looked at the ground for a moment, then up into his eyes as he spoke.

"We've got a tea leaf." He found the words difficult to say. They almost stuck in his throat. A thief in the barrack room was bad enough, but out here, at war, close to the enemy it was worse still.

"You sure?" Paul Cooper asked the question knowing full well that Fred would not have raised it unless it were so.

"Yeah." The response was emphatic, in a voice tinged with regret. "Too many blokes are missin' odd bits. I know, I know." He pre-empted the sergeant's scornful remark about soldiers' inability generally to look after their equipment and personal effects. "But these are good blokes who know the score and its just too much to be a coincidence."

"Anyone else spotted this?"

"No......No, I don't think so. Its the odd packet of fags, a couple of francs, a lighter. I mean, some of it ain't even got any value, like a pack of cards. I don' wanna make somethin' out of nothin', but I just think its somethin' we need to keep an eye on."

"Any ideas who it might be?"

"No, no I 'aven't. I mean, I suppose 'cos we 'aven't 'ad the problem before it could be one of the new blokes, but I don't know which one."

"Or it could be one of the regulars, whose circumstances might have changed." Paul Cooper had a look on his face that boded ill for someone; and he was pretty certain he knew who it was.

The weather on Saturday the twenty-second of August continued to be hot and sunny, and they looked forward with no great enthusiasm to more of the previous day's experience. This war was becoming dull, and very much more of this bleedin' marchin' would be gettin' on the bleedin' nerves. It was shortly before seven o'clock as the battalion began to move, on its way north, closer to the Belgian border and closer to the line that the BEF was forming along the Mons Canal. There had been tears before they left from Madame, who insisted on kissing each member of "her" platoon on each cheek. As they stepped back from the experience most of them felt a twinge of sadness, and in some cases loneliness, as they wiped the dampness of her tears from their faces. Peter Dakin looked away, hoping no one would see the moisture in his eyes as the memory of the Belfast dockyard came rushing back and he thought of Ma; and the pain in his throat became almost overpowering.

The two granddaughters, aged fifteen and thirteen, stood by Madame, shaking hands formally, curtseying with downcast eyes and a gentle "enchanté m'seiu." That was enough to soften the hardest of hearts, and there were lumps in many a throat as they moved off.

Madame was staying. She would not join the flood of refugees moving south. She had a farm to run, and when the men came back she had to have as much ready as she could for the spring planting or they would suffer next harvest.

"Good luck, love." Thomas was often a man of few words, but had a way of using them when he meant it.

The twenty-second of August was not, however, to be the same as its predecessors. There was to be a change, a shift in the tide that influences men's lives that was to affect them all. As they marched out of the village a squadron of the 4th Dragoon Guards, in an outpost position just north of Mons some twenty-two miles to the battalion's north-east, observed movement to their north-east. Corporal Drummer Thomas fired at a mounted figure; fired the first shot of the war by a British soldier and lit a spark that would fan in such a short time into an engulfing conflagration which would ultimately consume so many, friend and foe alike.

The talking was at an end, battle was joined, there was no going back; not that any of the young men moving up into the BEF's positions had any thought of turning back. They would give the Germans a bloody good hiding, kick 'em out of Belgium and stick old von Kluck and all the little Klucks just where it would do most good.

And on the way back 'ome they might jus' pop into Madame's farm an' see if she needed any more 'elp.

Chapter 6

The Rearguard at Elouges

Ted Ludgrove surveyed the scene around him, tensed his body, stretched, and shivered a little as he delivered himself of an enormous and satisfying yawn. What he saw gave him little pleasure. He looked both ways along the length of the factory wall, behind which, and within the empty sheds and workshops, the battalion had been billeted the previous afternoon when they arrived in Bois de Boussu. His eyes followed the line of the cobbled road, its surface slicked with water, glistening as the light of the post dawn began to create shadows and shapes around the drab brick houses strung together row on row in terraces; on the chimney stacks thrusting their snouts high towards the leaden heavens, the belching smoke of yesterday no longer present with it being Sunday morning; and on two young women as they walked to work in the small bakery on the corner near the factory gate, their shoes clattering loudly on the pavement of the otherwise silent street.

The early morning period on guard was one of the worst, and the misty, persistent rain that had fallen for the past hour or two had added to his misery, dampening the rough serge of his uniform, which was giving off a smell rather like that of a wet dog.

"What a bloody 'ole this is!"

An obvious statement which drew a silent nod of assent from Albert Carter whose mind was far away, on his wife and his children. The prospect of service and a little money had been attractive. If he was honest with himself he would also admit that escape from the constant drudge of making ends meet, of listening to the complaints and the moans and of trying to find work of any sort had also been a driving force in his desire to depart so swiftly when the telegram had arrived. Now he was thinking of a warm bed, the prospect of a lie in, of a walk to the small allotment they shared with a friend, of an illicit pint in the pub. Aye, 'e'd put up with a fair bit o' naggin' to be out of the situation in which he now found himself.

Ted looked at him. If the bugger would just smile a bit. Always bloody miserable; an' not very fit. 'E was goin' t' be trouble if they got involved in a real fight. "Suppose that's why Fred Smith's teamed 'im with Alfie; keep an eye on 'im, just in case."

He looked away again, at the vast pyramid of the slag heap which dominated the small collection of houses and offices at the edge of the coal pit head just a few hundred yards away. They had looked on with mounting concern during the previous day's march as the countryside had changed in character from the soft green and pleasant farmland that reminded so many of them of home into a strange alien landscape, dotted with man made mountains of slag, factories and foundries belching smoke, dirt and filth everywhere. Gone were the hedgerows set in banks of rich green grass dotted with wild flowers, multi coloured jewels set in a soft velvet cushion; the orchards, green and red with the colours of apples, pears and cherries; black and white Friesian cattle grazing contentedly in fields. Instead, they had found dirty ditches running alongside the roads, their stagnant contents supporting a scum of white and green filth in which the waste of urban life could be seen partially submerged. Odd bits of scrap metal were lying twisted and rusting, created for a purpose at which one could only guess, and discarded as useless by the uncaring denizens of a degenerate wasteland. Everywhere there was the black, all pervading presence of soot, marking the walls and roofs, staining the washing fluttering in grey lines in small back yards, discolouring the vegetation and mingling with the sweat as it ran down the faces of marching troops, streaking their faces as forearms were lifted to wipe away the moisture from their eyes.

They had noticed other changes as well. In France the only able-bodied men they had seen had been soldiers, and their first sighting had been only an hour after they left the farm the previous morning. That had given them something to talk about; and smile about once they were out of sight. The uniform being worn by the French Army was that which had been in use during the Franco-Prussian war some forty or so years earlier. The soldiers of the infantry detachment they had seen guarding a bridge had been dressed in dark blue with red trousers and a blue kepi. The blue top coat had looked cumbersome, folded back from the knees and buttoned in place. The uniform was made of wool, and the Frenchmen had looked very hot and uncomfortable in the August sunshine; and not unlike the chorus in a Gilbert and Sullivan operetta. But they had waved and shouted enthusiastically as the battalion wound its way north towards Mons.

Once in Belgium, however, things had changed. Everywhere there were young men, and not a few members of the battalion were heard to remark that they perhaps might be better employed removing the Germans from their soil rather than simply waiting for someone else to come and do it for them. 'Elpin' out was one thing, but doin' it all was gettin' beyond a soddin' joke; an' it might be a good idea if some o' them smilin' little bastards smiled a bit less, got off their bleedin' arses and did somethin'. No, France had been good; Belgium was a bit of a let down.

Thomas was not to know of course, even as these uncharitable thoughts passed through his mind, that in a valiant and courageous feat of arms the Belgians had, to the north and east, delayed an army vastly superior to their own in size and equipment, had inflicted on the Germans casualties they had never expected and had imposed the delay that was allowing the BEF at least to adopt some kind of defensive position before themselves receiving the onslaught of the Kaiser's huge war machine. But, even if he had known, it is likely that he would still have taken the view that the buggers could get off their backsides an'................!

There'd been a bit of excitement to liven up the day as they marched north. They had seen their first two aircraft, and confusion had been created. The first was clearly German. It had flown low enough for them to see the faces of the pilot and his observer, and the black crosses had stood out clearly on the underside of the wings. The second aircraft had been different, and higher, and also clearly German because they had seen the crosses again. The first aircraft, having caught them by surprise, had flown on uninterrupted. With more warning of the second some riflemen in the leading company had fired the battalion's first shots of the war; until they were told in no uncertain terms by the adjutant to stop.

"Why'd e' do that then?" Jack Waters' irritating nasal voice drew a sharp response from Paul Cooper.

"Because it's British is why!"

"No t'ain't!" Waters was not to be put off. "Bloody crosses under the wings there were, jus' like t'other one!"

"That, Private Waters, was a Union Jack you saw. A Union Jack. Our Union Jack. The one that has been the flag of the Realm for some time now. We do not fire at aeroplanes with Union Jacks on them because that means they are on our side."

Cooper's sarcasm was scathing, and it was a disgruntled Jack Waters who continued the march; muttering to Alfred Arbuckle beside him that a cross was a cross and if he saw one he was going to shoot at it and take the consequences. He continued moaning until Alfred, uncharacteristically, told him to shut up; which he did, much to the relief of those nearby who were more concerned about the effect of the cobbles on their feet and the proximity of the next brew of tea than Waters an' 'is bloody aeroplanes.

The fledgling Royal Flying Corps, formed only two and a half years earlier, having been part of the Royal Engineers for a year, was very worried about Jack Waters; and the many thousands like him who had shown they would shoot first and resolve the consequences later. The deaths of Lieutenant Cyril Hoskins and his observer, Captain Theodore Crean, from small arms fire whilst flying over their own lines had brought into sharp focus the need to resolve the problems of aircraft recognition. It was a French officer who demonstrated to the RFC that the red cross of the Union Jack was all that was clearly visible from below, and hence was sometimes mistaken for the German Maltese Cross. He suggested that the British adopt the same circular marking as the French, but here national pride was at stake. Consequently, although they accepted his idea in principle, the RFC painted them in reverse: a red centre and blue circumference. Before long all forty-seven remaining aircraft, the RFC's entire operational strength, were displaying the new markings; and everyone, on the ground and in the air, felt very much more secure.

"In yer go. Breakfast is on." Alfred Arbuckle's deep voice brought the welcome news that purgatory had at last come to an end, and he and Peter Dakin stepped up to take over the guard duty.

"'Bout bloody time." It was a standard response, was offered with no offence intended and none was taken. "C'mon Bert!" A last glance at the two girls, fiddling with the lock as they tried to get into the bakery, and they were heading for the soot blackened storage shed that had been home these past twenty-six hours or so.

Moving away from Carter and heading toward the urinals that had been set up behind the building, Ted stopped short as he turned the corner. Out of sight of most people, but just within his vision, tucked away behind an overflowing rubbish disposal area, he saw Paul Cooper, clearly angry, and Ned Preece standing rigidly to attention. Obviously something was up, it was bad, and he did not need to get involved. However, Ned was a mate.....!

Moving to the urinals, he unbuttoned his fly and undertook the normal rituals associated with peeing into a pipe inserted into the soil, whilst keeping an eye over his shoulder and at the same time ensuring that he would not be entering the messing area with a wet trouser leg. Cooper marched off from his altercation with Ned, and it was some minutes before his victim appeared into the courtyard looking white and shaken; and trembling visibly.

"What's up, mate? Need any 'elp?"

Despite the genuine concern in Ted's voice, Ned Preece's reaction was sharp and dismissive.

"No I bloody don't. Bugger off." He regretted it as he said it, but his pride would not allow him to retract. Instead he walked off in the direction of the front gate, where Alfred and Peter were to receive similar treatment as they asked after their obviously upset colleague and friend.

Ted twitched the corner of his mouth downwards in a rueful expression, and went to get whatever breakfast might be left to him. The mystery deepened, however, as he came back into the main courtyard and saw Mathew Jenkins and his sergeant standing together, and it was obvious that they were indulging in something more than a friendly chat. The stiff and formal salute given by Cooper as the conversation broke off made it clear to anyone who knew them that there had been a disagreement and Mathew Jenkins had made his displeasure known.

The platoon commander's briefing was due to take place at nine-thirty that morning, and prior to that they were involved with the post breakfast clear up and preparation for whatever activity the day might hold. At nine o'clock the section was sitting in a half circle. Before them on a small piece of rag was a brass cylindrical object some ten inches long and one and a half in diameter, with a sixteen inch wooden cane protruding from its base to which was attached a thirty-six inch silk braid tail. It was a grenade, the Number One Mark One; and was one of four issued to the battalion. All of them had come to the company because of its reserve role, and two were in the platoon.

They looked at it in wonder as Fred Smith explained yet again how it worked. He pointed out the solid drawn brass body, the hook for securing it to the waste belt and the serrated cast iron ring around the waist designed to fragment on bursting. He reminded them that it contained four ounces of explosive. He went over again the need to turn the brass cap until the word "remove" lay opposite the arrow painted on the body, to then take off the cap, insert the detonator, replace the cap and turn it again until the word "travel" lined up on the arrow.

He described the throwing procedure: the unwinding of the silk tail, the move of the cap so that the word "fire" lined up with the arrow, the removal of the safety pin and then throwing the grenade either under or over hand; ensuring that the tail could not entangle itself with the thrower or anything near him. It was to be thrown upwards at an angle of thirty five degrees, thereby ensuring maximum range and hopefully a vertical drop onto the target. This would give the best chance of detonation on impact.

"Any questions?" And as he spoke there was the most enormous rumble of noise, accompanied by a vibration in the ground which they felt very clearly through their backsides seated on the cold concrete of the storehouse floor.

"What the bloody 'ell is that?" The noise was continuing unabated, the vibration increasing. Startled looks of consternation appeared on faces throughout the barn.

"That, Private James is artillery fire. Somethin' very big 'as just started." Fred Smith was unaware just how big.

The German barrage on the British position on the Mons canal had begun, off to the north-east, to their half right as they faced the canal running directly in a straight east-west line about two miles to the north. The Battle of Mons had started, with the Germans commencing their onslaught on the salient, forced on Smith-Dorrien by the lie of the ground, on the right of the British Second Corps position; and in particular on the Middlesex Regiment and the Royal Fusiliers.

Just as the barrage commenced Matthew Jenkins arrived to give his orders to the small group, comprising his section commanders and platoon sergeant, through which he passed his instructions to the platoon. Ted looked at them both, searching for signs of the dispute between them, but saw nothing. Ned Preece drew himself back into a dark corner, not wishing to be seen by either of them

Matthew Jenkins smiled grimly. “It’s begun then. Right, listen in. There is very little for me to tell you. The company commander knows nothing, which means neither does the commanding officer. Brigade HQ is unable to add anything to what was said yesterday. The big picture as we understand it is as I told you last night. Thirteen and Fourteen Brigades have been sent forward onto the canal, as far as we know prior to crossing and taking on the Germans in conjunction with the French over on our right. Our brigade remains in divisional reserve, and we sit here until we are told what to do. In the meantime, be ready at very short notice to move. Rest and relax, brew tea by all means, but kit and bodies ready to go at thirty minutes notice. Any questions?”

There were, and the conversation ebbed and flowed for fifteen more minutes as he listened to them, let them unburden themselves a little and shared with them the concerns they all felt at the uncertainty; and the unspoken apprehension stimulated by the first sounds of hostile artillery fire. Still, it wouldn’t be long before they were on their way over the canal and having at the Germans.

Some time later, as his soldiers continued to wonder what was to happen, Edward von Gleichen stood by the front window of the room in which his small command post was housed, his signallers in the next room busily keeping in touch with his battalions via the several miles of cable laid by his line detachments the night before. As he listened to the artillery he spared his signallers a thought. Remarkable really, scruffy lot, couldn’t possible mount a King’s Guard with anything like that. But, by heavens, they were diligent when it came to setting up and maintaining communications. Couldn’t do without them really. As he watched, two of them appeared trailing a cable drum.

“Soddin’ goats. If another one chews through the soddin’

wire again I'll give the bloody thing to the cookhouse; in joints. Mornin' sir!"

The Brigadier smiled an acknowledgement. "Morning. Lovely day."

They smiled back, bent to their work and permitted themselves a knowing glance at each other. Officers!

He was listening to the artillery working its way along the bank of the canal in a westerly direction, watching in mild disbelief as the residents of this ghastly little town made their way to church, dressed in their Sunday best, for all the world as if nothing were happening around them. By the sights and sounds he judged that the German artillery was creeping towards Thirteen Brigade, to his right front. Suddenly, he saw shells landing on the north bank of the canal opposite the general area occupied by his brigade. He glanced at his watch. It was twelve-forty in the early afternoon, and as he began to wonder whatever next, concerned that he had no idea what was going on around him and no one could tell him, his brigade major approached from the table set up in the corner of the room.

"Message from divisional HQ sir. We have been asked to dig a fall-back brigade defensive position down here at Halte." He pointed to the map. A glance showed the significance. A brigade dug in there would cover a withdrawal of the division, and possibly other elements of the Corps. He said nothing. How many to send? How much could he afford to push back without weakening himself too much, and yet dig the thing in time? And a withdrawal?

"Two companies from each battalion please. But I should like them back in billets by nightfall. Now, dispositions......" He described on the map the way he wished the dig to take place and left his brigade major to distribute the orders. A withdrawal. Surely not. The French were to attack, to drive the Germans from Belgium; and we with them. I wonder what has changed. Ah well, time would tell.

Unknown to Edward von Gleichen and to his soldiers was the true situation in which the BEF found itself. On its right the Fifth French Army was not preparing to advance across the canal and assist in the eviction of the Germans from Belgian soil. Indeed, it had been withdrawing for over twenty-four hours and there was a gap of some ten miles between it and the BEF on its left. Further to the BEF's left was nothing but a few scattered French territorial divisions. For reasons never properly explained, Sir John French had agreed to fight the BEF on the Mons Canal position for twenty-four hours, after which he proposed to consider the effects of the German move on his front and the French retreat to his right rear. The effect was simple: a BEF with both flanks exposed.

By mid afternoon a number of things had become obvious. To the Second Corps commander, General Smith-Dorrien, it was clear that he could no longer hold the extended position along the canal, and in particular the salient on his right where the casualties had become untenable and the German pressure too much to bear. He gave orders for the corps to withdraw back into a shortened line, already worked out with his commanders. To Edward von Gleichen, who had been told to expect up to a corps of two or three divisions on his part of the line, but was in fact facing three times that number, it was obvious that he might need the fall-back position that was being dug. To the soldiers of the Ninth it was obvious that something was not quite right; that two of their companies had been sent to dig a defensive position to the south, which seemed odd; that they didn't appear to be preparing to advance; and that a large number of casualties were being transported, or were making their way, down the road in Bois de Boussu towards the rear.

If the sound and vibration of the guns had caused pangs of apprehension to gnaw at the stomach, some of the sights they saw on stretchers and carts moving back to the Casualty Clearing Stations to the south only added to the concerns they felt, but would never admit. Perhaps even more telling than the casualties were those assisting or carrying them. The pale drawn faces showing clearly the shock of men exposed for the first time to the bruising, shattering impact of high explosive detonating all round them, of bullets flying through the air like swarming hornets, of shrapnel coughing out its deadly load from on high, inescapable and intrusive. They stared, without wishing to stare, at bandages stained red, where there had been the time and the means to apply them; at crude splints where limbs had been broken; at pained faces gasping to draw breath as the hole in their chests competed with the mouth and nose to draw oxygen into their lungs; at uniforms once clean and presentable, but which were now soiled with the blood, the filth, the unpleasantness that resulted from contact with the enemy.

Things, it appeared, were not going according to plan.

"What on earth was that?" The brigade commander looked at his watch. It was quarter to five in the afternoon.

"What the fuck was that?" Less restrained than their brigade commander the soldiers of the Ninth, along with many others, had their thoughts diverted by two enormous explosions to their west, and about two miles away they could see two columns of smoke and debris rising into the air.

"The two prepared demolitions on the bridges near Pommeroeul, I would suspect," said the brigade major, pointing with his pencil to the map. The brigadier pondered the implications, concerned about his left flank and how best he might respond if a threat should manifest itself.

"Buggered if I know," said Fred Smith, turning away to check that his kit was still in order. The corporal pondered the implications, concerned about his wife and daughter and the fact that whatever was happening it didn't look or sound good.

Ted looked around the barn. The officers were taking it all very calmly, talking as if nothing were going on. Close observation of one young officer, however, would have revealed that it had been some time since he had turned a page in the book he was so studiously reading. The soldiers were more forthcoming in their expressions of concern and excitement. Ted caught a knowing look from Alfie, and returned his grin; covering, he hoped effectively, the anxiety he felt regarding what might be about to befall them.

And one thousand six hundred British soldiers were already dead, wounded or missing

But that really was it for a while. Apart from the guard duties, they ate and went to their beds that night with no further idea of what was going on. They were learning early the lessons of war: that boredom and inactivity could form a major element of their lives, that not knowing what is going on is pretty much standard, and that when they did have to do anything it would be in a hurry, not what they expected, and likely to change whilst they were doing it. They slept a deep sleep through what was largely a quiet night with barely a shot fired, for although the day had been plagued by inactivity the inevitable tensions created by the circumstances were extremely debilitating. Many did not wake when, at three in the morning, two more bridges were blown as the last of the cavalry withdrew across the canal, and it was only the shaking of colleagues to rouse them for the pre-dawn stand-to that brought many back to wakefulness. As they moved sleepily to their positions the Germans opened fire with a tremendous barrage along the canal, but they were already getting used to the sound of guns and the explosion of shells, and as they had yet to have any of this unpleasantness directed towards them they were learning to put it to the back of their minds. Behind them, to the south, their own artillery responded, the shells making a whooshing noise as they passed overhead en route to their targets. In the distance, over the canal, they stared with some amazement at the flares put up by the German artillery, lighting the residual darkness that preceded the approaching day. This was something they had never seen before and there was nothing similar provisioned for the British Gunners.

By ten that morning, and after a snatched cold breakfast of bread and marmalade, with the added bonus of a good brew, the battalion was in position on the northern edge of the town watching the German artillery fire getting closer and closer. To their front were the Bedfordshires and the Dorsets, and the sound of their rifles and machine guns could be clearly heard as they engaged the advancing Germans. As yet the Norfolks had not seen a German, did not know what they looked like or what to expect; and they were getting impatient.

At eleven-fifteen it seemed their impatience was to be satisfied. The orders were to move north and attack the Germans on the canal. At last, this was it, moving up and on further north, deeper into Belgium to do the job they had been sent to do: chuck the bloody Germans out and get back home. Webbing was already on, packs were shouldered, rifles checked. Friends looked at each other with mixed feelings. This, then, was it. Nothin' to be scared of, but jus' don't make a fuckin' idiot of yerself. A grin, a nod, a touch and then attention to the matter of getting on and, as Wellington said to Thomas Creevy before Waterloo, "doing the business."

They marched north, heading towards the sound of the artillery, making for a position some three miles away on the Mons Canal which ran east to west at right angles to their line of march. They marched in columns by companies as if it were an exercise, certain that out in front were British units and that they would have adequate warning of any approaching Germans.

"Cumpnee halt!"

"Now what? Bloody hell, but they'd 'ardly been on the bloody road ten minutes an' already they were stoppin'."

Those near to battalion headquarters began to get some idea that something was up. A staff officer had appeared suddenly, his horse blown and lathered, with a written message for the commanding officer. Lieutenant Colonel Ballard was being directed personally by the divisional commander, Sir Charles Ferguson, to take under his command, in addition to his own battalion, the First Battalion of the Cheshire Regiment, 119 Battery Royal Field Artillery and a squadron of the 19th Hussars and to take up a position south of the village of Elouges, about three miles to the south-west of his present position. His task was to fill the gap between Elouges and Audregnies, a distance of about a mile and a half. The CO did not know it, but Sir

Charles Ferguson's decision was motivated by the premature withdrawal of Nineteen Brigade on the left of his division, thereby leaving his flank exposed.

Ballard looked at the map. The position would see him facing out towards the north-west and four miles south of the canal. He was not to know that von Kluck's First Army had already begun its enveloping left hook towards the south-east, seeking to cut off the rear of the BEF and force its surrender or destruction. He was not to know that his tiny force would be facing the spearhead of that move: the Seventh and Eighth German Divisions, a force of twenty-four battalions of infantry, supported by nine batteries of artillery. He was not told that he was all that stood between the BEF and a German victory.

"What's 'e mean turn about?" Alfie James was not the only soldier in the battalion to ask why it was they were now moving south, when they had been moving north, moving away from the enemy instead of towards them. There was disappointment and confusion, and no orders except to do as they were told and listen in for the next instructions.

They marched through Elouges, a small village typical of so many they had seen, and not heavily industrialised. They left it, heading to the south-west along the Audregnies road, emerging as they left Elouges into an area of open fields which reminded them very much of Norfolk. Those near the front of the battalion were in time to see the commanding officer conferring with the CO of the Cheshires, who had already arrived with his battalion. His soldiers were lying beside the road, looking north-west towards where they expected to see the enemy, and waiting patiently. The small conference, taking place beneath a railway bridge, broke up, officers strode purposefully about their business, and the Cheshires rose from their position by the road and began to move along the Audregnies road away from the Norfolks.

Ten minutes later and their own orders were clear. The two battalions were to occupy a position on the ridge which lay some two hundred yards to the right, the north-west, of the Audregnies road and to engage any Germans who sought to break through. The Cheshires would be on the left and the Norfolks on the right, strung out in a single line covering a ridiculously large frontage. 119 Battery would be on another ridge, south of the road and positioned in line behind the right hand company of the Norfolks. The distance between the ridges was some seven hundred yards with the gunners looking down into the valley wherein lay the Audgregnies road running right to left across their front, and up onto the other ridge beyond the road where the Norfolks would be positioned just out of their sight on the forward slope beyond the rim. It was a position which gave the Gunners a good shoot away to the north-west, towards Quiverain from where it was expected that the enemy would materialise. Their short range options were, however, limited by the line of the hill upon which the infantry were positioned and which restricted their view.

The company commander had called his officers together. They had moved forward, under the railway bridge and into an area some two hundred yards long where the road ran between two steep embankments before emerging onto the high ground away towards Audregnies. They were to remain in this area, to be prepared to cover the battalion's withdrawal, and to give support forward when called upon to do so. Two platoons, under the company commander's direct control were to remain in the sunken road, soldiers deployed along the top of the bank facing the enemy. The other two platoons, under Matthew's command, were to move back to the second ridge, to the south-east of the road and near where 119 Battery was deployed, in order to provide depth for any rearguard action. They were to make the best of whatever cover there was. Time was not available in which to dig trenches or take other protective measures.

Matthew's orders to the other platoon commander were clear and simple.

"I want you to move back to the ridge behind us, and occupy a position with your right on the railway line and its small embankment." As he spoke he pointed out the railway line which bridged the sunken road and formed the right flank of their company position, and, further forward, that of the battalion.

"Your left will be that tree." He pointed at an Elm, and in so doing marked a frontage of four hundred yards. "The company commander wishes to have an officer's view of what is going on in the rest of the battalion so that he can be prepared for whatever is coming. Consequently, I am taking a section forward to the corner of that field so that I can see and report back." The spot he indicated was on the ridge line facing Quiverain on the right of the battalion, which was, even as he spoke, deploying. It was a patch of rough ground with a few small trees, providing cover from view, but precious little else.

"When I withdraw it will be back alongside the railway line, making use of the cover and the dead ground." He used a term meaning that the ground would be out of direct enemy view. "That means you must put the remaining three sections of my platoon, commanded by Sergeant Cooper, on the right so that I can get to them easily when I need to. I'm likely to be in a hurry. Finally, if I could just stress one vital thing and that is surprise. To have the best effect the enemy must not know we are there. The two platoons on the bank here will already have engaged the enemy and, hopefully, stopped him. Our job will be to cover them as they withdraw behind us and we leapfrog our way back, guarding the battalion's rear. Clear?"

He looked at the young officer's white face, saw the consternation in his eyes; but there was no time or place for confidence building.

"Questions? No? Good, then let's be about it and good luck."

Taking Fred Smith's section, Matthew left the rest of his platoon with Sergeant Cooper and scrambled up the bank to where he could see the ridge line only two hundred yards ahead and only twenty or so feet higher than his present position. Being on the reverse slope, however, he couldn't see any further, and it was this lack of visibility that had caused the company commander to want his own observation post forward.

"Right, Corporal Smith, I shall go to the left with half your section. As you can see, that puts me in a position where I am still a little blind to the right where the railway runs. The 19th Hussars are out there, protecting our flank, but I want you to keep me informed about what is going on. Take the other half of your section with you."

"Sir." The single word of acknowledgement. "Right, Corporal Floyd, take riflemen one to four and go with Mr Jenkins. The rest of you with me." As he spoke he began crawling on his stomach over the bank and way to the right near the railway line, his rifle held across his body and out in front ready to fire at once should that be necessary. Crawling two hundred yards with one's stomach flat on the ground is no easy task, and when you are well the wrong side of thirty it is even harder. It was a very weary Fred Smith who arrived in the position that had been indicated to him, but by waving the rest of his men back and taking rather longer than was really necessary to look over the ground in front of him before bringing them forward he was able to regain most of his composure before they joined him.

Matthew's small group was also quickly in position, and although he and Fred Smith were only twenty yards apart he had been right to split his observation party. The trees in which he positioned himself obscured his view to the right and he would have had to risk unnecessary movement in order to cover it; thereby increasing the chance of exposure.

The sight before them was one that would live with them forever. Ted Ludgrove could not contain a gasp, whilst Ned Preece gripped his rifle so tightly his knuckles showed white under the dirt that encrusted them. Albert Carter pondered again on the wisdom of being here, and John Hayes decided that he was scared and was by no means certain that he wished to remain where he was; or for that matter on the Continent at all. Joseph Floyd thought about responsibility, and wished he were once more a private soldier.

Before them stretched wide open fields with the forward

slope descending gradually to the north-west in a natural glacis that led eventually to flat land running just south of the Mons canal. Over a distance of about one and a quarter miles in a line towards Audregnies, just visible to the south-west about mile and a half away, was the assembled power of two battalions of infantry. Allowing for reserves in the Cheshires, such as was the case with their company, and headquarters elements there were over one thousand men lying down to take up a prone firing position facing towards the likely enemy approach. There was no pretence at supports or firing lines. Every man was positioned where he could bring the full weight of fire upon the enemy, and all they had behind them was the Norfolk's reserve company and anything the Cheshires might have had.

For a moment Matthew's mind flashed back to South Africa: blistering sun, men exposed in the open, impossible odds. But his was different. Now it was the British who held the high ground, and were the better shots and were well trained and versed in more mobile war fighting skills. He blinked, and dismissed it from his thoughts.

On the right of their battalion, and clearly visible to them, was one of the Vickers Maxim machine guns. It was a water-cooled, belt-fed machine gun capable of firing five hundred rounds per minute out to a range of three thousand yards. Government financial restrictions had precluded the BEF deploying with the more modern Vickers Mark One machine gun, with its higher rate of fire and lighter construction; and had limited the numbers in battalions to two, rather than the six that had been recommended.

In the short time available the crew of six had done a first class job of making the entire thing resemble an innocuous bush. Ted looked across at them, and did not envy them one bit. Not only were they a prime target once the enemy had located the gun position, they were lumbered well and truly with some very heavy weights to carry. In addition to their personal equipment, weighing the same as everyone else's, the gun, carried by two of the crew, weighed twenty-eight and a half pounds; thirty-eight and a half with a full water jacket. The tripod, carried by another two members of the crew, was twenty pounds and the boxes of two hundred and fifty round belts carried by the others pitched in at around twelve pounds each.

It was one o'clock. They had all been given their arcs of observation and the reference points had been agreed. Apart from Matthew Jenkins, who had binoculars, they had to rely on the naked eye, but they had a good view and could draw his attention to anything they saw.

It was Ted who saw the first sign of movement, way over to the left of the Cheshires in the area of Audgregnies.

"Church tower, sir," he named the reference point in that area, "right, four o'clock two hundred yards, sir. I can see cavalry sir."

The sun was high and to their south. Looking that far left he would have to be wary of reflection off the lenses. He focused instantly on the point indicated by Ted, and was able very quickly to identify the soft peaked hats and khaki uniforms as British. What he did not know was that they were part of Major General Allenby's Second Cavalry Division, sent up on the left by the corps commander to help seal off the left flank. Neither did he have any idea of what they might be up to.

"Sir!" There was urgency in Colin Baxter's voice. As the runner, he had joined the small observation party; staying, as his job demanded, close to his officer. "Sir, Pine Copse, slightly right. It looks like infantry sir; an awful lot of infantry."

His reference brought Jenkins' eyes round to a point some two thousand yards to their north-west, in the area of the small town of Quiverain. Moving south-east from the town, and heading straight towards them were great, grey solid masses in large blocks crawling ant like across the open fields. He was looking at two divisions of German infantry on the move.

"My God" he thought, but did not say.

"Bugger!" Ned Preece was not so reticent as his officer.

Ted's mouth dropped open, and he shut it as quickly as he could, hoping that no one had noticed. His stomach turned to water as he saw the massed ranks of the enemy moving towards their position, and he held the cheeks of his backside together tightly so that the manifestation of his anxiety would be silent. Ned was not quick enough, and he grinned sheepishly as both the sound and the smell made themselves known. In the midst of his own concerns Ted recalled that this was the first time he'd seen Ned smile for some time.

Swiftly Matthew scribbled a note in his field note book, a small pad, serrated down the left hand side, comprising pages which were divided into small, faint blue squares to facilitate scaled drawing; and each one sequentially numbered. Passing the torn off page to Colin with orders to get it to the company commander, he returned to gazing at the advancing enemy.

"Cavalry's up to something sir!"

He looked across to the left, out over a battalion where officers were calling out the fire control orders that would bring the considerable punch of British infantry firepower to bear on the advancing enemy; delaying the executive order to actually open fire until the enemy was where they wanted him.

The small observation party watched in amazement as what looked like one regiment of cavalry moved north out of Audregnies and prepared to take the advancing German infantry in the flank. In fact, they were watching the 9th Lancers and a squadron of the 4th Dragoon Guards taking on six German infantry battalions and six batteries of artillery across two thousand yards of open space. However, what no one knew was that the area was festooned with low wire fences, small railway lines and little sunken culverts; all products of the mix of farming and mining that was the basis of life in that area. It was not the combined fire of the artillery, nor the less effective scattered shooting of infantry on the move, that did the damage. It was the terrain; and it damaged the charging horsemen mightily.

Matthew and his soldiers watched in horrified fascination as men and horses fell in all directions, scattered and broke up into small groups, charged the enemy where they could, or sought cover from fire when they could not come to grips with the Germans. Through his binoculars Matthew watched the head of a horse smashed into a bloody shambles by a full charge of shrapnel, its rider pitching sideways to the ground. The trooper never rose, probably hit by the same shrapnel. Elsewhere a horse screamed, a long and agonised scream that cut into the hearts of men as it struggled, impaled through the belly, on a steel fence support. Its rider lay helpless on the ground; even at that range the white of the broken shin was visible protruding though his bloodstained right trouser leg. Horses without riders swirled aimlessly about, riders without horses sought to catch them and recover themselves, on the ground injured animals writhed in pain, and all around were small, still, khaki humps.

But the day by no means went all against the cavalry. The German infantry was temporarily halted and forced in part to retire. Behind the Norfolks, on the other side of the road, 119 Battery was giving good account of itself, taking on the German batteries and the infantry in the open and causing considerable casualties. The sound of their firing was hard on the soldiers lying in front of the guns. Being in that position the crack of the guns was much louder and sharper, and pierced inside their eardrums like a hot needle.

Meanwhile, out across the fields some of the British horsemen were able to close in on their foes. Matthew could not hold back a gasp of horror as he watched first one and then another lancer each skewer a German soldier and force him wriggling to the ground. The one who had been running away simply went down as the British cavalryman rode past him, flicking and turning his wrist to withdraw the lance tip from the body as he moved on seeking other prey in a German formation that was fast beginning to lose its cohesion. The second German had tried to face his aggressor, and Matthew watched whilst his hands clutched despairingly round the shaft of the lance as its tip plunged into his chest, blood spurting in a final gore-spattered scream from his open mouth.

And then it was over. Three hundred horses and two hundred and fifty men lay dead or wounded, or were missing. What was left of the cavalry rode back towards the British lines, pursued by German artillery fire. Some came straight across the fields, passing between soldiers lying in wait for the enemy. Some skirted the flanks of the regiment, and moved on behind, trying to get away to the west and rejoin their formation. Meanwhile, out in the fields, dismounted horsemen sought refuge where they could, moving where possible to join the infantry on the ridge.

Matthew sent a second written report to his company commander. Colin Baxter, having only just returned, panting, from his first foray took the piece of paper, offered a rueful grin to Ted Ludgrove and headed back down the ridge towards the bank. As he arrived on the road he saw that there were a number of cavalry soldiers milling about, their horses looking blown after their ordeal. It was no easy task for these animals, carrying as they did a full eighteen stone in weight. As well as the rider and his equipment, this included spare horseshoes, two feed bags, each with seven pounds of oats, a waterproof cape, a greatcoat, a canvas bucket, and sixty rounds of ammunition in bandoliers around its neck.

For their part the riders looked flushed with the excitement of their recent foray against the enemy. Colin was mesmerised for a short while at the sight of a young 9th Lancer, the whole of the front third of his lance smeared with blood, already losing its freshness and drying to a muddy brown in the hot August sunshine, and a lump of something caking up just behind the lance tip. He was wiping his right hand, also covered in blood, on the leg of his jodhpurs, grinning self consciously with a mix of bravado and mild shock; his white face beading with sweat on his forehead.

The withdrawal of the cavalry through and around the infantry had brought artillery fire to bear on the ridge and the road. High explosive shell began to rain down, throwing up great gouts of earth and stones wherever they landed. Shrapnel began to cough out its deadly load. Men began to be hit, and along the line shouts, curses and groans marked the effects as this sustained fire began to make itself felt on the battalion.

The observation party, off to the right of the battalion, was on the periphery of any artillery fire, but that did not stop several high explosive shells landing within twenty or so yards of them. They heard the whirring noise of shell splinters passing overhead, felt occasionally the spatter as small pieces of earth came their way and smelt the distinctive acrid smell of detonating high explosive. For the first time some of them experienced the dreadful feeling of being exposed, unable to hide from a shell which could appear unannounced and kill or maim terribly. It was like lying naked and blindfold, knowing that there was someone nearby with a knife that could inflict terrible damage on the exposed body; and there was nothing that could be done about it.

On the ridge to the south-west of the road Paul Cooper watched 119 Battery responding to the German artillery fire. Their own position had already been identified, which made things uncomfortable for the two platoons of Norfolks nearby as the Germans brought down counter battery fire on the British gunners. Paul watched and marvelled as they continued to service their guns, despite the shattering impact of high explosive and the rain of death from shrapnel. It was as if they were on an artillery demonstration on Salisbury Plain, gun drills perfect, orders crisply shouted, responses clear and positive. And when a man went down someone stepped into his job, the crews reorganised themselves automatically to respond to the loss of the casualty, and the firing went on unabated. In one case he saw a layer literally cut in half by an exploding shell, which did virtually no other damage that he could see. Another gunner simply stepped forward, removed the lower half of the body from the layer's seat where it had remained sitting, wiped the gruesomeness from the gun sight, put his eye to it and carried on as if nothing had happened..

Beyond the guns and on the forward ridge officers prepared their men for the executive word of command to fire as, two thousand yards away, the Germans finished regrouping after the cavalry charge and resumed their ponderous march towards the British position.

Matthew was near the right hand platoon, watching as the riflemen checked their final firing positions. He saw them looking along the rifle, lining up the V sight which was situated just forward of the bolt housing with the foresight at the muzzle and with the chosen target. The rifle muzzles pointed high, since their sights were set for one thousand eight hundred yards, and this would provide the right trajectory for the bullet as it sped towards its target. Some nervousness was obvious, a little fidgeting here, a hand clasping and unclasping on the forestock of the rifle there.

He heard the platoon commander beginning to prepare his men to fire: "Steady, steady....wait."

"'Scuse me sir!" The platoon sergeant interjected, and in a voice that carried to the rest of the platoon observed to an unfortunate private called Harris that he was "'olding yer bleeding bund'ook like a virgin princess playin' with a vagabond's penis," and invited him to "get a fuckin' grip or ye'll be washin' bleedin' dixies for the rest o' the soddin' war."

Along the line soldiers looked at each other, and grinned. Harris squirmed a little, and then he too grinned. The fidgeting stopped; hands held firm on rifles, heads lay steady to one side looking through sights. Normality had been restored. "Jus' like bein' on the range back 'ome and gettin' yer arse kicked for nothin'." The platoon commander looked at his sergeant, saw him nod for the officer to carry on, and waited for the moment when he would order his platoon to fire.

Matthew watched the performance, and marvelled; not for the first time. "What would we ever do without them?"

"FIRE!"

Even though they had been waiting for it the small observation party was startled by the sound of over one thousand rifles firing in unison, and then again two or three seconds later, and then again, and again, and again............

Cartridge brass is made of thirty percent zinc and seventy

percent copper. It has unique qualities of expansion and contraction. When the trigger is squeezed the pin in the bolt is forced by a spring onto a cap which fires the small propellant charge inside the cartridge case. The pressure generated accelerates the bullet down the barrel, to exit the muzzle at a speed of nearly half a mile a second, carrying the .303 inch projectile out up to three thousand eight hundred yards.

To prevent any gas washing back round the lip of the cartridge case, which is both inefficient and damaging to the breech, the brass expands to fit flush against the wall of the breech in a gas tight seal; and then contracts to allow easy extraction of the empty case and its replacement with a complete round at a rate of up to thirty times a minute for the better rifleman; and five hundred times a minute in the machine gun.

Not that these scientific details were on the minds of the Norfolks, or the Cheshires, as they poured a withering fire into the massive blocks of German infantry marching ponderously towards them. But they paid a price. Although most of the German artillery fire went beyond the men lying in the fields without proper cover all along the ridge, small bloody humps were laying still, their numbers growing by the minute. Men were crawling to the rear, and being taken to the Regimental Aid Post set up by the medical officer in a small house just under the railway bridge on the other side of the line which formed the battalion's right flank.

Added to the fire of the British infantry, the gunners fired low burst shrapnel, cutting bloody swathes thorough the advancing German columns. They were not to know it, but the British were, effectively, destroying entire battalions with their accurate, sustained fire. The German advance eventually faltered and they withdrew back towards Quiverain. They had not come within a thousand yards of the two battalions, so effective had been the defence. Subsequently, prisoners would not believe that there were not some twenty machine guns in each battalion.

Half an hour later they tried again, and the result was the

same. For Ted Ludgrove the abiding memory would be the noise, the awful, ear-splitting crack of the guns on the other ridge just behind them, the thump of rifle fire, and the persistent rattle of the nearby machine gun. And then from the other direction the sharp crack as bullets passed overhead, the crump of high explosive detonating below the soil as German shells ploughed in, the cough of shrapnel. The cries of the wounded echoed through it all, and the last screams of men dying within seconds of being hit. He saw bodies ripped to bloody pieces as shells found their mark, heads punctured and bursting their contents onto the soil, blood pouring from a range of wounds; and everywhere the smell of cordite, blood, vomit, gunpowder and high explosive. He watched, as men he knew, people he had played football with, had been drunk with, had chased girls with, died, or were wounded, sometimes horribly. His stomach churned, his bowels turning to water, and the bitter taste of adrenaline washed through his mouth.

And through it all, on at least two occasions, he found himself thinking of red hair, soft lips, scarlet nails and a probing, insistent little tongue; and in his loins something stirred.

The German artillery fire was persistent and chipped away at the exposed infantry. Despite this, they would have stayed, for the Germans had taken a bloody nose and von Kluck's turning movement had been stopped by a force one twelfth its size. However, at five o'clock, to the west the CO saw signs of a wider turning movement and with more activity about to develop on his front decided the time had come to leave. Messages were sent to the companies to execute the withdrawal plan, and to the Cheshires and L Battery for them to do the same. 119 Battery was ordered to withdraw.

From his position looking down on the sunken road, Paul Cooper saw the runners leaving battalion headquarters, and he knew something was up. He watched as one of them, heading west towards the Cheshires, ran into a bursting shell and simply disappeared. More activity around the HQ and another runner set off in the same direction, and Paul watched him out of sight.

"Sergeant, look!"

The young officer commanding the other platoon had stayed near Cooper throughout the afternoon, taking comfort from the experienced man, and leaving his own sergeant to look after his platoon. Paul followed the line of his pointing finger. Matthew's party was on the move, back down the ridge at a run and slithering out of their sight into the sunken road. They would go under the bridge, and use the railway embankment as cover until they were level with the platoon position, and then cross it without skylining themselves. The battalion, on the ridge, began to withdraw, men staggering back with wounded comrades, others providing cover in an organised and well orchestrated move, operating in pairs or by half sections, each watching over the other as they moved, keeping one tactical foot, metaphorically speaking, on the ground at any one time.

The forward two platoons of the company remained in their reserve position, watching for any pursuit, determined to stave it off and allow their fellows who, up to then, had borne the brunt of the fighting, to get safely away.

"Over here sir!" Paul Cooper called out to Matthew as he appeared through the hedge to the right of the platoon position, having crawled across the railway tracks on his belly.

Swiftly, and while Matthew regained his breath, Paul Cooper placed Fred Smith's section in the position he had allocated, leaving the neighbouring section commander to point out arcs of fire and reference points, and to co-ordinate activity with the new arrivals. Both platoons were well settled along a line of trees and bushes, with an earth bank providing a natural firing platform; and some protection.

Matthew gave his orders, pointing out that as he had left the enemy were forming for another assault and before long would be moving onto the position which, until a few moments ago, had been occupied by the rest of the battalion. He directed that a delayed fire control order be given to bring fire down on the forward slope just beyond the Audregnies Road, but that, if anything were to happen to him, under no circumstances was it to be executed until the two platoons on the embankment had either left, or had failed to halt the enemy and were in danger of being overrun.

As he finished speaking he heard the shouts of German officers and NCOs, out of sight for the moment, ordering their men on. Behind him 119 Battery had already gone, but L Battery RHA, way over on the left behind the Cheshires' left rear, carried on firing. Part of Allenby's Division, it had been there to support the cavalry and had stayed. Forward, and to his left, Matthew could still hear the full weight of the Cheshires' fire being brought to bear on the enemy, and as he gave his orders to the platoon it crossed his mind that they were leaving it a bit late to get away.

"Platoon!" The word of command indicated that the order which was to follow applied to them all. "At five hundred yards!" All along the line right hands moved forward along the top of the rifle to set the rear sight, graduated in one hundred yard segments from two hundred yards out to a range of two thousand yards. Up to six hundred yards the trajectory of the bullet was flat, which meant the rifle was held level to the ground in a nice, steady, comfortable position.

"On the slope above the road to your front, half way down from the ridge line. Enemy in close formation, rapid.....await my order."

There it was, a simple clear order; and they all knew that when the word "FIRE" rang out they would commence to pour death and destruction on their unfortunate victims at a minimum of fifteen rounds per man per minute. Suddenly they were there. A long grey line appearing first as bobbing heads as they approached the line of the ridge. Not for the first time did the Norfolks pass a mental compliment to the courage of the men who were presented as such inviting targets yet kept on coming, and cursed the bleedin' officers who lacked the imagination and flair to handle their men properly. This was no way to treat a soldier; still that was their problem, not Thomas'.

They heard the familiar voice of their company commander, ordering his men to open fire, and the column on the hill positively reeled just as it crested the ridge. Men fell by the dozen, some rolling down, their limbs floppy in death like those of a rag doll. Others spun back, often hit by more than one bullet, crashing into their oncoming comrades and creating yet greater confusion. But this attack was short lived, and very swiftly they withdrew behind the safety of the reverse slope. To the company commander their next move was obvious: his sunken road was about to be saturated with artillery fire prior to another attack.

"Right sergeant major, lets get out of here. The orders please."

"Sir!" The CSM looked along the line of the road. "Platoon commanders." The officers looked inwards towards him. "Gentlemen, if you would bring your platoons, and follow me, please." And more quietly to the major: "And you'll bring company HQ sir?"

"I will Sar' Major, now be off with you. The second-in-command will be waiting." The withdrawal route had already been worked out and a reconnaissance undertaken during the afternoon. The company second-in-command was now back at the next tactical bound, about seven hundred yards behind Matthew Jenkins' men on the ridge, preparing the next phase of the leapfrogging moves that would break them clean from the enemy. As he watched his men move swiftly away the company commander heard the Cheshires firing steadily on his left. "They're leaving it a bit late" he said to no one in particular, and then dismissed the thought from his mind. He had other things to worry about.

"That's it, sir. They're clear now as far as I can see." Paul Cooper looked at his officer. "'Cept for some wounded I think."

"There are none on the embankment; are there?" As he spoke the thundering crash of artillery blotted out all other sounds, with the earth bank and the sunken road just five hundred yards away disappearing in a confusion of smoke, flame, shell fragments and debris. "Well….." A pause, and then in a soft, gentle voice: "Well, if there were there aren't any more." He felt sick, and hoped it didn't show.

"Stand by!" All along the line men settled into a final comfortable fire position. The right leg ran straight back, following a line directly from the muzzle of the rifle through the right shoulder and the right side of the body to the heel of the right foot. The left leg was splayed out to the left at an angle of about forty-five degrees. The elbows formed a bipod, and most of them had made use of cover in front of them, resting the back of their forward hand and supporting the forestock of the rifle. The rifle itself did not rest directly on such a support as that threw off the shot, making it go high.

They waited, expecting the German shell fire to creep its way toward them as their enemy sought to clear the ground over which he must advance. If they were going to carry on moving in blocks like that they were going to have to do something to reduce their casualties.

Ted looked to his right, saw Alfie and winked at his friend. He glanced down at the two clips of five rounds he had carefully laid on a large Maple leaf in order to keep them clean. It would make reloading easier if he didn't have to fish for the first reload in his pouches. As he watched, a large spider, with a very round body and very spindly legs, made its way sedately across the ammunition and disappeared into the safety of a nearby Dandelion.

Still the Cheshires were firing over to the left and Matthew was grateful, for whatever they were doing could only deflect some of the enemy fire from coming his way. He waited for it to reach out onto their position. Once it did there would be terrible casualties for they had no overhead cover. A pang of fear knifed into his stomach, and once again felt the naked exposure of a man in the open; a ready victim to the onslaught about to befall him.

Suddenly, to everyone's amazement, the artillery stopped without advancing its rain of death beyond the road. As the noise disappeared and the smoke and dust began to subside they first heard and then saw the Germans advancing again, breasting the rise on the other side of the road in a huge, massed wave. Along the line anticipation grew, stomachs tightened, throats went dry, hands sweated, the peculiar, and by now familiar, sharp taste of adrenaline appeared in mouths and hearts beat faster. Men broke wind as their apprehension had its effect on their bowels.

Matthew felt that apprehension, knew how important it was to time this correctly. Too late and they would be able to use the road to outflank them, too soon and the impact would not be enough to allow the battalion to break clean. He looked at his men, saw them tense and ready to fire, then looked back at the enemy. He drew breath, ready to shout, and then held it; pausing for just an instant to be sure he was right.

Cooper looked across to his platoon commander. Strangely, he felt no fear. Despite some of the terrible sights he had seen on the gun lines just behind him, the thought had not really entered his consciousness that he might soon be in a similar condition. He saw the officer look along the line of both platoons, pause, draw a deep breath, and appear to hesitate for a few seconds; and then:

"FIRE!"

The German formation was half way down the ridge towards the sunken road as the ambush was sprung with complete surprise. Fingers tightened on triggers, a target already selected from amongst the mass, first pressure taken, hold the breath, squeeze the trigger, keep a firm grip on the weapon, tight in the shoulder, to control the recoil. As soon as the shot is fired up with the right hand to the bolt, grasp it with the forefinger and thumb, up with the bolt handle, then draw it back to eject the spent cartridge. The head moves only ever so slightly to the left, to allow the bolt just to brush the right cheek as it is withdrawn. Slam it home, the head back in position looking along the rear and foresights to the next target, at the same time gripping the rifle tightly at the forestock and pushing it well back into the shoulder to ensure a well controlled shot.

"Count yer rounds; ten in the magazine. No point in

firing on an empty chamber, waste of time. Bugger, 'ow many's that I've fired. Soddin' 'ell." Right hand up, forefinger and thumb, head to one side, slam it forward, grip the bloody thing, next target, bloody smoke, can't see sod all. Tenth round gone, bolt open, stuff the cartridge clip into the guide at the rear of the bolt assembly, press down with the ball of the right thumb, flick out the clip and put in the second; press down, ram the bolt forward to throw out the second clip, new target, they're still comin', bugger, squeeze, right hand up grasp the bolt, reload, select a target, bloody hand 'urts, must 'ave snagged it on a cartridge clip; shit, still comin', keep countin' the bloody rounds.......

In the first minute, eighty riflemen poured twelve hundred aimed shots into the advancing masses, and then twelve hundred more and then twelve hundred more and then...............and then there was no more need. The destruction was complete. In front of them the equivalent of two entire battalions had ceased to exist. The slaughter was horrendous, wounded crying out in agony, trying to crawl away from the relentless, lethal rain of savagery coming their way. The slope was slippery with blood, and as men sought to escape they slid and fell among the dead and dying. An officer, miraculously untouched by it all, stood in the centre of the slope, looked to where the two platoons, which he still could not see, had fired from, shook his head, turned and walked back whence he had come, his head bowed.

Subsequently, he was to report British troops in overwhelming strength, for which at least a divisional assault was required.

In the silence that fell over the Norfolks once the order to cease fire had been given there was a short pause, time for reflection, a feeling of relief, before each of the two platoons, acting independently, moved back through the new position behind them now occupied by the rest of the company, and on back to the next tactical bound beyond that.

Matthew looked at the carnage his fire order had generated, mesmerised for the briefest instant by the destruction they had wreaked. Then his brain snapped back to the present, and the need to break contact.

"By half sections, move." Away they went, the platoon commanders leading the first four half-sections, adopting after a hundred yards a fire position to cover the move of the other half-sections commanded by the sergeants, which passed through them and on for another hundred yards. And so the process was repeated, legs aching, hearts pumping, adrenaline flowing; throwing themselves down facing the enemy, rifles in position in case targets appeared, sights adjusted to the new and increasing range; watching the other half of the platoon doubling back until they were through the new line; waiting to hear the screamed word, "move" from the rear line, up onto the knees, grab the rifle by the forestock, turn and, holding it at the trail, run back through the others, seeing their friend's rifles aimed forward to protect them as they ran; and then down and do it all over again. Thus it was, three or four times each, until they reached the new company line, gasping for breath, and were having their new position pointed out to them.

But they need not have worried. The Germans had been stopped, although Matthew could still hear the Cheshires firing away, and wondered yet again before moving off to attend to more pressing matters.

There had been no casualties in Matthew's small force, and although desperately tired it was an elated group of men that arrived at the bivouac for the night, in a field near the village of St Waast, seven miles south of Elouges. They were to spend the night without shelter, which was not a problem given the excellent weather; without water which was a problem given their exertions that day and the loss of fluid from their bodies; and without food as they carried no rations with them. Their last meal had been two slices of bread at breakfast. But for once they were too tired even to complain. That would come later, when they had slept the deep sleep that comes with mental and physical exhaustion.

In brigade headquarters Edward von Gleichen counted the cost. At last he had his brigade back together, but it was much depleted. In addition to the casualties in the Bedfords and Dorsets from their action near the canal, and the Norfolks at Elouges, he had lost almost the whole of the First Battalion the Cheshire Regiment. Paul Cooper had seen two attempts to get a message to them. They, and a third attempt, had all failed. So the Cheshires had stayed, had fought.....and had died. Only two hundred eventually came out, and the losses here included a complete platoon of Norfolks which had been way over to the left and which had also not received the order. Added to which, one hundred wounded Norfolks had been left in the aid post by the bridge, with the medical officer, out of the total killed, wounded or missing of two hundred and fifty. It was a deeply saddened man who went to his bed very late that night.

Across the BEF the twenty-fourth of August had seen more than two thousand casualties, bringing the total for the first two days to just less than four thousand. It had been a heavy price to pay, but the Germans had paid much more. The BEF slept that night unmolested because the Germans had suffered so much damage they needed time to recover. When the war was over there would be many an analysis of the German errors in prosecuting their assault on France. Blame would be laid on the younger Moltke for not adhering more firmly to Schlieffen's concept; others would say that the Belgian defence made a significant impact in imposing unexpected delay and casualties; and still more that the weakening of the move through Belgium towards the coast by drawing off troops to the east was the key.

Whatever conclusions might be drawn, the fact remained that von Kluck and his Army turned when they did and the BEF kept them at bay by dint of skill at arms and raw courage. And if the BEF kept von Kluck at the end of the garden path, it was the tiny action, which would be recorded simply in a few history books as the flank guard action at Elouges, which slammed the door in his face and slipped the latch.

Meanwhile, in the BEF's general headquarters, a mood of

defeatism began to pervade. General French's orders from Kitchener had been specific: do not lose the Army; do not undertake actions which will lead to its destruction. Consequently, even as the soldiers who had fought so hard slept in preparation for whatever the next day might bring, or remained awake guarding against German attacks or infiltration, their leader, not knowing the true situation with the Germans and not trusting the French, had his eyes on a point south-west of Paris to which he could withdraw the BEF and prepare it for return to England. He had virtually decided it was time to go.

Chapter 7

South to Le Cateau

No matter how hot the previous day, and no matter how hot the day to come, sleeping the night on bare ground in an open field with no blanket, and nothing between body and ground, is a chilly experience, to be avoided whenever possible. Such was the view of Ted Ludgrove and his colleagues as they lay waiting for the approaching day of the twenty-fifth of August 1914.

Ted had woken, he knew not the time; except that it was before the stand-to that would come with the earliest hint of the approach of dawn. Every bone, joint, muscle and sinew in his body ached. Elbows were sore, having been used for most of the previous day to prop up his chest whilst the rest of his body was in the prone position. Knees were painful from crawling over stubble and rough ground. His left hip was agony, brought on by the rock which had moved itself into an awkward position underneath him during the night. On waking he had found his right arm to have been rendered numb from the position in which he had been lying, and its return to normality was an agonising process which he wished to see ended as soon as possible.

As he sat up, every muscle in his back protesting at the effort, he clasped his arms around his drawn up knees and, resting his chin on them, his thoughts drifted back over the previous day. His mind's eye passed over the horrific sights he had seen, and his stomach churned yet again; partly, perhaps, due to lack of food. He dwelt for a moment on the first man he had killed. He recalled it with crystal clarity, his sight lined upon a point just above the German's belt buckle, thereby lifting the shot into his chest. He remembered picking him as he came over the hill, not looking at his face, but concentrating instead on the target presented by the expanse of his upper torso. He thought about the moment when the order had come to fire, the holding of breath, the taking up of first pressure on the trigger and then the squeeze which fired the shot. At that point he had broken the rules, pausing just briefly to see the effect, as his target, not his man, was hurled backwards by the force of the shot smashing into his sternum and began to roll down the hill, arms flopping and useless in his instantaneous death.

His left hand went up to his right cheek. That small loss of concentration had caused him to mishandle his rifle, and the recoil from the second shot had sent the rear of the bolt bashing painfully against his cheekbone. "Bloody idle that. Won't 'appen again. Wonder 'oo 'e was?" Time for further reflection was curtailed by the voice of Fred Smith, requiring them to fall in on the road and to be bloody quick about it.

"Somethin' to eat would be nice!"

"Fat chance!"

Lieutenant General Sir Horace Smith-Dorrien viewed his situation maps with some concern. He had been ordered to withdraw Second Corps, but the orders had been less than precise. Furthermore, he had been ordered to withdraw them down a dead straight road which placed a forest, the Forêt de Mirmal, between him and the other British Corps on his right, commanded by General Haig, thereby opening up a gap of some ten miles between their flanks. Hardly a recipe for co-ordinated action against a pursuing enemy.

As he looked at the map he saw the wide open ground to the south of the forest, and the town of Le Cateau through which he had to withdraw. He decided that the small town, lying in a steep little valley, was a death trap in which he did not wish to be embroiled. He also knew that he had to get his tired and battered Corps away from the Germans who, despite having received a bloody nose, would soon be after him. As he paused to reflect that some more specific and positive orders from on high might be of some assistance he recalled an earlier conversation with Field Marshall French as he took over Second Corps following the death of Grierson. His orders had been to "give battle on the line of the Condé Canal." On asking if this was to be a defensive or offensive action the Field Marshall's response had been simply that Smith-Dorrien should obey his orders. Small hope, therefore, that any vision or clarity of thought might emerge from that source.

Standing by a roadside in the small village of St Waast, the soldiers of the Ninth waited to be told what was to be their lot for the day, secure in the knowledge that someone must know what was going on; and wondering when breakfast might be.

Edward von Gleichen, looking out from the window of the small red brick Town Hall in St Waast, the sign above the door proclaiming its construction in 1892, turned to his brigade major and asked, not for the first time that hour, if there were any news or orders; anticipating the shaking of his head.

"Can no one tell me what is going on, or what is to happen?"

The fog of war enveloped them all, corps commander and corporal alike; and they would have to find their way through the gloom as best they could, each with the tools he had been given by God and by the government.

"Wassee mean, withdraw? We beat the buggers yesterday. We should be goin' back to give 'em more, not bloody runnin' away!" Alfie James was not alone in the battalion, or for that matter the BEF, in expressing his concern in a forthright manner about orders which saw them marching south, away from the enemy.

Fred Smith, loyal as he was, remained silent and allowed his soldiers to give vent to their feelings. He too failed to comprehend the reasons for the move south. There had been casualties, and that was to be expected, but this was not a beaten army and they had shown themselves to be the masters of the enemy. "Another couple o' hammerins like the Germans'd 'ad yesterday and things'd be lookin' very different."

He was led, however, by Field Marshall French, a man who had given up all idea of any future attack against the Germans. With Lanrezac's Fifth French Army retreating to his right and with only a few territorial units on his left he felt let down and exposed by his allies. And the enemy pressure had been far heavier than he had expected. No, this was not the war he had anticipated, and, not wishing to be the man who "lost" the British Army, he had proposed to Kitchener, the Minister for War, that he should withdraw as fast as possible along his Lines of Communication to a point somewhere south of Paris with a view to returning home. It was an extraordinary proposal, but the fact was that Field Marshall French had lost confidence not only in Lanrezac; not only in the French military as a whole; but, worst of all, he had lost confidence in himself.

And being quite unaware of this; and not lacking any confidence whatsoever; and being utterly pissed off at moving in the wrong direction; and having the lack of food for some twenty-four hours upon which to focus his discontent, it was a very disgruntled Thomas who headed along the road from Mons, south-west towards Le Cateau.

It was a different road from that along which they had travelled on the way north only a few days previously. Gone were the cheering French people, waving flags, offering drinks and food. Instead, the road was filled with the debris of war: refugees, discarded equipment, tired and wounded soldiers, the mass of an army's baggage in an apparently disorganised muddle. Those French who had not joined the flood of refugees stared with a mixture of disappointment and hostility at their retreating allies and from the tone of voice used as the BEF marched by it was clear that some of the locals felt let down.

"Don't need to speak the bloody language to unnerstan' wot 'e meant," muttered a disconsolate Ned Preece. Alfie looked at his friend, concerned about him since that time in the factory with the sergeant, then glanced at the old Frenchman leaning on his gate and nodded.

"Aye, it's a bugger this, an' no mistake!"

They watched the refugees, struggling with enormous burdens and wished they could help. They were under strict orders, however, not to depart from the line of march and delay the withdrawal. They had to get clear of the pursuing Germans, and cavalry reports were beginning to come in confirming that the enemy was on the move and close behind. As the sun rose high and the temperature increased in proportion the march became harder and harder. Lack of food was beginning to take its toll, and coupled with the heat of the day was causing more and more to drop out by the roadside, or require help from their comrades. Ted and Aflie were busy with Albert Carter, the least fit of them all, and he was in terrible trouble.

Spittle formed on his lips as he sought to survive in the heat, to draw breath, to regulate his body temperature in some way. His feet had never hurt like this before; the agony was indescribable with the right heel so painful that he could hardly bear to place the foot on the ground. By the time they reached Englefontaine, a small village just under half way along the forest road, he was almost beyond redemption and had become a burden his fellows could really no longer support.

In the village, however, they could rest; and food was obtainable. A few apples, some cheese, a little bread and some plums; it wasn't much, but to starving and exhausted men it gave a much needed lift. The quartermaster was there, and he was able to find space on the battalion's wagons for the most exhausted of the men; and Albert Carter was one of these. They were permitted a good half hour in which to improve their general condition before the march was resumed.

Edward von Gleichen was standing by the roadside, watching his soldiers as their morale gradually improved, noting their sense of grievance about the withdrawal. Tired they might be, but there was plenty of fight left in them yet. Beside him, the imperturbable figure of Captain St André, both of them viewing some of the other sights around them with alarm and distaste. The state of the refugees was distressing to say the least. Old men and women walked with huge burdens, far beyond their capacity to carry for any length of time, or pulled carts which it was obvious were overloaded. Here there was a child, clinging with the one hand to a mother's skirt, and with the other to a small teddy bear; there was the peasant woman and her husband, dressed quite incongruously in their Sunday best, he complete with a starched collar which stood little chance of survival in the heat of the day.

A dignified, middle aged man approached the brigadier, clearly bent on striking up a conversation. This was the last thing he needed, but, always a gentleman, von Gleichen resolved to be as civil, and as brief, as possible. The Frenchman, it transpired, was a doctor, deeply concerned about the condition of many of the civilians trudging down the road; worried about the effects of heat, lack of food and poor sanitation on old and young alike. He articulated his words clearly and at a sensible speed, conscious that von Gleichen's knowledge of French might be limited.

"Not unlike some of my own concerns regarding the state of my soldiers," thought the brigadier as he responded to the doctor's questions about the proximity of the Germans, their attitudes to civilians and the chances that proper treatment might be available for the sick and injured. There had, after all, been terrible stories about the behaviour of the Boche; and could they be true?

"I am sorry, doctor, but I am really unable to help you very much. Like you, I have heard the stories about German treatment of civilians, but I have yet to meet anyone who has had first hand experience and so I cannot say if it is a rumour or not. I have been advising the people who live in these cottages to remain with their property in order to have a better chance of protecting it from looters, but as you can see it has had little effect."

As he spoke, the residents of the house opposite were turning for a last, regretful, look at their home before stepping out to join the throng of refugees clogging up the way to the south. As was the case throughout, the family comprised no men of military age; they had all gone to the war.

The doctor turned and moved away down the road, his head shaking in despair. Von Gleichen felt a twinge of self-conscious regret as he wished he could have given a better answer; as he wished they were not retreating from an enemy he knew they really could not trust to behave decently towards these people; as he wished someone would tell him what precisely was going on.

It took the indefatigable St André to lift his spirits.

"Mon General, if you continue to speak French with such fluency it will not be long before I have no job." His accent was, deliberately, excruciating.

Not for the first time did von Gleichen wonder at the constant good humour of his friend. He was not certain he could have retained such *sang froid* had it been England that was being invaded, its population that was littering the road, its cities and towns that were under threat.

John Hayes was watching the stream of refugees flooding past, his mind not really registering the enormity of what he was seeing. His thoughts were on yesterday, and the fearsome sights he had seen. The dead had been one thing, and if it had been quick then good luck to them. But, some of the wounds had been horrific, and the pain being suffered by many of the men he had seen had clearly been appalling. His mind was fixed on one individual whom he had seen dragging himself back from the firing line with the whole of the back of his thigh blown away, his hand clamped firmly over the femoral artery trying to hold back the flow of blood which was draining out his life. Crippled; if he survived. Not a happy prospect.

He was just thinking that a bullet through the foot, which

could be arranged, might be an easy way out, and was beginning to work out the means of achieving it. He had just stretched his legs to ease a cramp when something smacked against his ankle, a voice said something he could not understand and a shapeless heap was lying on the road in front of him, clearly in pain.

"Sorry love; I didn't see you, honest." He could tell it was a woman from the skirts, and then stopped himself speaking as he realised she probably wouldn't understand him anyway.

Alfie and Ted saw what happened and were on their way to help as Hayes began to assist the woman to her feet. The wrist that he held onto was thin and delicate; the shoulder around which he put an arm to lift her was so slight he felt he had to take care not to break it. Her body felt as his grandmother's had felt just before she died; fragile beyond belief. His surprise, therefore, when he saw her face was complete. She was young, in her early twenties with a small face in which were set two deep brown eyes aside a nose which had clearly been broken and twisted at some stage; all framed in a red and white check scarf.

"It is OK, I am all right." As she spoke she revealed small, white teeth, set in a broad expanse of pink gum; and then she grimaced as the pain in her right hand and wrist shot up her arm. It took him a few seconds before he realised she had spoken English, at which point he stated the obvious.

"You speak English!"

"Oui...yes....yes, I do." She was looking as she spoke at the blood where she had grazed her hand in the fall, and then winced as she tried to flex a wrist that had obviously sustained some damage.

"Here, let me fix that. Either of you two got a clean handkerchief or a bandage?" Alfie and Ted both shook their heads. Clean kit was not something any of them had, and anything spare was on the QM's wagons, and God only knew when they'd see that again.

Taking his water bottle, he removed the girl's scarf, moistened a corner and, holding her hand, began to clean the dirt from the wounds. As he did so, he noted her short, boyish hairstyle, the locks soft and brown. By the time he had finished, and he did not hurry, he had her life story. Her English mother had met a sailor from Ostend and had moved with him to Belgium where she had been born; hence she was bilingual, and her name was Cecile. Her mother and father were now dead, but there were relatives in England to whom she could go. She could not stay and work in Belgium, not with the Germans there, and anyway, her firm had closed as a result of the invasion. Her accent was delightful, and as she spoke her eyes and mouth were full of expression.

"Voila, c'est fini." She smiled at him as, reluctantly, he let go of her hand. "Thank you, m'sieu. I think you must now go, n'est ce pas?" She was looking, as she spoke, at the battalion getting to its feet.

She was not especially pretty, and some of her features taken in isolation, such as her nose, were unfortunate. However, the package was captivating, and by now, John Hayes was completely smitten. He did not wish to leave her; but he had no choice. Thus it was that, with extreme reluctance, he rejoined his fellows, fell in and resumed the march south. He glanced regularly over his shoulder for as long as she was in sight, on each occasion receiving the benefit of a coquettish little smile and raised eyebrow, with the head tilted slightly to one side; a look of utter provocation and promise. His obvious discomfort amused his colleagues hugely, and gave them something to think about for the next couple of miles until the pain in their feet and backs, lack of real food and general exhaustion stilled the banter.

Paul Cooper made a mental note.

The small town of Le Cateau is approached down a steep defile, following the valley of the River Selle. On either side of the town, running directly east to west, is a high ridge. It is a ridge which dominates for miles the ground to its north, the direction from which the BEF was now approaching, and over which their pursuing enemy must follow. The march up the steep hill from the valley bottom was the last of the many crests that the tired and dishevelled British Army had climbed during that long day; but their trials were not yet over.

Just to the west of Le Cateau is a cross-roads, where the Roman Road they had been following continues away to the south-west, intersecting with the road running out of Le Cateau, east to west along the ridgeline.

The Fifteenth Brigade was positioned to the left of the town, looking north. It was the left hand brigade of the three brigades in Fifth Division; each of them having been given a sector along the ridge line; Thirteen Brigade lying between Fifteen Brigade and the Roman Road, and Fourteen Brigade beyond the Roman Road, in the south-east corner formed by the cross-roads, facing towards Le Cateau, nearby to its north-east.

Fifteen Brigade was to be billeted about two thousand yards behind the ridge in the small village of Troisvilles, some three miles west of Le Cateau. As they arrived, the rich smell of a Bully Beef stew reached the Norfolks. The quartermaster had, as quartermasters are wont to do, found the time to set the battalion's cooks to work, having obtained from somewhere, and mere mortals would never know quite from where, the means to constitute and then cook a meal. Broken down into hayboxes by company lots it was quickly issued out, and with bread and hot tea the battalion was, in a very short space of time, feeling significantly better. As the soldiers were enjoying their food, however, the officers were busy elsewhere. The CO had conducted his reconnaissance of the defensive position allocated by the brigade commander. The orders were not clear, but then von Gleichen himself had no clear orders; he was simply taking sensible precautions. He had no idea what was happening, but his divisional commander's view had been that this would just be a temporary halt, prior to continuing the retreat once men had rested. They would, therefore, have to be on their guard against the German pursuit which might bump up against them.

Consequently, a defensive position was laid out, but defensive works were to be limited to preparation of simple scrapes or good cover for firing positions, in case they were caught by surprise. The important thing was to rest and feed men as much as possible, to prepare them for the rigours to come; and for a long march south.

Von Gleichen was alarmed at the clear message of defeatism which General Fergusson was translating from GHQ. It was in stark contrast to the attitude of his men, who failed completely to comprehend why they were running from their inferiors, and wished to know when they were going to stop and fight.

"Right, I've shown you your positions." Matthew Jenkins was slurring his speech, almost like a drunkard. He could not recall having been so tired in his life, and he was aching to remove his boots and do something to the sticky, painful appendages just below his ankles. However, there were matters requiring his attention before he could afford that luxury, or any other for that matter. The position he had laid out for the platoon was along a sunken, dirt road, level with Troisvilles and running east to west, parallel to the ridge line some two thousand yards to their front. Just behind them was a huge Elm tree, an excellent reference point if they had to find it in the dark. Immediately to the battalion's front, and on the ridge line, at the right front of the brigade were the Bedfordshires, and on their left the Dorsets. The much depleted Cheshires were to the left of the Norfolks, and forward of the sunken road, just on the edge of Troisvilles.

"Once I have taken your questions I want you to bring your men along here, show them their positions and the reference points and allocate arcs of fire. I do not know if we shall have to defend this place, the CO seems to think these are just precautions in case the enemy bump us, but I really do not know."

"I'll do that sir." Paul Cooper's voice was firm as he spoke to his officer. "Time you sorted out some scoff, sir."

Matthew looked at him. The altercation over Preece still smarted with him, and he was sure that Cooper had committed an error of judgement, but they could not afford to let relatively trivial matters interfere with their relationship.

"We must sort out sentries, and...."

"Sir," the voice was firmer. "Leave it with me, sir please." The last two words ran together, being pronounced almost as one, and left Matthew in no doubt that he was being sent on his way; and he was grateful. "Corporal Smith, if one of yours could fix a cup of tea for Mr Jenkins, and perhaps something to eat?"

"I'll do that!" Colin Baxter spoke. "If sir, that is, if you don't need me for anything else?"

Matthew smiled his thanks. There was nothing subservient in Baxter's offer of help. He knew, they all knew, that their lives might depend on this man whom they had all grown to respect. They also knew that his responsibilities far outweighed their own, and that he was just as tired as they were; and they'd been fed and watered, whilst he hadn't stopped. God knew, he'd walked every bloody mile they had.

"Sir, if you would follow Private Baxter, sir, he will look after you." Paul Cooper looked sternly at Colin. "Mug of hot water for a shave wouldn't hurt either." As he spoke, there was a clap of thunder louder than any of the artillery they had experienced, and the threatened storm began to rain down the first large, warm droplets of water. The sergeant looked at his watch; it was exactly five o'clock in the evening, and they were going to be very wet by the time they got back to shelter in Troisvilles. And what of the Germans, he pondered; where were they, and how long before they were here.

The Germans, however, were every bit as tired as their British counterparts. They had tasted the British reaction to their assaults, and were in no hurry to continue the pursuit until they could co-ordinate something overpowering. Their reluctance gave the BEF, and Second Corps in particular, some much needed time.

So it was then, that with rearguards drawn at dusk into the main position, with sentries posted, with runners in the forward battalions to bring back news of enemy approaching, the brigade slept deeply and soundly. Matthew Jenkins, refreshed with tea and stew and revived by a very welcome shave, had completely collapsed, on his side, on a pile of straw. Just near him was Colin Baxter, who cleaned his own rifle, and then his officer's pistol before turning in for the night. The rest of the platoon, having looked to their weapons, did the same; and only Ted and Alfie had sentry go to do, on the three to four o'clock in the morning shift.

Paul Cooper sat for a while, looking out into the village street in the moonlight. The thunder clouds had long since passed, and the damp ground was giving off a freshly washed smell. The dust had settled, and with his uniform now dry, he felt a strange contentment. The platoon had done well, and they had been lucky not to take any casualties in their first contact with the enemy. That was unlikely to last, and he thought briefly of who might be the first to go, and what the effects might be. He hoped, fervently, that Matthew Jenkins would remain at their head, and he needed the steadying influence of people like Fred Smith, and some of the old sweats who had come back with the influx of reservists.

His spat with the platoon commander still rankled. He was so certain he was right; bloody Preece was a liability, and even more so now. Why the officer had a blind spot for the man he simply did not know. The sooner he was gone the better, and if that was on the back of a court martial so be it. The rest of them weren't doing too badly though. Steady bunch of lads, really, although Hayes is looking a bit odd, and Carter is a bloody nuisance. His mind began to drift as the tiredness wafted over him. His last thoughts, as he slid into unconsciousness, were a mix of anxiety that he hadn't forgotten anything; that they were ready for whatever tomorrow might bring; and a feeling of gratitude that he had controlled his fear well, and done his job properly. Well, they were all still here, weren't they?

As they slept, things were happening; things which would bear not simply on what would befall them tomorrow, but for several weeks to come.

In Koblenz, in Germany, General von Moltke was somewhat concerned. He was receiving from his generals glowing reports of the progress being made by their armies. However, he could see precious little evidence of the results. Delay upon delay was being built in to the original timetable for the Schlieffen Plan, with no adequate explanation. And where were the captured guns and equipment? Where were the prisoners? But, the Kaiser was now certain, with the progress being made, that it was possible to move two corps to the Russian Front. This having been done, and with two corps tied up watching a defiant Antwerp, still clinging on and another two containing the fortresses at Givet and Mauberg, an utterly pointless and futile waste, there were only eleven of the original seventeen corps which von Schlieffen had prescribed as being necessary for the success of his plan. There were no longer enough grenadiers left for the right sleeve of the right hand man to brush the English Channel. The German enveloping movement was going to have to make its inwards left turn sooner and sooner.

At around the same time, General Joffre, commanding the French armies, viewed his situation maps with concern. The news from everywhere was depressing, and a lesser man might have contemplated the prospect of defeat. He was, however, made of sterner stuff than many of his subordinates, and certainly his British counterpart; paradoxically named French. Despite the difficulties he faced on his southern and eastern borders with Germany, he was confident he could hold against that onslaught. He took the decision, therefore, to redeploy two corps from the south to join the four territorial divisions on the BEF left flank in order to beef up his counter to the much more dangerous situation he saw to the north. They would form up, just north of Paris, under General Manoury, to form a new army; the Sixth French Army.

Closer to hand, General Smith Dorrien, also not a defeatist, was very worried about the ability of his corps to gather itself, and continue the withdrawal the next day in any sort of order. In Five Division, whilst Fifteen Brigade may have been in billets, fed and watered, by sundown it was only then, in the gathering darkness, that Thirteen Brigade had begun to trickle in; followed very much later by an exhausted Fourteen Brigade. Elsewhere, the situation was as bad. The centre of Le Cateau was a mess, as motor lorries, wagons, units, refugees, individuals, ambulances and the whole panoply of an army on the move mingled in a disordered mess on the defiles leading into and out of the town. Had just a few shells dropped in amongst them, the chaos would have been complete.

General Smith-Dorrien was on the horns of a dilemma. His orders from GHQ were clear: he was to maintain the pace of the withdrawal, and was not to risk further losses by engaging the enemy. The reports from his divisional commanders, however, were not encouraging. The Fourth Division newly arrived from England and now holding the left of his line, was in good order; Fifth Division on its right far less so; and Third Division's commander was emphatic: he could not be ready to continue before nine o'clock the next morning. Across the Corps area, men slept where they stopped, too tired even to think. Hunger and thirst plagued most of them, but the tiredness swamped everything. In the centre of the town the traffic jam continued all night as men in groups of varying sizes gradually found their way to their units. The Norfolks, asleep and fed in Troisvilles, were very much among the fortunate that night.

Smith-Dorrien felt he could make only one decision, and shortly after two o'clock on the morning of the twenty-sixth of August he issued his orders for a defensive battle which would allow him to hit the Germans hard so that he could break clean and continue the withdrawal. Regrettably, the last order that commanders had received had instructed them to continue the withdrawal the next day. It was five o'clock in the morning before von Gleichen was told that he was to stand and fight, and he was by no means the last to hear. It was precious little time in which to prepare.

Ted and Alfie were engaged in that most unpleasant of morning rituals: waking those who did not wish to be woken. Foul language mingled with the foul smells generated by sweating, unwashed bodies, over-ripe feet and unsettled stomachs. Their orders, however, had been that they should be ready by five o'clock to march further south, and reveille at four was therefore the latest they could leave it with any chance of a brew or breakfast. The two men had set a fire under a dixie of water a good half hour earlier, tea leaves had been thrown in as it boiled, and a tin of condensed milk, which had appeared from the QM the night before, had been added. Breakfast would be cobbled together from the remnants of a cartload of very smelly cheese and some fruit which had supplemented their meal the previous evening.

"Sir......sir, its time!" Paul Cooper gently shook his officer awake. Matthew started, and sat up in too much of a hurry, straw clinging incongruously to the side of his face, red weals marking him where the stalks had pressed against flesh. He looked at his watch, the luminous face standing out in the dark. "Gone four thirty; damn them, they've let me sleep on."

"Cup of tea, sir." Colin handed him the steaming mug. "Breakfast's not up to much I'm afraid," he added apologetically, as he passed over some very healthy Brie, two hard-tack biscuits and a plum.

Matthew took the offerings gratefully. "You shouldn't have let me sleep." He chastised his sergeant, without any real enthusiasm.

Cooper ignored him, launching instead into a short update on the state of the platoon, and confirming that they were to be formed up outside ready to move in twenty minutes. As he spoke, Matthew caught sight of Albert Carter, limping a little, but looking a great deal better than yesterday.

The sergeant caught the glance, and looked to see Carter moving through the barn door with the rest of Fred's section. "He's a lot better. Just needed some food and a bit o' rest. His feet were in a bad way, but we sorted those last night. We'll just have to watch 'im 'til they harden up a bit more, and then 'e should be all right."

He thought, briefly, about raising the Preece issue again,

but decided this was neither the time nor the place. "That's it then, sir." He had finished his short briefing. "Anything else I can do?"

Matthew shook his head, his mouth too full of cheese and biscuit to risk a reply. He stood, ready to leave, his right hand checking his pistol, whilst he brushed crumbs from the corner of his mouth with the knuckle of his left forefinger.

"Pistol's been cleaned, sir; and reloaded." Colin Baxter spoke from the shadows formed on the edges of the early morning shafts of sunlight breaking through the huge barn door. Matthew paused, and smiled his gratitude, with a small nod of his head.

The company had just marched off, ready to head south once more, when they were told to halt, and await further orders.

"Bleedin' 'ell, it's 'appened again. First one way then the other. Can't they make up their bloody minds?"

"They", in this case, translated into the CO and his senior company commander; the second-in-command and the adjutant both having been killed at Elouges. They were busy translating the latest order from brigade HQ, instructing them that they were to stay and fight, that they were to thicken up the defensive position they had been given the previous evening, and they were to await further orders.

In brigade HQ, Edward von Gleichen was as frustrated as his soldiers, but he at least was in a position to understand his corps commander's vision, and make some sense of what they were about to do. The Germans had to be so firmly stopped that the idea of pursuit was driven from their minds long enough for the corps to escape them. Having halted his brigade and sent his battalions to their positions with enough orders to get them working, he set about clarifying his thoughts and setting out something more specific, so that the brigade could operate in a co-ordinated and effective manner; and be as well protected as possible.

Troisvilles, at his left rear, was a linchpin, and by turning it into a stronghold it could become a bastion around which the enemy tide would wash in disarray. He permitted himself a brief smile as he thought of Hougoumont Farm at Waterloo, not far to their north, where Guardsmen in a previous era had excelled themselves. "Deja vu?" and then he dismissed the ridiculous thought from his mind. The Cheshires would occupy the village, supported by elements of the Dorsets. The rest would dig in on the open ground, and wait to repel the massed attacks of German infantry. Having discussed with his artillery officers the fire plan for the guns, and given guidance on the siting of machine guns he left his brigade major to turn his instructions into written orders and to issue them; whereupon he went to see how his brigade was getting on.

"D'you see that tree?" Sergeant Cooper's question to the section commanders was really superfluous, since the tree in question, right beside the dirt road along which the company was positioned, was positively enormous and could be seen for miles around. Indeed, it was its very visibility that had sealed its fate.

"Well, it's got to come down."

"Come down?" Jim Collis, the junior of the section commanders, and the most outspoken, voiced the incredulity that they all felt. "Come down," he repeated. "You mean chop the thing down?"

"That, Corporal Collis, is exactly what I mean." Paul Cooper could entwine a vicious note of sarcasm into his voice when the mood took him; as was usually the case when he had been given something stupid to do, but had to convince his sceptical subordinates that it was a spiffing idea. It was actually an idea sent down by the Gunners, who were concerned that enemy artillery could use it as a reference point from miles away, and the brigade commander had concurred.

"I want you to go into the village. Yes......you Corporal Collis. Go into the village and requisition a couple of axes, and I'm not sure that I didn't see a dirty great logging saw in that farm we were in last night. Bring 'em back here, and then set to work bringing this thing down."

"But, 'ow do I requisition? I got no authority or nuthin'." Corporal Collis was feeling uncertain and aggrieved.

"Use yer notebook, write it down, sign for it an' tell 'em they'll get it back when we've finished with it."

"But....., but I can't speak the friggin' language."

"Stop bloody arguin'." It was always time to stop anything when Paul Cooper swore; a real danger sign. "Take Baxter with you, get the axes and the saw, an' remember the orders about bein' kind to the natives. I don't want any lootin' or pillagin',...clear?"

The silence was his reply.

The company position along the road had them facing due north, and two thousand yards to their front, just on the crown of the ridge running left to right, east to west, they could see the Bedfords digging in. Just to the Bedfords' right, and distinguishable by their glengarries, were the Kings Own Scottish Borderers of Thirteen Brigade. The British approach onto the position had been masked by the thick mist, generated from the results of last night's thunderstorm and the cool of the morning. A sense of urgency was imparted to them by the sound of firing from the direction of Le Cateau town, a couple of miles or so away to the north-east, where some German scouts had appeared. They were in position by seven o'clock, but for those not exerting themselves, such as the sentries, woollen jumpers were a good idea.

They began work on the tree by half sections, using men from only two sections at a time. That way they could put maximum effort into preparing their defences whilst still meeting their obligation to remove the tree. However, it was no easy task, and after nearly an hour they had made little impression. Their efforts were not helped by the high northerly winds which began to develop as the morning wore on, and the fact that the tree had to fall to the south in order not to block the dirt road which was a critical lateral route for the move of troops and supplies along the rear of the divisional area.

By about nine o'clock the German artillery was beginning to make itself felt away over to the left of the Norfolks, on the ridge in the area of a small village called Inchy. Further away and off to their right, to the north-east, beyond the Roman Road and to the south-west of Le Cateau, Fourteen Brigade began, at around ten o'clock, to feel the effects of sustained German artillery fire. This was to form the pattern for the morning, and marked the essential difference between Le Cateau and the battles a couple of days earlier at Mons. It was to be an artillery battle, and there were three reasons for this: the more concentrated layout of the BEF position made German use of artillery more potent and effective; the ground was open and suited the use of artillery for suppression of an enemy that had little cover; and, perhaps most importantly, the Germans had experienced a taste of British infantry firepower, and were seeking to reduce its effectiveness as far as possible before engaging their own foot soldiers. It was not an equal contest, the Germans having some five hundred and fifty guns to the British two hundred and twenty eight.

"Right, bugger off you lot. We'll sort this out. Bleedin' amateurs." The pioneer sergeant's disparaging remarks had no effect on Fred Smith, or the others trying to bring down the tree. The axes and the saw obtained by their erstwhile colleague had not been of the best, and by half past nine they had made little impact. Lieutenant Colonel Ballard, impatient to see the task completed, had ordered the pioneer platoon to address the matter with more despatch than was being achieved by the riflemen.

The pioneers are a commanding officer's own small engineering element, giving him a limited capacity for undertaking simple tasks requiring artisan skills; and a knowledge of the use of explosives. The pioneer sergeant is often a man of great experience, of an enormously practical bent and with little, if any, intellectual vision. His soldiers were usually the workhorses of the battalion, often derided by their colleagues in the rifle companies in that paradoxical way that Thomas has of insulting others as a mark of grudging respect.

"All yours mate," said Fred with some gratitude. The pioneer sergeant was another of those whose uniform bore the symbols of service in South Africa, and they had known each other for years. It was with some gratitude that he re-assembled his section and they set about putting the finishing touches to the limited defensive works they had been able to construct along the sunken road.

Alfie James was watching with fascination the bombardment on Inchy, and was beginning to comprehend that a similar bombardment seemed to be getting under way to his right. He still carried with him the excitement of the action at Elouges. He had been amazed at his reaction; the fear of course, but then the sense of exhilaration as he worked the bolt of his rifle and watched man after man go down. This was what they had trained him for, and he was very good at it. And now they were attacking again, and he could barely wait for the opportunity once more to bring his rifle to bear with the same deadly effect.

It would be some time, however, before he would realise his ambition, as the Germans were clearly bent on pulverising everything before committing themselves to an attack. The Norfolks, though, were spared much of the unpleasantness as the German attacks continued to concentrate on the right and the left of the line; and their position in the centre was left virtually unscathed. This gave them the opportunity to concentrate their thoughts on the efforts of the pioneers to remove the tree.

"They've got tha' wrong." Alfred Arbuckle viewed the efforts disdainfully. "The way they're cuttin' tha' tis goin' t' fall this way;" which meant across the track.

"Aye." Peter Dakin could not but agree, having himself gained some experience in these matters as a young man doing odd jobs.

Matthew, lying close by, was alternately watching his men and his front. He too was fascinated by the tree, but more so because of the ludicrous situation in which they found themselves. Here they were, in the middle of a battle with heavy artillery fire raining down not far away and possibly soon on them. Yet here was a senior NCO, giving orders to men with axes as if he were preparing fences at a county show, quite oblivious to the mayhem around him. He watched Hayes as he reacted to the shellfire. He had gradually become concerned about the man. Having expected him to be a leading light in the platoon once he had settled down, he had been disappointed. Instead of taking the lead by example, he had become gradually more withdrawn; and there was a serious doubt about his aggressiveness. Matthew was being careful with himself when choosing his thoughts; cowardice was something he did not wish to consider until there were no other alternatives. However, he would have to watch him closely, for if he was going to break, and he chose the wrong time to do so, it could be very dangerous.

Suddenly, to the front there was a massive surge in the bombardment of Inchy. As he looked he heard the Pioneer Sergeant shouting, presuming it to be an instruction for the tree cutters to take cover. Watching to the front he waited for the German infantry to attack, prepared to move to counter any breakthrough. For several minutes, he concentrated on watching and waiting, but it soon became obvious that nothing would materialise. Turning back to the tree, he realised that the shout had not had anything to do with taking cover. The wind was now very strong, and the tree risked being blown down in the wrong direction: across the road. He watched as one pioneer, who had climbed the tree, threw down a rope which a colleague pegged to the ground.

This was ridiculous; first they were trying to cut the damn thing down, the next they were trying to hold it up. This had all the elements of a farce, the more compelling because of the battle raging around them.

Edward von Gleichen waited and wondered. His orders were to defend, but he was not being attacked. His brigade seemed to bear a charmed life that morning. The Bedfords had fired a few shots at some German patrols, and the Dorsets had suffered a little from a machine gun they had allowed to get too close. They'd mistaken it for a party carrying stretchers, so had, quite rightly, left it alone; until it opened fire on them. He made a mental note to warn about the possibility for such confusion, and turned as his brigade major approached.

"Nine Brigade on our left is having a hard time in Inchy. They've been heavily shelled, and Germans are getting into the village. There's been hand to hand fighting and its all rather unpleasant. On our right, you heard Fourteen Brigade beginning to get it in the neck about early mid-morning. Well, its getting worse for them. There are reports of German infantry coming round the eastern edge of Le Cateau, trying to outflank them. In the meantime, Thirteen Brigade on our immediate right is gradually coming under more pressure. We, it appears, are being spared for the time being."

"Thank you." Von Gleichen paused, as if thinking, then repeated: "Thank you."

There was an enormous cheer as the tree suddenly gave up its unequal struggle, and crashed, sedately, into the field to the south of the sunken road. It was accompanied by hoots of laughter from those who saw one unfortunate lance corporal of the pioneer platoon running for his life having misjudged just where it was the tree would fall. He made it with his body intact, but not his dignity.

"Thank God that's over," muttered Matthew to no one in particular.

"Sir!" Matthew looked round to see a runner from company HQ trotting towards him. "Sir," the soldier called out again as he realised he had the officer's attention. "Orders in ten minutes, sir."

"Thank you." He waved to confirm he had heard. Perhaps now we might get some idea of what is going on. He looked over at Cooper, who wore a look of curiosity and anticipation on his face, and received a smile in response to his own raised eyebrow.

"Well, the battalion clearly did such a splendid job of being divisional reserve the day before yesterday, that they want us to do it again." The company commander's voice held a note of mild sarcasm, designed more to draw a smile out of his tired officers than to imply criticism of the decision. The situation is that we have managed to get clear the transport, ambulances and a whole raft of other kit that was clogging up the town last night and early this morning and it is now away to the south. The Germans are pressing on the left, in the Nine Brigade area, and Fourteen Brigade, over to our right and nearest the town, is suffering. But so are the Germans. Their casualties are, reportedly, enormous."

He paused to look around, glancing briefly into the eyes of all of them. "They are, however, outgunning us. They seem to have twice as much artillery, and limitless ammunition, and are using it to good effect. It appears that their point of main effort is over on our right, and it is round to the east of the town and into our right flank that their efforts look to be concentrated. We, therefore, shall depart, in one hour, at two o'clock. Our destination is the small village of Hannechy, just to the right of the Roman Road, behind Fourteen Brigade, ready to assist them and Nineteen Brigade on their right."

He looked at Matthew. "I shall be leaving in fifteen minutes. I want you to provide a section to act as guides and for some protection, and each of the rest of you..." he paused again, looking at each of his officers in turn...."will each provide me with one junior NCO to act as guides, and to assist you onto the position when you arrive."

Having agreed the rendezvous at which the rest of the company would meet him some time after two o'clock, and having issued other guidance, he dismissed his officers and set about getting ready to move. He did not have much to do. His batman, knowing his major well, had anticipated his wishes and was sitting in the cover offered by the bank running along the sunken road, looking a little sheepish, with the officer's kit packed and ready to go, and a mug of tea to drink before they departed. It was a drink they shared, the mug passing between them.

"Look on the bright side." Alfie James was reacting to the inevitable moan from Jack Waters; and even as he spoke was wishing he hadn't bothered. "At least we're doin' somethin' an' not just 'angin' around 'ere an' gettin' shot at."

"I bet 'e bloody volunteered for this." Waters cast an accusing look in the direction of his platoon commander. "Jus' the sort o' thing 'e'd do is that."

"Waters, if I 'ave to tell you just once more about bein' disrespectful I shan't bother to warn you, an' I shan't bother to charge you. I'll take you away somewhere quiet and I'll kick the livin' bloody daylights out of you." There was vehemence in Fred's voice as he hissed the words, his mouth close to Waters' right ear. "'Ave I, for the last time, made myself clear?"

Waters was shocked by the obvious fact that Fred was clearly quite determined to do as he said.

"Yes, Corporal," he muttered quietly, hoping that no one else had noticed him getting such a vicious rocket. He'd overstepped the mark with Smith, and he'd have to watch it. Fred, for his part, had seen the destructive effect of a serious dissenter in South Africa, knew the damage it could do to the cohesiveness of a small group like theirs and was determined to stamp it out before it got out of hand.

By one-thirty in the afternoon the company commander had led them along the road from Troisvilles to the south-east, to a point where it joined the tarmac Roman Road in Reumont, just north of Hannechy, and where they crossed over to the eastern side well out of sight of the enemy. A short march south down the line of the Roman Road and they were at the cross-roads in Maurois where a sharp left turn had them moving through Hannechy, climbing the steady incline through the village, winding round to the north as they approached the ridge on the northern edge of the village where they were to take up their reserve position

It was typical of villages in that area. Red brick buildings in the squared Flemish style, castellated facades, straight chimneys and neat gardens. The farms they passed were walled off, with the wrought iron gates they had come to recognise as almost de rigeur. The church stood out, being of grey stone with a grey slate roof, its pointed spire sporting a weather vane. It offered the impression of a great, mother hen watching carefully over her brood with faint disapproval permanently etched on her features. Soon they were moving up the hill, towards the northern edge of the village to the point where they could see the ridge line just ahead.

The major stopped them about a hundred yards short of the crest, where a dirt road, set between banks some three to four feet high, ran away directly east, along the top of the ridge. He left Fred at the junction with the dirt road, hidden in the bushes with most of the party, watching east and west for any sign of an enemy that might cut them off. Asked to provide two men to accompany the officer he had nominated Ted and Alfie, both having already demonstrated that they were steady under fire, reliable in a crisis and very good shots. Fred could trust them to do the right thing by the officer.

Moving forward, the three of them approached carefully the crest, anxious not to be skylined and give away their presence. Crawling the last twenty yards the two privates held back behind the major until he was content that it was safe to motion them forward. As they began to look out over the valley below them, Ted could not help noticing that the village cemetery was just forty yards away to their left. He thought about remarking on the fact, and then, unsure of the major's sense of humour, decided to keep quiet.

The valley of the River Selle was laid out before them, a wide open expanse of fields, some yellow with stubble from harvested corn, others still green with sugar beet waiting to be gathered in. The fields were large, much larger than they were used to in Norfolk; hedgerows were not a feature, but there were stands of Elm, Poplar and Horse Chestnut scattered about. The slope stretched away to Le Cateau itself, some three miles north-east. Closer, some two miles away down in the valley bottom, the village of St. Benin stood out, with its dark church spire silhouetted against the green fields. The red roofs and white walls of the houses were in stark contrast to the natural colours of the countryside, and whilst the detail was lost to them, they had seen enough settlements of its type to be able to imagine just what it was like. The main road, running south-west from Le Cateau, and parallel to the Roman Road a half mile to their left, by-passed St Benin and ran within half a mile of their position to the right; to a point where the dirt road on which Fred was waiting, a hundred yards behind them, met it at a small cross-roads.

In the distance fighting was still going on around Le Cateau, but there were visible signs in the valley that the British were slowly being forced back. Wounded, some walking, some on carts, others on horses and a few on stretchers, were moving up the tracks and small roads which focused in on the Roman Road, the Second Corps' lifeline to the south. From where they were the sound of firing was clear, and they could see the fall of high explosive shell, the grey puffs of shrapnel bursts and the smoke from their own artillery as it returned fire. The crackle of small arms fire was constant, although at this range the effects could neither be seen nor felt.

Ted watched fascinated as four teams of horses were hitched up to guns in a battery just away to his right, about a mile. At that distance the figures were almost ant-like, but their frantic activity was obvious, as was the fire of German artillery landing around them. He touched the major's arm, something that he would not have dreamed of a few weeks ago, but now it seemed almost natural.

"Look, sir. They're gettin' out; the guns that is."

The company commander had other things to think about. The commanding officer had entrusted him with the task of identifying just where to deploy the battalion when it arrived. However, it was impossible not to be fascinated by the activity below, and he watched as the four guns moved to the rear, presumably to a new position.

"He's left two behind!" The major's voice held a quizzical note.

"Not 'nuff 'orses." Alfie offered his opinion, and the silence that followed indicated mutual acceptance that this was the most likely reason.

The silence continued, the two privates lying quiet whilst the major made his assessment of the situation, and how best the Norfolks might carry out their task. By now, Smith-Dorrien's soldiers had held out for over six hours, and were reaching the point where they could not do much more. Far from being beaten in spirit, they were simply being overwhelmed by the vast array of artillery and infantry power that the enemy was able to throw against them.

General Fergusson had seen by about midday the first signs that his front would not withstand the strain much longer. As he had ordered the Norfolks once more into divisional reserve he had sent a message to Smith-Dorrien, saying it was time to leave. But the corps commander needed more time, all the time he could get; all the time that the sacrifices being made by Fergusson's division could buy him.

The price of that was already evident to the small party of Norfolks overlooking the Selle valley. Damaged and destroyed equipment lay everywhere. Guns, overturned by the power of German shells landing among them; the skeletal finger of a split barrel facing the sky; a gun limber on its side, the wheel turning gently in the slight breeze that blew across the battlefield; a horse its leg shattered beyond redemption trying to rise, its rider dead beside it and incapable of putting the beast out of its misery. Here and there the now familiar khaki hump showing a British soldier either dead or unable to move unaided. Small parties of men were making their way to the rear. Some of them were assisting wounded, and some were clearly wounded themselves. More and more, however, the groups contained men who had simply taken more than they could bear, who had seen at close hand the terrible destruction being wreaked on their fellows and who had determined that now was the time to move off; to fight another day.

Fergusson was right; it was time to go. But Smith-Dorrien had been clear: the division's withdrawal had to be properly controlled, and steadily undertaken. Any rush would become a route, any congestion a bottleneck; either would be a disaster. The Norfolks were once more to man the last line that would hold the Germans whilst the rest escaped.

"Yes sir!" Fred came crawling forward, behind Alfie who had been sent by the major to collect him.

Swiftly, the company commander gave out orders which positioned guides on the Roman Road, and at the turnings through the village which would lead the battalion up onto the position. As each company arrived, he would point out where, along the dirt road, they were to be sited; there to await the enemy and to give him as bloody a nose as possible before falling back. Fred, knowing the importance of the task he had been given, nodded soberly.

"Right, sir!" And he was gone, crawling away so as not to expose himself on the sky line, before collecting his small party around him, and running down the hill, rifles at the trail, into the village to meet the battalion. Their boots clattered on the pavé road, gradually developing into a rhythm as they, almost subconsciously, came into step. Speed was of the essence; they reckoned on having only ten minutes before the rest of the battalion arrived.

"My God, they're going for the other two!"

The major had been scanning the valley with his binoculars, trying to work out the most likely spot at which the battalion would have to engage the enemy.

Ted and Alfie followed the line of his field glasses to where the two guns had been left by the battery they had seen withdrawing. Two teams, each of three pairs of horses and each pair controlled by a single rider, were heading toward the two 4.5 inch Howitzers that had been left on the old gun position. The gun limbers bounced and clattered behind them as they started galloping forward from a point about three hundred yards from where the guns lay.

German infantry was by now well in sight, waving and shouting, but taking no further action.

At first the Gunners bore a charmed life, as the two teams of horses swung round the front of the stationary guns to bring the rear of the limber alongside the trail so as to hook up the howitzer and haul it away. The lead horseman of each team remained in the saddle to control the horses; his two colleagues dismounting to manhandle the heavy gun onto the limber hook, one each side of the short box trail, heaving and straining to force the two large wheels to move from the ruts into which they had become embedded. Normally done by six men, it seemed an impossible task; impossible that is under normal conditions, and these were far from normal.

German artillery was holding off, for fear of hitting their own troops nearby, but the infantry suddenly awoke to what was happening. Either that or they had been awaiting orders before doing anything; as was the German character. From their vantage point on the hill the three Englishmen could make out the overwhelming sound of rifle fire; not certain who was firing, and whether or not their own infantry was taking on the Germans in order to assist the Gunners. At that range they could do nothing themselves to help.

The two teams completed the hooking up, almost together, and set off. As the first one away was approaching the track along which they would make their way back to Reumont, the driver of the second pair of horses threw up his hands and fell to the ground. All the while, the officer who had led them out sat astride his horse, calmly as if on a Hyde Park review. Now he waved his hand around his head, and as he turned his horse away into the gallop the two teams began to follow. The volume of fire seemed to increase. Again, the watching Norfolks knew not from which side. Suddenly, the leading horses of one team went down, throwing the rider; and the rest of the team, limber gun and all went crashing down in a flailing tangle of arms and legs.

"Aaaaah!" As he breathed his utter disappointment the

major watched one of the riders from the downed gun stagger to his feet and begin to look around him. As he did so he was caught by what must have been the fire of several men for his body jerked visibly several times before finally slumping to the ground. German infantry, encouraged by their success against one gun began to run forward, trying to head off the second. A machine gun team tried to set up its gun in order to bring fire to bear; an act which clearly caught the eye of some British infantrymen who took exception to the process. The German gun team was dead or wounded within seconds, a fate which also befell several of their colleagues who tried to take over the machine gun.

But the second team rode on, and despite the tragedy they had just witnessed the three men on the hill were captivated by the magnificence of the sight beneath them. As they drew away from the German infantry the enemy artillery tried to range in on the fleeing Gunners, and from all sides there poured in a withering fire. Through the smoke and the dust the riders lay low over their horses' necks, left hands on the reins of the horse they were riding, right hands controlling the right hand, riderless, horses; beside them the officer waving and yelling as the distance between them and the enemy lengthened. The limber and the gun bucked and bounced across the ruts and furrows as they headed across country, overhead, shrapnel coughed its deadly load, and around them huge gouts of earth were thrown up as German artillery tried to stop them with high explosive shell. But they bore a charmed life, passing through clouds of smoke and flying debris so close it seemed they could never survive; on and on, horses lathered, their mouths wide open in fear and in the attempt to draw as much breath as they could; further and further, until they passed from the view of the men on the hill and into safety.

They heard the major expel his breath, as if he had been holding it for several minutes; and it felt to him as if he had. "Well done," he muttered quietly to himself, with feeling.

"Good effort, that." Alfie, for once, was almost lost for words.

"Aye, fer Gunners." Thus was respect afforded by two

privates of the Infantry of the Line to an officer and two drivers of the Royal Artillery.

"Here they come!" One of the soldiers left by Fred by the dirt road called out to the major, and as he turned he saw the commanding officer leading his first company up the hill at a brisk pace.

Swiftly, the major explained the position, and the CO, nodding his assent to the plan, stepped back and allowed the first company to be shown where it should take up position. The process was repeated for the second company, and then the major smiled as he saw his second-in-command bringing along some familiar faces. His own company went into position on the left, near where the major had himself been overviewing the valley. The last company would, for the time being, remain in Reumont, in a small quarry, about half a mile to the north-east; and the guides were to remain in place in Hennechy to bring them in when the time came.

As the battalion took up its position it became clear to all that the withdrawal was on in a big way. German artillery was falling thick and fast, and the response from the British guns was growing progressively less as casualties and shortage of ammunition began to take their toll. The size of groups moving to the rear was increasing, and there were more and more of them. The rearguards of the forward brigades were beginning to pull back, relying on divisional reserves, if there were any, to allow them to break from the enemy.

At about five-thirty, the company of Norfolks in the quarry spotted enemy to their north-east, at about one thousand eight hundred yards range. Immediately, the company commander brought the full weight of his company's firepower to bear, and the Germans disappeared from sight, leaving a number who had fallen. Obeying his last order, to hit and break clean, the officer then led his soldiers swiftly down the Roman Road to where Fred was waiting to guide him to the rest of the battalion in Hennechy.

As they moved up the road through the village Fred collected in the guides. Arriving at the junction with the dirt road, he ordered the men from other companies to go back to them, and began to draw his section together before rejoining the platoon. They were still in good order, Carter apart. His feet had improved, but even the short brisk step up the hill in Hennechy had winded him.

"Gotta do sumthin' about 'im," he thought to himself.

The battalion was, by now, strung along the ridge, from where they obtained a clear view of the valley below. There was general amazement at the carnage they witnessed, and a determination that the Germans they could see in the distance would pay dearly for it. Moving from Le Cateau, along the road just to their right in the direction of Busigny to their south were columns of German infantry and guns. Orders were swiftly given, and, as the Norfolks were about to fire, the single 60-Pounder left in 108 Battery opened up with high explosive. Meanwhile, over in Reumont, just to their north-west, 122 Battery with two 18-Pounders joined in. There had been no co-ordinated plan; the three sets of fire were coincidental; and casualties began to mount among the advancing Germans.

The German columns, which were actually two battalions of Seventh German Division, part of Third German Corps, disappeared into dead ground near a cross-roads to the Norfolks' half right, and as they did so the battalion prepared to take them on again as they emerged into the open; but they never appeared. The orders to those German battalions had been to clear the way for a Third Corps pursuit, but they had been punished enough. They had neither the energy, the heart nor the motivation to pursue an enemy who seemed never to know when he was beaten, and whose terrible firepower did such consistently awful damage.

"Right, you lot." Fred addressed his section as the battalion ceased firing, "Get on up there and join the platoon, now!" He paused, watching them rise to their feet, and begin running towards the platoon about a hundred yards away on the ridge, to where they could see Matthew Jenkins busily checking the state of his men as they waited to fire on the Germans when they emerged from the dead ground.

Fred looked down the hill, in time to see a company of British soldiers, he knew not which regiment, moving into the northern edge of the village; into a position behind the Norfolks. He raised his hand in acknowledgement, saw the company commander respond, and briefly felt an overwhelming sense of belonging. It was a wonderful feeling: that they were all in this together, and the common goal was more important than the trivia of peacetime soldiering.

He turned, and began to move up the hill towards where his section had just reached Matthew.

Shrapnel, ammunition designed so that a single shell would deliver a scattering of sub-projectiles upon the enemy, thereby killing and wounding many of them, had been around for just over one hundred years. There had been changes in that time, and a modern shrapnel shell was basically a large shotgun cartridge. The shell body would be of forged steel, usually with the front portion annealed so it would open slightly on bursting. In the base of the shell casing would be a gunpowder burster charge, and for a seventy-five millimetre calibre shell this would typically be about one and a half ounces. Running from this burster would be a tube, passing up the centre of the shell cavity to join the base of the fuze at the shell's mouth. This tube would be filled with gunpowder pellets. Filling the space around the tube, and packed in tightly with resin, were bullets, each of them just under half an ounce in weight. For a middle calibre round, some three hundred would be the norm, and they would be made of lead and antimony, about seven parts to one. The fuze would then be screwed into the shell's nose, its base flush with the top of the central, gunpowder-pellet filled, tube.

The fuze designer would have made use of centrifugal force and the effects of gravity and built-in springs to release safety devices which started the time mechanism working as the projectile was about fifty feet from the muzzle of the gun from which it had been fired. The time element was a slow burning gunpowder train, with the time set by the gunner before loading. When the gunpowder train reached its end it ignited a flash pellet in the base of the fuze. This in turn ignited the pellets in the central tube, and they ignited the one and a half ounces of gunpowder in the shell base. The explosion of this gunpowder was sufficient to force off the fuze at the mouth of the projectile, and eject the bullets from inside the casing, in whatever direction the shell was facing, as if fired from a gun. Timing was, of course critical: set the fuze too short and the effect was significantly reduced as it burst too high; set it too long and the effect was lost as the shell ploughed into the ground without discharging its load.

Having discharged its load the empty shell casing was left to fly on; a hole in its nose where once had been a fuze; an empty cavity in its centre which had once been filled with bullets and gunpowder; and a shell body that was undamaged by the small gunpowder charge that had ejected the contents. Destabilised and tumbling, the empty steel shell would carry on for some distance until it eventually came to land.

The German gunners had the range of the crest upon which the Norfolks had taken up their position. Albert Carter was the right hand man of the section moving forward to join Matthew when a shrapnel shell burst just ahead of the running men, and slightly to their right. The lobe of his right ear was neatly removed by one of the bullets, causing a gout of bright, fresh blood to run down the side of his head and onto his neck, staining heavily the collar and right shoulder of his uniform and webbing.

He never felt the wound, however, for a second bullet from the same shell smashed into his sternum, pushing shattered bone back into his lungs and severing the Aorta, the great artery which carried the blood from his heart throughout his body. One large bone splinter peeled off, puncturing the wall of his heart. As blood welled instantly out of the wound in his torso, the greater volume of the red, sticky fluid escaped into his chest cavity, flooding his lungs. With his heart having stopped, and with the pressure thereby reduced, the blood poured from the wrecked artery in a steady, sustained stream. The bullet, bouncing off the sternum and flattened by the impact, sliced a large hole in his left lung, adding to the damage caused by the smashed breastbone. He hit the ground, flat on his back, and in the three seconds that followed, as the pain began to bite, he thought of his allotment, the gathering of the autumn crop and who would do it. Then the mist descended over his brain and the light of the sky above faded from his consciousness.

"Bugger!"

Alfred Arbuckle and Peter Dakin both heard Fred call out as Carter went down beside them. They both stopped, unsure what to do; although it was obvious to anyone that Albert Carter was quite dead.

"Come on!" Looking up they saw Paul Cooper beckoning them over, gesticulating fiercely with his right arm. Assuming that Fred's expletive had been to do with Carter being hit they carried on, and flopped, breathless and shocked, into the positions indicated.

"Where's Corporal Smith?"

"Coming, sergeant. He was just behind us."

"No 'e bloody isn't!" Ned Preece had looked over his shoulder as Carter was hit, and had seen Fred go down shortly after.

"Sir?" Cooper looked at his officer.

"Go......go on. Get him and look after him!" The concern in Jenkins' voice was clear for all to hear.

As the sergeant moved away, Alfred Arbuckle, unbidden, came along beside him.

"Where the bloody hell do you think you're going? Get back in the bloody line."

"I can carry 'im, sergeant, you can't." Calmly spoken in a steady, deep voice, it was a statement of fact. Cooper, briefly regretting his outburst, grimaced, nodded his assent and the two moved away to where Fred Smith lay on the ground.

His had been a great misfortune. The shell body, part of whose contents had seen the end of Albert Carter, had continued on its path toward the earth, whereupon it had struck a large rock, beside the road. It had then bounced off, twisted and bent by the impact, and had struck Fred Smith on the right ankle. Weighing almost ten pounds and travelling very fast it had shattered bone in the foot and the ankle joint itself. A creased edge of the fuze cavity, sharpened when it had smashed against the rock, had sliced flesh and tendon just above the ankle. His boot and puttee hid some of the damage from view, but the sight of white bone protruding from cuts in the boot leather together with blood oozing out of the lace holes, and from the puttee above his ankle, made it obvious that the damage was severe. The pain had clearly been excruciating; Fred Smith had lapsed, mercifully, into unconsciousness.

Paul attempted to lift the injured leg in order to place Fred's hat beneath the damaged area as a cushion. He flinched, briefly, as more shrapnel burst over their heads, the bullets raising small clouds of dust as they sprayed the dirt road just a few feet away. The foot flopped and twisted strangely as he tried to make it more comfortable. He gave silent thanks that Fred was out of it, and could not feel the pain.

"'Ave t' splint the ankle and then tie 'is legs t'gether. Cannut do it any other way." Alfred, common sense personified, made his views known. Paul nodded, grateful somehow for the big man's steadiness beside him. They worked together, gently removing the puttee from Fred's other leg, taking his bayonet and using it as a splint. Half the puttee went on the splint, and the other half to bandage the two limbs together, immobilising the damaged area. Blood still oozed, but they dare not remove the boot or puttee to staunch the flow. Best let nature take its course, and leave the rest to the doctors.

"How is he?"

They looked up at Matthew. Around them the rest of the battalion was getting ready to move away. Having stopped the Germans their work was done, and it was time to leave, to pass through the company of Royal Welsh Fusiliers, for that was who Fred had seen moving into the village, and on south to rejoin the brigade on the Roman Road.

"Foot's buggered. Ankle's gawn." Alfred summed it up, a tone of deep regret in his voice.

"Let me see." As he bent down Fred's eyes flickered and he drifted out of the faint into which he had lapsed. He saw Paul and Matthew, and groaned as the pain swept over him. Matthew saw the damage, the ripped boot leather, the blood, the small segments of white bone, the mud and dirt from the road. A doctor would have initially assessed a comminuted compound fracture, coupled with a likely severing of the Achilles Tendon. Matthew could only imagine what it looked like inside the boot. He felt sick.

"Right, we carry him until we can get him to a doctor!"

"Leave me." Fred heard himself speaking as if from a distance; not wishing to be left, but knowing that he would be a dreadful burden.

Matthew looked around at the rest of his platoon, waiting to follow. Three would not be with them, they lay dead on the ridge, and two more nursed minor shrapnel wounds. He glanced at his watch. Six o'clock. It was dull, and a drizzle was developing.

"Don't be silly." His voice brooked no argument. "Can you carry him on your own?" He addressed Alfred.

"Aye, sir, if summ'n'll carry me kit." Peter Dakin stepped forward as Alfred unbuckled his webbing.

"Sit up, corporal." Alfred lifted Fred to a sitting position as he spoke and removed the older man's webbing. He placed his left hand under the splinted legs, his right under Fred's arms, took the strain, stood with a straight back and then held him in his arms like a baby.

"Carter?" Fred muttered the word, the question was obvious.

"Dead!" Matthew was matter-of-fact.

As he lapsed back into unconsciousness it crossed Fred's mind, just very briefly, that he would not now have to do anything about Albert Carter.

"There's a wheelbarrow, sir, in the farm about two

hundred yards on the right, near that big red building with the village name painted on the side. We can use that." Colin Baxter was already on the move as he was speaking, and by the time Alfred reached the farmyard gate, Colin was waiting. Gently, they laid the comatose body into the barrow, Fred's legs tied to a plank put in place by Colin, and began wheeling him along as the rest of the platoon made their way, in the rear of the company, down the hill, through the village and onto the Roman Road.

Behind them, the Royal Welsh Fusiliers waited to fight a rearguard action that was never to be. The Germans had been stopped.

Von Kluck had misjudged it yet again. He had thought he was doing battle with the whole of the BEF, not knowing of the split caused by the forest, and having allowed Haig's First Corps, on Smith-Dorrien's right, to escape. He had also thought the BEF to be withdrawing in a more westerly line, rather than the generally southwards direction in which they were headed.

Smith-Dorrien had won the time he needed. It would be midnight before the leading battalions of Third German Corps entered Hennechy, and four o'clock in the morning before they would continue the pursuit. When they did so it would be to the south-west, chasing shadows. Smith-Dorrien had a twelve hour start, and an entire British Corps, Haig's First Corps, which had not been engaged, both at Mons or Le Cateau, remained virtually untouched and at full strength.

But the price? Since that first contact near Mons on the twenty-third of August the BEF had suffered fourteen thousand eight hundred casualties; almost entirely from among Smith-Dorrien's men.

Chapter 8

The Retreat Continues Southward

"What are we waiting for?"

The drizzle was getting worse, developing into a steadier downpour. Paul Cooper was voicing the concern they all felt, wanting to get on, to break from the Germans, to get Fred to a doctor.

"For the rest of the brigade. At least that is what I have been told. They came off the position late and they'll be here shortly." Paul Cooper was looking away up the road as Matthew spoke; not so much for the approach of the rest of Fifteen Brigade, but for some form of ambulance.

"We've got to get him to a doctor!" Cooper stated the obvious. Fred was still in his wheelbarrow, lapsing in and out of consciousness, but gradually spending more time than was good for him awake; and in pain.

Around them the platoon sat by the roadside, their collective attitude becoming progressively more morose as the wetness permeated their clothing and dribbles of water ran down their necks. The loss of four of their colleagues had hit them hard. They had no right to expect that they would be spared casualties, but their success on the ridge at Elouges had built their confidence to such a high degree that the gaps in their ranks were a burden they found especially difficult to bear. Albert Carter's death had been bad enough, but, for the section, it was the loss of Fred Smith that was having the greatest impact. He had become a real father figure to them, and the younger ones in particular were already beginning to feel his loss.

Alfie, who had retained through thick and thin the bottle of Bushmills from the dockside in Belfast, pulled it out of his pack. Unscrewing the cap he held it gently against Fred's mouth, spilling a drop of the fluid into his mouth. Fred gagged and choked as the spirit slid into his throat. Then, looking gratefully into Alfie's eyes, he motioned with his head for more, and this time took a good long pull before collapsing back into the wheelbarrow. The pain in his foot had by now reduced to an excruciating ache, but was just bearable. As he wondered what was to be his fate, he was dimly aware of a conversation taking place nearby, with heated voices raised.

Paul Cooper had seen a group of King's Own Scottish Borderers pulling a cart loaded with wounded. He had stopped them to see if there was any value in putting Fred onto it, or whether he should wait for something else. The cart would normally have been pulled by two horses rather than a group of men; and what Fred could hear was Paul being treated to an explanation by the very angry old soldier, a private, who was the commonly accepted leader of the group.

In very clear, soldierly language he was explaining how this "fookin' wee civvie" had removed the "fookin' hooerses" from the "fookin" carrrt" and had "fooked off wi' 'em" with no concern whatsoever for the "fookin' blokes" in the "fookin' back." He went on to explain in "fookin'" detail his views on civilians in general, and described graphically the fate that awaited this particular "fookin' wee civvie" if he ever laid hands upon him. He also expressed his remorse that he was unable to carry Fred, taking Paul to the back of the cart and pointing out that, much as he would like to help, there was "nae fookin' room".

It was to be another three hours before Fred was placed in an ambulance. By this time the battalion had been well along on the road from Le Cateau towards Estrées, some fifteen miles away to the south. Edward von Gleichen had given the CO permission to try and slip through the jam of traffic, soldiers and refugees and make his way at best speed to the rendezvous. It was, however, no use, for every time they seemed to be making progress they came up against yet another blockage which impeded their progress. It was during one of the attempts to force their way through that Matthew saw the red cross on the side of a wheeled ambulance, lit by the glow from the window of the cottage outside which it had ground to a halt.

"Sir, I'm sorry; there is just no room in here!" The Medical Corps sergeant was being as emphatic as he could be, in the face of a very determined lieutenant, older than usual, and a group of fierce looking, bedraggled soldiers who clearly were not in a mood to listen to reason.

"Put him on the floor, man. You've got room there haven't you?" The impatience showed through clearly in Matthew's voice.

"Yes, but.....!" His voice tailed off as Peter Dakin pulled back the blanket which had been covering Fred's leg. The look on the young Norfolk lad's face said everything.

"Bloody hell," muttered the medical sergeant under his breath, looking at the congealed bloody mass that was the remains of Fred's lower leg, with bones protruding. "Right," a firm and positive note in his voice. "Get 'im in here." Swiftly he bent and picked up the kit that was lying about in the well of the ambulance. Some was shoved under stretchers, and yet more was placed, gently, on the comatose shapes inside the vehicle. Matthew put his head inside, about to assist, and caught a whiff of the smell. It was a mix of body odour, vomit and disinfectant; coupled with a sickly, sweet odour which dragged those days in South Africa back into his consciousness, and the memory of the man wounded in the shoulder; it was gangrene. If a casualty is not with a surgeon within six hours of wounding his treatment is made more complex, and if it extends to twelve hours or more gangrene is often one of the complications. One of the men in the ambulance had been hit the previous day, and it was now getting on towards midnight; his condition did not bear thinking about. Fred was well into the six hours, and little prospect in this chaos of the ambulance making much headway at all. Still, Matthew reasoned, he was better off in the ambulance than in a wheelbarrow, in the rain.

Gently, they lifted him and carried him to the back of the vehicle. Such was the care and tenderness with which they handled him there was no hint of undue discomfort as they laid him on a spare stretcher in the well of the ambulance.

"Be all right, Fred." Ted's voice, with its reassuring note, came to him through the mist of pain, and the beginnings of delirium as his temperature began to rise. Later Fred would remember the gentleness in the voice, and the thought in his own mind at the time: that he didn't think it would be anything like all right. He felt a hand resting on the back of his own hand. Looking up he was aware of Matthew staring down at him.

"Take care, my friend. You're better off here. There's nothing more we can do for you. I'll see you when we get back."

Fred smiled. "Thanks, sir. I'll be seein' yer."

"Yes, yes you will." Matthew, by now, had a huge lump in his throat, and simply had no words left which he felt might be in any way appropriate. Swiftly, he turned away. Squeezing Fred's hand he said, simply, "goodbye," before leading the small group which had gathered around the ambulance back to the platoon, hoping the darkness hid the moisture that was welling in his eyes.

As Matthew left, Fred felt a great surge of empty loneliness welling up inside him. Tears pricked at his eyes, and he looked away from the enquiring gaze of the medical sergeant. As he drifted away into unconsciousness once more his thoughts were of Aggie and his baby daughter.

"Transport and mounted troops straight on! Three Division infantry to the right, Five Division infantry to the left!" Staff officers, repeating the call endlessly, stood at the cross-roads, two miles south of Estrées, which Second Corps had reached after a long wet and exhausting march. Tired, cold, soaked and hungry, they turned obediently to their left and carried on marching, down the hill in the direction of

Joncourt. Barely half a mile on and the cry went up: "Fifteen Brigade straight on, Thirteen Brigade in the field to your right, Fourteen Brigade to your left." The battalions were then called into bivouac areas.

The system was to carry on all night, and as the stragglers found their way in they followed the calling voices and arrived in their battalion locations. Fifteen Brigade had come through the whole process quite well, and was a reasonably cohesive formation by two in the morning of the twenty-seventh of August. The march had not been easy, but they had been helped by the road, which was as straight as a die. Lights had been on in some of the cottages as they had marched past, reflecting off the droplets as the rain continued to pour down. The pace had been steady, with no sign of panic. Indeed, there was a prevailing sense of annoyance at being asked yet again to fall back. However, they were very tired, as were their horses. Whenever there was a halt, men had slept, and had to be roused in order to get them moving again.

Ted Ludgrove had been detailed off, with Peter Dakin, to provide the rendezvous guides for stragglers coming in. They were exhausted beyond belief, almost unable to stand, and they cursed their luck that it was they who had been "volunteered" for such a miserable duty. Leaning against the gate post at the edge of the field in which the battalion had been billeted they watched the divisional staff as they brought people in and pushed them in the right direction.

"Over there, mate." My, but if they had a pound for every time they'd said that over the couple of hours they'd stood by the gate. Gradually, stragglers from the battalion trickled in and made their way slowly to where the RSM was running a collection point to identify them and pass them back to their companies.

As the frequency at which their colleagues were returning to the fold began to reduce, they fell victim to the torpor that comes with their state of exhaustion. Virtually asleep on their feet, they had never felt so tired in their lives. Ted jerked his head up for the umpteenth time, reaching up with his hand to wipe away the saliva that had dribbled from the corner of his mouth.

"You, you little bastard. Come here!"

The voice was sharp, pitched high and with a slight nasal twang. Ted leapt fully awake, recognising instantly who it was. Peter, startled, turned with his friend to face the direction from which the voice had come.

"'Oo, sir? Me sir?" Peter knew authority when he heard it, had confirmed this on recognising a captain's uniform, and had assumed that he was the subject of the officer's somewhat belligerent attentions.

"No, not you, you bloody idiot. Him. Ludgrove, the bastard. Get over here when I tell you, and look sharp about it!"

This was the moment Ted had been dreading. Now he would be exposed, charged with assault and probably sent to prison. With a dry mouth, his hands moist from his fear, he straightened himself and marched as best he could across the tussocks that separated him by fifteen feet or so from where Edward Snell stood. Snell's hands were on his hips, his mouth grimacing a vicious leer that exposed teeth, still in need of cleaning, and with moistness on his lips from the spittle that had splashed from his mouth with the violence of his outburst. Snell had been waiting for this moment since the time he saw Ludgrove at the cottage. He had known he would find him in time, and when he did Ludgrove was going to be sorry.

Thought you could get away with it did you? Bastard. How dare you strike me the way you did? You will pay for it, and I will see to it that you do, do you understand me?" Snell's face was very close to Ted's, spittle flying as he spoke, the stink of his breath repugnant in Ted's nostrils.

Silence. It was his only course of action. Snell was an officer, and any response he might make would simply get him into even more trouble.

"Well, say something! You were quick enough when that little cow made a fuss. No, nothing? Well, that won't help you now. I've got you, and you'll bloody well suffer."

"Quite what do you mean?" Ted recognised the company

commander's well modulated tones. He also recognised that subtle steeliness which always meant trouble for someone. Ted's stomach turned to water. This was it. Silence; just keep quiet.

Snell's head snapped round.

"Yes, you." The major was looking directly at him. "I should like to know what right you feel you have to address one of my soldiers in such an unseemly fashion. Has he done something wrong?" Ted glanced to his right, and saw that Matthew was standing behind the major, his face grim.

"Yes, yes, he has." Snell began to explain, very well aware that his language and behaviour had been of a sort unlikely to gain favour with a bloody upper class twit dressed in army uniform. "Two years ago he......"

"Ah!" The major interjected. "So he hasn't done anything wrong tonight? Wasn't diligent in his duties or anything like that, if you see what I mean?"

"Well.......no, but he......."

"Good, well that's that then. So you don't mind if I let his platoon commander send him off for some sleep then? Terribly tired they are, these two, you know?"

Matthew was trying not to smile. When the Major acted out the bemused aristocrat he was always amusing, and frequently lethal.

"Yes, yes, of course." Snell had lost the initiative and he knew it.

"And if ever, and I mean ever, you wish to speak to one of my soldiers you will first seek my permission." The words lashed out, seemingly enveloped in ice, quite different to the tone he had been using and in a voice low enough that the two soldiers could not hear; for that would be intolerable. "And if it is a matter related to discipline in any way, you will do it in my presence. Have I made myself clear?"

His teeth grinding in fury, lips tightly compressed, facial muscles rigid, Snell nodded and turned away. Now was not the time to pursue this. He would get him later.

"Right, you two, off to your platoon and get some sleep. We'll be on our way at four o'clock."

"Thank you, sir." It was a despondent mumble from Ted,

and his state of mind was not lost on his company commander. As the two soldiers moved slowly away, he turned to Matthew.

"Find out what that was all about; in slow time. We have, I suspect, more to worry about for the time being than whatever it was that happened two years ago."

As day broke, Fifth Division was already on the move. The chill of dawn on their damp clothing was assuaged by the sun as it rose on what was to be a warm and sunny day. Steam rose from wet uniforms as men plodded back up the road to the Estrées cross-roads, turned left and resumed the southwards march. The signpost informed them that Paris lay one hundred and fifty two kilometres to the south, but none had any idea they might travel so far that they might soon be within a short day's march of the French capital.

The damp and cold had stiffened their clothing and their equipment. Wearing it was an unpleasant experience, especially on the tender areas inside the crotch and under the arms. Morale was not high. There had been no food since the day before, and not everyone had eaten then; and their general discomfort was also a factor. There was, however, the overpowering sense of desolation that they were still retreating, and they did not know why, and this more than anything had them thoroughly browned off.

They would have been concerned, and ashamed, had they been privy to a conversation taking place that morning in Smith-Dorrien's headquarters. An order had been issued by General Wilson at GHQ instructing the two corps commanders to throw away all their excess equipment, load their lame ducks on carts and make best possible speed to escape the Germans. It was the language of defeat, and it rankled especially with Smith-Dorrien whose corps had suffered so much in order to give the BEF its chance to withdraw, and fight another day.

"How dare they issue me with such an outrageous directive!" The corps commander was very angry.

"It appears, sir, that GHQ is of the view that your corps has been decimated, and is no longer a formation capable of conducting operations against the enemy." The Brigadier General Staff's voice was icily urbane. Brigadier General Forestier-Walker shared his corps commander's view. Indeed, only an hour or so previously they had been together on the road near Bellenglise watching Fifth Division on the move. They had seen tired men, wounded men, hungry men, disgruntled men. But they had seen whole units, weapons cleaned, heads up, here and there pipes being puffed, soldiers trying to smarten their appearance. All they had heard were the questions, and there had been two: why are we going this way and not back at the Germans; and when is breakfast? No, battered they might be; finished they were not.

"Well, it might help General Wilson if he, or one of his staff, were to get off their backsides and come down here to see what is really going on. Under no circumstances whatsoever is any whiff of that order to reach the divisions." He turned to his BGS, speaking now more gently.

"Can you see to it, ... please?" He sat back and closed his eyes, the thumb and forefinger of his right hand pinching the bridge of his nose as he allowed himself to sink back into his chair, lost in his thoughts.

"Of course, sir." The BGS left.

The march south was a long slog. The road was hot and dusty, and whenever there was a halt men fell asleep at once. Some of the feet were in a terrible state, and these men were loaded on carts and gun limbers whenever possible. When they reached Bellenglise they were turned south-east, towards St Quentin. Von Kluck still believed they were heading south-west, and gradually the distance between the BEF and the Germans increased. Smith-Dorrien had bought the time, and deceived the enemy as to his true intentions. His success at Le Cateau was a model, but it would cost him dearly. Field Marshall French, whilst publicly extolling the excellent work of Second Corps, was privately furious at their success; at their proving that defeat was not inevitable. It was almost as if he would have preferred the corps to be wiped out.

Unaware of all this, Thomas marched on. On every rise in the road, away to their half left and drawing ever closer, they could see the square shape of the cathedral in St Quentin, with its ridiculously small spire in the centre seeming so out of proportion. There, they were being promised, would be food, and transport for the sick and injured.

The young French captain put his right hand into the small of his back, pressed it against his spine and arched his body so as to give some relief from the stiffness caused by riding for most of the night. Behind him, the soldiers of his squadron slumped in their saddles, exhausted; and to his left his only remaining senior NCO, a sergeant, was trying to discover from one of the local peasants just precisely where they were, and where was the nearest place they might find something to eat.

The squadron's war had commenced with mobilisation on the fourth of August, just over three weeks ago. Part of Sordet's corps they had ridden hard and fast into Belgium, to come to the assistance of their Allies. In truth, of course, they had been trying to fight the war on someone else's territory, but no matter. They had bumped the enemy a few times, and taken some casualties; but really the war for them up to that point had been one of riding endlessly, patrolling, observing, providing screens and flank protection. Now they had been ordered to the west, to reinforce the territorial divisions which were to become part of the newly forming Sixth French Army, to provide them with a reconnaissance capability, to become their eyes.

He looked around him at the rolling countryside, and wondered for a moment at what might become of his homeland if *les boches* were to achieve their objectives, if they were to repeat their success in the Franco-Prussian war, less than fifty years ago. He recalled his orders, the sense of urgency that had been imparted and the concern that all was not going well for *la France*. He had been advised that he would be crossing the line of the British, but he was to pay them no heed. They had sent a ridiculously small army, which had played no significant part in the fighting and was even now in headlong retreat, leaving the French to resolve their own problems. So much for allies; perfidious Albion again.

On the St Quentin road Fifth Division had sorted itself out quite well during the morning. Tired as they were, shape and order were clearly back, and spirits were lifting as the sun warmed their damp, chilled bodies. The company was leading the Ninth, with Matthew's platoon out in front. In front, that is, of the fit and healthy. The CO had determined not to leave any more men by the roadside if he could possibly avoid it, and had placed all his walking wounded at the head of the column. They would set the pace, and the battalion would stay together. It might slow them down, but the benefits would show later, of that he was certain. They were clearly going to have to fight the Germans again and he would need every man he could keep.

"Les tommies, les tommies!" The young captain looked up from the map he and his sergeant were poring over as two of his scouts came cantering back from their appointed task of forward reconnaissance. The senior of the two leant down from his saddle, his forefinger pointing at the map in his officer's hand, marking a spot on the road some eight hundred metres to the west.

Ordering his sergeant to mount, the officer climbed onto his own horse, half turned in the saddle, nodded to the NCO and moved off. Behind him he heard the words of command that would have the squadron following him in two files, side by side. He was curious to see these British. The mood in General Lanrezac's Fifth French Army had been hostile. It was clear that these people had promised much, and had failed to deliver, but that was only to be expected, surely. However, it was not only the very poor opinion held by the French Army that aroused his curiosity, but also that the captain's great grandfather had died at the hands of the British, at Waterloo.

Commanding his regiment, he had been part of Marshall

Ney's grand, and doomed, cavalry extravaganza in the middle of the afternoon on that fateful eighteenth of June in 1815. The story had it that he had slid from his dying horse in front of a square, formed of kilted, bonneted Highlanders, and had finished up within a metre of the front rank - alive. As he had tried to rise one of the Scottish heathens had picked up a fallen officer's claymore and with one swipe of the straight, heavy blade had cleaved the Frenchman's skull in two. The soldier had then been seen rifling the dead man's clothes, looking for booty. The story was told over and over again at family gatherings, taking on the force of a legend as it passed down through the ages; and gaining in passion with the passing of time.

Oh yes, he was anxious indeed to see these men, of whom he had heard so much; none of it good. Riding on at a steady canter, he left his soldiers behind him, their horses walking.

Matthew looked up. Off to his left he could see a horseman skylined beside the road. He was not British, the BEF's cavalry being clad all in khaki. This man wore a mid-blue jacket, his red trousers tucked into black boots. The distinctive shape of his blue kepi stood out very clearly. No, this was French cavalry.

What the young captain saw took him by surprise. He saw a British battalion that had clearly been in something of a fight. Out in front there were many tens of men bearing the obvious signs of wounding and injury. Behind them were others, divided out into company groupings, officers, some riding some marching beside their men, NCOs chivvying, and the steady tramp, tramp of feet marching in unison. Every man had his weapon, including the wounded. Clearly very tired, there was, nonetheless, a manner about them. These were not defeated men. These were soldiers; soldiers who had been in a hard fight, and who would fight again. As they saw the young Frenchman looking towards them chests lifted, heads came up higher and the sound of marching grew crisper. Even the wounded retained their military dignity. It was an impressive sight.

Something stirred inside him. He saw their obvious pride; saw no sign of defeatism here; saw something which made him think that perhaps all he had been led to believe might not be entirely true; saw brave men who had suffered, and were prepared to suffer again. Confused, he paused for a few seconds; and then came to a decision. He turned, his right hand holding the rear of his saddle as he caught his sergeant's eye. Turning back to his front he drew his sabre and held out his arms in the silent signal that would bring his squadron into line abreast, and stationary, just behind him. The sergeant was completely bemused. He had no idea what was going on. The soldiers did not care; they were too tired to care. With his squadron stilled the captain stood in his stirrups, waiting to gauge the moment when the battalion would be level with him. His soldiers, following the line of their officer's eyes, saw the British for the first time, saw the wounded, realised what the battalion had suffered, began to wonder what was going on.

The captain called his squadron to attention. They sat erect in their saddles, facing to the front.

"Sabre à la main!" There was a scraping noise as sabres left scabbards in unison.

"Portez sabre!" Even more erect now, the sabres were held upright, right hands close to the hip, the tip of the sabre running up vertically past the right shoulder.

"Presentez sabre!" Into the present, and looking straight at their allies as they marched past. Heads lifted, chests swelled, and even the horses, sensing perhaps the occasion, seemed to stand more proud and erect. With his men at the present, the captain swept his own sabre gracefully down and away to the right: the salute, the ultimate acknowledgement of honour and respect between soldiers.

Matthew could now see the white band around the Frenchman's kepi, the brass, or was it gold, chinstrap, and the little green pommel on the front, at the top. The epaulettes were white, and there was a number, which he could not see clearly, on the jacket collar. Behind him he could hear the CSM.

"Look up now. Steady. By the left, eyeeeeees left!"

Matthew snapped his head off to the left, his right arm whipping up to return the salute, looking straight into the eyes of the young officer. Their gaze stayed locked, as if by some indiscernible force, for what appeared an age, but could not have been longer than a few seconds. Matthew read pride and doubt in the younger man's eyes. The Frenchman read pride and thanks in Matthew's.

"Eyeeeeeees front!" The moment had passed, a moment in which a bond had forged between two people who knew not each others' names, and would never meet again. And a young French officer had perhaps taken his first step on the road to realising that stories should be taken for what they are, whilst the truth may lie somewhere else.

St Quentin was a railway town of some significance in the region, with its main station lying to the south of the town beside the canal that ran directly west to east along the southern edge. Marching through the town they passed the terraced houses and small shops that they had come to know as being typical of the region, red brick being the dominant building material, dulled and blackened by the pollutants from the local industrial plants.

The sight that greeted them as they arrived at the station, its large forecourt set off to the right of the main road heading south, was one of apparent chaos. Everywhere there were trucks, carts, ambulances and weary soldiers on foot. Those cavalry that were not away to the north, watching for Smith-Dorrien lest the Germans realised they had been fooled and resumed their pursuit, were walking their horses to save their energy. But there was order in the chaos. Trains were in the station and there was a constant stream of wounded, either sitting or on stretchers, being loaded prior to being moved away to the south, to the hospitals that had been set up in Nantes, St Nazaire and Rouen. Some bread was available, and tired, hungry men were sitting beside the road, leaning against the walls of gardens and houses, chewing slowly and washing down their meagre meal with whatever water they could get. In some cases, local civilians were offering drink and some food, but the exuberance and generosity of a few days ago were gone. Those who had decided to remain in their homes knew they would have to hoard all they could. There was little to spare for a retreating, defeated ally, whose contribution to the war effort was, at best, questionable.

Looking around them they could see the variety of trucks that the Army had pressed into use, and the range of company logos painted on the sides. Houses of Parliament Sauce, Waring and Gillow Removals and Storage, Harrods and many more. This was the result of a far sighted policy, established by the War Office in 1912. It had been determined that the supply of the army as far forward as divisional rear boundaries would be done most efficiently by wheeled vehicles. However, further forward it was likely that some form of off-road capability would be necessary, which the automobile did not possess. Consequently, transport at this level was to be by horse-drawn carts. There would be exchange points in the rear of the divisional area where supplies could be cross-loaded between the different means of transport for onward delivery.

The Thornycroft J Type lorry had been designed for the War Office to fill the role of the load carrying vehicle between the logistic bases, railheads and ports to the fighting formations. With its four cylinder side valve engine generating forty horsepower, it had a speed of fourteen and a half miles per hour. Its canvas driver and passenger doors and solid rubber wheels did not offer a comfortable ride, but its wooden planked cargo deck carried a worthwhile load. The War Office had, however, determined that it would not require these vehicles in peace, and arrangements had been made with firms across the country that they would purchase them for their own use. The difference between the military specification and that required for normal commercial business was paid by the Army, on the condition that in time of war the firms concerned would turn the vehicles, instantly, over to the military authorities. Thus had over eight hundred vehicles been available well within mobilisation time to re-supply the army in the field;

albeit with a wide range of different, and singularly unmilitary, markings.

Thomas, being unaware of the good sense behind the policy which had led to the panoply of colour before him, simply assumed it to be the result of yet another cock up in an army which was a by word for cock ups, and which couldn't even organise a bit 'o breakfast or, looking at the clock above the station entrance, lunch for that matter.

"Back in a minute."

Joseph Floyd looked up from his rifle, the bolt in his lap as he cleaned and oiled the weapon. He'd suffered a considerable shock with the loss of Fred Smith and the sudden responsibility it placed upon his shoulders. It was not something he welcomed particularly, but the time he had spent in the Army had not been for nothing, and something deep inside was motivating him to set an example, to maintain his standards, to make an effort. He watched John Hayes walking away towards the railway bridge, purposefully, as if he were looking for something, or had found something.

"Don' be long, mind," he called out. "Dunno when we're movin'." There was no answer. The lance corporal looked along the line of his section, and saw them all fast asleep. As he drove the bolt home and fitted the magazine with its ten rounds into the magazine housing his own eyelids were drooping, leaden with tiredness. He did not see the red and white chequered headscarf among the crowd of refugees near the southern edge of the bridge.

The march south commenced again, about two hours later. By now it was a stiflingly hot August day and the rough serge of their uniforms was doing little to help their morale. Had there been a slight breeze the movement of air through clothing soaked with sweat might at least have had a cooling effect. As it was, the air was still and the sweat ran into every nook and cranny in irritating rivulets. Even the most hardened felt the pain of sore feet, sore backs, sore crotches; and hunger together with a general shortage of water combined with the other physical discomforts to produce sore tempers. Paul Cooper's had been especially sore when he had asked Joseph Floyd the whereabouts of John Hayes and had been rewarded with a blank, uncomprehending look. In fairness to Floyd, he had just woken from a very deep sleep and had been trying very hard to remember when he had last seen Hayes. However, Cooper was in no mood to wait, and having torn the unfortunate lance corporal off a strip he marched away to report to Matthew Jenkins that the platoon was complete less one man who could not be found.

Edward von Gleichen viewed his brigade with some pride as it assembled and began to move off. They had done well. Mercifully spared some of the more vicious and intense fighting around Le Cateau, they had held together as a formation and were generally in as good an order as one could expect given the circumstances. They had some twelve to fourteen miles to march to their destination for that evening, on the south bank of a river, rather unprepossessingly called the Somme.

"Will they stay or go?" He referred to the townspeople as he turned to St André. "I mean, there are so many. If they all take to the road we shall get nowhere, they will simply flood us off."

"Who can say, mon General?" The questioning note in his voice as he shrugged his shoulders; that peculiarly Gallic expression which can mean so many different things. "They 'ear the stories of the violence against the civilian population and they are afraid. What we are told 'appened in Belgium is 'orreeble, truly 'orreeble. But then, as you said yesterday, if they leave they lose everything. Some will stay, some will go. Eet is not a good answer, but I 'ave no other to give you; but you knew that, n'est ce pas?"

The brigade commander nodded, smiled a rueful smile at his friend and turned to his horse. As he mounted he wondered how true these stories of brutality were. He had no illusions about the Germans and what they might be capable of, but they were a civilised race, and, after all, there were limits.

It would be some time before the British learned of the policy of "furchtbarheit", of terrorisation, which the German high command had impressed upon its soldiery. There was to be no sympathy shown to the civilian population. They were to be ground down, and any suggestion of resistance was to be dealt with swiftly and harshly; pour encouragé les autres.

As witness, at that very moment in a small farm somewhere to the north-west, in a village with a name unpronounceable to the average soldier, a woman was being savagely beaten by a feldwebel from the artillery battery which had been billeted there. Her two granddaughters, having screamed themselves into exhaustion, were slumped, cowed with terror, in the steely grip of two German soldiers. They watched, helplessly, as the woman's head was smashed from side to side by the heavy blows, blood spraying from her shattered nose and her bruised lips, spotting the uniforms of the two soldiers who held her up in order that their senior NCO could get an unobstructed view of his target.

It had been bad enough when the Germans had arrived in the first place. Arrogant and domineering, they had simply taken what they wanted, without payment or question. The family's crime however, had been the discovery in the bedroom occupied by the two girls of two British cap badges, each with Britannia seated proudly in the centre. This had formed the justification for the interrogation which was taking place in the farm kitchen. After only a few minutes, the woman had been beyond answering, so badly smashed was her mouth. She could taste the blood in her throat, not realising that some of it was being coughed up from her lung, punctured by a rib broken by the repeated blows to her chest and abdomen.

The eldest of the two girls began to recoil as she felt the hand of the soldier holding her begin to work its way in between her thighs; felt the stench of his quickening breath as he watched the beating with a look of anticipation on his broad, flat face. Her sister was blessed with a younger captor, whose own sister was a similar age and who watched with mixed fascination and disgust as his colleague completed his assault by forcing a thick, dirt-blackened finger into the cavity between her legs and began to work it from side to side, grinning horribly as he did so. She screamed, and then gagged as she smelt once again the stench of alcohol on his breath. Suddenly, the finger was withdrawn, and she looked beyond him to the door where an officer stood.

Ignoring the two girls, he walked over to where the woman, held erect, was choking as the NCO held her chin in his hand and yelled questions, in very poor French, directly into her face.

"Keine!" The feldwebel responded to his officer's questioning look. She had not been able to tell them anything useful.

The officer shrugged, a look of acute disinterest on his face. "Also, fahren wir. Lassen Sie die Frauen los!" They were going, and the women were to be left as they were.

In the farmyard he looked around him at his battery, a feeling of mild disgust causing a tightening of his stomach. They were mostly the worse for drink, but by this stage in the war the German Army was pouring alcohol into its soldiers, partly to assuage the tiredness they all felt and partly to offset the impact that the unexpectedly high casualty rate was having. It was judged by many officers as being the only way they could keep them going. Boorish at the best of times, he found the common soldier, in drink, an unpleasant creature. He had chosen not to see what his man had been doing to that young girl in the corner of the kitchen, and had recoiled as the soldier moved to his horse, drawing a smelly finger under his nose with an appreciative leer which brought hoots of laughter from his friends.

They rode away. Behind them a barn in which hay was stored flared as they set fire to it, apples lay on the ground where barrels had been smashed and a stack of sugar beet lay spread about the place where their horses had eaten their fill, and trampled much of the rest. A year's work destroyed in a fit of wanton vandalism. A family wrecked in a drunken orgy of violence.

The next morning, having elicited the help of a friend from a nearby farm to bury their grandmother, and refusing any other offer of assistance or succour, two young girls headed, in tears, south and west, seeking the protection of the French Army, or their British allies; hoping to avoid the Germans en route. They had no family other than their father who had gone off to war; a war of which they were now part of the flotsam.

"Well, this is all right."

Peter Dakin pronounced himself satisfied with his part of the barn in a farm set in one corner of the small village of Eaucort, on the north bank of the Somme, just four miles east of the small town of Ham. They were settling down in their billet, having enjoyed their first decent meal in some time, and anxious to get to sleep. Joseph Floyd had returned from Matthew Jenkins' orders group to inform them that they would be on the move at three-thirty the next morning. Every moment, therefore, counted; and anyway, the sooner they were bedded down the less chance there was of someone dreaming up something for them to do.

The meal they had eaten had been a result of the far sightedness of Major General "Wully" Robertson, the BEF's Quartermaster General. A Scot who had risen from the rank of private, "oor Wully" was every inch a soldier's soldier and he knew just what men would be needing on a long withdrawal; and what commanders would need to maintain their men's morale. Predicting the likelihood of the retreat, and the route it would follow, he had dumped stocks of food and fodder beside the roads for men to pick from as they passed. Fifteen Brigade had been ordered not to go near them, as von Gleichen was concerned for discipline on the march and the effect that a disorganised scrabble for rations might have on the cohesiveness which his brigade had managed to retain. However, he had made sure that unit quartermasters extracted all they required from the dumps and that proper meals were available in billets in good time to allow his men to get some much needed sleep.

"Yep." Ted, as he agreed with his friend, was already snuggling himself down into a pile of straw, his eyelids drooping even as his head lay back against the pillow he had made from his pack. Weapons had been cleaned, boots had been removed, feet sorted as best they could, bristly faces had been shaved and standards had improved all round. As he fell asleep he heard the contented snores of Alfie James, sharing the same pile of straw, and with a last vision of red hair and the fragrance of cigarette smoke on the breath teasing his senses he plummeted into the depths of a deep and dreamless sleep.

"Where do you think he's gone?" Matthew Jenkins was sharing a last few moments with Paul Cooper before they too turned in for the night. They were discussing the disappearance of Hayes, an event as yet unreported since Matthew had entertained all day the thought that he had become inadvertently detached and would join them in due course.

"I don't know." Cooper's voice told its own story. He might not know, but, whatever it was Hayes, was once more ploughing his own furrow, regardless of the consequences.

"You're suspicious? Do you think he's gone for good?"

"Deserted you mean? Well, he's done it before, as you know; except that was just absence without leave, and for a woman who probably wasn't worth it anyway. This is war, and a few hours, or days, adrift is a lot more serious. With a court martial and a firing squad at the end of it a man'd have t' think very carefully before he took 'imself off. With a bit of luck he's fallen asleep somewhere and he'll catch us up in good time."

"I hope you're right." Matthew's voice held a note of uncertainty.

"You don't seem sure?" The questioning note in Cooper's voice.

"Like I am about Preece you mean?" The officer smiled. "I know we don't agree there, but I am pretty certain that

Preece is not your thief. There's no record of him having been anything but honest since his time in the Army, and we know of nothing before that. I know he's been a problem, but never a dishonest one; and if anything our present circumstances strengthen a man's integrity rather than weaken it. No, I think we shall have to look elsewhere for our thief; but Hayes.........well Hayes is a different story. I've been growing progressively more uncomfortable with him since we got to France." A pause. "Ah well, we'll see. Time for bed I think. See you in the morning. Goodnight Sar'nt Cooper."

Watching his platoon commander head for his billet Cooper wondered briefly about Preece. If it wasn't him, then who was it? And as for Hayes, they could do little more than wait for him to turn up. As he turned towards his own resting place he stopped briefly, looking to the north, towards the enemy, and wondered what tomorrow might bring.

His question was soon answered: more of the same. The weather was stiflingly hot, the roads were long and seemingly unending, the halts were frequent, and, after a time, irritating; and still they were moving away from an enemy who had not had the beating of them. It was at one of these halts that they saw their commander-in-chief. Field Marshall French, his mind still fixed on the need to continue the retreat, had decided to see for himself the state his army was in.

"Stand up!" Paul Cooper had seen the panoply of khaki, red, gold braid and polished Sam Browne belts heading his way and, without waiting to find out what it comprised, he did the sensible thing and stood his platoon to attention. Mercifully, they had simply halted by the roadside for what had been planned as a five minute halt. Consequently, they were in reasonable order and still had on their webbing.

"Stand them at ease, please sergeant." The Field Marshal's well modulated voice held a note of kindness. He was a dignified man, his round face and wide set eyes offering to his soldiers a feeling of confidence which belied the innermost feelings of the man himself.

"Not a bad bloke, really." Alfie James offered his view to those around him as they continued the march southward.

"Seemed alright to me." Peter Dakin confirmed his friend's impression. "Nice what 'e said about us at Lee Catow, and about 'ow well old Smiff-Doreen'd done."

"Didn't answer the question, though, did 'e?" Alfred Arbuckle's voice came from behind above the sound of marching feet.

"Wa's that then?" A note of hostility in Alfie's voice as his opinion was challenged.

"Didn't tell us why we's goin' this way an' the Germans is t'other way." Alfred might be slow of speech, but he was not slow on the uptake. The Field Marshall had indeed, diplomatically and skilfully, avoided the question of the retreat and his own motives for it. Thomas, however, was not a diplomat; and he knew when bullshit was about the place; and it had been; and it had not gone unnoticed. Nonetheless, they felt more cheerful as a result of the encounter, buoyed by the knowledge that they had, as the Field Marshall told them, saved the left flank of Lanrezac's Fifth French Army by dint of their efforts at Le Cateau.

That afternoon they marched into Noyon, where GHQ had until recently been billeted. The distinctive twin spires of the cathedral, grey with their black slate roofs looking so much like priestly caps perched upon clerical heads, had been their guide as they came down off the plateau from Guiscard. Before them lay the wide flat plain of the valley of the River Oise, the woods through which it ran offering a final objective towards which they moved with the prospect not only of billets for the night, but also of a day's rest. Smith-Dorrien now knew for certain that his ploy had worked. The German pursuit away to the south-west had allowed him to break completely clean. He could now take a much needed day for rest and recuperation of his battered corps. Moving east of Noyon by about a mile, they crossed the Canal Lateral de l'Oise and then the river itself by means of the two distinctive concrete arched bridges just south of Morlincourt before moving on through Varesnes to their billets in the small village of Pointoise, a short distance south of the river.

"Nice 'ere, innit?" Ned Preece voiced the view of them all. There had been, as they crossed the river, a perceptible change in the countryside and the architecture. Gone were the wide open fields, vast expanses of crops and scattered stands of trees. Here was much closer country, woods predominating. Fields were bordered by hedgerows, birds fluttered and sang in the branches, wind rustled the leaves and the sunlight, dappled by the intervening foliage, scattered around the cooling shade offered by Birch, Larch and Elm. Gone, also, was the red brick that had dominated further north. Houses were now built from a grey stone, so much like that to be found in the villages around Salisbury Plain and to its west that for a moment it was almost possible to believe that they were on one of the exercises that the battalion had undertaken in the centre of southern England.

"Right, listen in!" Joe Floyd's voice broke into their thoughts. "We shall be 'ere for a few days. Mr Jenkins wants us t' get a good night's sleep ternight and to spend tomorrer sortin' our kit so we can be ready to move quickly if we 'ave to. Weapons are top priority. 'E will inspect all rifles tomorrow mornin' at eight o'clock. 'E's not worried too much about cleanliness, 'e reckons we're doin' alright with that, but 'e wants to make sure they work prop'ly an' that they 'aven't been damaged or summat. Evenin' meal is at six.........." He carried on with the rest of his orders. They listened in patient silence, aware that somehow the loss of Fred Smith had brought out something in his erstwhile deputy which meant he might not do a half bad job, given a decent chance.

That night, after their meal and in the fading light of evening, they sat quietly preparing their rifles for the inspection that would come in the morning and would, they had no doubt, be rigorous in the extreme. Ted looked over to where Colin Baxter sat beneath a tree. He could not remember ever having seen him write a letter in all the time they had been together, but just after supper he had responded to his friend's request and had passed over paper and an envelope from his own meagre stock. Colin had turned his face away, unable to respond to the questioning look in Ted's eyes, and had moved off in silence to be by himself.

The next morning, after a breakfast of bacon, bread and jam, washed down with tea, they were formed up awaiting the check of their rifles.

"Form yourselves into sections, dismantle your rifles and lay them out for inspection. The battalion armourer is with the company for the next hour, and he will do what he can to put right any damage." They looked at the small, wiry man standing behind Paul Cooper, the shield of the Board of Ordnance adorning his forage cap, with the three cannon in the centre of the shield surmounted by three cannon balls. Rumour abounded in the Army that the balls on the badge were too big for the cannon beneath them, and this was the basis of many a rude remark about the inability of the Army in general, and the Army Ordnance Corps in particular, to get anything right.

The general businesslike air which could be found among the highly professional soldiers who were gradually sorting themselves out, without any bidding, was not one which manifested itself further up the chain of command. Among the French there was bickering and dispute as Joffre attempted to get the uncooperative Lanrezac to stand and fight with his Fifth Army. Among the British there was bickering and dispute as Haig attempted to persuade French that he should assist Lanrezac in his enforced endeavour. French, obsessed by the desire to retreat, and believing Haig's Corps to be as badly mauled as Smith-Dorrien's, refused. In fact, Haig had fought only three small rearguard actions and had sustained only one thousand six hundred and thirty six casualties; a fact of which French should have been acutely aware.

So Thomas sat in the sunshine, whilst the political battles roared above his head, and got on with the business of basic, honest soldiering.

"Sorry, can't fix that. You'll 'ave to wait until I can get a spare sight, or replace the rifle." The Armourer pronounced his view on Jack Waters' rifle. The rear sight had been damaged at some stage, and the sighting cursor could not sight the rifle beyond two hundred yards. "Ye'll just 'ave to aim off for the longer ranges, or 'old yer fire 'till yer see the whites of their eyes."

"Come on, staff," the persistent whining note always present in Waters' voice. "Surely yer can do sumfin'?"

"Sorry, don' carry spares fer sumthin' like that, and we 'ave t' wait 'till we get back to a base before we can fix it. 'S'not the end of the world. You can work round it." There was no hint in his voice of any sympathy for Waters' predicament. It was the system, and there was bugger all the artificer staff sergeant could do about it.

Resupply of an army in the forward areas was a task carried out by the Army Service Corps. Educated at Sandhurst, along with the infantry and cavalry, officers of the Army Service Corps felt themselves a cut above the rest of the support structure then in place to sustain an army in the field, whose officers tended to be drawn from a less esoteric background; "from trade" as more than one cynic was heard to remark. The role of their corps was the delivery forward and the distribution of ammunition, food and fodder. The replacement of stores, weapons, clothing and equipment, together with any necessary repairs, was a task undertaken by the Army Ordnance Department and Corps, collectively referred to as Army Ordnance Services; and it was only done when a formation was withdrawn from the line into a rear area, well away from the enemy. The prospect of a conflict such as they were presently embarked upon, with an enemy so overwhelming that such reconstitution was impossible, had been foreseen only by a few; almost all of them Ordnance officers, and their protests had gone unheeded. Consequently, there was no system in place of forward replenishment of spares and equipment, or of forward repair; and the replenishment system that did exist, such as it was, had never been practised on peacetime exercises.

Not that it would have mattered, for even as the platoon sat in the peace and calm of a small orchard, chewing on freshly baked bread with a mid morning brew of tea, the entire logistic support of the BEF was in turmoil. Originally based on Le Havre, Rouen and Boulogne, an additional, forward, base depot had been established at Amiens, directly west of St Quentin by just over thirty miles. Not a helpful decision; it was too far to the rear in the event of an advance, much too close to the front in the event of a withdrawal, and had swiftly been threatened by the German advance. With von Kluck heading generally south-west, and the BEF moving a little east of south, something needed to be done to reposition the depots.

Consequently, three days earlier, on the twenty-seventh of August, the stocks in Amiens had been moved to Rouen, and the contents of Boulogne by sea to Le Havre on the SS Inventor. By the twenty-ninth of August the gravity of the situation had meant the original line of communication needed to be abandoned and moved to a fresh line based on Nantes and St Nazaire, with Le Mans as the headquarters of the Inspector General of Communications. At Rouen the contents of an ammunition park that had just landed, some hospital equipment and nine hundred tons of stores was to be shipped down the river Loire that night and an advanced depot was opened at Le Mans.

There was a rush to evacuate Le Havre, but the outload was not configured to suit the requirements of the operational plan. This was not a problem caused by Army Ordnance Services, but by the base commandant who was not an Ordnance officer since it was common practice at the time not to entrust a member of the Army Ordnance Department with command. The effect was to be significant. When the BEF began to scream, a few days hence, for machine guns to replace losses sustained on the retreat they would find most of them to be at sea. Just a few were saved, to go by rail to Le Mans, but they would not be enough.

Meanwhile, St Nazaire and Nantes were not proving to be good locations for Ordnance Depots. The dispersed sites and the fact that ships from England were diverted in no particular order, and were mixed with stores coming down from Le Havre and Boulogne, caused confusion. Uniforms, caps, spare parts, bales of horse rugs, blankets and ammunition, much of it in broken packages, were mixed with forage, medical, veterinary and other stores. Chaos reigned, and yet soon the BEF would need all the support it could get.

"I thought 'e said we'd be 'ere a couple o' days!" Eyes were raised to the heavens. The patience of the section with Waters and his moaning was wearing very thin. 'Avin' a grouse were one thing, but this bleeder were carryin' it a bit too bloody far.

"Well, we're bloody not!" Ned Preece was angry and he let it show. Ted and Alfie looked concerned as their friend's ill humour, which they had thought to be improving, returned once more. They were not to know they were the cause of it.

"Wassamatter, Ned. C'mon, you can tell us, we're yer mates fer Gawd's sake."

"Nuffink," had been the terse response.

Silence returned as they marched at a steady pace across the high open plateaux, descended down steep little roads into densely wooded valleys and then shortened their pace as they leant into the hill to climb the other side. Wherever possible they timed halts for the valley bottoms, offering the opportunity for shade from the persistent and scorching sun and a chance to replenish water from the clear bubbling streams and sedately flowing rivers. Behind them Fergusson's sappers blew the bridges over the Oise and the canal.

Ted looked up at the imposing Chateau in the small village of Pierrepont, its grey towers with their black slate roofs reaching up into the sky from its position on the rocky outcrop above the market place, dominating the road into and out of the village. He was standing beside the road with Alfie, having been detailed off to direct traffic and warn approaching lorries and ambulances that there were troops stopped beside the road.

"Quite somethin' that, eh?"

"Yep." His friend responded. "Nice place this. Be nice to come somewhere like this for a spot o' leave when all this is over. I mean, 's'not difficult to get over 'ere, an' if we save our money......well, could be a bit of all right......couldn't it?"

"Aye, could be." He wondered if Alfie really meant it. The way this war was goin' 'olidays was the last thing 'e was thinkin' of. He changed the subject. "Oo d'ye think it is then?" He returned to the subject of their conversation the night before, not knowing it had been overheard by a distressed Ned Preece. It had not required the brain of an archbishop to determine that there was a thief about. Too much had gone missing. It was just small things, but to be without something like a torch, or a sewing kit, created so much frustration and anger given the limited comfort they had that the impact was out of all proportion to the loss.

"Dunno, but it can't be anyone in the section. Anyone else in the platoon lose anythin'?"

They continued discussing the problem until they were ordered back into column to resume the march. They were at a loss, but they knew something wasn't right. They had nothing upon which they could base any action, and, as Ted so rightly pointed out, everyone was losing bits of kit left right and centre. There was, after all, a war on.

Meanwhile, von Kluck, away to their north, was deliberating on an equally vexed problem. He no longer had sufficient manpower to follow the edict of the original Schlieffen Plan. His casualties and the drawing off of formations by the Kaiser to undertake other tasks had so depleted his ranks that he was having to contemplate alternatives. He was under the illusion that the BEF had ceased to exist, for he had seen nothing of it now for two days. He believed, therefore, that the left flank of Lanrezac's Fifth Army was exposed, and that the Germans could make their swing to the left early, passing to the north of Paris rather than enveloping the city. They would still be taking the main French forces, along the German border, in the rear, and victory would still be theirs.

He knew nothing of the true position of the BEF, nor did he know of Joffre's decision to form the Sixth French Army, based on the Paris garrison reinforced by other formations from the east of France. He did not, therefore, know of the significant force, British and French, which lay to the north and east of Paris and to which he was about to expose the right flank of his army as it swung to the east. If some of his earlier decisions had not actually cost Germany the war, this one was about to.

Thomas continued his march southward. His mood was bloody, and getting bloodier by the hour. Conditions were awful, with the heat and the dust affecting everything. And all the while there was no sign of the enemy, and nobody to explain why they were moving at such a rate in the wrong direction. For four days the pattern was the same. Their only respite was the halts on the march and some sleep on their overnight stops. This was not, however, always of the best. Bivouacs were often in fields, and in Attichy they slept in the streets, on the pavement and in gardens. On, on south; across the Aisne and on down to the Marne.

Meanwhile, Kitchener, concerned by the reports he had been receiving from French, travelled to France and met the BEF Commander in the British Embassy in Paris. The pattern of the meeting remains unknown, but the result was a very angry Field Marshall French. He was angered by the fact that Kitchener had worn field marshall's uniform, despite the fact that he was quite entitled so to do; French felt he was making a quite unnecessary gesture in his position as minister for war. He was also angered by his orders: that he was not to consider leaving France and that he was to conform closely with Joffre. Regrettably, he was also told that he was not to expose his flanks, and he was to follow this edict to the letter, to the great frustration of his allies and his subordinates.

On the afternoon of Thursday the third of September 1914, just a month after mobilisation, the BEF crossed the Marne east of Paris. Passing over the bridge at Isles de la Villenoy, Fifth Division moved south-east as, once more, Fergusson's sappers blew the bridges behind the division. As they did so, air reconnaissance confirmed the start of von Kluck's eastward move and the fact that the right flank of his army was exposed and ripe for assault; Joffre had decided to replace Lanrezac with the much more effective, and co-operative, General Franchet; French continued to be defeatist and contemplated a retreat yet further to the south; and Thomas was becoming more bloody minded than ever, with no one, it seemed, able or willing to tell him what was going on.

The BEF had been mobilised for thirty-one days, at war for thirteen days, withdrawing for eleven days, had marched over two hundred miles and sustained something like fifteen thousand casualties, including those missing. Now the scene was being set for a change, and if the high command of the British Army entertained doubts about whither next, there was no doubt at all in the minds of the common soldiery. It was, they opined, to be hoped that the brass didn't blow all the soddin' bridges over the Marne or they might 'ave t' get their soddin' feet wet goin' back over the bleedin' river to get at the buggers.

Chapter 9

Battle on the Marne

It was the fourth of September 1914 when von Moltke finally abandoned the Schlieffen Plan and decided to concentrate the whole of the German effort in the east along the French border and around Verdun. The two armies in the west, those of von Kluck and Blülow, were to face west and protect the flank. It was a ridiculous order, given by a man who was out of touch with events; and, one might almost say, with reality. Von Kluck, the most westerly of von Moltke's army commanders, simply ignored the instruction and carried on in his headlong pursuit of the French in a south-easterly direction, leaving Paris away to his right, to his south-west, buttressing his own open right flank and ignoring Blülow to his left.

Among the Allies the great men were also heavily involved in plans that would affect the armies they commanded over the next few days and, some would later argue, the next few years. The garrison commander in Paris knew he faced an open and vulnerable German flank and sought the BEF's assistance in attacking both the flank and the German rear; thereby protecting Paris. He met prevarication and delay at GHQ, largely because Field Marshall French was out visiting the troops and no one would take a decision. Franchet, Lanrezac's replacement, approached General Wilson seeking his support for an attack by the Fifth French Army. He was under pressure from Joffre to return his army to the fray as an effective instrument of war, and he needed the British to support him if he was to be successful. He had a plan, which included the BEF, for a battle on the Marne on the sixth of September; just two days away.

Having been told on his return by his wholly inadequate Chief of Staff, Lieutenant General Sir Archibald Murray, of the visit of the Paris Garrison Commander, and by his sub-Chief of Staff, Major General Wilson, of the plea from Franchet, Field Marshall French's diary entry for that evening said it all:

> *"I have ordered the British Forces to retire some 12 miles towards Melun tonight and have given no decided answer to the Generals."*

This southward move would result in the exposure of the flanks of the Fifth French Army on his right, and the newly formed Sixth Army on his left. It would not affect the Germans in any way whatsoever: von Kluck didn't even know the BEF still existed; neither did he have any idea that the French were planning an assault from the left of their line against his own right.

Had Thomas known of his CinC's diary entry he would have been deeply ashamed. As it was he wearily prepared to hoist himself to his feet and carry on as ordered, moving south. He had not rested since that day on the Oise and he was completely exhausted.

"Sir." Paul Cooper addressed his platoon commander. "What shall I do with this?"

That day had seen the arrival of the first mail from home, and the platoon had gained a sprinkling of letters and parcels. Matthew had just opened a letter from his mother, and was anticipating a read of the Times she had sent him, when Paul Cooper approached.

"It's a letter to Fred.....to Corporal Smith; it's from Aggie." He responded to his officer's questioning look.

Matthew simply did not want to make a decision. He was tired, fed up with the constant withdrawal and had just found something to lift his spirits in the form of a letter from home. He would rather Sergeant Cooper simply went away.

"I'm sure there is a rule somewhere to cover things like that. Send it back to battalion HQ!" His answer was sharp, and he saw the frosty look of formality flash across Cooper's face.

"Very well, sir!" The emphasis on the last word. The sergeant turned on his heel and marched away. Matthew instantly regretted the tenor of his response, but it was too late; the moment had passed into history, and there would now be a tension between them for a while that he would not relish. He turned back to his letter, tried to forget what had happened, and as he did so he caught a flash in his mind's eye of a mangled foot and could smell again in his nostrils the odour of the ambulance. He shuddered.

"I am afraid that's all I can tell you. We continue to the south, and whither then I know not." Edward von Gleichen looked at the faces of the officers gathered around him and sipped at a glass of claret as he awaited any reaction. The commanding officers of his four infantry battalions, their faces a mixture of resigned disappointment and tiredness, stared back at him, shifting uncomfortably in their seats as they sought to assuage the ache in what seemed to be every bone in their bodies.

"Well then, I am afraid there is one more thing I must mention. It is, I fear, an unpleasant matter, but we appear to be beset by something of a plague of looting and irregularity. It is something that has been drawn to the attention of the CinC by the corps commander, and reportedly the Fifth Division is the worst offender."

Glancing at each other, the commanding officers, together with the brigade staff, awaited what they knew must come.

"The corps commander's view, shared by the divisional commander, is that the shortage of officers is to blame. I reserve my judgement, but I am afraid whatever the cause it is not something I can accept in the Fifteenth Brigade. Would you all, therefore, please look to your own stewardship, and if you do find any perpetrators, especially of looting or other crimes against the civilian population, put a stop to it; at once. Proper standards must be maintained or we deteriorate to a rabble."

Despite the languid, apparently insouciant, manner adopted by von Gleichen they all knew they had just received a blistering rocket. Something would have to be done.

The brigade commander sat back in his chair, took another sip of his wine and invited his brigade major to give the orders for the move that would see them marching overnight to Gagny.

The battalion marched through the silence of the night, a silence broken by the steady tramp of boots in unison on the road. Typically for that time of the year, there was a coolness which kept men fresh on the march and made the galling process under way somehow more acceptable. From time to time they heard a Tawny Owl off in the distance, its fluttering, mournful call seeming to echo off the moon as it hung low in the sky.

"Good morning, sah."

Matthew had known someone was behind him, catching him slowly. He resented the intrusion. His platoon was leading the battalion and he was relishing the opportunity to be just a little way in front, stretching his legs and consumed with his own thoughts. If he had hoped for any clarity of vision he was disappointed. The mix of emotions, thoughts and pictures running through his head were anything but orderly: South Africa, the letter from home, Fred Smith's foot, the deaths of his men, the wounding of others, the sights he had witnessed, the fear he had felt, and the exhilaration.

"RSM?" The questioning note in his voice as he saw with surprise who it was had caught him up.

"RSM, what can I do for you?" Junior officers, even those as mature as Matthew, walked in awe of the Regimental Sergeant Major, the only warrant officer in the battalion; a man respected by all, and feared by many. Matthew wondered to what purpose he had been accorded the honour, dubious though it might be, of sharing the RSM's company.

"Just felt like stretching the legs a bit. Doesn't do me any harm, and they..." he inclined his head to the rear "..need to see I can still set the pace." He smiled beneath his perfectly trimmed moustache, his teeth showing off-white in the moonlight. "Lovely night for it, isn't it sah."

Not being quite certain what "it" was, Matthew could not but agree with him. They marched on together for several minutes, exchanging polite conversation. Eventually, the RSM came to what Matthew realised must be the point.

"I'm just wondering how you're managing to look after your kit, and administer yourself when you have so much else to do. I mean, your officer commanding places additional burdens on you, and it can't be easy."

So that was it. The question of a batman. He could not help it, the thought of a rifleman being made to cook and clean and wait on him was an anathema. Indeed, it struck at the very heart of what he, as a young officer in South Africa, had felt was wrong with the Army.

"RSM, I really don't think....."

The warrant officer interrupted, his voice gentle, but firm.

"Sir, I know how you feel, and why you feel it; but look at it from the men's point of view. They know you're knackered, much more so than they, and a man can only do so much. You owe it to them to have someone to help you; they know that and they also know that their lives could depend on you not making the wrong decisions because you can't give all your attention to your main task: commanding your platoon."

"Yes, but...." Matthew began to respond, albeit half heartedly.

"Look, sir, you had Baxter helping you out at Le Cateau, and again when we stopped on the Oise; and both he and Ludgrove were digging your kit out yesterday when you slept. It's not demeaning, sir, really it isn't. They know you need someone, and so do you if you're honest with yourself."

"Yes, well I suppose....."

"Good!" The RSM seized on the chink which Matthew had exposed in his position and resumed the more formal, stern manner he used in public. "I'll speak to your platoon sergeant and see that he organises the right man."

He was about to turn away when Matthew's voice drew him back.

"No,.....no RSM. I will take your advice and regularise the position. However, I will make the choice......please." The last word was less of a plea and more a firm statement that he was not to be trifled with.

The RSM smiled. "As you wish, sir," and slowed his pace to let the column catch him up, leaving Matthew to his solitary position. He paused to speak to Sergeant Cooper before rejoining the battalion HQ in the centre of the column. The company commander smiled an acknowledgement as the warrant officer passed him.

As Matthew made his decision, out in front of his platoon, there was another decision being made not far away. Just at that very moment, three o'clock in the morning, Joffre sent a copy of his Order Number Six to Field Marshall French. It was the order for the Battle of the Marne, and the BEF had a major role in it. French's decision was not positive; all he promised was further consideration of Joffre's proposals. As Joffre received this discouraging news, at about seven-thirty in the morning, the Ninth were entering Gagny, and the bivouacs allocated to them. They brewed their tea and contemplated a morning cleaning rifles and sleeping. Joffre sipped his coffee and contemplated a meeting with the British CinC.

"I'm sorry, sir. You really cannot be serious!" Paul Cooper had taken his platoon commander to one side, to where he hoped the rest of the platoon could not see them and was making his views known in no uncertain fashion.

"But I am.......quite serious."

"Sir, I really cannot allow you to do this. I mean, for Heaven's sake, it really could not be a worse......"

Matthew smiled. He knew the man only had his best interests at heart, and like the rest of them was trying to do a decent job despite being absolutely exhausted. He determined not to prolong the agony. A change of subject was required.

"Did I see you get a letter from Mrs Cooper?" He broke into the sergeant's frustrated plea, knowing that mention of his wife would draw him back down to earth.

Matthew had met her two evenings before they left Belfast. Paul had simply arranged for her to be at the front of their married quarter as the two men had passed nearby; quite by chance of course. The pride had been evident in his voice as he introduced them. Clearly, he had told her all about their time together in South Africa; equally clearly he was besotted by her, and it was no surprise. Jane Cooper was a stunningly pretty woman of about twenty-three. Long, dark hair framed a face that no man could have passed without looking twice. Wide, deep blue eyes contrasted with the colour of her hair and captured the attention whilst her faintly quizzical smile gave a hint of flirtatious mischief which made her irresistible. Matthew had found himself shaking her hand for rather longer than due propriety allowed; but she was very, very pretty.

As he had expected, his sergeant calmed at once. "Yes...yes, I did. Yes, she's well, and asked me to pass you her best wishes. I'd have done it earlier, but......"

But,.... things had not been quite right between the officer and his sergeant for a couple of days, and they both knew it. Matthew let him of the hook, interrupting him as he faltered with what he was trying to say:

"But things haven't been easy; is that what you were trying to say?"

Cooper smiled, acknowledging the help.

"Yes, I suppose you could say that, sir." He continued talking for several more minutes, telling him about his wife and what she had written. Matthew let him monopolise their meeting until he judged the moment right to return to the original topic of conversation.

"Will you tell him, or shall I?"

Cooper looked at his officer. He clearly was not going to change his mind, and the RSM had made his views very clear to the sergeant. "I'll tell 'im, sir. Leave it to me. He's asleep now; I'll let 'im know when he wakes up; if that's all right with you?"

"Perfectly, thank you!"

At two o'clock in the afternoon of Saturday the fifth of September the battalion, less those on essential duties, was sleeping the deep, coma-like sleep that comes with complete exhaustion. As he had wound his way, at about nine in the morning, to his billet the company commander had been heard to remark that he would not have believed it possible for men to be so tired or so hungry and yet still have the will to live.

Not very far away from where the Norfolks were taking their well-earned rest another man who had slept little these past few days was on a mission of vital national importance. Tired of the indecision emanating from the British GHQ, and of the failure of his senior staff to pin down the elusive Field Marshall French, General Joffre had taken the trouble to find out exactly when his English colleague would be present, and at two p.m. precisely he entered French's headquarters.

There is no written transcript of what took place, but those who witnessed the event record the quiet passion with which Joffre spoke, revealing an emotion of which he had not previously been thought capable. He successfully reduced the British field marshall to tears, convincing him that the BEF's participation was necessary for the survival of France and won from him a promise that he would move his troops into position on the sixth, on the proviso that his exhausted army could rest for the whole of the fifth.

Joffre returned to his headquarters, a much happier man. As he did so, it is unlikely that he noticed the rich smell of corned beef stew emanating from British encampments, for the general was a man in love with his food; and what Thomas ate routinely was not something the

Frenchman would have described as such. However, the smell wafting through the orchard beside the farm in which the company was asleep soon had men stirring from their beds. As the movement turned into a bustle, with more and more soldiers coming awake and setting about their personal administration, there was a general air of purpose about the place.

"The evening meal will be at four-thirty!" Throughout the unit's lines NCOs spread the word. "And there will be mail from England at the same time." Grins of expectation all round.

Matthew walked round eating an apple given to him by the farmer, watching his men sort out their equipment and, as Cooper would have said, their bodies. Arbuckle stood beside a bucket he had filled with water from a pump just outside the farm. Stripped to the waist, his huge torso, white for want of the sun, showed the innate strength of the man. As Matthew watched, he lifted the bucket and doused its contents over his head. He saw Ludgrove and James laughing as they watched him, imitating a shiver as they imagined the cold water running all over the massive frame. Preece was sitting off to one side, still a loner despite attempts by the regulars in the platoon to bring him into the fold. Matthew wondered what damage Cooper might have done to him, and hoped it was retrievable.

His thoughts were distracted by the sound of Lance Corporal Floyd calling them together. He had been pleased with the way Floyd had taken on his new responsibilities, and, whilst Fred Smith was a hard act to follow, the lance corporal was making a decent fist of it. Certainly, his soldiers were listening to him, and without any obvious grudge.

He had a hand full of mail. Matthew looked at his watch. Only four o'clock. "Must have arrived early," he muttered to himself. "Good of him to go and get it." He knew how important it was for them to get mail promptly and, it was to be hoped, regularly. The trick was to spot those who never received anything and to make sure it did not get under their skin. Baxter might well prove to be a case in point.

Ned Preece looked up as Floyd approached. He had not responded to the Lance Corporal's call for he had seen the letters in his hand and had not expected anything.

"One for you, Ned." Floyd smiled down at him. Much of the man's lewdness seemed to have vanished over the past few days, or maybe they were all so bloody knackered no one either noticed, or cared.

The look on Ned's face was one of suspicion, tinged with expectation. He reached up from where he sat, his back against a tree, and took the envelope. It was made of cheap paper, and whatever was in it was not unduly thick. He smiled, his eyes flickering away from direct contact with Floyd's face as he self consciously looked away into the middle distance. "Fanks," a pause. "Fanks very much."

Floyd turned as if to leave, and then stopped as he remembered. "Oh yes, the platoon sergeant wants t' see yer afore the evenin' meal. Its ten past now, so you'd better look sharp about it." He carried on walking away, the last few words having been thrown over his shoulder, and therefore did not see the look of fear that crossed Ned Preece's pimply, slightly grubby and, frankly, unattractive face.

His mind was in turmoil. He did not know what to do, and he had no idea where, or to whom, he could turn. He considered running, then and there. He had no thought of where he might go, but there had to be somewhere that would offer him an escape. He knew what the price might be, he had heard people talking about Hayes and his possible fate if they ever found him. Anything, however, would be preferable to the certainty of what Cooper would see done to him if he ever got his way. In fact, he could not understand for the life of him why Cooper had not already done as he had promised he would on that dreadful morning in the factory. But the choice, if indeed choices there were in the tangled mess that was then passing for his brain, was removed by the sound of a voice; a voice he knew only too well.

"Private Preece, c'mere!"

He turned his head, and saw his bête noir standing just a few yards away. Swiftly stuffing the envelope he had just received into his jacket pocket he scrambled to his feet and, wondering if he might ever get the chance to see what was inside it, approached the sergeant. Standing to attention a few feet in front of him he awaited the worst.

"Private Preece!" A pause for effect. "Private Preece, you will no doubt be aware that Mr Jenkins is entitled to have a batman." Yet another pause, perhaps to see whether or not Ned might be foolish enough to think he had been asked to venture an opinion; but he had been around too long to fall into that trap. However, this encounter with Cooper was not following the pattern he had expected, and the trepidation was gradually beginning to dissipate. He swallowed, and tried to lubricate his dry mouth with saliva.

"For reasons which Mr Jenkins has chosen not to share with me he has decided that he wishes you to undertake the position." It was perfectly clear that Cooper did not approve. Ned's mind was racing. Surely to God they'd discussed him, and surely, therefore, he, Ned Preece, was the last one the officer would choose as his batman. But here it was, the offer of a position of trust, and of something that lifted him out of the routine dross associated with being a private soldier in one of His Majesty's Regiments of the Line. He knew he would have to wait until Cooper had finished, but his mind was already made up; he would take it.

With Ned's mind in something of a turmoil most of what Cooper subsequently said was lost, so much so that he actually missed the final part of the Sergeant's monologue.

"Well?" The Sergeant's face was getting dangerously close.

"Well what, sergeant?"

"I said do you 'ave any questions?"

"No......no, nuffink,....'onest."

"That's it then. You report to Mr Jenkins after you've eaten and he'll explain your duties as he wishes them to be carried out." Ned was about to turn away, but Cooper brought him to a stop with a jerk. "But don't you think I've finished with you Preece. I'll be watching you like a bloody hawk, an' if I get one sniff, just one bloody sniff of...."

"Private Preece, Sergeant Cooper; good evening." Matthew appeared round the corner of the barn.

"Evening sir!" The sergeant joined the private in standing to attention as their platoon commander approached.

"Has Sergeant Cooper explained to you what it is you'll be doing?" Matthew spoke directly to Ned.

"Yessir!" Very formal.

"And you are quite happy?"

"Yessir!" Just as formal. "I'll get crackin' straight after me scran....., er , me evenin' meal, sir; if that's all right with you sir?"

"Perfectly, thank you. Right, off you go, and I'll see you later." Ned was carrying his rifle in the position known as the "shoulder", vertically against his right side, tucked in under the arm and held by two fingers of his right hand through the trigger guard. He saluted, bringing his left hand across his body so that the forearm was parallel to the ground and the extended fingers of his left hand slapped against the forestock of his rifle just above his right elbow. He turned smartly to his right and moved away to where his friends were queuing for their food, straight into the ambush of their inquisitive stares.

"Ave you seen this?" Alfie James' incredulous voice emanated from behind a newspaper he had acquired, and the Lord only knew how, from the officers' mess.

"Seen what?" was the grumpy response from Joseph Floyd. He forbore to say that since the only person to have had sight of the 'paper had been Alfie it would have been impossible for any of them to see anything anyway.

"This,....the 'eadline; bleedin' cheek!" By now he had an audience and people were moving to gather round him. He laid the copy of the Daily Mail, from the thirty-first of August, on the rough plank that had served as a dining table.

"FINE RECOVERY BY THE MILITARY IN FRANCE"

The headline came as a complete shock to them. Some had seen earlier copies of the Daily Herald, and especially the edition printed on the twenty-seventh of August, where the newspaper had spoken of the heavy casualties that had been inflicted on the BEF, and the reverses they had suffered. What they were seeing now was a lie.

"Look," said Alfie, his voice shaking with anger. "It ses 'ere 'Germans fought to a standstill. British Army complete and undaunted. Our casualties only five to six thousand up to date. Reinforcements have already doubled the amount lost'. Well that's bollocks that is, must be loads more 'n that. An' wassee mean only five to six thousand." The emphasis lay heavy on the word "only".

"Some bloody good blokes gone, an' 'e ses 'only'." Ted had become as angry as his friend, and grew angrier yet as he read the rest of the article.

"I suppose," said Colin Baxter, "they are appealing to a particular kind of readership." He was about to expand when an irritated Ted Ludgrove cut across his dissertation.

"Whadderymean by that? 'Cos they're all toffs that read it that's the sort of rubbish they wanner read? Is that wot yer mean?" He was going to go on to mention "middle class idiots", but remembered that there were a number in that category of whom he thought quite highly, including Colin, and bit the words off just in time.

"I was about to say that there is an element in our society which has never experienced anything like we are experiencing, and they think its all derring do and tally ho chaps. There is also the fact that this rag is read by large sections of the female population and the editor would not wish to upset them by exposing the realities of life. After all, he is in the business of selling his newspaper and this does not always sit easily with reporting the truth. Anyway, the idiot who wrote this has almost certainly never heard a shot fired, except on a Grouse moor, and certainly hasn't been out here these past few weeks."

Peter Dakin sat a little apart from the group gathered round the newspaper, a slightly puzzled look on his face. He didn't really understand what was being said, but he noticed, for the first time, a funny sort of tone in the voices of his friends. Had he been asked to describe it he probably wouldn't have had the words, and since bitterness was not a sensation he felt, despite the rough hand of cards that life had dealt him, it wasn't something he'd ever thought about.

"Orders in ten minutes!" Paul Cooper's voice broke into their conversation. "Section commanders to me; the rest of you sort your kit and be ready to move at an hour's notice."

"Move where, I wonder?" mused Colin as the sergeant passed out of earshot. "If we keep on at this rate we shall be in Spain before the week's out."

Matthew was in a buoyant mood as he briefed his section commanders. He watched the smiles cross their faces as they realised that the orders he was giving would send them back up north; back against a German Army that they had been told was at worst halted and at best in retreat. "'Bout bloody time!" was the comment from two of them. Even the warning he gave them about looting and the dire consequences of anyone being caught indulging in such a thoroughly reprehensible activity would not serve to dampen the delight they displayed at the possibility of having another go at the Germans. As he gave that warning, Matthew chose not to notice the meaningful look flashed at him by Cooper. He and the Sergeant would have to continue to disagree.

"We're goin' back north. Ready to move at five o'clock tomorrow morning." Joe Floyd's enthusiasm came through clearly as he went into the detail of his orders to the section. Odd really, if any of them had paused to think about it; how he had changed so much with the responsibility that had been forced upon him. He passed on the warning about looting, very much as an afterthought, and thought no more of it.

At four-thirty on the morning of the sixth of September

Matthew was woken by a hand on his shoulder. He looked up to see Private Preece fully dressed and ready to go, offering a cup of steaming hot chocolate to his officer.

"Breakfast's not much, sir, but I'll 'ave it in fifteen minutes if that's all right. 'Ot water's there for shavin'." He pointed to an enamel bowl just a few feet away set in some straw.

Matthew smiled his thanks, and sipped at the chocolate. He lifted his head, a look of surprise on his face. This was not made with milk and water, but with thick creamy milk, and probably cream as well.

"How did you get.......?" But it was too late; Ned was already on his way to the cooks to collect the food.

By the time he got back, Matthew was pulling on his freshly cleaned boots. He looked around to pack the last of his kit, but that had already been done. He took the proffered bacon sandwich, with a fried egg squeezed into its centre, bit into it and then was unable to protest as Ned took his washing kit, rolled it into the canvas holdall and placed it inside his pack. Ned heard the grunt, looked up, smiled and went back to his work. As he finished off the last of his officer's administration he thought back to the letter he'd read by the light of a candle the night before. She hadn't had the best education, but then neither had he. When she wrote of love and need she couldn't really articulate the words properly, and the spelling was atrocious; even he could see that. But there was a joy in what she wrote that he had at last got in touch through the granting of his allotment; and a tenderness which shone through that affected him as he had never been affected before.

There had been two photographs. One showed a girl of about nineteen looking up into the camera and bending slightly as she held the hand of a baby just starting to try to walk; the second showed that same baby held in the arms of the same young woman, this time in close up. Her features were thin, and the nose was a little too pointed, but the smile said everything as she looked straight into her baby's eyes. Ned's own eyes had misted as he had looked for the first time at his daughter. Suddenly he had started in surprise as he heard a noise behind him. Looking up he had seen Ted and Colin patrolling as sentries, standing just a few feet away, looking down at him.

At first he had tried to hide the pictures, but Colin had dropped down on one knee beside him and had reached out with his hand, pulling Ned's own hand towards him with the pictures in it. Ned had hesitated, suspicious as always of the motives of others; but he need not have worried. Colin had looked at the pictures for a few seconds, then glanced up to at Ted, angling them so he too could see. The two of them smiled, saying nothing, and as Colin released Ned's hand he reached across and squeezed, and then patted, his shoulder. Looking into his eyes Ned had seen a look of understanding, and sorrow. As he thought about it whilst packing his officer's kit he realised that the Army, and perhaps the dreadful circumstances in which they found themselves, had brought him things he never realised he might have: among these men might be friends who actually cared. Fastening the last buckle, he hefted Matthew's pack and moved away to place it on the company cart where it would be carried.

"This forest we're going through is called the Forest of Crecy, isn't it?" By now they had been on the march for six hours or so, and had been enjoying their third halt of the day; and were very much looking forward to a decent meal when they reached their billets.

"So?" Ted's response to Colin's question was a little abrupt, due in large part to the fact that his thoughts had been by a dockyard railing in Belfast and he hadn't wished to be dragged away from them.

Unperturbed, Colin continued. "Well, if it is the English gave the French a real hiding here way back in the Middle Ages."

"Wrong Crecy." Matthew, sitting nearby, had overheard the conversation. "The Crecy in question is north of here, near Abbeville in the region of France known as Picardy. Hopefully, we shan't end up near there, or things will have gone wrong."

"See, clever sod," muttered Ted, and went back to his thoughts. Colin's face wore a slightly troubled look.

Rather than marching north, as Joe Floyd had told them, they were actually marching almost due east. Having come south of the Marne, Second Corps was moving along almost parallel to the river, heading for a crossing which would put it in position with the rest of the BEF between the two French armies, the Fifth on their right and the Sixth on their left. It would be a couple of days march before they would cross the Marne, if all went according to plan. But the countryside was attractive, the people were friendly, and, whilst the euphoria might not have matched that of their approach march to Mons, at least they were heading the right way and it showed on everyone's faces; civil and military alike.

As Thomas slogged steadily on, admiring the local women, accepting small gifts of food and wondering when he would actually see a German again, great men were once again having an effect the like of which he could not begin to imagine. By the time the Ninth had marched off that morning, von Kluck actually had four army corps and two cavalry divisions south across the Marne; and in the east von Moltke had ordered powerful attacks against the French armies defending the border with Germany.

Late the night before, however, von Kluck had heard of the attack on his right flank, had reacted immediately and had ordered his forces to withdraw. At Peçy, less than twenty miles due east of where the Norfolks had been billeted, and almost as they had moved off, a squadron of the 4th Dragoon Guards had watched as a column of German infantry halted on the road and then turned about and marched back the way it had come. The Fourth and Second German Corps were being withdrawn in order to secure the right flank and the rear of German First Army. Von Kluck was by now seriously concerned about the course of events.

The BEF was actually making quite slow progress. Having promised to help, the CinC was determined that his flanks should not be exposed as they had been on the retreat and was, therefore, determined to proceed with caution. This was one factor which was to lead to a series of wasted opportunities for which Thomas would ultimately suffer. Meanwhile, the Ninth, having marched all day, were billeted comfortably in the small village of La Celle, just on the River Grand Morin, by the railway station.

"Two for you, Corporal Floyd!" Paul Cooper's voice rang out above the sounds of Joe's section cleaning its mess tins and sorting itself out after a meal of stew and potatoes. As he spoke he chose not to notice the two empty wine bottles laying off to one side; neither did he bother to speculate how they might have obtained them since the locals in this village were being reasonably generous.

The whole section looked up as he spoke, having been warned in advance that the first reinforcements had arrived in the base area two days before and they could expect replacements for their losses. The two men beside Paul Cooper stared back, their faces a mixture of apprehension, eagerness and belligerence.

"You eaten?" Joe's question.

"Yurse." The taller one of the two spoke for them both. Not from Norfolk, but from East Anglia somewhere. The accent was the first indicator in the process they would go through of pigeon-holing their new colleagues so that their position in life and in the section could be determined.

"Yes, corporal." Joe established his position at once. Jack Waters smirked contemptuously, and looked for silent support from his colleagues. Finding none, he turned away and continued fitting his belongings into his pack in the secretive manner he usually adopted. Very public with his views, he was a man very private with his possessions.

With the moves of Colin and Ned to platoon HQ, and the loss of Fred and Albert, and having been one man down anyway, Joe Floyd had been reduced to only five riflemen instead of the eight he should have had. These two brought him up to seven, and by including himself he could pair everyone off.

"Names?" Some of them thought he was being a bit stern, unnecessarily so; but he had shown up well as their section commander, so no one really minded - except perhaps Jack Waters.

"Private Macleary." The taller one spoke again. "Eddie Macleary." Joe nodded, and then turned his gaze on the other man, awaiting his answer.

"Private Terry Smith."

Both men were in their mid to late twenties, with Macleary the older by a couple of years. They looked experienced and both bore themselves with a look of competence and soldierliness; and both were clearly uncomfortable as the new boys. Sensing their discomfort, Alfie looked at Joe Floyd, decided he was going to continue to be a bit stuffy as befitted his role as the man in charge, and so he seized the initiative.

"Alfie James." He grinned up at the two men. "Grab a seat."

"Cup of tea?" They both looked surprised at the well modulated tones of Colin Baxter's voice.

"Platoon commander's runner." Ever the one with a quick response, Alfie butted in. "Rubs off on yer, after a while." He dodged the piece of dried horse manure that Colin kicked in his direction, grinned widely and set about dismantling his rifle to clean it.

The two newcomers were quickly drawn into conversation and the probing began as the old soldiers, for that is what they now felt themselves to be, began the process of finding out where and how their recently arrived colleagues would fit in.

"A Lincoln?" Alfie was really enjoying himself as the life and soul of the little party that was developing. "Wassa bleedin' Poacher doin' in the Norfolks." He was responding to Macleary's assertion that his time with the colours had been spent with the Tenth of Foot, the neighbouring Lincolnshire Regiment, whose nickname was the Poachers.

"Buggered if I know. I jus' reported in an' did wot I wus told." That was an indisputable piece of military logic with which each of them could empathise.

"So, where you from, then?" Peter Dakin's accent was thickly Norfolk, as if to emphasise the point.

"Lincoln. Live on the edge of the city I do. Worked as a builder." Alfred Arbuckle's ears pricked up. "Not so much a builder, as a builder's labourer. No skill ye see. Been in the Army. Only good for diggin' 'oles. Did a lot of that. Wife works, mind. Dressmakin'. Works in the big 'ouses doin' specials for the ladies. More money tha' way."

"Kids?" Terry Smith asked the question, not having encountered his new friend until they had both appeared in the group that was to march from the base at Rouen up to join the regiment.

"Yurse, two of 'em. Cuppla lads. Buggers they are, but they'll look out fer their ma. While oi'm 'ere loik."

All eyes turned to Terry, seeking his life story, but two interruptions appeared. The first was a pleasant distraction in the form of two ladies in their mid twenties who were clearly looking to entertain them, but only in exchange for money and only one at a time. They had neither the money, nor the time, and it was with great regret that they saw the two clatter away with their shoes rattling on the pavé. In most minds were the thoughts of what they might have wished to do had things been different, but any ideas they may have had were disturbed by the second distraction which was the arrival of Joe Floyd to give the orders he had received at Matthew's evening briefing.

Joe watched the women until they disappeared around the corner of the station and out of sight, part of a contingent of girls who had come out of Paris on the trains to where the soldiers were, in search of business. For a brief instant the old, lascivious smirk returned to his face, but he had dismissed it by the time he turned to face the section.

The next day would involve more marching, turning further round to the north-east. They would hope to cross the River Grand Morin during the day and carry on towards a river called the Marne, which they had crossed a few days ago going south. Some of them nodded, remembering the name plate on the bridge. He had no answer to when they might meet the Germans. There were no reports of BEF units in contact that had been passed to him, and he had no idea what the French were up to.

Matthew was normally very good at keeping his soldiers informed. He felt strongly that it helped them to do their job better if they could put it in context. Therefore, they assumed, there was nothing more to be told.

That was it then. Turn in for the night, but first pair off the section for the new arrivals so they were ready at once if the need arose. Joe took Alfred Arbuckle as his pair, and spilt the newcomers with Ted and Alfie, Ted being allocated Macleary. As their section commander moved away to sort out his bed Ted and Alfie motioned to Eddie and Terry to come over and join them, at which point they went through the process of confirming the drills and routines they would follow as pairs; a process which took about half an hour until, all four of them satisfied, they went to bed.

Ted was pleased with what he had gleaned from Eddie. He was sorry that his partnership with Alfie had been broken up, but it made sense to put two regulars with two reservists. Macleary had known what he was on, and Ted felt quite comfortable. He glanced at Alfie as they lay down on the stone floor of the old railway storehouse that was their billet for the night.

"All right?"

"Yup." Alfie confirmed that he was happy with the arrangements.

"Night."

"Night."

They slept as well as was possible given the very hard ground and the complete lack of anything to cushion their bodies, or to protect them from the cold that seeped up from the concrete floor. At some point, as he turned over to make himself more comfortable, Ted saw Joe Floyd returning to his bed having been out for some reason, probably for a pee. He went back to sleep wondering whether or not he also had the energy to get up and relieve the pressure he could begin to feel building up inside. In the end, sleep won.

"I am really gettin' fed up with this!" Alfie, as was so often the case, spoke for them all. "We've been fartin' about fer bleedin hours now. Every time we get going, we stop again."

They could all hear shelling and machine gun fire away to the east. Something must be happening, but they seemed to spend all their time sitting by the side of the road waiting to march a half mile or so and then sit by the side of the road again. Thomas was not to know that the cause of his problem was, once again, his commander-in-chief. Having been obsessed by the business of retreat, French was now taking the small print of Kitchener's instructions very seriously. He was so determined to ensure that his flank was not exposed that he was limiting the pace at which the BEF advanced. Regrettably, over the next few days this approach was to mean that where advantage might have been gained by swift action it was lost; where victory might have been seized by zest and panache it was lacking; and the moments passed - never to return.

"An' tonight we's on bloody outpost. Wot a bastard!"

She climbed the stairs of the decrepit apartment block to the small room she shared with her widowed mother and the six month old baby. Born of a red haired father and a flaxen haired French girl, the child's colour and appearance, with ginger locks and pale skin, demonstrated its heritage very clearly. The father had vanished immediately after the sexual encounter that had conceived the child. It could hardly have been construed as love making, having been a lustful succumbing to passion and curiosity. He had been an attractive man, over two meters in height and taughtly muscled from the daily hard work on the barges that plied the Seine. She had already lost her virginity, but her conquests had been local boys who had fumbled and stumbled their way through the process; always leaving her frustrated and in need of something else, but she wasn't sure quite what that was.

He had been older, and had clearly taken a fancy to her from the outset; the long blonde hair being a special attraction. Her flirting eyes had led him to follow her as she had moved away from her mother's market stall in the gathering gloom of a June evening. Unashamedly, she had allowed him to come after her into the small workmen's shelter by the factory wall where so many of her friends undertook their assignations. Her curiosity, and her passion, was driving her wild by the time she had got through the door.

As he entered, and before his eyes could grow accustomed to the poor light, she had reached out and taken him towards the mattress in the corner. As she had stooped to kneel, and then sit and then lie down, her hand had brushed his trousers and she had felt the tingling of fear at the size of what she encountered. He had not been subtle, for that had not been what they were about. Neither had he been quick; she was not his first and he had developed the stamina to prolong his performance. She had been unable to believe the effect that the size, speed and power of his attack, for that really was what it had been, was having on her body. The sense of being filled to capacity as he had entered her and then the tingling pleasure as he had slammed repeatedly into her had almost driven her mad, writhing with excitement. The first orgasm had taken her by surprise, throwing back her head and calling out. He had paused briefly, looking to see if she was all right, before carrying on at the same unbelievable speed. As she had sensed the change, as he had grown even harder and the pace a little sharper, she had opened her eyes, looked up and seen his face contort as his own contractions began, sweat beading on his brow and dripping onto her upper body. She had felt a tinge of fear as the power had increased, not knowing what to expect. Then he had gasped, pushing into her deeper than she had ever thought possible whilst she shoved up against him trying to take every centimetre she could. The deep groan as she felt her second orgasm wash over her had come from somewhere down in her stomach, her legs had kicked and drummed against the wall at the end of the mattress, her hands scrabbling at his waist as she had pulled him into her; and she had felt the spurt of his ejaculation against her womb.

Lying exhausted she had felt him move, had felt empty as he withdrew from her sooner than she had wanted him to, had felt lonely and scared as he had quickly dressed and left. As she had rolled over she had felt, in the half dark, some paper near her right shoulder. Looking down she had seen that it was money; he had paid her; he had thought she was a prostitute; she had thought that she ought to feel dirty and used, but she hadn't.

Whilst that might have been her first payment, it was not to be her last. Within a few weeks she had realised that the spurt of his ejaculate against her womb had preceded by a few short hours the moment of conception of her bastard child. Once the birth was over, there had been few ways open to a girl of her class and with her lack of education to earn money, and she now needed to support them both; and help her mother with money whilst she acted as baby-sitter for her wayward daughter's frequent absences in pursuit of her new found profession.

It had been her profession that had drawn her to La Celle. Business, however, had not been good. British soldiers really did not earn enough money to make it worth her while to travel that far in search of custom. By the time she had paid the train fare she had barely made anything on the three encounters she had endured. The first two had not been too bad, older men, with wives, who weren't as frightened as the younger ones to take the plunge. Pity really, she quite liked the younger ones. They were so eager, and it was always fun to see if she could make them last a little longer than two quick shoves and a gasp. It had been the third one that had upset her. There had been something unpleasant about him and, even as he had approached her at the edge of the small copse in which she had been holding court, she had felt tempted to say no.

She had listened to him gasping as he went through the ritual, laying back with her eyes closed to give the appearance of enjoyment whilst at the same time avoiding looking at him and being able to think of other things. She had begun to sense the quickening and the hardening as he approached the end, and as she did so felt something moist on her chin. Remembering the sweat as it had dripped on her upper body that time in the workmen's shelter, she had looked up, half expecting to see a sweating, contorted face surmounted by flaming red hair, wishing briefly that she could experience yet again the heady passion of that memorable encounter; and she had recoiled as she had seen him dribbling at the moment of his climax.

Her first act on reaching her cramped home had been to wash her face; still able to feel where the rivulets of saliva had run even though they had dried hours ago; feeling, for the first time in any of her sexual liaisons, dirty and used.

"That's nice, innit?" Peter Dakin was moved to observe, unusually for him, on the rather imposing yellow stone church on the bank above the road at the north end of the bridge over the River Marne at Saacy. Its tower dominated the approach to the bridge, reaching up into the sky, capped by a pointed roof of grey slate, the whole thing standing out starkly against the green backdrop of the high bank upon which it stood. His observation caused a few heads to be raised, eyes to glance at the stone edifice and then to get the head down again and get on with the business of marching. Over to the east they could still hear the sounds of firing, heavy artillery thundering in the distance told its own story, whilst from time to time small arms could be heard, but quite some way off. There was silence as they marched, most of them consumed with their own thoughts; many wondering what lay in store for clearly something was happening around them; others thought of home and family; Colin thought of letters and replies; Ned thought of the two pictures he could feel pressing against his chest from within his left breast pocket; and Eddie Macleary wondered what he had done with the silver crucifix his Roman Catholic wife had given him before he departed - for the life of him he had been unable to find it.

The night before they had slept just south of Saacy, prior to the crossing. That had revived them after the previous night's duty as outposts. Providing the screen, and the immediate defence, for the rest of the sleeping brigade was always tiresome. The section had spent an uncomfortable night in a thicket watching out for enemy incursion, snatching sleep when they could in less than comfortable conditions.

But by now they had been marching east and north for three days, and they seemed no nearer to encountering Germans than had been the case when they started. They were tired, and the euphoria of their move back against the Germans had worn off. They were badly in need of haircuts all round. Their equipment showed the ravages of the conditions they had endured, and none more so than their boots. Despite their best efforts to keep them in good order, some had already resorted to binding the soles to the uppers with strips of rag, old puttee or baling wire; and there was no prospect of replacements so far as anyone could see.

To add to their misery, the weather had broken. The refreshing showers of the early morning, which had been quite welcome, had turned to a steady downpour and they were feeling bloody tired and bloody fed up. An' this bleedin' 'ill they were climbin' was a right sod!

Suddenly, however, as they stopped for their midday break, the atmosphere changed. Officers assumed an aura of gravity and purposefulness, members of the brigade staff were with the CO, and he was deep in conversation with the CO of the Dorsets. Aye, no doubt about it, sommat wus up.

"There is a hill, called Hill 189 from the trigonometric point which marks its summit." Matthew was giving his orders after a two hour delay during which time officers had conducted their reconnaissance of the ground before making plans.

"Two roads, both running just west of north, run up either side of it, to its east and west. Those roads lead on to Dhuisy and then further north. It is believed that the Germans are occupying the crest of the hill, but the reports are uncertain. Consequently, we are to clear the hill in a two-battalion attack, the Norfolks on the right and the Dorsets on the left. We will be supported by artillery, and there will be cavalry to our right and left providing screens.

If, therefore, you do see horsemen, please be sure who they are before deciding whether or not to open fire."

There were grim smiles all round. Professional as they were, it was still possible to make mistakes like that and they all knew it.

He had made up a small model of the ground as it had been described to him. As he spoke, he pointed out the salient features whilst his section commanders scribbled furiously those parts of his orders that related to their part in the attack. They would be moving from Bezu, where the battalion was currently loitering in the shelter of walls and trees, round the southern edge of the long feature whose summit was Point 189. Using the Bois des Essertis as cover they would approach the summit from the west. The woods would get them to within some eight hundred to twelve hundred yards of the objective and then they would be in open country. Unfortunately, the line of the woods lay at an odd angle to the preferred line of attack, and they would have to undertake what was effectively a left wheel, with those on the right having to sweep out much further than the rest, and then come round in order to be attacking directly north.

And yes, they were the right hand of the two Norfolk companies in the firing line, with the furthest to march on the sweep round into the attack. Bleedin' typical.

Machine gun fire would come over their heads from the Norfolk's guns which would take up position some two thousand yards south of the objective. The Dorsets would have their guns with them, and they would be on the left, trying to enfilade the German position. This involved placing the guns in what was called a defilade position, so they could hit the enemy from a flank and divert him from his main purpose of defending to his front. Easier said than done; and if the German commander had half a brain, which most of them did, he would have looked for the defilade positions and have catered for them.

Within the company, the platoon was to retain its normal reserve role, two platoons being in the firing line and one in the supports.

"'Ang on, wassat?" Eddie Macleary had hold of Ned Preece as he spoke. The two men had been near each other in the shade of the grey stone wall of a barn. Ned had just been about to sort his own pack, having looked out for Matthew's, when he had felt the hand on his arm.

"Woss wot?"

"That, this 'ere wot jus' dropped out o' yer pack. Me cross it is." Macleary bent down and retrieved the small silver object he had picked off the ground from where he had seen it fall from Ned's pack.

"Dunno; never seen it." Something was wrong, he did not like it and the defensive note in his voice was obvious to the small group who had already begun to take an interest in what was happening. Neither did it take Matthew and Paul long to realise that something was adrift, and as they reached the two men, and the small circle gradually forming around them, they were in time to hear Jack Waters loudly proclaiming the finding of a horse brass which he had last seen in the house in La Celle in which Matthew had been billeted.

By this time Ned was white with fear. He knew not where to put himself, or to whom he could turn. He looked wildly around him for some sign of support, but saw only confusion and dismay on the faces of his friends, hostility from some of the platoon, malevolence from Jack Waters and a gloating smile of satisfaction which made Paul Cooper look ugly. Matthew was the only one who remained calm, and poker faced.

"Sir, I'll.........!"

"You'll do nothing for the time being, sergeant." He did not look at Paul as he spoke, but instead concentrated his gaze on Ned, as if trying to read what was going on inside his brain. Ned was too terrified to have any idea what might be going on inside his brain and couldn't have answered a question of any sort; no matter how simple.

"We have a battle to fight, and when it's over we'll address this issue."

"Yessir, but h'ell 'ave to be charged with theft and looting. I'll put him back in a section and then we'll….."

"I said….." a pause for impact as he emphasised the words, "we shall do nothing yet. Private Preece is my batman and will remain as such. There is in our country a presumption of innocence, and I have not had the time to investigate this, nor will I for some time. Sergeant Cooper, you and I will quickly search Private Preece and his equipment, and we shall form up at the corner of the road, where we agreed, on time in ten minutes. The rest of you, get about your business!" The last phrase cracked like a whiplash.

Fifteen minutes later they were on their way, following the pavé road as it curved south down into the valley and then up along the left hand side of the spur which emanated southward from Point 189. On either side of them were stands of trees, interspersed with vineyards, their fruit hanging in great dark bunches awaiting the harvest.

The search of Ned Preece and his equipment, conducted by Cooper and witnessed by Matthew, had revealed nothing untoward. Matthew thought the boy had borne it well, for Cooper had not been gentle. He had seen him flinch when the pictures had been removed from his jacket and examined, and sigh with relief when they had been handed back.

Suddenly, in front, a hand was raised. They stopped and stepped into the side of the road. Lost in thought about the incident involving his batman and the implications, Matthew had not realised how far they had gone. As the reserve platoon in the right hand company of the assault they were a long way back in the column so they could enter the woods at the right time and in the right place, and this was it.

On a hand signal they turned to the right and began to make their way into the woods, following the guides who had been part of the reconnaissance party, using the logging tracks where they could, or struggling through undergrowth, to their positions on the forward edge of the wood. Try as they might to move quietly there was inevitably some noise. Whilst the enemy would not have heard the cracking of a branch or the sound of feet on dead leaves and twigs which had lain undisturbed on the ground for years, they certainly would have spotted the pigeons clattering out of the trees as they flew in alarm before the unintending beaters in the woods beneath them.

By the time they reached the forward edge of the wood, and Matthew could see the clump of trees some six hundred yards way which was to be the right marker for the right hand company, the enemy artillery was already bringing down sporadic speculative fire on what the German commander had deduced as being the most likely forming up points for an attack. They were using high explosive shell and the shock waves from the detonations brought leaves and branches clattering down. Here and there the blast or the splinters from a shell found targets, and screams and yells could be heard all along the line. Matthew, looking to his left and right, could see his platoon as they obeyed his signal to lie down. He glanced at Ned, just beside him, and smiled as reassuringly as he could at the troubled youngster.

As they lay waiting for the order to move they tried to relate the ground in front to the model Matthew had made. None of them had expected the hill to be so steep, nor had they realised that there was a dip into which they would have to descend before making the final climb. That would help a bit, as once they were in it they would not be in direct line of sight until about a hundred and twenty yards from the enemy; time then for the final assault. But getting there across open country was not going to be funny. Going downhill for part of the time with an enemy above them would make them an easy target and unable to return fire effectively due to the angle they would have to hold their rifles; and where was the bloody artillery.

Fifteen minutes later, and still no artillery. Sod 'em, can't they get anythin' right?

Suddenly the machine guns opened fire, from their left, manned by the Dorsets, and way down the spur to their right their own guns. Only four altogether, but at least it was better than nothing. They had no idea of the impact of the machine gun fire on the enemy, but hoped it would keep their heads down as, despairing of timely artillery support and with the day getting on, the two COs moved into the attack with only their own battalion firepower.

The orders had been clear: keep well spaced out, don't lie down and get to the assault line as fast as possible. Accurate aimed fire at long range was difficult, and because of the trajectory of the bullet over long distances the projectiles rained down from above; not unlike popular pictures of the rain of English arrows at Agincourt. Therefore, moving in rushes would not save casualties, neither would lying down. As they drew nearer the basic fire unit was to be the section and platoons would advance in rushes two sections at a time, seeking to dominate the ground and win the fire fight against the enemy before the final assault.

Matthew could not remember feeling so exposed as he stepped out into the open with two sections on his right and two on his left. Up to now they had been involved in defensive actions, and whilst there had been risks at least they'd had some advantages. Now they were in the open, and where German attacks, certainly at Le Cateau, were accompanied by masses of artillery, here the Norfolks had none. He looked ahead as men in the forward companies doubled forward, their rifles held loosely at the trail, in the left or right hand and parallel to the ground, five yards between each man just as the book said. He could still hear the machine guns, but had no idea of the effect. Some small arms fire was coming their way; he could hear the crack as it passed overhead, and from the front edge of the green wood on Point 189 he could see smoke. So they were there, but in what numbers it was impossible to tell. So far the German artillery had not bothered the infantry in the open too much. High explosive was still falling on the wood, but it wouldn't be very long before they realised they were now empty and that the attack was materialising.

For a moment there was a pause in the shelling. Then the woods to Matthew's north, just to the west of Point 189, erupted in smoke and flame. The artillery battery in a small village called Sabblonnière over the valley to the north had focused in on one of the German infantry's selected and rehearsed target areas and were giving the Dorset's machine guns a very hard time. For the time being, support from them ceased, and as it did so the German gunners loaded with shrapnel, which is much more effective against troops in the open, and began to concentrate their attentions on the infantry moving into the assault. Soon the sky overhead was redolent with the coughing sound as the fuzes worked and the filling projected the lethal balls down on the heads of the infantry below. Here and there men fell, some screaming, some silently, others like a sack of potatoes collapsing, yet more throwing up their arms and twisting as projectiles of varying sorts hit them.

Ted was feeling really quite frightened and trying desperately not to show it. He felt constantly as if something was going to impact his body, and found himself flinching with almost every step he took. Looking at him, Alfie was impressed by how calm his friend looked, clearly unfussed by all that was going on around him, whilst he, the life and soul of the platoon, no longer felt quite the same sense of elation as when he had been picking off Germans at long range at Mons and Le Cateau. Macleary, watching Ted looking to his left and right to ensure he kept position, thought him a fine example; Ted was checking to see if the line was holding as he was scared stiff of being out there on his own and not being able to get back.

Matthew, looking around him to see what was happening, suddenly tripped and as he put his hand down it landed in mush. Believing it to be cow manure, for there was a lot of it lying around, he looked down, and was aghast to see that his hand was resting on the neck of a decapitated soldier from one of the forward platoons, the hard lump of his spinal column, which Matthew had thought to be a stone, the blood still pumping from his arteries and the body still twitching with nervous reaction. His yell of horror was involuntary, as he whipped his hand away from the revolting mess; and then the bile rose in his throat as he saw the wide open eyes in the severed head, lying in the grass a couple of feet away. Suddenly he was lifted up, a hand under the shoulder strap of his Sam Browne belt.

"C'mon, sir. You all right?" He looked up to see Ned with a look of anguish on his face, so much so his first thought was that the boy had been hit; then he realised it was concern for his own safety that wreathed Preece's face. "Gimme yer 'and." Taking the arm just above the wrist, Ned wiped the gore on his own trousers, looking swiftly to see that there was no injury to the officer. "'E's fine." The remark was addressed to Cooper's enquiring look. Matthew, looking to see where his platoon had reached, stood and followed on to where Cooper had led them after he had fallen. White and shaken, he joined his small headquarters. As he did so, Colin gasped.

"Look, sir, look. That shell just got Number One Section!" Looking over to his left Matthew saw the section commander get to his feet. Five of his seven men were still advancing, two were not moving and the Corporal was holding the blood soaked sleeve of his left arm against his chest. Even at that distance Matthew could see the whiteness of the man's face as he turned back the way they had come in order to seek medical help.

As he watched, the senior private among the five began shouting orders, and the men adjusted positions as they continued moving forward. Matthew felt a mix of despair and pride as he thought of the loss and at the same time the response of the survivors. The drills were working, the discipline shone through, the effect was rock steadiness in the face of serious unpleasantness. Over to his right he could see that the right forward platoon was now approaching the copse which was their objective before they swung up the hill directly toward the enemy.

"Fuck!"

Ned Preece yelled as the bullet whipped across his back, between his pack and his body, drawing blood as it tracked the surface of the skin, the reaction throwing him to the ground. Matthew looked down, fearing the worst, and was about to bend when he saw Colin kneel beside his friend. The stream of invective emanating from Ned was all the assurance Matthew needed to know that he was not seriously hurt, but there was a fair amount of bleeding. Ned stood, arched his back and collected his rifle from the ground. Matthew moved off, looking back to see his batman following, refusing Colin's offers of help.

Now they were square onto the enemy, and in front he could see the platoons had reverted to moving with their sections as fire units. Two would go down to provide covering fire on the enemy position, and the other two would dash forward only to repeat the process as their colleagues moved forward. Watching as the company moved Matthew could see the gaps that had occurred in the ranks. Occasionally he would see a body here, a wounded man there as the platoon advanced in open formation. Not for the reserve the rushing by sections; they needed to be ready for anything.

Suddenly there was the whooshing overhead of passing artillery; British artillery.

"Silly sods've missed the soddin' 'ill." It was a very frightened Jack Waters who sought to assuage some of his fear by taking it out on some anonymous gunner.

"Goin' fer the German artillery first." Ted, who had no great love for Waters, cut him dead. "Get the infantry later." His breath came in short gasps as they had been moving quite fast, and anyway he was frightened.

About a hundred yards in front he saw the Firing Line go down on what looked like a small bank. Thinking about it he realised it was the lip of the little ridge which marked the end of the dead ground, and the beginning of the last one hundred and twenty yards to the objective. He wondered why they had stopped; 'gainst orders that were.

They had stopped because, with no artillery, the loss of the Dorset machine guns to the left and the fact that the Norfolk's machine guns had now to stop for fear of hitting their own men, there was nothing to keep the German defenders heads down. The casualties in the firing line had been considerable and the long slog in the open had been exhausting. They had little left with which to prosecute their attack. Lying just out of sight of the German infantry the message went back to get the "bloody artillery to sort themselves out and put some fire on that bloody hill."

The number of men fallen had reduced as they moved into the lee of the ridge, for the German infantry fire could not reach them. Casualties were only being caused by artillery, and the British counter battery fire was now dealing with that. For once, with the Germans retreating, the number of British guns in range of German batteries was in a more favourable proportion. Responding to Matthew's hand signal, they knelt, and then lay down, awaiting orders. Cooper, by now a very tired, and, like them all, frightened man, watched as Ned Preece, flinching with the pain in his back, bound the shattered right hand of a corporal from one of the forward platoons, and then laid him down close beside him to try and keep the man warm. The heavy rain of the earlier part of the day had eased, but the ground was wet and cold, and that would do the wounded no good at all. Relatively safe as they were in the dip, they could not risk going back to the wood and exposing themselves yet again. They were stuck, it was late afternoon and it looked like being a very long night.

"Chaaaaarge!"

The platoon commanders on the ridge screamed out the command, as much to assuage their fear as to encourage their men. The forward platoons had moved off to coincide with the delivery of artillery fire on the objective and once the men had risen and were moving the order to charge had been given. Climbing up to the ridge behind them, Matthew signalled his platoon to halt, and to await developments. Ahead of him he could see men running towards the enemy, well spaced out, and making hard targets, he could see the shrapnel bursting forward of the tree line and he could see smoke from the trees as the defenders sought to stave off the assault.

Suddenly, the attack ground to a halt; the forward line had encountered a previously unseen barbed wire fence at waist height which stopped the charging men in their tracks. Those who attempted to cross it made stable and inviting targets. Matthew saw one platoon commander, exhorting his men to go on, twist round with his hand half raised as a bullet entered his head and removed the top half in a spray of brains and blood which covered the man next to him. The individual recoiled, and began slowly to move back away from the obstacle; and as if by telepathy, that trend continued along the line as men returned to the relative safety of the ridge.

"Wot're they doin'?" Terry Smith was incredulous. For some reason he did not understand he was feeling no fear, simply a burning desire to get on and get to grips with an enemy he could see for the first time.

"Get down, yer stupid sod." Alfie James was not sympathetic. This was bloody dangerous, and until there was a bit more support it was fairly obvious that what the Germans had on that hill was more than could be coped with by two battalions on their own. As he spoke, Terry was lifting himself up to see what was going on, at which point a bullet entered his face just to the left of his mouth, passing between his open jaws at a slight downward angle, and smashing into his lower jaw just by his right lower wisdom tooth, whereupon it exited his face, causing considerable damage to the lower jaw, and ploughed into the ground some distance away. He yelled, and then gurgled as the blood flowed down his throat, causing him to choke and convulse. The pain was beyond belief, and Aflie, seeing the mess, rolled over to him as he fell.

"Silly sod, wot yer do that fer?" His hand reached out at once to stem the flow of blood, drawing a cry as he applied pressure to damage tissue. Alfred was also on his way, having been sent by Joe Floyd, crawling on his stomach to reach the pair as quickly as he could. Dressings were quickly applied, and Terry was laid on his front, his head to one side, to stop blood flowing down his throat. He lay there whimpering as Eddie went, in response to Matthew's bidding, to try and find a medical orderly; but with express instructions not to expose himself and become another casualty.

And there they stayed. The fighting gradually petered out. The British had no strength left to continue the assault for the time being. Orders were given for shell scrapes to be dug and to wait until reinforcements could come up and assist with taking the position. Any food with them could be consumed cold. Wounded were to be tended to as well as could be, and recovery of casualties back to the regimental aid post in the woods was to be attempted only with great caution, remembering the flares which the German artillery could put up and the British could not and which would expose men in the open at night.

They did not know it, but the last shots in the three day old Battle of the Marne had been fired. The Germans moved away to the north, evacuating the position, their delaying task complete. Patrols going forward in the small hours had detected German movement away from them and by three in the morning they were certain that the German position was empty.

The small action against a German covering force outpost on Hill 189 did not rate a mention in the history books; it was an event of no real consequence. However, a major victory had been won on the Marne, and they had, in theory at least, made their contribution. The result of that contribution lay in the dozens of dead men from Dorset and Norfolk, lying on a hillside so far from home and whose lives had been given for an event of no real consequence.

Cold, damp and dispirited they moved, unopposed, onto the objective at dawn to find forty-seven dead Germans and evidence that many had been wounded. Looking down at their dead adversaries with a mix of curiosity and emptiness, those who were on their feet hefted their rifles and headed for the road, just a hundred yards east of the position, to which they were being called by their NCOs and where, with luck, breakfast might be forthcoming.

Terry Smith died during the night from a blocked airway caused by accumulated blood and fragments of broken teeth.

Chapter 10

Battle on the Aisne

The River Aisne flows wide and deep from its source in the mountains of eastern France, running west through the centre of the country to Soissons, on to Campiègne where it joins the Oise to head south-west, to the west of Paris, to the Seine and then the English Channel. A twig dropped by a passing soldier might, as with his dreams, float on down the highway of water toward the home he wished to see once more; but was beginning to think he might not, and certainly not by Christmas.

The weather was foul. Most, if asked, could have offered an opinion on what they would rather be doing on a Sunday morning. Marching through rain, driven by a cold and wintry north-easterly wind, did not draw favourable comparison with a pint of ale and Sunday lunch at home followed by a game of football or a walk with the family. It had been like this since that morning on the tenth of September when they had moved off Point 189, past the bodies of their dead foes, and resumed their northward progress in pursuit of a retreating enemy, leaving their own dead and wounded behind.

The rain had been almost incessant; it had slowed them on the march as the mud on the roads grew even deeper and more glutinous. It had slowed their re-supply, which had caused even more delay. It had dulled their edge, making tired men even more tired; physical exhaustion to a point which some had felt they could never sink and survive, and mental exhaustion too - more insidious as it crept up unnoticed until, suddenly, it became too much to bear.

They were still cursing the brigade staff for Friday night's debacle. The countryside across which they had marched had been especially difficult. Setting aside the mud and the rain, it was a region of high plateaux interspersed with deep valleys. This meant long slogs across the top with no shelter from the elements, descending into and marching up out of the valleys, cut by a succession of streams and small rivers. There was some debate about which was worse, "floggin' down the bloody things or back up t'other side." The balance of opinion was probably about even; beyond dispute was the general agreement that it was an inconvenience they could live without.

It had been at about five o'clock in the morning that they had halted the brigade in the area of a large farm called L'Epitaph. Colin Baxter had been busy explaining to anyone who was prepared to listen, which wasn't many, the significance of the word in English when the Norfolks and the Cheshires had both been turned about and marched back down into the valley of the Crise into billets in Nampteuil. The air was blue, and had any of them been given the opportunity to offer a view on brigade headquarters' epitaph it would have been succinct, and composed largely of four letter, single syllable words.

And now here they were, in another deep valley in a small village called Serches, being told that they were about to move north, just a few miles, to the Aisne whereupon they were to cross it. However, since the Germans had blown the bridges they would be crossing on rafts constructed by the Royal Engineers.

When the company commander, having given out his orders for the move, asked if there were any questions he feigned surprise when Matthew asked what they would be doing once they got to the other side, and what, if anything, was the expected German reaction. The major's look of surprise had nothing to do with the questions for, indeed, they were perfectly reasonable. His mock astonishment was more to do with the fact that they had been asked at all.

Consequently, looking carefully at Matthew as he spoke, his response was unfailingly courteous, but abrupt:

"I am afraid I haven't the faintest idea. Now, unless there is anything else ..... no? Good. Thank you, gentlemen," and with that the orders group dispersed.

"S'all very well for 'im to say 'e don't bloody know, but I bloody do. I bet them buggers is waiting f'rus, an' it won't be like a Sunday on the Broads an no mistake." Alfie was, once again, expressing, on behalf of his colleagues, the view that most of them held. They had just received from Joe Floyd their platoon commander's orders and, despite the enormous respect Matthew had earned from them, they were unhappy that they were not being given the full story; whatever that might be.

The French and British perspectives of what might be about to happen were, not for the first time, at variance. General Joffre had his eyes beyond the Aisne, north into open country where he could take on the enemy on terms of his, Joffre's, own choosing. For his part, Field Marshall French continued to be obsessed by his flanks, moving north at the steady pace required not to expose himself, rather than at the cracking pace required to conquer a fleeing enemy.

Edward von Gleichen took the second cup of coffee poured for him by his French hostess, a lady of middle years, middle class and exquisite charm who had been only too delighted to have a true English gentleman "imposed" upon her; even if his name did sound somewhat ...... well ..... Germanic. Still, one never knew with the English. Patting her hair carefully into place she left to return to her kitchen.

"My friend." he turned to St André who immediately broke from his conversation with the brigade major. "Have you noticed, we have not seen our enemy, not hide or hair of him, for four days?"

"Oui, mon General. Zat causes you concern?" His accent was always more inexorable when he was trying to lighten his commander's mood, and clearly von Gleichen was troubled.

"Oui, mon ami. It troubles me, for if we have not encountered him since Point 189 then he has broken clean. We are no longer in contact - he could be anywhere."

Without waiting for a response he stood from the table, motioning to his colleagues to remain seated as good manners caused them to begin to rise, and moved to the window. Staring into the inky blackness as the wind howled through the eaves of the house and round the outbuildings, and the rain clattered against the glass of the window panes, he stood, alone with his thoughts. "I wonder where you are, and what you are up to." Consumed by the tiredness that was affecting them all he turned, smiled briefly and wished his fellow officers goodnight. This time, as he left the room, they rose to their feet, waited until he had gone, smiled ruefully at each other and, having quaffed the last of their drinks, headed off to sleep.

But no one knew where the Germans were or what they were doing. The terrible weather had grounded all air reconnaissance and blinded all ground reconnaissance, and von Kluck and Blülow were free to move as they saw fit. The lost opportunities at the Marne, where robust speed and action might have sent the Germans reeling back home, were about to be repeated. There was a complete lack in the higher echelons of the BEF of mental and physical momentum.

"This is beyond a bleedin' joke!" Alfie's views on the river crossing were explicit, and forthrightly spelt out. In fairness, the move that night down to the raft crossing at Moulin des Roches was well organised and went smoothly. Alfie's problem, which he would admit to no one, was that he could not swim and the prospect of drowning filled him with horror.

"Shurrup!" Joe Floyd's voice hissed out the command, to the immense gratitude of many of the rest of the section. Despite the fact that there was already a fair bit of noise with bumping rafts, groaning ropes and creaking timbers there was a general, if somewhat illogical, view that the sound of a voice was what would give them away. Ted, sensing his friend's fear, used the cover of darkness to hold Alfie's left arm, just above the elbow, and offer a squeeze, which he hoped would be reassuring. He saw a flash of white as Alfie's face turned towards him and the grin, never absent for long, was back again.

Matthew was at the front of the raft as they approached the bank. Beside him, one either side, were Colin and Ned. Paul Cooper was at the rear to shepherd everybody off. Ahead they could see the flat river plain stretching about seven hundred and fifty yards to the main road running east to west at ninety degrees to their front with the inky blackness of an escarpment beyond. Once on the shore they would head into Saint Marguerite, a small village like so many others in the region, to their left and just over half a mile west of the point where they would join the main road.

He glanced at Ned, unable to read his face in the darkness. The boy had completely withdrawn into a shell. The penalty for the charges of theft and of looting, in this case the horse brass, which had been brought against him were severe, and likely to be all the more so because of the circumstances in which the incidents had occurred. Clearly it was playing on his mind. Matthew had kept him as his servant, partly because he still could not bring himself to believe that Preece was a thief, and partly because he could at least keep an eye on him. It was this latter point that had won over the company commander, given that there was no means by which Ned could be incarcerated and everyone who could fire a rifle was needed where he could bring that fire to bear on the enemy. Paul Cooper's disapproval had been thunderously silent, and the gap had once more opened between them. But the search of Ned's kit had revealed nothing more than Macleary's St Christopher medal; so where, Matthew asked himself, was the rest of the stuff that had gone missing?

The scraping of the raft on the north bank caught him by surprise and he stepped off it into water that was about ankle deep. He grimaced, for even though his feet were wet from days of rain the infusion of yet more cold water into his boots was unwelcome. He contented himself with the thought that at least some of the mud with which they had become encrusted would be washed off. Wet and uncomfortable, with the cold of the night accentuating the dampness of his clothing, and feeling utterly miserable, he led his platoon along the route he had been given to the rendezvous in St Marguerite. As he did so he glanced up at the blackness ahead, wondering what the ground would look like once the dawn broke; and wondering also what that dawn might bring.

The valley of the Aisne is quite broad, but the north bank has a high escarpment dominating it. Along the top of the escarpment, and between a mile and mile and a half from the river, runs the Chemin des Dames, a lateral road built by Louis XVI for the ladies of the court the better to speed their carriages as they headed from Paris in the heat of the summer to the cooler high country to the east. Pointing south, like the udders of a dormant sow, were five promontories, each of which needed to be taken if the high ground north of the river was to be held and become a launching platform for subsequent operations as Joffre envisaged. Needless to say, the Germans were only too aware of the importance of the high ground north of the river and had used their time out of contact wisely in preparing their defences. Thomas was going to have to shift them; and it looked like an uphill struggle in every sense of the word.

St Marguerite lay south-west of the line of the Chivres spur, the left hand of the promontories to be taken by the BEF; and the task lay with the Fifth Division. It was a matter of some regret that the point from which the attack needed to be launched was from the village of Missy-sur-Aisne which lay due south of the spur and about a mile east of St Marguerite along a road that was covered by very large amounts of German weaponry from vantage points high on the hill. Still, as Thomas was quick to point out, "yer carn't 'ave everythin' right all the bleedin' time, can yer?" But it would have been nice to have been sent to the right spot in the first place.

"We are to be part of an attack by ten companies drawn

from three battalions. Three of them will be from the East Surreys from Fourteen Brigade on our left. We shall provide another three, and the Bedfords will attack as a complete battalion with all four companies. The Norfolks will be on the right of the attack with two companies in the firing line and our company as supports."

The section commanders glanced at each other. This sounded complicated, and, on the basis that no plan ever survived first contact with the enemy, ran counter to the golden rule that simplest was usually best. Matthew caught their look, shared their unspoken concern and carried on with his orders. He turned back to the small model he had made. It was his trademark, but a picture really did paint a thousand words, and the models also provided a sound basis for questions at the end.

"Our objective is the Fort du Condé on the top of the spur. It is protected by woods all along its southern face with an open gap between the edge of the woods and the fort itself of about two hundred yards. The woods themselves are quite dense and several hundred yards deep." He pointed to the model. "We get into them up the open hillside here, just above Missy into this opening here." His pointer, a stripped birch twig, hovered over an opening into the wood, simulated by a handful of grass.

They went on to discuss control in dense woodland, the need to keep reasonably close to each other in order to retain cohesion and the importance of being able to regroup prior to any final assault on the fort from the northern edge of the woods. When it was all over they returned to their sections to give a set of orders they knew they would have some difficulty delivering with any sense of conviction. After all, it was pretty simple really: advance across open country to the next village along roads swept by enemy machine gun and artillery fire; move into a village none of them had ever seen; pass through the village onto a start line no one had marked; from there attack up a steep hill, over open ground into dense woodland with no reconnaissance against an enemy who'd had ample time to construct his defences. "Nuthin' to it!"

Breakfast comprised some cold bacon they'd brought over the river that night, washed down with water; save the enterprising souls who by dint of cash or winning smile inveigled coffee from some of the families who, despite the prospect of becoming embroiled in a battle, had remained in their homes. Matthew watched his men as they ate, and as they received their orders. He admired the professional resignation on their faces as they were told what was about to happen, but couldn't fail also to notice the weariness in their eyes, and the general air of debilitation brought about by tiredness, equipment, especially boots, in need of replacement and, to be honest, fear. They were about to embark on their fourth battle in less than a month, with many of their friends having been killed or wounded, and they would be less than human if the prospect of their own mortality had not crossed their minds. Matthew grimaced, the thought emerging briefly that perhaps it was just him who was scared and that the rest of them were just taking it in their stride. He wondered if he had communicated that fear to the Major with his questions about likely German reaction. He shrugged his shoulders, and looked at Cooper who, despite their rift over Preece, had been a tower of strength, apparently unperturbed by all that went on around him.

He glanced down the village street towards brigade headquarters, and stiffened briefly as he saw Snell entering the cottage in which they were housed. "An unpleasant creature," he thought, and then reminded himself that he still had to speak to Ludgrove regarding the incident after Le Cateau; but now was not the time for that.

"Lissen!" Joe Floyd looked round the section. "Now, jus' you lissen t'wot I'm sayin'!" The force of his oratory was driven by an aura of disgruntlement at what seemed on the face of it to be a foolhardy and dangerous undertaking. "Jus' remember yer drills, keep close in yer pairs an' stay within 'earin' o' me voice. That way we stays tergether an' we gets aht of it tergether." There was general assent, offered more in attitude then in words. The man was talking sense.

"Good, right; well we should be movin' off about 'arf ten.

Coupl'hour's kip won' 'urt so get yer 'eads down." They needed no second bidding, and despite the dampness and the cold permeating their bodies most of them were dead to the world in a very few minutes. They were lucky. The move to Missy was delayed and the couple of hours became four. It was midday before they were dragged, reluctantly, from sleep and assembled ready to move.

"This is goin' t' be fun," Alfie remarked to no one in particular. Ted wasn't listening; he was too busy trying to work out how he might fit the heel back on his left boot. After two minutes he gave up and threw it away. He looked up and saw Peter Dakin watching him, quite unsympathetically. He had not had heels on either boot for three days now, and was in danger of losing the sole on one of them. By comparison, Ted's problems "were nuthin'."

Alfred Arbuckle bent and picked up the discarded piece of boot, and handed it back to Ted.

"Never know when yer might find an 'ammer an' a nail or two," he remarked, with ponderous disapproval at Ted's profligate discarding of a potentially repairable piece of equipment. Ted thought of arguing, then thought better of it and then heard Paul Cooper exhorting them to get ready to move. Stuffing the heel piece into his jacket pocket, he rose to his feet and fell into his place in the section.

The move to Missy was a masterpiece of subtle tactics. The obvious route was ignored and they moved carefully through village streets, along lines of trees, through small clumps of woodland, beside the walls of vineyards and through into the centre of Missy. One company stayed out to the left of the moving line of soldiers, acting as a screen lest the Germans gained a hint of what was going on and sought to disrupt the move by launching an assault. By two o'clock the battalion was passing through Missy towards the right hand, eastern, end in preparation for their assault up the hill which lay to their left as they walked through the streets of grey stone cottages. Many of them glanced upwards with more than just a little apprehension as they saw the size of the task facing them.

"Gawdon Bennett," breathed Ned Preece, just loud

enough for Matthew to hear. Colin Baxter glanced at his friend, smiled ruefully and then asked Matthew at what time the attack would be. As he spoke they could all hear the whisper of artillery shells passing overhead, the rumble of their guns to the south and the typical crump crump of high explosive detonating in the distance on the hill above them beyond the woods. Paul Cooper's immediate reaction was to tell Baxter to mind his own business, but he thought better of it. What might have held good on the square at Palace Barracks didn't always have its place in the conditions in which they now found themselves.

Matthew, thinking as he heard the high explosive that at last they were doing a proper job of softening the enemy, responded vaguely to the effect that he really didn't know. At this point they were just passing the church with its tall tower with the black slate of the rounded tower dome in marked contrast to the red slate of the roof of the main part of the building. The village appeared to be constructed in a series of terraces, the church being in the one above the road along which they were walking. The walls of the terraces and the large walled farm complexes provided excellent cover from view and from fire as long as they kept well into their left and did not expose themselves.

"Company commander's compliments, sir," the runner was speaking to Matthew. "Pull yooer platoon in boi that thur farm gate over thur an' bide yer toim till 'e 'as more t' tell ee."

Matthew nodded, and glanced at Cooper who, taking the unspoken instruction, began to marshal the sections into place, two each side of platoon headquarters and seated on the ground with their backs to the high farm wall. Above them, further up the hill, the battalion's screen company was on outpost. The whole of the attacking force had moved into the village with no loss, save a few casualties from some speculative long range shrapnel fire which the Germans were lobbing into the villages along the north bank of the river. None of those had occurred in the company.

Before long people began to doze as the tiredness overcame them again. Ted, with his back to the wall looking out through a gap in the houses on the other side of the road to the river beyond, was thinking of home. Such thoughts he had tried to banish from his mind, and in Belfast he had begun to succeed. Certainly, in the move up through France and the retreat, and despite his meeting on the boat with Allsop, there had barely been time. Now, as he faced again the prospect of attacking a well defended position, homesickness began to gnaw at his stomach. A picture came into his mind of Betty Chalmers, swiftly to be replaced by reddish hair, scarlet lips and the imagined smell of cigarette smoke. His eyelids were drooping, and he jerked himself awake, dragging his thoughts back to the things he'd been forced to leave. Although he'd been a churchgoer, because of his mother and because of the Army and its church parades, he had never been a "God fearin'" man; but for a reason he could not have explained, as the tiredness swooped down on him again, he began to say, quietly, to himself:

"Our Father, which art in heaven, hallowed be thy name ....."

Alfred, seated beside him, heard Ted's almost inaudible whispering and understood, from the rhythm of the prayer, what was being said. Nodding his approval he began, silently, to join in; and they both fell asleep before "thine is the Kingdom......"

It was quarter to four by the time Edward von Gleichen arrived at his headquarters in Missy. He was, briefly, apologetic before getting briskly down to business.

"I'm sorry, but I am afraid my discussion with Fourteen Brigade regarding co-operation for our forthcoming attack took rather longer than I had planned. However, no matter - where are we now?"

The brigade major explained, quickly, the layout in the village, offering the view that it would take the attacking force some ten to fifteen minutes to move up into position to commence the assault, and that really they were as ready as they were ever likely to be.

The brigadier glanced at his watch. "Good, right; we'll cross the start line at quarter past four. Artillery" - he turned to Edward Snell standing in the corner of the room - "to commence firing on the forward edge of the wood and the fort at four o'clock?" There was a questioning tone in his voice. Snell nodded his assent, turned and went into the room next door where his artillery signallers would pass the message along the line that had been laid from St Marguerite and from there back to the guns.

"Good, that's settled. Inform the battalions." And with that he turned to his map.

It was shortly after four p.m. that the orders reached the Norfolks, who had the farthest to go to get to their start line, and it was in something of an unseemly haste that men, many doped with sleep, were dragged, cajoled and hauled to their feet and set off up the steep and narrow alleys in Missy to the northern edge of the village. There was some advantage in that they had no time to consider what was about to befall them and steam could be let off cursing about officers and NCOs who clearly were incapable of organising a "piss up in a soddin' brewery!" It was not, however, only steam that was let off as apprehension and fear had its effect on many a stomach and wind was broken, both noisily and silently.

Alfie looked apologetically at Ted. "Sorry!" Ted grinned.

"Fartin's one thing, but two bleedin' verses o' Rule Britannia's a bit much." They both laughed, as did two or three others nearby. It was a much needed and welcome relief.

They moved to the sound of the guns, hearing the whisper as their own artillery passed overhead. High explosive was now falling on the forward edge of the woods on the hill, mixed with shrapnel. Further up, and on the fort itself, only shrapnel was available to try and keep the German heads down and disrupt their defensive efforts. In silence they moved into line along the lane that ran above the village, and which was to be their start line. Even the quickest wit among them could find nothing to enliven the proceedings. To their left they could hear musketry and the sound of British machine guns as the Bedfords and East Surreys commenced their attack. The Norfolks were late; it had taken them longer than planned to get into position. Ahead they could see great gouts of flame and black smoke as high explosive from 60-Pounders and a battery of four, obsolete, 6-inch guns, which had just arrived from England, pounded the woods. Above the tree line were the familiar puffs of greenish grey smoke as the shrapnel shells disgorged their contents, the familiar coughing sound being largely subsumed in the noise created by the heavier shells as they detonated.

Matthew watched the two leading companies move up the hill in extended line, well spaced, to get as close to the enemy as possible before having to indulge in the much slower process of fire and manoeuvre. He looked inwards; the company commander raised his hand and executed a forward motion as, pistol in hand, he set off up the hill. At first it was relatively easy, but then, as the artillery began to lift, the Germans in the woods began to fire on the advancing British, and their artillery began to find its mark. In the centre, and well forward watching the attack, Edward von Gleichen winced as, looking through his binoculars, he saw the impact of shrapnel and rifle fire on the flesh of his soldiers.

Ted looked around him, at Alfie on his right and beyond him Jack Waters. To his left was Peter Dakin and, just a little way away with platoon headquarters, Ned Preece and Colin. They were all sweating with the effort of climbing the steep hill, and grim faced, looking to their front. His legs ached with the effort of pushing uphill, the tops of his thighs tight with the strain. The back of his neck hurt as he sought to look up at what was going on ahead whilst at the same time leaning into the hill to make the climb easier. He tried not to look at the body he passed, stitched across the chest by machine gun fire with the front of his tunic a mashed, bloody mess. He avoided the eyes of young Jonesy from one of the forward companies, a fellow footballer in the battalion team, as he staggered back to seek medical assistance for a hand that was hanging just by a tendon, and which would see an amputation halfway up the right forearm before the evening was out.

"Jus' concentrate on gettin' up the sodding' 'ill!" Around them swallows swooped and dived, feeding voraciously off the insects flying up from the grass as the feet of advancing men disturbed them and forced them out of cover to their deaths in the beaks of their waiting enemies.

"Sir, have you seen what's happening?" Cooper moved up alongside Matthew. "Our forward companies are being pushed across to the left as we go into the re-entrant. We're bunching up and they'll be mixing it with the Bedfords soon." He flinched as a rifle bullet cracked past his head, hoping no one noticed the reaction.

"I know, I've seen it." Matthew was shouting above the din of high explosive detonation, shrapnel shells, the whiplash crack of bullets passing close by and the screams and yells of men. "But we're nearly in the woods now." He was watching the firing line of the leading companies flushing a few remaining Germans out at the point of the bayonet and prisoners were beginning to drift back into Missy under guard. Looking round he could see his platoon still with him, and so far as he could see no more than a couple had become casualties, but they were bunching as the ground forced them further into the centre. There were just too many men trying to get into too small a space.

"I hope they remember what I said about keeping tight in these woods!" yelled Matthew. His platoon sergeant nodded in silent agreement, looking to his left and right as he did so. They were still in one piece, but the woods were very much thicker than he had thought. This had all the hallmarks of a nightmare.

They stepped into the shadow of the trees, and despite the obvious difficulties the woods were about to present there was general relief that they were off the open ground and less exposed. Stepping round the bodies of German soldiers, rent asunder by high explosive, they tried not to look at these shattered and torn reminders of their own mortality. They stepped to one side as the steady trickle of their own wounded made its way back down the hill, and then moved on. Ahead they could hear the confused sounds of fighting as the withdrawing German screen clashed with the forward elements of the British attack.

Suddenly, bullets crackled all around them. To his left Matthew heard an expletive and looked to see a lance corporal holding an arm, flapping uselessly and already wet with blood. Looking ahead he could not identify the source of the enemy fire, but he needed, now, to gain control of his platoon.

"Take cover!" The order passed along the line.

"Thank the Lord for that," Ted heard Peter say, rather too loudly, as they dived to the ground and then crawled forward to a point where they could see forward. Behind them the rest of the company had also gone to ground and the major was up with Matthew trying to find out what lay ahead. By now the firing no longer appeared to be directed at them, so, acting on Matthew's hand signal, they rose as one and moved forward; at least they hoped it was forward and not off to the left again, or even the right, for by now they were losing track of direction.

"Roit bugger's muddle, this!" was Alfie's expressed view.

"Shuddup!" was Joe Floyd's response, followed by "bugger!" as he snagged his hand on yet another bramble in undergrowth that was growing denser as they moved further into the wood. By now the only line they had to follow was uphill on the basis that the fort was somewhere up there at the top. Then they were under fire again, and once more went to ground.

"Where on earth is that coming from?" The major was once more up with Matthew.

"If you'll forgive me, sir." Colin was a little reluctant to broach anything to the company commander. "I think it's from over there to our half left, and I don't think its Germans."

"What!" A pause. They all listened. "By George yer right. It's our own lot firing at us. Where's yer runner?" The question to Matthew.

"It's me, sir." Colin answered at once, and nodded his acknowledgement of the unspoken order, moving away to his left. Ned, lying beside a tree next to Matthew, suddenly fired two shots in quick succession and was rewarded with the sight of a German sniper tumbling from a tree, his limbs slack and gangly in death. The major looked down. "Thank you, Preece. Was he .....?" He left the question unfinished.

"Mitabeen, sir, mitabeen." Ned was looking forward as he spoke, his face expressionless. Matthew smiled at the major who responded with a grimace.

After a few minutes the firing ceased again, and once more they rose, trying to move further into the wood with the going becoming progressively more difficult. Ahead they could see shadows moving in the trees, unable to discern who or what they were. Overhead, shrapnel began to cough out its deadly load once more, the balls spattering on the leaves and branches of the trees.

Watching proceedings from his vantage point Edward von Gleichen decided enough was enough and that the confusion was too great. He would call it off, and runners were sent with orders for bugles to be used to sound the recall. As he did so he was aware of a commotion a short distance away where some of his staff were gathered.

"What is going on?" His commanding voice broke through the babble.

"Beg yer pardon, sir," the corporal was out of breath. "Colonel Ballard's compliments sir, but 'e finks that shrapnel's ours not theirs an' we're takin' casualties, sir!"

The commander reminded himself, briefly, how lucky it was that British soldiers could be trusted not to be overawed by generals, as he snapped at his brigade major.

"See to it!"

Turning back he was in time to see the corporal running up the hill into the maelstrom in the woods, his duty done and more to do. Not for the first time he felt humble.

"Hold it here." The word passed along the platoon. They were to hold their ground to provide cover for withdrawing units in front of them and delay any response by the Germans. It wasn't easy, for it was gloomy in the woods and identifying friend from foe was difficult. They had found themselves by a horseshoe shaped track deep in the woods and that at least gave them some sort of clearing, offering the opportunity to make an identification, hopefully in time. German shells were raining down by now as they sensed an enemy on the run and sought to harass.

"Time to go," muttered Joe Floyd to no one in particular.

"Too bloody true." Eddie Macleary, normally taciturn, was only too happy to agree.

As if the telepathy had worked, the order came to move back. Ted, bending one knee and preparing to stand, suddenly saw movement ahead and brought his rifle to the aim. What he saw was two soldiers running hard down the hill through the trees. They had no weapons and were throwing fearful looks over their shoulders as they ran.

"Stand still!" Paul Cooper's voice rang out. They stopped, as if they had run into a wall. Suddenly, just as Paul was about to call them forward, there was a huge flash and an explosion as a German shell detonated against a tree trunk about ten feet above the ground. The blast blew both soldiers over, the right hand of the two being thrown backwards never to rise. The other man was also hit, a long shard of shattered trunk driving directly downwards from the tree and carving off the right hand side of his head before smashing into the collar bone and penetrating the upper chest.

The force threw the man forward, rolling down the hill across the clearing towards the area occupied by Joe Floyd's section. Ted, having ducked as the shell detonated, looked up to see a body sliding and rolling towards him. He recoiled as it slithered to a halt in front of him, the smashed head just a few inches from his face, the smell of exposed brain and arterial blood filling his nostrils, the dislodged right eye dangling sightless on the optic nerve. The man must have been dead, but he twitched as he lay there. Ted saw from the shoulder title that he was a Bedford. Believing there might be some life, and having slid away a few feet from the horrific sight before him, he reached over and touched the man who rolled over onto his back, the lie of the hill providing additional momentum. Ted need not have wasted his time, he was dead. He looked down at the small star shaped scar on the left, undamaged, cheek and realised that he was looking at the twitching, mangled, mortal remains of Lance Corporal John Allsop.

"We go again!" The orders percolated down. Come the dawn and they were to try once more to take the fort, following the same route as yesterday. The difference this time would be that only two battalions of Fifteen Brigade would make the attempt, the Norfolks and the Bedfords, with the Norfolks leading. The rest of the brigade would be in reserve. Thirteen Brigade on the right would attack the spur from the south-east. The theory was that fewer men would be easier to control and using whole battalions rather than the somewhat amorphous collection of companies used in the first attempt would result in success.

It was an hour before dawn when the final orders were given. Reconnaissance patrols during the night had identified new defences thrown up by the Germans, but the artillery would be trying to knock them out. They listened almost as if in a trance. Casualties the day before had not been heavy, only a hundred or so across the whole of the attacking force, but it had been a shocking experience for many of them and if they had thought themselves tired on previous days there was now a form of dulled exhaustion which was beyond description.

Colin Baxter, who had become lost after delivering his message to the Bedfords, inviting them to stop firing on their own side, rejoined the platoon only an hour before the orders for the next attack. He had no time to share with his friends the unpleasantness he had endured, merely enough to clean his rifle and replenish his ammunition. His stomach had sunk at the prospect of revisiting the hills; and he was desperately hungry, but hot food was a luxury they would all do without.

Ted had been very quiet, and awake, all night. Once they had recovered, in quite good order, down the hill and back into Missy the reaction had set in and he had withdrawn into himself. The vision of Allsop's injuries simply would not leave his mind's eye. He consoled himself with the thought that the man had almost certainly suffered no pain, and he probably got no more than he deserved, running away as he had been. When he heard that they were to go back up again an uncontrollable shiver passed through his body.

The grey of the dawn edging its way into the blackness in the east found them damp, cold, hungry and very fed up, lying on the ground by the lane at the north of the village where they had been the previous afternoon. Matthew wondered if they had noticed that on the way they had turned right to follow the track and in so doing had passed the village cemetery off to their left. He shook himself, wondering briefly if he was becoming too morbid, and then looked left and right, seeing the shapes of his men in the gloom. His belly ached for want of food and his eyes itched for want of sleep. There was a feeling of nausea associated with biliousness which was acutely uncomfortable, and potentially embarrassing. One thing for a soldier to "shit 'is pants" as some had done, but an officer ....?

Cooper, trying to stay awake, moved nearer to Matthew. The officer, looking round, motioned in the growing light for him to remain where he was. Initially offended, he was mollified by Matthew's smile of reassurance; but he was still cold and afraid; and missing Jane terribly. He was jerked from his loneliness by the woosh of passing artillery shells and the crash as they detonated on the tree line ahead. If the Germans hadn't known they would attack again, they certainly did now.

As the day grew clear they rose, shook themselves to free stiff joints, hefted their rifles with the long bayonets fitted and, heads lifted so they could look up the hill, moved off together to try once more. The German response was shrapnel, and they had the range and altitude just right. Their effectiveness was limited by the disciplined spacing of the Norfolks, but casualties could not be avoided. By now they were getting used to the indiscriminate toll levied by enemy fire, the sudden shout of pain, the thwack of metal impacting and penetrating flesh, the slack, disjointed crumpling of a dead man, the cries as the agony sometimes became too much to bear. After what seemed an age they were there, up against the tree line and moving into it.

"What on earth ......?" Matthew's question tailed off as he viewed a six foot high fence in the dense undergrowth.

"How the hell do we get through this?" Paul Cooper was angry, frightened and perplexed. How on earth had yesterday's attack and last night's reconnaissance missed this sodding thing?

"There's a gap here." Alfred Arbuckle's deep voice echoed down to Matthew.

"Baxter, go and tell the major what has happened. We cannot funnel everyone through a small gap. Tell him I am putting half the platoon through as a screen, and we shall need to make other gaps with wire cutters." Matthew knew that the company had a section of pioneers with them for just such an eventuality. Colin ran back to company headquarters. "Sergeant, take two sections through that gap and hold the ground on that small bank," he pointed fifty yards ahead, "to give us a foothold on the other side."

"Sir!" Paul was up in an instant and on his way. Corporal Floyd, Corporal Collis, your sections follow me and take position to my left and right when we reach the bank by the brown bush." They looked up, acknowledged their destination and ordered their sections to "prepare to move!"

Joe Floyd leading, they dashed through the gap in the fence whilst along the company frontage men with wire cutters began to hack at dense undergrowth to get at the wire barring their progress. With the British artillery lifting so as not to hit their own side they began to suffer from small arms fire as the Germans surfaced in the woods beyond.

Gasping from their dash, and with a heart rate also increased by apprehension, they threw themselves onto the bank in fire positions watching for an approaching enemy whilst at their backs the attack stalled on the wire. Over to the east, and unknown to them, Thirteen Brigade's supporting attack had run into stiff opposition and had faltered.

"Divisional HQ has ordered a cessation of the attack." The brigade major handed the message to von Gleichen.

"Thirteen Brigade has been stopped, and Fourteen Brigade over to the left is having trouble."

The brigade commander's face was inscrutable. "Give the order." He turned away and looked up the hill to where the Norfolks were suffering under shrapnel and small arms fire of a gradually growing intensity. Behind them, in the open, the Bedfords lay, also taking casualties, their supporting role never to be undertaken. "What a waste." He looked round to see if anyone had noticed his muttered comment, but, if they had, they showed no sign.

"Sergeant Cooper!" Matthew's voice bellowed across the space which still lay between them, the wire unbreached. "We are to retire. Back you come!"

Paul nodded his assent. "Hear that?" He looked at his two section commanders who nodded. "Corporal Collis, you first, and I'll bring the rest."

Jim Collis nodded, looked left and right: "Prepare to move, back through the gap after me." A pause, a look round as his men slid back out of their fire position so they would not rise from where they had lain. "Move!" They were up and dashing back. A few twigs crashed down as bullets flew over their heads, but they were safely through.

Paul was on his feet as he looked to his left and saw Joe with his section ready to follow him. He turned and ran as fast as he could at the gap and burst through towards the rest of the platoon. He stopped to watch all of Joe's section through.

"Sarge!" He heard Preece's voice call out, a note of great urgency in it. "Sarge, behind you!" He turned, just in time to see a group of Germans only a few yards away bursting through the undergrowth. The leader, and the largest of them, was on him before he could raise his rifle. He was smashed back against a tree, the breath taken from his body, the man's forearm against his throat, and the sharp pain in his larynx as the strangulation began. The look of anticipation in the German's eyes as his own began to mist, the smell of his assailant's breath, stinking of tobacco and alcohol.

Suddenly there was a woosh as the German exhaled, and

the pressure released. Blood spurted from his mouth and spattered the front of Paul's uniform. He jerked his head away in disgust and, looking down, saw Ned Preece at the bottom of the small bank on which the tree stood, his rifle with the bayonet slanted upwards into the man's belly, through the lung and into the heart, blood running down the forestock onto Ned's hand, his face white with shock at the enormity of what he had just done. Paul pushed the German away, and there was a sucking noise as Ned heaved the bayonet out.

"Thanks!" Paul was gasping for breath.

"S'alright," grunted Ned, feeling sick.

Two of the Germans in the group were down, both killed. The other two had surrendered. Ted was lying in a small bush where he had fallen, looking shocked and holding his side low down near his left hip.

"You all right?" A nod. "Right, well c'mon, let's go; and bring those two with you." Paul gestured at the cowering Germans.

When a bullet strikes human flesh the damage is caused by the transfer of energy from the bullet, a function of its mass times the square of its velocity on impact. The severity of the wound depends on the amount of energy that is transferred and the rate of transfer. For the worst kind, the effect inside the flesh is one of "cavitation", or "explosive wounding", so called because of the large, macerated partial cavity that is created looking just as if a mild explosion has taken place.

Often the German seven point nine two millimetre bullet would pass through a body, thereby limiting the amount of energy transferred. However, the one that struck Jack Waters low in the right shoulder had been deflected by a small branch. Consequently, it was tumbling and therefore offering a larger surface area than the bullet point when it impacted; hence it remained in his body with all its energy very swiftly transferred. He was thrown on his back, emitting a loud gasp as he hit the ground. Turning away from the German he had just killed, Ned saw Jack fall and raced across to him. Looking up the hill he could see more Germans, and Waters was still alive. Ned rolled him over and, grabbing the cross-straps of the man's webbing, began to run down the slope towards the village and safety. Despite his slight frame he was tough and wiry and fear lent him strength. Dragging and bumping his screaming burden he fought and struggled his way down into the open and on to the village. Just as he thought he had made it he felt the burning sensation as a bullet passed through his left calf. Tumbling as he went down he surfaced near a long stone wall at the top of the village. Trying to rise he found his leg would not support him. Dragging himself up by pulling against the wall he reached down to haul Waters over, not sure how he would achieve it.

"Leave 'im. I've got 'im." It was Alfred, his huge frame looming through the mist of pain and sweat that seemed to have clouded Ned's vision.

"C'mon, I've got you." He heard Paul Cooper's voice and felt a strong arm under his own, taking the weight off the damaged leg. He winced and yelled as he was hauled over the wall whereupon Ted and Alfie grabbed him and moved him into the relative safety of the terraced village streets. Ahead he could see Alfred carrying Waters as if he were a child.

"Put 'em down 'ere!" Joe Floyd was taking control. Paul didn't argue; he could leave them there and get about helping Matthew pull the platoon together. Most of them were nearby, grouped by the wall beneath the church.

"Stuff somethin' in that wound. 'E's bleedin' like a stuck pig!" Joe Floyd addressed himself to a white faced Peter Dakin. Waters was passing in and out of consciousness as Peter fumbled at the straps of the man's pack looking for socks or underwear to pad the wound and help congeal the blood flow. Waters' own shell dressing, which he would normally have used, had been ripped away during the tumble down the hill. Ted pulled a knife and cut through Waters' webbing straps, and Peter emptied the contents onto the ground.

"That'll do," said Joe, pointing at a scarf.

"'Ey, wassat?" Alfie picked up a pack of cards. "These are mine. I lost these weeks ago."

Joe Floyd looked down, and saw a number of other small items that he knew from section chatter had been "misplaced" over the past few weeks. "Sergeant! Mr Jenkins!" The two men turned as he called and came over to where Ned and Jack Waters lay side by side against the wall.

"See!" Ned Preece's voice was very aggressive as he watched Paul looking at the contents of Waters' pack. "It bloody wasn't me, and you wouldn't bloody believe me."

"Preece!" Paul's voice was sharp, with a defensive note to it. "You just watch your bloody tongue!" He looked at Matthew, his face a mix of emotions.

Ned was about to ignore Paul's order and return to the attack when a word from Matthew silenced him.

"Preece!" Matthew had a serious look on his face, conscious that his sergeant's credibility was on the line. "We shall take account of all this. It seems we may have found our thief, but we still need to explain the medallion in your kit. We shall take this one step at a time. Sergeant Cooper, gather all this up and I will discuss it with the major."

"Bastard prob'ly planted it." Alfie had never liked Waters, and resented the mental agony his friend had been through over the past few weeks.

Silently, Matthew agreed with him and resolved to prosecute that line with the major. He hoped he could make it work, and he was glad that his trust in Preece had been vindicated. He was dragged from his thoughts by a series of huge explosions in the village, several hundred yards to the east. The earth vibrated with the shock of the detonations, and he watched open mouthed as great clouds of black smoke with debris intermingled rose into the sky. He had never heard artillery fire of such power before.

The Germans had deployed on the hills above the river some of their siege artillery. Brought with them in order to attack the French forts, they were using 210 millimetre guns whose shell, eight inches in calibre, would very quickly reduce to rubble buildings of the sort to be found in Missy. The guns were deployed in batteries of three and had a slow rate of fire of something like one and a half minutes between each round. Indeed, it was about ninety seconds later, with no movement by the British, and for the moment no thought other than to wonder what had caused the damage and whether there were any more, that the next three arrived. They looked on in horror as, landing closer this time, three massive explosions took place in the area occupied by the company to their left. Paul Cooper watched as a khaki clad object spiralled lazily into the air, recognising from the black object at one end that it was a man's leg. Ted and Peter, both having seen the same thing, turned back to attend to Ned, Peter catching Ted's eye as he did with a look on his white face that showed the strain they were all under.

"Move away, down to the south, towards the river." The order flashed along the line. "And hurry." The sense of urgency in everyone's voices as NCOs chivvied men and men cajoled each other.

"C'mon Ned, le's go." Alfred Arbuckle towered over the diminutive Preece holding his hand downwards with the unspoken offer to help him to his feet and then assist him down the hill. Meanwhile, Joe Floyd had ambushed two of the battalion's stretcher bearers as they were running towards the carnage left by the German barrage and was supervising the loading of Jack Waters onto the canvas carrier. The man screamed out as he was lifted, with some haste given the probability of impending German heavy artillery fire, and then fainted into silence.

Further along the road to their right they heard some sporadic rifle fire, and for a moment there was a concern that Germans may have penetrated into the village. Paul was about to direct a section to guard their withdrawal when he heard the sound of an aircraft and tilting his head skywards found himself looking at the cause of the firing; a German spotter aircraft. No wonder they had the artillery smack on.

Dragging and carrying their wounded they made haste

away from the village whose buildings, with shells that size, would offer little protection, to the hedgerows and open fields between the river and the village. Equipment clattered as packs bumped up and down on men's backs, water bottles slapped against bodies, rifle slings chinked. Boots clattered on roads and offered only muffled thuds as men chose, where they could, to run on grass and save their feet. As they reached the southern edge of the village there were three more rounds from the big howitzers, to be followed by yet three more.

"They keep this up an' there'll be no soddin' village left." Joe Floyd was gasping for breath as the section threw themselves to the ground on Paul Cooper's order. But they did not keep it up. It was as if the Germans knew they had moved out, and they began hunting for them in the open country using shrapnel.

They were lying with their backs to a hedgerow, using the bank as cover from direct enemy fire, and from view. However, they were growing increasingly concerned about the effectiveness of the German artillery, and they were faced with very few options. The village was not a nice place to be with the howitzers having its range, and they would take serious casualties trying to dig in here under fire, and the plain through which the river flowed offered very little cover indeed. Alfred was bandaging Ned's leg. The bullet had passed right through, but it was impossible to say how much damage had been done.

"Could be a Blighty one, this'n Ned." He grinned at Ned Preece who, the stigma of being the platoon thief having been lifted from him, simply grinned back. If it was a Blighty wound and he got home on the strength of it he knew precisely what it was he was going to do.

"Ted, wot're ye doin?" It was Alfred again who, looking up from his labours on Ned's leg, could see Ted examining the old boot heel Alfred had made him keep, and comparing it to a hole in his tunic. His hands were shaking a little as he looked up and spoke not just to Alfred, but to Peter and Alfie who were also watching him.

"Remember that second German up thur, the one who

came through jus' where Ned stuck the other one?" Nods of understanding prompted him to carry on. "Well, 'e wen' fer me with 'is bayonet an' I was off balance an' tripped back over sommat, a log or sommat, I don' know what." More nods. This was making a good story, regardless of the mayhem that was surrounding them. "Well, as I wen' down 'e wen' t' stick me in the stomach an' 'is bayonet got stuck in this." He held up the heel showing the deep gouge where the German bayonet had embedded in the leather. "'E were standin' there tryin' t' pull the bloody thing out and I was 'anging on to 'is rifle trying to stop 'im when Jack shot the bugger roit through the 'ead. Lifted the top of 'is bonce right off it did." He looked away to where the stretcher bearers were carrying Waters and other casualties towards ambulances which were braving the shrapnel fire. "Owe the bastard me loif, thievin' sod!"

"Sir, sir!" Any prospect of debating the vagaries of life and the strange twist which made them grateful to a man they now despised was lost in the urgent call from Eddie Macleary as he drew Matthew's attention. "Sir, c'mere!" Unusual as might have been for officers to obey the orders of a private soldier it was clear that Macleary had seen something untoward and to which attention required to be paid. "There sir, look, can y' not see it?"

"See what, man?"

"In that 'aystack, sir. Look, jus' there at the back. It don't settle the way the rest of 'em do, and unless I'm mistaken, sir, an' I don' think I am, I saw somethin' movin' in there. Black it were."

"Well, there's nothing there now. And as for a settling haystack, what is that supposed to mean? What are you saying?"

"I'm sayin' it's worth a look. I think there's sommat there." He ducked his head as a shrapnel round coughed just overhead. "An' sommat is making darn sure them buggers know where they be firing them guns."

The haystack was three hundred yards away, and Macleary, thought Matthew, must have very good eyesight indeed if he thought he saw anything in there.

"'Ang on, sir. Jus' a minnit. Alfie, mate, you jus' 'old yerself still." Eddie rested his rifle on Alfie's shoulder, and Alfie, trained professional that he was, asked no questions, but assumed that another professional knew what he was doing. Eddie took very careful aim, whilst Matthew watched fascinated. "Wan' the bugger alive, don' we sir?" Matthew could scarce believe he was hearing what he was hearing. He watched as Eddie took a deep breath, settled his rifle into his shoulder, the forestock on Alfie's shoulder as a support to aid accuracy, steadied his breathing, took first pressure on the trigger until it was firm against the seer, and then squeezed. The rifle bucked into his shoulder, but his head had already moved to one side, the look of satisfaction on his face making it clear that he knew a second shot would not be required. Automatically, without thinking, he worked the bolt to eject the spent cartridge and chamber the new, making a mental note that there were now seven rounds in the magazine and one up the spout.

In the haystack there was sudden movement as something inside disturbed the hay. "Gottim." Alfie looked round sheepishly as he spoke, hoping no one thought he was claiming the credit.

"Corporal Floyd, take your section and bring back whatever is in there! Baxter, go and tell the major we have what might be a German spy." Matthew was grinning hugely at the prospect of what they might have done. Joe Floyd took with him Alfie, Ted, Peter, Eddie and Alfred, all that was left of his section, and ran down to the haystack, impervious, so it seemed, to the continuing German artillery fire. As they arrived it was obvious that someone was in there.

"Come on out, y' bugger!" Joe was not feeling charitable. There was a groan from the top of the stack.

"I said come out, an' I mean now!" The thought that the occupant of the haystack might either not speak English, or had been rendered incapable of speech of any sort by his wound, had not crossed Joe's mind.

"Ich bin verletzt. Ich brauche hilfe, hilfeeee...." The last word trailed off, but it was obvious that someone was in pain, and needed help. They were, however, mindful of several stories of Germans waving white flags and then firing on any British soldier who exposed himself to take the offer of surrender. The decision was made for them by the collapse of the back part of the haystack and the appearance, in an uncontrolled slide, of a German officer clutching a smashed kneecap and clearly in very great pain.

"Good shot that," muttered Ted.

"Aye." Eddie Macleary was clearly satisfied with his work. "An' look 'ere, the bugger 'ad a telephone. An' look 'ere, the wires've been buried. They mus' go all the way up the 'ill."

Satisfied with their work, and unceremoniously dragging their prey, who was yelling in agony, they headed back to the platoon position to be greeted by a delighted commanding officer and brigade commander.

"Who spotted him?" The CO was clearly very pleased.

"Me sir." Eddie looked sheepish. "An' I shot 'im too." His face lit up as he said it, proud of his skill with a rifle. "An' the bugger's still aloive. Can answer a few questions I shouldn't wonder." The grin was growing broader.

"Well done." The brigade commander's urbane tones cut through the conversation. "Very well done indeed." Eddie assumed the look of serious attention, looking into the middle distance, that soldiers always adopted when faced with officers of seniority, and he responded with the single word: "Sir!"

"Ballard, if you would now get your battalion back into the village and hold the line of this morning's start line whilst I determine what it is we must do next. Thank you." He looked around him as he said the last two words, clearly addressing them to everybody, with his gaze lingering on Eddie. Smiling, he turned away back to his headquarters as two military policemen escorted the German away to see a medical officer.

The German artillery fire having slackened the battalion moved back up through the village, leaving behind their wounded to be cared for by the stretcher bearers and then the Medical Corps once they reached a dressing station. Ned Preece was one, as was Jack Waters. The unscathed survivors spent a very wet and uncomfortable day lying in shell scrapes as the rain descended waiting for the possibility of a German attack which never materialised. There they remained until dusk, when orders were passed to them that they would be relieved that night by Fourteen Brigade, and they were to move back out of the line into billets at a place called Le Mernil; which meant crossing back south of the river again.

It was not an easy withdrawal, handing over in pitch dark to the incoming brigade and then moving south, in order, and in pouring rain, to the crossing site. The Norfolks were the last to leave, and shortly before they were due to move the Germans decided something was amiss and used searchlights and starshell in an attempt to light up the area. They also brought heavy small arms fire to bear on the general area of Missy. The Norfolks responded with machine guns, and wet soldiers, who could not get any wetter, operated the bolts of their rifles and fired into the enemy positions, the droplets of rain water hissing as they struck the hot muzzles of the rifles. After a short while the Germans desisted and the withdrawal resumed in peace, but it was dawn before the brigade, or rather what was left of it, was complete on the south side of the river.

It was around eight o'clock in the morning before they found themselves at their billets, not in Le Mernil which was actually their crossing point over the river, but in Jury; and were faced with some prospect of drying out. Stew might not be every man's idea of the ideal breakfast menu, but the one served up to them as they arrived was probably the most welcome sight any of them could ever remember. Washed down with hot tea, they were just coming to the end of their meal when an artillery duel commenced. By now they were impervious to the whisper of shells passing overhead, and even to their detonation not too far away. They had learned that the one which kills or maims is the one you haven't heard and whilst they were still apprehensive at the game of chance which seemed to rule who was hit and who not, they were now better able to cope with it.

Consequently, since none of the unpleasantness was directed at them, the Norfolks enjoyed a peaceful day, sharing their billets with the Dorsets. As they rested, Sir John French ordered the line to be strongly entrenched, whilst indicating at the same time that he intended to continue the advance at the first opportunity. However, from that day, the sixteenth of September, there were no more daily operations orders; they were only issued when necessary. The brains had stagnated, the line had stagnated and initiative had stagnated. The order to dig in was, de facto, the first notification of the onset of trench warfare.

Consumed with their own thoughts, it was an exhausted group of men who lit a fire in an attempt to dry out. Ted was very quiet, the horror of his brush with death at the hands of the German and the memory of Allsop's mangled remains very fresh in his mind. He felt he wanted to write a letter to his mother, but he was too wet and too tired. He looked around at his friends, and most of them seemed also to be withdrawn, each consumed with his own thoughts. He watched Joe Floyd, trying to sort the contents of his pack into some semblance of order, and wondered at the man. In Belfast he had been a bit of a joke, considered by most to be weak, and a fearful lecher. However, the responsibility foisted on him by the departure of Fred Smith had certainly brought out the best in him. He'd done a good job up on that hill.

Matthew, with Colin now doubling as runner and servant, lay back on the bed he had been allocated in the farmhouse. His mind was in turmoil, the images of the last two days crowding in with those that had accumulated from the time when they had first encountered the enemy near Mons; was it only a few weeks ago? It seemed an age. He had spoken to Cooper about Preece, and the sergeant had, sheepishly, admitted his error. Their relationship was now back on an even keel, for which he was thankful. He was feeling very lonely, and a little afraid. He worried about how he might react if he were to be seriously injured, or how he might respond if asked, once more, to undertake the sort of venture on which they had been embarked these past two days. Cooper's presence he found reassuring. He drifted off to sleep, a vision in his mind of a black tunnel; and he could see no light at the end of it.

Chapter 11

The Race to the Sea

They were having some difficulty coming to terms with the pronunciation of the name of the town in whose general direction they were heading. "Wipers" was the nearest anyone had got because that's what it looked as if it ought to sound like when they saw it written down, although for some reason officers persisted in calling it "Eeepra".

"Sounds like 'e's got bleedin' 'iccups," muttered one signaller in brigade HQ, having had his pronunciation corrected a dozen times by the brigade major.

The cause of it all was the stalemate that had developed on the Aisne. The Allies could not move north, but the Germans, despite strenuous efforts, had been unable to dislodge them from their hold on the river line. At the same time Falkenhayn, the German Chief of Staff, determined that the only unoccupied battle ground lay to the north, between the River Oise and the sea. For his part, Joffre, having realised he could not break through by frontal assault, decided his best chance of success lay in a wide, sweeping move out to his left, behind the Sixth French Army lying north of Paris, and attacking the enemy's right flank.

Ypres, as the most westerly town in Belgian Flanders, was a vital centre of communications and as such was the focus of attention for the Allies, and for the Germans in their new endeavours to break the deadlock into which they were settling on the Aisne. Whoever held Ypres held the key to Calais and Boulogne. For the Germans there was also an obsession that this was the shortest route to victory. Their objective was to close with the enemy in that part of Flanders and gain Calais.

Field Marshall Sir John French viewed the intentions of his ally with some trepidation, fearing that the BEF would find itself exposed and once more victim to the whim of the French whose principal concern lay with the sovereignty of their territory and not with the survival of the small British Army. He also knew that Churchill was planning a raid on Antwerp to support the Belgians who continued to occupy it, thereby providing a diversion on the German right. French wished to be nearby when it happened. He was also very keen that he be near Calais or Boulogne so that he could run for home should the need arise.

Reluctant to offer the British a position from which they could more easily desert back to their homeland, and short of transport given his own desire to move in the same direction, Joffre, nonetheless, acquiesced to the British CinC's request that he be given part of the line to the left of the French Army, and, consequently, just over three weeks after their bloody encounter on the hill above Missy, the Ninth found themselves part of a huge, and unmolested, move away south-east from the line of the river and then north, by rail, to a detraining area at Abbeville. It remains a massive tribute to the skill of British staff work and the professionalism of the regular British Army that the Germans had no inkling of their move, and were still reporting six British divisions on the Aisne long after most of them had gone.

Ted sat with his back to the wooden walls of the cattle truck, his buttocks resting comfortably on a decent pile of straw. One of the new lads had just opened the dixie of tea, and, in company with a sandwich of cold beef and pickle, he was trying to remember when a cup of tea had tasted quite so good. He looked across at Colin and smiled as his friend caught his eye with a glance. They hadn't talked about it, but a couple of days ago there had been two letters from England. Watching him open them Ted had seen the colour drain from his face as he had read the first, and his hands tremble as he had hurriedly opened the second, only to display a completely different set of emotions. His face had re-established its colour, and he had flushed red as tears sprang into his eyes. Embarrassed, he had looked around to see who was watching, and on seeing Ted had risen to his feet and left the derelict cottage in which they had been billeted.

"'E'll tell me when 'e's ready." The thought flashed through his mind as he began a review of the past few weeks, and the unpleasantness that had followed their rapid withdrawal from Missy to the south of the river. Really, it hadn't been too bad. They had moved between billets in a number of the local villages into trenches and back out again; and there had been times when the German shelling had been pretty intense. The twenty-fifth of September stuck out in his mind, partly because that was also the day that letters began to come in from home in response to the first ones they had sent after arriving in France.

His mother had been glad he'd met "Mr Allsop", and had been brought up to date on what was happening in the village. She was pleased that he knew the secret was out about him being in the Army. Betty Chalmers, now called Smith, was back in the village living with her ma and pa while her husband was away training for the war. He was going to be an officer, and everyone was very proud of him. Ted had grunted as he read that, drawing inquisitorial looks from his chums to which he had not responded. Mention of "Mr Allsop" had brought back the memory of the man's death and its particularly gruesome nature. He had shuddered, and wondered if he should do anything, like write or something.

The weather had been typically Septemberish, with something of an Indian summer from about the twentieth. The nights, of course, were cold; and getting colder as the days shortened into the autumn. Leaves on the trees in the valley had begun to drift from green into the transitions of yellow and brown which preceded their descent to the ground. There was a dampness about the place which, at night especially, chilled the bones.

They had not seen anything of Ned Preece since he had been loaded on a stretcher and carried off to the clearing station. Word had filtered back that his injury was not too serious, but he had fractured a bone in his leg, to whit the fibula, and he would need to spend some time plastered up before he could walk properly. He would be back, but not for some time and not until after he had indulged in some convalescent leave in England.

"Lucky sod!" Sympathy, as Colin Baxter had once so eloquently put it, is a word found in Thomas' dictionary somewhere between shit and syphilis.

Jack Waters had been dead within a couple of hours. His shoulder had, essentially, been destroyed by the impact of the German rifle bullet. A lump of flesh was found to be missing from the entry area where the bullet had struck, and there had been a fist sized hole driven through the shoulder blade. As they had sought to stem the flow of blood with dressings they had seen bits of his uniform and equipment protruding from the wound where they had been driven into his body by the impact, and small, white pieces of bone could clearly be seen. Despite their best efforts, however, he had suffered massive blood loss, and his condition had been complicated by extreme pain and shock. His passing was not considered a loss. A search of the rest of his kit, held by the QM in B Echelon, had revealed yet more booty, including stuff looted from some of the billets in which they had stayed. Ned had been cleared, and Ted would never forget the look on Cooper's face as the man realised he had been wrong all along. Watching him, across the other side of the wagon, Ted wondered how the Sergeant felt. There had been no comment on the matter, and no apparent change in his demeanour, but that was to have been expected. The man was more machine than human, but he knew his job and those who had survived thus far owed him that.

No more, however, than Cooper owed Ned Preece. He

could still feel the pressure of the German's forearm on his throat and remembered the panic as he had tried to fight him off, and the realisation that he might not be able to achieve it. Preece had saved his life, and he knew it; and he felt so incredibly foolish that he had taken such a stand regarding the man's guilt. Matthew had been a complete gentleman about the whole affair, making it clear that no one was to blame given the quite clear attempt by Waters to implicate Preece, and given Preece's less than soldierly history in the regiment. However, the fact remained that he had been a bloody fool, and he owed his life to the man he had victimised. He looked round at the platoon spread around the wagon, and for a second imagined that they were all talking about him behind his back.

"Prob'ly did that already anyway," he thought, and then shook himself as if to rid his psyche once and for all of the recurring embarrassment. He looked down at the letter from Jane. He had been stunned by the news of her pregnancy, yet to be confirmed, but about as positive as could be. She was three weeks overdue, and up to now it had been possible to set a watch by her menstrual cycle. That night when he had first heard he was off to war had been the cause. She had clung to him so tightly he had feared he might have hurt her. At least, if he didn't make it back, there was something else for her to hold on to. He hadn't mentioned it yet, not certain that he was close enough to anyone to really want to share a moment of such intimacy and joy; but something inside him was bursting to let it out and he knew it was only a question of time. A few beers in the sergeants' mess, if they ever got together as a mess again, was probably the answer.

There were a dozen new faces to get to know, reservists drafted in and Special Reserve soldiers brought onto the active list, plus a few from Britannia Barracks, their Norwich depot, who had been on detached duty or with the second battalion. They'd come out under command of a young officer, arriving just after the Missy affair, feeling, as with all newcomers, out of place among men who had already experienced the ghastliness of battle and who, inevitably, felt and acted somewhat superior. The newcomers' morale had not been helped when the new officer had come forward with his allocation of men to reinforce the company and had walked straight into a Jack Johnson. This was the name being given to the German 150 millimetre mortar, which gave off a significant cloud of black smoke when it detonated. Jack Johnson being a black American boxer it was perfectly natural for Thomas to think of him when seeking to attach a label to some common occurrence.

The cause of the black smoke lay with an inadequacy in the chemical composition of the explosive. A high explosive molecule comprises, typically, atoms of Carbon, Nitrogen, Sulphur and Oxygen. When a shock wave, greater than the speed of sound in the compound, is imparted to the explosive by a detonating mixture such as, say, Fulminate of Mercury, the molecule breaks up into its constituent atoms and then reforms again as new compounds. These might be Nitrous Oxides and Carbon Dioxide or Monoxide. It is the dissipation of the energy bonding the original molecule, the heat of deformation and reformation and the sound of the shock wave which deliver the shattering effect and the blast of high explosive, the flash which causes such terrible burns and the ear splitting noise.

If there is insufficient Oxygen in the molecule to create complete, new, simple molecules then there is waste and inefficiency, and in early explosives not all the Carbon could recombine to make Carbon Dioxide and Monoxide due to a lack of Oxygen in the high explosive molecular structure. Hence the black cloud of unconsumed Carbon which was a feature of so many detonations, and the Jack Johnson in particular. Nonetheless, however inefficient it might have been, the effect on the young officer's body had been to inflict the most horrific injuries, flayed by shell splinters, dirt and gravel; and his arm had been ripped from his body and thrown some distance to land in a waste food pit. They had not even got to know him, and with his face having ceased to exist in a recognisable form, they would not even carry his memory in their mind's eye.

One of the new arrivals had been violently sick at the sight, and Cooper remembered with a grim smile that although the rest of the platoon had held their stomachs in place it had not been without difficulty for some. He looked across at Peter Dakin, asleep in the corner of the wagon. He'd be stiff when he woke, although they had been roughing it now for so long they could probably sleep anywhere and in any conditions and still not feel the effects too badly. He'd been with the boy when the first letter had come out from Belfast. "Dear Son." Dakin had hardly been able to contain himself as he read it. Cooper could remember the contents, not in the detail of the words, but in the emotions and thoughts expressed for the boy had shared it with them all. For all the world it was as if Peter had just acquired the mother and father he had never known. The closing words, "with our love, Ma and Pa," had brought a huge grin to his face and he had set down at once to write a response. That he had found difficult, and the Sergeant had seen him discussing it with Colin Baxter. How to write about normal things that wouldn't frighten them, when all around was abnormality.

Matthew Jenkins put down the three-day-old copy of the Times he was reading, and, with his hands in his lap, looked out of the window of the carriage in which the officers were being transported at the French countryside as the train ambled its sedate way north from the Oise and the small town of Rivercourt from where they had entrained. They had left their overnight billets in Bethuy St Pierre at seven in the morning and marched to Rivercourt, where the train had departed at two in the afternoon. Apart from some tea laid on by the movements control organisation, and some sandwiches provided before they left, there had been no refreshment and the pangs of hunger were gnawing at his stomach. No matter, there would be food at a halt somewhere up ahead, and he would have to put up with it until then. He smiled his thanks as the major passed round segments of a bar of chocolate to the occupants of the carriage. Amazing how such a small intake of food could instantly curb tummy rumblings, albeit only for a short while. He watched the major, marvelling not for the first time at his sang froid, and the charmed life he had borne in all that had passed these past few weeks. Once more his stomach tightened and churned at the thought of death or injury. Opposite him sat the second of the two young officers who had joined them on the Aisne. The young man looked at Matthew, grinned weakly and marvelled at the coolness of the senior subaltern whose reputation for courage and skill in battle was already something of a talking point.

They had been on the march for a few days, having left behind them the awfulness on the Aisne with not one tinge of regret. They had all been dirty and in many cases unkempt, although there had been that occasion in Chasigny, just a week ago, where there had been the opportunity for a proper shave and a haircut. The results had been a bit slapdash, with one pair of clippers to two hundred men and a razor between twenty; and woe betide the twentieth man to use it. However, they had all felt very much better for a clean up.

He thought over the events of the past few months and pondered the conversation he had undertaken with the major the previous day. The casualties among officers had meant that there would have to be some redistribution, and he was being considered for promotion to captain and command of a company. Hardly surprising really, given his age and maturity; and the consensus among his brother officers was that he had done a good job and could be relied upon. He was in part flattered and in part saddened at the prospect of leaving the platoon, for he had built up a good rapport with them; and he was now back on an even keel with Cooper. He was also apprehensive, for the added responsibility was something with which one ought not to trifle, and he was, frankly, scared. Scared of what, he was not entirely sure; of death itself; of maiming or of some terrible wound whereby he could not contain his own screams of agony; or simply of failure or perhaps the public expression of that fear in some way. In short, he wondered very much if he could face very much more of what he had already endured, let alone take on even greater responsibility.

He was considering his options for the future structure of his platoon, and the promotions he wished to discuss with the company commander. Colin Baxter had done well, and should be given a section early, even if protocol only allowed promotion to lance corporal. Similarly, Alfie James had potential, but lacked the maturity to hold the responsibilities of corporal. A single tape and second in command of a section would suit him for the time being. Joseph Floyd should be made up to corporal; he had done surprisingly well, and James would be good as his deputy. Of the rest, Ludgrove was also worth a stripe, but behind his other two friends. He was honest and straight, and a good soldier, but he lacked a little flair and needed some time just to round off his personality; if he survived that long. Had he still been here, he would have seriously considered Preece for promotion. Despite his shortcomings, the man had courage and an inner strength which seemed to grow day by day; and he was respected by his fellows. In fairness, Preece deserved a Distinguished Conduct Medal for what he had done on the hill at Missy, but, given the cloud that had been hanging over him, that might have been just a touch too far to push and he had decided not to mention it to the major. Nonetheless, he had a citation written in his field note book in case the moment arose when it might be opportune to present it.

As Matthew turned his thoughts back to the Times the object of the last thread of his thoughts was sitting comfortably in an armchair, enjoying a brisk, fresh, sunny autumn day in Sussex as he looked out of his ward onto the public park beyond the hospital wall. His eyes focused briefly on a couple of lads throwing sticks at a Horse Chestnut, its leaves turning to a mass of yellows and browns, as they sought to bring down conkers. He turned back to the captain seated in the chair next to him. There was a look of determination on Ned's face.

"Yessir, I'm certain. It's wot's right an' it's wot I needs t' do. 'Onest, sir. It's proper, an' they'll 'ave me back over there afor long an' that might be it."

"If you are certain," emphasis on the "are", "then it can be arranged, and I'll see to it for you if you wish?" There was still a questioning note in the officer's voice.

"Yessir, 'onest." Ned's wholly unattractive face creased into what he hoped was his most winning smile. Unconvinced, the captain, nonetheless, nodded firmly and got up to leave. "I'll be in touch," he said as he left the ward. Ned grinned, and returned his gaze to the two boys who were just running off in response to a call from a woman on the path that circumnavigated the park. He winced as the wound in his leg twinged. Soddin' thing!

The eighth of October would not go down as one of those remembered with any affection. They had left the train at Abbeville at four in the morning, without breakfast, and had marched all day and most of the evening. By eleven o'clock that night they were in the small town of Boufflers, eating a cold meal that had gone dry with the waiting, and doing their best to wash it down with lukewarm tea. There'd been worse cock ups, but many were trying to remember when it had been as, grumbling at their discomfort, they rolled into blankets and fell asleep.

The good news the next morning was that they were to march a short way to another town, Haravesnes, where there would be buses to take them the rest of their journey. Quite why the buses could not come to them was a question they did not bother to ask. Assuredly, there was some military logic somewhere that simply made the obvious too difficult and they weren't prepared to argue. So far as the Norfolks were concerned, the really good news was that they did not have to move off until two o'clock and so they could catch up on sleep and on sorting themselves out.

Colin sat in the sun of a warm early Autumn day, watching Matthew read a newspaper. He had taken over the servant's duties left by the absence of Ned Preece, and had not found them a great burden. Matthew placed very few

The march proved, in the end, to be fruitless for when they arrived the buses had not appeared, and did not appear. Neither did their supply wagons which had gone on to where the buses were to have dropped them off. So it was, with no food, no blankets and no idea what was happening, they slept in a field. Indeed, it was not until eleven o'clock the next morning when the buses arrived, and when they did there were not enough.

They were treated to the incongruous sight of double deckers of the London General Omnibus Company in their original livery. They were not to know that they were among the forty-eight that had escaped south from Antwerp where they had formed part of the abortive British attempt to prevent the city falling to the Germans, that they had only just arrived and that they and their drivers had undergone some fairly hair raising adventures. They knew only, with that simple clarity of thought that Thomas so often demonstrates, that they were "bloody late" and they should either "get sorted" or "not bloody bother."

As it was, they were paraded in two ranks and told off by elevens so that twenty-two men boarded each bus for the journey to Doeval and their billets in the Chateau at La Thienloye. They would have been there earlier had they marched from Boufflers in the first place, as many were quick to remark, and the dampness of the billets did nothing to assuage their grumbling.

The next couple of days did little to improve matters. More marching, still heading north, with their progress impeded time and again by British and French cavalry moving at right angles across the line of the march. As they halted at Bethune for a couple of hours they could hear the familiar sound of shellfire in the distance. The veterans among them feigned not to notice, smiling patronisingly as they watched the newcomers raise their heads to listen to the sounds in the distance.

Charlie Marshall had joined from Belfast, where he had been left behind to clear up the residual difficulties imposed on his mobility by an ankle broken during the summer training. He had been in another company in Ireland, but as a replacement he simply went where the numbers dictated. Alfred Arbuckle had taken him under his wing, Joe Floyd having paired them off. Alfred, although a reservist, had shown himself to be a man to be reckoned with and someone upon whom they could rely. Hector Noakes, a man who railed at the unfortunate name chosen by unimaginative parents, liked to be known as Noaksie; and having let it be known, thus was he christened. After all, "'oo'd want t' be called bleedin' 'ector?" He was another who had done his time between the South African war and this one, and therefore fitted in quite quickly. Certainly, the protracted move from the Aisne, shortly after they'd joined, had helped greatly with the settling in process. Nonetheless, both men were conscious of being very new.

Festubert is a small French town, unprepossessing like many others in the area of northern France around Lille, very close to the Belgian border. It is built around the cross-roads in the centre, running away to Givenchy in the south and heading east in the general direction of the large industrial city of Lille a few kilometres away. As is the case with most villages of its type, the church occupied a dominant position in the centre. The British Army was moving onto a defensive line facing east, running from the canal at La Bassée, about one an a half miles south of Festubert, north through Houplines. Second Corps was on the right. The purpose was to halt the advance of the German Army which was seeking to take Ypres and then to reach and control the coast of southern Belgium and northern France. The force deployed in Festubert was almost the right of the British line, and to their right they could hear the French Eleventh Corps in Vermelles under attack from advancing German forces.

The Norfolks arrived there at dusk on the twelfth of October and as darkness fell commenced digging in. The next morning they were bombarded by the Germans. It was speculative shooting as the thick mist which prevented the Norfolks from seeing their new home also prevented the Germans bringing down aimed fire.

The section spent the day in an old blacksmith's forge just behind where they had dug their trenches the night before. It was a sensible move, given the dreadful weather and pouring rain and they could be in the trenches very quickly if need be. They had no idea what was going on, but they could hear the sounds of fighting coming from a small town, Givenchy, to their half right. The Bedfords and the Dorsets were both defending the area and there was bitter hand-to-hand fighting. Ultimately, the German pressure was so great that von Gleichen, who had positioned himself well forward in order to stay in touch with events, was forced to withdraw the two battalions back to a new line west of the town. He got 11 Battery of the Royal Field Artillery out just in time. They had been firing shrapnel from their 18-Pounders over open sights down the town's streets, cutting great swathes through Germans advancing en masse. As it was, they lost two guns. The Dorsets, who hung on just a little too long, had been enfiladed by the Germans and suffered four hundred casualties.

Stood to throughout with mayhem and death all around them, but not playing any part in it, they sat in the dry gloom of the old forge and wondered what the day might bring and whether or not they might become involved in whatever was going on. Ted was glad he'd eventually written to Mrs Allsop. He'd chosen his moment the other morning whilst waiting for the buses. It had been on his mind for some time, and in the several letters he had penned to his family had had thought of mentioning it, but had balked. He'd somehow felt that any words he might use would sound wrong, and anyway, he had only seen Mrs Allsop once and wondered if it was his place. In the end, he had decided, in consultation with Colin to gain advantage from his command of English, that it was and he should.

He had begun by pointing out that he had seen her only once, in the pub; and that she might not remember him and he hoped she wouldn't mind him writing. He had written of the battle, saying only briefly that they had all been attacking a German hilltop position. He had explained that he had been present when Mr Allsop had been hit, and he knew for certain he could have felt no pain. Death, he was sure, had been instantaneous. That much at least was true, but the bit about him dying a hero's death in the face of daunting enemy fire had rankled somewhat. Still, the bloke was dead and doin' 'im down weren't goin' t' solve anythin'. He had expressed his condolences, offered his sympathy and signed himself "yours respectfully and in deep sorrow," the last bit being Colin's idea, "Edward Ludgrove, Private." It had gone back the previous day with the empty ration cart to B echelon where someone from battalion HQ would see that it got to the Royal Engineers postal service. It would be with Thurza Allsop within three days.

As the afternoon began to draw to a close and the fighting began to die down with the onset of evening, Matthew drew them all together; still in the old forge.

"I am afraid I have to tell you that I shall be leaving you this evening." He looked around at their faces. The originals, who had been with him since the beginning, looked dismayed; although they had heard rumours and his departure was not unexpected.

"I am to be promoted." Murmurs of congratulation sounded from the thirty or so men seated before him on the ground. "And I am to take over command of another company most of whose officers have been killed or wounded. Their own company commander has been moved to another position." He paused, watching their faces for further reaction. "Sergeant Cooper will remain with you, and you will have a new platoon commander from tomorrow. He is here already, and will join us tonight so that I can brief him. Before that happens, however, I have to make some changes that I wish to have in place before he takes over. I have discussed with the company commander a number of promotions needed to fill gaps, and he has agreed the following."

Looks of anticipation in their eyes, and one or two looking down or away into the distance; hoping their names were on the list, believing they should be, determined not to show disappointment if they were not, and to congratulate their successful colleagues.

"Lance Corporal Floyd is to be made up to corporal and to remain in command of his section." Murmurs of approval, the man had done unexpectedly well. "Private James is to be made lance corporal and is to be Corporal Floyd's second in command. More murmurs of approval. "Private Baxter is to be made lance corporal and is to take command of number one section." More nods of approval, although Cooper, ever watchful, saw the look of disappointment cross the face of the senior soldier in the section, who had commanded it these past few days. Young Baxter would have his work cut out there. Matthew nominated another soldier in number two section for promotion, and paused as if he had finished, looking round to see the effect of his announcements. "Finally, having lost Private Preece and Lance Corporal Baxter from platoon HQ I shall be advising my replacement to take Private Ludgrove as his runner. More murmurs of approval. Ted was a good bloke, he had proved himself and they knew they could rely on him. Ted smiled. He was a little disappointed seeing his friends promoted and wishing he was with them, but runner was an important job and, done well, would see a stripe on his arm before long.

"That's all then, unless anyone has any questions?" A pause. "No, good, well then, I shall see you later with Second Lieutenant Hawthorn who will be leading you from now on. I know I can rely on you to give him the excellent support you have given me, and I wish you all the very best of luck." He felt self conscious as he went through the ritual of saying farewell to men he had grown to know and admire, and upon whom he had come to depend. Already he felt a pang of loneliness gnaw at his stomach.

"Good luck to you too, sir." Cooper spoke for them all, and there were more nods and sounds of approval from around the room.

"The corps is to dig in along this line here." The brigade major was pointing out on the map the line they were to take; Givenchy-Festubert-Estaires. Von Gleichen looked down at the table on which it was spread. That would mean recapturing the village from which they had been beaten back by the Germans. There was no natural line save for a road running from La Bassée due north, laying a couple of thousand yards forward of the position. It would be an untidy mess, across fields and through villages. Sighing, he bent his back over the map, and his mind to the task that lay before him.

"Right, tomorrow morning we dig in to the west of this town just in front of us."

"Yer mean the one we couldn't see t'day 'cos of the mist and rain?" Alfie was at it again, his confidence buoyed by the bright new chevrons he had sewn onto his uniform.

"Corporal James, will you, for once, shut up!" Paul Cooper, giving out orders in the absence of his platoon commander, yet to be brought forward, was not at his most patient. He continued without giving Alfie the opportunity to respond, but as he carried on he noticed with satisfaction that the grin was still there. They were going to need every ounce of good humour they could get, and Alfie was a past master at making people laugh.

"West means this side of it, in case any of you didn't quite know where you were. The town is called Festubert, and the Germans are in part of it. To our half right," he pointed to the south-west and then to the model made in the dirt of the forge floor, "is Givenchy, and the Germans have all of that. The brigade will drive the Germans from Givenchy and stabilise our line from there, up through Festubert to the north. Once we have that line we may exploit it forward. Any questions so far?"

He looked round, seeing apprehension on most faces. In the case of the experienced ones there was the inevitable concern about yet another attack against a strong enemy position; for the newcomers it was the concern of not knowing what to expect or how they might react.

"We shall not form part of the attack. It will be done by other battalions in the brigade. We shall hold a secure position here to protect their flank from German envelopment. We begin digging at two in the morning so we can be in position by first light." As he finished he heard a noise behind him, and looking round saw Matthew with a young second lieutenant whom he did not recognise, but assumed to be their new officer. His reaction was instantaneous.

"Stand up!"

They responded at once, scrambling to their feet and standing to attention. Matthew spoke.

"At ease please, Sergeant Cooper." The command was swiftly given. "Sergeant Cooper, let me introduce Mr Hawthorn who is to be your new platoon commander."

"Pleased t' meet you, sir." Cooper held out his hand. The young man smiled hesitantly, and in silence shook his Sergeant's hand. Cooper kept a straight face, but noticed at once the clammy, weak handshake and the lack of positive response from the young man. "Bloody hell," he thought, "I've got my work cut out here."

"Well, Charles, they are all yours, and you could not have a finer body of men as your first command." He smiled reassuringly at Hawthorn. "If you will excuse me, I should like a word with Sergeant Cooper before I go. I'll leave you with the platoon. Sergeant Cooper?" The questioning note in his voice. "Would you mind joining me outside?"

"Sir!" Together they stepped out of the old forge and walked a few paces. Around them the wind blew in gusts and overhead clouds chased each other like blackened chariots across the darkened night sky, their shadows from time to time being reflected down by the brightness of a full moon. As they left, the platoon looked expectantly, and with some mounting concern, at the nervous, silent, young man before them. In the distance was the sound of sporadic rifle fire, and the rattle of machine guns seeking out targets in the dark.

Matthew looked at Cooper, his face clearly visible in the moonlight. "Well?"

Cooper hoped the darkness would hide his expression, but was unlucky. However, years of training forced the answer. "Bit young, sir, but he'll be all right."

Matthew smiled, his teeth showing off-white against the

darker shape of his face. "I'm sure he will, but you will have to look after him. He is straight from training at the Royal Military College and has much to learn; very quickly." He tried hard to keep any note of despair or concern from his voice at the prospect he faced of handing his men, his sergeant, over to a virtual schoolboy with the power of life and death over them.

"You take great care now." Matthew held out his hand. "And please give my very best wishes to your wife when you next write."

Paul held the officer's hand in a firm grip. "She's pregnant, sir." Now he had said it the grin seemed almost to split his face.

Matthew shared his delight, and the handshake went on. "Oh, very well done. I am delighted for you both. How long have you known?"

"A few days, sir, just a few days. We weren't certain, but today's letter said it fer sure." They stayed talking for a few more minutes, both of them conscious of the nervous young man in the forge behind them and the need to get him sorted out. Finally, it had to end.

"Bye, sir. Thanks for everything." Cooper whacked up a cracking salute, which Matthew returned.

"Goodbye, Sergeant Cooper." He stood there as the man who could never be his friend, but was probably his best friend, turned and went back to take a firm grip of his new platoon commander.

They were not to know it at this stage, but they were already a part of what would become known as the Battle of La Bassée, and which would officially be designated as having started on the tenth of October 1914. They were responding to the British CinC's Operation Order Number Thirty-three, issued at Abbeville, in which he stated his intention to "advance to meet the enemy, prolonging the French left." Stretching away to the north the BEF was deploying at Armentieres and even further north in a sort of bulge, described as a salient, north and east of the middle sized town of Ypres. It was just six weeks since they had left the canal at Mons.

The whole of the next two days were spent digging themselves in to trenches at the western edge of Festubert. They were as complete as they felt they might be by the evening of the fifteenth of October; and on that day to their north began the First Battle of Ypres. The routines of digging a position were well practised. Guards were posted, men worked in pairs, food arrived at regular intervals, stand-to was at dusk, no lights were shown at night, and sentries kept watch as men slept, woke with the dawn, stood to and then carried on. They were sufficiently far from the Germans for sniping and rifle fire not to be a problem. However, speculative artillery fire and long range exploratory machine gun fire was a constant hazard, and took its toll.

During all this Charles Hawthorn began to try to get to know his men. His difficulty lay with his own sense of inferiority. He knew he was their social superior and that a gracious King had endowed him with a commission giving him authority over them. They would do as he said because he told them to, whether they wanted to or not. However, they had been to places he had not, suffered experiences he could only begin to imagine and developed a bond which would make any newcomer feel like an outsider. Neither did he have the escape of the officers' mess, which would have been available in peacetime, at lunch time and during the evening. True, they gathered from time to time for orders, and when together would take a glass of whiskey. Other than that he was left alone with his platoon. He could not escape them, there were no weekends at home, no dinner parties, and no social equals with whom he could chat and forget the daily grind of his present life.

"Sir!"

He looked up to see Cooper approaching along a communication trench. He was in awe of this man, and felt unaccountably nervous whenever they were together. He seemed to know so much, to be so imperturbable, so indestructible; and yet he resented his experience and superior knowledge. And why wasn't he scared too?

"Sir, there is to be an orders group in half an hour." Hawthorne looked at his watch; it was four in the afternoon. "According to what I know we shall be moving forward against the Germans, either tonight or tomorrow." As he spoke, Cooper felt his stomach churn at the prospect of yet more exposure in the open to enemy shell, shrapnel and machine gun fire. His face remained inscrutable as he watched the already pale face of the young officer grow a shade paler at the prospect of what was about to come.

"'Ere y'are, sir." Ted handed Hawthorne an enamel mug of tea, with a few dark leaves floating on the surface. The officer smiled, uncertainly grateful. Ted smiled back, trying to build some confidence in the young man, no older than he, who carried with him the very difficult burden of not being allowed to be scared like the rest of them, or, if he was, never to show it. The orders group at around six in the evening, to which his position as runner placed him in attendance, had not been the slick affair that Mr Jenkins used to conduct. There were no models, no discussion of drills or of tactics. They had simply been told they were to advance forward beyond Festubert about two thousand yards and slightly south-east to a feature of high ground marked on the maps as Chapelle St Roche. The capture of Givenchy to the right was to be undertaken by the Bedfords and the Dorsets, despite their heavy losses when they were driven out. Sighs of relief all round when that was made clear. Chapelle St Roche, being forward of Givenchy, would secure them a launching platform for further attacks beyond, towards Lille. It was still the CinC's intention to "advance to meet the enemy", and they were about to be a part of it. Charles Hawthorn did not know it, but his soldiers were already compensating for the shortcomings in his briefing by using their own experience to work out how to handle matters, and briefing the newcomers accordingly.

It was a cold damp night as they tried to get what sleep they could before the dawn and their advance into enemy territory, and most of them would be glad to get away from the trenches they had dug. The Germans had the range, the ground was wet and muddy, they were filthy and itched all over and the intermittent shellfire during the day had been unpleasant. Other parts of the battalion had suffered more than they, the sum total of the platoon's discomfort being several gouts of earth from detonating high explosive shell which had plastered them with yet more mud in addition to that which had accrued about their persons and on their feet from the digging of trenches. Two trenches in a neighbouring platoon took direct hits, and the complete platoon HQ was eliminated in a sudden gore-drenched, mud-spattered mess; so sudden that not so much as a cry or a scream had been heard. The officer and his sergeant had been two of the originals; they would be missed. Charles Hawthorn had been sick, Paul Cooper had watched with concern as he vomited the contents of his stomach on the floor of the trench, and Ted had covered the mess, as surreptitiously as he could, with some loose soil. Both he and Cooper hoped that the young man would soon come to grips with what would be expected of him; for all their sakes.

Several hours passed, and most of them had drifted into an uncomfortable sleep. Suddenly the cry went up along the line: "Stand to!" Stiff, wet and cold, they jerked themselves into wakefulness. Ted had his rifle in his hand, checking that the bolt action had not been obstructed by dirt during the night, whilst at the same time keeping an eye on his officer. Suddenly, the sentry was there, panting and gasping with the exertion of his dash along the trench and apprehension at what was about to befall them.

"Germans, sir. Lots of 'em, look......see?" He pointed over the lip of the trench to a point where, some three hundred yards away, shapes could be seen moving. The British Army had no star shell, unlike their opponents, so there was no means of lighting up the area. It was only the flames from a few burning buildings which broke the inky blackness of a starless, overcast night.

"But, there's been no artillery." The incredulity was clear in Hawthorn's voice.

"There wouldn't be, not if they want to surprise us." Paul Cooper looked at Hawthorn. "I'll give the fire order, sir, if you wish. And the runner to the company commander, sir."

"What?" He looked bemused. "Yes.......yes.....yes, do that." A note of concern in his voice as he realised the Germans were getting nearer and he had done nothing about it. "What should he do? Cooper would know, blast him." Cooper looked at Ted, who was already moving, unbidden, towards company HQ.

"Platoon, three hundred." Most of them already had their sights set to that very convenient range which actually gave them a good degree of accuracy between one hundred and five hundred yards. It saved fishing around in the dark. "Enemy in mass to your front. Rapid....." He paused. "Fire!"

Once again they were back doing what they did best; destroying the enemy in droves. Hawthorn looked on in amazement. He had seen men firing in training, and knew the speed at which many of them could operate, but he had never realised the firepower that a platoon or company could put down in a concerted effort. He watched as men squeezed the triggers of their rifles, absorbed the recoil, flicked open the bolt in a smooth action, head slightly to one side to avoid impacting the bolt on the cheek, bolt forward and squeeze again. From a flank he heard the sound of the battalion machine guns pouring forth yet more destruction on the enemy. To his front he could see the grey shapes taking form as they grew closer, could see them twisting and falling as the hundred and forty grain bullets found their mark, could hear screams and groans as men tried to bear the agony of their wounds. Above all the noise was a sound he could not recognise, a whiplash crack which penetrated his eardrums, adding more to the pain caused by the assault of the noise from his soldiers' weapons. Nearby he heard a thud, and looked to see the inert form of a man in Lance Corporal Baxter's section, struck by enemy fire.

"They've got their machine guns in support." Cooper was talking to him as if from a distance. So that was it, the cracking was the noise of enemy bullets passing close by. "They'll keep their artillery off for fear of hitting their own, but they'll go for us to cover a withdrawal." He looked at the officer. "We shall need to be smart about getting our heads down before that happens." Hawthorn nodded, and then winced as he saw brains and blood spray from the back of a man's head; a man whose name he did not even know, yet he commanded him.

Ned Preece walked through the lamp lit streets from Hoe Street railway station towards the house. His pace was limited by the crutches he used to bear his weight, long wooden affairs with a pad to cushion the area beneath his armpits and surgical tape binding the stem, showing white against the yellowish glow of the street lighting. His mouth was dry, and his hands sweaty. He was nervous, and with just cause. The telegram he had sent two days ago had warned her that he would be coming; and he knew, thereby, that others would also have been warned. He had received no reply, and he knew not what response he might expect when he reached the door. On his back was a small pack, containing all he needed for the next few days, whatever the outcome.

There was silence as he moved down the street, now within fifty yards of his destination. The only sound was that of his boots on the pavement and the noise made by his crutches as they supported him on his way. Looking ahead, he could see the house with the short pathway from the gate set in the privet hedge leading to the front door. Then he could see them, moving out of the shadows to confront him. He recognised the large, bulky shape of his father, and beside him his uncle Jack, his father's brother.

"So y've come back, 'ave yer?" Colin Baxter would instantly have noted the banality of such a question when the answer lay so self-evidently before the speaker; but he was some way away at the moment, facing problems of his own. Ned remained silent. This was the hiding he had run away from two years ago, and his brute of a father was clearly bent on delivering it now. He glanced over his father's shoulder and saw the door of her house open slightly, saw a curtain flicker in an upstairs window; and thought he saw a pale face behind it.

"This 'ain't none o' your business." He carried on moving towards them, aiming slightly left as if to go round them to his destination.

He was prepared for a tirade of foul mouthed invective from his father, for that had been the man's stock in trade ever since Ned could remember; but the depth of it, and the extent of the man's hatred for his own son, took him by surprise. However, where in the past fear might have been the dominant effect now it was anger and hurt. This man, who had bullied him all his life, was standing, foul mouthing and threatening, between him and something he wanted more than he could remember wanting anything: to hold his baby daughter and her mother in his arms. He watched as the two of them came towards him. Jack had always followed his brother's lead, and the pair had a reputation locally as bullies with whom it did not pay to argue.

It was a direct, frontal assault. Regardless of his injury they had but one plan; to knock him to the ground and then beat him senseless. To this end, Ned's father had brought with him a two foot wooden stave which in another life would have been the top of a fence post. It was probably the gloom, and the fact that they were expecting an easy victory against a young man who had taken after his diminutive mother in stature, and consequently had never been able to counter the beatings inflicted on him in his youth. They missed, therefore, the fact that his body had filled out, hardened by the Army and by what he had endured during August and September. The weeks in hospital had not adversely affected the wiry toughness. Neither did they notice, as they began to move, that he was no longer relying on the crutches to hold him erect, but was nicely balanced with his feet slightly apart.

Jack was in front of his brother, aiming to the side with a view to getting round behind Ned to his right. Suddenly, he screamed and, bending double, collapsed on the pavement, his hands clutching his nether regions. Ned withdrew the crutch from between the man's legs, his strong right arm having swung the tip in a viciously swift arc to connect with Jack's genitalia. Normally, of course, a wooden crutch would not have too undue an effect, even in a sensitive area such as that. However, the white surgical tape had been used to bind onto the crutch, and at the same time disguise, a two foot length of steel angle iron. Swung upwards by a deceptively strong right arm to which anger had given renewed power, it was a potent weapon, the effect of which was to completely crush one testicle, lacerate the penis and break a chip off the lower part of the pelvic girdle. The shock hit Jack instantly, and he began to vomit the contents of his beer swollen belly onto the pavement.

Ignoring one enemy already down, Ned dropped the crutch from his left hand, and held the one which had just done so much damage to Jack forward to face his father in the classic bayonet fighting stance drilled into him over so many months; and which he had used in anger against the German trying to strangle Cooper. In front of him, his father leered.

"Wassup. Carn't y' fight fair?" This from a man with a wooden stave in his hand.

Ned grinned. "Nope." As he spoke he lunged, with perfect timing and watched with satisfaction as the tip of the crutch sank into his father's swollen stomach. He had taken great care to ensure that the end of the implement was well bound and padded, so there was no risk of penetration. As his father bent forward in reaction to the pain in his midriff, Ned stepped back, reversed the crutch and, as with a rifle butt, smashed the shoulder pad into the man's face. Flat on his back, Preece the elder was treated to the sight of his son standing over him, his booted foot squarely on his throat, the pressure being applied. Choking, he struggled, reaching up with his hands to grab the "boy" by the ankles to dislodge him. He screamed as the metal bar cracked onto his arm, snapping both the Ulna and the Radius of his right wrist neatly and cleanly, and as his mouth opened with the scream he felt the tip of the crutch inserted into it. He gagged and choked as it went back into his throat, and then was released back a little. Looking up, he saw not a hint of pity in the eyes of the young soldier he had once known as his son.

"You lissenin'?" He nodded, unable to do more than grunt with a mouth full of wood, broken teeth, steel bar and surgical tape.

"Try anythin' again an' yer dead, clear?" Another nod. "An' try anything wiv 'er," a nod in the direction of the house "an' yer get the same. Questions? No? Good, then fuck off, an' don' let me or 'er ever see yer again."

He stepped back, glanced at Jack groaning in the gutter, the spreading stain around his crotch a mixture of blood and urine, the puddle of vomit on the pavement, and turned to walk up the path. If her father and mother had planned to have a go at him for leaving their daughter pregnant then all thought of it had left their minds. They stepped aside as he walked into the house. She had seen the events outside from her bedroom window, and was at the bottom of the stairs as he entered, holding a sleepy baby, clad in night-clothes, in her arms. Slowly he walked over. He knew exactly what to do; he had been planning this for days, including the anticipated punch up. He reached out, looked into her eyes, held her shoulders gently and pulled her towards him. His arms tight round them both, he rocked gently from side to side, never wanting to let go; and he cried.

The Germans had worked their way in very close to the trench line. They were brave and determined men. Small parties were within grenade throwing range, and the British Number One Grenade was not proving an effective counter. The trenches did not permit a good swing of the tapes, and the ground was too soft for the percussion fuze to function. These small bombing teams had to be flushed out with the rifle and bayonet. Responding to Paul Cooper's "c'mon, sir," Charles Hawthorn led a two section attack against one of the bombing parties. Working in close, with covering fire from the other two sections they headed for the shell hole from where Colin Baxter had reported the grenades being thrown. Reaching the lip at the crawl they heard the guttural sound of a German speaking. Infused with the excitement of the moment, Hawthorn forgot his fear. Looking to left and right he knew his men could see him in the flickering light of a burning cottage. He raised an arm and hooked it over, pointing down into the hole. They rose as one and leapt in onto their enemy, beating and smashing and bayoneting anything that moved. Seeing one try to run, Charles lifted his pistol and, quite deliberately, shot him. He watched, transfixed, as the body of his victim flopped in death's sloppiness back down into the hole. He looked round at panting men, the reaction setting in, a sense of shame in some at what they had done, in others a sense of exhilaration.

"Pick him up." He heard himself giving the order as he pointed at a newly joined private who had been spiked in the leg by a German bayonet. "And bring those with you." He addressed Joe Floyd as he pointed to half a dozen German grenades. "Right, let's get back." Brimming with new found confidence he began to move back up the side of the shell hole.

"I'll jus' give the signal to Corporal Baxter to give coverin' fire, sir."

"'Er, yes, thank you Sergeant Cooper." He looked at the senior NCO expecting an expression of rebuke, but instead saw a smile, almost of welcome. He realised he had crossed a personal Rubicon, and felt a temporary glow of satisfaction. Crawling, he led his men back to their trenches, covered in mud and the blood of the enemies they had, literally, slaughtered, beneath the covering fire provided by two sections of riflemen.

Ned sat in the peace and quiet of the front room. Retained only for guests on special occasions, her mother had bustled in and lit the fire which was always laid, ready for such an eventuality. She had scolded her husband into going upstairs and putting on a collar and tie, and had shooed the other children into the back kitchen which was where most of the normal business of day to day living was conducted. Sat on the sofa, Ned was half turned towards her, his less than attractive face blotchy from the tears. She faced him, complete with her own blotches, holding both his hands in hers. They had both now stopped crying, and she could barely believe what she was hearing.

"It'll be in Sussex, near the 'ospital." He looked at her mother apologetically. "That were the only way I could fix it wiv the special licence an' all." He did not mention that arranging the wedding as far away from Walthamstow as he could was intended to keep his family well away lest they seek to spoil it. "Yer can get there on the train if yer wanna come, like."

She looked at him, so strong, so brave, the father of their daughter and she loved him so much it hurt. Whatever more could a girl want than him as her husband?

Outside, on the street, two injured men tried to make their way to a hospital. No one came to help, and the police would find no one who had seen anything.

The advance was postponed at the last minute, for just twenty-four hours. Consequently, they spent the rest of the day up to their ankles in mud in trenches that were not equipped to stave off the ravages of the weather. It was a damp, depressing experience, made all the more so by the persistent German artillery fire which took it's gradual, steady toll of casualties. Peter Dakin wrote another letter to Ma and Pa, Paul Cooper to Jane and Colin Baxter changed his mind about writing again to his mother. Charles Hawthorn spent the day thinking about the night before, and trembled a little with excitement at the thought that he had killed someone.

The night was quiet, and after the dawn stand-to they moved forward out of their trenches towards the enemy positions. On their right, and earlier, the two battalions designated for the attack on Givenchy had moved forward into the outskirts of the village. The sound of sporadic firing assailed their ears, but nothing like the volume of the last few days. As they moved forward they expected at any time to come under fire, but it never materialised. They moved through Festubert, past the church with its neatly kept graveyard, the Café de la Renaissance opposite offering the prospect of *café et croissant* if only they had the time to stop. On out beyond the village the ground began to rise up onto the Chapelle St Roche feature; only a small rise, but in the flat countryside of that part of northern France it offered a major advantage. Nowhere were the Germans to be seen. On the hill, they dug in. The site for their position had been a beet field, and the ground around was scattered with the residue of the harvest, limp green leaves everywhere. They were part of a general advance, ordered by French, designed to attack the enemy wherever they might be met, but he had based his order on a gross underestimation of the true enemy strength facing the BEF.

By now, the battlefield in Flanders had assumed the shape that was to remain for the next four weeks, with essentially two battles being fought: south and north, separated by the River Lys.

The next morning the company was ordered forward to a position about five hundred yards further east, around a collection of farm buildings known as Canteleaux. Their objective was to act as a forward position in the event of an enemy advance, and to secure a start line for any further advance eastwards by Fifteen Brigade. As they awaited their orders, the battles to their north were developing, and already the emphasis was beginning to be placed there; around Ypres.

Tired men dug in once more and awaited what the day would bring. On their left, about three quarters of a mile to the north, the rest of the brigade, having successfully taken Givenchy the day before, captured the town of Violaines as part of a move by Smith-Dorrien to wheel towards the south-east. Joe Floyd's section was forward of the position, well ensconced in a haystack which gave them good observation from the front, good rest at the back and no protection whatsoever from enemy fire. Behind them, in a trench at the forward edge of the farm, Ted looked at the position occupied by his friends and for a moment felt a pang of loneliness. Paul Cooper watched over them all, but was too late to stop his new platoon commander using his binoculars to scan to the south. The flash from the lenses as they reflected the sun was all the German artillery observers required and within a few minutes their life was being made very uncomfortable by the attentions of a couple of batteries of howitzers.

In the haystack they were safe from all this as the Germans concentrated on the farm behind. Very soon, however, they noticed that shrapnel was falling round them. Joe Floyd simply could not understand it. He was certain they had not exposed themselves to view. That was a basic mistake and none of them would have made it. It was Alfie who spotted the cause.

"Look at the bleedin' angle. It's our own soddin' artillery. Will someone sort the bastards out?" Squirming to the back of the tent he waited for the Germans to stop firing before seeking to gain someone's attention. Waving furiously he saw Paul Cooper raising his head to see what might follow the lull in German fire, for the shrapnel was not affecting them. Watching Alfie's frantic gestures he looked up and realised at once what was happening. Explaining the position to Charles Hawthorn he recommended a runner to battalion HQ to try and get them to stop, and another to company HQ on the other side of the road to tell them what they had done. Feeling very foolish about his stupidity with the binoculars, and feeling he had lost all the gains he had made, especially since he now had three wounded men on his hands, he agreed at once on the basis that the runners would also seek advice on evacuating the injured men.

Ted, listening in, nodded as Cooper looked at him. Taking a deep breath, he hefted his rifle, slipped out of the back of the farm, nipped across the road, into the ditch opposite and followed it to the north around a bend in the road to where a hedgerow ran up across the field. By following its northern edge he was able to keep in cover from the enemy away south-east in La Bassée, protected to his right by the Fifteenth Brigade occupation of Violanes. Charles Hawthorn, watching him go, suppressed his embarrassment and his desire not to appear too much the new boy, and, turning to Cooper he asked him how Ludgrove had picked his route and had known what to do.

There was no condescension in Cooper's response. The young man needed to learn, and if he was prepared to ask questions so much the better. "He's a good lad, sir, and he's got a countryman's eye for ground. He's learned fast since we left Belfast, so I suppose the answer is he just knew. He'll be all right, and if you need another lance corporal he's probably your best choice; and then Arbuckle." He saw the questioning look on the officer's face. "The big bloke out in the haystack."

"Ah yes, I remember. I'm sorry, I'm not good with names and there are so many of them." As was expected of him, he had learned them by heart, but matching the right face to the right name was not always possible.

"Now, sir, the runner for company HQ, might I suggest........"

Just behind him, Colin Baxter was trying to stem the flow of blood from one of his injured men, a white hot splinter from a high explosive shell having almost ripped the calf muscle from his shin bone. It was not an easy task and his hands were sticky with the groaning man's blood. It was three o'clock in the afternoon, they had not eaten since dawn, and the Germans had begun shelling again. Hawthorn winced as he heard a prolonged scream and went to see the cause, conscious that he had brought this on his men; and they knew it.

Ned Preece looked at the clock in the Registry Office. He was nervous, and his nerves were not helped by the fact that she was now late for a ceremony due to start promptly at three o'clock in the afternoon. He glanced at the two witnesses, the captain of the Army Chaplain's Department who had organised the affair at Ned's insistence, and the sister from his ward. He grinned, self consciously and nervously, glancing at the registrar who, having seen it all before, was a picture of benign, patient understanding. One minute later, escorted by her father, with her mother a couple of paces behind carrying the baby, she entered.

Neither of them had much money, neither had they had a lot of time to plan; but both were determined to make this an occasion. She wore a two piece suit of beige with black trimming and black shoes. Her hair had been fashioned in a salon in the town that morning, with a little floral decoration that sat neatly to one side. She carried a posy, organised by her mother. Her slight, little figure neatly set off the outfit and her thin face was a radiant picture. She was the loveliest thing he could imagine, she loved him, she was his and he hers, and he, standing in his uniform without crutches, had never felt so happy or complete in his life. Looking at their faces, the captain realised that his concern about the suitability of Ned's course of action had been ill judged. These two were entitled to each other, and given what he would have to go back to in a few weeks, or even days, this was a perfect arrangement.

The registrar began: "Ladies and gentlemen, we are assembled here this afternoon..........."

Paul Cooper had his hands over the man's belly, trying to stem the flow of blood, and keep his intestines within the wall of the abdomen as internal pressure sought to push them out through the cavity ripped open by a shell splinter. The young man's eyes were wide open, the fear and the pain so clear to see, the whiteness of his face and the sweat on his brow, the breaths coming in short gasps as he panted to try and ease the pain, the groans coming as he failed so to do. Hawthorn was fiddling with the morphia phial he carried and the hypodermic. Paul, motioned to him to place his hand over the man's stomach, a feat he undertook with great reluctance, especially as he touched the warm sliminess of the intestines. Hawthorn watched as his sergeant competently filled the barrel of the syringe with the clear liquid and injected it deep into the young soldier's thigh. Gradually, over a period of several minutes, the panting had stopped as the drug took over and he lay back. Dressings were applied, binding tight to the abdomen, and, in response to Hawtorn's questioning look, Cooper answered:

"Probably not, unless we evacuate him now."

The runner had come back from company HQ with the instruction that casualties with life threatening wounds should be recovered by stretcher bearer to the regimental aid post behind the Chapelle St Roche feature, just under a mile away. It was a long carry, and, on Paul's advice, Charles Hawthorn detached the whole of Colin Baxter's section for the task; which left him twenty-five percent down in firepower. He was learning some hard lessons; fast.

Ted Ludgrove reached battalion HQ and gasped out his message to the adjutant. The lines were down to brigade HQ, having been severed by German artillery fire. Pointing out the HQ, near Violaines to the north, the adjutant told him to get on a bicycle parked nearby and cycle there with his message. As he cycled off he heard the RSM advising him, as only RSMs can, that he was on a battalion HQ bicycle, he was required to bring it back and woe betide him if he did not. Within ten minutes he had arrived, but having arrived was unsure where to go.

"In there mate." An obliging signaller pointed into a doorway. "If'n yer've got a message yer takes 'em in there." Passing through the doorway, he entered a room full of officers and clerks; and instantly felt nervous.

"Yes?" The brigade major looked up from the message he was reading. Ted squared his shoulders.

"Private Ludgrove, sir, Norfolks. We's in the farm at Cantaloo an' we's bein' shelled by our own guns. Shrapnel it is, sir." He saluted, realising he had forgotten to do so earlier.

"You sure?" He looked over Ted's shoulder. "Is this right?"

"Possibly, but very unlikely." Ted flinched as he heard the voice; Edward Snell's voice. "Can we be certain he is telling the truth?"

"Well?" The brigade major looked at him.

"It's ours sir, 'onest. Yer can tell from the angle of the stroike and the position of the smoke. It's comin' in from behind sir, and tha's the truth. Oi've jus' come from thur." His heart was in his mouth at the close proximity of Snell.

"All right, we'll look at it. Snell, could you........?"

"I really dont' see why, on the word of a ...."

"I think you should see to it at once!" A well modulated voice from the doorway attracted all their attention. "Young man," he looked at Ted. "Thank you for your information. Is the fire causing casualties?"

"'Ard t' tell, sir. We's bein' 'it by Germans as well. But we're losin' blokes, sir, an' a lot of the shrapnel is goin' off over us."

"Thank you. Right, cut about your business." He acknowledged Ted's salute as he left, sparing a glance at Snell whose malevolent hatred showed through in the look he gave the young soldier. It was not a look that was lost on Edward von Gleichen. "Right, Snell, if we could now......." Ted was gone, on his way back with the bicycle, the RSM's last message at the front of his thoughts, blotting out the concern caused by the presence of his enemy.

Ned had drawn out all his credits from his pay book, and had enough to buy them all a cream tea in a tea shop in the town before his new parents-in-law took the train, and the baby, back to Walthamstow. They were left alone. They dined in a public house and returned to the bed and breakfast he had organised with one of the nurses from the hospital whose mother owned a cottage on the edge of the village. It was eighteenth century, thatched and perfect for the occasion. The bed was large, with a soft mattress into which they both sank, and fluffy pillows upon which tired heads could sleep the deepest of sleeps. They held each other tight, fumbled a little at the newness of what they were about, then gave themselves completely to each other, and slept the dreamless sleep of pure contentment.

They slept in the wet and the cold, showing no lights. Food had been cold, with only water to drink. They were damp, miserable and apprehensive about the next day. Sleep was difficult; they were expecting a German infantry attack at any moment. It was a tired and dishevelled bunch who peered into the distance at stand to as the grey of the first light turned to the softer pinks of a growing dawn from the east, where their enemy sat. There was no breakfast, save for some cold bacon, and a brew which they made themselves as the opportunity arose.

Ned sat at the breakfast table, his new wife opposite and the picture of modest embarrassment since their landlady would know what they had been at the night before. She need not have worried, an ex-nurse herself their landlady had seen it all. Being honeymooners, she made a special effort, with flowers on the table and a huge spread of bacon, fresh farm eggs, sausage, tomatoes from the garden and toast with home-made marmalade. After all, 'twasn't every day you got married, was it?

Nothing happened that day, save for the arrival of battalion HQ in their farm as the rest of the battalion moved forward ready to continue the general eastward move of Second Corps. The German batteries that had caused so many problems the previous day had been taken on by British counter battery fire and had either moved or found more interesting prey. They had deployed some snipers, who were becoming a real nuisance, and orders were issued to each platoon to take them on. Eddie Macleary had demonstrated his ability as a shot on more than one occasion since he had taken the German observation post out of the haystack on the Aisne. Taking Peter Dakin with him as spotter they eased forward into a hedgerow where they could obtain a good field of view. Well camouflaged they watched with the naked eye for any sign of movement. The rest of the platoon had open season on anything that moved, but Eddie and Peter were there to get the good ones who were hard to spot.

Forty minutes of lying completely still brought its reward. "Split Elm," Peter used one of their agreed references. "Left, two o'clock, fifty yards, gap in hedge. Left of the gap twenty yards is a mound. 'E's there."

"Gottim!" Eddy eased himself slowly, oh so slowly, to bring his rifle to bear. Carefully, determined not to display any of the movement, however slight, that had given away the German's position, he aimed, drew in his breath and squeezed the trigger. He was treated to the sight of a rifle flying a couple of feet in the air and part of an arched body as his bullet struck home.

"Certainly did." Peter grinned and, remaining perfectly still, continued his vigil. They stayed there for the rest of the day, finding no other targets, and left only when darkness permitted a safe withdrawal.

As it was getting dark, Ned sat with his new wife on the train, heading back to her parents' house where he would remain until called back to Britannia Barracks in Norwich to be sent back to the front. He did not know how long that would be, and however long it was he would make the best of it. Beside him she slept in the crook of his arm, their second child already growing deep inside her womb.

In the regimental aid post the young soldier with the ruptured abdomen slipped, in a morphia induced sleep, into death.

Chapter 12

In The Line

On the twentieth of October the Norfolks were pulled back to Chapelle St Roche in the face of enemy artillery fire and concentrated infantry attacks; and as part of a general withdrawal onto a more secure line just east of Festubert. The enemy pressure had simply become too intense, and weakened battalions could not advance against an enemy of the strength their patrols had indicated and with the firepower they were now experiencing from Prince Ruprecht's Sixth German Army, which enjoyed a two-to-one superiority on the "southern" battlefield.

It was on this day that Falkenhayn, the German Chief of Staff, decided to counter-attack across the whole front. He had gathered together the resources he felt he needed in order to achieve success, and the assaults he set in motion ran from La Bassée in the south, northwards, beyond Ypres, to the coast. It was this act which generated a change in the operation orders emanating from GHQ. No longer were they to advance to attack the enemy; they were now to contain him.

At first, the fighting was off to the Norfolk's left, involving the Cheshires and Fourteen Brigade. As was so often the case, carnage reigned a short distance away, whilst they remained safe in relative calm. None, however, had any doubts that their turn would soon come. And come it did. On the twenty-second of October infantry and artillery were unleashed on them in gargantuan proportions. It was more of the same, the same as Mons and Le Cateau: masses of grey clad infantry advancing in huge blocks designed to batter their way through weaker defences already pulverised by artillery. And they were weak. Many battalions were below half strength, and what was left bled away yet more as the casualties mounted. However, this was still the remnant of the old, professional British Army, and the reservists who had been part of it before the war were once again every bit as much a part of it. The firepower they unleashed was phenomenal. Tiredness, the cold, the wet, the mud; all were overcome by a heady mix of professionalism, exhilaration and fear.

They fired their rifles until they were too hot to handle. The platoon was well forward in the firing line, and in the thick of it. Charles Hawthorn and Paul Cooper simply made their way up and down the trench, offering encouragement and being seen to be there. Ted, staying always with his officer, saw things for the first time at a level more then six inches off the ground through a rifle sight; and saw with it a new perspective. Giving orders was pointless: no one would hear them and the targets were obvious. Men fired at anything that moved, and section commanders controlled the fire at their level whenever they could make themselves heard.

He watched Colin Baxter screaming orders like a man possessed, directing the fire of his declining group of men onto those enemy targets closest to him. He saw first one man then another go down; some wounded, some never to rise again. In Joe Floyd's section he looked on as Alfie James grabbed Noaksie and shoved him back into the front of his trench, bawling into his ear to keep on firing. Peter Dakin looked round as he rammed another charger into his rifle, forcing five fresh rounds into his magazine. Ted saw the look of fear on his white face as it seemed nothing they could do would stop the mass of grey to their front.

It was too much, not just for them, but all along the line. Orders were given at eleven o'clock that night to pull back off the Chapelle St Roche feature to a line nearer Festubert, but still to its east. They buried their dead as best they could in the trenches they had occupied, and moved silently to their new positions where the trench lines had been marked out by the battalion advance party. By now they were used to exhaustion, and continued to handle it as they always had: with dogged determination, but not all of them. The pressure was becoming too much for some, and it was beginning to show. Volunteers to accompany wounded to the rear were too readily available, their return often delayed by "circumstances beyond their control." Their general condition was not helped by the bruising of their bodies from constant firing and fighting, the wounds some had sustained whilst remaining at their posts, the impact of the noise on their eardrums and on their capacity to think straight. Charlie Marshall, who had just been settling down in the section, was an early casualty, his ear being seemingly virtually ripped off by a shell splinter. The same shell burst gashed Joe Floyd's forehead, but he remained where he was once Alfred had bound it with a field dressing. Eddie Macleary took a bad hit high on his left shoulder, and swiftly found himself on his way back to the casualty clearing station which was further back, treating casualties too bad to be dealt with by the regimental aid post. In another section, three men went down to an unlucky shell burst, two, mercifully, dying at once and the third screaming out his agony until exhaustion and shock forced him into a stupor. He died thirty minutes later. Colin Baxter lost his third since he had taken command, killed by a bullet straight through his head.

The night turned to day as they dug in on the new line, were shelled by heavy artillery, carried on digging, took more casualties and then the day began its descent once more into night. By the evening they were firmly dug in, and still resisting constant pressure from infantry and artillery attacks. There was, however, a lessening of the pressure, because of the resources being used by the Germans in their attack on the village of Neuve Chapelle, sitting roughly on the junction between the Third and Fifth Divisions and some distance away to their north. It was an attack that was to last four days, through to the twenty-eighth of October. It would consume vast resources, inflict huge casualties and offer no advantage to either side; and the Norfolks would only hear it, not see it and not be a part of it.

The Norfolks used the respite to feed, strengthen their defences, replenish ammunition and water and prepare as best they could, in straightened circumstances, for what might be to come. Part of this process was the manufacture of hand grenades to supplement their meagre supplies of the Number One Grenade. The CinC had already asked London for four thousand hand grenades and two thousand rifle grenades per month, but there was precious little chance of them ever arriving. Instead, they turned to their own ingenuity and created, at unit level, the "Jam Pot" Grenade. This involved a tin jam pot, filled with shredded Gun Cotton and "tenpenny" nails for fragmentation, a Number Eight detonator and short length of "Bickford's" fuze. It was not a sophisticated instrument, and lighting the fuze was a nightmare in difficult conditions. It was best achieved by "scarfing" the fuze, which meant cutting it at an oblique angle, taping Swan Vestas to it and striking them against a match box when the time came to light them. The delay before detonation was determined by the length of the fuze and its measured burning time, which was at a rate of thirty seconds a foot, plus or minus a second or so.

It wasn't much, but it gave them something with which they could counter German attacks and the difficulties being imposed upon them by the seemingly limitless supplies their foes had of hand grenades. Capturing some was a much sought after prize, and they were used with great gusto on their former owners whenever the opportunity arose.

The platoon watched in fascination as a corporal from the pioneer platoon gave demonstrations on how to build the home made grenades. He left them with the wherewithal to construct their own, and the advice that there was plenty of explosive back with the quartermaster should they need to make more. Before long, there was a nice little stock resting on shelves, dug into the side of the trenches, and under the control of section commanders.

Paul Cooper, who really was dominating the platoon, began to talk softly to his young officer about the sort of orders he might give for the use of the grenades. Apart from one or two flashes of spirit, Charles Hawthorn had really not grasped the nettle of his role as platoon leader and he deferred more and more to his experienced senior NCO. It had not gone unnoticed in the platoon, and more than one was heard to say that things would be all right for so long as they had Cooper, but if he were to go, and anybody's turn could be next, they'd be in a right bugger's muddle. His weakness had not been lost on the major, who watched with concern as the boy drew more and more into a shell of his own making. "Thank God for Cooper" was a thought that was passing all too often through his mind.

The night of the twenty-fourth and fifth of October brought the first real frost of the year. As the dawn broke and stand to ended they saw that it had nipped the bulk of the ailing brown leaves, and most of them had descended to form a rustling carpet over large parts of the countryside, drifting in the wind up against fences around where fields abutted against woods and copses. The trees looked naked and exposed, the first shivering sign of the onset of real winter. Men stamped their feet and rubbed their hands up and down on their upper arms in order to expel the chill from their extremities.

At the same time there came hot tea from the cooks, breakfast and the mail. As had become the custom, Paul Cooper passed it to Ted, once he had extracted his own and his officer's, for him to distribute among the sections. Barely had Ted got his hands on the sandbag full of parcels and letters when the first German shell arrived, pitching into the ground about ten feet in front of his trench, the force of it throwing him backwards in a mud spattered heap on the ground. Beside him he heard Paul Cooper calling for stand to, and from the corner of his eye saw his platoon commander picking himself up, a look of abject misery on his face. Standing, he looked forward, ducking his head as more and more high explosive fell around and, in some cases, in trenches. In the latter instances there was very little for stretcher bearers to find, and unless they could hear any noises they generally did not bother investigating what they knew would be a gruesomely horrid sight. Mixed in with all this was the shrapnel coughing above them to keep their heads even further down for when the German infantry advanced under the cover of its artillery.

The artillery barrage lasted almost an hour, and by the end of it men were crouched in the bottom of whatever was left of their trenches, many of them with their hands covering their ears to blot out the noise of the shells, the ear splitting crack of bullets from long range German machine gun fire passing close over their heads and the ghastly sounds of their friends and colleagues screaming and coughing in the agony of their wounds. Their brains had reached the stage when they were no longer capable of lucid thought. Some were crying, and Joe Floyd watched with mounting concern, on those few occasions when he had his eyes open, the shaking image of Hector Noakes as his fear overcame him in gibbering waves of tears.

"Stand up, and face yer front!" The screaming, parade ground voice of Paul Cooper transcended everything. He, almost alone among them, had managed to maintain some sort of observation of their front, having told Hawthorne, who had become inarticulate with the pounding in his ears and the assault on his brain, to stay down.

"I said," a short pause "stand up; and get a bloody move on." His voice raised an octave. "They're coming!"

All along the line the cry went up as officers and NCOs reacted to the new threat from German infantry, massed to their front and only a couple of hundred yards away. Befuddled men dragged themselves to their feet, the fitter ones helping their less robust colleagues, or those who, despite being wounded, were fit and able to fire their rifles. Peter Dakin grabbed Noaksie, and yelled in his ear for him to start firing, but the man simply collapsed again at the bottom of the trench. Glancing at Alfred and Alfie James, Peter shrugged, lifted his rifle into his shoulder and prepared to fire.

"At the enemy in front......rapid.......fire!"

Sporadic at first, the familiar sound of rapid rifle fire soon began to pick up as, all along the line, officers and NCOs forced their men to fight through the fear, pain, atrocious headaches made worse by the sound of firing rifles and disorientation and respond as their training had taught them. This was where hours of boring drill in classrooms and on ranges bore fruit. The German method of attack played right into their hands. There was no fire and manoeuvre as the BEF practised in order to dominate the enemy firing line by winning the fire fight; just great chunks of humanity coming their way. Apart from some fire from the hip from the front ranks, which was inherently inaccurate, poorly focused and of no real use, the German covering fire had gone with the lifting of their artillery. There was nothing to keep the British heads down, and the Germans paid for it dearly.

Ted, beside his officer, and flanked on the other side by Cooper, fired his rifle until the barrel simply became too hot to hold. The opportunity to rest it for a few seconds as he rammed home new clips of ammunition came as a welcome relief to the burning pain in his hands. He was not needed as a runner; there were no orders save that they fire as fast as they could into the huge grey target before them.

It was not long before the screams and yells of their wounded foes mingled with those of their own, in a dreadful bilingual cacophony of misery and pain. Of all the sounds he heard, it was this that affected Charles Hawthorn the most. Would it never stop?

And then it was over, almost as suddenly as it had begun. The rifle and machine gun fire was too much for the Germans and they did not pursue the attack, despite having come very close to the British trench. They withdrew, and as they made to collect those wounded they could, the firing slowly ceased along the British line. There was no more threat, and their foes should be allowed to collect their casualties as best they could.

Charles Hawthorne heard the order come down from the company to cease firing, and, his mouth open and gasping for air, he leaned back against the rear of his trench looking to the heavens as if for solace.

"Sir!" Cooper's voice penetrated his brain. "Would the bloody man never go away; always on to him to do things. Why did he have to do so much; why did it have to be like this?" "Sir, the casualties, sir. We must get a count of the casualties, get 'em out and replenish ammunition at once, sir. They might come back, and soon."

Dragging himself upright, he drew a deep breath, looked Cooper straight in the eye and said: "Carry on sergeant, since you know what to do. I shall go and see the company commander." It was an escape from a reality he could not face.

Cooper, wiping blood from his face where a flying stone had gashed his cheek, turned away, his expression grim, and began issuing the necessary orders to the section commanders who had congregated at his command. Only three of them were there, together with the one surviving member of Number One section, a private of just twenty years of age. Ted looked at his filthy, unshaven appearance, and the deep shock etched on his white face, and wondered how he himself must look. They stepped back to allow a stretcher to pass, bearing the twisted wreckage of the boy's section commander, his left leg and left arm both missing and the side of his body a mess of blood, mud and filth, the rattle of liquid in his throat as blood welled from somewhere deep within.

Joe Floyd reported four left on their feet, two dead and two wounded. His face was expressionless as he spoke. Ted looked at Colin, and the look that passed between them asked the question about who had survived, but it was never spoken. They would find out soon enough, but within both there was a tightening of stomachs as they wondered who might be left.

"Right, that's it. Any questions?" Paul Cooper was coming to the end. "Good, Private Ludgrove has the mail, so you'd better take that back with you and hand it out. Corporal, Floyd, to me please." Joe approached, not without trepidation. Cooper spoke quietly. "Joe." The look of surprise on his face as Cooper used, for the first time ever, his Christian name. "Take the lad," he nodded towards the lone private "and look after 'im." Joe nodded, and saw a tight lipped smile of gratitude on the Sergeant's face. His heart skipped a beat; he had been accepted into the fold for his seniority, his experience and his performance under fire. He felt, for almost the first time in his life, an immense surge of pride.

The short delay meant Joe was the last to collect the mail. There were three letters and a parcel. He took them, and scanned the addresses. Cooper, standing close by, watched carefully. Wordlessly, his face a crumpled picture of remorse, Joe handed back to Ted a letter and a parcel, both bearing a Belfast postmark. Peter Dakin would not need them.

Ted felt the lump in his throat, rising so fast and causing so much pain he thought he would never be able to speak. "How?" His voice barely more than a whisper. As he spoke, Colin Baxter who had hung back, moved alongside him, realising what must have happened, sharing his pain, wishing to share the grief. Joe Floyd was trying to be the imperturbable NCO, and not being very successful. Everyone had liked young Peter and losing him was bloody hard, and no mistake. He managed to speak, but long sentences were beyond him before his voice cracked.

"Bullet in the 'ead. Rifle bullet towards the end. Right in the fore'ead. Never felt a thing." As he said it he realised that was what they all said in letters home. He looked straight into Ted's eyes. "'Onest, never felt a thing as Gawd's me witness."

Ted, holding a letter and a parcel, turned to Cooper in his distress and confusion. "What do I do wiv....." He held out the mail, the question unfinished, a pathetic gesture of supplication; tears welling in his eyes.

"Give them to me." Colin's trembling voice broke through before Cooper could respond. He too, although it never showed, was having trouble with his emotions. There hadn't been an ounce of bad in that lad; it was just bloody unfair. "I'll write," Colin said in response to a look from the sergeant.

"The regulation is......"

"I know the regulation." Colin's interruption drew looks of surprise. His tone softened as he saw anger flare in his sergeant's face. "But, sergeant, we cannot simply return these to sender. They are not his official next of kin; they'll get no telegram or official notification." His voice now very gentle, he concluded. "It's best someone writes, and I'm probably best equipped to do so."

"Aye." Cooper spoke with a deep sigh. "Aye, yer right. Where is he?" The question to Joe Floyd.

"We'll get 'im." Ted heard himself speak as if from a long way off. "S'roit fer us t' get 'im an' take 'im back."

As he spoke, the German artillery opened fire again, and by now they had the range pretty well. High explosive began, once more, to rain down on them. Paul ordered stand to yet again and they rushed to their positions, just as their platoon commander came into view from company HQ; from where he had been sent packing by the company commander.

Joe Floyd stopped short as he entered his part of the trench system to see a section of it caved in. They would not need to bury Peter Dakin, the German artillery had done it for them. Bawling out orders, he sorted what was left of his men into two halves, with Alfie commanding one half, and then had them crouching in the bottom of the trench taking as much shelter as they could. Ted, who had followed him in order to see his dead friend, turned and went back to his officer, a look of abject misery on his face, and a feeling of anger of such intensity he could not remember having suffered such an emotion before in the whole of his young life.

This continued to be the pattern for the next few days. Quiet would descend from time to time, but always the Germans would pound away with artillery so there was no sleep, no rest; and no time or facility for any sort of personal administration. Men became filthy, plastered in mud and grease. They stank, but no one noticed since they all smelt as bad as each other. Lice bred in the warm, moist seams of their clothing and then invaded the soft flesh of their bodies, between the legs, under the arms; an infusion of itching irritation. Teeth went uncleaned, washing simply did not happen, shaving was a luxury almost impossible to achieve and hair grew long and ragged; a perfect nesting place for yet more vermin.

Rats began to migrate into the trenches from surrounding farm buildings, drawn there by the prospect of food where flesh, in varying states of decay, lay uncollected as debris in and around the trenches. At first men would seek to kill them with a well aimed boot heel or a rifle butt. Before long, however, it just became too much effort, and the rats became a part of their daily lives, to be tolerated with all the other intolerable things they were enduring.

The ending of the assault on Neuve Chapelle brought no respite. The Germans continued their battering. At one stage they were within sixty yards of the trenches and were lobbing what appeared to be grenades, but at a range far beyond that which allowed the Norfolks to respond in kind.

"What are they?" Charles Hawthorne's strained voice asked the question they all wished answered.

"They" were trench mortars, which the Germans possessed in considerable profusion. Having prepared themselves to fight a war which would involve investing and then fighting for and within large fortresses, the Germans had ensured they were equipped properly so to do. It was their good fortune that the very equipment required for this role was also ideally suited to trench warfare of the kind that had developed on the Aisne and now on the Western Front. The mortar was a tube, about two inches in diameter and a couple of feet long, which fired a small bomb containing a few ounces of high explosive out to about one hundred yards. Its arrival was always preceded by the cough of its firing and, given the chance to look up, it was possible to track the bomb through its flight. Avoiding action, should it be judged to be coming your way, was virtually impossible: head down and hope was the best that could be achieved.

By the end of October they were sorely depleted in

numbers; and those who were left were ill and weak with the cold, the wet and the lack of proper food - to say nothing of the impact of the constant pounding they had received over such a long time. Consequently, there was no question of forays into the open to take on the trench mortar positions. They had not the physical strength, nor could they afford the numbers of casualties such a venture might accrue. Artillery was the only option they felt they could use. However, it was the same day that some fifty percent of the British artillery was withdrawn from the line for want of ammunition, and the rest had their firing severely curtailed. They would just have to put up with the trench mortars unless they could silence them themselves; which they could not.

"Brigadier, we are to be relieved."

Von Gleichen, caught in the middle of his morning ablutions, paused, the razor in his right hand, lather covering half his face. Well aware that his men were faring much less well than he, it was his view that he had to maintain standards as well as he could in difficult circumstances. If they all ended up looking like ragamuffins there would be no order, and with no order there was chaos; and then defeat. Inwardly, he sighed his thanks to God. Outwardly, he remained imperturbable. "Go on."

"The corps is to be withdrawn. We are to be replaced in the line by the Lahore and Meerut Divisions of the Indian Corps."

"When?"

"Starting today." It was the thirtieth of October.

"Good. See to the orders please," and with that the commander returned to his morning toilet, saving his expression of relief until he was alone.

"The brigade is to be relieved." The company commander was giving out his orders. Looks of expectation on the faces of his platoon commanders, two of whom, by now, were sergeants and one of those had been a corporal the day before.

"However," his voice held a sombre note, "we shall not be going immediately. The Indian Corps, which is to replace us, will need time to settle and therefore some will have to remain behind, for a time, to guide them. That will be our task." He watched the crestfallen looks on the faces around him, disappearing quickly in all cases except young Hawthorn. The boy had held on much better than expected, but was still too withdrawn and detached, still lacked the spark that was needed to make him stand out as an officer should. He continued with his orders, winding up as always with the request for questions. However, this time he had additional news to impart, which he had saved until the end.

"This is not a good time for change, however, I am afraid I shall be leaving you in a few days. I am to move onto the staff at divisional HQ." They looked aghast. The man with the charmed life, the man who had remained an icon for them all, never wavering, never in doubt, always there when needed, the guiding hand to which those who had survived owed their lives, was going.

The major went on. His relief was to be a captain who had been wounded on the Aisne and was returning to duty. They were mollified just a little when they heard the name. He was an experienced man, and well regarded, certainly by the sergeants' mess.

The second piece of news hit Charles even harder. Cooper was to be replaced. The CSM had been wounded a couple of days earlier, would not be returning and a successor was required. The new company commander would need a strong man to assist, especially since there was no longer a second in command in the company, and little prospect of the post being filled. That person was to be Paul Cooper, and he was to be promoted accordingly.

Corporal Jim Collis, the only one of the platoon's original section commanders left, was to be promoted and replace Cooper as platoon sergeant. This brought nods of approval from those who knew him, but did nothing to assuage Charles Hawthorn's feelings of trepidation and misery. He may not have liked Cooper, he may have resented the man's knowledge, his obvious courage and his experience, but he knew he needed him, relied on him totally and was now faced with the prospect of being in serious difficulty without him.

They were also informed that a new draft of men was on its way from England, and they could expect their strength to be increased within a day or so.

They stayed in the line for two days whilst the rest of the brigade moved back and the Indians began to move in. Their arrival coincided with a perceptible slackening in the pressure from the Germans as their efforts to reach the coast began to falter all along the front, but principally in the south. The Norfolks watched their British colleagues leaving with feelings of considerable envy. Second Corps had been promised by GHQ that there would be ten days rest, and they, the Ninth, did not appear to be about to get their share.

They watched as the Indians arrived. Led by British officers, they were a mix the like of which most of the young soldiers in the trenches had not seen before. Some of the reservists had done time in India, and resorted at once to the vernacular they had used when serving there. For the rest, there was the sight of Sikhs, Dogras, Bengalis, Ghurkhas and a whole raft of others with varying forms of headress, facial hair and regimental accoutrements. They heard the strange sounds of new tongues and smelt the spicy odour as they cooked their rations in the trenches. Some of the more adventurous were tempted to try new tastes, whilst some of the old hands revelled in eating food they had enjoyed so much all those years ago.

The slackening of the German effort was a great boon to the settling in of the new troops, and on the second of November it was judged time for the Norfolks to retire to billets. In the dark of the early part of the night, at eight o'clock, they were relieved by the 8th Sikhs, and filed quietly away to the rear to march the two and a half miles due west to their billets in the small village of Gorre.

The second of November was the official end of the Battles south of the Lys; the battles of Armentières and La

Bassée. Technically at an end, this did not stop the fighting which continued throughout Flanders, both in the south, and to the north at Ypres where the second of November coincided with what was probably the climax of that battle: First Ypres. Neither should it be thought that those in the south had suffered any less than their compatriots to the north, in the infamous salient. The casualties had been enormous, and the Norfolks had suffered grievously With Cooper gone, Ted looked around as they arrived in the billets. Apart from Jim Collis, who was exerting his new found authority in settling people in, there was Colin Baxter and two from his section, Joe Floyd, Alfie James, Alfred Arbuckle and Ted himself who were all that was left in the platoon of those who had boarded the ship in Belfast just eleven weeks earlier. Apart from Alfie and Alfred, all Joe had left was the young lad he had been asked to look after by Cooper. Noaksie had become a gibbering wreck days ago, or was it weeks, he couldn't remember. They'd shifted him back, and God knew what might happen to him.

Ted felt a wave of emptiness wash over him, a sick physical pain wrenching at his stomach as he thought of the loss of so many. He made a move towards Colin, to try and talk to him, to just get close to someone he knew and could trust. As he did so there was a commotion at the door of the barn in which they were to sleep.

"It's the new draft, sir," said Jim Collis, responding to Charles Hawthorn's look of enquiry. "Shall I bring 'em in and sort 'em out later?"

Charles thought, briefly, that Cooper would have done it without asking. Oh dear, he would miss him. He spoke.

"Yes please Sergeant Collis. We need to get cleaned up, and to know what we have been given, before we make any decisions about what to do with them." If they had not been quite so tired they might have noticed a new ring of confidence, however imperceptible, in the young officer's voice.

"Sir! Right you lot, inside." And as he spoke they began to file through the door.

"Ted, that you?" Ned Preece could barely recognise his

friend as the begrimed, filthy, bearded, long haired creature with which he was faced. "Ted, wot the fuck's been goin' on mate? Where's Cooper, an' where's the rest of 'em?"

The sight of Ned Preece looking fit and healthy, and wearing a lance corporal's stripe, brought a grin to Ted's face and a delighted yell from Colin Baxter. They shook his hand and thumped him on the back so soundly he thought he might suffer permanent injury. Within seconds he was surrounded by others, Floyd, James, Arbuckle, all asking how he was and what news there was.

"An' Pete?" There was a questioning tone in his voice, and a look on his face which said he didn't want to hear the answer. Ted stared at the ground and shook his head, unable to look his friend in the eye. "Bastard!" was Ned's response, said with a vehemence that sought to dampen the acute pain he felt.

"Ted! Ted, is that you?" Ted looked round.

"Oh yeah," Ned's voice in his ear, "there's a bloke come out on the boat wiv us reckons 'e knows you from back 'ome." As he spoke, Ted recognised the smiling, open face of James Woolford as his old friend approached across the open space between the barn door and the corner in which he had been about to settle.

"James. Jim. Wot 're you doin' 'ere?" His emotions ran riot, the enormous pleasure at seeing his old friend again combining with dread at the prospect of what might befall him in the cauldron of the Western Front. Grinning so widely his face hurt he grabbed Jim's right hand in his and his right forearm with his left hand and just pumped and pumped until Jim, laughing, asked if he could have his arm back. The laughter, however, soon disappeared from Jim's face and voice as he took in the state in which he found his friend. "My God, Ted, what on earth do you look like? What has been happening?"

As he spoke, mugs appeared brimming with hot tea from a dixie bubbling on a fire just outside the door. "Food in ten minutes," was Alfie James announcement. "'Allo mate." He offered his hand to Jim. "Nice t' meet yer. You a mate o' Ted's then?"

Within minutes they were sitting in a corner of the barn, shovelling down hot stew, the like of which they had not tasted for ages. There was fresh bread with which to mop it up, and as much tea as they could drink. Outside, at the back of the barn, there were Soya Stoves, large wood burning affairs, about the size of a forty-five gallon oil drum, in the bottom of which a fire could be lit. Within a very short time each one would produce several gallons of hot water with which they could wash.

The QM had appeared with B echelon, and they had been able to sort out the kit they had left with him for safe keeping since before they had gone into the farm at Canteleux. It was midnight as the section began to shave and wash. Others had already succumbed to extreme tiredness and had fallen asleep, almost where they stood, but the exchange of news had kept them awake, together with Joe's recommendation that they would sleep better, and certainly wake better, clean. As he said it, Joe paused to think that, had Cooper been the sergeant, they would have done that anyway, as a matter of course. No one could be sure what the morrow would bring. Charlie Marshall was back, his ear having been sewn up, and Eddie Macleary was with him, the shoulder wound having been less serious than had been thought, and certainly not a "Blighty"; much to his chagrin.

Shaved, clean, and feeling better than he could remember feeling for a very long time, Ted lay back on the hard barn floor and, as he drifted off to sleep, ran over in his mind the events of the evening.

There had been a deal of banter, set off, despite their sombre mood, by the news of Ned Preece's wedding and the pictures he had circulated of his wife and daughter. His story of the courtship, including the damage to his uncles "working parts", had brought forth grim chuckles. He had described the wedding, and the ten days they had been able to enjoy together before he had returned, as bid by a telegram, to Britannia Barracks in order to form part of a draft to the Continent. He did not describe the tearful farewell, the pain as he had left, and the agony of his loneliness as he missed so much, so very much, something so precious he had not the words to describe it.

The draft had arrived in the battalion that morning and had been hanging around waiting for the withdrawal into billets. The RSM had seen Ned, had, in the past, spoken of him with Cooper, they had needed some NCOs and he had been promoted on the spot. He had, immediately, changed his allotment to his wife, passing on to her the whole of the pay increase.

He gave them the good wishes of Fred Smith whom he had seen in Norwich. The foot had been amputated; indeed, the amputation was half way up his calf. However, he now had an artificial limb, was walking well on crutches, and Aggie had moved down from Belfast to join him in quarters by the barracks. He was working in the stores for the time being, on paper work, but when the leg was good enough he would be going on to train new recruits. He had shared with Ned the news that he had been told he would serve on to pension since he could still make a useful contribution, certainly with a war on, and that sergeant was not impossible.

There had been nods of approval all round. "Good ol' Fred, dives in a bucket o' shit an' comes out smellin' like a bleeding rose."

Ted had managed a few minutes with James Woolford, to find out what had brought him here. James had not stayed away from Norfolk for long after his father's looms had closed. He had returned to Norwich to take up a post in an insurance company, called the Norwich Union. It had been Charlie's assertion that the weaving trade was dying fast, no matter where he took his business, and his son would be better off with a profession to sustain him. With his contacts in the county it had not been difficult to fix James with something appropriate.

James had fallen in with a group of young men in the firm who were members of the Special Reserve, and, out of a mix of boredom and curiosity, he had gone along with them to some of the training. He had found himself enjoying it, and had joined. They had been in for the fun, and despite their obvious qualities, none of them had wished, initially at least, to try for a commission. He had damaged an ankle during summer camp, and had not been fit to join up until now. Hence, he was now in France, a private soldier. His friends had left home soon after hostilities had commenced, were out here already and he knew not what might have happened to them.

By this stage Ted had been slurring his speech with tiredness, and James stopped talking as he watched the eyelids droop. Not having been allocated a section he lay down beside his friend to try to sleep. It did not come easily. The state in which he had seen Ted initially had been a terrible shock. He had looked almost sub-human. And there was a look about him, a hardness, a tiredness, a something upon which he could not put his finger, but found disturbing. He was certainly not the young man who had left the village just over two years ago.

They woke the next morning, late, having been allowed to sleep on. As he woke, James saw Ted was reading a letter, delivered that morning with the rations.

"Who's that from?" James had not yet learned that some questions were simply just not asked. Ted swallowed the initial feeling of resentment at the intrusion into his privacy. James would learn.

"It's from Mrs Allsop." He saw the questioning look on James' face. "Yer prob'ly don't remember. She were married to that Allsop bloke 'oo came back t' the village jus' afore I left. Been in the Army 'e 'ad. I met 'er once." He then proceeded to explain how he had come to write to her, and as he did James remarked, mentally to himself, and not for the first time, how badly Ted's accent and quality of speech had deteriorated since he had been in the Army.

"Oh, right....I see." His curiosity satisfied, he returned to cleaning his rifle whilst Ted returned to reading his letter. It was nicely written, in a firm, round hand. She thanked him for writing to her, and apologised for any delay in responding, but felt sure he would understand. She wrote of her deep shock, and her sense of loss, but also of the need for life to go on. She hoped he was well, and that her reply would find him in good health; and she mentioned that she would like it if he could see her if he was home on leave. She signed it: yours sincerely, Thurza Allsop.

Breakfast was available at nine o'clock and those who were awake woke those who were not, on the basis that a decent meal was not to be missed. The time at which they were busying themselves with rifle cleaning, person cleaning, kit cleaning, eating and reading their delivery of letters also coincided with the arrival of the morning delivery of mail in most of the homes across most of the United Kingdom.

So it was in Belfast. She did not recognise the writing as she collected the single envelope that had plopped on the mat, and as she opened it could sense something was wrong.

The cry of anguish came from the very depths of her being, the cry of the she-animal at the loss of its child, at the extinguishing of the life of the product of its womb. It was a cry primeval in its origins. Neighbours in the neat terraced houses heard the call echoing along the street and came to find the cause. There was no reply from the front, so those who knew went round the back where the door was always open. They found her, knees tight together, hands clenched on her lap, shoulders hunched, tears streaming down her face, and gut wrenching sobs that shook her whole body to its core; and which her diminutive husband had no hope of curbing. The letter was held, damp and crumpled, in her hand.

"'Oi'll make d' tay." Sleeves rolled up and pinny securely round her middle, the responsibility for making tea was taken, determinedly, by one. Others went and shooed away the curious, one more went for the priest and yet another sat beside her on the sofa, arms round her shoulders offering what support she could to them both in their grief; not by talking, but simply by being there.

Colin Baxter's letter had been beautifully written. He had agonised over it, and had done his very best to get it right. But, however much he had tried, the brutal fact was that Peter was dead, and there were no words that could assuage the pain. Peter had died believing he had found the mother and father he had never known. He would never know that he had become the child they had never been able to have, or that a room in their small house had been set aside as his room for when he came back. That news had been in the letter Joe Floyd had returned to Ted.

"We are going back into the line, this afternoon!"

Charles Hawthorn had recovered his composure in the walk from company HQ, having attended the orders given by his new company commander, the recently arrived captain. The few days which the major had believed would elapse before he moved on had reduced, typically, to a few hours. There had been no time for farewells other than to those in company headquarters and his officers. The first his soldiers knew of his departure was when they were told by their platoon commanders.

They received the news in silence. There was nothing to say. The company had now ceased to exist as they had known it just a short time ago. The old hands suffered emotions which could best be described as desolation and foreboding, whilst the new arrivals, as was always the case, suffered the apprehension borne of ignorance about what might befall them. The sights they had seen since their arrival, however, did not give them strong feelings of confidence about the immediate future.

Charles went on to describe the position, and to advise them that they would be joined in the line by the 8th Ghurkhas. He also ordered Jim Collis to issue out a supply of Battye Bombs which had just been brought forward. There were enough for two per section and they were to supplement the Jam Pot Grenades which would continue to be manufactured by the troops as and when necessary.

Battye Bombs, however, were a bit more reliable than their home-made counterparts. Named after Captain B C Battye of the Royal Engineers, this initial production run had emerged from the ironworks in Bethune, a medium sized industrial town about a mile and a half south-west of Gorre and some five miles behind the line. The bomb was based on a design by Major R L McLintock of the Royal Engineers, developed in Bangalore, in India before the war. It comprised a cast iron cylinder, four inches long and two inches in diameter. It was closed at one end, and the outer casing was segmented by half inch serrations to aid fragmentation. The filling was high explosive, generally Ammonal. The open end was closed by a wooden plug into which went the detonator and the fuze which was lit by a Nobel's igniter, the same one as used in the Pas de Calais coal mines. This was ignited by a soft blow, so, as a safety device, a cap and safety pin were added in order to prevent accidental initiation.

"'Ow d' we use these, then?" It was Joe Floyd who asked the question.

"You'll find out when we get up inter the line." Jim Collis was asserting his new found authority, and received a withering look from Joe for his pains.

On returning to his section Joe handed the two bombs to Alfie, and told him to add them to the collection of Jam Pots they would be taking forward. Alfie voiced a similar question regarding training, and was advised, grumpily, that it would be done "on the fuckin' job!"

They moved up in file, slipping into their new positions as the Indian battalion occupying them moved back out. The company was on the right of the battalion, and the platoon found itself with the Ghurkhas immediately to their right. They listened with a mix of amusement and confusion to the guttural sound of the language, they admired the white officers who spoke with such fluency the native language and they responded with smiles to the irrepressible grins of the small hill men from Nepal. They looked with interest at the kukri each of them wore on his belt, tucked into the small of the back and readily available to be whipped out, right handed, whenever the need arose. They wondered at the stories, embellished no doubt, told to them by the old India hands about the use of the kukri in close quarter fighting; and trembled a little at the thoughts created by the imagination.

As it grew dark they waited for the order to stand down and leave out sentries. As it came they were also told that the Ghurkhas were to mount a raid to test the strength of the enemy, and bring back information about the opposition facing them in the German trenches not far away across no man's land. They would be going out after midnight, and were to be in by dawn, and there would be about twenty of them. Sentries were briefed and the word passed on during the night so that when the return came they would be expected and would not be fired upon by their own side.

The night passed quietly. Charles Hawthorn could not sleep, and with Ted he moved along the trench to lean, looking out over the open ground to the Germans, beside the sentry. It was James Woolford, and Charles returned the smile of welcome which he was just able to discern in the light of a moon that exposed itself only occasionally from behind scudding clouds which were being propelled by a freshening wind. James, of course, had no qualms about equality or his place in the pecking order; private he was, Hawthorne's social and intellectual equal he also was.

"Hallo, sir." The whispered welcome. "Ted." He acknowledged his friend's presence. "I've not seen or heard anything."

Hawthorne nodded, and in silence, shivering in the cold, they continued watching out to the front. As they stared, trying to discern activity, the shadows took on a life and shape of their own, dancing before their eyes so that they had to blink and refocus in order to convince themselves that they were not seeing either returning Ghurkhas or approaching enemy. There was no sound from around them save the rustling of dried, fallen leaves on the ground, the creak and shuffle of branches in the wind, a snore or a snuffle from a sleeping man. In the middle distance there was the sound of sporadic shooting, probably mostly due to nervous sentries, and here and there a flare was put up over the battlefield. To their north they could hear the sounds of heavy shell fire and see the flashes on the horizon, the flickering light dancing through the shadows of trees, bushes and small buildings. To their front, all was quiet.

Suddenly, as Hawthorne's eyelids were beginning to droop with fatigue, there was a commotion from the area of the German trenches. It was just beginning to show light in the east, a couple of minutes to go to the dawn stand to, and the deep boom of a grenade was accompanied by a flash which, briefly, lit up their surroundings. It also showed a gaggle of figures on the edge of the German trenches. They heard commands being shouted, unable to determine who was giving them. Then there were bursts of fire from rifles. A German machine gun began to fire and then stopped as suddenly as it had begun.

"Stand to the platoon, Ludgrove; but quietly please. No shouting." Hawthorn felt very calm, and in charge of things. He picked up the field telephone positioned nearby. "I will tell company HQ what has happened. Let Sergeant Collis know where I am and tell him I shall remain here for the time being." He stepped to one side as Joe, having just woken, moved into place in the trench and the rest of the section fell in on either side of him.

"Wassup?" Joe's question to James, known to the rest as Jim, and he listened, impressed, to a lucid explanation of events.

"Right." He looked along the section. "Them Goorkas is expected back around 'ere, so watch for 'em an' no firin' less I tells yer. Clear?" The question went unanswered, and he assumed a positive reply. He watched as the old hands checked their sights for three hundred yards, checked the bolts, tapped their pouches to confirm the presence of ammunition and settled in comfortably to a watching position. He smiled as he saw the newcomers copying. Charles, taking his lead from the corporal, moved along a few yards to Jim Collis and gave him a similar order for the platoon before returning to watch with Joe's section the events to their front.

As suddenly as it had begun, the commotion ceased and they saw shadows beginning to come their way. The Germans put up three flares, and as they burst into life, casting a flickering yellowish glow over the ground beneath, the section could see the Ghurkha patrol making its way back. As soon as the flares popped, half of them turned and began to fire on the enemy, whilst the rest carried on for a few yards before turning and firing themselves to give their comrades the covering fire through which they could move. Thus, they leapfrogged back in good order towards their own lines. The rate of fire was well up to standard, and there were grim smiles of approval from the British in their trenches. From away to their left and right their own machine guns, trained on the area in case covering fire were needed, began to fire in long, sweeping bursts.

"Bleedin' artillery'll get 'em if they don't get a move on." Ted's voice broke the human silence in the trench.

"Aye," breathed Joe.

But it never came. The Germans really had no idea what had hit them, and simply did not know what to fire at. Their local command and control had been completely disabled. The Ghurkha patrol had actually been crawling around their lines for quite a long time. The sentries were dead, as were the three officers who had been in that section of trench. They would be found in the growing light of dawn with their heads neatly severed from their bodies, lying in great puddles of congealed, arterial blood with no epaulettes or insignia; these having been removed for intelligence purposes. The explosion had been caused by a booby trapped grenade on the lip of a trench, which had killed two of the Nepalese. Those Germans in the immediate area who had woken had found themselves being bayoneted and shot by men who had got in amongst them with such stealth there had been no inkling of their coming.

Unable to fire in support of the withdrawal because of the angle, the section watched admiringly the highly professional withdrawal being executed by the patrol, control being exercised by a senior NCO. They looked on as they drew closer, clearly visible in the light of the flares, but seemingly untroubled.

"Wot's 'e carryin'?" Alfie was referring to the senior NCO,

now approaching quite close to the position, rifle in his right hand and something pale in the left.

James Woolford vomited into the trench as the realisation struck him. Charles looked away, his face a picture of repugnant horror, trying desperately to hold onto the contents of his stomach. Joe's mouth dropped open as he stared, and the rest of them displayed assorted looks of shock and disbelief.

"Fuckin' 'ell!" The expletive from Eddie Macleary, echoed by Alfie. Alfred Arbuckle retained his customary composure, but looked very pale in the light of the flares.

The luckless German machine gunner who had managed to fire only one short burst had not had time to look up from his sitting position behind the gun, even though he had realised someone, appearing from nowhere, was standing above him. He barely registered the grunt as the man prepared for a strenuous physical exertion, but had not felt the pain as the kukri sliced his head vertically from top to bottom along a line running just behind the temples. He was already dead as the bloody remains of his head slumped forward, what was left of his exposed brain impaling itself on the firing handles of the gun. It was his face that the Ghurkha NCO was bringing back as a trophy, with a huge grin on his face as he demonstrated the results of his prowess to his cheering regiment.

The white officer, seeing Charles' distress, smiled sympathetically, and then, feigning not to notice the cause of the commotion as the patrol returned, took himself off for an early breakfast.

The reduction in activity on their front was not being mirrored further to the north. Here, in the salient on the eastern edge of Ypres, the battles continued to rage. Such had been the intensity of the fighting, by the second of November, the day the Norfolks had been undergoing their very short rest in Gorre, there was barely a single unit north of the Lys fighting with its original formation. Platoons had ceased to exist, the company structure they had trained in had disappeared. It was not unusual to find companies whose strength did not run to double figures, commanded by corporals. What was left of battalions were commanded, in many cases, by subalterns or sergeants. They had fought to a standstill that had taken them beyond exhaustion into a trance-like state where normality had no place. It was a form of insanity, and without it many of them would not have survived for it anaesthetised them to the horror and the immediate prospect of death or maiming.

Seventh Division had been withdrawn from the line in the salient, a division in name only, depleted beyond belief. Its place had been taken by a collection of battalions, fifteen of them drawn from Second Corps. The trickle north of these battalions had commenced on the thirtieth of October, the day they had been pulled out of the line in the south on the promise of ten days rest. So much for promises. Five of the battalions went up onto Messines ridge, south of Ypres, and the other ten to Hooge, just to the east. As they did so, the Germans threw in a series of limited attacks in order to disrupt the reinforcement; and by the sixth of November, General Smith-Dorrien, his HQ still south of the Lys, no longer had a corps to command.

The Norfolks remained at Festubert, in the trenches. The enemy continued to harass them, becoming more and more adept with trench mortars and grenades, day and night. People were ill from exposure to the elements and from the strain on everyone's nerves. They watched as regiments they had fought alongside for weeks vanished away to the north. Daily, they waited for relief, but in vain.

The eleventh of November dawned grey and foggy, with a light wind blowing away from them towards the enemy. As the greyness lightened with the approaching day, they heard to the north a phenomenal barrage. Given the limitations on their own artillery ammunition consumption, they assumed it, correctly, to be German. It was the most violent bombardment yet delivered in the war, and it preceded the final German attempt to break through the British Army and reach the coast. On a front of nine miles from Messines to Polygon wood, the Germans had assembled twelve and a half divisions and some two hundred and twenty eight guns, finally to destroy what was left of the British. The Kaiser was behind them, waiting in Courlot to lead the victory parade through Ypres when his victorious troops swatted the irritating British fly to their front.

Regrettably, no one had informed Thomas of the Kaiser's plans. Dug in, short of ammunition, starving, filthy and decimated, there was nowhere to go; so he decided to stay. And stay he did, firing his rifle seemingly faster than ever, crying out as he was wounded, lying where he fell as he died. By six o'clock that evening, as it began to rain, the Germans had given up, and the Kaiser had left to return to Germany, his victory parade an unfulfilled dream. He had not succeeded in breaking through the line of the insignificant little army he had despised; but he had succeeded in destroying it. On average, there were only thirty soldiers per battalion left of those who had landed in France in August. The old, professional British Army had ceased to exist; it had fought itself into oblivion.

At Festubert, the pioneer platoon, assisting some Sappers, had blown the old trenches to render them uninhabitable as the battalion moved back to a new line which had been dug by some of those from other regiments in reserve. The next day they were relieved by the 7th Dragoon Guards acting as infantry; and they would not see their horses again for the rest of the war. The Norfolks moved back into Gorre once more, into billets.

As they fell out, on Jim Collis' command, Ted saw a group of officers talking, some fifty or so yards away. He paused, seeing Edward Snell and James, standing beside him, followed the line of his friend's gaze.

"Isn't that....?" He asked.

"Aye," said Ted, and as he spoke saw that the officer Snell was talking to was their new company commander; and as he watched they both glanced in his direction.

His heart sinking, and fear in the pit of his stomach, he moved miserably into the pigsty to which they had been allocated.

Chapter 13

A Deserter Returns

On the seventeenth of November 1914 they marched north in the direction of Ypres, to join those regiments of Second Corps that had left over the past couple of weeks, all heading in the same direction. The march was hard, for their feet had suffered terribly in the wet conditions of the trenches. The long period of immersion leading up to their first break on the second of November had taken its toll.

That one night out of the line had offered the first opportunity for a long time to remove their boots and change their socks. Actually, socks was hardly a fair description of the encrusted remnants, oily and greasy with sweat and stinking beyond belief, that had emerged into the light as they removed their boots. Feet were blackened with encrusted dirt, sticking, rock hard, to the soft flesh. Removing the dirt had involved bathing gently in hot water, carefully separating the toes and removing lumps of dead flesh and sweaty deposits. Swathes of skin, leaf like and translucent, fell in layers from the undersides. Drying them, sleeping without the boots on and exposing them to the air had gone some way to remedying the damage, but it had not been until the 7th Dragoon Guards had relieved them on the twelfth of November that they had been granted a few days rest, in Gorre once more, to really sort themselves out. Many had been within an ace of contracting Trench Foot, but this was not something about which they knew very much; and had not been taught its causes, its prevention or its cure.

But on the way to Estaires, my how the road took its toll. Feet, hardened by the long marches they had undertaken at the beginning of the campaign, now blistered and hurt in their softened state in stiffened boots, tramping along the pavé roads. It wasn't a long march, but it was a footsore and weary band that went into billets, having travelled only the six miles from Festubert. That night they had the best sleep many of them could remember for a very long time, but woke with feet in agony. Placing them in boots, turned to rock hardness by constant soaking, was hell; to walk on them was torture.

Then it was more of the same, a five mile march north to Bailleul, and then on to the small village of Dranouter lying north-east of the town, just over the border into Belgium; and only seven or eight miles south-west of Ypres. In the distance they could hear the thud of sporadic artillery fire; and given the state of their own ammunition supply they knew that most, if not all, of it was German. They shivered, and blamed the biting wind for it; but for many it was more than just the wind causing the shivers.

The morning of the nineteenth of November dawned with the coldest frost they had thus far endured, and to give a foretaste of unpleasantness to come they suffered the first snowfall of the year. Their boots turned the white, soft expanse into muddy trails as they marched off, at four that afternoon, to relieve a French unit at Kemmel, just a couple of miles away to the east. It was a quiet relief, and the trenches were in good order, well dug and well maintained. They were not to know it, but they were part of a process whereby Foch had agreed to take over responsibility for the Ypres salient for the time being, given the casualties suffered by the BEF in holding their line. Over the next couple of days there was a general redeployment, which found the BEF covering a front of about twenty-one miles between Givenchy and Kemmel; which placed the Norfolks somewhere on the very left of the British line.

From the twelfth of October, when the brigade had gone

firm in Festubert, the British and Indian casualties had been almost sixty thousand in just six weeks, the bulk having fallen to the First, Third and Seventh Divisions. German casualties are given as more than twice that number. Whatever else it was, First Ypres was a human tragedy on the grand scale.

“Lance Corporal Baxter and Private Woolford, commanding officer’s interviews at ten o’clock!” Jim Collis looked at the two men, seeing the concern registering on their faces, hoping the curiosity did not register on his. They had either done something very right, or very wrong. No one had reported either to him, and he was at a loss to work out the reason. And if Charles Hawthorn knew anything he was not telling.

The rest of them wondered also, shivering in the freezing cold of a sharp frost, the snow from four days ago still masking the damage caused by exploding shells, the brown earth peeping through where the covering had either been insufficient or had been blown away in the biting wind. The mist of their breath gathered in small clouds above their heads, to be whipped away by the fresh breeze, dispersed never to be seen again, like the ghosts of the fallen seeking their peace in a world beyond anything they might ever imagine. To their front, looking out over the ruptured land before them, they saw the stiff frozen bodies of the dead. The only blessing of the cold was that the rate of decomposition slowed, and the smell was less; but in the snow they could see the tracks of rodents and other scavengers who used the night to feast on the bounty of flesh that man had lain before them

“Lef’ right lef’ right lef’ right!” The pace at which the regimental sergeant major wished them to march as he moved them smartly into the farm kitchen that was the commanding officer’s office was somewhat faster than any normal human being was capable of contemplating.

“Maaaaark tooooime! Lef’ right lef’ right!” Their knees moving so rapidly, seeking to get the thigh parallel to the ground, the speed at which they were marking time defeating their aspiration, making it look as if they were dancing on the spot rather than marching on the spot.

"'Alt! Roooooit tarn!" They were still, their feet hurt terribly, but they dared not show it. Their breath came in short pants as they recovered their composure, looking directly at the wall to their front, and not at the officer seated before them. It was some time, therefore, before they realised they were dealing with Major Done and not Lieutenant Colonel Ballard.

"The commanding officer has left the battalion to take up a new appointment with Seventh Brigade." That explained it then. "I have been appointed in his place." The major neglected to mention that he would not be promoted; but then it was none of their business. "Before he went we discussed the matter of commissioning soldiers whom he felt might aspire to be good officers, and based on the views of your former company commander," he glanced at Colin, "and on the reports and recommendations that have followed you from England and the fact that you took, and passed, the entrance examination for Sandhurst," he glanced at James, "I wish you two to consider going for officer training."

Silence. They were both taken aback; James less so since he had been half expecting it, Colin completely.

"Well?" There was an impatient questioning note in the Major's voice.

"Will that mean a commission in the regiment, sir?" James was the first to speak.

"In your case, yes." Colin was quick to spot the inference. He, having only attended a minor public school and being of indeterminate background, but able to speak well, and clearly a natural leader, would find himself sent off somewhere else to do he knew not what. "Sir, do I have the opportunity to think this over, or must I give you a decision now?" Colin heard the RSM behind him draw in his breath at the impertinence.

"You have until six this evening, at which point you will

go back to take the train to officer training school; or not, the choice is yours."

"I'll go sir." James did not wait a second as the major finished speaking to Colin. The eagerness in his voice was not lost, either on the major or the RSM. He glanced at Colin. "Come on, Colin, come with me. It's a wonderful opportunity."

"You're right, it is. But it isn't for me." In just a few seconds he had made up his mind, and, conscious that he might regret it for the rest of his life, however long that might be, he knew that the cynical rebel in him would not make for a comfortable life in the officers' mess. He drew himself more stiffly and formally to attention. "Sir, thank you very much for the privilege you have offered me, but I am afraid I must decline." He did not mention the overpowering feeling that he would be running out on his friends, the few that were left alive, and the impact that a strong wave of emotion had made on his decision.

"Very well." The major was not going to argue. He was not, in any event, too keen on selecting potential officers from the ranks in this fashion, so Baxter's refusal gave him no hardship whatsoever. "RSM, that will be all." They left, in response to the RSM's utterances, just as rapidly as they had entered. Outside the office, James was advised to pack his kit and be ready to move by six that evening, and Colin was given the RSM's views on wasted opportunity, and on half-witted lance corporals who knew not on which side their bread was buttered, before being sent back to his section.

James Woolford left that evening, having been bade a warm farewell by his colleagues in the platoon. For most of them it was the fact that he would be out of the firing line for quite some time that made them jealous. For Ted, there was relief that his friend had survived thus far and would survive longer, but it was accompanied by a pang of loneliness. It had been wonderful having him around, and to have someone to whom he could talk about his fears for what Snell might try to do. James had sought throughout to reassure him. The incident had been years ago, no one had pursued it even though he appeared now to be trying to make trouble, and anyway, the officers had much more to worry about than one man's attempt to be difficult

Watching James go Colin suffered a twinge of regret as he wondered about the good sense of what he had done. Charles Hawthorn shook his hand, and wished him luck.

For those who remained behind the next seven days were awful. The only saving grace of the intense cold was that the water in the bottom of the trenches froze, and so their feet were not immersed in it; they simply froze as well. It continued to snow heavily, a soft blanket covering the ground in front of them, forming humps where it lay gently on bodies left from the fighting, piling up against them, making small dune-like formations and delicate sculptures as the drifts were fashioned by the wind.

They remained there, in acute discomfort, until the first of December, whence they were sent back to Dranouter into billets. A typical, small French village of the area, it had been largely evacuated by its population, but some entrepreneurs had either remained or had drifted in from elsewhere to take advantage of the spending power of the soldiers. Individually, that power was not great, but taken together there were significant profits to be had. Several estaminets had appeared, offering a warm fire, food, hot drinks, alcohol and strong French cigarettes. By a stroke of luck there was one immediately beside the old tractor workshop in which the platoon found itself billeted. True, it was noisy trying to sleep there, given the revelry in the bar, but to men used to artillery bombardments of the sort they had suffered it was nothing. Much more important was proximity to the pleasures it offered.

"Deux biere pour mes amis, mais pour moi une verre de vin rouge, s'il vous plait." Colin's accent was impeccable as he placed his order with the waitress, his smile as devastating as he could make it given the conditions under which he had laboured in order to make himself presentable. She looked straight back at him, her expression one of someone who had seen it all before, despite a quiet stirring as she realised that this young man was just a cut above the rest of them.

"Oui, m'sieu. C'est tout?" The questioning note in her voice as she asked if they required anything else.

"Pour le moment." She was a poppet, and he did not want to let this go. "Mais peut être vous avez une menu?"

She smiled, and as she did the dimples in her cheeks showed clearly. "C'est ca." She pointed to a slate propped up by the bar, on which was chalked the offerings for the day. He grinned back, the ice was broken. "Merci, pour le moment, seulement les bieres et du vin." She turned to move back behind the bar, with just a little extra swing of her hips as she did so; purely for his benefit, but it was not lost on Ted or Alfie, or on Joe Floyd seated at the next table.

By the time they left, a couple of hours later, they had sunk a few beers and consumed a plate of Pommes de Terre Frites, christened "Bombardier Fritz" by Thomas, and felt the better for it. Colin, to the amusement and, quite frankly, envy of his chums had clearly made an impression on the waitress and had determined where she lived and the times at which she was free. All he now needed was some free time of his own and there was potential here. She really was very nice, long brown hair tied in a plait which sat neatly in the nape of her neck, the rest of her hair framing a gentle round face. The eyes were brown, and her wide smile reached deep into them. Tall, at about five feet eight inches in height, she wore long flowing frocks that accentuated the roundness of a very nice bottom and a long sleeved smock which left entirely to the imagination what might lie underneath. Colin's imagination was running riot.

Opposite, on the other side of the road, was a different sort of emporium. What had become known as "Red Lamp Establishments" had grown up all over the area behind the battlefields. The best was, apparently, in Amiens, but was extremely expensive. There were others of a higher quality in places like Béthune and St Omer, but all of these were out of the reach of Thomas's pocket. In the villages, however, they could satisfy their needs for just two francs, the equivalent of one shilling and seven pence; something approaching two days pay for a private, after stoppages. Colin, however, was quite clear, he had his eyes set on higher things; well, better things.

Unfortunately, he was to have very little time in which to pursue his quarry, as, within two days, they were back in the trenches again relieving the Dorsets near Wulverghem, a couple of miles just south of east of their billets. The trenches, by now, were beginning to form the structure and pattern that would remain for some time to come, although they had no idea of that. They were formed in three lines: the Front Line, the Support Line and the Reserve Line. They were built in right angled dog tooth fashion, and each section within them was called a fire bay. The bends were called traverses and there was a fire step on the enemy side of the front line. When the water table was too high they built up rather than digging down. An access trench led into the system by entering into the reserve trench, and then each of the lines was connected by a communications trench. The whole thing could be several hundred yards deep.

A good standing trench was about six feet deep so soldiers could walk safe from snipers, with the firing step being two feet high. The Dorsets had commenced work, aided by some sappers, but there was still much to do. In particular, they had to work hard with duckboards and brushwood to combat the wet and to lift themselves above the water table. Pervading everything was the cold and the damp.

A trench routine was now becoming standard along the line. Stand to was always thirty minutes before dawn and lasted an hour, after which they would have breakfast and shave. Sentry duty was always a two hour stint, usually singly by day and in pairs by night. Sentries in the trenches stood, at night, with head and shoulders above the parapet so that they could see and not be surprised. Not surprisingly, this was not the most popular order they had been given, and adverse comment was, from time to time, passed: “bollocks to this!”

There was an almost constant traffic of carrying parties

going back to pick up supplies which had been brought forward by transport. This would include ammunition, food and defence stores, such as sandbags and wire, with which to make the approaches to their trenches more difficult and to provide them with the wherewithal to construct shelters and latrines in the sides of the trenches. At dusk there was another stand to, and this would often be followed by patrols going out to test the enemy, find out more about them, disrupt their routines; and to repair their own defences.

In the evening they would have a hot meal, with most of their food being canned. Maconochie's was a form of tinned stew, containing meat, potatoes, beans and vegetables, and this was the name given to all such tins of stew, even though they were actually made by a number of different manufacturers. It could be eaten cold, but this was generally unappetising, and wherever possible they would fry it in a tin over a fire. There were iron rations as well, but these could only be consumed on the orders of a superior officer.

"Wassamaarer wiv you?" Lance Corporal Preece was looking at the object before him, a newly joined private soldier, as he inspected the contents of his mess tin. "Somefin' wrong?"

"S' bloody awful this, corp. S'all soddin' gristle an' no meat." He poked disconsolately at the cooling slush with a fork.

"Lessee, gi's it 'ere." He reached out for the mess tin and inspected the contents closely. "S'not good issit? Where's the tin yer got it from then?" He held out his hand as the offending receptacle was passed to him for inspection.

"That explains it. S'not made by Maconochie or Moir Wilson. They're the only ones 'oo put decent stuff in the tins. The rest of 'em is bleedin' crooks. Stuff anythin' in they do. Bastards they are. Don't give a shit abaht us." Ned's views on contractors who let down the Army by failing in their obligations were not uncommon among his colleagues. The British Army had thought it had learned its lesson in the Crimea, where the complete failure of civilian contractors to provide that for which they had been paid made the Army swear that it would never again be reliant upon them. It was for this reason that the distribution and supply corps of the Army were made a part of the uniformed service and still were at this stage in the Army's history, in the form of the Army Service Corps and the Army Ordnance Department and Corps.

Regrettably, however, supplies had to be sourced from industry, and not everyone had the scruples to ensure that what they provided met the government specification. In the case of tinned stew, made by firms other than Maconochie or Moir Wilson, it was too often rice and pieces of gristly meat.

The newly joined private looked up from his unappetising repast. "Bastards should be soddin' well shot!"

"Aye." Ned could not but agree. "Where's yer water bottle?"

"S'ere, corp." The young man pointed to it hanging on his webbing.

"'Ow much yer got in there, then?" Ned reached down and shook it. It felt about three quarters full. "Jus' make sure yer go careful. S'gotta last yer a full day that 'as. There'll be no more."

The young man looked back, an expression of incredulous indignation on his face at having had something so basic explained to him. "Yes, corp!" Ned paused. He didn't know what "patronising" meant, but the little bastard sounded insubordinate. Consequently, he fixed him with a severe glare and reminded him that the correct form of address was "corporal" before moving on to check some of the other new men just arrived from England.

Ted was making a pudding by boiling jam and biscuits in a tin, over a fire made of charcoal, dug into a small pit in order to hide the light. Regimental cooks were back with the transport in Dranouter, and only cooked for the battalion when it was out of action. Otherwise, soldiers were their own cooks, and the only way to make hard tack biscuits edible was to soften them down somehow. Thomas had to improvise in the absence of trained culinary expertise, but would argue, often vehemently, that he did a far better job than the professionals.

Actually, it was worth conserving the jam, for the French loved it, and the marmalade; and would buy four of the one pound tins for a franc. Ted's mind was, however, on greater things. He looked up at Charles Hawthorn watching him, smiled as if to offer him some of the sticky mess in the jam tin and acknowledged the hand held up, palm outwards, as the young officer declined the unspoken offer. Colin came and sat beside him.

"Everything all right?"

"Aye."

"I see you received another letter today, and I presume it was from Mrs Allsop." They were close, these two, and knew too much about each other for privacy to be a barrier between them.

"'Ow'd you know that, then?"

"It isn't difficult. The ones from home you read once or twice, and hers you read somewhat more often."

Ted flushed. "Nuthin' wrong in that, then, is there?"

Colin smiled. "Are you going to eat all of that yourself, or is there enough to go round?" He proffered a cup of tea he had just made, which would go down well with the biscuit and jam mash. Ted grinned, and spooned a large helping into an old bully beef tin for his friend. Colin checked it carefully, since it was the habit, in the absence of proper latrines, to use old bully beef tins in which to urinate before tossing the contents over the back of the trench. He felt fairly safe with Ted, since it was his habit to use a German Picklehaub helmet for the purpose. Consequently there was every likelihood that this particular tin had only ever contained bully beef.

Ted sat back, savouring the tea. He had written twice now to Mrs Allsop, and received a reply each time, each one slightly faster than its predecessor. They were formal letters, both his and hers, but he enjoyed reading her version of events in the village, and she was putting him in touch with things his mother missed out. Her handwriting was very clear and easy to read, and in the last letter there had been just a touch of mischief in her description of an event involving a churchwarden and a lady from Norwich. His chuckle had lifted a few heads as they wondered what it might be that anyone would wish to chuckle about given their present wet, cold and miserable circumstances. She always finished formally: "yours sincerely, Thurza Allsop."

On the eighth of December they were relieved of the horrid tedium that had been their lot this past week, by the Bedfords. The sight of their successors, looking smart and clean in their freshened uniforms, gave them a sense of anticipation of what was about to come their way. They had been offered the prospect of a bath and a change of kit, and were very much looking forward to it, back in Dranouter. Colin was also looking forward very much to renewing an acquaintanceship in the village, and Ted was reminded of the death of John Allsop as he saw the familiar Bedford cap badge passing by. He also suffered yet another twinge as he wondered what might happen if Snell ever got his way. The bloody man was still preying on his mind, although logic, and Colin, Ned, Alfred and Alfie, told him that as time passed the likelihood of anything happening grew less and less.

As the battalion moved with keen anticipation to the delights of Dranouter there were ten who would not be joining them; they formed the casualty list that was the price of that week in the trenches; caused by sporadic artillery fire and a couple of snipers, one of whom had paid the price of exposing himself to Eddie Macleary's amazing prowess with a rifle.

Their arrival in Dranouter was, however, to be a disappointment. The baths were not ready, their billets were cold and damp and they had only one day before they were to go into divisional reserve with the brigade at a place called Jean St Chapelle, just over the border in France, and about three and a half miles west of Dranouter. They had just one evening in which to sort themselves out, and they were on their way again. Most of them slept, some drank in the estaminet, and one or two went to the brothel, returning sheepishly to the billets to suffer the ribald remarks of their colleagues. Colin Baxter spent as much time as he could with Jacqueline, for that was her name, whilst Joe Floyd watched furtively the comings and goings at the establishment across the road, and envied Baxter the smashin' bit o' crumpet 'e'd snared. "Wot 'e wouldn't do ter......!"

St Jean Chapelle was not, however, the disaster they had thought it might be. A little further from the line, it was somewhat better organised, and the baths were working. They were run by the Royal Army Medical Corps and staffed by French women whose job was to iron the bugs out of uniforms. They did their best, but the lice laid their eggs in the seams and within an hour or so of them being put back on new lice had hatched in the warmth generated by the body and it was back to scratching all over again. Nonetheless, the bath itself was a welcome relief, their first since they had arrived in France; which for a few meant August.

"Silly cow. Wass she laughin' at?" Ned Preece, the cleanest of them all since he had last bathed a few weeks ago, stared venomously at a group of giggling French women as they stripped to their underwear prior to handing over their filthy uniforms.

"Not very much, probably." Colin could barely contain his own mirth at the sight of Ned's penis poking out of the hole in the front of his filthy underpants. "Come on, get in the bath."

The bath was, in fact, a series of huge vats into which ten of them at a time lowered themselves, assorted looks of rapture and pain on their faces as the hot water soothed their aching muscles, whilst the soap found the cracks and splits in their skin and the sores on their bodies, stinging, in most cases, quite painfully. It took an hour to put the whole company through, and there was extreme reluctance to leave the hot tubs when the time came. It was only the threat of cold hoses, brandished menacingly by the bath attendants, that forced them out, to move to a changing room where they collected a new issue of underwear, and cleaned, ironed uniforms. The effect on morale was huge, and it was a very much happier band of men that left to return to their billets.

The next three days were to be a period of personal administration as they fulfilled their reserve role by simply being ready, at short notice, to move wherever they might be required. Haircuts were organised, equipment was cleaned and there was a generally purposeful air about the place. Paul Cooper was very much in evidence, his role as company sergeant major keeping him well to the fore; and he was clearly enjoying the opportunity to "get things sorted."

It was on the second day that she appeared. Ted saw her, looking around the village and clearly seeking out Colin. She smiled in recognition as he approached and, in passable English, asked where Colin might be. Ted explained, as best he could, that he was away on duty, but was expected back in an hour; and he invited her to wait. He was sitting by a glowing brazier cleaning his rifle, and was about to start on his boots. There was tea, it was a bright December day with a weak sun sitting low in a clear blue sky, and there were worse ways for her to while away the time.

As her confidence grew, so her English improved. Ted was a nice man, and he very soon had her at her ease. Being a country girl, they had a lot in common, and could talk about the land, the farming and the local way of life before the war. They stumbled along, laughing from time to time as they tripped over each other's language, and hardly noticed the hour pass. It was only when her eyes opened a little wider and he saw the smile of anticipation on her face that he knew Colin must be approaching. He turned, seeing his friend walking towards them, grinning at the sight of the two of them. As he did so, Colin saw the look of consternation cross Ted's face and, glancing over his shoulder, saw Edward Snell watching. Ted stared, wondering how long the man had been there, and then turned back to Jacqueline as Colin joined them, his heart pounding inside his chest. The bastard would get him one day, and no mistake; and there was nothing he could do about it.

Very soon they were joined by Alfie and Alfred, and then a little later by Ned. Before long he had forgotten his woes as the banter circulated round the glowing brazier, and tea was brewed. Jacqueline had trouble understanding most of what was said, but enjoyed the good humour for an hour or so before she had to make her way back to Dranouter. A short visit, but she had made her point: it was worth Colin Baxter continuing to try and see her. There were grins all round as he walked her to the horse and trap that would transport her back, the driver, an old man of around sixty years of age, having completed his business.

It was beginning to get cold as the sun dropped closer to the horizon, and they gathered nearer to the brazier for warmth. Others watched them, men recently arrived, and others who had been there a long while, but no one sought to join them. These were the real soldiers, men who had come out at the beginning and were still here, alive and fighting when over ninety percent of their colleagues were either dead, wounded, missing or prisoners. No, these were special, and they were best left on their own. Joe Floyd, entitled by dint of the same shared experience to be a part of them, kept himself to himself, his growing confidence in his own ability still insufficient to allow him easy access to the group of friends given his long term track record of being just a bit seedy and unpleasant.

"Private Ludgrove, Lance Corporal Preece, Lance Corporal Baxter, Lance Corporal James….." Jim Collis was calling out their names, and as he came round the end of the building outside which they were seated he stopped. "Right, since yer all 'ere I can save me breath. All of yer, platoon commander wants ter see yer, now; an' that means the lot of yer; you too Arbuckle."

"Gawdon Bennet, wa's this abaht." Ned Preece, despite realising that he was now highly regarded, still had not lost his suspicion of authority; and when called to its presence he remained sceptical until he knew the actual outcome of the encounter.

A pitying look and a note of sarcasm. "If I knew I wouldn't be tellin' yer. 'E's in company headquarters and that's where you'll be within the next two minutes; clear?"

Nods and mutterings, and they assembled themselves in a presentable form to head in the direction of whatever might be about to befall them; Jim Collis in attendance. As they approached the former café that the company headquarters shared with battalion headquarters, Ted recoiled at the sight of Snell leaving and coming straight towards them. Jim, on the alert, gave a quick "left right left right" to get them in step before giving "eyes left" and saluting the officer as he passed. Snell returned the salute, half-heartedly, and then, as the sergeant gave "eyes front", noticed Ted in the group. His mouth opened, but before he could say anything the moment had passed and they were halted outside the headquarters and about to be dismissed to file inside. Ted's heart was in his mouth. This then was finally it, he was going to be charged and probably sent to prison, and he could see no way out of it. Snell's presence in the headquarters confirmed it all: he had complained, and without Matthew or the major to protect him Snell had won the day. His mouth was dry and his palms oozed sweat as he stood waiting to be told his fate.

Charles Hawthorn appeared with Paul Cooper, looked at them and then, his face serious, turned to Paul.

"Carry on, please sergeant major."

"Sir!" Paul's voice fairly bounced off the walls. "Right you lot, on my word of command you will......." And he proceeded to explain how it was they would deliver them into the presence of their company commander, how they would be dressed, how unimpressed he was with their turnout, their demeanour and, frankly, the mere fact that they existed at all, what precisely would happen to them if they made a cock of it, and just because they were engaged in the middle of a war made absolutely no difference whatsoever. Asked if they understood, their silence assured him that they had; perfectly. Within a few seconds they found themselves, slightly out of breath, in the presence of the captain; aware that there were others in the room, but not daring to look away from a point on the wall two feet above the captain's head.

"Stand them at ease, please, sergeant major." Paul complied, and the flimsy wooden walls of the building shook as they responded with great stamping of feet. This was a better sign; remaining at attention would have meant serious grief; this was a lightening of the situation. Ted simply could not work out how they were all involved in this, when Snell was his problem, and had nothing to do with his friends.

The captain had several sheets of paper in front of him, and made a show of reading them most carefully, dragging out the tension.

"Lance Corporal Preece?"

"Sir!"

"Stand to attention when the company commander speaks to you!" Paul Cooper's voice shook the office, and the stamp of Ned's left foot driving in alongside the right followed it instantly.

The Captain paused, and then looked up. "Awarded the Distinguished Conduct Medal for courage under fire at Missy." He saw the look of shock register on Ned's face, and allowed his own stern expression to slip. He smiled. "Very well done, Lance Corporal Preece."

Ned, on the right of the line, could barely contain himself, and as he wondered what to say he was conscious of a movement to his right.

"Well done." He heard the familiar voice, and turned half to his right, to see Matthew's outstretched hand. As soon as the major had left he had submitted the record of the incident as he had recorded it in his notebook, and the award had been made. Ned reached out and clasped the officer's hand. "Fanks, sir, fanks very much."

"Face yer front!" He swung his eyes to the front on Paul's command.

Lance Corporal Baxter, you are to be promoted to Corporal, as are you Lance Corporal James. We have sufficient manpower for only three sections in Mr Hawthorn's platoon, and with Corporal Floyd you will be the section commanders." He went on to impress upon them the importance of the task, and the need to train and bring up to standard the new men coming in as reinforcements. They nodded, looking stern and responsible.

Along at the left hand end of the line, Alfred and Ted were wondering by now why it was they were present. They were not to know that the company commander had deliberately pulled in most of the surviving originals, and made a show of it, in order to make the point to the rest that they were set apart from them and were the new junior leaders; not that the rest of the platoon needed telling.

Private Arbuckle, you will become the second in command of Corporal Floyd's section, as a Lance Corporal. Corporal James, you will have Lance Corporal Preece in Two Section." Alfie nodded, delighted.

"As for you, Private Ludgrove, you will no longer be your platoon commander's runner." This then was it. All the others promoted and him dismissed, back to being just a bloody rifleman or worse. "You are to be promoted to Lance Corporal and will be in Corporal Baxter's section. Clear?" Ted, numbstruck, could only mumble a reply, his mind a confused turmoil. How, if Snell had been able to get his way, had this happened? Something was wrong and he couldn't work it out.

"Thank you, sergeant major." The captain indicated that interviews were over, and once again the office shook at the sound of Paul's voice and the accompanying drill movements of the party of newly promoted and decorated soldiers as they left the presence of their company commander.

"Halt! Stand still. Will advance, leeeeeeeft tarn!" They were facing him outside in the cramped corridor, panting for breath, their backs to the wall.

"Corporal Preece?"

"Sir!"

"Well done, Ned, bloody well done." The sergeant major reached out and shook Ned's hand. "You earned that, and everyone knows it." Ned, lost for words, simply grinned.

"As for the rest of you, you're all improperly dressed. Get to the QM an' get yerselves sorted." No movement. "Now!" His voice raised an octave and they scattered.

"Corporal Ludgrove!" He called Ted back from the chattering group that had stopped outside the company office, mainly to congratulate Ned.

"Sir!"

"A word." Ted approached with some trepidation. Paul's voice dropped, and became almost conspiratorial. "Listen laddie, we know that gunner officer is after your blood, and we know what happened back home." He held up his hand to quell Ted's question even before it was spoken. There was no need to tell the lad that Colin Baxter, articulate as ever, had approached him and Matthew one dark night at Festubert to see if anything could be done.

"Captain Jenkins has had a word with the new OC. You're a good soldier, you've earned yer tape and that bastard can't touch yer as long as we're around. Ye'll have t' watch yer back a bit if yer ever get near him, but you should be able to keep yer distance. Go on now, cut along with that bloody lot out there."

Ted was barely able to contain his relief, and he walked out into the weak December sunshine feeling as if a great weight had been lifted from his shoulders to join his chattering friends. He grinned like a Cheshire cat as Alfie pounded him on the shoulder, and he reached out and held Ned's hand in congratulation. They straightened and stood to attention as Charles Hawthorn came out of the building, and added his congratulations to the rest, but stopped short of shaking hands. That was a barrier he just didn't feel he could cross.

"C'mon, let's go and get the tapes." Alfie, always to the front, started to walk towards the old barn where the QM had set up his stores.

"And the medal ribbon," said Colin. Ned blushed; something he could not ever remember having done before.

"What the fuck..............?" They stopped, dead in their tracks, Alfie's epithet trailing off, incomplete. Walking towards them, heading towards battalion headquarters, flanked by two very stern military policeman, was a bearded figure with unkempt straggly hair, clad in scruffy civilian clothes, limping slightly and looking very apprehensive. John Hayes, the deserter, was returning to the battalion.

They were gradually sorting out their kit, and trying to replenish the many items of clothing, stores and equipment that had been lost since they landed in France. It had not really been possible until now, with the opportunity presented by the stabilisation of the lines. Furthermore, since there had existed no system of forward replenishment of stores other than fuel, fodder, food, medical supplies and ammunition, which were delivered by the Army Service Corps, there had been no way to get the stuff up to them from the base areas.

The Army Ordnance Department had been highlighting this problem for many years before the war, but it had not been until October that the CinC had ruled that something had to be done since the planned method of reconstitution, by withdrawing formations from the line, was clearly out of the question. He pointed out that the difficulties being experienced were a lesson of war, and since the system had always been considered too difficult to practice on exercise in peace, that was, arguably, true. He was, however, to experience some difficulty in changing attitudes. The Army Service Corps, seeing themselves very much as the cavalry arm of the support services, were very unhappy at the prospect of soiling their hands with tradesmen's work. So much so that the Director of Supply and Transportation at GHQ referred to the "bugbear of Ordnance stores" in a letter to his headquarters in the War Office. However, common sense prevailed, and eventually a system of consolidated demands, by telegraph, was set up from the Deputy Assistant Director of Ordnance Services or DADOS, usually a major, on the staff of each divisional headquarters to the base. Items were then forwarded in specific commodity groups on specific days. Eventually, the DADOS was given a dedicated lorry for this work, and the system began to work effectively.

It could, however, only work effectively if it had the right kit to deliver in the first place. The decision, for example, taken in the middle of December, to double the number of machine guns in battalions from two to four could not be implemented since there were only twenty-three in the Ordnance Depots in France. It would be some time before British industry could catch up with the military requirement and meet the highly specialised demand for large quantities of new Vickers Maxim machine guns, or, indeed, other equipment of a specifically military nature.

"Wot d'yer think'll 'appen to 'im then?" One of the young privates, having gained some courage from a glass or two of Ving Blong, sought Ted's opinion on the likely fate of John Hayes.

Ted, trying to write, was less than communicative. This young brat hadn't yet learned when to leave a body alone. "Dunno. Shoot 'im I suppose."

"Shoot 'im?" Not to be put off, the young man's voice rose a note or two in incredulity.

"'S no more than the bugger deserves." Ted felt no sympathy. Hayes had wandered off and left them to face the music. He deserved everything that was coming to him. He looked up. "You cleaned that rifle today?" It was enough to cause the young man to scuttle away to where he could hide from the gaze of the fearsome lance corporal. Ted went back to his letter.

He was writing home to explain what had been happening, and to share the news of his promotion, to say how delighted he was about Ned being awarded his medal. He also wanted to write a little about what it was really like, carefully so that it would pass the censor, but he did not feel he could write that to his mother and father. Consequently, his first letter had commenced: "Dear Mrs Allsop."

He sat back against the wall of the dugout. They had been in these trenches now for a couple of days, just near Messines; about five miles east of Dranouter and six miles due south of Ypres, having relieved the Duke of Cornwall's Light Infantry. The trenches were damp and cold and the approaches to them were very wet. Carrying parties were a real chore, and life, as they approached Christmas Day, was far from pleasant. All this, however, was lost on Ted as he revelled in the thought that Snell had been exposed and that he was safe. He really could not believe his luck, and wondered just how much he had worried, unnecessarily, over the weeks since he had first seen the man. What he could not fathom was how they had found out. Neither would he ever know that Snell had approached the new company commander at the earliest opportunity after the major had gone. However, despite being a firm disciplinarian, the captain also had a strong sense of fair play, had seen Ted in action and had not liked Edward Snell at all. He had done what all sensible company commanders do when faced with a problem, and had discussed it with his sergeant major, who knew the story as told by Colin. A quick chat with Matthew had confirmed the initial impression that Ludgrove was as sound as a bell, and should be promoted, rather than pilloried to satisfy the whim of a thoroughly unpleasant creature, and that had been that.

"Post's 'ere!" The call went up from Eddie Macleary who had replaced Ted as the runner. "Christmas card from Princess Mary!"

"Stone me, we'll be gettin' a soddin' present from 'er next." There was always a wag, and the new draft had brought one in with it.

"Funny you should say that," responded Macleary, with the smug sarcasm of one who possessed information, and who was about to capitalise on it. As he spoke, Alfie James walked round the corner wearing a piece of white cotton wool on his chin, and, in a deep voice, called "Ho, ho, ho," imitating a rolling gait as he walked and carrying a sack which obviously contained packages of some sort.

"Silly sod," muttered Ned. He was feeling very homesick for his wife and daughter, especially so with Christmas coming on; and he did not need reminding. He had just heard the news of the impending arrival of his second child in about seven months or so and desperately wanted to be home.

Charlie Marshall opened the white envelope containing the small card. Princess Mary's monogram was on the front, a crown above the initial "M", and beneath it the date: "1914". All the lettering was in red. On opening it he saw, on the top left hand corner of the inside page, a picture of a sprig of holly, and beneath it the words:

"With best Wishes for a Happy Christmas and a Victorious New Year"

written in blue with the first letter of key words picked out in red. On the right hand page was the greeting:

"From Princess Mary and Friends at Home"

with a picture of the Princess, looking serene in a white dress and showing her right profile, her hands in her lap holding a white fan. She was seated on a regency stool, and her signature, "Mary" was at the bottom left of the page.

Feelings were mixed. Ned's sense of bitterness increased at the sight of someone in such luxury and comfort, when his idea of comfort at that stage was not to be suffering a wet backside. Ted also felt an upsurge of loneliness and anger, or was it envy. For others it meant nothing, and many more were heard to remark that it was "nice of 'er to remember."

They shared out the small tins of cigarettes and sweets and other gifts that had been sent out under the auspices of the royal family. Some of them had also received some early parcels from home and, where the contents did not meet individual taste, some of the items were passed round. Ted had opened his, and, typical of his mother, there were socks, a knitted balaclava, gloves, mince pies, which had crumbled a bit, a small Christmas pudding and boiled sweets. There were cards from his sisters, and a note from his mother and father saying they both hoped the parcel would find him well. He felt very emotional as he looked through what they had sent. They couldn't afford much, and this would have been the very best they could have done, given that there was a limit to what could be sent through the post. He smiled, sadly, and wished he were somewhere else, a long way from Belgium.

Colin's parcel was two in one, from mother and aunt and postmarked Cromer. He also had a letter from his mother, and another, hand delivered to the post corporal in Dranouter, written in French. This he read several times over; and not because of any difficulty in translating the contents. Ned stayed very quiet as he investigated the contents of what he had been sent. There was nothing from his family, but the love and affection bound up in the simple contents and misspelled words in her offering to him had a lump in his throat he could not swallow, and tears he could not hide. Colin and Ted spent quite a lot of their time just sitting with him.

Their life in the trenches settled into the tiresome routines to which they were becoming used. The Germans were only a couple of hundred yards away and, from time to time, and especially at night, they could hear the guttural sound of the language as orders were shouted or people called out to each other. The Germans were a noisy lot, and they, the British, were under strict orders to avoid shouting at all in order not to give anything away.

There was occasional artillery fire, just a few rounds here and there, some mortaring and from time to time some rifle or machine gun fire. They kept their heads well down most of the time to avoid offering snipers a target. The order for sentries to keep head and shoulders above the trench line was being interpreted liberally, and experienced men were telling newcomers how best to make use of cover and see the enemy without being seen. It was open season on snipers, and anyone who had the chance of a shot was empowered to take it. The platoon left this work to Eddie Macleary, who could sit for hours just watching. Suddenly, they would see him moving his head very slightly and taking aim before a shot despatched yet another careless member of the opposition and he moved to a new fire position.

Charles Hawthorn had relaxed a little, the reduced activity making it easier for him to tolerate the responsibilities laid upon him, chiefly because he could escape more often to the comfort of a shack, built into the wall of a trench, with fellow officers, rather than spending all his time in the trench with his men. He didn't dislike them, and certainly did not despise them. Indeed, he was fond of many of them, and almost in awe of the few who were still there from the beginning. It was simply that he found it so hard to relate to them, so difficult to maintain his distance yet remain a part of them. Sometimes, when alone, he prayed quietly for deliverance in some form from his present circumstances; not from the risk of death, but from the responsibilities of command. God alone knew, there were times when he wished he were one of them; then he could show fear and give vent to his feelings - and have someone with whom to share the joys and the sorrows of their present existence. He looked at Ted, Colin and Ned, Alfred and Alfie, and he envied them their closeness.

Ted's second parcel arrived on Christmas eve, in the middle of the afternoon. The cooks had been doing their best to improve morale and celebrate the season, and they had eaten roast pork, mashed potato and cabbage; and there had been plum duff to follow, with a rum issue to finish it off. He recognised the writing, and knew it was from Thurza Allsop. It was with a peculiar feeling of apprehension that he tore off the string, having first broken the red sealing wax on the knots, and ripped off the paper. Inside was yet another balaclava, he smiled, but on checking he found it to be wrapped round a half bottle of Brandy. He grinned. Further investigation revealed home made fudge with nuts and dried fruit and flavoured with rum, a bottle of stout wrapped in a scarf, some good stilton cheese and a little stone bottle which, on investigation, contained port. Tucked in a corner was a packet of Woodbine cigarettes. It was, in character, a quite different parcel from that he had received from his parents.

The note was placed at the bottom, to be seen after he had found all the contents. He smiled as he read it. She had sent the balaclava because she thought she could remember how big his head was. Socks and gloves she had left to those better qualified to know his size. She hoped the rest would also help to keep him warm, and she would toast his Christmas with her glass of port at midday; if he wished to join her. This was a cheeky letter, quite unlike the rest, and was signed, simply, "yours, Thurza." He felt a pang of consternation, and his mouth dried a little as he pondered the implications. However, he had little time to dwell on them as Colin Baxter came over to discuss the sentries for the night.

It was a cold, clear night, and most of them found it difficult to sleep. The raw cold, exacerbated by the dampness in the trench, made the process physically difficult. For most of them, however, no longer exhausted as they had been a couple of weeks ago, it was the mental images of home which kept them awake. Christmas Eve was a time when they should all be with their families, mothers and fathers, wives and children. Fathers with young children imagined the stockings being filled at home, and the silent expedition upstairs in the hope that the little blighters had gone to sleep; and that they wouldn't wake until a decent hour in the morning. Sons missed their mothers beavering in the kitchen and the smells of cinnamon and roast goose that would be emanating from them, and a glass of Stones' Ginger Wine to set them up for the midnight service in the village church.

Ted had a kaleidoscope of pictures in his mind, a tumbled mix of imagined smells and memories that he had managed to bury quite well in his two years in the Army, but which now came flooding back. He ran his mind's eye over the family, his mother and his sisters in particular, over Betty Chalmers, trying to visualise her pregnant. Alice Bartram flashed before him, to be followed by red hair and scarlet lips between a dockyard railing, a peculiar tremble in his loins and then finally there was an attractive lady, with a round, softly moulded face, a wide mouth, but not overly so, and delicate brown eyes framed by a soft pile of brown hair, with just a subtle hint of reddishness. She was a little older than him, and had a slightly offset front tooth.

"Lissen!" Ned's voice broke into his thoughts. "Wassat?"

Ted looked up. It was midnight, and all along the trench

men were cocking their ears to listen to the noise emanating from the direction of the German trenches. It was a deep, melodious sound of men singing, and if they did not recognise the words they certainly knew the tune. They had all learned "Silent Night" at their mother's knee and had sung it in countless carol concerts over the years. Surely, for it was a favourite in every church in the land, they should be able to remember the words.

Thomas, however, could be quite self conscious at times; and every army padre could wax lyrical on the difficulties of actually getting him to sing in church with any degree of enthusiasm, if at all. This was quite unlike continental armies, where singing was a fine and much loved tradition, as their enemies were proving just at that moment. Some of them began to hum, gently, so as not to be overheard, whilst others just listened, quietly, to the beautiful, wistful sounds of the hymn wafting across no man's land.

> *"Stille nacht, heilige nacht, alle schläft, einsam wacht........."*

Charles Hawthorn was standing with his hand on a trench ladder, his head lifted, looking at the stars high above in the clear night sky. Trained as a choirboy in one of England's great musical church schools he had developed a mellow, well pitched, alto voice which rose high above the tenors and the deep bases of the Germans opposite. In harmony with them, he filled his lungs and sang as if seeking to reach the very heavens himself.

> *"Stille nacht, heilige nacht, hierten erst, kund gemacht........."*

They looked on in amazement, wondering how he knew the words in a foreign language, not realising that to sing it in its original German was to sing it in its most beautiful form. They were astounded at the clarity and strength of his voice, and the deep feeling with which he sang. Across the nightmare that lay between them, the Germans heard the young voice raised in supplication to God, marvelled themselves at its beauty and joined in the joy of it, giving thanks in mutual adoration for the coming of Christ, for the birth of the Saviour. The paradox lay, of course, in the prayers offered by both sides to the same God, that they might prevail, each over the other. Not for nothing did the German Army march into battle with the epithet "Gott Mit Uns" embossed on every soldier's belt buckle.

Charles leaned back against the wall of the trench, still looking skywards in the calm that followed the carol. He breathed gently, feeling at peace for the first time. He realised something that had been growing within him for a long while, since before he joined the Army. He knew now, with absolute certainty, that he wished to be a priest. He had come finally to his faith in God at that moment, a moment of absolute clarity, and was now quite clear as to the direction his life would take. The joy of it, the relief, the depth of his feelings, brought tears to his eyes and he slumped, pressing the bridge of his nose between the forefinger and thumb of his right hand in an attempt to assuage them.

He was not the only one with tears in his eyes. The impact of the moment, the singing and the closeness it had brought had affected them all. Men sat silently, consumed with their own thoughts. The captain looked across at Charles, and smiled to himself. Soldiers looked up at him from their own reflections and respect for him suddenly grew. It was as if they sensed he had found himself. Hearing a movement to his left, Charles looked round to see Colin, an enamel mug proffered and in his left hand, held flat and open, a piece of cake. "Happy Christmas, sir." The smile spoke volumes, clearly visible in the bright moonlight. Charles smiled in return.

"Thank you Corporal Baxter. Macleary?"

"Sir?" Eddie confirmed his presence, as was his duty, right beside his officer.

"Macleary. There are two hampers in my kit. Will you bring them out here please?"

Within a very few minutes they had arrived, one of them from Fortnum and Mason, the other from a local store in

Norwich. Sentries remained posted, but on fifteen minute rotations for about the next hour, and were replenished in situ with cake, sweets and duff. Across the divide between the trench systems they could see flickering lights as the Germans, in keeping with their Christmas traditions, lit candles and exchanged gifts. Charles sat among his soldiers, on a piece of duckboard, freezing in the below zero temperatures, sharing all he had with his men, and they with him. It was a moment to treasure, and he could not remember having felt so content.

Above the noise they heard a shout. "Shurrup!" Joe Collis's voice bade them be silent whilst they listened.

"Hey, Tommeee. Happy Christmas."

"Same t' you Fritz," yelled back a sentry, without waiting to be told; or told not to.

Charles sat back and grinned. They would never believe this back home.

Christmas day dawned with a thick mist that had descended in the early hours of the morning. It prevented what little sun there was from reaching through to begin warming them, and by midday they were feeling pretty miserable. Despite the cooks' best efforts, lunch was not going to be what they might have expected at home, and it was turning into just another day in the trenches; except that a tacit cease-fire was clearly in place, and no one was shooting. The frost was very hard, and they were very cold indeed, but by midday it was well on its way to clearing and people were a little more cheerful. Ted, remembering Thurza's letter, poured a good measure of port into his mug, and as Colin's watch showed twelve o'clock he proffered a silent toast in the rough direction of Norfolk. He smiled, a secret smile, and ignored Colin's questioning look.

"Stop! Stay where you are." It was just two o'clock in the afternoon as the sentry yelled his command to someone they could not see. "I said stand still. Sir, sir, come and look at this."

One glance told Charles that there was a German officer

approaching their trenches, followed by others. "Macleary, can you see that?"

"Yessir."

"Right, report it to the company commander, and tell him.........tell him.......tell him I'm going out to meet them. If they get any closer they'll be able to look into our trenches and we don't want that," he glanced at his runner, smiled, and finished, "do we?"

"No, sir." Eddie smiled and headed away towards company headquarters as Charles stepped up the ladder and walked across no man's land to meet his enemies.

"Come on." Colin's exhortation to the platoon to follow him as he put his first foot on the rung of the trench ladder. Jim Collis' command for them to stay where they were was lost in the moment as Colin's natural leadership took over and they followed him out into the open of a bright, clear winter's day, their rifles slung over their shoulders as they picked their way through the mud, ruts and shell craters towards men it was their duty to destroy; but not just now.

Within a very few minutes Charles was part of a choir singing, once more, the favourite German hymn: Stille Nacht. Colin and Ted were chatting amiably to a German gefreiter, a rank equivalent to their own, and swapping cigarettes as well as schnapps for whiskey. Language was not a problem, since he had worked in the London Hilton as a waiter for four years before the war. He knew London far better than they. The captain, who spoke quite reasonable German, was in conversation with a couple of typical caricatures of the German officer, smoking a large cigar and apologising every time he uttered a wrong declension. They, in return, were trying out their very best English, happily informing him that the prevalent view on their side was that the war would last just another two months, and they would all be home in time for the spring. He responded that he hoped that would be so, but kept to himself the doubts he harboured.

Joe Floyd was having difficulty exchanging views with the group into which he had entered, for small talk never came easily to him and he always found it difficult to relate comfortably with his fellow men. Alfie James, on the other hand, acting the fool, had them all laughing across the divides of language and culture. Alfred, looking on, was keeping a very close eye on his friend lest he overstep the mark and needed rescuing. He needn't have worried. Alfie could make anyone laugh without making them uncomfortable, and his impression of a typical German officer, wearing the necessary accoutrements, which he had borrowed, went down just as well as his emulation of those from his own side.

For a good half hour the conversation and singing continued at a pace, and then, as the afternoon wore on, they became more reflective and the groups split to drink coffee and tea, gin and korn, cherry brandy and kirschwasser; to eat duff and fudge, and to try black bread and stollen. It was gone four o'clock before, with the temperature dropping and by an unspoken mutual consent, they all drifted back to their trenches. Ted's new found friend offered one last thought as they parted: "Tonight, my friend, no shooting, eh?"

Ted nodded, his face sombre as they shook hands. "Aye."

Charles spoke to the captain as they slid down the ladder, back into their own trenches.

"Did you notice how many there were? I didn't realise they had half that number over there."

"I know," said the captain, ruefully. "I'm just off to talk to the CO about that very thing. Charles, look after your men. We shall need to get them firmly back on track after all this. The war is by no means over, and before very long it will be business as usual."

Hawthorn nodded, and smiled. He felt such inner contentment; and wondered when he should broach the subject of leaving in order to enter the priesthood. He was unsure of the regulations in war. Ah, well. Time enough in the next day or two.

The patrol was to be led by an officer. It was one of many over the next few days that would be sent out in order to remind Thomas and the Germans alike that they were still at war. The news of the meeting on Christmas Day in no man's land, and there had been many up and down the line, had not been well received at GHQ and stern messages of rebuke had issued forth about the need to preserve the fighting spirit of the men, and to avoid any fraternisation which might diminish it.

Ostensibly, the reason for the patrol was to determine the true strength of enemy opposition and the structure of the defensive works to their front. That, at least, gave it a degree of credence, but Thomas wasn't stupid. He already knew pretty well the information that would be coming back, and there would be little added value in risking lives in order to prove it. But, orders were orders, and they would have to get on with it.

Charles gave his orders to the fifteen men who were to accompany him. He broke them down into two fire support teams, each of four men commanded by a corporal: Joe Floyd and Colin Baxter. The assault team, which he would lead, comprised a lance corporal and four privates. Sensibly, he chose his biggest and strongest men for that task, and Alfred Arbuckle was to be the NCO. They would attempt to snatch a German for interrogation. It was a cloudy night so there would be no moon, which was to their advantage. He went through the ritual of the orders. The drills involved were well known to the experienced men, but needed to be impressed on the newer people. Lives depended on the proper wearing of kit, the tying down of rifle slings, the elimination of rattles and noises, the preparation of ammunition and grenades, the orders for their use, the signals to be used, the rendezvous points, the action on ambush or on enemy lights, fire control in the dark, routes in and out, the password and a whole raft of other detail. The process of getting ready took several hours, and included rehearsals in the support trenches. They were due to leave their own lines at ten o'clock, and be back by two the next morning. There would be some artillery and machine gun fire from time to time in order to cover noise.

"Careful!" Colin nodded his response to Ted's warning as

he prepared to leave. He took no pleasure in what they were about to do; he could see no point in it."

"See you later." He tried to sound as if he meant it, which was difficult, being as scared as he was.

Slowly, in extended line, they moved out towards the Germans. A light mist had formed, which meant they could proceed the first few yards beyond the trench in a crouched walk, but from then on it was down on the stomach and crawling. After a short distance the two fire support teams spread out, one either side of the axis of advance they had set themselves by lining up on the silhouette of a dead tree, each moving alternately so that there was always one group ready to fire. Behind them the assault group moved just behind the nearest of the two fire teams, whichever one it was at the time. Slowly, very slowly, they inched their way across the muddy expanse between the lines, the ground, hardened by the freezing conditions, rubbing harshly against their limbs, taking great care not to put weight on any of the ice lest it crack and give them away. Their bodies stiff and chilled, the slow pace of their advance did nothing to warm them, and the cold from the ground beneath worked its way into their bones. Silently, they moved on until the left hand fire support team was within fifteen yards of the German trench and behind a small rise, at which point Colin stopped, and touched the man to his right on the shoulder to indicate that they had arrived at their destination. The touch was passed to the right hand man of the team who, waiting for them to draw level, reached out to the left hand man of the right hand fire support team and they too came to a stop.

His heart beating nineteen to the dozen, Charles moved slowly forward. He felt the fear in his stomach, but a strange peace of mind overshadowed it. Easing himself to the top of the very tiny rise, and bareheaded, he was able to look for signs of German activity. Nothing; everything was still, but there had to be sentries. The trick was to spot one and make him the target of the snatch, whilst his colleagues took their time waking and coming out of their bunkers. This was likely to be complicated if the Germans, as they usually did, posted sentries in pairs by night. Alfred's team each had a sock filled with stones, known as a sap, with which to silence any opposition. Whilst they were snatching, Charles was to get as good an impression as he could of numbers and trench structure to take back with him.

He felt a hand on his arm. Turning his head he saw Alfred who, having obtained the officer's attention, pointed a finger away to his right. There was a slight movement, and listening carefully they could hear the sound of a man adjusting his position in some way. He became their target. Charles held up his hand. They would wait for one of the artillery shoots before making a move. They all knew this to be the plan, and settled down silently to wait.

Charlie Marshall, in Joe Floyd's section, contracted his stomach and held the cheeks of his backside together as hard as he could, terrified that the fart, were it to transpire, would be sufficiently noisy to alert the enemy. If he could get away with a silent one and just the smell then the wind direction, blowing back towards the British trenches, meant it would not give them away. Glancing silently to his left and right he envied the rest of them their calmness; his stomach felt as if it were on the boil. "Wot a bloody night t' get the soddin' shits." Around him, the rest of them just tried to hold themselves still against the all pervading cold, fearing that a violent bout of shivering would offer sufficient noise to give them away. One of them, only a couple of weeks in the line, looked at Charlie and envied the calmness of a veteran who had suffered the terrible battles around Festubert before Christmas.

The rumble to the west heralded the rushing sound as British artillery searched out targets just behind the German lines in their area, and the battalion's machine guns took on targets a couple of hundred yards either side of the patrol's objective. Over no man's land, a few hundred yards to their south, the Germans put up a star shell, the flickering light of the flare casting an orange glow over the earth beneath, sending shadows skittering in all directions as it descended slowly, born by the wind towards the British; and away from the patrol.

Taking the cue, Alfred and three men scrambled to their feet, and leapt towards where the sentries had last been heard. The fourth of the privates in the group stayed with Charles as protection for his reconnaissance of the trench system. As he reached the lip of the trench, Alfred looked down to see a pair of white faces looking up at him. He saw the glint of a bayonet, and the barrel of a rifle being pointed up towards him. Abandoning any thought or caution, he simply jumped into the trench between the two white blobs, his mass and their fear sufficient to give him the advantage. Savagely, he lashed out at the man on his right with his sap, catching him square in the face and sending him flying backwards.

Aware that the noise of the bombardment was covering any they might be making, he turned to the man on his left and shoved him back against the trench wall with his forearm against the man's throat, seeking to prevent the yell of alarm that might give them away. So far it had all happened so quickly they were on top of the situation. Ripping off his victim's Pickelhaub by pulling it forward over his face, Alfie nodded to the soldier who had appeared on his left to hit the man, an instruction which he carried out, with his sap, with great gusto. The German went limp. Glancing to his right Alfie saw the other sentry still down and not moving very much, and the other two members of his team watching along the trench to their right. He slipped the rope from round his waist, tied it under the unconscious German's armpits, and motioned the two of them up a nearby ladder, one of them taking one end of the rope. Once they were up, they began to drag their victim with them, being aided by the third of their number pushing from below. Alfred, his work complete, looked to his left to see what was happening to Charles Hawthorn, who had vanished round a bend in the trench. As he did so he heard the shot, a pistol by the sound of it, followed about ten seconds later by another two shots and the explosion of a grenade.

"Blast!" Strong language indeed from Alfred as he ran to see what was happening. As he came round the corner there, on the ground, was the private who had gone with Charles, obviously dead. Leaning against the trench wall, his pistol in his hand was Charles Hawthorn, looking towards where a portion of the trench wall had been brought down by the explosion and beyond which came the sounds of a man, or maybe two, in agony. What was also coming from beyond the debris, and from back where Alfred had been by the sentries, was the sound of waking Germans.

"C'mon, sir. We've gotta go!" Grabbing the young officer Alfred suddenly realised he was wounded, in the leg, and was in great pain."

"Go on, go without me!" A note of desperation in Hawthorn's voice.

"Sorry, sir. Can't." This was no time to argue. Using a German stick grenade he had brought with him, Alfred added to the confusion Charles had created by lobbing it beyond the fallen area of the trench and at the same time dragged Charles back round the corner. As he did so, he saw the private who had been pushing the injured German up out of the trench locked in a hand to hand struggle with the other sentry, who had clearly recovered sufficiently well to make a fight of it; and they were between Alfred, Charles and the ladder. Dragging Charles with him Alfred moved forward to help move the revitalised German sentry out of the way. Behind him he could hear more mayhem as the left hand fire support team above the trench lobbed Battye Bombs down into the carnage created by the first two grenades.

Suddenly, the private fighting with the German let out a gurgling scream, hunched forward and lifted up onto his toes, his hands, which had been round his adversary's throat, dropping to clutch at his stomach into which the German had embedded a stiletto dagger that he had retained tucked into the top of his boot for just such an occasion. Alfred, already with his blood well up, saw red. More flares were now lighting up the sky, and his eye fell upon a metal shape lying embedded in the trench wall beside him. It was a British entrenching tool, clearly obtained by some nefarious means by the Germans and put to use. Grasping the wooden handle he swung it at the sentry, the whole strength of his brawny right arm and shoulder behind it, coming upwards from about waist height. It caught the German, edge uppermost, beneath his chin, and cleaved a straight line up through the lower jawbone, splitting the tongue asunder, and out through the bridge of his nose. Blood spurted everywhere, and a keening note of agony came screaming out from the back of a throat fast filling with blood from the shattered buccal cavity. Grabbing Charles' pistol from his right hand, Alfred held it at arm's length, sighted it quickly, and shot the screaming German straight through his wide open right eye.

Stuffing the pistol into his belt, he glanced at the young British soldier groaning weakly on the trench floor, and at Charles standing, also weak from his wound and some loss of blood, by the ladder. He made a decision. For the lad he could do nothing, and with luck the Germans would get him to a doctor. He could only get one away, and Charles was the one with whom he was most likely to be successful. Pushing him to the ladder, he shoved his right hand under the officer's Sam Browne belt and hoiked him up the first few rungs, allowing Charles to use his good leg for propulsion whilst he, Alfred, supported the one that was damaged. The bullet had entered Charles's thigh from the front, about eight inches above the knee. It had missed the bone, but was lodged, painfully, deep into the muscle having carved a track just to the left of the femur and on beyond it towards the back of the leg.

Joe Floyd saw Charles' head appear above the line of the trench and then disappear again. He did not realise it, but Alfred, who had been pushing his officer with a shoulder under his backside, had been diverted by Germans coming from his right and had to fire upon them with the officer's pistol, and had lobbed his second stick grenade in that direction. Whilst he couldn't see, it was clear that considerable support was required, and fast. Swiftly, he gave his orders.

"You two," he called to his two right hand men, "bombs into that end. All yer've got, an' mind Alfred. You two," speaking to the two on his left, "with me."

He scrambled forward, hearing Colin give orders on his left for covering fire, and at the top of the trench bent forward to lift out his platoon commander. Alfred, panting with exertion, followed very swiftly and flopped onto the ground as German machine gun fire from a depth trench began to crackle all around them.

"Get down. Withdraw!" Joe's command, as the designated senior non commissioned officer on the patrol, rang out. It rang out too late, however, for Charlie Marshall. Leaning over the top of the trench to view the damage caused by his bombs and to see what help was needed he was silhouetted against the light of a flare above him, his head cocked to the right looking lengthways along the trench. A wounded German, looking up, fired his rifle and the bullet entered Charlie's face by the left cheekbone, exploding the brain and blowing the remnants out of a large exit hole, taking with it completely the right ear that the surgeons had so lovingly stitched back on just a few weeks ago.

The young man with him recoiled in horror and, not realising that he was in the cone of fire of a German machine gun, stood to turn and run. He took four rounds in the legs and fell back into the trench where he was pounced upon by two Germans who, with relish, set about beating him to death with their rifle butts. His screams echoed in the ears of the patrol for what seemed like an age as they worked their way back towards their own trenches.

Colin and Joe, both very experienced, orchestrated the fire and movement between them. Joe took the remaining two men from the assault team under his wing, together with their unconscious German prisoner whom they were having to drag. He left Alfred to assist Charles, dragging him along over the hard, muddy ground in time with the covering fire being provided, despite his protests that they go on without him. Beyond them, in their own trenches, fire support was also forthcoming, whilst, overhead, artillery whooshed past on its way towards their enemy. Either side of them they could hear the battalion's machine guns pouring fire in on the area from which they were withdrawing.

On the fire step Ted looked both ways at the two men to his left and the one to his right. His briefing to them had been clear and succinct: "Hit one of ours an' yer fuckin' dead." Conscious of his huge experience, they determined that he probably meant it and they did not wish to test the theory. "Listen in." He gave the fire control order. "Section, at close range." He watched as two of them checked their sights at three hundred yards, the battle setting, then nudged the third, combining it with a look that would have frozen hell, to remind him. "Get the soddin' drills right. 'Ow many times durse I 'ave t' tell yer," he hissed. "Right, at close range, enemy infantry as individual targets. Watch and shoot." That meant open season on any identifiable enemy infantryman trying to pursue their colleagues.

But they had no need to fire. The Germans had no desire to pursue. They would use their artillery to resolve the problem, and simply make it as slow a return as possible for the men out there to give the artillery the best possible chance of killing the maximum number. Knowing this, and under quite sustained fire from those Germans brave enough to stick their heads above the parapet, the patrol was making the best speed it could. First to arrive was Joe's fire support team, with the prisoner, rolling over the edge of the trench and flopping, exhausted, onto its floor some six feet below them.

To their left, Colin was slightly slower getting back as he was providing cover on the final bound. Looking to his right he saw Alfred at the edge of the trench with Charles Hawthorn, and he motioned his right hand two men over the edge. They needed no second bidding. Sliding back to the edge, he had just yelled "now" to his two left hand riflemen when a barrage of light artillery shells landed to the left of his position. The nearest shell landed precisely between the two men as they prepared to move back, instantly turning the left hand of the two into a mud spattered, blackened, gory mess, whilst at the same time lifting the other and throwing him onto Colin. His mouth and eyes full of mud and other things he did not wish to think about, Colin felt himself pulled as he slid backwards towards the trench, taking his wounded man with him. Ted, releasing his friend's foot once he was sure he was on his way down to safety, turned to Alfred, who was just a few feet away, trying to pull Charles behind him into the trench.

As he watched, and Ted would never afterwards be able to explain why, Hawthorn, with his backside on the edge of the trench, sat up to look back the way he had come. Then, after just a second, with his back to the Germans and looking down at Alfred, he was about to slide to safety when the machine gun bullet struck. It smashed through the sixth and seventh cervical vertebrae, severing the spinal cord and killing him instantly. It exited through his throat, ripping out the larynx and creating a gaping fist sized hole beneath his chin. Blood and flesh sprayed onto Alfred's upturned face, seeking as he was to exhort his officer to "get down!" Hawthorn was thrown forward, his arms outstretched, to smash, arms splayed in a parody of the crucifixion, against the rear wall of the trench. He remained there for what seemed like an age as they all looked on in horror before sliding face down into the dirt and filth at the bottom of the trench.

Ted, sickened and distraught, looked away. Colin, picking himself up from beside his badly wounded soldier, bent over the man to start first aid, looking up as he did into the shocked white face of his second-in-command.

"Bastard!" said Ted. Colin nodded, and bent to his work. Alfred sat slumped in misery and exhaustion, wiping his face. Alfie, who had stayed in reserve throughout, got his men sorting tea and something to eat whilst he went round with the rum bottle; in silence.

The patrol had cost one officer and four soldiers killed, one badly wounded and taken prisoner, to die from his wounds in captivity three days later, and one soldier badly wounded, who would survive with the loss of both legs. The German prisoner died, the soldier in the assault party having been a touch too exuberant with the sap when seeking to render him unconscious.

The next day, the twenty-ninth of December, they were relieved in the trenches by the King's Own Yorkshire Light Infantry, and moved back into divisional reserve in Bailleul. On the thirtieth, Edward von Gleichen left for a month's leave.

By the end of December 1914 the Western Front was a static trench system over three hundred and fifty miles long, stretching from the Swiss border to the North Sea.

Chapter 14

Execution and Leave

John Hayes looked out of the window of his cell towards the greyness of the early morning. Behind him, on a bare wooden table, was the slowly congealing mess of the special breakfast they had brought him on this, his last day on earth. In the corner the military policeman, who had been his constant companion since the sentence of death had been pronounced, sat on a plain wooden chair, silently watching him. Hayes had no watch, but he knew it was just about half past seven and that they would be coming for him shortly.

He bent his head forward and rested it on his right forearm which lay across the ledge of the window, his fist clenched. He was in a cottage which had been pressed into use as a prison, with security having been provided by a stout wooden door and barbed wire stretched in a criss-cross pattern across the window and nailed into the frame. He closed his eyes and tried to rationalise his feelings. For the moment he felt no fear, but was certain that would come. He prayed, briefly, not for salvation, but that he might retain his dignity up to the final moment. He felt no bitterness, for he knew perfectly well that he had no one to blame but himself for his current predicament. He had known when he had left with her from the bridge in St Quentin that they would get him for absence, if he was lucky, provided he was back within twenty-four hours. Longer than that and it would be desertion, whether he kept hold of his military kit or not; and that meant death if convicted.

He thought of Paul Cooper. He was glad he was still alive, and that he had been promoted. He would go on further, if he lived, and make the success they had both been predicted all those years ago. He cast his mind back to their meeting that day in battalion headquarters. Cooper's face had been a mix of incredulity, anger, sorrow, pity and he knew not what else. He hadn't seen him since, just that one brief meeting, and he wondered whether or not he would be there today. It was the custom for the regiment of the miscreant, or parts of it, to be paraded to bear witness to an execution, especially for a crime like desertion; pour encourager les autres, lest they be foolish enough to contemplate something similar.

A picture of Cecile flashed before him. He smiled, and this time there was bitterness. She had captivated him so and it had ended in disaster, just like all his relationships with women, except that this time it was terminal. She had been delighted to see him when he had approached her in St Quentin; even more so when he had offered to escort her safely towards the south. He had told her that the British were defeated, and their orders were to try and escape the best they could. Those with a little French, and he had a schoolboy smattering, had been told they should try and blend in by adopting French dress where they could. It had been an improbable story, but she had accepted it, apparently without qualm.

They had taken a cross country route, and on the first night had found an abandoned cottage in which to shelter. There had been a few clothes, left by the former occupants, and he had managed to make up enough to be able to shed his uniform. His initial impression of Cecile had been reinforced. Coquettish, with twinkling eyes and a lovely smile that lit up her face, she had completely captured his heart. She, for her part, had quite clear motives: this young man would be her protector and help her get away to the south and on to safety, for she had no desire to be left in a ditch, having been raped and butchered by the advancing

Germans; the stories being spread around of their brutality were truly terrible. It was helpful that Hayes was presentable, appeared to be nice and she found him attractive; and it was clear that he was very attracted to her.

Consequently, on that first night, she had cemented his attachment to her. They had lain down to sleep on separate cots on either side of the room, Hayes being determined not to wreck his chances by making unwarranted advances. As his breathing had levelled and it had been clear he was about to drop off to sleep she had slipped out from under her blanket and padded softly across the room. Kneeling on the floor beside the bed she had slid her hand gently under the covers. He had returned to full wakefulness with a start as her hand had begun to caress him between his legs, and within seconds he had grown to full, and fully extended, hardness. He had not been able to see her face, for all was complete darkness, but he felt her mouth seeking his, and the vigorous insertion of her tongue once she had found it. His back had arched as the tremors rushed through him, and he had reached out to grab her, only to be gently pushed away. Slowly, she had undressed him, kissing him as she did on face, hands and body. Determined to make him a part of it, and to get herself to a point where she could respond without faking it too much, she had guided his hand to her sensitive areas and gently started him massaging.

He had been, despite his relative maturity, quite inexperienced, but very soon he had set up a rhythm with his hand that had her squirming quite nicely, gasping quietly as she did so. She, for her part, had brought him on as gently as she could, not wanting him to be too quick when the moment came. Laying back, she had groaned as he had entered, enjoying, as she always had, the moment, the sense of being filled and of tightness round a man's member; and then she had begun to move against him as he thrust into her, rotating her bottom on the bed as he did so, feeling the familiar tingling sensation passing around her nether regions and focusing around her clitoris as he rubbed against it. The rhythm had grown faster and faster, and the noise from the beadhead of the cot banging against the wall behind her head had been enough to wake the dead. Propped up on his arms, he had looked down to where he knew her face must be, seeing its outline in the gloom as his night vision improved, hearing her grunt and gasp with every smack of his lower tummy on hers.

She had timed her move perfectly, and as the final hardness came and his explosion was imminent she had given a little squirm of her bottom and with her right hand had deftly removed him from within her, hearing him pant in the dark, feeling the pumping in her hand as his buttocks contracted time and again, and the wet warmth on her tummy, up almost to her breasts, as he had spilled his seed where it would do no harm. It wasn't by any means a perfect method of birth control, but she had not been caught out yet, and neither would she be this time.

He had lain in the dark, her head cradled on his shoulder and, looking up at the dark expanse of the ceiling above, had affirmed the decision which would ultimately cost him his life: he would not be seeking to return the next day, or ever, to the British Army. As he had drifted off to sleep that night it had never crossed his mind to consider how she had acquired the experience she had so dextrously demonstrated that night.

He never knew if she had believed his story about being ordered to escape, and as the news had developed of the reverse of German fortunes followed by the stalemate of the trenches and the huge battles of late 1914 she had made no mention of his possible return to the Army. Their life together had, at the beginning, been exciting; a heady mix of the adrenaline rush of being escapees, combined with quite regular bouts of sexual athletics which kept him firmly on the hook. However, as time moved on Cecile had become more and more petulant and, consequently, less compliant, especially at night. Her plans for a move to England had been unsuccessful, and it had been Paris, once it was safe, where their journey had led them. More and more, Hayes had become a liability. With virtually no French, she had to do everything for them; and she had been the only one who could make money. He had no idea where she obtained the funds to keep them fed and in the small apartment they had managed to find; except that she worked afternoons and evenings, sometimes late. He, for his part, had been virtually a prisoner, unable to risk being apprehended by the Gendarmerie who were on the lookout for deserters of any nationality.

Finally, it had come to a head. He had discovered that the source of her income had been as a bar girl, with a little extra on the side in order to top up her earnings. She had contemptuously asked him where he thought their money had come from. There had been a blazing row, in which he had learned of her true background in Ostend, it having been precisely the profession she had been pursuing in Paris; and accounted for her high degree of dexterity and competence in bed. She had pointed out that she, in any event, was tired of being encumbered by a hopeless case, who had deserted his own army and was clearly a coward. That had been the first time anyone had said such a thing to him, and it had hurt; and he had lashed out, catching her a stinging blow on the face. At that point, the concièrge had called a passing policeman, blurted out her suspicions about the man in apartment seven, suspicions she had harboured for several weeks, and asked him to resolve the noisy domestic incident currently in progress. It had not taken the policeman long to work out what was happening, assisted by a flurry of rapid French from Cecile as she blurted out the truth; or at least her version of it. Hayes hadn't understood a word, but he had gone quietly when the Gendarme motioned him down the stairs, resignedly accepting his fate in the realisation that he had once more, stupidly, wrecked his life for a woman who simply had not been worth it.

The door opened, and the Padre, whose services he had already rejected, stood there with the escort party waiting to lead him away. Stepping out of the cottage, he gasped as the cold air struck him, and shivered involuntarily in the thin uniform. Looking around, he could see soldiers drawn up in two ranks, and, a hundred yards away, a single wooden post standing vertically from the ground. His eyes watering from the cold, he obeyed the instructions given to him, oddly feeling no fear as he did. He knew one thing for certain, he had been about to crack up after Le Cateau, and it would only have been a question of time before had had given way to his terror. Mind you, he might have been diagnosed as a psychiatric case and put in a loony bin, which was happening to more and more soldiers as the war took its toll on the less resilient; but, knowing his luck............! At least this would be quick, no ghastly maiming, and no screaming as he writhed on the ground; just quick and clean, and he wouldn't even hear the bang since the bullets would reach him before the sound of the firing.

Paul Cooper watched as they manacled his friend to the post, saw his head jerk as they blotted out the daylight with the hood, watched him shiver in the biting wind as his last few seconds passed, saw the spreading stain in his crotch as the eventual realisation of imminent death had its impact on his bladder and his bowels. As if in a trance he heard the words of command, culminating in the order to fire. Even his iron self discipline was not sufficient for him to keep his eyes fixed to his front. He turned his head away, looking down to the ground, as the bullets ripped the life out of John Hayes, his body sagging, supported by his bonds, in a clown-like parody of death. There was no dignity in this. Better to go like a soldier. Paul flinched at the sound of the single shot as the officer administered the coup de grace with his pistol, spreading John Hayes' brains onto the ground, staining the hoar frost which had whitened even the mud at the base of the execution stake.

Paul took refuge in the comfort of routine as, in response to the captain's nod, he turned about and gave the orders which would march the company back to its billets in Dranouter. Falling them out after a three quarter of a mile march, he watched as they went into their huddles and headed, in some cases, for the estaminet. The faces of the new arrivals, and many of the younger ones, reflected their shock at the brutality of what they had just witnessed. The old sweats were showing no reaction, other than to look a bit grim faced.

"No more than the bugger deserved," muttered Ted; expressing his view with somewhat less conviction than had been the case in the days leading up to the morning's events.

"Right." Ned added his four pennorth.

Colin looked up as Jacqueline appeared with cups of chocolate for the five of them. He smiled a distant look as if he were not really there. He had explained to her a few days ago the background, and her hand reached down to hold, gently, the back of his in a gesture of understanding. By now, they were both very fond of each other, and very aware that the vagaries of their present lives did not make for permanence in a relationship. Consequently, they had yet to cross any physical boundaries, but not without considerable effort and self control. He was a mixture of feelings, his emotions in turmoil, as she moved away to go about her business in the kitchen.

"This is bleedin' awful!" The young soldier looked aghast at the trench they were taking over from the Cheshires. The soldiers they were to replace were climbing out of freezing water that was waist deep. His expression of revulsion drew no sympathy from the departing occupants, and as the ribald remarks came his way he made a mental note to shut up in future; a view reinforced as an unsympathetic Ned Preece shoved him forward into the mire and then stood there, looking at him.

"Jus' wanned t'see 'ow deep it were." He grinned. "Right, the rest of yer, get in 'ere." He managed to maintain his grin, despite the creeping cold as the water ascended up to and then beyond his nether regions. The sleeveless, goatskin jerkin he wore, as did so many others, as protection against the cold draped into the water despite his best efforts to keep it dry. Looking along the line of the platoon he could see his chums chivvying and marshalling reluctant soldiers into their new positions, doing their best to make it all seem as normal as could be. He grinned, watching Alfie berate a young soldier who had dropped his rifle, and watched as Ted drew his face close to the ear of a young man who had clearly earned his displeasure, and whispered endearments of some sort to him.

And there they stayed, for two days of pure purgatory. They made the best they could of a bad job, and with brushwood and by improving the parapet they made it a little less unbearable. They were shelled on the second day, and two men in another company were killed, and it rained heavily on the third day. It was with great relief, on the tenth of January, that they handed the trenches back to the Cheshires, who showed no particular delight at returning to them, whilst the Norfolks headed back to Dranouter to dry out.

Their relief only lasted two days before they were once again back into the misery of the same trenches, for another two days before handing over, wet through, freezing cold, utterly exhausted having had no sleep for the whole of their occupancy, and dishevelled, to the West Kents. The two days cost them one killed and one wounded, although not from the platoon. They lost, however, a number from the effects of hypothermia, evacuating them to recover in the warmth and dryness of a casualty clearing station further to the rear. The trick in these cases was to spot the symptoms early and get the man out before he became sufficiently advanced to threaten life. Generally, they were successful, and would expect to see the casualty returned to the unit within about three days.

The next fortnight, up to the twenty-fourth of January, they were in trenches in reserve. Life was not much more comfortable, but at least they were not bothered unduly by enemy indirect fire, and they did not have to worry about snipers as was always the case in the forward trenches. It was at the end of this that they moved once more into Dranouter, but this time into billets that were very much less satisfactory than on earlier occasions. A leaking roof, damp floors and an all pervading cold were not something they welcomed. However, they could relax, and once their weapons were cleaned and their kit sorted their time was their own.

The estaminet was the obvious destination for Colin, and

he made his way there as soon as his duties permitted; Ted and Alfred went with him. A couple of cups of hot chocolate later and Ted and Alfred felt very much better, but Colin was the worse for wear. Shivering and cold, he was clearly quite ill and Jacqueline would hear nothing of their suggestions that they take him back to the billet. It was raining outside and he would only get worse. Under her firm direction, and she was clearly not going to brook any insubordination from them, Ted and Alfred helped their sick friend upstairs to a bedroom. It was with some envy that they left him, naked and asleep between clean sheets. Jacqueline, modestly, averted her eyes as they went through the ritual of undressing him and then, when it was safe for her to do so, she swept up his filthy clothes and headed, determinedly, towards the wash house.

They reported him sick, and cleared his absence with Paul Cooper. The next morning they went back and found him dozing, but better, and once more found themselves under command of a very determined young lady, whose knowledge of English was growing daily better and better; especially some of the vernacular. Consequently, and following clear directions, they carried the tin bath up to the room, ferried gallons of hot water, removed him from the bed and set about bathing him. She stood in the doorway, arms folded, eyes averted, making quite sure they did things properly, and ensured that Colin was safely back in bed, properly dried, before leaving them to strip off their own clothes and bathe, each in his turn, in the gradually cooling water. The reward for their pains when they went downstairs was a cup of hot coffee, a baguette with cheese and a winning smile that had the power to stop an army in its tracks. "My, but Colin were a lucky sod."

He was back with them by the next morning, looking very much better, and the following day they were off yet again for more of the same, taking over once more from the Cheshires, near Wulvergem. The next few days were difficult, with enemy sniping becoming a real problem. Casualties amounted to six killed and ten wounded in freezing conditions, with very hard frosts, and a heavy dump of snow on Sunday the thirty-first of January. Ted was aware that Colin seemed unusually distant. As usual, he simply waited for what would eventually come out when his friend was ready. Colin, for his part, was a mixture of joy and misery. On that last night, Jacqueline had come to his bed with a contraceptive she had acquired, and which her mother had taught her to use, and they had finally broken through the physical barrier that they had both known would collapse at some time. It had been the most marvellous thing, planned by her so that she would be safe, and he could not have imagined in his wildest dreams the pleasure involved. Afterwards, they had talked long into the night, and had agreed that to plan too far was madness, but that love was something they both had to acknowledge, and that they would have to work around what the war might bring; hence the misery competing with the joy in his heart.

Their billets after this stint in the trenches were in Bailleul, where they stayed until the ninth of February. Their relaxation was spoiled towards the end by an inspection of the brigade undertaken by His Majesty, the King of the Belgians, for which there was a fair amount of bull. Colin was less concerned by this than by the fact that his chances of seeing Jacqueline were severely impaired by distance. Furthermore, he was determined to keep as much private as he could, and whilst everyone knew that they were fond of each other, none had any idea that they had consummated their relationship. None, that is, except Ted to whom Colin had eventually confided that he and his lady had declared their feelings for each other on that last night in the estaminet. Ted, who had been brewing tea at the time, had looked up from under the brim of his cap at his friend standing above him, and had grinned.

"Leave? Wadder yer mean, leave?" Ted was incredulous, and Colin, standing beside him, speechless.

Jim Collis gave them the pitying look reserved by all senior NCOs of the British Army for lesser mortals; a lesser mortal being any creature, military or civilian, who was not a member of either the sergeants' or officers' messes of the

British Army, in that order. “Yes, leave. Yer get five days, including travel, back in Blighty and you are goin’ on the tenth of February. You will be back on the morning of the fifteenth.” A few quick questions determined that they could depart at about four in the evening, which would get them home by about nine o’clock the next day, depending on trains from Liverpool Street. A card, sent today, would, with luck, arrive in time to warn those at home; Colin’s went to Cromer and Ted’s to his parents. Alfred and Alfie were also advised that leave was coming their way, as was Ned; and all would see it completed during February. Joe Floyd too, but his would come towards the end of the month. That way, the experience was balanced throughout the platoon whilst they were away.

The two friends looked at each other in delight. “Bloody marvellous!” Ted was, unusually for him, ecstatic. He had been thinking more and more of home these past few weeks, especially with the interest Thurza had tickled. The thought of being there within a few days and of seeing his family again, roused tremendous feelings of homesickness in him.

They had little time to prepare, and in the meantime had moved to Dranouter. Colin had thought that Jacqueline would be saddened at his going, but her delight that there were five days in which he would be in no danger was infectious; and suddenly he was looking forward to it. He and Ted waited by the estaminet to depart with the squad that would march to the station, and she was there to see them off. Colin was inside the door, being kissed goodbye, when Ted called that it was time for them to go, and Colin decided he had to go to the toilet. Leaving him, Jacqueline stepped outside to talk with Ted as they walked towards where the squad was forming up. As they approached the group of men they stopped, she wished him a happy holiday and he thanked her. Her hand reached out to shake his, and she leaned forward to kiss him, gently, not once, not twice, but thrice on alternate cheeks, as was the local custom between friends. She was fond of her man’s friend, and she knew how close they were. In the distance neither of them noticed Edward Snell turning away, the anger and hatred etched in his face as he stumped off on his way to brigade headquarters. Ted, for his part, suffered the ribald hoots and whistles of the squad as he moved to join them, knowing that they would be even louder for Colin's farewell kisses; which they were.

The Commander-in-Chief had been worried for some time about the state of his war stocks and his ability to sustain action against a hugely powerful enemy when he had virtually no ammunition and very little prospect of obtaining any more. They had started from a poor basis before the war, when the re-equipping the Royal Artillery with quick firing guns like the 13 and 18-Pounder had not been accompanied by a commensurate increase in ammunition scales. They could fire faster, but had been given, or scaled, to use the military term, the same number of rounds as the slower firing guns they had replaced. The general staff had increased provision for small arms ammunition, but there had been an all round disinclination to face the costs of an increase in artillery ammunition or in the transport required to carry it. Consequently, for the first year of the war, the availability and re-supply of ammunition was a major problem. Furthermore, lack of staff in the War Office meant that there were inadequate means to manage the contracts for weapons and ammunition.

Consequently, despite some increases in manufacturing, there remained shortages, and he was in the process of issuing an order limiting the 18-Pounder to just ten rounds per gun per day; but only shrapnel, not high explosive. The 4.7 Inch Howitzer was limited also, to just eight rounds per gun per day. French was in the process of urging, yet again, the authorities in England to strive yet harder to provide him with the wherewithal to conduct effective operations. Newspapers, such as the Daily Mail, were becoming aware of the situation, and were beginning to mount campaigns in order to achieve improved factory output. Not all of them were especially complimentary about the British workforce who, in the eyes of many, were guilty of letting down their fellow countrymen fighting the might of the brutish Hun on the Western Front.

It was a fact that factories still were undermanned, and employment of women, which might have gone some way to remedy the problem, was limited in Britain by Trade Union rules; unlike France and Germany. In addition to the prohibition of women doing men's work, it was also prohibited for unskilled or semi-skilled men to do the work of skilled men. There was a limitation of one man per machine and yet further limitations imposed on a man's output. Trade demarcations were endemic, and there could be no question of union men working with non-union men. Attempts to resolve this were foundering in February 1915 due to industrial unrest caused by a demand for increased wages by reason of the profits employers were believed to be making, and by rises in the price of food. As Ted and Colin boarded their train with a copy of each of the Daily Mail and the Daily Herald between them they were able to read the two differing perspectives. They quickly dismissed the average British workman as a fly-by-night and a charlatan, with no thought for anyone but himself, there being nothing wrong with him that a dose of the trenches would not put right. The thought that they quibbled over money when good men, earning far less than they, were dying hourly by the dozen was anathema to a soldier. "Bleedin' civvies!"

That they were about to meet up with family who were themselves members of the civilian population was rather lost on them both, but anyway, "that were different." They chatted and planned all the way by train to Boulogne, and then, on the packet steamer across the Channel, they fell into a deep sleep, sat against a bulkhead, side by side, Ted's head on Colin's shoulder. They were rudely wakened by a sailor, surely after only a few minutes dozing, to be told that the boat had docked and if they didn't get a move on they would be heading back to France. Grabbing packs and equipment, they scrambled up in time to see soldiers still walking down the gangplank, and a grin on the matelot's face. Grinning back, they headed along the deck and walked down the gang plank to set their feet on English soil for the first time in getting on for three years, if you included the time in Ireland.

As they stood, bemused at first, they heard a voice calling that there was tea available, and bacon sandwiches for those who wanted them. They moved over to where a group of women had set up a stall from which the smell of frying bacon wafted in what seemed the most appetising smell ever. Colin had learned to love the soft French lilt that his Jacqueline brought to the English language, but, my, it sounded good to hear an English lady speaking for the first time since,....since,....well, forever. Thanking her, they followed the instructions of the NCO directing them to the station in Dover Western Docks wherein stood the train that would take them up to London. Sitting back in the carriage they looked out of the window at the green fields of Kent sailing gently by as the train made its sedate way towards the capital. The uninterrupted greenness of it all struck them both: no shell craters, no trenches, no wire; and no bodies. Serried rows of apple trees, bare of leaves, reached away into the distance, planted in straight lines in their orchards. Hop poles reached upwards, their crops having long been carted for drying to the Oast Houses whose conical roofs dotted the countryside. They passed through Ashford, Marden, Staplehurst, Paddock Wood, Tonbridge; clickety clack, clickety clack. As they entered Charing Cross they had been asleep for some time and woke again, this time to the gentle shaking of an elderly lady, enquiring if they were all right and asking if there was anything she could do.

Declining politely, they left the train, walking out of the station to board a bus in the Strand that would take them to Liverpool Street and the train to Norwich. Ted would alight before the county town, at a station only a couple of miles from the village; Colin would go on to Norwich where he would change and take the train out to the coast, to Cromer. His mother would join him there that afternoon. As the rain reached his station, Ted looked across at his friend, reached out and shook his hand. Colin looked back at him, his face uncertain.

"Have a good leave." Their grip was firm as he spoke, as if neither wished to be the first to let go.

"See yer, Liverpool Street, Tuesday night in toime t' get the boat train from Charin' Cross. Enjoy yer leave," and with a last grin Ted was gone, the train door slamming behind him. Colin sat back, smiled at the lady in the far corner of the carriage and then stared out from the window, consumed with his thoughts.

There was no public transport that would get Ted from the station to his village, but it was only just over three miles along the roads, and this was not a distance of any consequence. It was a cold, crisp morning, and a good day for a walk. Before long he was swinging along the lane, his legs stretching out to eat up the miles. In just under forty five minutes he was in sight of the southern edge of the village, the black slate roof of the church standing out among the Elm trees in the flat Norfolk countryside. His breathing had shortened and his pulse was racing, as much to do with the anticipation as with the exercise he had been taking. The light breeze whipped away the vapour from his mouth as his hot, moist breath condensed in the cold February morning air. As he entered the village there were a couple of boys playing in a garden, off to his right. As soon as they saw him they were on the road, marching alongside him in a parody of the military style. Ted grinned at them, suppressing the mild irritation he felt that they did not have anything better to do; and, being suddenly aware that they did not know him, began to realise just how long he had been away. Swiftly, and without warning, an overpowering sense of loneliness swept over him, making him feel sick to his stomach; he felt like a stranger in an alien land.

Tiring of their fun, the two boys returned to their game, and Ted marched on up the main road through the village to the terraced cottage that was the new family home. On the way he saw a couple of women he knew, and watched from the corner of his eye as they talked about him, not at all sure if they recognised him. And then, suddenly, he was there, a small wooden gate at the start of a short path leading to a nice, brick cottage with a black slate roof on the left of the road as you look north. My, but dad had done well to get this. Things must really be looking up. As he walked up the path, the heels of his boots clicking on the cobbles, the front door was flung open and a tall, slender young woman stared out at him, her face wreathed in a smile of huge anticipation. He barely recognised his sister; and certainly had no idea which of the twins it was.

"Ted! Ted, is it really you?" "Darft question, 'oo else'll it be? Steady now, remember, this ain't the Army."

Looking over her shoulder she screamed out to an unseen gathering within the house: "It's him......, he's here......, he's arrived," and with that she was running down the path to throw her arms round his neck and hug him so tight he thought at one stage that she might throttle him. Over her shoulder he saw her mirror image appear in the doorway, and head towards him at the same pace as her sister. Then there was his mother, framed in the doorway, his father behind. There were smiles on their faces, but he felt a look of uncertainty on his mother's face that he could not explain, and then thought of it no more. The two girls had him, one on each arm, propelling him towards the doorway and the waiting arms of his family. As he approached he wondered why he did not quite feel the overpowering sense of joy he had anticipated. Neither did he yet know which of his sisters was holding which arm

His parents watched the approach along the path. "My gosh," breathed his father, "he's changed....., he's grown." He looked down at his wife as she nodded up to him and they both stepped forward to greet a son they weren't sure they knew. Ted's hug for his mother was long and sustained, and when he drew back from it there were tears in his eyes and hers. She kissed his cheek. "I've kept breakfast for ye." She smiled, remembering that the arms which just entwined her had been like hoops of steel, and the chest against which she had been pressed had been like a wall. The young man who had left her home two or more years ago had grown beyond recognition. The handshake for his father had the man wondering at its strength, and at the calluses which bore the evidence of the hard work they had endured. Looking into his son's eyes he was not sure what he read.

Ted stepped into the neat hallway, and looked around in wonder. They had done very well for themselves, and clearly Bert Chalmers was a good employer. His mother smiled with pride at the obvious impression her new home had created. As he stepped into the kitchen a young man of roughly his age rose to his feet. Ted looked at him, and the self conscious way in which he stood.

"Ruth, introduce Bernard. Bernard is Ruth's young man, Ted," said his mother. Well that cleared up one thing; as Ruth advanced to stand, somewhat protectively, beside Bernard it gave Ted the opportunity to separate her from Eliza. Ted shook hands as the introductions were made, squeezing a bit harder than was strictly necessary. He was about to say something, and then thought better of it, especially given the obvious effort his mother had put into the breakfast that sat before him on the table and cooking on the hob. Within a few minutes they were all gathered round the table, the two girls talking nineteen to the dozen, his father smiling, his mother bustling about cooking and serving, Bernard sitting quietly and Ted trying to squeeze a word in where he could.

After a few minutes his father asked the pointless open ended question that Ted had half anticipated. "What's it loik, then, out there I mean. Ye know, what's it loik?" Looking up over his fork he gave the only answer he could: "Bloody awful." His mother looked shocked.

"Is it true, then, what they say?"

"Wot do they say," the emphasis on the "do". 'Oo the bloody 'ell're "they" any way', he thought to himself.

His father was uncertain, put off by the tinge of belligerence in his son's voice. "Well, y' know, in the papers an' that, about the Germans an' the shortage of ammunition an' the food an' everythin'?" Ted saw that the man was trying to come to terms with something he had no hope of understanding, and felt a little ashamed of his own antagonism. He softened.

"Aye, dad," his voice gentler now. "It's a bastard an' no mistake. Sorry mum." He looked up at her disapproving expression and realised that he would have to break the habit of soldierly vernacular that had become so natural these past few years, and especially the last six months or so. He turned back to his father and began to talk; but barely had a few sentences been spoken, hardly had he begun to describe the filth, the cold, the wet and the smell when his mother shooed them away from the table and sent his father packing off to work. Ted looked at her, and she would not catch his eye. He turned to Bernard, sitting in a corner, having remained silent throughout the meal. Eliza was trying to talk to Ted, but it was clear his mother did not want to know, and so he responded in monosyllables. Eventually, he spoke to Bernard.

"Got no work then," a note of sympathy in his voice.

Ruth replied for him, a defensive note in her voice. "Bernard's in a protected trade."

"What would that be, then," asked Ted, feeling a little less charitable.

"Munitions." The single word, no embellishment, from Bernard.

"Munitions," said Ted, a slight questioning note in his voice. "They be the munitions we ain't got enough of by any chance?"

Bernard looked uncomfortable. "Anyway," Ted was not to be put off, "why's 'e not at work?" He addressed his question to Ruth since she seemed to be the one doing all the talking.

Again the defensive note. "They're stroikin'"

"They're what?" The note of incredulity in Ted's voice.

"Stroikin'." By now Bernard was looking distinctly uncomfortable. Ruth carried on. "Bernard's firm makes special bits for guns, an' the bosses is takin' all the profits an nuthin' ain't goin' t' the workers, so they're stroikin' fer more pay. An' t' keep prices down they's employin' unskilled labour doin' skilled men's work an' doin' good men out of their just reward." Her voice had risen in pitch as she spoke. Ted, barely able to believe his ears, and determined not to upset his mother who was clearly in a dither over all this, got up from his chair and walked across to the kitchen where he picked up a tea towel, put his arm round a frail shoulder, squeezed it and gave her a kiss. Little shit weren't worth a light, an' certainly not to upset the old lady. Ruth's got 'erself a right toe-rag there. Ruth, her face a confused picture of distress and defiance, took Bernard by the hand and led him out into the garden where they sat on a small wooden bench in strained silence.

They washed and wiped in silence, the mother and her son. He had grown beyond belief, and not just physically. There was a sense of age, of maturity, of wisdom beyond his years, of hardness. She had remembered him as the boy who had run away in those dark days over three years ago, and he had returned to her in days even darker; a young man she did not know and with whom she had nothing more in common.

She broke the silence. "I'm goin' shoppin' in a bit. Fancy a walk, an ' y' can choose what y' want fer yer dinner." She smiled, reached out to touch his cheek, and tried to draw herself close to him. "Strong young man like you, y' can carry me bag."

"Love to, mum; love to." He smiled back at her.

It was ten minutes before she was ready, and he held the front door open for her. She smiled up at him as she stepped past him. As he closed the door behind them he remembered, for the first time since he had arrived in the house, and spoke:

"Oh, by the way, oive gotta see Thurza,.....I mean Mrs Allsop, afore I go back. Like t' do that t'day or t'morra if I can." His mother looked round swiftly, and there was a sharp note in her voice.

"What for?" He was surprised at her tone, and once more felt the rebellion rising up inside him. He didn't know what the problem was, but it seemed she couldn't stop treating him as if he were a child.

"I saw 'er husband killed, 'e died two feet away from me;

and she wants t' talk t' me." He stared back at her suspicious face before his belligerence subsided and he finished, lamely: "It's the least I can do." His mother nodded, apparently mollified, and turned to stride purposefully down the path and through the gate before turning right towards the village shop. Ted walked beside her, looking round for people he knew, not sure now that he really wanted to see anyone.

The shop had hardly changed, the green door with its clear glass panels, each obscured by an advertisement for a range of products, including Oxo, Bovril, Sunlight Soap, Players Navy Cigarettes and Bryant and May matches. She pressed down on the brass handle and pushed the door to step inside, the tinkling of the bell on the lintel alerting the occupants to the presence of a new customer.

"Marnin' Martha." There was only one other customer and she turned to greet the new arrival. "My an' oo's this with ye? Its not young Ted is it? Surely not, it can't be.....my, but 'e's grown. An' 'ow is 'e then?"

"'E's fine, thank you fine." Ted stood to one side, wondering if he would ever be invited to speak. He was busy looking round for something in which he could take an interest in order to cover his embarrassment when he heard a movement as someone came through the door behind Agnes Chalmers, who was serving.

"Hallo, Ted." There was no mistaking the voice, and his heart lurched as he turned to face what he had really known had been inevitable since the day he was told he would get leave. Betty Chalmers suited pregnancy. She was something like seven months gone, and she was absolutely radiant, a look on her face that spoke of her pleasure at seeing him, and a small suggestion of reproof, even after all this time, presumably at the way he had left. She came round from behind the counter, stood on tip toes and kissed him, briefly, on the cheek. Ted ignored the indrawn breath from his mother and her companion, and did not look at Agnes, as he returned the kiss, on her other cheek, just as he would have done with Jacqueline.

"'Lo Betty. Good t' see yer." And it was. She had long

ceased to be a feature of his life, his dreams, his fantasies; but she was a lovely girl and it would have been a fool and a liar who denied it, or denied that it was a pleasure to be in her company; or so he thought.

Within seconds she was talking about her new life as the wife of a banker, of the house they shared and of the imminent arrival of her baby in just two months time. She cared not what it was, just that it would be all right. She chattered about the nursery they were building and the swing crib being made to go under the apple tree. She looked despondent when she pointed out that her Reginald was missing a great deal of this as he had signed up for Kitchener's new army, and he spent much of his time training. She did not want him to go to war, but it was his duty and she understood that. Anyway, by the time he got out there the war would be over. There was every prospect of that, she was sure; wasn't that so?

Ted, who by now had not inserted so much as a word edgeways, tried to speak, thought better of it and simply inclined his head in a half hearted nod.

"See, I told you so." She turned, excited to her mother. "See, Ted agrees, don't you Ted?" Before he could say a word she was off again. He didn't know who Reginald was, and he did not remember her natterin' like this before, but bloody 'ell, she could yak fer every wife in the soddin' regiment. "Anyway, Reginald is going to be an officer, and they don't have to take the same risks, do they. I mean they're further back, aren't they. There's much less chance of them being hurt, isn't that right?" The words spilled out in a rush, directed at Ted in particular, but also at the assembled throng. The look on Agnes' face was of despair.

Ted didn't know whether to be insulted or not, having just been relegated to nothing more than cannon fodder, in existence for the protection of officers. Images flashed across his mind: the young officer on the wire at Point 189, his brains spread liberally over those around him as his head exploded; the newcomer on the Aisne whose face he had never seen, and whose arm had finished up in a pit of composting waste; Charles Hawthorn, spread-eagled against the wall of a trench, his throat ripped out by a high velocity bullet. Silly cow. Only 'ad to look at the casualty lists in the papers t' see what officers do: they bloody die loik the rest of us, an' more of 'em seein' as 'ow few of 'em there were. Briefly, whilst seeking a response, he wondered what Matthew might say about officers and their responsibility for leading their men. Sensibly, he decided he didn't have the words, and that if she wished to harbour an illusion then best he didn't shatter it.

"Aye," was all he could mumble, and then, to his mother, "I'll be outside." Agnes smiled, briefly, nervously and with thanks that the boy had sense.

He sat on the wooden bench in front of the shop window, and lit a Woodbine. As he leaned back and inhaled the smoke he offered the thought to God that the sooner leave was over and he was back where he belonged the better. Inside, the women decided that he had been away a long time, that the war was obviously having its effect on him, poor boy, and what he needed was some good home cooking and sleep in a proper bed and he would be back to normal soon. As he was sitting, wondering how long his mother would be since the cold was beginning to get to him, the door opened and Agnes stepped out.

"Jus' a second," she called over her shoulder. "That'll be a shillin' an' tuppence farthin' fer Mrs Ludgrove, Betty, if y'd take it." Turning to Ted she smiled. Reaching out she pressed a packet of Players into his hand. Quietly, she spoke: "Thanks, Ted. She can't 'elp it. She's scared, y' see. Scared of bein' alone when the baby comes; an' she don' want t' be a widder afore she's a mother. Take these, son," pressing the packet firmly into his hand, "an' good luck t' yer." With that she returned to the shop, whilst Ted continued sitting, thinking over what had just transpired, deciding that Mrs Chalmers was a sensible lady and safely stowing the cigarettes in his left breast pocket.

Lunch at home was a quiet affair, Ted sitting alone with his mother over bread and cheese. Nice t' 'ave a good bit 'o cheese after that soft, 'orrible French stuff. He tried to talk to her, but matters beyond that which transpired within the parish boundary were not really for discussion; and events in France were simply not mentioned. He enquired after Thurza Allsop, receiving a slightly frosty response, but nonetheless was able to determine that she continued her work as a seamstress from her cottage, taking in work and employing a couple of village girls in a shed at the back. Most of her stuff was sold in the market in Norwich, where there was a man with whom she dealt. There was some emphasis on the word "man", the disapproval clear; and he felt a tiny inner shock that he could not explain. However, after lunch, he headed in the direction of the small, thatched cottage she had shared with her late husband, and in which she had begun to build her own business once she had realised he was a waster, and that children did not appear as though they were going to be a feature of her life.

He knocked on the door, nervous for reasons he could not explain. His mouth dry, the palms of his hands sweaty despite the cold, he waited as he heard footsteps approaching the door, and it opened. He stepped back a pace as she stood there, the weak, February sun lying low behind him against the horizon reflected off the auburn tints in her hair, sending her face partly into shadow. She smiled, a wide smile with the slightly offset front tooth that he remembered from that first meeting in The Bull. Her face wore a look of surprise at the unexpected visitor.

"I'm sorry," she spoke hesitantly as if trying to gather her thoughts. "Do I........," a questioning tone in her voice. Then the realisation. "Ted!" Her voice rose in surprised delight. "Ted Ludgrove, well this is very unexpected." She reached out and shook his hand, her own feeling cool and dry to the touch. "When did you know you were coming home, why didn't you tell me, oh, don't just stand there, come in." He stepped over the threshold into a neat, well kept front room. "I'll make some tea, do sit down." He sat, his hat screwed up in his hand, stiffly on the edge of his seat as she busied herself in the kitchen. Within a few minutes she had returned with a tray of tea, a plate of home made biscuits nestling amongst the empty cups, the sugar bowl and the milk jug. The crockery was plain, simple and white. No frills and no fuss.

An hour later and he was making excuses to leave, not because he wanted to, but because propriety forced it upon him. It was getting dark and they were not properly chaperoned, and although things had changed in society he did have her reputation to think about. Odd really, when considering what it was they got up to in France, but this was rural England, and one had to be careful. The time had flown by, relaxed conversation about the village and a little about the war in France, but only so much as he was prepared to reveal. It seemed she had a natural sense of when to move the subject around. They did not discuss her husband's death, and he was conscious of that as he stood to take his leave.

"You must come back." He could not remember having heard such welcome words. "There are still.....well," she hesitated briefly, searching for the right words, "things we need to talk about."

"Aye, we never quite got round to that did we?"

"No." She glanced down at the floor. "No,....... now was not the time. We have the weekend, and I'm my own mistress here and can take my time as I wish. Can you come to lunch, tomorrow or Sunday, without upsetting your family? I mean, they will all want to see you, won't they?"

"Aye," he grinned, "but they can get too much of a good thing." Ted was, by nature, a touch reserved, but her personality brought out the little bit of the devil that lurked within him. Sunday lunch, after church, which he presumed he would have to attend, was a bit of a ritual and one in which he would have to take part. Saturday was different, hence his response:

"Termorrer alright?"

"Perfect, twelve o'clock." She smiled. "And I'll have one of my girls here, working." He grinned again. This lady thought of everything.

He walked down the short path that led to the road, a spring in his step, and feeling better than he had since he had arrived back in the village. On his way home he wondered how Colin was faring, and would have been pleased to know that he had spent the afternoon with his mother, just holding her hand and talking gently about how he had missed her. He had also broached the subject of Jacqueline, at which his mother had smiled, comfortingly. She was certainly not going to make an issue of it, well aware that the circumstances in which he found himself were wholly unusual, and the chances of him, the French girl or their love surviving the war were remote indeed. The few days she had with him were too precious for her to wish to risk marring them with anything contentious. There had been too much of that already.

After supper, old Ted offered to take young Ted to the pub for a pint. Martha shooed them off; she had enough to do and they'd be better off out of her way. The two girls sat in the corner, sewing a dress for Ruth, looking enviously at the men as they left. What they would not give for a night out in the pub, but..........!

The door opened to reveal a smoke filled room, with most of the customers middle aged or older. Hardly surprising really, with so many of the young men having moved off to join up. Curious faces turned to see who had entered, and most of them made a double take before they recognised the boy who had left, in something of a hurry, over two years ago now. The well built, purposeful young man they saw was not the Ted Ludgrove they had known, and there was a hardness in his eyes that many noticed once he got close enough for them to see clearly into his face. His handshake was firm and hard, and the hands bore witness to hard work over long periods.

"Pint?" His father looked at him quizzically.

"Aye, thanks dad." This was the first pint his father had ever bought him; it was a moment to treasure. He was glad when his father refused Uncle Henry's offer to "buy one fer the lad." This one was important. He raised the glass, looking across the top into his father's eyes. "Good t' see y', dad. Cheers." And with that he took a deep swallow, wiping the back of his hand across his mouth to remove the thin film of foam that had collected there.

Henry leaned on the bar, a couple of his cronies on either side, and engaged the Ludgroves in conversation; directing most of his remarks to young Ted. Questions were asked about what it was like "over there", but no one waited to hear the answers. Within minutes, Henry was regaling them all with stories of his own exploits, pitched such that it was obvious that anything Ted had been up to could not possibly match with anything he, Henry, might have undertaken. Ted, who tried to put his four pennorth in at the beginning, soon gave up the unequal struggle and watched as his father laughed at Henry's stories; and Ted sank rather more beer than was good for him. And the more he drank the lonelier he became.

"Bit quiet, your lad," remarked Henry as the Ludgroves left the pub just before closing time.

"Aye," old Ted responded. "Been a bit like that since 'e got 'ome. Don' unnerstan' wot's got into 'im really." With that he left, walking alongside his son the three hundred yards home. They said nothing, young Ted could see no point.

"Lunch? With Thurza Allsop? Why?" His mother was incredulous.

Ted was taken aback. This were gettin' daft. "'Ere 'e were, a grown man oo'd butchered other men and 'ad friends butchered and maimed around 'im, 'ad fought a bleedin' war fer six months, an' 'ere 'e were bein' asked why 'e'd accepted an invitation to lunch. An' wot were the problem, anyway, with Thurza?"

"Wassa problem?" Despite his best efforts he could not prevent the note of truculence creeping into his voice. His father looked up, detecting the warning signs. "Yer mother's a bit concerned, Ted, that yer get looked after proper, loik, while yer on leave, y' know?" He nodded conspiratorially at his son, hoping that the man-to-man approach would take the heat out of the situation.

Ted, desperate not to overstep the mark and upset his mother, although it appeared he had already done so, looked out of the window, his face a sullen mask. This was not going the way he had planned and dreamed it would in those horrid days and nights in the trenches. Up to his waist in freezing water, numb from the backside downwards, in an agony of exhaustion when sleep was impossible, hearing the rats rummaging in the bodies of the dead just a few feet in front of the trench. These were the times he had read his letters over and over, had dreamed of home and its comforts and had missed his family. Now, it wasn't working; and he could not understand why.

Martha, for her part, had lost a son, a boy, a few years ago, had missed him terribly, and had retained an image of what and who he was. The young man in her kitchen had the physical characteristics of her Ted, but he was different. He was hard, he had about him a sense of impatience and intolerance, he smiled, but it didn't always reach his eyes. Above all, perhaps, he was no longer dependent upon her, no longer needed her. They had almost nothing left in common and he would go his own way no matter what she said. The loss of control hurt, and there was now another woman, an older woman, an experienced woman, who could take her boy away; forever!

Old Ted understood none of this; he only knew he had a problem; he had no idea how to redress it. As he was trying to think of something to say there was a knock at the door. Eliza opened it, and stood back when she saw who was there, a look of apprehension on her face. After all, it was most unusual to have the constable visit the house.

Old Ted went to the door, and invited him in. The constable stepped across the threshold, removing his helmet as he did so. "I understand young Ted is back from the Army." His voice sounded deep and official; which meant he was on business. Martha saw her son's face turn white, and saw the fear in his eyes. Her heart went out to him. Whatever he had become, whatever he had been through, he was still her son and the sight of his anxiety brought out the protective instinct in her. For his part, Ted felt sick to his stomach. He knew what this was about: Snell had reached out from France through his father and would get him whilst he was on leave.

"He's over there." Ted's father pointed towards him. "Fancy a cuppa tea then George?"

"No thanks, Ted," his voice sounding ponderously official, "I'm afraid this is duty. Now then, young man, I should like to talk to you." Ted remained silent. The constable sat at the table and took out his notebook. Martha and old Ted stood behind their son, fearing the worst, whilst Eliza, having been flashed a look by her mother, left and went up to her room.

"Right then." He thumbed his book slowly until he reached the page he was seeking, before settling himself and looking straight at Ted. "I am 'ere to investigate an allegation of assault by a young man on the person of Edward Snell in the summer of 1912." Ted made as if to respond, but a look from the constable shut him up before he had even started. "The accusation is that a young 'ooligan by the name of Ted Ludgrove beat Mr Snell severely, causin' 'im considerable personal injury, requiring 'im to seek medical treatment for cuts, bruises and," he paused over the long word, "lacerations." Having finished he looked up from his book straight into Ted's eyes.

"Look, I..." There was a note of desperation in Ted's voice as he began to speak.

"'Owever," the ponderous voice cut him off again, "the only Ted Ludgrove oi've bin able t' find is one 'oo's fightin' fer his King an' 'is country, which is more than can be said fer some." Ted, glancing at the medal ribbons from South Africa on the policeman's tunic, realised he was dealing with an old soldier. His hopes began to rise, his spirits to lift. "I know of no...," a pause as he consulted his notebook in a very deliberate manner.... "young 'ooligan by this name, only a young soldier, so this carnt be roit. Must 'ave the wrong Ted Ludgrove. That settles it then." He reached across the table and shook Ted's hand. "Good ter see yer young feller, an' well done fer keeping yer soddin' 'ead down. Sorry, Martha, slip o' the tongue." He looked at old Ted. "Best oi 'ave that cuppa tea now, an' a piece of Martha's seed cake if'n it ain't too much ter arsk." He turned back to Ted, one old soldier to a younger one. "Ow's it goin', then?

Bit rough?" The understatement was language Ted could comprehend so clearly.

"Aye." He looked him in the eyes as he spoke, a flash of understanding between them. Ted's father, watching from the side, saw the look and envied them their shared experience. Still unsure of where he stood, he carried on. "This business with Snell, what's goin' t'....?"

"Ferget it son. The man's a cut 'n dried bastard,....sorry Martha. I know wot 'appened out there that day." He held up a hand as he saw Ted's unspoken question. "Oi've got me means. You jus' concentrate on enjoyin' yer leave an' stayin' alive over there; they ain't goin' ter bother yer. My, Martha, but this'ns the best yer've ever made." His last sentence was spoken through a mouthful of seed cake. Opposite him Ted grinned, and attacked his own slice of cake, the relief in his face plain for all to see,

Ted left in good time to walk the couple of hundred yards to Thurza's home. Following George's visit, and the relief they all expressed when he had gone, the morning had been mostly silent, broken by Eliza chattering from time to time about nothing in particular. His mother was still frosty about his visit to "the widow Allsop", and he had heard mention, again, of the "man" who visited from Norwich. This clearly preyed on Martha's mind, and Ted resolved to find out the truth, and perhaps try to set her mind at rest. As he turned out of his parent's front gate he bumped into Bernard, Ruth clutching his arm. For a second they faced each other in silence, Ted's blue eyes staring, cold as ice, straight into the face of his future brother-in-law.

"Not working then?" The question went unanswered. "Still, don't suppose it matters." Ruth looked shocked at the naked hostility in her brother's voice. Bernard made to speak, thought better of it, and guided Ruth to one side as he made way for the openly contemptuous soldier. With his fellow union members he could excuse his actions; faced with a victim of the outcome of those actions it was not so easy.

She was waiting as he walked up the path, the door open as he reached within a couple of yards of it. The smile was open and welcoming, and her eyes seemed to sparkle as she greeted him and bade him enter. For his own part, he had become a little tense once more, a manifestation partly of the altercation he had just endured with Bernard and Ruth and partly of the nervousness he felt in the presence of Thurza Allsop. She was, after all, a very attractive and experienced lady. Asked what he would like to drink, he asked if she had a glass of beer, and followed her into the kitchen as she went to find a bottle. The smell of roasting lamb, which had struck him as he entered the front door, was yet more powerful. Seated at the table, on which plates and serving dishes were stacked ready for the meal, was a young woman sewing a shirt, one of a number from a pile in the basket beside her.

"This is Mary," explained Thurza. "She's doin' a bit of extra work for me today, and you'll be here as long as we need you, won't you love?" The last part of the sentence was addressed to the young woman, who, smiling sheepishly, nodded and bent back to her work, her eyes lingering briefly on Ted. Ted's own grin was a bit sheepish as he took the pottery mug full of beer from Thurza, whilst she poured two cups of tea from a large, brown pot, leaving one with Mary as she led Ted from the kitchen with the words: "lunch will be in about twenty minutes."

The conversation continued where it had left off the day before, although by some form of unspoken mutual consent they avoided the war and the death of John Allsop. Time enough for that later. Thurza Allsop was a good cook. The lamb was as good as he had ever tasted, and the roast potatoes had crispened beautifully on the outside whilst retaining their soft centres. Cabbage, carrots and peas were a perfect accompaniment, and the gravy was a rich concoction derived from good stock and the juices of the meat. Treacle pudding followed, with smooth, yellow custard. Unable to say no, he weakened for a third helping, wondering, just briefly, if she had known it was his very favourite. Bloated and very content he moved over to sit before the crackling fire as she went to make tea, feeling sleepy, but determined not to give in to it. He felt so relaxed, so content in her company, he simply did not wish the occasion to end. If he could only preserve this forever. She returned, smiling as she saw his eyelids drooping and then starting into wakefulness as he saw her coming through the door.

"Sorry." He grinned. "Fed too well." He sat back on the settee, the cup in his hand whilst she took up position in the chair beside the fireplace a few feet away. She looked at him.

"Tell me about John." Her voice was gentle, sad, a note of pleading behind it as if she knew what she was asking, knew she needed to know and knew she did not want to know. His head jerked, his mind dragged from the pleasant surroundings of her parlour to a bloody face just a few inches from his own, an eye dangling on its optic nerve, a body quivering in the nervous reaction of sudden death. He had known this moment would come, but more and more he had been hoping she would not wish to mention it, would not wish to break the magic that seemed to be surrounding them. He hesitated, then looked as if he were about to speak. As he did so, she got in first.

"The truth, mind. I want the truth, Ted." There was a firm note in her voice that he had not heard before. He looked directly at her, determined that he should do as she asked, but wondering how far he should go."

"I always do tell the truth." He said it not defensively, not angrily, but simply as a statement of fact. "He was killed by......," he hesitated. "He was killed while we were in a wood trying to......" Again the hesitation. He took a deep breath. This was not easy. Suddenly she was closer to him, sitting on the footstool in front of him, her cup and saucer relegated to the tiled hearth. She took his from his right hand and placed it alongside her own on the hearth and then, holding his hands in hers, she looked up at him, her hazel and green eyes staring directly into his face.

"Tell me, Ted." She spoke gently, comfortingly. Suddenly it began to pour out, not in a flood, but simple measured words describing the death of her husband. He spoke as if he were not there in her parlour, as if he were far away in a place and at a time removed from their present surroundings. He talked of the shell, the splintered tree, the suddenness of it all, the certainty he felt that if John Allsop had known what had happened, or had felt pain, then it could not have been for long."

"Was he running away?"

He looked at her. Gently he said: "Yes."

She closed her eyes briefly, a tremor passing through her body. In her heart she had known it, for she knew he was a waster. She opened them again and looked back at Ted, squeezing his hands gently as if to thank him. It was as if she had pressed a switch for he began to talk again, once more from that far distant place and time into which he had taken himself. She sat and she listened. From time to time she cried at what he said, tears drifting unrestricted down her face. He told of Peter Dakin, of Colin Baxter and his mother, of Charles Hawthorn and his awful, wasteful death. He talked of things that had lain hidden within him, and she interrupted only to prod him a little more, to ease him into the next phase of his unburdening. It was as if she were lancing a boil that had festered for too long, and was squeezing the last drop of puss from the infected tissue. It grew dark, but she would not let go to put on the lights. It grew cold, but she would not let go to feed wood to the fire. She grew thirsty, and knew that he must be also, but she would not let go to brew tea for them both. Mary put her head round the door, and in the twilight looked at them. She caught Thurza's eye, and lit the lamps around them, half listening herself as the young man talked, and joined her mistress in tears as he told of other young men in their prime screaming to be put out of their misery, screaming as they were bayoneted, screaming as they were dismembered, disembowelled or flayed alive by exploding shell, screaming their fear in their dreams as they slept.

He sat back, in silence, drained. She stood, reached out and ran her hand across his brow. "I'll make some tea." His eyes were closed. He was exhausted, and had not known until then just how much. She came back and set the tray on a small table.

"I'm sorry. Shouldn't 'ave talked so much. Didn't mean to upset you." He hadn't noticed, but his accent and speech had improved in her company. She smiled.

"You haven't." She poured his tea, handing it to him with a biscuit in the saucer. "Thank you for telling me about John, and as for the rest.....well, you needed to get that out of your system." Privately, she wondered if he ever would; if anyone ever could.

It was nine in the evening before he took his leave, Mary having sewed many, many shirts in the kitchen. As he stood in the doorway, about to go, she leaned forward and kissed him gently on the cheek. "Can you come back and see me again before you go? He had thought she would never ask.

"I'd like to, if yer don't mind."

She smiled. "'Course not. When?" She sounded almost anxious, as if there were not enough time left; and so far as he was concerned there was not. He was beginning to believe there never could be.

He felt the apprehension in his stomach as he spoke, wondering what her response might be. "Can Mary do some more sewin' from about four o'clock termorrer?" She giggled and, standing with her feet together, swayed her shoulders back and forth like a small child, her hands clasped together up at her breast.

His reception at breakfast the next morning was frosty. He had not gone straight home, but had stopped off at The Bull for a pint, half wondering if it would be any different from the night before. It had not been, and he had rolled in at about ten o'clock and had gone straight to his bed. That night his sleep had been deep and dreamless. Martha had heard him come in and had stayed awake to listen for the cries of the previous nights as he lived his nightmares. There had been nothing, and she wondered at how that might be.

Sunday then followed the pattern it always had, and whilst at church he met many of the people he had not been able to see up to then. Several already knew he had spent time with the widow Allsop, but none mentioned it. One or two thought about raising it, but were close enough to see into his eyes, and thought better of it. The vicar welcomed him heartily, pumping his hand and booming out how good it was to see him there. Alice Bartram was in church, which surprised him. She was with a young man he had not seen before, who, it transpired, was from a God fearin' family in the next village whose parents were none too happy that he had taken up with a young lady of Alice's background. Alice, for her part, was determined to drag herself from the trough into which her well-meaning mother could so easily dump her; and if that meant going to church and smarming up to his parents and showing that she was a reformed character then so be it.

She and Ted chatted briefly, but he had never been terribly interested in her and, even though she had been the cause of his hurried departure, they had nothing really to say to each other. In any event, he was going back to the Army, she had her life to build and, anyway, she had heard about the two visits to Thurza Allsop's cottage. Even so, as he moved away, his shoulders broad and square in his uniform, the slight swagger as he walked, the innate toughness in his demeanour, she cast a wistful eye to the heavens and wondered, not for the first time, what might have been. Ted thought of what might happen once the poor sod she'd taken up with was in the Army as surely he must be one day.

As he exited the church gate leading onto the main road he came face to face with Alfred Snell, a look of malevolent dislike on the man's face. It was easy to see from where his son derived his own character. Ted, now certain that the issue was dead and buried, simply looked him straight in the eye. "Marnin' Mr Snell, noice day, ain't it." Deliberately thickening his Norfolk drawl he waited only briefly for a response before saying: "No?... well,.... suit yerself," before turning his back and walking away, leaving the man spluttering and fuming with anger.

Heading home he found his parents making a real effort to chat and to make Sunday lunch as normal as possible. His father was talking about his work, and the way the business was performing; and even suggesting that Ted might think about working with him again when "all this were over." Lunch was a pleasure. He had relaxed, Bernard and Ruth were not there, his mother had cooked a super meal and his father was finding it easier to talk. By three they had finished and washed up, by three forty five his parents were asleep in front of the fire and by four he was sitting at the kitchen table with Thurza and Mary. By nine he was back home, to be greeted by a suspicious stare from his mother, but no questions, and a look from his father that he interpreted to mean it was his life, but be careful. He grinned. He was going to be careful, very careful not to lose a woman for whom he now harboured feelings beyond measure. As they sat and drank cocoa he allowed the subject of Thurza to be raised, pointing out that he had now told her of the manner of her husband's death, and how unpleasant the whole business had been. His father, listening carefully, began to probe a little, but as he did so Martha made it clear she did not want to listen and changed the subject. Ted, feeling trapped again, and unable to express himself, finished his drink. As he was about to get up and leave he spoke of the "man from Norwich." He was, it transpired, her brother-in-law and he ran a clothing business and he was helping her find her feet following the death of her husband. And it was London he came up from, not Norwich; which is why, from time to time, he stayed the night. It was, after all, a very long way for a day trip.

Martha pursed her lips and looked studiously into the fire as Ted leaned down and kissed her good night on the top of her forehead, just above her hairline. He glanced at his father, seeing the look of exasperation mingled with despair on his face at the attitude his mother was taking.

At breakfast on Monday he made his announcement. He pointed out to them that he would be going back on Tuesday, and would have to catch the twelve-seventeen train if he were to get to Liverpool Street on time. He very much wanted to be able to say goodbye properly to them, but he also needed to say goodbye to Thurza and spend a little time with her. Consequently, he would be going there for tea that afternoon, but would be home in time to have supper with the family at seven o'clock; if that were all right. His father accepted enthusiastically, and it seemed he had been speaking to Martha, for she agreed with reasonable grace. Eliza clapped her hands with delight, partly because she thought it was lovely if her brother might be forming an interest in Thurza Allsop, whom she liked very much indeed. Ruth smiled a sad smile for she loved her brother and hated the rift this war and its effects seemed to be causing.

At Thurza's cottage that afternoon, Mary, now quite settled in her role as chaperone, made the tea as the two of them sat in the parlour. Mary could not remember when she had heard two people so able to talk to each other with such ease, or sit in such comfort in silence. Ted occupied his customary place on the settee, but this time Thurza sat beside him rather than on her chair.

Faced with the prospect of leaving, and maybe never returning, Ted found conversation difficult. There were things he wanted to say, and didn't know if it were the time or the place, and did not want their last meeting do be marred in any way lest he overstep the mark. Sensing his mood, and understanding his difficulty, Thurza eased the conversation along with talk of inconsequentials, before realising that this was the wrong route. He wanted something else from this afternoon, and she felt she knew what it might be. She switched to asking how he felt about going back, and that opened him up yet again. He now had complete confidence in her, and once more he began to talk. She was the only person to whom he had ever exposed his fear, and the raw nakedness of it frightened her.

She reached out, and with her hand behind his head pulled his face down onto her shoulder, stroking the back of his head. The warmth of the fire, the fresh smell of her soap, the softness of her hand-knitted cardigan all had their effect on him, and he felt the rousing of his passion. He had harboured such thoughts of her before, but now, so close, things began to develop a momentum of their own. She knew what was happening, sensed it almost before it started, had known that it might and had already laid her plans.

Lifting his head gently she looked into his eyes. “No, Ted, not now;...... not yet.” She had her free arm holding his right wrist, preventing his arm from looping round her in an embrace. She kissed him gently on the forehead. “Not now my duck. C’mon, let’s squeeze that second cup of tea out of the pot.”

“I’m sorry, I’m very sorry.” He was getting up, making to leave. Damn, why had he had to overstep the mark?

“Ted!” That note of firmness in the voice again. She held his hand. “Ted, sit down.” He complied. She had one hand on his lower thigh and another holding his left hand. “Ted, don’t be silly.” She smiled. “It’s only natural, there’s nothin’ t’ be ashamed of. It’s a complement that you find me so attractive.”

Attractive? She was the most attractive thing he could remember ever having seen. As the thought passed through his mind so did red lips, red nails and Belfast dockside railings; but he dismissed those very swiftly. “I....” He began to speak, but she cut him off.

“This tea’s had it. I’ll make some fresh.”

An hour later and it was time to leave. Neither of them wished it to be so, but time moved relentlessly on, and he had his obligation to his family. He stood, about to open the door, and unsure of how to finish it. She, knowing his discomfort and uncertainty, sought to help.

“You’ll write, won’t you; and more than you have been?” She was smiling, wickedly.

He wanted to say so much, to declare his love, to ask her to be his wife; but throughout they had skated round any permanence in what, up to then, they had referred to as their friendship. Finally, he plucked up courage, and began to speak: “Thurza, will you...., I mean, if I was to...., well. Will you....”

She held up her hand, palm outwards, and placed the tips of her fingers on his mouth. “I’ll be here, Ted, when you get back.” She raised herself on her toes and, for the first time, kissed him on the lips; a soft, warm, dry kiss. As she did so she thought, privately, "if you get back."

Tears in his eyes he turned and walked down the path, his mind, and some parts of his body, in turmoil. She watched him go, until he was out of sight, waving until he disappeared. Mary, standing behind her saw the tears in her mistress's eyes as she turned back into the house, and she headed straight for the kitchen and the kettle. Thurza sat in front of the dying fire. "Aye, Ted, I'll be yer wife if yer make it back." She had known that since the Sunday afternoon, but had determined not to make any final commitment, physical or spiritual, until this war was over and she could be certain of a future. One disaster in her life was enough. It would be bad enough if he was killed now, but to have committed herself, in any form, would have just made it worse.

The cart was parked outside the cottage. Bert Chalmers, at Agnes' insistence, had supplied it and old Ted would drive his son to the station. The hugs and farewells seemed as if they would go on forever, but eventually he climbed onto the cart and they headed south, towards the church and on out of the village. As he passed Thurza's cottage she was there in the doorway, waving, and blowing him a kiss. He sat back as they all passed out of sight, a sharp pain in his stomach and a lump in his throat that prevented speech. In silence they moved on, the horses' hooves clip clopping on the cobbled road, the cart lurching along over the uneven surface.

He thought back to the previous evening, and the very special effort everyone had made to make sure he was properly sent off. Ruth's contribution had been to tell Bernard not to be there. As he had gone to bed, Martha had held him long and hard in a hug, and as he kissed her goodnight he had tasted the salt in the wet tears on her face. Lying in bed he had cried, and had felt very much afraid.

The train was on time. As it drew in old Ted looked at his son. "Look after yerself, son." It was trite, but there really was nothing else to be said.

"Aye, dad, I will." Equally trite.

The guard, impatient to be on time, was moving their way in order to shut the door. Ted did it for him. Leaning out of the window he looked at his father as the train began to move away. "Give my love to mum!"

He saw, but did not hear: "I will. Take care now," and then he was gone. Ted sat down on the hard, third class seat and, ignoring his fellow passengers, stared out of the window at the passing Norfolk countryside, consumed with his own thoughts.

"Hallo, Ted, how did it go?" Colin's voice was unmistakable. He looked really buoyed up, as if he had really had a marvellous time; which he had. He had been mollycoddled completely by an adoring mother and aunt, eaten well, drunk well and slept as well as any of them could with the horrors that were implanted in their minds. And now he was heading back to the woman he loved.

"Fine, it were all right."

"And Mrs Allsop, how was she? Did you meet her? How much time did you spend with her? And how are your parents?"

"Fine, fine. 'Ang on a minute, mate, one question at a time." Ted seemed a little grumpy. No matter, Colin was quite happy that his friend would tell him what had happened in his own good time, if he felt the need.

"Come on then, we've got a bus to catch. The train leaves from Charing Cross at four o'clock on the dot. Mustn't be late."

Ted fell in alongside his friend and they headed out under the archway of Liverpool Street station into Bishopsgate to catch the bus that would start their journey together back to the war they had managed to escape for all too brief a period. The thought of not returning had not entered their heads, neither of them, not once.

Chapter 15

Gassed

Something was wrong, and for the life of him Colin Baxter could not work out what it was. They had arrived back on the train on time, accompanied by a new draft for the battalion, commanded by a young officer. Accordingly, transport was waiting to meet them, and they boarded one of a couple of double-decker buses for the journey. With the buses, as a guide, had been a corporal from battalion headquarters, whom Colin knew quite well. Colin's cheerful greeting had, however, been met with a look of uncertainty, and then one of clear relief as the young officer asked what was happening and he could get on with organising the party. It had been no accident that he had made sure he was on a different bus to Colin and Ted.

Arriving in battalion HQ the mystery deepened. Several people whom they knew barely acknowledged them, and the response from the orderly room quartermaster sergeant when they asked the whereabouts of the company was cursory and, so it seemed, embarrassed. Ted, looking round as they walked towards where their platoon was apparently located, grew more alarmed as he saw a small group of soldiers pointing them out and clearly talking about them. "Sommat were up, an' that were fer sure."

As they walked into the company area there were a couple of soldiers undergoing Number One Field Punishment, and in particular that element of it which involved being tied to a wagon wheel for a couple of hours, exposed to the elements. It was meant to be uncomfortable and undignified, and it was. There had been more and more of it dished out as the old regular soldiers were disappearing and the replacements did not posses the same sense of discipline. Colin had always found it barbaric, and chose to look away as they walked past. He wondered what petty crime they had perpetrated.

Looking at the equipment and the preparation being undertaken by men around them they were quickly aware that they would be heading for the trenches very shortly. A wrench of their guts as the spasm of anxiety passed through them; but it had only been what they might have expected. They passed the estaminet on their way to the billet, Colin knowing that he would have to report in and see to his duties before anything else, but desperate nonetheless to see Jacqueline. Ted wondered if Colin had noticed that the estaminet, which would normally be open and doing a brisk trade, was, in fact, quiet and apparently deserted. Jim Collis looked up as they entered, the smile that had been on his face wiped clear as he saw who it was. Scrambling to his feet, the bolt of his rifle, which he had been cleaning, falling carelessly to the floor, he rubbed his hands down the sides of his hips and outer thighs. His tongue ran across his lips, and he appeared nervous. In the gloom behind him there was movement and Colin saw Alfie, Alfred and Ned heading his way.

Ted wondered if Colin had noticed the two chevrons of a corporal freshly sewn onto Ned Preece's jacket. Probably not, as he was concentrating all his attention on Collis. At the back of the billet someone spoke quietly, and someone laughed, a dirty laugh. One look from Alfie James was enough to silence whoever it had been, and the miscreant was invited to present himself after the evening meal for a discussion about his future, which at that stage in the proceedings did not look too rosy.

"Sergeant, what on earth is going on?" Colin's voice held a real note of concern, for it was clear that something had happened that affected him. All sorts of thoughts were passing through his mind, and it was as Collis was about to say something, and as he noticed the new chevrons on Ned's sleeve, that he heard Paul Cooper's voice behind him.

"Corporal Baxter," the tone direct and matter-of-fact. He turned.

"Sir!"

"Corporal Baxter, come over into my quarters,....... Now!" The last word cut off the question that was framing on Colin's lips. He fell in behind the sergeant major and remained silent until the door of the small room, at the end of a large barn, closed behind him.

Ted looked at Alfie, conscious of the silence that had pervaded since Cooper had appeared. "Wot the fookin' 'ell is goin' on?" Briefly it crossed his mind how swiftly he had slipped into the vernacular now he was back with the Army.

"It's Jacqueline." It was Alfred who spoke up after a brief, awkward silence. "She's been raped." A simple matter-of-fact statement, spoken gently and quietly, almost as if it were Ted's girl of whom they were talking.

"She's been what?" Each word rising in pitch as he spoke, and then sat down on a bale of hay, the shock having taken the strength from his legs. "My Gawd," and as he spoke he thought of his friend receiving the news from Cooper, for that was surely why he had been called to his presence. "When did it,...I mean oo'd do such a thing?" He looked up at Alfie, towering above him, his face a picture of misery. Somehow, despite the horror they faced daily, and the fact that many of them joked about sex and some even went with the prostitutes in the Red Lamp Establishments, the defiling of a young girl, especially one they knew, liked and respected, was a matter of great regret.

"It happened the night you went on leave, about eight that evening." Jim Collis had taken the initiative. "It was Joe Floyd."

"It was who?" The note of incredulity in his voice. "Joe? Is that why Ned's been made up?"

Jim nodded. "Aye, put 'em up yesterday, after the court martial." He paused, and then carried on in response to the unspoken question on Ted's face. "Yep, they acted bloody fast once they knew 'oo it was. Captain sez it were t' keep the locals 'appy that justice were done quick an' positive, like."

"How.....?" As he asked the question he knew his friend would need him as soon as he came out of Cooper's billet.

"She were out the back, in the dark, collecting sommat from that shed they 'ave just at the back by the trees. She said a soldier attacked 'er, dragged 'er onter a coupla crates, biffed 'er with sommat so she were aht o' it. She remembered 'er skirt bein' lifted and the next thing 'e were at it, like." He saw the look on Ted's face. Embarrassed, he continued: "Got all that from me mate 'oo were in charge o' the escort."

"Is she.....?" He felt guilty at not having asked the question earlier.

"Yeah, she's awlroit. 'Er mum and dad've taken 'er away fer a coupla days, 'cos she were knackered after the court. That's why the pub's shut. Anyway, after this bloke's finished she staggers back inter the pub, cryin loik, and there's a coupla military police in there. They rushes aht the back and lo an' be'old there, wiv is clovin' in disarray," he emulated a policeman at his most pompous, "were Joe Floyd."

He carried on with his story, more relaxed now he was in full flow. Joe had not had an alibi of any sort and on the basis of that, of his disarranged clothing and of the girl's testimony that it had been a soldier, although she could not swear which one and had no means of so doing, he had been tried and found guilty. It appeared that, apart from grunts, he had remained silent throughout the attack except for the one word, hissed in spite: "bitch!" As she had given her evidence she had wiped her hand across her face, for not only had he spat out the word with his mouth close to her face, but as her ordeal was ending he had dribbled onto her face, over her nose, her eyes and her lips and for all the world she wished to wipe away that particular part of the memory. She shuddered every time the recollection of it came back, but had not mentioned it in her evidence; it had not seemed relevant.

"Fifteen years 'ard labour 'e got." The tale was ended,

and just at that moment the door to Paul's billet opened and a white, shaking Colin Baxter emerged, with Cooper in the doorway behind him. They saw the look in his eyes as he motioned them towards Colin, and as one they headed in his direction, Ted in front and trying desperately to work out what to say. In the end they all stopped in front of him, speechless in their shared hurt and embarrassment. Ted smelt a whiff of rum, obviously provided by the sergeant major, and it gave him his entrée.

"C'mon, we'll get yer some more o' that," and taking his friend's arm he escorted him over to the barn in which they were billeted. Alfie, having gone ahead, had the rum bottle and a half full enamel mug, one in each hand, as Colin sat, slumped, on the same bale of hay upon which Ted had received the news. He looked up, saw Ned and grinned, a bitter, horrid travesty of his normal smile.

"Well, at least one useful thing came out of it." He glanced at the stripes on his friend's arm. Ned looked acutely embarrassed and turned away.

"I'm sorry, I didn't mean to....."

"Salright." Ned turned back. Never finding it easy to show his emotions he responded in the only way he knew: "Bastard, innit?" It was inarticulate, but the sincerity of his friend's concern was clear for Colin to see.

"Yes, Ned, it's a bastard." And there they sat, in silence for much of the time, only talking when it was obvious that was what Colin wanted. Ted, whilst this was all going on, from time to time left his friend to go and sort out the new member of the section who had arrived in the draft that had travelled over with them on the boat. He had been less than charitable with the poor chap on their first meeting.

"Name?" The man to whom he spoke was hardly a callow youth, his age being somewhere in the mid twenties and he jerked a little in surprise at the terseness of the greeting, although he should have known what he might expect. After all, the NCOs at the depot had hardly been models of Christian charity, nor had they demonstrated any degree of sympathy for their charges.

"Curry. Private Edgar Curry." The voice was cultured,

and Ted was instantly reminded of Colin and of their first meeting way back in Belfast. Ted looked him up and down, regretting the tone of his initial greeting, and conscious that his friend needed him. He glanced at Colin, and Edgar Curry caught the look, feeling sympathy for the man who he did not yet know, but whose young lady had been defiled by some brute. He had heard nothing but good of Colin and Ted, and it had been made clear to him that he was lucky to be in their section. On balance, the treatment he had received was understandable.

Ted spent a couple of minutes talking to him before handing over to the senior private in the section with orders to "get 'im sorted", but did so in a much friendlier fashion. As for Colin, in the space of the next few hours his emotions passed through disbelief, anger, sadness, back to anger, resolve to do the right thing, whatever that was, back to anger; and then, finally, he dropped into an exhausted sleep, his last thought being that he had to find Jacqueline as soon as he could, and before the Army interspersed its authority and moved them back into the trenches. The only good news was that tomorrow's impending move into the line had been postponed for a few days; at least that was how long rumour said the delay would be.

Colin was right to be concerned that time might not be on his side, for as he slept the great men were contemplating moves that would affect the lives of tens of thousands; in many cases ending them.

Sir John French was unhappy, the War Council in London was unhappy and General Joffre was unhappy. French felt his plans to progress the war were being adversely affected by circumstances outside his control, not the least of which was the complete inability of the War Council to drive British industry into producing the equipment, weapons and ammunition he judged necessary to prosecute the war properly. For their part, the War Council were staggered by the huge losses and the lack of success on the Western Front, and the prospect of more to come. So bad had matters become that they had considered withdrawing the BEF back to England and "doing something else"; although no one was quite certain what that might be. Joffre believed that the BEF was too small and ineffectual to be of real value, and had been disappointed with its performance in December, when it had incurred huge casualties for what he considered to have been little effect. Furthermore, his agreement to plug the line at Ypres after the battle there in November was weakening him elsewhere and adversely affecting his plans for further offensives against the Germans. It did not help that the Germans had spent the winter digging in and strengthening their defences on higher, and consequently drier, ground and would be even harder to dislodge.

Joffre was developing plans to undertake attacks on the vulnerable German lines of communication stretching back through the occupied territories to the homeland. If he could cut these he would, as he saw it, force the capitulation of the Germans and their withdrawal from French soil. At the same time, French was contemplating an attack in the area of Neuve Chapelle, south of Ypres, on the British right, in order to take and hold the Aubers Ridge. Only fourteen miles long, and barely high enough to be called a ridge, it was, nonetheless, a feature offering considerable tactical advantage to the possessor and French determined to make it his. His problem was that Joffre's plans required the withdrawal of the French Army from the Ypres salient and their replacement by British troops. To do this, reinforcements were required and although some arrived the balance of those promised were diverted to support a naval expedition planned for the Dardanelles. He would, therefore, need to plug his gaps using his own resources; and the Norfolks would form a part of that move into the line around the beleaguered city; but not just yet.

He approached the back door of the estaminet, his mouth dry and his palms sweating with the apprehension of what might be about to befall him. He could not recall feeling in such a funk, even at the moment before an attack when that sense of naked vulnerability to the randomness of enemy artillery and small arms fire made one want to curl into a tiny ball until the badness had passed away. He knocked and heard a responding movement beyond the door, with a male voice calling out to someone else that he would answer it. It was her father's voice. The door opened and there he stood. Concerned that his daughter had taken up with a soldier, and an English one at that, he had always maintained his distance from Colin; and as he recognised who it was a look of naked hostility crossed his face. After all, it was one of his kind, one of his comrades, who had violated his Jacqueline.

"M'sieu, je......" He tried to speak, but before he could really begin to say anything his words were drowned in a torrent of vitriolic French, condemning the whole of the British Army, and him and his friends in particular, and with a special mention for Joe Floyd for whom public castration and starving to death, naked in the open in a cage, would have been the soft option.

He was about to turn away and close the door, leaving Colin outside, when Jacqueline's mother appeared in the doorway, her tiny frame squeezing round in front of her husband. She saw the look of abject misery on the boy's face, turned her face up towards her husband and, gently, bade him cease. He ignored her. The next time she asked there was a somewhat firmer note in her voice and he, spotting what was obviously a losing wicket, lapsed into silence with a scowl. Turning to Colin she held out her hand to take hold of his and lead him into the relative dimness of the back kitchen of the estaminet. She knew what her husband did not: that these two had cemented something, and they both needed to confront each other in the new circumstances.

"Asseyez vous." She indicated the chair by the scrubbed oak table and he took a seat. A cup of coffee appeared and then she was gone, leaving him to sip his drink and stare disconsolately at the half loaf of bread and two or three slices of smoked bacon lying on the table, and which had been forming the basis of an early lunch. He carefully avoided looking at her father, who remained in the room, a menacing figure in the corner, facing the wall and doing something with a rabbit that would see it in the pot for supper.

He heard a noise on the stairs, and, half standing, looked in anticipation at the doorway, disappointment registering when he saw it was Madame. Then she stepped to one side, to be replaced by Jacqueline. She wore a dress buttoned to the neck, a handkerchief in her left hand held up against her mouth, her right forearm across her body supporting the left elbow. It was a picture of a young woman in a state of unbearable tension, facing something she had no wish to face and terrified of the outcome. She looked closely at him as he stared back at her, searching out the accusation in his eyes, the laying of blame at her feet, the revulsion as he inspected a woman defiled whom he would no longer wish to touch or have anything to do with.

She watched as he stood, slowly, placing his cup on the table as he did. He was looking directly into her eyes, but the shadow hid what was in them; and there was no smile on his face. With a heart rending sob she turned away, and made as to move back up the stairs. In a second he was there, his hand lightly, but firmly, on her arm, a gentle pressure to turn her back, to face him. His hands were on her shoulders, trying to bring her face square onto him as she resisted. The pressure was just enough to bring her round, without causing any pain. She felt a hand alongside her right cheek, bringing her head reluctantly to the point where her eyes would have no choice but to meet his; unless she kept them closed, which she did. She felt the gentle touch of his lips just below her eyes as he kissed at the tears. She lifted her eyelids and saw before her a face displaying such tenderness and such misery, with tears of its own trailing in floods to fall unchecked somewhere on the floor below.

"Je t'aime." It was simple, it was all it needed: the unembellished statement of his unequivocal love for her, with no conditions. With a sob that poured from the depths of her soul she threw her arms around his neck and cried and cried. Standing there for what seemed an age, and was certainly several minutes, he just held her and let it all pour out. When she was ready, he disentangled himself and led her gently to the small sofa in the corner of the room by the fire, making sure he held onto her hand as he did so. He somehow felt that if he let go her fragility would cause the magic of this moment to shatter. Mother placed two glasses of cognac on the small table near where they sat, and headed for Father with another. The man was leaning back against the workbench, the entrails of the rabbit discarded in a bucket at his feet. Not one given to great bouts of emotion where human relations were concerned, even he had been moved by the obvious feeling these two had for each other. Quaffing his brandy in a single gulp he paused and glanced at Mother. This was not the raw spirit they sold to their unsophisticated customers; she had broken out the good stuff, and he regretted the speed with which he had swallowed some very fine cognac. Holding out his glass he motioned for a refill, and turned back to the rabbit, wondering if it would feed four, since that was clearly what it was going to have to do. On the sofa Jacqueline was still crying and trying to explain to Colin, between sobs, what had transpired on that dreadful night just under a week ago.

As it was, a week was to pass before they moved back up into the line, to replace the Dorsets in the trenches. It had been a good break, but it was not uncommon for units to spend quite long periods out of the line. There were twelve thousand men in a British division, and at any one time only a quarter of them would expect to be in the front line. During the week a great deal of time was put into training new arrivals and bringing new officers up to the mark, although the platoon would continue for the time being with Jim Collis in command. Ned Preece, Alfie and Alfred took their leave, and returned within the five days, Ned with the news that he was to be a father for the second time. He had known before he left, but, never one to risk exposing himself to any ridicule, had had kept it to himself until he was certain. Of the three, he was the one who was morose, having left something more than chums in the pub, as in

Alfie's case, and aged parents, as in Alfred's case. Ted left him to the other two, concentrating his attentions on Colin whenever necessary. The rest looked on as the five musketeers, so christened by some wag in January, watched over each other.

Joe Floyd's time was spent much less productively, or pleasantly. He had been incarcerated since the moment of his conviction in a small building not unlike that in which John Hayes had spent his last few hours on earth. Exercise had been denied him, largely because there was a fair amount of adverse feeling about the place, in both the military and civilian population, and it was easier to keep him out of sight. The window had been blocked other than for a slit at the top, as much to prevent others looking in as to stop him looking out.

He was a bitter and frustrated man, and had been proclaiming his innocence of the crime ever since that terrible moment when two military policemen had emerged in a great rush from the back of the estaminet and fallen on him like avenging angels. He could scarcely believe his ears as the evidence had mounted against him: how he had been found with his clothing in disarray; how he had been seen on various occasions looking covetously at the victim; how he had been seen to leave the estaminet some little time before she had left to go out back, and on the way had tried to put his arm round her, and been rebuffed.

No one would listen as he had tried to explain that he had tripped and fallen into her. No one was interested in the fact that he had gone out for a pee, although he did not add in his evidence that the event had been prolonged a little in order to relieve a different kind of pressure. No one paused to consider that, having raped her, he was hardly likely to have hung around the back of the pub, or that he was on his way to it and not away from it.

Instead, they had charged him under the Army Act in that he, at Dranouter, on the tenth of February 1915, had, contrary to Section 48 of the Offences Against the Person Act of 1861, raped Jacqueline La Saint. The trial had been over almost before it had started, and he had been sent down for fifteen years hard labour. He had been scarcely able to believe any of it, and certainly not do anything about it. Anger, bitterness and frustration tore at his very insides, but he could see no way out; there was no way out.

The morning Joe Floyd began his journey back to England, to the fearsome prison on Dartmoor, Colin moved off with the platoon, following a tearful farewell. He promised to write every day and to get back when he could; but they both knew that billeting in Dranouter could not continue forever and that the war would pull them apart as it had so many. As he left, he was conscious of the effect of the rape on her and that he had a great deal of building to do before their relationship could get back to normal. They had all agreed that once he moved from the area so should she, to stay with an aunt in the seaside town and port of Boulogne. She would not be, could not be, exposed to the lascivious leers of estaminet customers, or be placed at any risk that someone might try his luck on a pretty French girl. The question of what might happen if the assault had resulted in conception had not been discussed, but Madame, in selecting which of her several sisters to look after her daughter, had chosen the midwife; a midwife who had access to means whereby pregnancies could be terminated cleanly and without fuss. Her letter of explanation had covered all eventualities; there would be no adverse consequences.

They remained in the trenches for three days before being relieved by the Northumberland Fusiliers, whereupon they marched to Bailleul and went into divisional reserve, where they were to remain until the second of March. There was no opportunity for the lovers to meet, and on the third of March, as they left to go to Ouderdom, Colin wrote to Jacqueline to say that now was the time for her to head west. He could not say, but he had heard from contacts in the battalion headquarters that they were on their way into the Ypres salient and they would not be coming back this way for some time. From Ouderdom they moved forward to Kruistraat, just a mile or so to the south-west of Ypres town centre, and, after a couple of days in brigade reserve, took over a trench line to the south-east of Ypres from the Cheshires.

This remained the pattern for weeks to come: constantly moving between Ouderdom, Kruistraat and the trenches, in brigade and divisional reserve or holding the line. The holding of the line varied in its difficulty, depending on the attitude of the Germans and the high command. One huge benefit had been the introduction, in February, of a periscope with which to view the enemy. This had greatly improved morale, and significantly reduced casualties from enemy snipers. It was now possible to see without being exposed. Apart from one day, the fourteenth of March, where an attack in another part of the line had brought shelling down onto them, there had been few casualties; not that the fourteenth had not been bad enough. The medical officer, Lieutenant McCurry, had been killed along with six others, together with nineteen wounded.

As they conducted their business in relative quiet, further to the south the attack on Neuve Chapelle and on to the Aubers ridge had been launched and had failed. It had not failed for want of impetus by Thomas, or the desire by commanding officers to push on beyond early objectives they had seized swiftly and with gusto. It had failed because poor communications had hampered the staff in making their decisions and irresolute command and control at the higher, operational, level had imposed delay after frustrating delay. As usual it was Thomas who paid the price, and who summed up the outcome in his own way. His officers, at regimental level, were no less scathing, if perhaps somewhat more eloquent, in their condemnation of a shambles that need not have been. Despite a Times leader that proclaimed six thousand dead Germans and two thousand prisoners; despite the fact that the British had demonstrated to the French that they could assault as well as they could defend; despite the fact that they had penetrated formidable German defences and broken the enemy line, they did not have possession of Aubers ridge. It was, therefore, a “bleedin’ cock up!”

The trench was foul. It looked out over a wide expanse of muddy ground, pock marked with shell holes and smothered in barbed wire entanglements, established by both sides. It was the last day of March and the weather was showing a distinct improvement. At least it was not so cold, especially at night, even if it was still very wet. Daffodils and Crocuses could be seen growing at the front of houses as they moved into the line, the birds were getting progressively more and more boisterous and there was a general feeling of spring in the air. Ted was standing on the fire step beside Edgar Curry. Over the few weeks he had been with the section they had got to know each other well, and Ted found him easy to talk to. They were taking turns at peering through the periscope at the German positions only a hundred or so yards away from their own, and discussing the news, heard an hour or so ago, that their new platoon commander was to join them that morning. Ted reflected that it seemed an age since Charles Hawthorn had been killed, but such was the shortage of officers extended gaps had to be accepted.

“Ugh!” Ted started as he heard the exclamation of disgust from Edgar.

“Wot?” He looked away from his periscope and watched as the other man withdrew his hand from the front wall of the trench where a part of it had given way. Looking down at the excavation Ted could see the decomposing remains of a human face embedded in the mud, an empty eye socket staring back at them both, a worm crawling around the rotted aperture. Even with his experience of horror, Ted recoiled; and Edgar vomited up his breakfast into the back of the trench. Ted, swiftly filling soil into the hole with his entrenching tool, turned to pat him on the back as he rose from bending forward, supporting himself with his hand on the back wall of the trench.

“Sorlroit. ‘T’appens. Sometimes there’s no toim t’ bury

'em an' they stays in the trench, or around somewhere, an gets dug up agin. You all roit?"

Edgar wiped his mouth with the back of his hand, and shuddered. "Surely we can do better than that? Surely a man is entitled to a decent burial if we can give him one. I mean, shouldn't we be digging him up and doing something?"

"Yeah, an' yer'd be doin' it every bleedin' day fer the rest o' the soddin' war. Best leave 'im, an' keep 'im covered or yer'll 'ave the bleedin' rats in 'ere afore ye can say Jack Robinson. Down!" The last word was emphatic and direct as the artillery fire began to fall around them. Ted, squinting into the periscope, sought out the enemy positions, looking for any sign of an attack, but there was nothing. It was simply speculative artillery fire to disrupt the pattern of life and to inflict a few casualties; in much the same way as the pestilential snipers sought to do.

"Gerrout, and get up in there!" Ted heard Alfie's voice and turned with interest to see his friend, for he had been sent back to collect the new officer. The recipient of his invective was one of the new soldiers in his section who, on hearing the artillery fire whilst in the communication trench, had taken cover, without being given an order to do so, in the nearest available spot. Regrettably, he had chosen a latrine trench and when he emerged from his hiding place he smelt rather less attractive than when he had entered it. The rest of his section could simply not contain their mirth, and as Ted watched them, and joined in the general laughter, he saw the new platoon commander out of the corner of his eye.

"Good morning Lance Corporal Ludgrove."

Barely able to believe the evidence of his own ears he turned, his right hand moving into a salute yet stopping before it had gone half way. His mouth half open and a look of complete surprise on his face he stared into the cornflower blue eyes of Second Lieutenant James Woolford.

The next morning, the thirty-first of March, they handed over their trenches to the King's Own Yorkshire Light

Infantry to move back to Ouderdom as part of the divisional reserve. During the night Ted had not been able to talk to his old friend as the new officer had so much to do, and, frankly, he found that something of a relief for he did not know how to handle the situation. The respite overnight had given him time to collect his thoughts. Really, he had no choice and knew he would have to stick with the formalities of the situation. However, he had seen the closeness between Paul Cooper and Matthew and knew it was possible to maintain friendship and mutual respect at a distance and well within the bounds of professional discipline. Indeed, in very many cases that was the basis of the relationship between good officers and good NCOs.

He had thought briefly of Cooper and Captain Jenkins. Cooper had left just after the rape incident to go back and be RSM in a training unit somewhere on the coast, and they had last heard of Matthew being sent back on sick leave a couple of weeks ago with a bad chill that had got to his chest. Eddie Macleary had fallen into a trench during renovation work and had broken his leg, so he was gone too. It was one of those moments when he felt an ache of loneliness in the pit of his stomach: so many of them were gone, or going; and what chance was there for the few of them left that they might survive. His mouth dried as the fear shot briefly through him, then he shook himself into action and chivvied a couple of soldiers for no real reason at all.

The first of April dawned a bright Spring day, and they received the good news that they were to be in reserve for a good ten days. Time to reconstitute, to bed in some of the new drafts of reinforcements that were arriving and to do some training. New equipment was entering service, such as rifle grenades and trench mortars, and skills needed to be developed so that they could be properly used. The first duty, however, that day was rather more sombre. During the hand over there had been German speculative fire and the adjutant, Captain Megaw, a very popular officer, had been killed. His funeral was held on the ramparts of the city of

Ypres, and following it many of the veterans were in reflective mood as they set about the business of the day.

James Woolford's problem was that he was about to lose his platoon sergeant. Jim Collis had a very bad case of Trench Foot, and would have to be evacuated and hospitalised for some considerable time.

"But I thought you only contracted this in the cold, and with constantly wet feet?" James was looking down as the sergeant from the medical section examined his fellow NCO's feet as he lay back on the stretcher. Looking over his shoulder James could see that the flesh was pale and lifeless and really looked liked the early onset of frostbite, which he had seen once before.

"No sir, no, not at all. It's caused by damp conditions, but it usually happens when the temperature is above freezing. It doesn't help if boots or puttees are too tight." He looked up into James' enquiring eyes. "Restricts the blood flow sir, and that aggravates the condition. The trick is to catch it early." As he spoke he looked away from James and accusingly into Jim Collis' eyes. Collis looked away. He knew what was going through the man's mind: he'd encouraged the condition and not reported it until it was so bad he would have to be sent home, for a while at least.

"How long…?" James left the question unfinished.

"Could be weeks," said the medical orderly. "In fact, if he develops gangrene, which he might when it's this bad, he'll lose a foot or two and you'll never get him back. Still," he looked meaningfully at Collis, "no loss is it?" and as he turned to face James he was smiling, as if he had been joking. Jim Collis lay back on the stretcher looking up at the dugout roof above him, not sure if he was afraid, elated or ashamed. Probably he was all three, in turn; but at least he was out of it.

"As you know, the rest of the battalion moved up yesterday, the tenth of April, into the line outside Ypres at a place called Verbranden Molen." James consulted his notebook and read the complicated name slowly and deliberately. Our company is to go forward today to join them, and to begin with we shall be in battalion reserve. Sergeant Baxter."

"Sir." Colin looked up from his notebook, the chevrons still new on his sleeve from yesterday when the RSM had called him in, advised him that he was not fit to walk this earth with other human beings, discussed with him, in a one sided sort of way, whether or not both of his parents had been subnormal to have produced an object such as him, warned him that his life was about to become very complicated, largely due to the fact that he was improperly dressed and he only had fifteen minutes in which to sort himself out with a needle and thread before he would have the opportunity to accompany the RSM to the sergeants' mess and buy him a drink with the proceeds of his newly inflated salary.

It was, in the judgement of all right thinking men in the battalion, the best thing that could have happened, and there had been a huge chorus of approval from his friends when he had returned, somewhat the worse for wear, to the platoon of which he was now the sergeant. Equally good news, so far as they were concerned, had been Ted's elevation to corporal to command the section, and letters had already gone to an aunt in Cromer, a French girl in Boulogne and a Mrs Allsop in a Norfolk village. A letter to Ted's parents would follow when he had a bit more time. And James could count himself lucky to have such a collection of experienced NCOs to provide him with the support he was going to need; and he knew it.

Having got his sergeant's attention, James went on to explain how he wanted the move organised, and before a couple of hours had passed they were in Verbranden Molen, a small village, typical of the many they now knew. It lay beside the railway that runs south-east out of Ypres through Comines to Lille, at a point where it enters a long railway cutting and just five hundred yards from where the road to Zwarte-Leen, running roughly east to west, bridges the cutting. The Verbranden Molen to Hollebeke road, running south-east and pretty well parallel to the railway bisected the Norfolk's position and provided the axis against which all movement was marked, and, in many cases, targets indicated.

The German trenches were, on average, about two hundred yards from their own, up, for the most part, a gradient which, whilst by no means steep, offered their enemies the ability to direct fire onto the British trenches from either rifles and machine guns or artillery. They could also see very clearly soldiers in the open should the British choose to attack, for the lie of the hill gave them nowhere to hide. It was an exposed killing ground.

The railway formed the left boundary of the battalion and just over the railway bridge, and dominating the cutting and that part of the line held by the rest of the brigade, was a feature known as Hill 60, so called because of its height in metres as shown on the local maps. It was artificial, formed from the spoil resulting from the digging of the cutting when the railway was being built. It was occupied by the Germans, and it gave them a huge advantage. On the right of the cutting, immediately in front of the Norfolk's left hand company who were occupying the euphemistically named Trench 37 was another artificial hill, from the same source, known as the Caterpillar due to its elongated shape. Also a dominant feature, it was further away, very long and narrow, at ninety degrees to the line of the trenches and well wooded.

Hill 60 was seen to be the crucial lynch pin to the German defence system, the hinge upon which the Ypres salient turned. From here the ridges wound north-east to circle the city, and to the south was the Messines Ridge, bending like a huge question mark and dominating the Flanders Plain. The British high command had wanted, ever since they took the area back off the French, to take and hold those ridges, but after a series of fruitless infantry attacks had decided upon more unconventional means. Since the beginning of March men had been tunnelling deep beneath the Hill, covertly digging out huge caverns which would eventually take massive quantities of explosives, to be detonated when the time was right. It had been a huge undertaking: just the logistics of soil removal had been a major problem in its own right, to say nothing of the need for silence, for secrecy and for the cunning and strength of the men working in airless, fetid darkness for weeks on end. But now it was finished, and ready for its intended purpose.

The high command, however, received something of a shock on the fourteenth of April, as did the Norfolks and everyone else in the area, when, forty-five minutes before midnight, the night was shattered by the huge explosion of a German mine at St Eloi, some two and a half miles south of Ypres. It was followed by a methodical bombardment, the Germans having already preceded the mine with four days of pretty constant artillery fire. None of this had affected the Norfolks, whose time in their present trenches had been quiet, with really quite pleasant weather. The British artillery responded, assuming an attack to be imminent, but no enemy infantry appeared. The Germans had, however, drawn attention to that area, which may have been their intention, for that same day intelligence was received to say that:

> "a reliable agent of the detachment of the French Army in Belgium reports that an attack on the Ypres salient has been arranged for the night fifteenth/sixteenth of April. Reserves have been brought up and passages prepared to cross old trenches and to facilitate bringing forward artillery.
>
> The Germans intend making use of tubes with asphyxiating gas, placed in batteries of twenty tubes for every forty metres along the front of Twenty Sixth German Corps. This prisoner had in his possession a small sack filled with a kind of gauze or cotton waste which could be dipped in some solution to counteract the effect of the gas.
>
> The German morale is said to have much improved lately owing to the men having been told that there is not much in front of them. It is possible that the attack

may be postponed if the wind is not favourable so as to ensure that the gas blows over our trenches."

The amount of detailed knowledge imparted by this particular prisoner was in itself suspicious, and many were reluctant to place too much store by it, believing it to be disinformation, designed to confuse the British as to the German's true intent. The following day Number 6 Squadron of the Royal Flying Corps undertook a reconnaissance over the German lines and found nothing unusual, nor did there appear to be any concentration of troops; and the same would be true of subsequent flights over the next couple of days. The Norfolks remained in their trenches, and when he fell that evening to writing the regimental diary for the day the adjutant would simply record that they had experienced fine weather and that the situation was generally quiet.

That evening James returned from the captain's orders group with the news that an enemy attack was expected on the Ypres salient that night, and that a "demonstration" was to be delivered at one forty five in the morning in order to discourage them. At one thirty the whole company was to stand to, with grenadiers ready and rifle grenades primed on rifles but with the pins still in place.

The grenade in question was known, in military parlance, as the Grenade Rifle, Rodded, Percussion, Number Three, and to Thomas as the rifle grenade. Introduced into service on the sixteenth of February 1915, it had a steel cylindrical body, externally segmented over the whole of its surface. Its base was threaded to take a ten inch steel rod which fitted down the barrel of a rifle, and it was projected by a cartridge filled with ballastite, and with no bullet. The grenade became the "bullet", forced from the barrel by the gas pressure from the fired cartridge out to a range of two hundred yards. On hitting its target the grenade was set off by the force of impact driving forward a firing pin onto a detonator; and there was a safety pin in place to prevent that pin moving forward during normal handling. It was never removed until the grenade was firmly fixed in position in the rifle barrel.

The attack never materialised, and neither did the "demonstration", which had been planned as an artillery barrage. The next day dawned peacefully, and proceeded in much the same way as its predecessor. There was, however, some consternation in general headquarters when a report was received from the Belgians that twenty thousand mouth protectors were being manufactured in Ghent for the Germans. The implication was that gas, unused up to now, but always a fear, was about to be deployed. There was some speculative British artillery fire, but, since no German reinforcements seemed to have been brought up and no attack took place on the night of the fifteenth/sixteenth of April, GHQ paid no further attention to the suggestions or warnings of an attack, and especially one involving the use of gas. The French regarded them as a ruse to prevent troops being withdrawn from Ypres for their offensive which was in preparation near Arras; or an attempt to inspire terror by the threat of use of gas.

So far as the British were concerned the word "gas" meant little more to soldiers than a stink pot or the smell from bursting shrapnel or high explosive shell. It was presumed, no doubt, that the effects of "gas" would be trivial and local. Furthermore, at this stage no British officer believed that the enemy's leaders would depart from the usages of civilised warfare, and consequently dismissed the whole idea as fanciful.

That night, Thirteen Brigade took over part of the line opposite Hill 60 without attracting enemy attention, and this placed the Royal West Kents on the left of the Norfolks.

It was three in the afternoon when James called his platoon together, and from the excitement in his face it was clear that something was up. His section commanders felt a flicker of apprehension, having been at this for some time now they knew that an inexperienced officer's excitement often meant pain and grief for them. All working parties were drawn in so that everyone would hear what was going on.

"At seven this evening six mines will be fired under Hill 60 in three separate explosions. The first will be under the hill itself, the second in to the west of the hill, and opposite Trench 38, which is immediately to our left just over the railway. The third will go off opposite Trench 40, further away to the east. They will be fired at ten second intervals, so you must be prepared for them." He looked round his men. The younger ones were sharing his excitement, and whilst on the faces of his NCOs he read expectation, he also saw caution. He carried on.

"When the mines have exploded we will fire on the south-east corner of Hill 60. The rest of the company will be firing on the Caterpillar and into the trenches immediately to its front. Thirteen Brigade will assault the Hill immediately after the explosions, and then hold it. Any questions so far?" He looked round, and received only silence in reply.

"Shortly before seven, sections one and two on the left of the trench will close up to the right hand end in order to get away from the effects of the explosions, but will recover to their positions straight after the third one has gone off. There will be a company in the communications trench of Number 36 Trench, with a telephone link. All communications will be through them."

So it was, at six thirty five, having dined on tinned stew and tea, they were stood to in the trenches looking expectantly to their half left from where the explosions would come. James gave as much warning as he could, but his watch was slower than that of the man firing the charges and it was something of a shock when the earth surged and great gouts of mud, trees and rocks went flying into the air. Ted, watching in fascination, knew that there bits of men mixed up in that debris and tried not to think about it. Seconds later the second went off, this time much closer, and the ground in their trenches vibrated with the shock as bits fell off the breastworks and dropped onto their boots. All around them debris began to splatter on the ground, just as the third great explosion shook them.

"Back to your positions." James' voice, high pitched in its excitement, galvanised them into action as they squelched through newly arrived mud to take up their posts on the fire step. The targets had already been indicated and it was only necessary to shout "fire" for the familiar cacophony of noise that was British rapid rifle fire began pouring in to those few Germans who were left alive. Overhead the whoosh of British artillery competed with the noise of small arms, including machine guns, whilst trench mortars coughed their deadly little loads into what was left of the enemy trenches.

"Steady now." Colin's voice rang out above the noise. He had seen movement on their left. "Our boys are going in, aim away. Don't hit our own!"

The German response was immediately to inflict heavy artillery fire on the British, dropping shells all round the fire and support trenches; but there was practically no rifle fire. The attack roared in from their left, and very soon the Hill was in the hands of C Company the Royal West Kents. Surprise was complete. Those of the German garrison, a company of 172 Regiment of Fifteen German Corps, who had survived were overwhelmed. Some who resisted were bayoneted, the rest captured, with only seven British casualties. A supporting company of the Royal West Kents and two companies of the King's Own Scottish Borderers followed up as a carrying and working party, and with them followed the machine gun section of Queen Victoria's Rifles. James was beside himself with excitement.

"Gosh, just will you look at that." He was punching Ted on the upper arm as he spoke. Ted looked at him, and beyond to Colin on James' left.

"Aye, now they gotta bloody well stay there."

"And we need to straighten the line." The serious tone in Colin's voice caused James to calm down and look at him, preventing lasting damage to Ted's arm.

"Oh, you mean......?"

"Yes sir. Anything on that hill can now be enfiladed by Germans in those trenches," he pointed to the Caterpillar, "and anything on the other side beyond the railway." He paused, something had caught his eye and they looked away to their front to where some Germans were leaving their trenches, probably to escape.

"If I may, sir." Colin paused, barely waiting for a reply before issuing a flawless fire control order the result of which was a number of Germans toppling like rag dolls as the bullets tore into their bodies. It was swift and it was lethal, and James felt a little shocked by the ruthlessness of it.

At first the German artillery shot wildly and anywhere but at Hill 60. It then settled down to shelling the railway cutting south of the Hill, the trenches on either side, and continued in a sporadic fashion into the night until about ten o'clock when, supported by artillery, the enemy delivered three desperate counter attacks, coming in great waves. Some brave and determined individuals reached the parapet that the West Kents had thrown up. The fighting went on most of the night, with the Norfolks taking great care to keep their fire on areas where they knew they were targeting enemy; not an easy undertaking in the night and with the smoke and chaos caused by exploding artillery. They watched in the early morning as, by the light of flares, they saw two more companies heading onto the Hill.

"Poor bastards!" James looked reprovingly at Ned Preece, who showed no remorse. He had meant it; he knew what it was like up there.

As the dawn rose the German artillery fire on their trenches intensified, seeking to deny the troops on the hill the support available from the riflemen and machine guns. Slamming in all around them, they were forced to keep their heads down, feeling that familiar, dreadful nakedness, not knowing if, suddenly, they would be dismembered or destroyed in a blinding instant. James, whilst trying to maintain his composure, was feeling real fear. What had seemed to be something super, and a great adventure that would make a difference to the war, was already turning into a marathon of a slogging match, and they were deeply embroiled in it.

The inevitable casualties began to accrue, although a

direct hit inside a trench was necessary in order to do any serious damage. It was when heads were raised to try and fire at the enemy that the greatest risks were taken, and Ted lost a young soldier in his section, killed with a shot to the head, whilst Alfred saw two of his go down, one dead, one wounded, from the effects of a shell bursting near the front lip of the trench. James looked aghast at the side of one man's face, almost torn away and with the cheek and his teeth exposed for all to see. Alfie ripped the man's shell dressing from inside his pocket, and swiftly tied it round the wound, informing him that he ought to shut up and stop moaning, since the result of his injury would be to render him very much better looking, the victim having been an ugly bastard in the first place.

"Look up, and look to your front. Section commanders, get a grip." Colin's voice rang out. The inexperienced among them were beginning to focus on the wounded and forget the enemy. Instantly, Alfie, Ted, and Ned picked up the cry; and James learned a lesson.

Ted looked along the trench at his sergeant, his friend, with a conspiratorial grin on his face. The feeling of closeness, of being bonded in a team, of being a part of each other, had never seemed stronger; and the grin froze on his face. If there had been a change in the tone of Colin's voice he had not noticed it, but his friend was holding his right forearm with his left hand, or more properly the stump of his right forearm, and there was blood everywhere.

When a high explosive shell detonates the steel shell casing fragments into shards of razor sharp metal, blued by the heat of detonation and travelling at very high speed, propelled by the twenty thousand feet per second velocity of the detonating wave. Fitted with a time fuze, they can be made to detonate in the air, thereby sending their rain of deadly missiles down onto troops in the open or in trenches lacking overhead cover. Some of the shards are very small, and some can be quite large; the size, say, of a table knife. It was one such shard that had flashed down from above, and had severed Colin Baxter's right hand from his arm at a point three inches above the wrist; as neatly as a surgeon might have done it.

At first there had been no pain. Then the realisation struck him of what had happened, and the shock swept over him in waves, the feeling of nausea rising in his stomach, threatening to deploy the remnants of his last meal all over the bottom of the trench. He began to topple forward.

"Steady, mate, I've got yer." Alfie was there instantly. "Ned!" He looked up, seeing Ned acknowledge the call, and look aghast at Colin as he realised what had happened.

"Ned, keep these bastards lookin' t' the front." He saw the hesitation. "Go on, do it. Ted an me'll look after 'im. C'mon, mate." Gently the two men laid their friend on the ground. Ted, looking down, shifted the useless hand out of the way with his boot, shoving it into a small hole at the back of the trench. He would deal with that later, to keep the rats off it. He shuddered at the thought, as he held a brandy bottle against Colin's lips. James, looking on, felt completely useless.

"Leave them to that, you get back to your platoon."

He looked round to see the company commander standing behind him, looking grim faced.

"How is he?" said the captain as the young officer went back to where Ned Preece was filling his role as the most senior of the NCOs available to control the men.

Colin, looking up, smiled through his pain. "At least I'm left handed, which is helpful."

"Buggered yer salutin' arm, though, ain't it?" Ever quick witted, Alfie's black humour produced a smile from Colin who looked up at his officer. "You'll forgive me not standing, sir?"

"Of course, Sergeant Baxter, of course." Experience had taught the captain that the black humour, Thomas' anaesthetic from physical or mental pain, was something to play along with at times like this. "Corporal Ludgrove." Ted looked up from putting the final touches to a field dressing. "See he gets to the clearing station."

"Sir." A pause. "Thanks sir."

"Be sure you get back smartly now." He smiled. "Be off

with you. Corporal James, go and help Mr Woolford." He turned and went over to James, making a mental note that Corporal James was the next logical incumbent of the post now vacated by Colin Baxter.

The Norfolks' stretcher bearers were busy that day. The battalion lost two officers wounded, one mortally, eleven soldiers killed and another forty-six wounded. Ted accompanied the two men carrying Colin, and as they approached the regimental aid post he could see that it was crowded to overflowing, with wounded propped up against the trenches on either side of it. Colin, in that melée, stood little chance of swift attention, and he decided simply to move on the two miles to the casualty clearing station. Secure in his pocket was the piece of paper, torn from the Captain's note book, which cleared him to accompany the stretcher. Desertion was a charge too easy to lay, and too hard to deny for such precautions not to be necessary.

His approach to the CCS was no more encouraging than the RAP, but at least there were more doctors and orderlies and there was a chance of him being seen faster. However, getting there had extended their journey and by the time they arrived with their burden the two stretcher bearers were exhausted; and Colin was looking very pale and very much the worse for wear.

"Put 'im down there an' get back t' yer unit." The medical corps sergeant was in no mood for niceties.

"Will 'e........?"

Neither was he in a mood to answer questions.

"We'll get to 'im when we can, mate." He looked at Ted, a flash of sympathy crossing his face. "Chum, is 'e?"

"Aye. We'll get to 'im, but there's a queue an' 'e'll 'ave ter wait 'is turn."

Ted looked grim, but was resigned to the inevitable.

"Where will 'e go when yer've finished, loik. I mean, 'e's lost 'is arm so 'e's goin' 'ome, that's fer sure." He felt a wave of relief as the thought struck him, for the first time, that his friend was now safe if he could survive the ordeal of the wait and the surgery.

"Poperinge an' then Boulogne, that's where they're all goin'. Now bugger off an' let me get on wiv me work."

As Ted got back to the trench he nodded, with more confidence than he felt, at the enquiring looks of his friends. He would give them the details later. For the rest of the day there was very heavy shelling and fighting continued all day on the Hill. Reports of strange smells began once more to fuel the idea that gas was being used by the enemy, although no one exhibited any effects. During the day the Germans recovered part of the Hill, and at six in the evening the Norfolks bore witness to a counter attack by two battalions: the Royal West Kents and the King's Own Yorkshire Light Infantry. The commanding officer and second-in-command of the West Kents were killed as was the officer commanding the lead company. However, by the end of it Thirteen Brigade was once again in possession of the whole Hill.

As this was going on their attention was diverted from what was happening to their front by the opening of a bombardment of Ypres with huge German howitzers of seventeen inches in calibre. The enormous shells were fired in pairs, and passed through the air with a noise described by one of the soldiers as being "like a runaway tramcar on rusty rails." The fuzes being used by the Germans had a delayed action. It was for less than a second, but it meant that the shells had buried themselves quite a long way into the ground before detonating, and so the effect was much more destructive of land and buildings. The craters they made were enormous, and it was on this day that the destruction of Ypres really began. The Cloth Hall which, although roofless from the first Battle of Ypres, had retained a semblance of a structure enough to hold two battalions, now had to be evacuated completely. By the twenty-first of April the shops and cafes which had been re-opened were again closing down and the inhabitants leaving.

Meanwhile, the struggle for Hill 60 continued, and the Norfolks watched, almost as disinterested spectators. The new arrivals, including James, had become hardened to the noise and effects of battle, and were getting used to the fact that occasionally one or two of them would disappear, wounded or killed. Apart from some speculative fire against their trenches, seen as the closest which could give support to the Hill, life, whilst uncomfortable and from time to time dangerous, was not nearly so bad for them as it was for others. On the Hill itself, where men were fighting for their very existence, all traces of trenches had now disappeared. The surface was a medley of confluent mine and shell craters strewn with broken timber and wire and it was impossible to dig without disturbing the body of some British or German soldier.

In the meantime, the destruction of Ypres with the huge guns, accompanied by some smaller cannon, proceeded, the bigger shells being seen to lift whole houses into the air. Ypres was pronounced by Thomas as "eeps", but by now it was in such a state he was calling it "heaps".

The twenty-second of April was something of a landmark. A beautiful, sunny day and the Germans chose it to launch the first gas attack of the war, against the French in the north-east sector, away from the British. This was the opening move in what would become known as the Second Battle of Ypres; but for the Norfolks it was the ground around Hill 60 that was to absorb their attention. However, the gas attack did prompt the British into developing some form of protection and muslin gauze masks were made, with elastic to hold them in place, with instructions that they be wetted and placed over the mouth in the event of an attack. If possible they were to be dipped in a solution of bicarbonate of soda which was kept in buckets in the bottom of the trench for the purpose.

Only a small amount of the muslin flannel gauze and elastic was available to make the gas masks, and officers were despatched to Paris to purchase material which was made up in the small towns at the front. The Daily Mail called on the women of England to make a million, but whilst this was going on Thomas just carried on, lookin' to 'is front.

However, the emphasis of fighting had now moved round to the north of Ypres and to the battles round the Gravenstafel Ridge in late April, St Julien from the twenty-fourth of April to the fourth of May, Frezenberg Ridge between the eighth and thirteenth of May and Bellewaarde Ridge at the end of that month. Meanwhile, the fighting around Hill 60 just flogged interminably on, day after day for the rest of April, with the Norfolks being very much less involved than those on the other side of the railway cutting.

The first of May brought a major change, with the launch of a gas attack against Hill 60. Command of the Hill had shifted, and was now a Fifteen Brigade responsibility, Thirteen Brigade having been redeployed north to assist in repelling the German attacks on the salient. Consequently, it was the Dorsets now holding the Hill and the Norfolks remained in their trenches, thanking their lucky stars that they were not exposed on that ghastly, broken death-trap. At about seven o'clock, after a severe bombardment, the Germans, from less than one hundred yards, released gas on a front of four hundred yards. It shot over in volumes so quickly that very few men had time to adjust their extemporised masks, and one company was caught with them dry. Ted watched, numb with horror, as the cloud reached the men on the Hill, and as soon as it did the enemy opened rifle fire, attacked both flanks of the battalion with bombing parties and concentrated the guns to form a barrage on the approaches to the Hill.

A few of the Dorsets, all suffering from the effects of Chlorine, jumped onto the fire step and under the command of a young officer opened rapid fire. This, for the moment, saved the situation and just gave time for the supports of the Dorsets which were close at hand, together with the Devons, with the commanding officer working on his own initiative, and reinforcements of the First Bedfordshires, to charge through the gas cloud and reach the front before the Germans gained a footing. Bombers from the Devons and Dorsets drove them back.

The noise was horrendous, artillery fire crashing all around, rifle fire crackling, grenades detonating, men screaming and shouting. Close at hand was the sound of their own rifles, the high pitched noise of their firing hurting the eardrums of men on the fire step, pouring everything they had into the flanks of the enemy in order to assist their fellows on the Hill.

Unknowingly, they were watching the earning of a Victoria Cross: Private E Warner was awarded the decoration for conspicuous bravery in recovering and holding a vacated trench. He died shortly afterwards, from the effects of gas. But this part of the battle marked a stage in history as it was the first by which the enemy gained no advantage. Gas had been faced and defeated, although the Dorsets had suffered for it. Ninety men died from gas poisoning in the trenches or before they could be delivered to the dressing stations. Of the two hundred and seven who reached the dressing stations, forty-six died almost at once and twelve more after a long period of suffering.

James Woolford was beside himself with anger, and near him Alfie James was pounding the front edge of his trench in rage and frustration, the new sergeant's chevrons now muddied and dull after a week's wear in the trenches.

"Bastards," was a word heard routinely along the trench, and some younger ones were crying with rage as they saw the state to which their fellow soldiers had been reduced. Some of the Dorsets, blinded by the chlorine, staggered across the railway bridge and into the Norfolk trenches.

Chlorine has a powerful irritant effect on the respiratory system and all mucous membranes with which it comes into contact. It causes spasms of the glottis, a burning sensation in the eyes, nose and throat, followed by bronchitis and oedema of the lungs. Frequently there is evidence of corrosion of the mucous membranes, of the air channels and of the cornea.

Prolonged inhalation of a high concentration of the gas will cause death by asphyxia or, if not fatal, will produce cardiac dilation and cyanosis, or blueness of the skin. Translated into what was happening in front of them, they could see that the men caught by the fumes were in terrible pain; coughing and vomiting and rolling on the ground in agony. Some were already, at this stage, dying. Those with wet cloths round their mouths, breathing in through the mouth and out through the nose, were able to withstand it and keep going.

Ned Preece, bending over a Lance Corporal and trying to control the spasms of agony, feeling useless at his own inability to do anything, was heard to mutter that he would not, any more, be taking any prisoners. Bastards who could do this to a man did not deserve to live. He was not alone in his view, or in his expression of reluctance, in the future, to abide by the rules of war insofar as prisoners were concerned.

Their eyes and mouths stinging somewhat from the effects of the small amount of gas that had come their way, and once they had cleared the Dorset casualties, they waited to see what the rest of the day would bring, but it settled into the routine to which they had become accustomed. And so it was for several days to come: some German aggression, but nothing too serious, work to maintain the trenches, carrying parties to the rear for food and ammunition, battalion signallers coming forward and repairing telephone cable, watching out for snipers and trying to stay on their toes to meet the unexpected.

Ted and James had skated around each other for a while, neither of them sure of how to react to the other. They had been together in the platoon now for several weeks, and James had lost his schoolboy approach to the war. Their relationship really was as Ted had thought it might become, not unlike that between Matthew and Paul Cooper. As they became more attuned to their surroundings they had realised that it was possible to avoid the constant use of ranks and the word "sir", and by speaking in the third person they could maintain the strictures that they both knew the Army required of them, whilst at the same time regaining some of the closeness that had existed when they were children.

"You 'eard wot's 'appened t' Colin?" Ned Preece was

stirring a mug of tea, offering it to James and speaking to Ted as he did so.

"Nope. Last I 'eard was wot I told yer when I got back from the CCS. 'E'll write when 'e can." In his heart he hoped more than he could express that his friend was all right. He had written to Jacqueline, in very simple English, and with James' help to get the words right, telling her of the injury, and that she should try the British hospitals in Boulogne, for that was where he would be going. Ted had her address, Colin having entrusted it to him with orders to write if anything should happen to him.

"Wonder where 'e is." Alfie chipped in. "An' Mr Jenkins. You ever 'ear wots 'appenin' to 'im, sir?"

James looked up from the scalding fluid he was trying to sip without doing permanent damage to the surface of his tongue.

"Ah, there I can help you. A chum of mine came out from the depot yesterday, and he brought us all up to date on the gossip. He won't be coming back here. They needed extra officers in the second battalion, so he's gone off to join them, somewhere in the Mediterranean. Place called Gallipoli."

"'Ope 'e's better off there than 'e would be 'ere."

The young nursing auxiliary led Jacqueline through the echoing corridors of the hospital. As soon as she had received Ted's letter she had been badgering the staff, attempting to discover when and if a Sergeant Baxter of the Norfolk Regiment had been admitted. With the hospital only a ten minute walk from her aunt's house it was easy for her, and she was determined not to be put off by the bossy English ladies who ran the place. Playing every trick she could she focused on the men, knowing that a pretty smile would unlock doors, for there was always an inherent suspicion in these circumstances that a local girl was trying to cause trouble for the soldier, and therefore a natural antipathy towards helping with information.

Then came the day when the corporal she had been working on hardest came up with the news that a Sergeant Baxter had been admitted two days earlier, with an amputated right arm. She could barely contain her excitement, jumping up and down in little steps and clapping her hands together. Her joy was infectious, and even the corporal, who had harboured secret thoughts about how lucky he might get if this bloke Baxter didn't turn up, was captivated by her obvious pleasure.

The young girl who escorted her was French, only just over sixteen and working partly to keep herself and partly out of gratitude. She and her sister had fled the war, trying to keep away from the Germans who were doing such terrible things to the civilian population, and who had killed her grandmother. Never a strong girl, her sister had succumbed to a severe chill in the damp and cold of an abandoned hut in which they had taken shelter; and had died of pneumonia shortly before Christmas. Moving on, distraught at the loss of her grandmother and her sister in so short a time, she had entered the outskirts of Boulogne without any clear idea of where to go. Discovered by a British doctor asleep in the doorway of his billet, she had been taken to the hospital for a check up and a hot meal and there she had stayed.

As she led Jacqueline through the hospital she fingered the lucky charm in the pocket of her overall. It was a Norfolk cap badge, given to her by one of the soldiers who had descended on their farm at the very beginning of the war and had helped with the harvest. It was worn smooth with the constant rubbing over the past few months, and she treasured it as a link with the good things she had once had in her life, and of the lovely men who had been so kind. She wondered where they all were now, and feared for them.

"La bas." As she spoke she pointed to a bed in the corner of a ward containing upwards of twenty beds. She knew only the man's name, but had never approached him, had never seen what he looked like; he was just another patient among so many. Walking through the ward Jacqueline felt real fear, not knowing what to expect. As she passed the beds she tried not to look at the remnants of human beings in them, but curiosity, fascination, overcame propriety. The bandages masked much of the damage, but whole faces, eyes, stumps, heads and chests swathed in them told their own story, as did the groans and cries of some.

He was asleep as she approached, her mouth dry, her palms moist, the apprehension like a knot in her stomach. He was lying back on the pillow, both his arms above the blankets, all that was left of the right one swathed in a spotless bandage. Looking round she saw a chair and silently moved it so she could sit and look into his face without disturbing him. It was an hour later when she saw the first flickering of his eyelids as wakefulness set in. During that time she had been approached by one of those bossy Englishwomen, but a raising of the head, a finger to her lips and a look of such fierce determination had ensured silence and a tactical withdrawal. The female was protecting the lair, and woe betide anyone who attempted to breach the defences.

She had been rehearsing this ever since she had known he was injured: what to say the moment she saw him, knowing he would be distressed and in pain. She waited as his eyes opened, waited until she knew he was with her, saw the look of surprise begin to cross his face and then lent forward, whispering "je t'aime" as he had once done in her hour of need; and kissed him gently on the mouth. Then she wept; with relief, for he could no longer go back to the war. They were safe.

On the fifth of May, after a few days of relative quiet, the Norfolks were hit by gas directed at their trench line. The dawn stand to was behind them and they had just finished breakfast when, at seven-thirty, the gas came down from Hill 60, opposite Trenches 37 and 35. The greatest concentration was in 35 owing to the very close distance from which the gas was released from the cylinders.

It had become evident that men who stayed in their places suffered less than those who ran away, any movement making worse the effects of the gas. Those who stood on the fire step suffered less than those who lay down or sat at the bottom of the trench. Indeed, they often escaped any serious effects because the gas was denser nearer the ground. The worst sufferers were the wounded lying on stretchers, and those who went back with the crowd.

However, staying was often easier said than done, and in many cases fit men getting down to assist injured or gassed comrades were themselves also taken by the ghastly effects of the Chlorine; mask or no mask. Such it was with Alfred Arbuckle. It was the right hand end of Trench 37 which took the worst of the attack, and this was Alfred's position. The boy next to him was struck in the neck by a shell splinter, and began bleeding profusely. Experience had shown Alfred that a hand firmly place over a wound like that could apply enough pressure to stop bleeding, and as he bent to do so a great gout of dense gas rolled round the corner from the trench next door. Within seconds he was retching and coughing, the pain in his lungs indescribable. His huge bulk heaved and bucked as he sought to assuage the agony, his face buried in the mud as he fought the desire to scream; a process too painful for his tortured throat to endure. His eyes streamed, his suffering impossible to describe, but since to mix Chlorine with water is to create Hydrochloric Acid he was suffering the equivalent of acid poured into the soft mucous membranes of his eyes, mouth, nose and internal organs.

Ned Preece, seeing what had happened from further down the trench, moved as fast as he could to help his friend, conscious also of the youngster bleeding to death. Yelling to those above to stay on the fire step and out of the gas he bent to try and lift Alfred, knowing it was pointless. The man was already drowning in the fluid pouring into his lungs and he was far too large for Ned to lift or drag. Futile it was, but he had to do something, even if he ended up doing nothing. Within seconds he too was a victim of the gas. Lower in concentration, having dissipated, it nonetheless impacted straight into his eyes and rendered him blind within seconds. Screaming in pain, he held his friend, unable to see him, but feeling him weaken and then be still. He felt hands on his shoulders, felt a wet rag being pressed over his eyes, felt water pouring into them to try and clean out the acid, heard Ted calling out that he would be all right, felt himself led away along the trench, felt fear as he wondered if he would see again.

The Norfolks suffered seventy-five casualties from the gassing.

The mound, held by the Duke of Wellington's Regiment, was by now a rubbish heap of shell and mine torn earth, timber and dead bodies, and the fighting had churned it all up and pulverised the surface into a scene of complete desolation. The British trenches were shapeless cavities; there was no other kind of shelter and the enemy was less than one hundred yards away. The position which, with trenches on either side of the Hill, formed a front of one and a quarter miles was held exclusively by Fifteen Brigade with the Norfolks, The Duke of Wellington's Regiment from Thirteen Brigade and the Bedfords in the front line. The Dorsets were in local reserve in shelters in Larch Wood, four hundred yards behind Hill 60, near the railway cutting, and the Cheshires and the Sixth Battalion of the King's Regiment were in reserve in dugouts on the south-west bank of the Zillebeck lake.

It was quarter to nine, following the release of gas against the Norfolks, and, after a wakeful night, most of the trench garrison, other than the sentries, were asleep, tired out. The Germans released gas from two points against the Hill and with the wind in its favour it drifted not across, but along the trenches. Only one sentry saw the gas coming, and he at once sounded the alarm. Orders had been given that, in case of a gas attack, the men were to move to the flanks to avoid it and let the supports charge.

However, the release of gas from the flank scuppered this as it affected a great length of front. Furthermore, the gas hung around the trenches so thickly that even with a cotton respirator, that had constantly to be kept wet, it was impossible to stay in them. Some men ran back to the support line and those who remained were overcome. Thus when the Germans advanced after the gas had been flowing for a full fifteen minutes they secured all but a small portion of the front line on the lower slopes of the Hill.

The Dorsets sent their strongest company, supported by others, along the railway cutting to a trench on the right of the Dukes, whence they started bombing. They gained a communications trench leading to the Hill and became engaged in a combat that ebbed and flowed all day. The new commander of Fifteen Brigade, Brigadier General Notley, at once ordered up the Cheshires and the King's from the reserve, but before they could arrive on the scene the Germans, at eleven, released more gas, this time against the Bedfords to the north-east of the Hill. The right, in the Zwarteleen salient, yielded, thus increasing the gap left in the brigade frontage by the withdrawal of the Dukes. However, the left held on and sufficient men continued firing to keep the enemy at bay until gone midday. At this point, the Cheshires, who had been digging a second line near Hooge, arrived with a company of the King's and reinforced the line having marched up through a heavy gas cloud and gas that hung about. But it was only gradually and by repeated counter attacks that the Germans, who had pressed forward between the Dorsets and the Bedfords were forced back by the Dukes, Dorsets, Cheshires and King's and some of the lost trenches regained; the Dorsets holding the trenches they had originally seized.

However, the actual crest of the Hill remained in the enemy's hands. At seven that evening the Germans again released small quantities of gas, but it had little effect and the infantry attack that followed was repulsed by rifle fire. At nine o'clock Thirteen Brigade, with three battalions, namely the Royal West Kents, the second King's Own Scottish Borderers and the second King's Own Yorkshire Light Infantry, and which was just back from the fighting north-east of Ypres, was told to counter attack and retake the Hill.

At ten o'clock, in the dark and after twenty minutes bombardment, an attempt was made by the West Kents and the Borderers to take the top of the Hill. Darkness, broken ground and a well prepared enemy put paid to this, and although a party of Borderers actually got to the top, it was driven off at one in the morning by enfilade fire from the Caterpillar and Zwarteleen.

Throughout all this fighting the Norfolks were only spectators, holding the ground to the right, keeping possession of the important railway cutting and providing as much covering fire and succour to the "poor bastards trying' to get that soddin' 'ill" as they could. But in the end it was to no avail. Hill 60, even if it could be captured, could not be held unless a wide extent of the enemy's front on either side of it was also secured. Its loss was partly in consequence of the enfilade fire from the Caterpillar, which had never been attacked, but mainly in consequence of repeated gas attacks.

At the end of the struggle for Hill 60 the British had lost one hundred officers and three thousand men. Victoria Crosses had been awarded to three officers, one a territorial, and one private soldier; and, as the last of them moved off the Hill, men lay dying in the arms of others from the gas.

The next morning, the sixth of May, the Norfolks were relieved by the Middlesex and returned to the camp at Ouderdom. The regiment had been in the trenches for a continuous period of twenty-six days, and it was a group of completely exhausted men that slumped to the ground in their billets, the horrors of the past month etched deeply in their faces. Some drifted straight to sleep, some began to read letters, others to write, some cleaned their weapons like automatons, others put them to one side as if they never wanted to see them again.

"Let them sleep and we'll sort them out in the morning" had been the orders, and officers, every bit as tired as their men, headed for beds, meals, baths, anything that might bring oblivion for a few precious minutes or hours.

Ted, slumped against a wooden stall in the stable in which they were billeted, looked at Alfie sitting beside him. In his mind's eye was the picture of Ned being led away in a line, his eyes bandaged, his hand on the shoulder of the man in front of him as they were guided back for treatment, and of the vast bulk of Alfred, lying still with his face pressed in the mud, the pool of blood from the dead soldier next to him surrounding his head in a slowly coagulating mess, rats, also affected by the gas, squirming and wriggling in their death agonies among the blood and vomit in the bottom of the trench. Within days the five that had been left were now two; and he felt sick and afraid.

"Jus' you an' me then, Alfie."

"Aye." A silence, followed by a nudge to gain Ted's attention. Looking into his friend's eyes he said softly: "It's sergeant, an' don't you ferget it." With a lopsided grin he passed the hip flask to Ted. "Best we look after each other, then."

"Aye." As he drifted off to sleep Ted wondered when it would all end, wondered what would happen to him, wondered when, if, he would see Thurza again. Even as these thoughts were passing through his mind a plan was about to be put into effect to the south, a plan which had been germinating since the twenty-fourth of March, a plan which would affect them all.

Oblivious to this, the two friends sat slumped and asleep, side-by-side, the discarded flask lying on the ground beside them, its contents dribbling out onto the stable floor.

Chapter16

Festubert - Again

The idea was conceived by the French, and had its birth in a discussion with the British as early as the twenty-fourth of March, just a few days before the assault at Neuve Chapelle which had been intended to take the high ground of the Aubers Ridge, and which subsequently failed. The ninth of May, just three days after they had left the trenches at Hill 60, was the first day of the battle that matured from those early thoughts, although it would be some time yet before they became involved.

The basis of the idea was that the Central Powers, to whit Germany and her allies, had carried on activity throughout the winter on two fronts. In the winter battle of Masuria, between the fourth and the twenty-second of February the Germans had liberated East Prussia from the Russians, but had not broken the Russian front and so, strategically, had really gained nothing. In a campaign in the Carpathians in February and March the Austrians had re-occupied the Bukovina, but had not succeeded in relieving Przemsyl which capitulated on the twenty-second of March. As spring had approached it had appeared more and more certain that the German Supreme Command was preparing a great offensive on the Eastern Front, and in order to make it effective further reductions had been made in the German forces on the Western Front. During March and April eight new German divisions had been formed, made up from units drawn from all along the Western Front.

It seemed, therefore, that this might be turned to the advantage of the Allies, and that they might have the opportunity to drive the Germans out of France and Belgium whilst the enemy's reserves were engaged elsewhere. Consequently, it was in the interests of the Allies to afford what assistance they could to the Tsar by means of a speedy attack which would cause the Germans to look over their shoulder at an inconvenient time; or so the logic ran. There was no suggestion of any sympathy for the Tsar, but it was quite clearly important for the Allies to throw the Germans off balance, for, were they to defeat the Russians, this would allow them to concentrate the whole of their force against the Allies.

Joffre's plan, in those early discussions, was to use the Tenth French Army, on the right boundary of the British Army. It was to be on a four mile frontage with three corps, and another two and a half corps plus a cavalry division in reserve, with the crest of Vimy Ridge as its objective. This would allow them to overlook the plain of Douai, and this was step one in breaking the German line. The idea for the British element, a day after the French started, had been to extend still further the breach created by the French towards the Aubers Ridge and La Bassee; and the battles at Ypres to the north-east of the town and around Hill 60 had not induced General Joffre to make any change in his plans. In his view the best way to recover the initiative in the north, where the ground was unfavourable to the Allies, was to proceed with his carefully prepared offensive further south.

Came the ninth of May, and the Germans were well dug in with strong fortifications. British artillery barrages were only forty minutes long, and with limited quantities of heavy artillery they had little effect. The British plan was to use the same tactics they had employed at Neuve Chapelle where the short, sharp bombardment had worked against hastily prepared German defences, and the infantry had made gains. However, the Germans had also learned their lessons, and had dug in deeper and harder.

Their front trenches were shallow, necessarily so due to

the high water table. The chief protection in these forward trenches was the breastwork parapet, and they had built a similar construction in the rear of each trench, thereby protecting their backs. These and the traverses were almost entirely built of sandbags, each course being supported and strengthened by stretches of large mesh wire. The width of the parapet was doubled or trebled to measure at least fifteen to twenty feet across and lengthened to six or seven feet. It was then considered to be proof against the shell of all but the heaviest calibre British gun. The wire entanglement which, in conjunction with machine guns, made the position so formidable had been increased in breadth and in many places remade with stronger wire. Yet more wire was erected down in the excavations in front of the parapet, and this was carefully hidden so as not to be visible from the British trenches.

The Germans had then constructed dugouts every few yards in the parapets and the parados, the name given to the 'parapet' at the back of the trench. These consisted of large wooden boxes placed at ground level, filled with earth and covered with sandbags the height of the parapet or parado, and each of these wooden structures was sufficiently large for two men. Woven into these lines of dugouts were machine gun positions, every twenty yards or so, also comprehensively dug in with large "V" shaped wooden boxes with the point of the "V" at the outer edge of the breast work. From these, machine guns firing through steel rail loopholes near ground level were able to sweep the front with a grazing effect. Only a direct hit by a high explosive shell close to the machine gun could put it out of action. Reserves of ammunition and hand grenades were stored in yet more boxes dug in to the sides of the trenches.

A German regimental sector covered about two thousand yards, and in each of them one or more strong points had been built in salients, or bends, in the front line. From these positions, machine guns could enfilade lines of attacking infantry advancing against the main positions, ripping them apart from the flanks even as they were trying to assault the heavily entrenched and well protected positions to their front.

The trenches for supports, normally some two or three hundred yards behind the front line, had also been reconstructed and could be used as fire positions. They were wired, with gaps for communication trenches and their parapets, although not so strongly built as the front trench, offered sufficient protection to ensure that determined men could stop any infantry who may have got through the front line. Special attention had also been given to the communications trenches which, at the time of Neuve Chapelle, had been either inadequate or incomplete, or both. There was now in every regimental sector an up and a down trench, providing a one way system in order to avoid congestion. They had fire steps on the sides and were often covered by blinds or hurdles or other roofing which, whilst giving no protection from artillery, even shrapnel, at least had the advantage of offering cover from view from the prying eyes of the Royal Flying Corps.

It was a nightmare, and by the evening of the ninth of May the British had lost four hundred and fifty eight officers and eleven thousand men. The survivors were in such a state of disorientation and confusion that they would not again be in a position to fight for several days at least.

The French, on the other hand, had prepared their assault with a much heavier artillery bombardment and they had been very much more successful than their British counterparts. However, despite making nearly all their early objectives with their front line troops, they had retained their reserves too far back for them to be brought into the battle in time, and much of their impetus was lost. Joffre, nonetheless, was excited by his relative success, and was of the view that just one more good shove would send the Germans toppling.

This placed the British in an invidious position. With the lack of resources, and in particular heavy artillery complete with large quantities of high explosive ammunition, they should, really, have considered putting the Aubers Ridge assault down to experience and cutting their losses at the end of the first day. However, their activity on the French left was holding down German reserves, and national pride, if nothing else, meant they had to stay and continue the fight, despite the common sense approach of living to fight another day. There was, however, a light in Haig's darkness, for the First Division over on the British right, and in touch with the left flank of the French armies, had succeeded in pushing the line forward of Festubert. The Seventh Division, much to Thomas's delight, would, therefore, march south to Festubert whence they would be a part of a renewed assault on Aubers Ridge.

For the moment, after a couple of days rest and with the prospect of more time in billets before a return to the line, they were sorting themselves out after the horror of just short of a month in the firing line around Hill 60, oblivious of events to their south. Baths, clean uniforms, fresh food, the chance of a few wets in the estaminet, plenty of sleep and a programme to integrate the new arrivals into the battalion in line with the reorganisations that were necessary as a result of the casualties they had suffered.

"Seen this?" Alfie had obtained a copy of the Daily Herald of a day or so earlier, its headline blazing out the story of the sinking of the Lucitania, reporting the deaths of two thousand innocent civilians.

"Seen wot." Ted's reply was curt. Alfie was a mate, but could sometimes be a bit irritating when nothing seemed to get him down. Ted, having eaten a breakfast of a huge bacon sandwich, was enjoying a mug of tea and staring off into the distance, consumed by his thoughts. They had just lost three of their closest mates. Alfred's death had hit them all very hard. No man deserved to die the way he had, but for a gentle giant like him it had been so much worse to bear. Ned too, shuffling along with a wet rag round his eyes, perhaps blinded, perhaps worse with damage to his internal organs, his shoulders bowed, his knuckles white as he'd gripped his hands tightly to help fight the pain.

"Bastards," was his response when Alfie explained the sinking of the ship. First gas, and now innocent women and children. The anger welled up in him, and he threw the remnants of his tea to the ground in a gesture of hopeless defiance, resolving never again to even consider showing mercy of any kind, and wishing he had Colin there, the one with whom he could most easily share his pain. An image of his friend flashed before his eyes, and he wondered how he was, and whether or not his letter to Jacqueline had got through. He felt lonely, and he felt afraid - conscious more than ever of his own mortality. Reaching into his top pocket he removed the letter from Thurza that had been delivered with breakfast and read it, not for the first time. Her neat, round handwriting flowed across the page as she described the normalcy of the village, but with a hint of mischief as she got to the gossipy bits. Alice Bartram had married her young man, who had since been called to the Navy; which seemed to be safer than the Army, or so she thought. Betty Chalmers had given birth to a healthy little girl, and was pushing her around the village as pleased as punch. Her husband's unit was still in training and they had no idea yet where they might be going, but he managed to get home most weekends, which was nice.

He smiled bitterly. My, but it must be nice; anything would be nice to get away from this nightmare.

"C'mon, we're wanted." Alfie's voice cut into his thoughts. It was nine o'clock and at nine-fifteen they were due to join a group of the very few experienced NCOs left in the battalion for instruction on a new kind of hand grenade so that they could then instruct the platoon in its use.

The Grenade Number 5 had been christened the Mills Bomb after the name of its inventor, and it was one of a range of new grenades being introduced into service for use in trench warfare. These included a fragmentation hand grenade in a tin can; a much larger affair looking rather like a hair brush that contained a pound of explosive, as opposed to the couple of ounces in a hand grenade; and a cylindrical grenade also carrying a pound in weight of explosive. These latter two were really more small demolition charges than grenades, to be placed rather than thrown; but they were all part of a programme to try and redress the huge advantage that the Germans had in weaponry that was suitable for trench warfare.

"The Mills Bomb," the instructor held an oval cast iron object in his hand, its external surface segmented, "is a very much more effective weapon than the grenades we've been issued wiv up t' now." He went on to describe the features, in accordance with the approved lesson plan structure, pointing out the base plug which had to be unscrewed to fit in the detonator assembly, the spring loaded plunger which fired the detonator, and the way it was held in place by a lever which in turn was held in place by a safety pin with a ring on it to facilitate pulling. The detonator assembly comprised a short length of safety fuze with a detonator at one end and a .22 inch rimfire cap which, when struck by the spring loaded plunger, initiated the safety fuze. After a burning time of some five seconds the grenade would then detonate.

The instructor had their complete attention, the dreadful events of the past month drifting to the backs of their minds as they absorbed the advantages this new weapon had to offer. It no longer relied on a good strike on the ground for it to function, it was easier to carry, which meant they could carry more, and it was simple to operate, which made it much handier in awkward circumstances.

Alfie and Ted made their way back to the platoon, carrying with them several white painted grenades, known as "drill" grenades. These were actual grenade bodies which had never been filled with explosive, but came complete with pins, springs and levers and a dummy detonator assembly; all to be used in training. They had been given time on a range, specially set aside for training with the live grenade, for the day after tomorrow. Wasteful though it might seem with the prevalent shortages of ammunition, the British Army had always considered it important to train its soldiers with live rounds. It was especially important with grenades, for there was a propensity among the inexperienced to "freeze" once they had pulled the pin and simply stand there holding the thing in their hand. It was something to do with holding on to a "bomb". Much better they get little foibles like that out of their system on the range and not be faced with them on the battlefield.

Ted was feeling very much better. Concentration on something important associated with the job had allowed him to turn his thoughts away from the misery he had been feeling, and had acted as something of a tonic. It was further helped by the fact that he and Alfie would have to set up lessons for the platoon in time to get them all through the training before their morning on the range. Before long he was fully embroiled in it, and the professional in him took over. It wasn't until that night, as he tried to sleep, that the images, and the bitterness, began to drift back into his consciousness. He tried to dismiss them, and forced the picture of a face framed in reddish brown hair, and a pretty smile which displayed a slightly offset front tooth, into his mind's eye; and he managed to stay with that until he drifted off to sleep. When he woke the next morning he would not remember that Edgar Curry had twice in the night shaken him gently and calmed him as the crying out, and the thrashing of his arms and legs, in his nightmares woke those around him.

"'Ere, you read this?" Alfie, once more, had access to a newspaper and, as always, insisted on sharing its contents with those around him.

"Read wot?" responded Ted, wondering how it was he was supposed to have "read" anything since the newspaper had not been available to any of them until Alfie had appeared with it only two minutes ago.

"It ses 'ere that the Cabinet 're finking abaht usin' poison gas on the Germans, same way as they used it on us."

"Bloody good thing if yer ask me." A new arrival, just three days with the platoon, made his views known. Alfie and Ted each offered him a withering look.

"Well, I bloody didn't arsk you."

"Sorry sarge." The young man, who was trying to be an older man, recoiled at the vehemence in his sergeant's voice.

"Its sergeant t' you, an' don't you bloody ferget it, d'you 'ear?"

"Yes sarge...... sergeant. Sorry sergeant."

"Them buggers should've been at bleedin' 'ill sixty wiv us." The bitterness in Ted's voice was plain for all to hear, and it shocked James Woolford who was just about to enter the billet and heard it as he stood in the doorway. "If they saw wot that stuff did to a man they'd bloody think agin, an' that's fer sure. Bleedin' armchair warriors; they wants ter come out 'ere an see wot its really like afore they get their bleedin' bright ideas." James turned away, deciding that what he wanted to do, which was not important, could wait.

"Anythin' else in that paper then, loik some good news fer instance?"

"'Fraid not. There's quite a bit 'bout ammunition shortages an' they reckon it's about toim the Government did sumthin' 'bout it. 'Ere, Ted, didn't you 'ave someone 'oo worked in an ammunition factory 'oo was on strike fer more pay, or somethin'?"

"Aye, bastard wants ter spend a day or two out 'ere. I'd give the little squirt a soddin' stroik, an' not one 'e'd ferget in an 'urry eether."

They were not to know it, but the situation was actually more alarming than was being reported in the press. Essentially, there was a breakdown emerging in the relationship between Lord Kitchener, the Secretary for War, and Lloyd George and his Cabinet. Kitchener would not have made French his first choice as Commander in Chief of the BEF, and was not above permitting his personal view of the man to colour the pronouncements he made about the situation in France. It might be suggested, for instance, that the bleating from the front regarding lack of ammunition might easily be designed to cover the operational and tactical errors which were causing such huge casualties. Indeed, he denied emphatically that Sir John French had ever properly advised the War Office that a lack of ammunition was impeding offensive operations. Stretching pedanticity to its ultimate it might have been argued that there was a grain of truth in this, but it took no account of the many complaints sent back from France, nor of the fact that in planning his offensives French had done so on the basis of resources promised and never delivered.

The story really took off when a Times headline pronounced: "*British soldiers died last week on Aubers Ridge because the British Army is short of shells.*" The article was drawn from remarks made by Sir John French to a reporter when, trying to sort himself out after the first, failed, attempt on Aubers Ridge, he had received a message from London ordering twenty thousand shells to be sent to Gallipoli. He had simply exploded, and the reporter had received the full benefit of his views.

Regrettably, the article ran counter to the assurances, given three weeks earlier by Asquith in a speech in Newcastle, that the rumours of munitions shortages were incorrect. In the meantime, knowing that the article was to be published, French sent a memorandum to London in which he laid out the situation, stressing its gravity, and attached copies of all the correspondence that had been conducted with the War Office. There were three copies of the memorandum, one for Lloyd George and the other two for key members of the Opposition: Arthur Balfour and Bonar Law. Normally the politicians would have seen none of this, since, for reasons of "security", neither the War Office nor the Admiralty correspondence was passed on to the Cabinet. Until the arrival of these memoranda there had been no basis upon which anyone could challenge Kitchener's views and opinions.

And it was Kitchener's views and opinions that lay at the heart of the problem. Very much a soldier of the old school, he would not tolerate the interference of civilians in the conduct of war, believing it to be none of their business, and certainly outside their competence. In so doing he failed to face the reality that this war was no longer a brush fire in some distant land fought by a professional army, but instead had become a matter involving the whole nation at arms, and one in which politicians had to take an interest and play an active part.

The effect of the ammunition crisis was to force a change in the structure of government, with the formation of a coalition, a disbanding of the War Council, to which Kitchener paid no attention anyway, and the creation of a Ministry of Munitions with full powers. Asquith determined to dissolve his Cabinet, where in-fighting and quarrelling were common place, and forge a new team. However, it was not just the munitions crisis that was the cause of the fall of the Liberal government: the Dardanelles and the resignation of the First Sea Lord also played their part. But, even then, whilst seeking to create a new order there was no suggestion of the removal of Kitchener as Secretary of State for War. He was too closely identified with the nation's spirit, his picture appeared on all the recruiting posters, the new army under training was known as Kitchener's Army. No, he would have to stay and Asquith would have to work round him.

But, if anyone was prepared to listen, Thomas could have told them the real problem. It wasn't so much the shortage of ammunition, as the shortage of heavy guns. Even with high explosive shell the field guns would have little impact on the strongly dug in German positions. To break them up required a heavy shell that would drive through the structure on a delay fuze and wreck the positions from the inside. The British had one thousand two hundred and sixty three field pieces in France, and only one hundred and five heavy guns. It was more heavy guns they needed, as well as the ammunition.

Time dragged on, with relative inactivity broken by bouts of tedious work improving dugouts, filling sandbags and generally acting as forced labour for anyone who wanted a dirty job done; or at least that was how it seemed. The new arrivals grumbled, and Ted and Alfie kept telling them to shut up and to count their blessings. For his part, James Woolford could not suppress feelings of sadness as he saw the changes in his old friend, felt the bitterness, watched the hardness in the eyes; and he wondered if he, one day, would be like that.

It was the twentieth of May before they went back into the line, and resumed their old positions just short of Hill 60, relieving the Middlesex Regiment. They had received reinforcements, with three hundred men having arrived just a few days earlier, and news of another eighty-five or so due shortly. To Ted, looking around him, there was barely a face in the battalion that he knew. He had no idea how many of the originals were left, but it had to be many less than a hundred, and certainly there were only half a dozen or so left in the company. He stared out in front of him, watching for signs of enemy movement through the periscope, watching for the chance of a snipe at anyone foolish enough to show himself. They had been given carte blanche to take on anyone they saw, and he was relishing the thought of killing, of gaining revenge for the hatefulness these people had inflicted on their fellow men. As he had watched the Middlesex Regiment leaving with looks of relief on their faces he had moved forward to find himself in the trench where Alfred had died. Edgar Curry, who knew what had happened, could understand his attitude, but the newer ones who felt the rough edge of his tongue at every turn had decided the best thing to do was to keep out of his way whenever possible. The man to whom Ted paid the closest attention was the Wind Sentry whose job was to detect wind direction and to warn when it had turned to a direction that the enemy could use for gas attacks. It was not a job any of them relished, but crucially important given that the Germans could hit a trench with gas within three seconds.

As time went on they became more and more used to the routines of trench life, to the damp, the dirt and the discomfort, and within a day or two Ted was fairly happy with his section. Alfie, for his part, spent a great deal of time with James, making sure he understood the business they were about and ensuring he did not drop any clangers. Alfie was keen to ensure this did not happen, as young officers' clangers could cost lives, and, even for very trivial matters, would bring down on Alfie's head the wrath of the sergeant major for "not properly looking after his officer."

In Le Havre that day a young woman of twenty-three lay back on the bed, the bloodstained sheets half way down bearing witness to the birth of a child. The sweat rolled off her brow, and she lay passive as the midwife pummelled and massaged her stomach to force out the afterbirth. Her eyes were closed, afraid to look at the product of her womb, praying that when she did it would bear enough of a resemblance to her husband for her to be able to believe that it was his and not the result of an act of stupidity in a field on the hills above the town. As she lay there the anguish rolled over her once more. There had been no news of her husband for many months, and then in February, with her six months gone, she had heard of his death. A sergeant in a cavalry squadron, he had been part of Sordet's cavalry corps from the outset. Led by a young captain, the son of a local dignitary whose family links with the Army traced back to Napoleon, they had crossed the line of the British as they retreated from Mons and joined the Sixth Army as it formed on the left of the BEF. It had been whilst undertaking a deep reconnaissance to the north that they had been ambushed. Her husband had been shot dead by an Uhlan even as he was trying, in a vain attempt to save his life, to remove the lance that had impaled his young captain; so she had been told by a survivor.

She heard the midwife approaching, and forced her eyes open, fearing what she might see. The child was still purple, turning pink, a thick head of hair still matted down from the fluid in the womb. Her husband had possessed a thick head of dark hair, and at first glance the shape of its button nose resembled his. It was enough, she could believe it was his - she had no choice: she had to believe it was his.

Meanwhile, Sir John French was embroiled in resolving his embarrassment in the south, with a political crisis in London which, whilst it might solve some of his problems later on, would bring no immediate succour by way of additional resources to his hard pressed troops. General Foch was still engaged in the Second Battle of Artois, and was rather hoping that the British would co-operate on his left towards Loos. Sir Douglas Haig, commanding the First Army, was concerned at the open nature of the ground which made it difficult for him to form up his infantry and to establish proper gun positions for his artillery. He advocated, instead, a smaller operation north of the canal from Givenchy towards the higher ground approaching Violaines, which would embarrass the enemy, and be a useful step towards a larger operation later on; Sir John French agreed that there was merit in the plan.

Consequently, on the thirtieth of May First Army issued preliminary orders to Fourth Corps for an attack against the line Chapelle St Roch - Rue d'Overt, just west of Festubert, involving an advance of a quarter of a mile, which would straighten the line and remove a salient which was causing the British particular difficulty. The eleventh of June was provisionally selected as the day for the attack.

"Right you lot, listen in." Alfie's voice rose above the noise to bring them swiftly to silence, and then ordered them to sit to attention. James had called them all together, rather than briefing through the NCOs; and so far as Alfie was concerned that meant bad news. Not that he let it show. Turning to James he saluted smartly and advised him that all were present save one man who had gone sick and another who had been away on a detail and could not be found in time.

"Good, thank you, sit them at ease please sergeant." Alfie snapped out the words of command and they relaxed in their sitting positions.

"We are to be detached from the battalion for a short while. There is an attack being organised further south, in the area where the French are having some success in pushing the Germans back. Some of you will have read in the newspapers, or heard, of Aubers Ridge. It is to there we are to go, to a place called Festubert. Alfie's and Ted's heads jerked up at the mention of the name. They had a memory of a village in a valley with high ground beyond it on which Germans sat; and it was not a happy memory.

"Some of you know the place." He looked at the two men,

realising he had said the wrong thing. It was not some of them who knew, it was just two of them; all that was left.

Trying to cover his embarrassment he pressed on. "Part of the plan involves a divisional attack in an area of the trench where there is a salient pushing into our line, and a company is required to provide a junction point between two brigades. We are to be that company, and we are to have with us an artillery observation party, with signallers, to help call down fire when needed." He went on to explain the details of the move, and the fact that they would be leaving the next day, proceeding by a mix of marching and transportation in buses. They were to be looked after by a territorial battalion, the Fifth Seaforth Highlanders, and the rendezvous was in a place called "Indian Village".

"Quite like bein' 'ome," muttered Ted, and, catching James' flash of irritation at the interruption, looked down at his feet.

It was, however, inevitable that nothing went according to plan. There were times when the transport did not appear, or was delayed or was diverted. There was a lot of hanging around doing nothing, punctuated by occasions when NCOs had to chivvy the men hard to meet suddenly imposed deadlines. In the end it was the fourth of June before they arrived in the reserve trenches at Indian Village to a welcome that, whilst warm, was tinged with suspicion. There was just the hint of a feeling among the "jocks" that the regulars were there to help a territorial battalion judged incapable of undertaking the task itself. It did not take long for anyone to realise that the soldiers in the company were as new, in some cases newer, than the territorials. In any event, since they were all in the same "pile o' shit" they very soon found that common bonds drew them together.

One common bond they all shared was that of being "mucked about", and this was to be no exception for on the eighth of June General Haig was informed that Foch had to delay the time of his own attack. The British operation was, consequently, postponed, which brought mixed reaction. For some there was genuine disappointment, for there was still in them a an attitude of the "boy's own" adventure. For the more experienced there was relief that the evil day had been put off a little longer. There was time to visit the estaminet, to pop into the local Red Lamp establishment, although the queue of a couple of hundred men at the door should have been enough to put anyone off, to write letters, to play cards, to try to forget what was to come.

On the twelfth of June they were notified that the French attack was to take place on the fifteenth, in the evening; and by now everyone was really fed up with the waiting in the misery of muddy trenches where sleep was difficult, and dampness pervaded all, even though the weather was generally warm and sunny. The orders were that the bombardment would last for forty-eight hours at a slow rate, followed by twelve hours of heavy fire. The object of the slow fire was for wire cutting and trench breaking. The artillery of three divisions was involved, plus twenty 6 inch howitzers and three groups of French 75 millimetre artillery. It was on this day that the artillery observation party joined the company, and the signallers appeared in the platoon's trench, for it was with them that they would be going in to the attack.

Festooned with telephones and drums of jute-covered cable, they were a dishevelled sight after their long journey, and instantly offers of tea, stew and cigarettes were forthcoming. Their journey had not been helped by their officer, who, so it appeared, was a thoroughly nasty piece of work, and the sort they could well do without, with or without there being a war. Ted felt the hairs prickle on the backs of his arms as the thought struck him.

"Wot's 'is name, then?"

"Snell," replied the bombardier. "Right bastard 'e is too. Why, d'you know 'im?"

"You could say that," responded Ted grimly, gazing at a shocked Alfie James.

As they were talking, the object of their discussion was drinking tea with the captain and the rest of the company officers. It had come as something of a shock for him to see James Woolford there, and a swift inquiry had determined that Ted Ludgrove was also there with them. The look of malevolent spite on his face did not escape James, who made a mental note to take great care and to keep an eye on Ted.

That evening, as he retired to bed, Edward Snell was overcome by waves of hatred and bitterness. Once again, the hand of cards that he had been dealt by life had proved to fall against him, and the fire that burned deep inside him seemed about to engulf him in an exquisite pain that left him gasping for breath. "Why," he kept asking himself, "why did it have to happen to me. Why couldn't some other bastard be dragged down by it, why me?"

He cast his mind back to the time, a fortnight earlier, when he had taken some leave and, travelling alone as always, had journeyed to Paris. It had been his intention to pay for some form of sexual diversion, but he had only been granted three days and it had taken him some time to get his bearings. It had been whilst he was working out what to do on the second evening that he had taken a seat at a café in Montmartre, up on the hill near Sacré Coeur. At first, having ordered a glass of wine, he had paid no attention to the woman at the table next to his, although he was aware almost from the outset that she was frequently glancing up from her newspaper to look at him. She had not been particularly attractive, indeed, the reverse was true. Short, blonde hair framed a chubby face, and he had noticed, when she spoke to the waiter, that her teeth were not of the best. Well built and stocky, she had hardly been the picture of Parisienne chic, although there had been an air about her that, despite himself, he had found alluring. There were gold bracelets on her wrists, whilst the hands that held the newspaper had several rings; and the nails were unusually long and straight and painted a deep red.

It had not taken long for her to strike up a conversation, and not much longer for him to have joined her at her table. The waiter, if he had sensed anything, had been the picture of disinterest as he served them for the next couple of hours, and as he paid for the champagne Edward Snell had wondered just what it was he was letting himself in for. She had asked him to walk her to her apartment, some ten minutes away. Once clear of the square she had moved closer in to him, and eventually, as they were approaching where she lived, had slipped her arm into his.

"I will dismiss the maid." Her voice had sounded strangely husky, and he was beginning to believe that he might be about to avail himself of the most extraordinary stroke of luck. The door had opened, and he had felt a tinge of embarrassment as the young girl had looked straight into his face, obviously well aware of her mistress's intentions. He had wondered how many others there might have been, but he had been, by then, too deeply embroiled to be able to turn back or, indeed, to want to turn back. After a short conversation, very little of which he understood, the maid had collected her coat bobbed a curtsey to him and with a delicate "enchanté m'sieu" had slipped out of the door.

The maid had returned to the apartment she shared with her widowed mother and her red haired baby, its father long since gone on the barges that plied the Seine. Since that day when she had taken the train into the country she had turned away from her pursuit of the oldest profession, the experience with that British soldier having been something dirty which she never wished to repeat, no matter how desperate she had become for money. It had taken time, and she had found herself work as a washer woman and as a seamstress in a sweatshop, turning out clothes for twenty hours a day in order to make ends meet. But she had persevered, and had managed to find employment with Madame shortly after Christmas. Her former profession had meant that she had no difficulty tolerating the sexual mores of her employer, and they had developed a good working relationship. She always found it interesting that Madame did for free what she had done for money. Still it took all sorts.

As she had climbed the stairs and heard the baby crying, she had wondered, briefly, why it might have been that the man with her mistress had seemed familiar. Absentmindedly she had passed the back of her hand across her face as if to wipe something from it.

Having spent ten minutes in the apartment Edward Snell had consumed a glass of champagne, and had been waiting for her to appear from another room into the drawing room where he was sitting on a chaise langue, his belt and jacket removed. She had appeared wearing a loose fitting house coat of silk, coloured cream and hanging partly open to expose melon like breasts and wide hips. Without any preamble she had approached and begun to kiss him whilst at the same time removing his shirt. Deftly and with practised fingers she had stripped him to nakedness, halting his occasional protests which a stern “sshhhhh”. Still in silence she had raked her nails gently along the underside of his penis, bringing it to full erectness faster than he had ever known. Then she had pushed him back onto the couch and as he had tried to regain his composure had taken him directly with her warm, moist mouth. No one had ever done that to him before, and the feelings generated by her flickering tongue had been beyond description. Unable to control himself he had exploded within seconds and, completely unable to react as he always did, heard her gulping above the sound of his own groan as his loins contracted in huge spasms. Looking down he had seen her head lift as she raised her eyes to his, a trickle of moisture at the corner of her mouth, beginning to run down her chin. Slowly, she had picked up his shirt from the floor. Using the tail to dab her mouth dry, she had picked up her glass of champagne and, still looking straight at him, washed its contents round inside her mouth before swallowing. The look in her eyes had been one of absolute triumph.

The lady had been an expert. Within twenty minutes she had caused him to reach a stage when he would be able to perform again. This time the process had taken very much longer. She was hugely experienced and was not going to let him waste his energy until she was satisfied. There had been a range of positions, but after some time she had sat astride him, her thighs wrapped round his head, blocking sound, with the taste of her in his mouth as she wriggled and squirmed. When she had been ready, she had moved further down and impaled herself upon him, riding him to suit them both, slowly at first and then with gathering speed as the feelings became too much for them both. Finally, the explosions had started, but this time he had been ready and was able to react to orgasm as he always did. Turning his head to one side on the pillow he had dribbled saliva as the contractions had overpowered his loins.

He had left the next day, at around midday, in an ecstatic agony of tiredness, for there had been virtually no sleep; suffering pain and stiffness in his nether regions from the pounding he had received during the three bouts of lovemaking she had been able to generate; with soreness on his back, his sides and his stomach, for she had liked to use her nails, especially during her orgasms, and he was to bear those marks for some time to come.

But now the agony was something he could not bear, for whilst she had given him the night of his life he had brought away with him another legacy. The pains had commenced about four days after he had returned. He had risen to go to the toilet in the middle of the night, and it had been all he could do not to cry out as he sought to pass water. He had woken the next morning to find a stain in his pyjamas, and the remnants of a yellow, puss-like discharge on his penis. "The bitch had given him bloody gonorrhoea. Poxed, damn her. How the hell was he going to explain that to the doctors? The bastards would have to report him because it was treated as a self inflicted injury and subject to disciplinary action. It was bound to get out and then every bastard would be laughing at him. Sod the bloody woman."

In fact, it was more than simply gonorrhoea, for she had passed on gonorrhoeal epididymitis. Normally, gonorrhoea was painless except when trying to pass water. Snell, however, had contracted a disease which left him in almost permanent discomfort, and sometimes acute pain; with the added inconvenience of a swollen, painful testicle. It had been a week now since his first discovery, and he was reaching the point of desperation. Despite the implications, had been about to approach a doctor when this job had been dumped on him. Now it would have to wait.

The first hint that something might be wrong came the next morning. If there was to be a forty-eight hour bombardment, followed by twelve more hours, for an attack on the evening of the fifteenth it did not take a master mathematician to deduce that the shells should have been descending on the Germans on the morning of the thirteenth. Yet there was, relatively speaking, silence.

"Surely they will put down a proper barrage before we attack?" Edgar Curry was asking the question of no one in particular.

"If they've got the ammunition." Ted glanced at the older man. "An' it ain't jus' the ammunition, its the soize've it. Mr Woolford's told yer the artillery plan, and the only things with any punch in 'em is them 6-inch 'owitzers, an' there's only twenty o' them. Nah, its goin' t' be the poor bloody infantry agin, on their jack jones." He turned to his section, conscious that he had a responsibility.

"Roight, c'mon then. Let's get them rifles cleaned an' we'll sort out the ammunition an' grenades and then we'll go through some o' the drills fer foightin' in their trenches." Within a few minutes he had them around him, listening to him and drawing all they could on his vast experience. He, after all, was still alive, so he had to be doing something right; so ran the logic of the newer members of the section.

Eventually the news filtered down that the attack would now take place on the sixteenth of June, but by now they had stopped believing anything and simply got on with the daily grind. However, early on the morning of the fourteenth came confirmation of intent as the artillery began to fly over their heads in the direction of the German trenches and they watched and listened as it detonated on and around the trenches which lay only a hundred or so yards from their own firing line. Even from their positions in the reserve trenches they could get a good idea of what was going on.

"We are to occupy our trench in the firing line tomorrow evening, shortly after dark." James was giving the final orders before the move. "Our route will be away from the village here to the west and then south along the road into

Festubert; and that will be just less than two miles. We shall then turn directly east out of the village before entering the communication trench under cover of darkness. We are taking the long way round to delude the enemy as to our intentions, but I don't think the detour will tax you." He smiled as he spoke, hoping he radiated more confidence than he felt.

"Captain Snell and his party will be joining us." He nodded towards the other officer, sitting off to one side, with his men in front of him. Snell acknowledged the young officer with a curt nod, and then returned his gaze to where it had been focused for most of the briefing: on Ted Ludgrove. Ted was feeling uncomfortable, but confident that the man could not touch him in any way. The police in the village had made that clear, and there were enough left in regimental headquarters who knew the situation. No, he would be all right.

He might have been less confident had he known what was passing through Snell's mind: that in the heat of battle things could go wrong, accidents might happen, and it might be arranged that Ted Ludgrove did not return from this attack. A bitter and frustrated man, paranoid in his hatreds, consumed by the fires of discontent and self pity, he wanted more than anything to wreak revenge on Ted Ludgrove; and not just for what had happened in the village that afternoon, just three years ago, but for everything the world had done in conspiring to do down Edward Snell. As he plotted his evil the pain in his nether regions was a constant reminder to him of how unfair it all was; and the fires burned even hotter.

They left in the mid-afternoon, following a good lunch of bully beef stew and tea; the last hot meal they would see until the attack was over. The march was a gentle affair, and they moved at a sensible pace along a pavé road that had been torn up by shell fire and repaired with mud and gravel. Turning south they approached the village that Ted and Alfie could remember so clearly from those days in October and November last year, now over six months ago. My God, it seemed like yesterday, yet so much had happened in the meantime.

They had seen desolation on a grand scale over the past few months, but they were unprepared for the effect that sight of the village would have on them, the contrast with their memories making the damage seem so much starker. Many of the houses were raised to the ground, and most had no roof, or the walls were all holed. One house stood solitary, untouched. The poor church was a wreck, and only part of the walls stood. The graveyard was all ploughed up and stones thrown about, and here and there bones were uncovered. Amidst all this desolation stood a solitary crucifix, almost untouched, save for a part of its foot which was partially damaged.

As quietly as they could they moved through the communication trench, the company order of march placing the platoon at the rear, with the artillery party behind them. Ted, whose section was last of all, could feel Snell breathing down his neck, or so it seemed for the man was actually a good twenty yards behind. To their left the One Hundred and Fifty Third Brigade was moving into position for the assault, with the One Hundred and Fifty Fourth on their right. The third brigade in the division would continue to hold the divisional front, with the exception of the Fifth Seaforths who were to advance and connect up with the two advancing brigades in their new positions.

They passed a quiet night in the forward trenches. By now they were well used to the life style and they adapted very quickly, even though they had spent the hours of darkness doing everything by feel. To show a light was out of the question, although the odd flare from time to time gave them the opportunity to get a better idea of their surroundings. Ted and Alfie, the old soldiers, spent much of their time breathing an air of normality about them. Bitter and angry as he was, Ted was still a professional soldier, and he knew the importance of getting the balance of morale just right. A joke here, some cynicism there, judicious use of the rum ration and the odd growl to remind them who was in charge. James watched them, and marvelled at it. After all they had been through they retained that essential something, an intangible inner strength, a je ne sais quoi that set good British NCOs apart, in a class all of their own. God, but he was lucky to have those two; and as the thought crossed his mind he remembered that only a few weeks ago he had been counting himself lucky to have "those five". A twist of fear surged through him, like a knife into the stomach, and, as he wondered what tomorrow might bring, he offered a silent prayer.

"Smiff, if I sees you doin' that agin I'll 'ave your guts fer garters. Gawd save me from fools an' fuckin' idiots."

James smiled as he listened to Alfie James' forced whisper, and pondered briefly on what the unfortunate Smith might have done to incur his sergeant's wrath. Probably not very much from the sound of Alfie's voice, but it all helped to keep them on their toes; and the time would not be long coming when they would all need to be very much on their toes. He leaned back against the rear wall of the trench and wondered what the next day would bring. He shivered a little, for although the days were warm it was a cool night. There was a "plop" in the sky above them as a star shell burst and in its flickering yellow light he caught Ted's eye. They smiled, each acknowledging the other, their relationship secure, despite the gulf that divided them. Huddled on the ground, half asleep, sat Edgar Curry. After some thought James had, a few days earlier, taken him as his runner. The man was intelligent, had proved his ability under fire and could be trusted. Most people reckoned it was a good choice. Ted and Alfle certainly did, which was good enough for James.

The morning dawned sunny and bright, and for the first time they had the opportunity to observe the ground they would be crossing. The German trench was about two hundred and fifty yards away, over ground that was quite level. The grass lay green in front of them, pock marked by a number of shell holes, but not desolation on the scale they had seen up around Ypres and at Hill 60.

There are five hundred thousand seeds in a poppy pod,

and they can lie dormant for twenty years before ploughing brings them to the surface and they bloom. Virgin ground ploughed up by shell fire had released those seeds in great profusion, and beside ditches and tracks, along the tops of communication trenches and out in the open the red blooms spread all around them. Ted shivered, feeling the significance of the colour, as red as fresh, arterial blood. He touched his breast pocket containing the last letter from Thurza and, quietly, he prayed.

All along the German line the shells were bursting and great clouds of yellow, black and light coloured smoke rose from their positions. They could hear German shells landing behind them as the enemy sought to bring counter battery fire down on the British artillery positions. In the forward trenches they were, mercifully, left pretty well alone. There was nothing else for it but to settle down to a brew and some cold bacon for breakfast, and to clean their rifles and prepare the ammunition - again.

During the day the intensity of the bombardment increased, as had been promised. Ted, looking out with Alfie alongside him, offered the view that it did not look as if the wire had been cut, and how good it was of the artillery to speed things up so that the Germans would know they were coming. They kept their views to themselves: no point in bothering the platoon with such matters of detail. They'd find out soon enough, and they'd worked out the drills to cope with unbroken wire; assuming, that was, the Germans gave them the chance to carry them out.

At half past five they began the final preparations, James passed on his last words of encouragement and the section commanders got a grip of their men. Ted's was to be the last section over the top, and the platoon was to be the last in the company, acting as supports. The artillery party was to be just in front of Ted's section, protected as far as was possible in the middle of the platoon. In front of them they could hear their own artillery firing at even more intense rates. Ted looked at Alfie and smiled grimly. The bastards'd be expectin' 'em, an' that were fer sure.

Five minutes to six, and James was poised at the bottom

of the trench, whistle in hand, his eyes on his watch. Just three minutes later, at two minutes to six, a mine to their right, up at Chapelle St Roche, on a feature known to the troops as Duck's Bill, was fired. Looking left and right at his men James studied his watch and at precisely six o'clock blew his whistle.

Ted heard him shout, "come on chaps, off we go," and those were the last words he heard him utter as he vanished out of sight, leading the forward elements of his platoon behind the rest of the company. Ted suppressed an attack of panic, looked round at his men with a grin that demonstrated a humour he did not feel and then nodded to Edward Snell to lead his party ahead. "Oi'll be roight be'ind yer, sir." He was courteous; he had to be, despite despising the man.

With a vicious sneer, Snell responded: "Thank you, corporal, very kind of you, very kind indeed," and with that he was gone, leaping up the ladder like a man possessed. Ted, following up behind him, breasted the top of the trench to bear witness to carnage. In front of him the forward elements of the company had run into wire that had not been cut, and as he watched men struggling to fight their way through it they were being cut down by constant machine gun fire from the trenches to their front. In seconds he saw men doubling over as bullets ripped into their abdomen, throw up their hands as other rounds hit them in the head and upper body, stumble and fall as they were wounded in the legs or tripped on the uneven ground. Here and there section commanders were calling on their men to provide covering fire for each other as they approached different parts of the trench, trying to win their own local firefight. It was mayhem.

In front of him he could see Snell moving forward, his eyes fixed ahead, but for the life of him he could not see James. Then, just as Ted lifted out of the trench, he saw Edgar Curry, a few feet ahead, kneeling over something on the ground. As he drew level Ted saw that it was James, lying on his back. Aghast, he saw the flares that the young officer had been carrying burning inside his uniform. It was most probably a tracer bullet that had hit them and caused one or two to ignite. Edgar, being his runner and having been right beside him when he was hit, was beating uselessly at the flames, trying to put them out knowing full well that it was futile to try and extinguish a magnesium flare. James wasn't moving. He was either unconscious or dead from the impact of the bullet that had hit the flares, or from other shots. Ted could see no blood on his Service Dress jacket, but the flames and smoke obscured much. Edgar was calling out in desperation at the futility of his task, the pain in his hands and his anger at the loss of one so young and with so much to offer.

All this Ted's consciousness absorbed within a couple of seconds. He was about to grab Edgar and order him forward, there being nothing more that could be done for his friend, when there was a meaty "thwack!" It was a noise Ted had heard many times before: that of a bullet impacting on human flesh. Without uttering another sound Edgar Curry lifted from his knees half way into a standing position and fell forward, quite dead, across the body of his officer as if seeking to protect him in death as he had been unable to do in life.

Ted was temporarily in an agony of indecision, but only very briefly. He saw two of his own men go down and knew he had to get on. There was nothing whatever he could do here, they had to push forward. Almost blinded by tears of rage, hate and sadness he yelled for his remaining men to get sorted and follow him. To his front, and just slightly right he saw Snell heading for a spot in the wire where a gap had been created, and towards which some men were making their way, struggling against shell holes, machine gun bullets, rifle fire and shrapnel overhead from German artillery. It was a miracle that anyone was on their feet, but he had no time to think of that. By now they were within fifty yards of the trench, and as he looked around he still had three of his men with him. It wasn't much, but if they could get there they could do some damage.

Running forward he pulled one of the new Mills Bombs from his pocket. Ahead he saw Snell slip over the edge of the trench to slide down into it, two of his signallers with him. God knew where the rest were. Desperately Ted tried to remember how many there had been, and then dismissed the thought from his mind almost as soon as it had entered it. It didn't matter. There was no one in front of him, and he had seen no one go into the firing bay. Holding his rifle by the forestock he hooked a finger into the ring and removed the pin from the grenade. When he threw it there was a "ping" as the lever flew off into the air and the spring propelled the striker onto the cap that would ignite the fuze. He saw the blue smoke of the burning fuze emanating from the pressure release hole in the base plate as the grenade disappeared into the trench, to be followed by a most rewarding bang and a very satisfying scream as it found its mark. As he reached the lip two of his men were beside him and looking down he could see two Germans, one with the side of his head missing, and the other lying back and looking up at the British soldiers above him.

Ted did not hesitate for a second. As he looked at the German the visions of Alfred, retching up his lungs, of James on fire, of Colin with his severed hand, flashed into his mind's eye. In merciless silence he leapt into the trench, landing with both feet on the German's face, hearing bone crunch as teeth were smashed from the man's mouth, as his jaw broke and as his cheek caved in. Stepping back he viewed his handiwork, watching for just a second as his victim moved and bubbles of blood emerged from his shattered mouth before driving his bayonet so hard through the man's throat that it severed his spinal column at the neck and went through to the ground below. Looking up, Ted saw his two men staring aghast at what their corporal had done.

"Get down 'ere an' start flushin' the bastards out. When yer've cleared that firin' bay ter yer right one o' yez keep an eye on it and the other watch fer their bleedin' supports comin' in." As they rushed to obey him, he moved in the opposite direction, to where the artillery party were. The sight that greeted him as he rounded the bend was one of horror. Snell and his party had obviously landed among some Germans, and had not pre-empted their arrival with a hand grenade, or any form of suppressive fire. One of the signallers lay dead, shot at close range. Behind him the cable he had been unreeling from their own trench, and through which communications were to have been made, lay slack. It had already been broken in several places by enemy shell fire and was useless. The other had been bayoneted through the face, right through from one cheek to the other, and there was blood everywhere. Leaning back against the wall of the firing bay, a pistol in his hand, was Snell and it looked as if he had managed to use it to put down the two Germans in the trench. One of them, the nearest to Ted, had lost the top of his head, and his pickelhaub lay to one side with the contents of the top third of his cranium lying raw in it as it wobbled from side to side on the uneven ground. The second was lying still on the ground, and looked dead.

Snell was covered in the blood of his wounded signaller, and the man was lurching towards Ted, his hands on either side of his face trying to stem the flow of blood. Holding out his arms, his rifle in one hand, Ted sought to catch the man as he stumbled and almost fell. Looking past him he saw his enemy, a man who hated him beyond belief, staring straight into his eyes. The look was one of pure poison.

Snell could scarcely believe his bad luck. He had landed in a trench with two live Germans and there had been a fight which was clearly going to be to the death; but it was not going to be his death. He had seen the first German shoot the first of his two signallers, and as the man went down, clearly dead, the second signaller had shot the offending German. The second German, seeing that there was an officer in the party, had decided to go for the bigger game, and, having no ammunition in his rifle, had come for Snell with his bayonet. The other signaller, having dealt with the first German, and had been about to turn his attention to the second when Snell yanked him by the shoulder strap of his webbing and pulled him in the way of the oncoming bayonet attack. Stumbling as he had done so, it was his face that had collected the bayonet thrust intended for the officer. Taking his opportunity, Snell had then succeeded in shooting the German, which was when Ted appeared round the corner.

The noise all around was almost overpowering. Machine guns were still firing, shells were flying overhead, grenades were going off and there were screams and shouts as the few British who had reached the German trenches fought for its possession and for their lives.

As Ted looked at Snell he realised with horror that the man was raising his pistol to shoot. With his arms wrapped round a wounded soldier, the man's blood running down his uniform, his strangled breathing loud in his ear, there was nothing he could do. He watched Snell take the pressure on the trigger and as the shot fired he flinched, instinctively, waiting for the impact. A combination of Snell's hand shaking with shock, the sudden move of Ted's head and a sideways stumble by the wounded signaller and suddenly Ted was splattered with the man's brains as Snell's misdirected bullet ended the soldier's suffering.

"Bastard!" Snell spat out the words. As he spoke the pain in his loins reminded him of the disease he had contracted and of the agony to come. The pain was insufferable, as was this little shit in front of him. Now he could kill him. Up to now he'd only been able to screw that French whore of a girlfriend of his. All that lovey dovey when they were saying goodbye that day, nice little kisses on the cheeks. Bastard. Pity he hadn't caught the pox before, then he could have given that to the bitch as well. But she'd cried enough when he'd done it to her. Now the little bastard was going to die.

As he raised the pistol again he smiled as he saw Ted desperately trying to untangle himself from the dead signaller, revelling in the control he now had as his victim stood before him. Aaah, the pain in his crotch was so bad now, why him, why did it have to be him? Suddenly he gasped out loud, lifting up onto tip toes as the pain struck him, and so much worse than he had known it, biting deep into his vitals screwing and twisting. His hands weakened, and suddenly he could not hold the pistol, it began to slip from his fingers, and through a mist of pain he looked down to see the German soldier he had shot lying on his side, his bayonet rammed upwards into the Englishman's genitals, hacking through his scrotum and on up into his lower abdomen.

Snell's scream was enough to waken the dead. It was a scream borne as much of the frustration at the unfairness of life as of the pain. Ted was transfixed, unable to move, as he saw the threat of death pass by, and Snell impaled on the end of a Mauser rifle.

"Wot the fuck's goin' on. Ted, fer Gawd's sake get the fuck out o' 'ere. We're goin' back." The sound of Alfie's voice snapped him back to reality and he moved forward to yank the rifle from the German and remove the bayonet from the officer's body, dragging yet another scream from Snell as he did so. Looking down at the German he saw the man was in great pain, and a few moments ago would have killed him without a second thought. Now it somehow didn't seem so important. Looking at Alfie, he hefted the rifle and threw it over the parapet before turning to grab Snell and pull him towards a ladder.

"Ted, will yer stop farting about. Leave the bastard an' let's get back. 'E ain't worth a candle, an' yer know it."

"I seen wot the sod did, an' e's comin' back, an' I'm reportin' 'im an' you're me witness."

"I never seen anythin', an' anyway, they'll never listen ter you over 'im. Just leave 'im, an let's go. C'mon, let's get the lads back." With that he dived back into the firing bay from which he had come and began marshalling the survivors, giving orders that would ensure their withdrawal was orderly and effective. As he breasted the top of the trench he saw Ted to his right, and gave a despairing sigh as he saw Snell draped over his friend's shoulder, Ted stumbling along as he moved back towards their lines.

Evenings in June are long, and there were still a couple of hours daylight left as they tried to make their way back. The Germans, however, were determined to ensure that they did not do so without penalty, and it was not long before casualties began to occur among the few of them that were left. They had gone barely seventy yards when Alfie called out that they should take cover, and they went to ground in any one of a number of shell holes dotted around the still largely green swathe that was no man's land.

Ted slid and tumbled into a hole and found that he and Snell were the only live occupants, there being two dead Norfolks in the bottom. Leaving Snell where he had fallen, Ted crawled back up to the lip of the hole to where he could observe the enemy in order to avoid being taken by surprise by any sally they might make from their trenches. He need not have worried, for the Germans had taken enough punishment and were happy simply to recover their position. Glancing to his right he could see Alfie doing the same thing, and he lifted his hand in acknowledgement before a burst of rifle fire from the German trenches caused him to duck down.

And there they stayed, waiting for the darkness. Ted tried to bind a field dressing onto Snell's wound, but the man pushed him away with a groan of distaste.

"Suit yerself. Yer can bleed t' soddin' death fer all I care." His rifle at the ready he kept watch, and waited for the right time to make his move. A good hour after darkness fell, and at a time when, hopefully, the Germans would have stood down, and it was time to be off. Dragging Snell to the lip of the hole he stood, hauled him to his feet, bent, put his right shoulder down and his right arm through Snell's legs and lifted him. By now Snell was almost unconscious with pain and loss of blood. Even so, he groaned as his terribly injured abdominal area bounced against Ted's shoulder.

"Serve yer roight." Sympathy was not an emotion Ted was feeling as he made his way back to his own lines. His passage was not without difficulty, for the ground was rough, there was no light by which he could see clearly and Snell was a heavy burden. Staggering forward under the weight, he gritted his teeth with determination as the pain in his legs began to reach unbearable levels. His breath coming in short gasps, he was feeling sick with the sustained effort.

Suddenly he heard the familiar sound of a star shell. The orders on these occasions, when isolated in no man's land, were to either go to ground at once, before the light appeared, or to freeze absolutely still if caught by it in the open. Well, he was caught by it, and as its flickering yellow glow cast shadows across the land he saw that he was within twenty feet or so of the lip of his own trench. This, he decided, was no place to stop, and, although he needed no encouragement, he heard Alfie calling him.

"C'mon Ted, mate, yer've made it. Run!" Clearly his friend had returned from his shell hole a little earlier.

Dragging up reserves of strength he did not know he possessed from somewhere deep inside him he began to make his final dash as Alfie gave a fire order for those in the trench to put down covering fire. It was then it happened. Just eight feet from the lip when success was in his grasp and his foot went into a hole and he tripped, the weight of his own body and that of Snell bearing him down to the ground.

Alfie heard the scream as Ted vanished from view. "Bastards," he yelled, fearing the worst, and leapt to the lip of the trench seeking out his friend, dreading the thought that he might have been killed. Standing on the ladder he looked out, his face within a couple of feet of Ted's, Edward Snell lying beside him breathing harshly in short gasps.

"It's me leg, me knee."

"Well, yer can still talk so it can't be serious." Alfie's relief at hearing Ted's voice was almost overpowering. "C'mon, let's get yer in."

"I can't. I'm stuck on somethin'. Aaaahhh, sod it, that 'urts."

"Lessee." Alfie crawled out of the trench and in the dark ran his hands around Ted's right knee, having first ascertained that it was the one causing the problem. Ted, in falling, had twisted his knee, which in itself would not have been so bad, but had also fallen onto a metal spike, part of the support structure for some of the barbed wire and it had penetrated in from the left side behind his knee cap tearing at the ligaments, cracking the knee cap itself and chipping pieces of bone from the knuckle of the femur. Alfie was no specialist, but he knew three things: the injury was serious, getting him off the spike was going to be painful, and at that moment Ted needed to know neither of these things.

"'Ang on, yer silly sod, yer've got yerself stuck. 'Ere, old this." He placed Ted's rifle in his hand. "Now 'old it tight, cos this might 'urt a bit," and before Ted could protest he heaved his right leg as high as he could to clear the spike.

Ted almost fainted with the pain, and allowed himself to be dragged by Alfie towards the trench until he realised what was happening.

"'Old on. Just a minute." He could barely speak with the pain. "'E's comin' too," and rolling over he put his hand under Edward Snell's Sam Browne belt and heaved as they were both pulled by willing hands into the trench.

As he lay in the bottom he was conscious of Alfie's voice calling for stretcher bearers, and before a few minutes had passed he felt himself being lifted onto the canvas slung between two poles that was the standard British Army stretcher, followed by the gentle bouncing as the two men carrying him tried to negotiate the rough ground as best they could to the regimental aid post. However, although Ted was in agony, he was not the worst injured by any means, and he would have to wait his turn.

"Ye'll be fine, laddie." The corporal's voice came through a mist of pain, and he smelt the whiskey as a small cup was held to his lips. "The doctor'll get t' ye in a wee while." He felt a pin prick in his arm and within seconds he was asleep.

He woke to a dawn chorus provided by a pair of sparrows sitting on top of the dugout. Staring down at him was the young face of the regimental medical officer, a captain who barely looked old enough to be out of school, let alone out here dealing with this horror.

"We'll be sendin' ye back, laddie. There's nothing I can do here for your knee."

"What.......How.......I mean, how...?"

Ted was trying to frame the obvious question.

"It's a bad injury. Ye'll probably be able to walk on it, but it'll need quite a bit of surgery. Cheer up laddie, look on the bright side. It's a Blighty true enough, an' ye'll no be back t' this madness. As he lay back on the stretcher a wave of utter relief passed through him. It was finished. He'd done his duty, survived it all and now he was going home. It was over, and he was alive.

"Lucky sod." He looked up and saw Alfie standing looking down on him.

"Wot 're you.....?"

"Cut me 'and, see." He held up a bandaged right hand. "Did it unsnaggin' you from that spike yer got stuck on. Saw it this mornin' I did, after it got light. Nasty it is. Could do yerself a proper mischief on that spike, yer could."

"Jim? I mean Mr Woolford; and Curry. Did they....?"

Saddened and silent Alfie shook his head, which was enough to deliver the message. He did not go on to say that the bodies had yet to be recovered, and that thanks to some German artillery fire they might not be in a recognisable form. He held Ted's forearm, seeking to comfort him as a look of utter devastation wreathed his face.

"Hey up." Alfie's warning alerted Ted to the presence of an officer, in this case the CO of the Seaforths.

"That was a good piece of work ye did yesterday laddie, trying to save an officer's life the way ye did." Ted was at a loss to understand him.

"I'm sorry, sir, I don't.......?"

"The artillery officer, the one ye tried to save." The colonel was smiling, paternally, at the young man lying injured on the stretcher. "We all saw it, and it was marvellous what ye did. I'm afraid, however, it was to no avail. Captain Snell died a few hours ago. His injuries were too severe and he had lost too much blood. But as for you, I'm recommending ye for a Distinguished Conduct Medal, and if it's granted then it will have been richly deserved. Now, I understand that yer own injury gets ye back to England, and probably permanently. Well, in that case very good luck to ye, and well done." He reached down and shook Ted's hand, and with that he nodded to Alfie, who stood to attention, not saluting as he was without a hat, and moved on to talk to some of his own wounded soldiers.

"Well," said Alfie, "that is a turn up for the book. You lucky sod. I dunno, land in the shit an' come up every time smellin' o' roses." He looked up as the orderlies approached to take the stretcher to the ambulance, a lump in his throat as he realised his friend was leaving and would not be returning. He reached into his pocket.

"'Ere, the post came t'day, caught us up from the regiment. There's one from Colin, I got one too. 'Im an' Jacqueline're t'gether. She found 'im in the 'ospital." As he spoke he was walking along beside the stretcher as it was borne to the horse drawn ambulance for evacuation to the CCS and then beyond by motorised ambulance to the hospitals in the base area.

"That's good, I'm glad they got t'gether." The smile Ted offered his friend was tired, his energies drained by all that had happened to him in the last few hours. He tried to hold the envelopes and couldn't.

"'Ere," Alfie took them from Ted's limp fingers and stuffed them in his breast pocket. "There's one from Thurza too." Ted was about to be placed in the ambulance, and the lump in Alfie's throat was now precluding easy speech. "Give 'er my love when yer see 'er." He didn't know the woman, but could think of nothing else to say. "Bye mate."

As the stretcher was settled in the ambulance Ted heard his friend's parting words, and turning his head to one side he looked into Alfie's eyes as the doors closed, stared briefly at the last of them to be left, saw the loneliness etched on his normally cheerful face, felt a knife-like pang of remorse deep in his entrails; and then, as he lay back and began to drift into drug induced sleep, he caught a glimpse of reddish brown hair and a pretty smile made special by a slightly offset front tooth. As the blackness washed over him he whispered:

"Bye."

Epilogue

The End; and a New Beginning?

The fire warmed his legs, and whilst he dozed and dreamed the surface of the cup of tea beside him clouded over as it cooled, untouched and unwanted. From the kitchen came the noises associated with preparation of the Sunday lunch, and Jenny, having seen him sleep, decided to leave him be rather than remove his coat. She could use the peace and quiet, and there was no need to wake him until just before she was ready to serve up.

"C'mon Ted."

The voice came to him from the misty distance, as the figures approached. Shadowy at first, they gradually took shape and he saw the smiling open features of Alfie James. My, but the lad looked well, and young Dakin beside 'im too.

"Ted," a pause, "its been a long while Ted." Peter Dakin's voice had never lost its broad Norfolk drawl in all these years.

"'Allo Ted." Ned Preece's nasal twang sounded, as it always had, out of place among the softer brogues of his colleagues from the country. He was as scruffy as 'e'd always been, but 'is skin looked clean for the first time ever. "It's good t' see yer, mate."

Behind Ned loomed Alfred's vast shape. Invariably quiet, he just smiled an acknowledgement at his old friend.

"'Allo fellers."

In the kitchen Jenny started at the sound, and then realised he was still dreaming, talking in his sleep. "Poor old sod, who'd 'e ever find to talk to in these dreams of his?"

"Ted, it's time now." Colin was suddenly beside him, reaching out to touch his elbow with his right hand to guide him gently, Jacqueline standing just behind him with a smile of welcome on her pretty face. But Ted was afraid. The pang of fear was brief and unexpected, but it was there and he paused because of it, turning away from his chums and looking for a way out; and then it was he saw them.

"I've been looking after her for you." James Woolford looked every inch the young officer, his service dress fitting immaculately, his Sam Browne belt highly polished. He looked so young and fresh, so much as he had always been, and always would be. But the glance that took in James was no more than a brief flicker. His gaze fell on the lady on his arm, and even as he saw her she smiled gratefully at her escort, displaying a slightly offset front tooth, detached herself from his protective grasp and turned towards her husband.

"Its time now, Ted," the voice had never lost its slight nasal twang, even after all those years in Norfolk. "We've all been waiting a long time for you. Come on, take my hand my love, it's not far now."

Behind her James smiled his welcome, so pleased was he to see his friend again.

He reached out, felt the cool touch of her hand, the slight roughness to her skin that she'd never lost. My, but she looked so lovely. He stepped towards her, the pain in his leg had vanished, the right knee working as it hadn't done for years. She took his arm tucking, as she always had, her left hand into the crook of his right elbow and reaching across to clasp his forearm with her right hand, slipping her shoulder in against him, displaying the affectionate closeness that had always been a feature of their lives together. Then he was among them, listening to their voices, hearing their tales, surrounded again by those he held dearest, happier than he'd been since he could remember when.

Jenny had found him, quiet in the wheelchair, his head gently on one side, his right arm bent with his hand positioned as if it were holding on to something; something she could not see. The smile on his face had been gentler and more placid than she had ever seen; a man completely at peace.

The Royal British Legion had been in touch with the Regimental Headquarters of the Royal Norfolks, a regiment long since amalgamated as the British Army had reduced in size over the years to the point, in the November of 1994, that it was only just over half the size it had been on the fourth of August 1914; and God knew that had barely been enough, even for only the first few months.

The Royal Anglian Regiment, whose ancestors were not just the Norfolks, but also the Suffolks, the Bedfordshires, the Lincolns, the Northamptons, the Hertfordshires, the Leicesters and the Essex, had provided a guard of honour and pall bearers for the funeral of one of their own. They wouldn't have done it for everybody, but as the Legion Chairman had explained on the telephone to the Regimental Secretary, an Old Contemptible aged one hundred years was perhaps just a bit special.

So it was that six young soldiers lowered him gently into the grave, Corporal Ted Ludgrove, late of His Majesty's Ninth Regiment of Foot, awarded the Distinguished Conduct Medal for his courage under fire in seeking to save the life of an officer at Festubert on the sixteenth of June 1915. The Vicar intoned the words of the Book of Revelations, Chapter Twenty One: "There will be no more death, neither sorrow nor crying, nor shall there be any more pain, for the former things are passed away." The young bugler whipped the mouthpiece up to his lips, worked his tongue briefly into it and offered a short prayer that the cold would not cause him to cock it up; he'd be buying beer for the rest of them for the rest of the day if he did; and those high notes could be a right sod on a cold day like today.

The long, gentle call of the Last Post drifted away across the still November air, echoing through the treetops, drifting around past the church and wafting away into the heavens. The youngster put his heart and soul into it; and it showed. In the silence that followed, twelve young men standing to attention beside the open grave thought briefly about the drill movements they were about to execute, and then at greater length about how bloody cold it was, and how the white ceremonial gloves offered no protection against it, and how slippery they were in this kind of weather on the furniture of the modern SA 80 rifles they held at the "present", and just what that bastard of a colour sergeant would do if one of them did drop a weapon as they moved them with cold-stiffened arms in preparation for firing the salute.

"Poor old sod. Still, a hundred years was a good innings. Bloody hell, but two minutes at present arms is a bloody long time when it's this cold. Can't we get a bloody move on?"

Reveille echoed from the bugle, sounding the end of the period of silence. Feelings of relief in the firing party as they sloped arms in response to the colour sergeant's word of command.

"Guard of Honour!" The words rang out sharply, loud and clear, a warning that they were about to commence another drill movement; to fire the final salute to an old soldier.

"Thank God for that. Better do it properly mind, give the old boy a decent send off. Least we can do for him, 'specially with these bloody civvies lookin' on...."

"Guard of Honour!" The words of command repeated, but much longer drawn out preceded the sharp single executive word which would throw rifles forward in perfect unison, crash hands against weapons, scrape working parts as blank cartridges slid swiftly from the tops of magazines through lightly oiled mechanisms and into breeches.

"Present!" A pause. "Fire!"

Rooks flew from the surrounding treetops, their harsh cries echoing back down to earth as they fled in alarm from the sudden noise.

The movement was repeated twice more.

"Aye, but the drill weren't bad, not for young 'uns anyway. Nice rifle that though. My, but if we'd 'ad them at Mons or even at Le Cateau them buggers would never 'ave got to the Aisne, let alone the Marne. Ypres would've been a different story too, an' as for Festubert........"

"Right turn!" It was over, and twelve young men moved smartly away to their motor coach, faces pinched with the cold, eyes displaying an age beyond their years; memories still fresh of their time in Bosnia, only a few weeks ago now, around Sarajevo, eighty years on from when that city had been the source of another conflict. Memories of "ethnic cleansing", of butchery for butchery's sake, of political dogma prosecuted through the barrel of a gun; starving women and children, rape, pestilence, senseless killing........! Thomas was still at it: going where he was sent, doing what he was told and usually a bit more besides, and not for love of Queen or country or any special feeling of patriotism, nor was he terribly fussed about who was causing the problem he was there to solve. He did it because 'e was there, and he did it as well as he did because...., "well yer didn't let your mates down; and anyway, yer couldn't just jack it in....could yer?" Some things don't change with the passing of time; for which citizens of the United Kingdom can thank God as they sleep safe in their beds; and officers of the British Army can count their blessings.

The bus drove away. Jenny was the last to leave, the vicar gently holding her arm, and the grave diggers moved in to begin shovelling the earth that would place Ted Ludgrove firmly in the ground, beside his Thurza forever. It was a placid November day, not a breath of wind. Stillness hung in the air. Peace, perfect peace, and yet something fluttered in the trees, caused the leaves briefly to move. A gravedigger's dog looked round, sensing perhaps something beyond understanding; high in the branches of the Elms the Rooks silenced briefly their raucous calling, pausing perhaps to wonder briefly at what might just have passed; and maybe that was the sound of tinkling laughter wafting away to the heavens, or probably it was just a flock of Starlings calling out as they wheeled through the sky in close, and ever changing, formation.

....and there was no more pain.

Fact and Fiction

The genesis for this book came from research conducted into the death of a relative, Edgar Curry, a private soldier, at Festubert in northern France on the 16th of June 1915, resulting in a visit to stand on the spot where he had died, and to see where the machine-gun had been that had killed him. He was a soldier in the 5th Battalion The Seaforth Highlanders. A Londoner, a Glass and China Merchant, he joined the regiment in September 1914, when it was stationed in Bedford. There is no record that he had any particular affiliation to the Seaforths, and he had no Scottish connections; and there is evidence of others joining at that time from the London area.

However, the involvement of the Fifth Seaforths in the events of 1914 and 1915 did not provide me with the vehicle to tell the story I wished: to tell of the British regular army that went to war in 1914 and never returned; to describe events before the war degenerated into the mud and blood of Flanders with which it is so commonly associated; to tell a tale of raw courage and human weakness; to attempt to provide some character to the faceless thousands who met their deaths, to pay tribute to Thomas. Thus it was I chose the Norfolk Regiment, again due to family connections and research in the county. I have traced the regiment's war in those first ten months as closely as possible with information based on diaries, both personal and official, and a wide range of works on the history of the time, together with my own knowledge of military history and of the Army.

I have sought to tell the story from a soldier's perspective, and hope I have been successful in telling it as it was.

I remain true to history until the last chapter, where the task given in this book to a company of the Norfolks was actually carried out by C Company of the Fifth Seaforths. The description of Festubert in June 1915 is taken from the diary of Captain J H Mahon, 8th Battalion The King's Regiment. The regimental diary of the Seaforths records that the attack on Aubers Ridge cost the regiment two officers killed and six wounded, with thirty-two men killed and seventy wounded. Edgar Curry was one of those thirty-two, and his death occurred exactly as I describe it, based on an eyewitness account. He was 26 years old. The officer who died as Edgar sought to beat out the flames engulfing his body was Lieutenant J D L Mowat. Neither of them has a known grave.

It is my sincere hope that neither the Norfolks nor the Seaforths will object to my tinkering with history, for my objective was to tell a story of which they were both a part, and in which they can both take great pride. I hope even more that Thomas will feel I have done him justice

There was, of course, no Royal Artillery officer with the Company on the day. Edward Snell is an invention, as are all the other characters from the village. I have been at pains throughout the book never to refer to the company to which my characters belong by its title or to any of the officers by name; except Matthew Jenkins. He is also a character I have created, as is Paul Cooper and the members of the platoon. By retaining anonymity I make no reference to any man who actually took part, and, consequently, do no one any injustice.

Outside the company, however, the names are those of people who were a part of the events in Britain and Europe. Their characters, as I draw them, are derived from a range of historical works, and the perspective I offer through their eyes is what I have deduced from what has been written and said by them and about them. At whatever level they served they helped to mould history, and it was their decisions which had Thomas marching the length and breadth of

France and southern Belgium; it was they for whom Thomas fought and died and for whom he turned the run of play against a well equipped and very much larger German Army, against all the odds. It was they who owed Thomas their gratitude; as do we who live on in freedom thanks to him.

At the end of the book a number of the characters are still alive, and, since they are an invention, I can continue their story by describing what fate might have had in store for them as the war and their lives progressed. Matthew would be killed at Gallipoli. I would like to think, however, that among the one officer, the quartermaster and six warrant officers and non commissioned officers of the Ninth left at the end of the war from those who had marched out from Belfast in August 1914 there may have been a Paul Cooper and an Alfie James; and that they may have gone on to lead worthwhile lives after the war. Fred Smith and Aggie would have deserved to see out their days in contentment, bringing up their only daughter with his Army pension supplementing his wages running the household of one of the Norfolk nobility, he having reached the rank of sergeant.

Ned Preece would have suffered terribly from the effects of the gas on his lungs. It would mar the rest of his short life, for he would be dead before he was forty. Hopefully, however, he would have found work back with the railway, and would have lived in relative happiness, given his poor health, with a woman who adored him; and there would have been a brother for their daughter. He made himself something he could never have dreamed possible: a respected member of society, his status enhanced by his work for the war wounded in the newly founded British Legion. The small pension associated with his DCM would have helped meet the bills.

Colin would marry Jacqueline, and shortly after the war his father would die. This would leave his mother free to join her son and daughter-in-law in France, living out her days with them as her son tended the graves of the war dead being assembled into cemeteries by the newly formed Imperial War Graves Commission. Subsequently, Colin's son would be undertaking the same work when the German armies flooded once more into France. Joe Floyd, imprisoned for a crime he did not commit would be released from Dartmoor at the end of his fifteen-year sentence a broken man. He would die two years later in a gutter in the Isle of Dogs, drowned in his own vomit having fallen into a drunken sleep.

As for Ted Ludgrove, he of course outlived them all and carried the memory longest. It was he who grew old, whom age wearied, whom the years condemned. It was he who, at the going down of the sun and in the morning, was left to remember them. I hope his story, and the tale I have told of the rest of them, may help preserve that memory, and pay proper respect to the officers and men who created a legend.

The rank and file were ordinary men from every part of the country, from every walk of life, some despised, some criminals, often misunderstood, many times hurled from public houses or rejected by the local girls in garrison towns, mistrusted by many of their own class and routinely contemptuously condemned for "going for a common soldier". But, when asked to do their duty they did so, and in so doing showed that they truly were Very Exceptional Soldiers.

Printed in the United Kingdom
by Lightning Source UK Ltd.
104693UKS00001B/28-33